Books by Robert L Skidmore

The Satterfield Saga

If Genes Could Talk
Yankee Doodles in Black Hats
Green Eyes, Red Skies, Pale Ales, White Sails
Point of Rocks
The Drums, the Fog, the Terrible Shadows of War
The Sorry World
Did You Lose Your Elephant?
The Ballbreaker

The Inspector Richard Thatcher Series

The City of Lost Dreams
Cluster of Spies
The Hollow Men of Capitol Hill
The Distracting Splat at the Eiffel

The Conor Gifford Series

The Day the Mountain Cried
Circles within Circles
Keep A Happy Ghost, Or None
The Gods Are Talking
The Jealous Mistress With A Hubris Problem
The Accidental President

The Lieutenant Chase Mansfield Series

Mountain Mystery, Fairfax Miasma
Pay or Pray: The Odd Threesomes

Other

The Silicon Wizards
Which Way from Here? (Editor)

Pay or Pray

The Odd Threesomes

Robert L Skidmore

AuthorHouse™
1663 Liberty Drive
Bloomington, IN 47403
www.authorhouse.com
Phone: 1-800-839-8640

First published by AuthorHouse 7/12/2011

ISBN: 978-1-4634-2369-8 (dj)
ISBN: 978-1-4634-2370-4 (sc)
ISBN: 978-1-4634-3307-9 (ebk)

Library of Congress Control Number: 2011910536

Printed in the United States of America

This book is printed on acid-free paper.

For Margaret.

Prologue

Professor Thomas Hamid Jesperson greeted his distinguished guest at the front door to the Center for Arts Concert Hall with a relieved smile.

"Christ, Jes, I know I'm late, but I've just come from the White House," James Howard Townsend said as he held out his hand. "And traffic was horrendous. I'm so sorry. Did I keep many waiting?"

Jesperson shook his head. "No problem, Jimmy. We've got a full house, but everybody understands. We're all delighted you were able to work us into your busy schedule."

"Stop the bullshit, Jes. I'm the one who has to thank you for giving me the opportunity."

Jesperson stared at his old fraternity brother from Cornell just long enough to let him know that the common man demeanor and false humility were not working. They had never been peers, but at least they had been honest with each other. At Cornell Townsend had been a big man on campus, and Jesperson, despite his better grades, had stood with the hoi polloi. Both had risen in the world since then, but Jesperson had never caught up with Townsend. Jesperson had earned his doctorate, written three books–the last one a modest seller in the nonfiction world–but Townsend had taken off like a rocket. He had started small as an intern in the office of Congressman Arthur C. Featherstone who represented the 22nd District which included a sizeable portion of southern upstate New York. It had taken Townsend only two years to secure a position as a junior staffer on a House Armed Services subcommittee where he had specialized in foreign affairs. As Congressman Featherstone had climbed his career ladder, he had carried the bright and indefatigable junior staffer along with him. Ten years ago Featherstone had moved on to the Senate and had supported Townsend's campaign to replace him, keeping the 22nd District's seat in compatible hands. Townsend had won with a sizeable margin and had immediately used congressional contacts and national security affairs expertise to establish himself as a rising star. He had wisely continued his courtship of his mentor, Senator Featherstone, who had eventually climbed to the political summit, the presidency. Jesperson, then established as a tenured professor at George Mason University, a respected middle level academic mill in Fairfax, Virginia, had been mildly surprised and more than a little envious when President Featherstone had appointed his protégé to his first cabinet as Secretary of the Department of Homeland Security.

"Jimmie," Jesperson forced a chuckle. "I may be a minor academic, but I know what your schedule is like these days. Don't forget, I served as a contract consultant to the commoners who serve the high and mighty like yourself when I was young and innocent."

"Until two years ago when you abandoned your government and selfishly dedicated yourself to writing your next tome," Townsend laughed and rapped Jesperson on the shoulder hard enough to throw him off stride. "Are your budding geniuses going to give me a hard time tonight?"

"Nothing you can't handle, I'm sure, Mr. Secretary." A derisive tone crept into Jesperson's voice when he pronounced his college friend's current title, and he immediately feared he had inadvertently let his jealousy show.

Townsend caught the inflection and glanced at Jesperson who quickly lowered his eyes and looked away. Townsend read the embarrassment for what it was and decided to ignore the slip. He rather enjoyed having old friends jealous of his success.

"I should warn you, Jimmie, that you might find some of tonight's audience skeptical about a few of your department's policies," Jesperson said, trying to recover by putting Townsend on the defensive.

"Particularly those whose parents subsidize air travel and do not appreciate some of our enhanced security procedures like full body pat downs," Townsend laughed as he referred to a minor problem highlighted quite dramatically in a memo that had crossed his desk that morning. "I'll try not to embarrass you."

"Small chance," Jesperson smiled. "I'm sure I don't have to warn you, however, about academic types."

"Warn me, please. I know I'm in hostile waters, here, Jes."

"Intellectuals like to showcase their mental prowess at all times and tend to react a little too aggressively to outsiders who try to proselytize them, particularly ranking politicians."

"I know."

"I've got to apologize for one thing," Jesperson smiled.

Townsend glanced at his host and waited for an explanation.

"Some of the members of my seminar got so excited at the chance to meet with you that they shared the news of their good fortune with their friends. After the word got out, I had to invite a few others to share the opportunity."

"How many is a few Jes? I didn't prepare a speech."

"That's good," Jesperson said without answering the question.

"Jes, how many? No media, I hope, because I'm leaving if there is."

"No problem there. Just academic types. Members of my seminar, all bright young students, the best of our current crop, and a few of my colleagues."

Townsend stopped and waited for his old friend to get more specific.

"Thirty or forty, maybe fifty, or a couple more; I didn't actually count them," Jesperson tried to lessen the impact of his words with a laugh.

"I thought this was going to be an informal discussion with your seminar," Townsend said.

"I know. Informal it will be. I'll introduce you, give you the opportunity to say a few words to set the agenda, and we'll all chat about the world. You remember how it was when we were students."

"I sense an ambush," Townsend said.

"Nothing you can't handle,' Jesperson said. "Just be your usual, abrasive self. Some of the questions could get a little hostile, but don't let that bother you. There will be individuals in the audience who are quite vain about their intellects and won't be able to resist the opportunity to show off a little. They will be speaking to you but really challenging their peers."

"Your faculty colleagues."

"Yes, we have a few staff members with extreme views, but they have promised they will watch their manners. Some of the kids from the foreign students club will probably be more aggressive, which is understandable."

"You didn't mention the foreign students. That might pose a problem."

"Not for you, Jimmy. I didn't intend to include them, but when word about our little meeting leaked I had to invite them. I'm the club's faculty advisor."

Townsend stared at his host for a few seconds before relenting. "Let's get this over with," he said as he motioned for the smiling Jesperson to lead the way.

"Just keep your temper under control, Jimmy, and this will prove to be interesting. Treat them the way you do Congress."

"That will be difficult. As a member of the executive branch, I avoid my former colleagues whenever I can. It's amazing how one's views change when you join the real world. Politicians, like luminaries of the academic world, are blinded by an unhealthy preoccupation with themselves." Townsend fired a warning shot at his friend.

"I'm glad to hear that maturity has brought you around to my point of view," Jesperson counter-attacked.

Townsend glanced at his old roommate, accurately read the comment as critical, but dismissed it without dispute, deciding it was not worth the effort. Besides, he had other things on his mind for tonight.

"I'm confident this will be the highlight of these kids' academic year," Jesperson continued to play the host.

"Just so anything I say remains on campus," Townsend said. "I've got enough problems with the left wing weirdoes."

Jesperson shrugged. Within the hallowed, ivy-covered halls of academic freedom, he could guarantee nothing.

****

Two hours later the two friends retreated to Jesperson's second floor office in Robinson Hall A to chat while they waited for the audience to disperse.

"Can I offer you a drink?" Jesperson asked.

"Of course. After setting me up for that ambush, you owe me more than one."

Jesperson was not sure that was a complaint or a threat. He had fairly given Townsend advance warning. "I thought it went very well. You might even have acquired a convert or two."

"You've got to be kidding. Make that drink a stiff one."

Jesperson turned to hide his smile. His friend was still smarting from the academic assault he had just suffered. "I hope you have an acquired taste for Araq. That's all I have to offer," Jesperson said as he pretended to search in the top drawer of a file cabinet for a bottle.

Townsend stared at his host's back. "What in the hell is Araq?"

"I know you've been to Greece. Did you try the ouzo?"

"I'm strictly a whisky man, but bring on your Araq. I hope it has a bite."

"That I can guarantee," Jesperson grinned. "Araq and ouzo, like France's absinthe and Italy's sambuca, are aniseed-flavored drinks with a high alcohol content made from grapes."

"High alcohol content is just what I need. What does it taste like?"

"I can't believe you've never tried absinthe or ouzo," Jesperson said. "If I recall correctly, you never passed up a beer during your undergraduate days."

"Beer, pool, girls, movies," Townsend agreed. "Those were the days. Serve your Araq and we can reminisce. Christ, licorice flavored booze. You academics are too much."

Jesperson with an odd shaped bottle in hand sat down behind his desk, deposited the bottle in front of him, turned, retrieved two heavy glasses from a credenza drawer, opened a small fridge with a cupboard like wood front, added three ice cubes to each glass, and placed them on the desk next to the bottle.

"On the rocks OK?" He asked his guest who now sat in a chair facing him.

"I think you've already decided for me, Jes," Townsend said, an exaggerated skeptical expression on his face. "It's your booze."

Jesperson grabbed the thick, green-glass bottle by its short neck. "This is the good stuff."

"I sincerely hope so."

Jesperson made a show of unwrapping a stiff seal and pulled the fancy cork out of the bottle. "I picked this baby up in Istanbul, an indulgent stop after my last visit to the homeland."

"Persia, the ancestral home of the Cult of the Assassins, how appropriate," Townsend said, referring to Iran, Jesperson's mother's birthplace. "How are your mother and father?"

"You confuse me with your ambiguity," Jesperson said.

"I hope your academic colleagues feel the same way."

"To answer your question," Jesperson decided not to quibble. "Both are still alive and kicking. Dad's now emeritus, no longer teaching, and Mom's happy tending to her roses. She still hates the mullahs and what they've done to her homeland, and she refuses to visit as long as Iran is a theocracy. Boycott is her version of protest. I'm not sure who loses, certainly not the mullahs."

Jesperson's mother, Manujeh Tabatabai, had been born in Teheran, the daughter of one of the prominent thousand families who tabulated their wealth by the number of villages they owned in the hinterland. Manujeh had attended Wellesley College. Jesperson's father, Terrence Jesperson, the only son of a middle class New England family, had graced the Massachusetts Institute of Technology. Manujeh and Terrence had met as undergraduates, dated, and had fallen love. Neither of their families had enthusiastically approved of their marriage, but this had not inhibited the young couple. Terrence, an academic to the depths of his soul, had earned a PhD in Electrical Engineering and had devoted his career to teaching and research at his alma mater. The low point of their idyllic campus life had been Ayatollah Khomeini's 1979 Revolution.

Jesperson raised his ornate bottle into the air but held it poised over the first glass. "The natives prefer theirs with water."

"But you take yours only mildly diluted," Townsend said, referring to the ice.

"Naturally."

"On the rocks it is," Townsend said.

Jesperson smiled and poured one small glass half-full of a colorless liquid. He set the bottle down and lifted the glass. "Please note," Jesperson said as he gently swirled the ice cubes in the clear liquid. "As the ice melts, the Araq transforms itself."

Jesperson handed the drink to Townsend and poured an equal amount of Araq in his glass.

"It's turning milky," Townsend announced as he held his glass up to the light. "Are you sure it's safe for Homo Sapiens to consume?"

"It's an acquired taste, but I assure you it is perfectly safe, particularly after an intensive intellectual exchange." Jesperson raised his glass in toast. "To old friends," he declared.

"To old friends and heated debates," Townsend reciprocated.

Both sipped their drinks. Jesperson smiled in satisfaction.

"Christ, that's strong," Townsend said as he grimaced and swallowed. "And it tastes like licorice."

"I think I suggested it might."

Townsend risked a quick second sip and then a third, deeper.

"Take it slower. You are supposed to savor it," Jesperson ordered.

"It's not bad, but it will take some getting used to. Are you sure this is not just an after dinner liquor, something favored by the better classes, not the likes of bourgeoisie like you and me?"

"It is a staple of Mediterranean coffee houses where it is the solace of the downtrodden. It's served with mezza."

Townsend waited for his friend to explain.

"Mezza, little traditional dishes."

"We might as well go the whole way. Serve the little dishes."

"Sorry, all I have is Araq."

Townsend nodded, sipped some more, then slid his glass towards his host. "Give me some more of the good stuff."

"It's pretty strong," Jesperson said as he poured more Araq into Townsend's glass. "You might regret it when you wake in the morning or even sooner if you are driving."

"I'm driving, but don't let that bother you. This is my night out, and I don't have a DUI to my name."

"There's always a first time."

"I have friends in high places."

Townsend retrieved his glass and again pretended to be concentrating on the swirling liquid.

Jesperson raised his glass and toasted his visitor. "For medicinal purposes only," he smiled.

Townsend returned the casual salute, sipped the potent drink, and frowned. "I would say my critics had me outnumbered at least five to one. You were only half-right. The foreign students don't buy my pitch, but your colleagues were even more hostile."

"I know, Jimmie. I apologize. I was afraid that if I admitted that my fellow professors were waiting in ambush you would have advanced to the rear forthwith. I thought you handled them quite well."

"Well, you owe me for that, Jes."

The odd expression on Townsend's face made Jesperson wonder if the Araq was already having an effect on the Secretary of Homeland Security on his night out with the boys. He was almost smiling.

"When will your book be published?" Townsend abruptly changed the topic.

Jesperson stared at his friend, suddenly suspecting that the question revealed the real purpose behind Townsend's unprecedented offer to visit him on his home turf and expose himself to the critical academics. The expression stemmed not from the Araq but from Townsend preparing to ask his question. Not wanting to discuss his book, Jesperson hesitated.

Townsend laughed. "Don't be modest. I hear that it will be released next week. Do you have an advance copy?"

"Where did you hear that?" Jesperson answered with a question.

Townsend shrugged. "The publisher, of course."

"Jimmy, why are your people checking on me with my publisher?" Jesperson did not hide his irritation.

"We hear that your book contains some alarming insights into developments that impact on our country's national security," Townsend pressed. "If that's true, why didn't you share with us? You know the routine."

"Would it shock you if I said the American people have a right to know. If I had given you a heads up, you would have insisted that I not go public. I will not submit to censorship. That's why I terminated all my government contracts two years ago."

"Jes, you know as well as I do there is no such thing as the citizens right to know in the constitution."

"There should be."

"Let's not get sidetracked with a meaningless undergraduate debate," Townsend said. "Is it true that you've succeeded where the CIA failed and acquired a source willing to talk about Iran's nuclear program?"

Jesperson's silence told Townsend what he needed to know.

"How many bombs does that madman have and does he plan to use them?" Townsend referred to Mahmud Ahmadinejad, the President of Iran, who the late night comics cited as Ahmadnutjob.

"Read my book, Jimmie," Jesperson sipped his Araq. "Would you like another refill?" He glanced at the green bottle that set on the desk between them.

"I assume you know that Ahmadinejad has threatened to blow Israel off the face of the earth," Townsend ignored his old friend's attempt to return their conversation back to the mundane. "And the Israelis are determined to not let that happen. If the Iranians have the bomb, Israel will launch a preemptive strike."

"And you and your president will do nothing to stop them."

"Arthur C Featherstone is a good man. He is as much your president as mine," Townsend replied. "And please note one thing. The Israelis will have our tacit approval to take preemptive action."

"Preemptive action, Jimmie? Don't you mean trigger a nuclear holocaust?"

"This is not an undergraduate debate, Jes. You know as well as I do what it means for Ahmadnutjob to get his hands on a nuclear bomb. He will use it. The man truly believes the Mahdi will return sometime within the next two to three years and he is insane enough to do whatever he can to create the chaos that will trigger that grand occasion."

"Shit, Jimmie, don't lecture me. You don't even know what a Mahdi represents. That's just an argument you lifted from some kid analyst at the CIA or State."

Townsend did not reply because he knew he was in no position to debate Shiite beliefs with his friend.

Jesperson took Jimmie's silence as confirmation. "For your information we're talking about the return of the Twelfth Imam, Muhammad ibn Hassan, the twelfth descendent of the Prophet Muhammad's son-in-law. At the age of six in 874 he disappeared. The faithful believe he will return as the Mahdi, the Rightly Guided One, as a prelude to the Day of Judgment when Shiism will assume its rightful place as the true faith."

"Great, Jes, for your information, Ahmadinejad is one of those faithful believers you referred to, and he is prepared to do whatever is necessary to insure the Mahdi's return. He joined the Revolutionary Guard as a young man, served as a covert operative in Iran's war with Iraq. He rose through the ranks, participated in the takeover of our embassy in Teheran and the holding of our staff as hostages, and was eventually selected by the hardliners to serve as mayor of Teheran. In that office he implemented Revolutionary Guard policies: he turned cultural centers into prayer halls, closed fast food restaurants, required city employees to grow beards, segregated elevators for male only and female only use, and constructed women only parks. He is also the seer who described the Jewish holocaust as a myth."

"Jimmie, I am not a defender of Ahmadinejad. I know what his government stands for, and the threat it poses to the region and the world. That is one of the reasons I have worked so hard on this book, and I'm determined to share that information with my fellow citizens. You will have any insights I have acquired when the book is published. I know your intelligence community firsthand, and I refuse to let anyone censor my modest effort for any ostensible reason."

"Jes, I'm just trying to do the job that the president has handed me. It is imperative that we have access to information like that you have apparently acquired before it becomes public knowledge so that we can take preemptive action to protect this country. Days and hours of advance warning could be critical to our very survival."

"If I thought my modest effort contained the kind of information you seem to think it contains, of course I would share it with you immediately. I do not, however, know the date of the world's next Pearl Harbor."

"Excuse me, Jes, but you are in no position to make that judgment. You don't know what information we already have. You could have the last fragment of insight that provides us with a key that we so desperately need."

"And you, Jimmie, don't know that I have that key. You will realize that next week when my book is released. Please, let's change the subject." Jesperson calmly retrieved his old fraternity brother's glass, and dropped three more ice cubes in each glass before pouring the Araq.

"This will have to be my last, or I'll never make it home tonight," Townsend sighed.

Again, Jesperson raised his glass in toast. "I thank you one more time, Jimmie, for taking the time to visit our modest campus and giving the kids a chance to match wits with one of our country's leaders that they read and hear about every day in the media."

"I hope I didn't disappoint them," Townsend said. "I look back with great fondness on our innocent Cornell years together."

"Me too, Jimmie," Jes said. "Now can we stop bullshitting each other. How is Nancy Lou coping with your long hours?" Jes referred to Townsend's wife who he had once dated.

Chapter 1

"Wake up, lieutenant, your day is about to begin," Theresa, the major domo of the Criminal Investigation Bureau of the Fairfax Police Department, announced her presence.

Chase Mansfield, who had been dozing with his feet propped on his desk and his head braced against the wall behind his chair, opened his eyes, glanced at Theresa, blinked twice, and closed them again.

"Very well," Theresa smiled. "I'll call the chief back and tell him."

"Tell him what?"

"That you are not interested in responding to his order to appear forthwith in his office."

"What's he want?"

"I don't know."

"Then ask Barney," Chase referred to his ostensible superior, Major Barney Hopkins, the Chief of the CIB. Barney, once one of Chase's subordinates, had been elevated to the position after Chase who preferred investigations to managing the bureaucracy had declined the promotion. Chase now served in a position he had created, Special Assistant to the CIB commander. He handled sensitive investigations usually assigned directly by Chief Raymond Arthur when Chase did not stumble on them directly from his closet sized office adjacent to the CIB reception room dominated by Theresa.

"I can ask the chief to ask him if you wish," Theresa smiled.

Chase waited for Theresa to explain. Theresa did not. Instead, she turned and returned to her desk. Chase sighed and followed. He found Theresa posing with her hand on the phone.

"How long has Barney been in the chief's office?" Chase asked.

"Shall I tell them you are on your way?" Theresa asked, enjoying their role reversal. Usually, she was the one futilely trying to get Chase to tell her what was happening.

Chase shrugged and headed for the elevator.

"Go right in, lieutenant. They are waiting for you," the chief's secretary greeted him.

"Who's in there?" Chase asked.

The secretary answered by pointing her thumb at the closed door. Chase tapped once and entered to find the chief, Barney, and an oversized, muscular male sitting on the upholstered furniture in the chief's conversational corner that he reserved for conversations with visiting dignitaries.

Chief Raymond Arthur, who had commanded the CIB when Chase had first made detective some twenty years previously, nodded, and turned to the visitor, "Special Agent Cotton, Lieutenant Mansfield, finally."

The stranger turned and glanced at Chase. He inclined his head but did not speak or offer his hand. Chase nodded back, sat down in the last empty chair, and waited for someone to explain. Finally, the chief broke the silence.

"I assume you are aware of the incident at George Mason last night."

"No, sir," Chase answered honestly.

The chief frowned and turned to Barney. "Major, I assumed you discussed it at your morning staff meeting."

Barney deferred to Chase with a glance.

Chase who seldom attended Barney's morning staff meetings did not react.

"Packard and Whitten handled the call," Barney did not directly address the chief's remark.

"Both experienced detectives," the chief spoke to the silent visitor.

"Chief, as I noted, that is not an issue," Cotton said. "We will take over the investigation, and your department need not concern itself."

"And as I noted, Special Agent Cotton," the chief said. "George Mason University is located in Fairfax County, and we will handle the investigation. Given the Bureau and the Department of Homeland Security's tangential interest, you may assign one of your officers to work with Lieutenant Mansfield."

Chase looked at Barney who smiled.

"Now, if you will excuse me, I will leave you and the lieutenant to work out the details."

Chase, who did not have a clue what was happening, obediently stood up.

"Major," the chief grimaced. "If I could have a moment of your time."

Barney obediently remained seated.

Chase started for the door, where he paused with his hand on the knob. He turned and looked at the frowning visitor, waiting for him to recognize that he had been dismissed.

Cotton stared at the chief who ignored him. Chase opened the door and stepped into the reception room where he winked at the secretary. By the time he reached the door to the hall, the angry, red-faced visitor stormed out of the inner office.

"Special Agent Cotter," Chase said, deliberately using the wrong surname. "If you would join me in my office, we can discuss the parameters of our limited cooperation." Chase, like most of his fellow police officers, had a congenital dislike of federal officers.

"Cotton," the angry man corrected.

"Like the gin," Chase smiled.

"Lieutenant, you and your chief have just committed professional suicide," Cotton declared, ignoring Chase's feeble attempt at humor by referring to Eli Whitney's cotton gin, a local invention that stimulated an agricultural revolution.

As a native Virginian, Chase had learned of the cotton gin very early in his grade school education. Eli Whitney meant nothing to him personally; the name of the inventor had been the first thing that had popped into his mind when the visitor had made an issue of his surname.

The two secretaries greeted Cotton's comment with applause. Chase ignored the fact they were approving of Special Agent's Cotton's threat, bowed in the direction of the applause, and started for the elevator leaving the visitor in the chief's reception room. Officious FBI special agents ranked very low on his deference scale. Quite coincidentally, the elevator door opened before Chase could push the button. He waited for two smiling county employees to exit and entered. Just as the door started to close behind him, a huge paw caught it, and Major Barney Hopkins joined Chase in the elevator.

"That didn't take long," Chase said.

"It doesn't take the chief long to give a six word order."

Chase pushed the second floor button but did not ask the question he assumed Barney was waiting for him to ask.

They rode in silence until the door opened.

"Don't you really want to know?" Barney asked.

"Know what?" Chase asked innocently.

Barney shrugged and led the way down the hall to their CIB offices where Theresa greeted them with a smile and waited to be briefed.

"Please have Bruce and Charles join us," Barney ordered.

A disappointed Theresa frowned but pointed with a thumb in the direction of Barney's office on her right.

Barney turned left and Chase right, deliberately pretending he did not understand he was to participate.

"Please join us lieutenant," Barney called over his shoulder, ignoring Chase's gesture. "I'm confident the chief would want us to brief you forthwith."

Chase winked at Theresa as he followed Barney into his office and closed the door behind him, knowing that would aggravate Theresa even more. Barney sat down at his desk, nodded at the two detectives, Packard and Whitten, whose faces showed the wear of a long night. Barney sat behind his desk, waited for Chase to take a seat, and then spoke.

"The chief dismissed us with a terse command: 'Don't let Mansfield screw this investigation up,'" Barney smiled.

"That's seven words," Chase blurted.

"So who around here can count?" Barney countered.

"Do those seven little words mean we can dump this mess on the lieutenant's desk?" Packard asked. Both detectives knew that Mansfield preferred to work alone.

"Yes," Barney answered.

"I don't like sentences that end in a preposition," Chase observed.

"Take it with the chief up," Barney smiled.

Before Chase could think of a reply that ended in a preposition, the intercom buzzed.

"Yes, Theresa," Barney said, gracefully, aware that his secretary was dying to know what happened in the chief's office. He also knew that speaking to her was like using a loudspeaker. Confidentiality was not a word in Theresa's vocabulary. Her access to the department's secretarial grapevine was useful at times but required judicious management.

"Special Agent Cotton would like a word," Theresa announced.

"Please have Special Agent Cotton join us," Barney said.

The door opened, and the red-faced, heavy set Irishman with the physique of a NFL linebacker charged into the room. He glanced at the assembled detectives but did not acknowledge them. "We've got to establish some ground rules," he spoke directly to Barney, the Chief of the Fairfax CIB who presided from behind his scarred and paper littered desk.

"Special Agent Cotton, let me introduce Detectives Packard and Whitten who were first on the crime scene, and you may recall Lieutenant Mansfield, who you just met in the chief's office," Barney said, ignoring Cotton's attempt to establish an agenda. "I caution you that Lieutenant Mansfield is never the first at any scene."

Cotton frowned as he nodded at the others before he returned his attention to Barney. Before Cotton could speak, Barney continued: "Your sudden appearance, though unscheduled, is timely. Detectives Whitten and Packard were just about to brief Lieutenant Mansfield and me on the results of their investigation. You may join us and contribute as you wish."

"You're wasting your time. As I told your chief, this is now a federal case," Cotton declared.

"And as the chief told you, Lieutenant Mansfield will head the investigation and the Bureau can assign an officer to work with him if it chooses," Barney said.

"That's not the last word," Cotton said. He turned and stared defiantly at Chase, obviously expecting him to comment, but Chase ignored him and silently deferred to Barney.

Barney in turn waited for Cotton to react. Chase and the two detectives smiled as they watched the outnumbered but not intimidated Cotton, who clearly was a man accustomed to having his way. After a full minute of silence, Cotton sat heavily in a chair near the door. Although obviously furious, he said nothing more.

"Charles, James, the floor is yours," Barney ignored the visitor's brooding posturing.

Packard and Whitten exchanged amused glances; Whitten deferred to his senior partner with a nod.

Whitten took a notebook from his pocket, opened it, and addressed Chase.

"At exactly twelve thirty-five last night the George Mason campus police duty officer called to report a homicide. Pack and I were up next on the wheel, and we responded. The duty officer met us at the front gate and escorted us to," Whitten consulted his notebook, "Robinson Hall A, where," Whitten smiled, "we learned they indeed had a homicide on their hands. In a chair, actually. A cleaning lady a short time before entered a second floor office to do her thing and was shocked to find one of their professors slumped in a chair behind his desk with a bullet hole in his forehead and a second in his chest. She immediately retreated, called the campus police who in turn alerted us. As soon as we made our preliminary survey—it appears we have a pristine crime scene—we summoned the techs. The victim, a Professor Thomas Hamid Jesperson," Whitten smiled when he stressed the odd middle name, was a male who appeared to be in his late forties. We subsequently spoke with his chairman who had nothing but praise for Doctor Jesperson, describing him as a cornerstone of their department of history where he specialized in the Near East. Jesperson was a published author who in the past had served as an area consultant to the Congress and the White House; most recently he taught graduate seminars and concentrated on his writing. He has a book coming out soon which the department head anticipated would attract considerable attention."

Whitten paused and looked at Chase. "Of course you know a lot more about something like that than either Pack or I do."

Chase reacted coldly. Whitten referred to the fact that Chase was a published author, an avocation that Chase did not discuss at the office, and Whitten knew it. A confirmed bachelor, Chase enjoyed writing in his spare time and his modest success as an author of mystery novels was something that he tried to keep completely separate from his professional life as a police officer. Although he made a concerted effort never to let his writing intrude on his career, particularly never used actual cases as material for his creative efforts, he knew that others, either because they might be jealous of his success in either realm or because they did not like his admittedly difficult personality, would use the odd mixture to denigrate him. The chief was aware of Chase's literary output under the pseudonym Travis Crittenden, and, unfortunately, thanks probably to Theresa, many others in the department were also knowledgeable. Chase, however, determinedly never publicly admitted to the fact that his vocation and avocation coincided.

Whitten, Packard and Barney all smiled but did not comment. Barney considered Chase, who had once been his supervisor, a friend, and indulged him while Whitten and Packard enjoyed provoking Chase but never explicitly challenged him because no one knew how he might react. Cotton, despite his own personality shortcomings, was astute enough to recognize unspoken byplay when he heard it, did not know what was going on, but filed the observation away just in case it might prove useful as he anticipated that he and Mansfield would undoubtedly clash in the future.

"The department head told us that Jesperson was a bachelor who lived alone. He could not identify a single friend or associate who was close to the victim. He described Jesperson as an academic loner who lived for his work. In the chairman's opinion, Jesperson was not a natural teacher, did not particularly enjoy working the classroom, and merely tolerated the students. Research and writing were his milieu. He had over the past few years after the modest success of his early books had withdrawn to the point where he had reduced his classroom work to highly specialized graduate seminars. In fact, Jesperson had devoted the past academic year in Iran to researching his new book."

"Did the department head provide any interesting leads?" Barney asked.

"Just one. Last night Jesperson had a prominent guest. It seems that Jesperson and the current Secretary of the Department of Homeland Security, James Howard Townsend, were old college buddies, and Townsend responded to a Jesperson invitation to address a select group of graduate students and faculty members of George Mason last night. Townsend did so, and after the session the two retreated behind the closed door of Jesperson's office to share a drink and apparently rehash old times."

"What does Townsend say about that?" Barney asked.

"And this is where I come into the story," Cotton interrupted.

"Not yet," Whitten replied.

Cotton smiled but did not comment.

After a pause, Whitten continued. "There were two glasses and an almost empty bottle of something called Araq on the victim's desk, but no other sign of the alleged visitor, Townsend. The techs were preoccupied, and we were trying to make sense of the scene when two excited Feds who identified themselves as members of Townsend's security detail appeared demanding to see their boss." Whitten paused, obviously enjoying the enhanced interest of Barney and Chase, particularly the latter who was pretending to be bored by the process.

"And where was he?" Barney asked the obvious question.

"Who the hell knows?" Whitten answered. "I told the Feds we wanted to chat with Townsend too. When I observed that Townsend was our number one, our only suspect, they laughed and departed with their tails between their legs."

"Very funny," Cotton said. "After you inform the major that the Secretary of Homeland Security is missing, his wife is in hysterics, the White

House is involved, and we have a priority search underway, I will have something to say to this august group."

"Do you think the Honorable Secretary murdered the professor?" Barney asked with a straight face.

Cotton ignored the question.

"We definitely want to talk with Secretary Townsend when he reappears," Chase joined the discussion.

Cotton stared coldly at Mansfield while he digested the remark. Suddenly, he smiled as he realized the implications of what the Fairfax lieutenant had just said.

"Agreed," Cotton nodded. "Fairfax investigates the homicide, and we handle the secretary's disappearance. I'll give you a call when the secretary is ready to chat."

Whitten laughed. "Are you sure that won't strain the Bureau's resources? I've got ten bucks that says Townsend spent the night with a girlfriend and will arrive home exhausted with a terrible hangover by noon."

Cotton took his billfold from his picket, extracted a ten-dollar bill, and dropped it on Barney's desk. Whitten quickly placed two fives next to the ten.

"We can let the major hold the money," Whitten declared. He turned to his partner. "That's the easiest ten bucks I ever made."

"I'd like a little of the same, too," Pack said as he placed a ten dollar bill on the desk.

Cotton chuckled as he matched it. When he leaned back in his chair, Cotton looked at the two detectives and asked, "Do you think the secretary will arrive by taxi or will his girlfriend chauffeur him to his front door?"

"He'll arrive driving his own car," Whitten said. "His DHS detail said he drove his own car to George Mason and deliberately left them at home."

"That would be a neat trick. We found his little green Ford parked in the lot behind the professor's office. It has already been towed," Cotton smiled.

"The bet's off," Whitten said as he grabbed two of the tens from the desk and handed one to his partner. "You've been withholding valuable evidence from a Fairfax investigation."

Cotton stood up, retrieved his twenty dollars, and headed for the door where he paused and spoke to Chase. "Keep in touch. I've got a feeling we are going to be seeing a lot more of each other."

Chase nodded.

"And don't let the boys and girls from DHS agitate you unduly. They're new at the game and just lost their boss," Cotton said as he closed the door behind him.

Barney stared at the door only briefly before turning his attention back to his detectives. "Chase, do you want to start asking some questions now that we can get serious. If the Secretary of Homeland Security is really missing, and our dead professor was the last person to see him, the media is going to be all over our case."

"The leaks began too late for the morning papers, but the electronic media are already playing Chicken Little," Whitten said. "The satellite trucks were on campus when left to come here."

"Who do we have at the murder scene now?" Chase asked.

"Jane's minding the fort," Whitten said.

Chase nodded. Detective Jane Moscowitz was not his favorite person, but at least she was competent and tough. She would guarantee the site was closed tight and the media and the feds would not get a chance to contaminate it.

"What's the department head's name?" Chase asked.

"Doctor Wilfred Adams," Whitten replied after consulting his notebook. We only talked with him on the phone. His office is across the hall from the victim's. We planned on returning to Robinson Hall A this morning to interview him and anyone else there, students or faculty, who were present last night, and/or who could tell us something about Jesperson personally."

"I'll handle it," Chase said. "Who else did you interview?"

"We didn't interview Adams or anyone else," Whitten frowned. "There was no one in Robinson Hall or on campus at the time. The body wasn't found until after midnight, and the place was deserted. The maid and the campus cops knew nothing. We called Adams at home—he didn't appreciate our waking him out of a sound sleep—and after a brief chat agreed to continue the discussion at his office this morning."

"Did the fact that one of his professors had been murdered in his office concern him?" Chase smiled thinly as he asked his question.

"He said he was shocked. What would you expect him to say?" Whitten challenged, not liking Chase's attitude. "I already told you everything he told us."

"Don't get defensive, Whitten," Barney intervened before Chase could snap at him. "The lieutenant isn't criticizing your procedure, just trying to get a handle on where things stand."

"Major, we told you where things stand. We have a stiff, no leads, and the Feds and media crawling up our backsides," Whitten said.

"What do the techs and the coroner's office have to say?" Chase asked.

"We haven't had a chance to talk with them," Pack said. "The shooter used a .22 handgun, probably with a silencer because the maid who was in the building did not hear any shots. As best as we can tell, the place was deserted except for the maid, the victim, and of course the shooter. It's an office and classroom building not a dorm, so that's no surprise, given the time. Presumably, there was a pretty good crowd for the secretary's speech, but afterwards, according to the department head, Jesperson escorted his guest back to his office where they waited for the audience to clear."

"What time did the event end?" Chase asked.

Pack shrugged. "I'm sure there's a lot of people at Robinson Hall right now who can answer that question. There was sure nobody there when we arrived."

"Christ, I hope Jane is keeping the media out of Jesperson Hall and away from any potential witnesses," Chase said.

"Moscowitz knows the routine, and she has enough blue suits and the campus police to help her," Pack frowned.

Chase stood up. "I better get out there to make sure. Is there anything else you two can tell me?"

"We've been up all night, and we're beat," Whitten said. "You know everything we do, and the case is all yours. Good luck, you're going to need it. Just watch out for those Home Security stiffs."

Chase nodded. "I'm sure they're upset. Their principal went out without them and was last seen in the company of a homicide victim."

"You've got it," Whitten said. "All the same they're a pretty tough bunch and don't appear to be in a mood to listen or share."

"I doubt that we would be either if someone knocked off the chief or Barney," Chase laughed.

"The chief, I agree with you," Whitten chuckled. "But the major, that's something different. And you would be a cause for celebration."

Chase started for the door, and Barney called after him. "Keep me in the loop and let me know if you need anything."

Chase waved dismissively and closed the door behind him.

Whitten looked at his partner and then Barney. "This could get interesting. Mansfield has a unique style."

Pack laughed. “The media will love him.” After a slight hesitation he continued. “Cotton already does.”

Barney stared at Whitten and Pack. “You two get some sleep and leave this investigation with Chase.”

“With pleasure,” Whitten said as he pushed out of his chair.

Chapter 2

Chase paused at the entrance to the George Mason campus, flashed his credentials, and asked, "Is everything at Robinson Hall under control?"

The campus guard laughed. "Lieutenant, the media has it under siege. All the networks have satellite trucks on campus, and I'd estimate that at least fifty reporters are wandering about interviewing students, anyone who will talk with them, including each other."

"Is there any place nearby I can park?"

"Everything is chaotic; just leave it anyplace you want."

"I don't want to be towed."

"Try the staff lot at the end of the street."

Chase nodded, circled the campus, noted that the streets leading to Robinson Hall were jammed, and parked in Lot H as the guard suggested. He tossed his "Official Police Business" placard on the dash and started the short walk to his destination. Halfway there, he impulsively turned and entered a familiar building. On the second floor he tapped on a door and entered a small office where he found himself facing a familiar figure with her back to the door. He admired the shapely backside.

"Go away, I'm busy," Professor Barbara Jordan ordered without turning.

"Do you think it'll snow today?" Chase asked.

"Oh, shit," Jordan said without turning. "With you around, even in October, it probably will."

Chase waited. Barbara Jordan, a member of the English Department, was one of Chase's on and off intimate friends. Their relationship had been in an extended off phase for almost ten months, a consequence of Chase's involvement with a local attorney. Chase had mentioned snow in a feeble attempt at humor. Jordan had a morbid fear of snow in any form or amount, and a sudden West Virginia mountain storm had dropped a foot of the white stuff on them the previous December when Barbara had accompanied Chase on a spontaneous work/pleasure trip that had ended with a slippery return drive to Washington.

Finally, Jordan turned and confronted her visitor. "What are you doing here? Did you and Wacky Jacky finally come to your senses?" Barbara referred to Chase's current best friend, Jacky Rossi, the local defense attorney.

Chase knew better than touching the Jacky issue. "I was in the area and thought I would pay my respects to my best campus friend."

Barbara laughed. "Mansfield, you don't have any friends, not on campus or anyplace else. To know you is to despise you."

"I'm glad to see that you are in a good mood this morning, professor."

"Mood my ass. Nothing associated with me is any of your business, detective. Don't try to bullshit a bullshitter. You're in the neighborhood because of that," Barbara pointed a thumb in the direction of Robinson Hall. "I feared you might make an appearance. Why do you think I'm hiding in here behind a closed door?"

"I knocked."

"And I didn't invite you to come in. I saw you ambling down the street."

"You waved, and I didn't wave back. That's the reason for this hostile mood?"

"It's not a mood, and I didn't wave. I just don't like you."

"Anymore," Chase smiled. "I remember when…"

"Don't. I've cleansed my mind of all traces of you."

"I would be glad to help…"

"Please. Let me answer your questions so you can leave. I have a class starting in ten minutes and…" Barbara hesitated and smiled as she had a sudden thought. "And today we begin a section dealing with modern mystery writers. You wouldn't happen to know of any worth discussing, would you?"

Barbara was aware of Chase's Travis Crittenden avocation; one of his early books had been responsible for bringing them together. She had been researching a lecture on local authors.

"I'm helping out with the Robinson Hall thing," Chase said. "Did you by chance know Doctor Jesperson? I understand he was an author of some repute."

"My subject is American fiction. Doctor Jesperson was a serious writer of modern history." Barbara placed heavy emphasis on "serious writer" and smiled at Chase as she did so.

Chase ignored her petty effort to put him down. "How well did you know the good doctor?"

"Not intimately," Barbara said. "If you are interested in a list of my intimate friends, I have one here somewhere." She opened a desk drawer and pretended to search inside.

"I'm simply trying to find someone who knew Jesperson well enough to identify some of his friends and contacts," Chase said, weary of the fencing.

"I can't help you there, detective. I know, knew Doctor Jesperson by reputation, and I met him a few times, casually, at faculty receptions. That's all. I can't assist you, so leave."

"Could you point me in the direction of someone who might be of assistance," Chase persisted.

"Try the History Department in Robinson Hall. This is the English Department. You know the difference, don't you?"

Chase shook his head in frustration.

"I didn't think so," Barbara smiled as she pretended to take his head-shake as a negative response to her question. "In this department we treat with English as a subject. You know, rules of grammar, literature, all that good stuff. But, of course, that's not something that would interest a philosophy major and police detective like yourself. Certainly your prose indicates a complete disregard for grammar, style, and something called literature."

"What was your impression of Doctor Jesperson?" Chase persisted even though he knew he was wasting his time.

"He was a gentleman, polite, reserved, self-confident. Quite unlike some insecure and antediluvian males I have met."

"Don't you care if we catch his killer?"

"I do care, but I thought the shooter had already been identified. Isn't there a manhunt underway?"

"For whom?"

"For Secretary of Homeland Security James Howard Townsend."

"Where did you hear that absurdity?"

"Don't you ever watch television news?" Barbara smiled.

While Chase was trying to decide how to respond, Barbara stood up, turned off her computer, picked up a file from her desk, and strode past him. At the door she paused long enough to say, "Turn off the lights when you leave, Mansfield, and please don't take anything or I will have to call the cops."

Chase watched the door close behind her as he called, "Have a nice lecture, professor."

Chase exited the rear door of Barbara's building and made his way to the back of Robinson Hall. Since a phalanx of Fairfax uniformed police and campus security officers were keeping the media isolated in the front of the building, the area was relatively calm. Only a stream of students and faculty were allowed in the rear door. Chase flashed his credential case and followed the hall to the front door where he approached a uniformed Fairfax Officer who was blocking access.

"Where's Detective Moscowitz?" He asked.

"Crime Scene, second floor, lieutenant," the officer wearing sergeant's stripes answered. "Just follow the parade," he indicated a stream of uniforms and civilians flowing up and down the stairs to his right.

Chase climbed the stairs and was approaching a mid-floor office guarded by two sober faced patrolmen when he heard a loud, strident female voice.

"Detective, I don't care who you represent, it's time you learned that there's a big world out there where your rank, that of your chief, and all those petty little autocrats in between don't carry any more weight than a flea on a donkey's sorry ass." After a brief pause, the attack continued. "The fact that I moved the secretary's personal vehicle without your permission and its current whereabouts are none of your goddamned business. I will decide if and when you will have access to it."

Chase winked at one of the patrolmen who guarded the door and entered to find the speaker, an attractive brunette in her thirties, glaring at a scowling Detective Sergeant Jane Moscowitz. The two women, standing inches apart, ignored Chase.

"That's what you think, you skinny little bitch," an angry Moscowitz got personal.

Chase, who had his own problems with Detective Jane Moscowitz, listened with amusement, waiting to see how the brunette responded to that sally.

Moscowitz didn't give the brunette a chance; she took a deep breath and continued, "Without authority, you moved a critical piece of evidence, and if you don't tell me forthwith where it is, I'm going to charge you with obstructing a Fairfax County police investigation and have one of those uniforms you see in the hallway haul your sorry little ass off to the county jail."

Enjoying the moment, Chase silently watched, waiting to see how Moscowitz's protagonist handled that patently shallow threat. Moscowitz was not one of his favorites; their professional relationship was marked by a running bellicose confrontation that amused him more than it irritated him. He considered Moscowitz one of those who had exploited the tendency of today's working environment to overcompensate women for past professional injustice; unluckily for her, she had been too successful and had advanced one-step beyond her ability. Her unfortunate personality in no way qualified her for her current sergeant rank. Besides, one glance told him that her judgment had failed her in the current impasse. Her antagonist in no way qualified for the epithet skinny. Standing near the heavy-set, wide shouldered, overweight Moscowitz whose ill-fitting suit made her look like a linebacker in drag, the other woman projected the appearance of a professional model. Her expensive tailored blue suit and white blouse went well with the short hair, bright-blue eyes and attractive face. She looked more like a successful K Street lawyer than a government bureaucrat. She glanced at Chase and smiled before turning her focus back on Moscowitz.

"Sergeant, you can huff and puff if it makes you feel better," the woman said. "But the end result will be a phone call from the White House to your superiors and a reprimand and reassignment back to the traffic detail for you."

Chase silently applauded that threat. If implemented, it would do wonders for the CIB's morale in general and Chase's in particular.

"May I be of assistance, sergeant?" Chase announced his presence.

Moscowitz turned, glared at Chase, and muttered, "Shit, I should have expected you to show up; you are neither needed nor welcome."

Chase ignored Moscowitz and grinned at her protagonist. "I am Lieutenant Mansfield, and I am in charge of this investigation. I gather you two have a slight problem."

"Slight my ass," Moscowitz declared. "This..." She hesitated, forced herself to calm down a little, and continued. "This...I'm not sure what she is, but she claims to represent the Department of Homeland Security who..."

"Lieutenant, my name is Claris Gore," the brunette interrupted Moscowitz. "I'm a senior investigator assigned to the Department of Homeland

Security's Office of Security. I report to the DHS Chief of Staff who in turn reports to the secretary."

"I'm impressed Ms. Gore," Chase said, ignoring Moscowitz who muttered, "Big fucking deal."

"I am responsible for determining what happened to…for locating our missing secretary. We're concerned as is Mrs. Townsend, and, of course, President Featherstone," Gore smiled as she attempted to steamroller Chase.

"I'm sure Mrs. Townsend and the president are quite concerned," Chase said. "Are you confident that the secretary didn't decide to take a brief holiday from all the pressures of his important position, and somebody forgot to relay the message for him. If I'm not mistaken, he has only been out of touch for a few hours, certainly not the twenty-four hours that the law…"

"Don't be ridiculous, lieutenant," Gore interrupted. "The secretary is a man whose job keeps him on call twenty-four hours a day."

Chase nodded but did not react in time to keep Gore from continuing.

"But that's not a concern of yours. DHS is responsible for Secretary Townsend's security," Gore declared.

"I understand," Chase replied amiably, ignoring her offensive style. "Have you by chance coordinated your inquiry with Special Agent Cotton?"

"Cotton? Who the hell is he? And why should I coordinate anything with him? I assume Special Agent means he works for the Bureau."

"Yes," Chase said. "I was slightly delayed this morning because I was meeting with Special Agent Cotton to work out the parameters of his investigation. Special Agent Cotton," Chase rather enjoyed stressing the title because it seemed to distress Gore, "informed us that the White House had charged the Bureau with locating Secretary Townsend."

Gore took a deep breath before reacting.

"That's bullshit! You don't need to worry about that little bureaucratic misunderstanding. I will handle the search for Secretary Townsend, and I will deal with Special Agent Cotton who obviously overstated his position. The damned Bureau has a tendency to do that. If the Fairfax Police have any questions about Secretary Townsend, you can address them to me." Gore pulled a card from her suit coat pocket and handed it to Chase who reciprocated.

"I have no trouble with that," Chase smiled. "But I did work out a little jurisdictional agreement with Cotton," Chase dropped the Special Agent title to give Gore the impression he was agreeing with her.

"And what was that?" Gore demanded, her tone making it clear that Chase was not succeeding if he was trying to hustle her.

"That we would have no objection to the Bureau trying to locate their missing secretary as long as it did not impede our investigation of the murder of Doctor Jesperson which is a Fairfax police matter. Would agreeing to that allocation of responsibilities cause difficulty for you?"

"I don't give a shit about your little jurisdictional agreement with Cotton," Gore declared. "You can agree to anything you like as long as the Fairfax Police leave the search for Secretary Townsend to DHS."

"And you will deal with the Bureau?"

"Certainly," Gore smiled. "We can be sure the White House will give Cotton his marching orders."

"And you will assist us with our investigation as needed?" Chase asked.

"What does that mean?"

"Secretary Townsend was one of the last to talk with Doctor Jesperson last night in this very office," Chase said. "And we need to ask him a few questions about Doctor Jesperson's last hours."

"That will be a matter for Secretary Townsend to address," Gore did not commit herself.

Chase nodded agreeably.

"Since Professor Jesperson is in no position to reciprocate," Gore smiled in the direction of the chair behind Jesperson's desk to buttress her point. "I'll leave you to your investigation, lieutenant," Gore said, nodding coldly at Moscowitz before turning for the door.

"Oh there is just one more thing, Ms. Gore," Chase called after her.

Gore stopped and looked at Chase.

"I need access to Secretary Townsend's vehicle," Chase said.

"What on earth for, lieutenant?"

"We must determine if our victim was recently in the vehicle. It was prematurely removed from our crime scene. Surely, you can't object to that."

"I don't understand why the secretary's personal vehicle is of any pertinence to your investigation."

"We could easily get a warrant from a Fairfax judge," Chase said. "But I'm reluctant to do so. God knows what that media mob out front might do with that."

Gore glared at Chase, recognizing the not so implicit threat. "Oh very well," Gore acquiesced. "The vehicle is locked in the Townsend garage in McLean. I'll instruct the secretary's security team to give you access."

"That wasn't so difficult, was it?" Moscowitz muttered as Gore started for the door.

Gore ignored Moscowitz as she paused for a final shot at Chase. "But please don't harass Mrs. Townsend. She is quite distressed."

Chase made no commitment.

As soon as the door closed behind Gore, Chase turned to Moscowitz.

"Brief me."

"Have you talked with Packard and Whitten?" Moscowitz asked, not concealing her disinterest in doing what Chase ordered.

"Brief me," Chase repeated.

The fact that the surly Moscowitz didn't like him amused Chase, but he couldn't ignore her insubordination. He treated her coolly, refused to grant her a special respect solely because of her sex, something that Moscowitz seemed to expect, and demanded that she perform like her peers regardless of gender.

"I've only been on the scene for two hours. Packard and Whitten were here all night," Moscowitz retreated.

Chase waited.

"We don't have dog shit," Moscowitz capitulated. "Not a single suspect. As best as I can tell at this point, Jesperson was a weirdo who didn't have a friend, male or female."

"Certainly he had enemies, at least one," Chase referred to the shooter.

Moscowitz, missing Chase's point, shrugged. "He kept to himself."

"Not completely," Chase glanced at the chair behind the desk where Jesperson had died.

"Very funny."

"Who have you interviewed?" Chase persisted.

Moscowitz scowled as she consulted her notebook. "You've met Ms. Gore. I wasted a good half hour conferring with her. The department chairman is Doctor William Addams. He could only spare me five minutes. I have an appointment with him after his first class which is in session as we speak. I chatted briefly with Jesperson's graduate assistant. I suspect he spent more time with the victim than anyone else around here, but he also is in class. He's down the hall meeting with Jesperson's graduate seminar and has a quiz section later. I planned on tracking down the other members of the history faculty when Gore and then you descended on me."

"What did the techs find?"

"In here?" Moscowitz offered Chase her most sarcastic expression.

Chase waited.

"The body," Moscowitz smiled.

"What else?"

"Not much. The arms of that chair," she nodded in the direction of the solitary visitor's chair facing the desk, "was covered with prints. I doubt they will be of much use. Any prints the techs can identify will probably belong to nervous students."

"And Secretary Townsend and maybe the shooter," Chase said.

"There were two glasses on the desk. The techs took those with them. I predict they will find prints belonging to the secretary on one of them, if that is what you're worried about, and Jesperson on the other."

"I'm not worried. I'm just trying to get caught up."

"While making certain that the rest of us remember how to suck eggs," Moscowitz grumbled.

"Has anyone contacted Doctor Jesperson's next of kin?"

"We have yet to determine who that might be."

"I'll handle it," Chase said.

"I intend to meet with Addams, the department chairman, at ten," Moscowitz said, her tone daring Chase to react.

"Leave that to me," Chase said.

"Since you don't need me around here, I'll get back to headquarters where I am sure I can find some dishes to wash or floors to scrub," Moscowitz directly challenged Chase.

Chase assumed she quite predictably was getting ready to threaten him with a sexual harassment charge of some kind. That was Moscowitz's usual fallback position.

"No, you stay here and secure the crime scene."

"You've got enough help here, lieutenant; you don't need me. It's no secret you like to work unimpeded by marginal detectives like the rest of us."

Chase ignored the complaint about his investigative style. It was pure Moscowitz. "You take charge of the crime scene. I'm going to start moving around," Chase ordered.

"Do you want me to deal with that mob out there," Moscowitz nodded defiantly in the direction of the front of the building.

"No. We'll leave the media to public affairs. Give Sally a call," Chase said, referring to Sally Patrone, the Director of the Office of Public Affairs for the Fairfax Police Department.

"She will just say they'll want a briefing by the officer in charge of the investigation," Moscowitz complained. "That's you, allegedly."

"Tell Sally I said I'm busy. She can confer with Barney and the chief who might want to handle the formal briefing themselves."

"They'll need to know what you want them to say."

"Detective, when I know, I'll tell them. Let Sally stall the media for now. What is the name of Jesperson's graduate assistant?"

Moscowitz consulted her notebook. "Nicholas Dizekes."

"Know where his seminar is meeting?"

"No."

"Where is the history department office?"

"You don't know anything, do you?"

Chase waited.

"Directly across the hall," Moscowitz capitulated.

"Thank you."

"I thought you were intimately acquainted with this place," Moscowitz waspishly referred to Chase's past relationship with Barbara Jordan.

"Have you checked the desk and Jesperson's files?" Chase asked, ignoring Moscowitz's tasteless comment.

"You're kidding. There's a ton of paper in this place." She glanced at the two large file cabinets to the right of the desk and the loaded book shelves that lined the walls.

Chase waited.

"I glanced at the desk. There's a small address book in the top drawer." Moscowitz watched Chase step behind the desk. He did not sit in the chair where they had found the victim. "But I don't think you will find it very useful," Moscowitz smiled thinly. "It only has a handful of names in it."

Chase, still standing, opened the drawer and took out the small notebook that was right in the front."

"You can sit in the chair, if you're not squeamish," Moscowitz said as she turned for the door. "The techs are finished in here."

Chase sat down. Before he could open the address book and as Moscowitz was reaching for the knob, someone rapped on the door. A uniformed patrolman, one of the two who controlled access to the crime scene, opened it and poked his head in.

"There's a guy out here who wants to see the sergeant," he spoke to Chase and nodded in Moscowitz's direction.

"Let him in," Chase answered.

A young man in his mid-twenties with long, shaggy hair, a Mediterranean nose, and a worried expression materialized.

"You told me to report back as soon as I finished with the seminar," he addressed Moscowitz.

"This is Doctor Jesperson's assistant," Moscowitz announced for Chase's benefit.

"That will be all, sergeant," Chase dismissed Moscowitz. "Come in, I'm Lieutenant Mansfield, and I'm in charge of the investigation," Chase smiled at the nervous assistant.

"Sir, my name is Nicholas Dizekes, and I am, was, Doctor Jesperson's graduate assistant."

Chase waved in the direction of the chair facing the desk and waited for Moscowitz to depart. She glanced at Dizekes and then at Chase, obviously preferring to remain to hear whatever the assistant had to say. Chase did not invite her to do so, and she finally turned and departed, slamming the door behind her.

"Who did this terrible thing?" Dizekes asked with a tremble in his voice as he sat down.

"That's what we hope you can help us learn, Mr. Dizekes. I understand you were close to Doctor Jesperson."

"I worked for him. I wouldn't say we were close," Dizekes said.

"I know how that is," Chase said, trying to relax the nervous young man. "As hard as it may be to believe, I was once a graduate assistant myself."

"Here? In the history department?"

"No, in the philosophy department at William and Mary," Chase chuckled. Most found the idea of a cop with a philosophy major background amusing. Chase did not, but he pretended he did, and he used the ostensible absurdity of the concept to establish rapport with a witness when feasible.

Dizekes smiled. "A philosophy major," he said. "What made you decide to…" Dizekes hesitated.

"...become a cop," Chase completed the obvious question for him. "It's a big leap and a long story; we'll have to save it for another time," Chase said, ending the rapport building phase. "We're having a little difficulty identifying the professor's close friends and confidants," Chase jumped to the subject that interested him. "This isn't very helpful," Chase held up the little address book without admitting he had not even opened it.

"Doctor Jesperson was a very private person. I don't think he had many friends," Dizekes squirmed in his chair, and he spoke softly, clearly not wanting to be heard saying anything that might be construed as critical of his advisor.

"Not even close associates on the faculty?"

Dizekes shook his head negatively. "No sir. Doctor Jesperson spent most of his time at his desk or in a library somewhere, usually here or at the Library of Congress. He's only been back from his sabbatical since May."

"His sabbatical?"

"Yes, he stayed almost a year in Iran doing research for his new book, and since he returned he has been busy writing. He even ate his lunch at the desk. Between you and me," Dizekes leaned forward. "Some of his students had begun to complain. They resented me filling in for the professor at his seminars. You know, they felt that they were paying for him and getting only a graduate assistant, me."

"How many classes did the professor teach?" Chase asked, wondering if it would be worthwhile questioning the students. He was not confident that Dizekes was going to be much help. Chase suspected that Dizekes was another loner like his mentor.

"Only two seminars, three times a week each."

"Six hours a week? That's good work if you can get it. Obviously, I chose the wrong profession." Chase smiled, and Dizekes relaxed slightly before Chase hit him with his next question. "How did Jesperson get along with the students?"

"They all respected him, except for the problem I mentioned—you know, the professor skipping classes so to speak--and they like, liked, being able to brag about having earned a place in one of his seminars. Professor Jesperson didn't accept everyone, just the A students. Like everyone else around here, they were looking forward to reading his new book. We all assumed it would be a best seller and to be honest wanted to bask in his glory."

"Did he discuss the book?"

"With me?" The question seemed to surprise the nervous young man. "Of course, I worked on it every day."

"Really? Did you write any of the chapters? I know a lot of professors use their assistants to do a lot more than basic research."

"Oh no. I researched some of the historical chapters, but Jesperson, Doctor Jesperson, did all the writing."

"You didn't do any first drafts?"

"No, sir. I proof read everything, just for typos and spelling, that sort of thing."

"Is there an advance copy I can read?" Chase asked.

"Oh no," Dizekes reacted. "Doctor Jesperson was quite clear about that. Nobody was to have access until the release date."

"But you worked on the book."

"Only the drafts, and not every chapter. Three of the key chapters Jesperson let nobody see. I only read them once without permission when Doctor Jesperson went to class and forgot to shut down his computer. He said they were too sensitive to allow others to read them in advance."

"Sensitive, but he included them in his book?"

The young man nodded.

"Then other people had to have access to the key chapters, the ones with the sensitive information."

Dizekes frowned. "I'm not lying, sir."

"I don't doubt you, son," Chase said. "I refer to those in the business, not here, his agent, publisher, editor, printers."

After a pause, Dizekes nodded. "You're correct. I misspoke, but I know that Jesperson refused to let the agent or publisher release advance copies to journalists, that kind of thing, to promote advance sales. He said they weren't happy about it, but he was adamant."

"What was so sensitive?"

Dizekes hesitated and squirmed. "I'm not sure I can tell you, lieutenant. The professor felt very strongly about it."

"If the material was so sensitive, don't you think its release might have provided a motive for someone to do what happened here? I would hate to have to arrest you as a material witness and take you to headquarters and force you to answer my questions." Chase regretted having to pressure the young man, but he needed to know what was in the book. Its content represented the first hint of a motive for the shooting.

"I can say that certainly the Iranian Government is not going to like the book," Dizekes equivocated. "And I am sure that our own government will be anxious to read those chapters. They scared me."

"That's interesting," Chase said, wondering if gaining access to the book's information was why the Secretary of Homeland Security had visited Jesperson. "Now show me a draft of the book. There has to be a draft copy somewhere."

"I don't have a copy. I assume it's still on that computer," he nodded at the credenza behind Chase, but I don't know the password."

"How did you work on it?"

"Professor Jesperson would make a copy of whatever chapter he wanted me to work on and send it to my computer. I was not allowed to keep a copy or print one out. I made my suggested corrections and sent the chapter back to him. Then, I had to delete it from my computer."

"And you never made a copy for yourself? Tell me the truth."

"I am, sir. There was no reason for me to keep a copy. Besides, I never had the sensitive chapters."

"I need to know what was in them," Chase pressed.

"Why don't you call his agent or the publisher? They have to be told what happened. Maybe they won't want to release the book now."

"Nicholas," Chase used the young man's name for the first time. "I'll call them. That's a good idea. Who are they and what are their numbers?"

"I'm sure they are in that address book," Dizekes said. "I've seen the professor check it before calling them. Want me to look for you?"

Chase handed the address book to Dizekes. He quickly found the names and pointed them out to Chase.

"Now tell me what was in those chapters, Nicholas, or I will have to call Detective Moscowitz back in here and have her take you in and charge you. That's not something you will enjoy." Chase leaned back in his chair and waited.

As fate would have it, Moscowitz opened the door without knocking at that very moment. "Will you be much longer? I need to talk with you," Moscowitz said.

Chase looked at Nicholas who turned, glanced at the sour faced Moscowitz, and then back at Chase. "OK, I'll tell you" Dizekes capitulated.

"Give me a few more minutes, detective," Chase said.

An irritated Moscowitz slammed the door behind her.

"You made a good decision, Nicholas," Chase said. "Detective Moscowitz has a terrible temper.

"The Iranians have the bomb and Jesperson's sources told him that they are preparing to use it," Dizekes blurted.

"What bomb? Against whom?" Chase sat up straight.

"An atomic bomb," Dizekes said. "Against us."

"That's not very good news," Chase said, concealing his real reaction with bland words. Dealing with foreign governments and atomic bomb threats were way out of his league, but if Dizekes's allegations were true they certainly explained Homeland Security and FBI interest in Jesperson.

"Do you have any idea how reliable the professor's sources were?" Chase asked the first question that popped into his mind.

"I just know what I told you because I once scanned those chapters. I never did it again because I was afraid Jesperson would fire me if he caught me. We never discussed sources, but I assume they were reliable. Doctor Jesperson was a very careful researcher."

"And that's all you know."

"Yes sir, but I'll tell you one thing. After reading those chapters I always kept a close eye on those Iranians in the foreign students club."

"Are you a member?"

"No sir, but Doctor Jesperson, who was the club's advisor, used to have me help with the schedule for meetings and planning for speakers, but I never attended meetings. They don't invite American students to participate, not that anyone wants to bother."

"Do you have a list of members?"

"The professor has a club file in there," Dizekes pointed at one of the two file cabinets.

"Is there anything else about that book that you can tell me?"

"Not about those chapters. You'll have to ask his agent or publisher or wait until next Wednesday and buy a copy. Jesperson said his agent was confident it was going to be a best seller, and he warned the professor he was going to be busy dealing with the media and the government."

"Did the professor have a friend or faculty associate he might have discussed the book's content with?" Chase asked.

Dizekes shook his head. "I know more than any of the professors, and Jesperson didn't have any friends that I know of."

"No girl friends?"

"Not to my knowledge."

"Who might be able to answer these questions?"

"Just me."

"Where did Jesperson live?"

"He had a condominium on Waples Mill Road just off Route 50."

Chase opened the desk drawer, took out a pad and ballpoint, and slid them toward Dizekes who grabbed them and wrote down the address.

"What do you know about his family background?" Chase asked as Dizekes was writing.

Dizekes looked up. "His father and mother are still alive. His father is a Professor Emeritus of MIT, and they live in Cambridge. His mother is the Iranian connection. She was born in Iran but attended school here, at Wellesley, met his father through a roommate, married him, and moved here. I met them both once. She said she has an extended family in Iran, and I always suspected they are the ones who helped with the research."

"The bomb business?"

"I don't know, but as I said he spent last year in Iran."

"Why didn't you tell me this when I asked about sources?"

Dizekes shrugged. "You just asked me if I thought they were reliable, and I answered honestly. I never met them and don't know how reliable they are."

Chase stared at Dizekes but said nothing. Chase nodded his head as he privately acknowledged that he was the one who had asked the wrong question. Moving on without admitting that this was not the first time, Chase asked, "Do you know where the parents live in Cambridge?"

Dizekes shrugged.

Chased checked the small phone book and found a number for the parents and tossed it back on the desk.

"Is there anything else you think I should know?" Chase asked.

Dizekes shook his head. "Please don't tell anybody I told you about that bomb business," he pleaded.

"Don't worry, I won't," Chase said. "You can imagine what the media outside would do with that kind of sensational allegation, and neither of us need that hanging over our heads. I will want to talk with you again later. Don't leave town."

"Don't worry. I'm still working on my dissertation and will be slaving here for another year," Dizekes said. "Can I go now?"

Chase waved a hand in dismissal. As Dizekes approached the door, Chase called after him. "If you see Detective Moscowitz out there, ask her to come in."

Dizekes hurriedly left the room. The door had just closed behind him, and Chase was reaching for the phone when the door reopened and a frowning Moscowitz appeared.

"What?" She demanded.

"What yourself, detective," Chase answered. "Did you have something on your mind?" He referred to her earlier interruption.

"Yes. How much longer do I have to waste my time hanging around out here in the hallway?"

"You can sit down in that chair if you wish," Chase smiled as he pointed at the chair Dizekes had just vacated. "What did you learn from the victim's colleagues?"

"Not a damned thing, lieutenant," Moscowitz muttered as she lowered her bulky frame into the chair.

"Because?"

"Because they are all busy elsewhere. At least their offices are empty. I talked with the department chairman who claims he told Packard and Whitten everything he knows. The vic was a loner who had no friends, spent all of his time on his research, and that you were talking with the only person who was even minimally close with him. I interrupted because I expected you to invite me to join you like any partner should."

"I don't have a partner, Sergeant Moscowitz, certainly not you, and you know that, so quit whining."

"I'm not whining; I'm just stating the truth" Moscowitz challenged Chase.

Chase smiled but did not respond.

"Since you are so damned independent—I would describe it differently myself--you don't need me here," Moscowitz continued her tirade. "I'm returning to headquarters where I will ask the major to reassign me."

"Stay where you are," Chase ordered. "I'm going to make two phone calls, one to the next of kin to inform them of what happened, and one to Jesperson's book agent in New York. You may listen if you wish."

"So I can learn how it's done," Moscowitz said sourly.

"Then I will leave you in charge of the crime scene where you can act like an investigating officer while I visit the victim's residence to see what I can learn there. Later, we can meet to share information, if you have no objections. If acting like a detective doesn't satisfy your career ambitions, I'm confident that, like that DHS lady, I can arrange for your return to the traffic patrol."

Moscowitz glared her response at the waiting Chase but did not speak. She remained seated, however.

Chase reached for the phone and dialed the Cambridge home of Jesperson's parents.

"Hello," a deep male voice answered on the fourth ring.

"Professor Jesperson?" Chase asked.

"You are calling from my son's office. Who am I speaking with?" Jesperson asked.

Chase hesitated, never comfortable with informing a family member that a loved one had died precipitously. "Professor Jesperson, I am Lieutenant Mansfield, a Fairfax police officer."

"Has something happened to my son?" Jesperson demanded.

"I apologize for having to contact you in this manner, but I must advise you that your son, Doctor Thomas Jesperson, was found dead in his office early this morning." Chase paused, waiting for a reaction. A heavy silence followed.

"Professor..." Chase said. He heard the shocked father take a deep breath. In the background, a woman's voice sounded. "Terrence, what is wrong?"

"What happened?" Jesperson asked, apparently not replying to his wife's question.

"We don't know exactly," Chase said. "A cleaning lady found him slumped in his chair."

"You identified yourself as a police lieutenant," Jesperson declared sharply. "Are you involved because his death was not due to natural causes?"

"Yes sir, he was shot twice by a party or parties unknown."

"Did he suffer?"

"That is difficult for me to say, sir, but he was shot once in the head and once in the chest. I would say no."

"God-damn-it,' Jesperson reacted angrily. "It was that damned book. I knew this was going to happen. I told him to be careful."

Chase heard a woman shout, "Something has happened to Thomas."

"Lieutenant, I'll call you back in a few minutes," Jesperson said and hung up.

Chase put the phone down and stared at Moscowitz who had a silly smirk on her face. The expression irritated him, but he ignored it. He was in no mood to quibble with her over her facial expressions.

"These calls are never easy," Moscowitz surprised him by commiserating with him. "I assume he did not take it well."

The words suggested that Moscowitz's odd expression had been simply a nervous reaction. "Would you?" Chase asked. Still irritated by her previous unprofessional behavior, Chase did not share the professor's angry comment about having anticipated something like this happening. "He said he would call back. His wife was present, and he had to share the bad news with her."

"What now?" Moscowitz asked.

"While you interview the other staff members and students who knew Doctor Jesperson, particularly those who were in the building last night, I will call his agent and publisher."

"May I ask why?"

"The professor's new book is scheduled for release for next week, and I want to know if the pending event has generated any controversy."

Moscowitz nodded and started for the door.

"Don't bother questioning Dizekes, his graduate assistant," Chase called after her.

Moscowitz stopped immediately and stared at Chase.

"I've already started his debriefing, so leave him to me," Chase said, not bothering to answer Moscowitz's unspoken question.

She waited for Chase to explain, but he picked up the address book and ignored her.

Finally, a frowning Moscowitz departed.

Chase found a listing under the D's, Doris Dunlop, agent, NYC. He dialed the number, and it was answered promptly by a high-pitched male voice. "Dunlop Agency."

"May I speak with Ms. Dunlop please?" Chase said. The male's very effeminate voice threw him off stride.

"Who is calling, please?"

"This is Lieutenant Mansfield of the Fairfax police."

"Where in the world is Fairfax?" The man asked with an amused lilt.

"Fairfax, Virginia," Chase replied curtly.

"Oh my, I've never heard of it. May I ask, sir, the nature of your call?"

"A private matter," Chase replied.

"Oh dear," the man said. "Are you sure I can't help you?"

The man's tone made Chase wonder if he were trying to flirt with him, a thought that irritated him even more.

"I need to talk with Ms. Dunlop personally," Chase said.

"If you are calling about a book, I'm sure I could serve you, sir," the man said.

"This is an official call. Please put Ms. Dunlop on line," Chase ordered.

"Oh well, if you insist," the man giggled and put Chase on hold.

A long two minutes later, a woman came on line. "Doris Dunlop, how can I assist you, Lieutenant Mansfield? I should warn you that we are not currently taking on any new clients."

"As I informed your secretary this is an official police call," Chase said.

Dunlop surprised him by laughing. "Don't let Charles' manner offend you, lieutenant. He likes to flirt with all my male callers. I assure you. He's harmless."

"Ms. Dunlop," Chase ignored the frivolous comment. "I understand that Doctor Thomas Jesperson is one of your clients."

"If you are from the media or the government and playing games with me, Mansfield, I'm not interested. I have already made it perfectly clear that Thomas's book will be released next Wednesday and not before."

Sensing that she was about to hang up on him, Chase said, "Ms. Dunlop, wait. I am a police officer, and I have something of extreme importance to discuss with you that may impact on the book release."

"I'm sure Charles told you that we are not taking on any more clients, Mr. Mansfield."

Chase hesitated, briefly wondering if Dunlop was so self-centered that she did not focus on a word he said.

"Well?" Dunlop demanded.

"I am sitting behind Doctor Jesperson's desk holding his phone as we talk," Chase said, testing to see if Dunlop were listening.

"Good for you, lieutenant. Let me speak with Thomas directly. If you are harassing him about a parking ticket or speeding, I assure you that Thomas did not do it. That simply is not his style."

"I regret to say, Ms. Dunlop, that you cannot speak directly with Doctor Jesperson. That is why I am calling."

"Oh don't worry. I will handle any fine. Just put him on line. I don't have the time to play games with you. If that is what you want to do, I'll put Charles back on the phone."

"Ms. Dunlop, Doctor Jesperson was found dead in his office early this morning with two bullets in him," Chase said bluntly.

A brief silence greeted that declaration. "Was it suicide?" Dunlop finally asked.

"One shot to the head and a second to the chest indicate otherwise," Chase said.

"Who did it?" Dunlop demanded.

"That is what I'm trying to determine. Can you help me?"

"Oh Christ, it's got to be that damned book. Poor Thomas. This is going to lift it right to the top of the *Times* best seller list. Look, I can't say it has been pleasant talking with you, lieutenant, but this just makes me busier than before. I've got to talk with the publisher. Thank God the printer has the book ready for immediate release."

"Ms. Dunlop, I can't help you with that, but I need you to answer a few questions for me."

"I don't have the time, lieutenant. Call me tomorrow. Better yet, come and see me when it's convenient."

"Who's publishing the book?" Chase asked.

"Wilson & Wilson. I'm sure you've heard of them."

Chase had. Wilson & Wilson was a top three publisher who along with its two competitors had rejected Chase's early attempts to get his own first book in print. Thinking about those rejections still made him angry.

"Who at Wilson & Wilson is handling Doctor Jesperson's book?" Chase asked.

"Clarence Fisher. Who else?"

Chase had never heard of the man. He hadn't got past the secretaries who answered the phone and who sent the form reject letters along with the unread manuscripts submitted by unknown, aspirant authors.

"Goodbye,' Dunlop said curtly.

"Ms. Dunlop, what in the book was sensational enough to inspire someone to murder Doctor Jesperson?"

"Great question, lieutenant. You are going to have to do what everyone else will have to do, buy a copy, and read it. Thomas expressly ordered me to hold all comment until the release date. If I answered your question I would lose my best author."

"You've already lost him. Now help me apprehend his killer."

"You do your job, lieutenant, and I will do mine."

"I'll subpoena you."

"Good luck. Talk to my lawyer, and he'll brief you on the Bill of Rights, free speech, and all that good stuff."

"Where should I start my investigation?" Chase sounded too contrite for his own ears.

"I would start with Iran," Dunlop said and hung up.

"Iran's a big country and far away," Chase complained to the dead receiver.

Chase leaned back in the chair and looked around the room wondering what to do next. He needed to talk with the father, but he wanted to give him a little time to recover from the initial shock and to console his spouse. Before he could decide what to do in the interim, the door opened and Moscowitz again intruded.

"I talked with a couple of his seminar students, and they didn't know dickshit about the professor's personal life. According to them, Jesperson was a monk whose only interest was his research," Moscowitz said. "They didn't have a clue about possible boyfriends or any of that good stuff. How did you make out with the agent?"

"I got nowhere," Chase admitted. "She was so excited about the murder and how it would help sales that she didn't have time to chat."

"Did you mention the big secret?" Moscowitz asked.

"Big secret?"

"Wait until she hears about the Secretary of Homeland Security's involvement and disappearance."

'What do you mean involvement?" Chase asked, not willing to admit he had lost Townsend's disappearance somewhere in the back of his mind. "Do you know something I don't?"

"They towed Townsend's car out of here, and he was one of the last if not the last person to see the good professor sitting in that chair you now occupy. So where is he? And how did he get there."

"Townsend's disappearance is none of our business. It's a federal matter," Chase said.

"Until one of us comes up with information that indicates he was the shooter. That would make him our perp no matter what the Feds want or think."

"Let's take this one step at a time," Chase frowned. "We concentrate on the professor. You interview his colleagues and students."

"And what are you going to do while I spin my wheels?"

"I'm waiting for the father to call me back. Then, …" Chase hesitated, not sure what to say next. A sudden thought struck him. "And then I'm going to visit the victim's home. Who has his keys and wallet?"

"I do," Moscowitz smiled. "They are in plastic bags in my briefcase in the trunk of my car which is parked right out front under police guard."

"Bring the wallet and keys to me," Chase ordered.

"Do you want me to come with you to his place?"

"Just get me the wallet and keys and then concentrate on your interviews here."

Moscowitz frowned and departed. Chase noted that this time she did not slam the door, possibly a sign she was getting her temper under control, a very dubious omen.

Chase was sitting at the professor's desk examining the contents of the wallet when the phone rang.

"Hello," Chase answered.

"Lieutenant Mansfield?" The senior Jesperson asked.

Chase smiled, pleased that the father had remembered that Chase was waiting in his son's office.

"Yes, sir," Chase said.

"Where is my son now?" Jesperson immediately got to the important stuff.

"He is now at the Coroner's Office. If you like, I can have them contact you, sir."

"When can we have him?" Jesperson demanded. "We of course want him returned to Cambridge."

"I will make sure that the coroner's office is cooperative. It will, of course, be a few days."

"Just a minute," Jesperson said, and Chase listened as the distraught father softly briefed his wife.

"Now, how can I help you?" Jesperson asked when he returned his attention to Chase who was impressed with the old man's composure.

"Just before we ended our last conversation, you mentioned your son's book," Chase said. "You said you warned your son about something in the book."

"Yes, have you read it?"

""No."

"Well I have. Thomas sent me the printer's proof copy. Would you like me to send it to you?"

"Yes sir. Please send it by registered priority mail. Address it to:

Lieutenant Chase Mansfield
Criminal Investigations Bureau
4100 Chain Bridge Road
Fairfax, Virginia 22030

The professor noted the address and read it back to Chase.

"It's important lieutenant and you should read it immediately," the professor said.

"I will, sir," Chase promised.

"I will FedEx it as soon as I get off the phone," Jesperson said.

"I apologize for putting you to the trouble at this difficult time," Chase said. "I know you and your wife need some quiet time."

"Don't worry about that," Jesperson said. "You concentrate on finding my son's killer. Anything we can do to help, we will."

"That's right. Make sure he understands we will do anything to help," Mrs. Jesperson said in the background.

"Did you hear that?" Jesperson asked Chase.

"I did. Please assure your wife that catching your son's murderer is my number one priority."

"I'll hold you to that son, particularly after you read the book. Remember, just tell us if we can help."

Chase thought briefly about asking about the younger Jesperson's relationship with Secretary of DHS Townsend but decided against opening that subject at this time. Instead, he asked about the book.

"Could you summarize any passages in the book that you think might have provoked the attack on your son? Surely the killer couldn't have thought that killing your son at this stage would have kept the book out of print and the public view."

"You are very perceptive, lieutenant. The book, damn it, will be an instant best seller. If Thomas had discussed it with me, I would have ordered him to give his information to the government. I don't know what he was thinking."

"What worried you most about the book?"

"Thomas obviously had sources in Iran in a position to report on the Iranian Government's nuclear research. The bastards without question have the bomb and intend to use it."

"Did your son say where or when?"

"Not explicitly. His sources appear to be somewhere in the research end of things. Clearly they have the bomb. Where and how the government intends to use it remains a question. My son and his sources speculate that it will be either against Israel or here in Washington or both."

"Jesus. How can the publisher sit on this information?" Chase asked.

"My son told me that he had given them explicit written instructions on the book's release."

"Why didn't he share his information with his government?"

"I am embarrassed to say I do not know. We did not discuss any of this bomb business. I received the printer's proof copy only yesterday; spent the night reading it, and did not have a chance to discuss it with him. I planned to do that today."

"Professor, this is too important to wait for the mail. Would you object if I asked the FBI to ask their local office to visit you, retrieve the book, and hand-carry it to Washington?"

"Fine by me."

"Professor, I will have more questions for you. If you don't object, I will phone you later in the day. Now, I should contact the Bureau."

"Good," Jesperson said and hung up.

Chase took out the card Special Agent Cotton had given him, dialed Cotton's cell phone, briefed him succinctly on his conversation with the senior Jesperson, and hung up realizing that by putting the book in Bureau hands he had lost the opportunity to be the first to read it. He also assumed he had lost complete control of a potentially important facet of his murder investigation.

Chase resumed his examination of the wallet, noted it contained three hundred and twenty dollars, three credit cards, and a Virginia driver's license. Clearly, robbery had not been a motive. Since the shooter had used a silencer and ignored the cash and credit cards, Chase doubted that the perpetrator had been a simple student. Unless...unless, he considered that thought for a moment. Unless the student had a more personal motive, a perceived slight like a bad grade, a denigrating comment in front of others, an unwanted sexual advance, or was acting at the behest of others. That thought brought Chase back to the father's comments about Iran and the yet to be released book. Recognizing that he did not have enough information to reach any kind of conclusion about the shooter's motive, Chase stuffed Jesperson's wallet in his pocket and stood up, still holding the car keys in his hands. He looked about the office, thought about the file cabinets and the computer, and decided to leave them to Moscowitz and her crew.

Chase exited Robinson Hall via the route he had entered, avoiding the clamor of the media in the front. At the back door, he greeted two Fairfax uniformed officers who were chatting with a member of the university security force.

"Where do the faculty members park their cars?" Chase asked the George Mason officer.

"Lot H to your right," the officer replied.

Chase expressed his thanks and turned right. He was relieved to note that the media had been effectively contained on the other side of

Robinson and the only street traffic he encountered were students apparently preoccupied with their own problems as they made their way to morning classes.

Chase had no trouble finding Lot H; that was where he had parked the Prius. The lot was only half filled, but Chase hesitated at the entrance.

"Dumb shit," he grumbled. He had been so pleased with having escaped Robinson Hall without encountering the media that he hadn't taken the trouble to find out what kind of car that Jesperson drove. He considered returning but quickly dismissed the thought. He took Jesperson's keys from his pocket, was disappointed to note that they carried no identifying seals, and was turning to retrace his steps when he noted that the ignition key was one of those that contained three buttons, lock, unlock, and alarm.

Chase smiled and pressed the alarm button. A horn obediently sounded near the end of the second row. Chase immediately headed in that direction, twice pressing the button, until he identified the responding vehicle, a top of the line, late model Lexus, not bad wheels for a university professor.

Chase pressed the unlock button and climbed behind the wheel. The Lexus surprised him. It was unlittered and spotless. The rear seat appeared unused, and only one thick book rested on the front seat. Chase picked it up and read the title, *The Rise of Nuclear Iran: How Iran Defies the West* by Dore Gold. Those words gave Chase pause. After a few seconds, he decided the book represented routine background research. *Don't jump to conclusions!* He cautioned himself. *Let the Feds worry about national security. Your job is to identify the shooter.*

He opened the glove compartment. It contained two items, a small flashlight and a plastic folder. He shook his head as he thought of his Prius's dashboard compartments stuffed full with old maps, copies of billings for past visits to service centers and inspection stations, outdated letters from his insurance company, directions to God knows where, stale candy bars, detritus of an indifferent owner. Jesperson, by contrast, had been a neat freak, a fussy bachelor. Chase wondered what that meant to his investigation and decided nothing; it indicated only that the professor had preferred an ordered life. Chase opened the plastic folder. It contained the vehicle registration; the car was two years old, and Thomas Hamid Jesperson was listed as the sole owner. Chase assumed that made Jesperson appear rather sad and lonely until he remembered that was exactly how his registration read; he immediately dismissed his initial conclusion about Jesperson's personality. Preferring to live alone did not make him a misanthrope, a person to be pitied. Chase leafed through the old insurance cards before carefully returning the case and its contents back to the dashboard compartment exactly as he had found them, case on the bottom and flash on top, squarely aligned. Chase lowered the sun visors, checked the door pockets, popped the trunk lid and climbed out. The Lexus looked brand new, not two years old. All it lacked was the new car smell. If he didn't like his Prius so much, Chase would have considered offering to take it off the older Jesperson's hands.

The trunk like the car's interior was immaculate. The mat appeared new without a trace of lint or dirt accumulated over time from past loads. Chase lifted the cover under the mat and found a small chest of new tools and a spare tire that had never touched the road. Chase shook his head, closed the trunk, retrieved the book from the front seat with the intention of checking out what Jesperson was reading at the time of his death, relocked the car, and made his way back to his Prius.

His passage went unnoted by the media whose eyes were concentrated on the front door of Robinson Hall and each other.

Chapter 3

Chase, following the directions given him by Dizekes, Jesperson's graduate assistant, had no difficulty locating the professor's Waples Mill condominium. The building appeared to be relatively new, and the sign out front advertised apartments starting at $350,000. Chase assumed that meant a one-bedroom model with larger versions going for up to $600,000, a range he considered fairly reasonable for a full professor. He knew that his friend Barbara, who was an associate professor in the George Mason English Department, had paid $500 thousand for her townhouse in Fairfax.

The lobby was clean and well maintained but had no reception desk and no doorman. Chase took the elevator to the sixth floor, the penthouse level, and easily found 604. Like the entrance, the hallway was deserted, and Chase assumed that most of the residents were working couples. At least, he saw no sign of children, another plus in his mind. Chase unlocked the door and entered to find himself in a large room that served as a combination living and dining combo. A polished, round, dark wood table with six chairs set immediately to his left under an imposing crystal chandelier. A fabric covered couch and two end tables were separated from a bookcase and two matching chairs by a shiny five-foot mahogany coffee table. The bookcase was filled neatly with books, but the coffee table, like the dining room table, was bare. Two oversized brass lamps dominated the end tables. The far wall had a ceiling to floor glass window with a door at one end that led out to a balcony that overlooked a wooded area filled with hundred-year old oak trees. Chase admired the view if not the pristine furnishings before turning to the doorway on his right that led to a kitchen and an adjacent sunroom. A large bar with a granite top separated the kitchen from the sunroom that the professor had obviously used as his den. The kitchen, again uncluttered and shiny clean, had aluminum faced appliances and dark wood cabinets. The walls of the sunroom were lined with floor to ceiling bookcases. A single leather recliner faced a large high definition television set. A table lamp stood next to the chair; a solitary remote cluttered the lamp's table.

Despite having cautioned himself to reserve judgment, Chase decided that the professor was a highly disciplined neatness freak. Every item in every room clearly had its place. The apartment looked like a model not a home for a bachelor. Obviously, Jesperson had washed every dish and restored every possession to its assigned location before leaving for the office. Moving on, Chase checked out the master bedroom. Like the kitchen, the order there was impressive. The bed was made with military attention to detail. He lifted the spread and was not surprised to find the starched sheets tightly anchored under the mattress. Chase wondered where the professor parked his feet.

Chase opened the drawer on the bedside stand expecting to find a weapon of some sort. Chase kept a well-oiled but never fired thirty-eight, a gift from his father, within easy reach. He found Jesperson's drawer empty. The walk-in closet reflected the owner's fastidiousness. A row of suits were carefully aligned an exact one inch apart. Even the shirts and slacks showed the same discipline. Chase, whose own style ran to informal indifference, shook his head in amazement. Returning to the bedroom, he opened the top two drawers of the dresser. Carefully rolled socks and neatly folded T-shirts and boxer shorts were exactly where Chase expected to find them, all in a tight parade formation.

Ignoring the bottom two drawers, Chase continued on to the second bedroom which Jesperson had converted into a home office. Tall bookcases lined three walls, leaving space only for a small closet. The fourth wall had two large windows framed by green drapes. A credenza with two desktop computers and an oblong monitor supported by the usual peripherals, a keyboard, mouse, modem, router, printer/copier, and Belkin switch, stood in front of the windows. A massive desk and leather covered executive quality chair with a high back faced the door. Chase opened the closet and found it completely occupied by a file cabinet. He tugged at a drawer, but it did not budge. Chase shrugged indifferently, assuming that the key was hidden in a desk drawer. Not interested in wading through reams of paper detailing Jesperson's finances and daily routines, Chase had reached the point in his professional career where he cheerfully delegated such tedious tasks to others with personalities equipped to deal with minutiae. He made a mental note to place a detailed apartment search next on Detective Moscowitz's agenda.

Chase sat down at the desk, opened the laptop which set directly in front of him, and turned it on. While it started up, he coaxed the two desktop computers on the credenza to do the same. He glanced out the window as he waited and again admired the view. The laptop pinged to get his attention, and he turned to find it demanding a password. Not surprised, he checked the two desktop computers and found similar needs. Again, Chase deferred to others, this time the computer techs; he switched off the computers and checked the top desk drawer where he found multiple pens, pencils, post-it notepads, and blank tablets, all neatly stacked. He smiled when he saw a single key which he placed on the desk to the right of the laptop. Chase peeked into the other desk drawers, found nothing of interest, just a dictionary, a thesaurus, blank envelopes and a couple of reams of copy paper.

He glanced at the small table on his right. The miniature CD player looked expensive. Curious about Jesperson's taste in music, Chase turned it on. Satchmo's rasping voice caught him by surprise. Chase checked the CD's on the lower shelf and found them all jazz and big band. At least he and Jesperson shared one thing in common, their music; he decided that had to be a generational thing. Other than the music and cars, they had nothing in common. Chase turned off the CD player and continued on to the third bedroom, which made Jesperson's home as large as Chase's townhouse, an observation that made Chase wonder if it were not time to give up all his stairs for the convenience of a condominium like this one.

The smallest bedroom surprised Chase a little. The single bed was carelessly covered. It looked like Jesperson or whoever had made it had done so hastily without any attention to detail, quite unlike the order of the other rooms. Chase opened the closet and found two pair of slightly worn Nikes; they looked almost new. Chase did not bother to pick them up to check. Two pair of jeans, one pair still bearing the original sales tag, and several sports shirts, no suits, hung in the closet. His curiosity engaged, Chase opened the small dresser and found a tangled jumble of T-shirts and jockey shorts, not boxer shorts like the master bedroom. The bottom drawers were empty. He checked the bedside stand and in the top drawer found a bottle of Vicks and a paperback mystery with a picture of a shapely redhead in bra and torn panties on the cover. Although Chase, a mystery writer himself, kept current with his more successful competitors, he had never heard of the author or this title.

This room and its scant paraphernalia definitely was not Jesperson. The furniture was that of a typical guestroom, but not the personal stuff.

He made another mental note for the techs. Check it carefully for prints. Chase was considering what to do next when a ringing phone surprised him. He hurried back into Jesperson's office, sat down behind the desk, and picked up the phone on the credenza.

"Hello," he said in a tone that was as neutral as he could make it.

The caller did not respond, but Chase could hear someone breathing.

"Yes?" Chase said, not wanting the caller to hang up before identifying him or herself.

After another brief hesitation, a woman spoke. "Who is this?" Chase detected a thick accent that he could not identify.

"This is Lieutenant Chase Mansfield of the Fairfax County Police Department," Chase said. "May I ask who is calling?"

Silence again greeted that question.

Chase waited.

"What are you doing there?" The voice finally demanded.

"Madam, if you will please identify yourself, I will explain," Chase said.

"Is there anyone with you?" The woman asked.

Chase found the question an odd one. "Madam, you might as well tell me who is calling, and then I will answer your questions. Tracing this call is a simple matter so you are not hiding anything from me."

The woman took a deep breath before responding. "You are in my son's apartment," the caller said. "What are you doing there?"

"Mrs. Jesperson?" Chase asked as he leaned back in his chair wondering why or rather who Jesperson's mother was calling. Chase had heard Mrs. Jesperson's voice in the background when he had called her husband, so she knew her son was dead.

"Yes."

"And you know I called your husband." Chase was reluctant to refer to Mrs. Jesperson's son's death in a way that added to her grief.

"Yes."

"Then you know I am conducting an investigation," Chase said softly. "Is there anything that you can tell me that might be of assistance? I'm having difficulty identifying your son's friends. Did you son have any close female companions?"

"We never discussed it," Mrs. Jesperson said.

Since Mrs. Jesperson's voice was firm, Chase decided that he could continue. "It would really be a help if I could talk with someone who is familiar with your son's life in Virginia," Chase said."

Mrs. Jesperson did not respond.

"Mrs. Jesperson, why did you call?" Chase tried another approach.

"Because…because I wanted to talk with...with someone. Is that wrong?"

This time Jesperson's accent was so strong that Chase had difficulty grasping what she was saying. "No ma'am, I understand. Is your husband there?"

"No. Goodbye."

"Wait, please," Chase said, trying to keep her from hanging up.

After a brief pause, Jesperson asked, "What?"

Chase was not sure what he could say that would not cause her to terminate the conversation.

"Well?" Mrs. Jesperson demanded.

"Where did your son stay when he visited Iran on his sabbatical?" Chase asked the first question that came to mind, just trying to keep her talking. He hoped that mentioning her native country might help.

"Here and there. I don't know. He moved around and seldom wrote," Mrs. Jesperson said.

"Did he visit with relatives?"

"Probably. I don't know. I haven't seen him since he returned. He hasn't been home in over a year."

Chase had difficulty coping with that comment. "I assume he was very busy working on his book," Chase said.

"I assume so. Hamid is just like his father. No one ever tells me anything," Jesperson complained.

Chase required a few seconds to realize that Jesperson was referring to her son by using his middle name. "Hamid is a very unique name," Chase said, not caring, simply chatting.

"Not in Iran," Jesperson said.

"Mrs. Jesperson did Hamid," he used the name trying to establish rapport with the very difficult woman, "have any close friends in Cambridge?"

"My son was a solitary person," Jesperson said.

Chase did not comment, afraid anything he said would be misconstrued.

"Goodbye, don't steal anything," Jesperson said and hung up.

"Who was sleeping in the guest bedroom?" Chase spoke into the dead phone. When he realized nobody was going to answer his question he hung up.

Chase left the bedroom, walked though the house a second time, and was on the way to the elevator when he changed his mind and decided to try knocking ,on a few doors in an effort to see if any of Jesperson's neighbors had spent time with him. There were six apartments on the floor and rapping on the doors of the three nearest 604 produced only silence. Chase was reaching for the knocker on 606 when the door opened suddenly, surprising him.

"If you don't go away, I'm going to call the police. Salesmen are not allowed on the premises," a gray haired little lady who Chase judged to be in her mid-seventies waved a cell phone at him.

"Ma'am, I apologize for disturbing you. I am Lieutenant Mansfield of the Fairfax police," Chase displayed his credentials, trying to reassure her.

She stared at Chase and then studied his credentials. Chase waited as she perused every line before examining his picture and peering again at his face. To his surprise, she suddenly relaxed and asked a question, "Are you investigating my neighbor's murder?"

"Yes ma'am," Chase answered, assuming that candor would work best with the tough, old lady.

"And you are canvassing the neighbors looking for clues," the old lady declared primly. "It won't do you any good. I'm the only one home during the day, and none of us knew Mr. Jesperson. He lived like a hermit."

"Ma'am could I come in for a few minutes. Anything you might be able to tell me would be helpful. I have yet to talk with anyone who can identify a single friend or acquaintance of the professor."

The old lady stepped back allowing Chase to enter.

"Coffee?" The old lady asked as he followed her into a small living room.

"I wouldn't want to be a bother," Chase answered.

"I've got a fresh pot brewed, and I don't like to drink alone, something my current status requires me to do," the old lady said, turning towards a small kitchen on the left. "This is my purgatory," she waved her hand in the air and chuckled.

Her words and now friendly demeanor gave Chase the impression that the old lady truly welcomed the company.

"Sit over by the window," the old lady ordered.

Chase glanced at the furniture, all antiques dating to the late1890's, treasures accumulated over a lifetime. Two relatively modern, identical rockers, both overstuffed and covered with a heavy fabric that featured large pink roses, were turned so that the occupants could view each other and the small forest behind the building.

"Sit down, lieutenant," the old lady insisted as she handed him a brimming mug.

"Black will have to do. The cream is soured," she said. "Too old, just like me."

"Black is fine, ma'am," Chase said as sat down. He didn't particularly like coffee and seldom indulged after breakfast, but he assumed that the coffee would buy him the opportunity to ask a few questions.

"And stop calling me ma'am. My name is Marsha Hillencotter, and I'm a single woman, now."

"Yes, Mrs. Hillencotter," Chase said.

"What do you want to know?"

"What can you tell me about Professor Jesperson?" Chase sipped his coffee.

"Like I said, none of us really knew the Hermit. That's what we called him, the Hermit. He left the apartment every morning at exactly eight AM, spent his day at the university, returned home at five, a little later if he did any shopping. He ate at home, did his own cooking, and spent his evenings working on his book. What kind of life is that?"

Chase shook his head negatively, but he did not comment. Except for the truncated workday, the schedule sounded pretty much like his own. "Did he ever take an evening off?" Chase asked. He allotted himself two nights a week with female companionship, of late usually Jacky Rossi, previously with Barbara Jordan. He made a mental note to follow up with Barbara, given the fact that she knew Jesperson and could probably be cajoled into being more forthcoming than she had been to date. He really needed more help with understanding the victim.

"Take an evening off?" Hillencotter repeated the question. "Never, not even on weekends."

"You don't know the names of any of his friends?"

"Friends, he didn't have any," Hillencotter laughed. After a pause, she continued, "except … maybe."

Chase waited, now alert, no longer just going through the motions.

"Who am I to say anything?" Hillencotter clamped her thin lips tight. "Times change; life styles change, but really some things today are reprehensible. Are you a church going man, lieutenant?"

Chase reacted with an involuntary shake of his head. He was not a religious man, in fact, the exact opposite, but this was no time to indulge himself by noting that he considered religion to be a gigantic crime, a hoax imposed on naive people over the centuries, exploited them really. "I don't attend church as often as some think I should," Chase equivocated.

"Neither do I, lieutenant," the old lady smiled, clearly seeing through his words. "Still, as a lawman, I'm sure you see much more of the darker side of people than is good for you."

"Yes, ma'am," Chase answered.

"I'm no prude," Hillencotter said. "Still, people today have no morals."

"Are you referring specifically to Professor Jesperson?" Chase asked, leaning forward to stress interest.

"It's not for me to say," Hillencotter smiled.

Chase deliberately did not react, using silence as a lever.

"Did you chat with that young man?" Hillencotter asked suddenly, surprising Chase.

"Young man?"

"Yes, the young man who has been living with the Hermit for the past two weeks."

"Do you know the young man's name?"

"Never met him. Said hello to him in the hall one time. He nodded but did not have the grace to speak."

"How do you know he has been living in the professor's apartment?"

"I keep an eye on things. Some of my neighbors are more friendly than others, so I reciprocate when they are at work."

"Did any of the others have much to do with Professor Jesperson?"

"No."

"Or the young man?"

"No. I'm the only one who has even seen him."

"Could you describe him for me?"

"Not really. He was rather common looking, always dressed in sneakers, sports shirt, and jeans. He looked like a typical college student."

"Do you know that he was a college student?"

"No, lieutenant. Don't put words in my mouth. He looked like one."

"Did he go off in the morning and return in the evening with the professor in his car."

"Only for the first days. A week ago he got his own car. A real junker."

"Do you know the make?"

"No. I'm not a car person. I still drive my husband's old Ford, and he died six years ago."

"Would you say the junker is older than your Ford?"

"Yes."

"What color?"

"Black."

"Can you tell me anything else about it?"

"It's small, one of those little foreign cars, the kind they call a bug or something."

"A Beetle?"

"Probably. The right front fender has been in an accident."

"Dented?"

"Dented and rusted. I never looked closely at it, but once it was parked right next to my Ford, and I didn't like that. Didn't complain though."

"How old would you say the young man is?"

"Young, college age. Too young to be playing games with a man the professor's age."

"Games."

"I shouldn't have said that. What people do in their own homes is none of my business."

"Why do you say games?"

"What else do you call it. The young man has dark skin."

"How dark?"

"He isn't a black man, if that is what you're thinking."

"A Hispanic?"

"Something like that. Maybe he just spent a lot of time in the sun. I should have said he has a deep tan."

"What color is his hair?"

"Black. He needs a haircut."

"How tall is he?"

"Shorter than you?"

"How much shorter?" Chase asked.

Hillencotter held up her frail hand with the thumb and forefinger separated about four inches. Chase estimated the young man would stand about five foot eight.

"How much would you say he weighs?"

"No idea."

"Is he pudgy, muscular, skinny?"

"Skinny."

"Is there anything else you can tell me about him?"

"I probably have already said too much. Sometimes he wears a knapsack like students use to carry the books."

"Did you ever see the young man and the professor together?"

"Not after the boy got his bug."

"Did either the professor or young man ever have any visitors?"

"Never."

"When was the last time you saw the young man?"

"Last night, about six. He came home at his usual time."

"And the professor?"

"Last week. Don't remember which day."

Chase set his coffee mug, still three quarters full, on the table beside his chair. "Mrs. Hillencotter is there anything else you can tell me about your neighbors?"

She responded with a negative twitch of her head. "As I said, I don't know a thing."

Chase stood up and took a card from his suit coat pocket. "Mrs. Hillencotter, please give me a call if you think of anything else. I am going to arrange for some officers to come over and inspect the professor's apartment. Don't worry about them. When the young man or anyone else enters the apartment, please call me immediately if that would not be inconvenient."

"You want me to stake out the apartment for you?" The old lady laughed.

"Nothing so dramatic, Mrs. Hillencotter," Chase smiled. "If by chance you should remember or see anything you think I should know, just give me a call."

The old lady nodded, thought for a few seconds, and said, "I have another request."

"Of course."

"Please call me Ms. Hillencotter. It makes me feel a little less ancient."

"Of course, Ms. Hillencotter," Chase laughed. "But you are one lady who doesn't have to worry about appearing ancient."

The old lady winked as she closed the door behind Chase.

Chapter 4

Chase planned on a quick stop at headquarters to brief Barney, just enough to keep the chief off his back. Then, on this, one of his nights out, he planned to arrange a date with Doctor Barbara Jordan, his first in over six months. He recognized this could prove contentious. Barbara was one thing and risking a chance meeting with Jacky Rossi was another. He rationalized, however, that consulting with Barbara was virtually an official interview mandated by the Jesperson investigation.

Theresa greeted him with a frown and a thumb pointed to her right.

"Is Barney busy?" Chase glanced at the closed door leading to the CIB commander's office.

Theresa smiled, playing one of her little games.

Chase glanced at the wall clock. Five o'clock. He had a phone call to make and a couple of housekeeping errands to run before heading for his townhouse. He was running late and had no time to humor Theresa.

"Theresa, please," Chase surrendered.

"Sergeant Moscowitz, her team of investigators, and the major started without you," Theresa belatedly answered his question.

"Thank you, Ms. D'Angelo," Chase spoke formally, trying to put Theresa in her place.

"You are welcome, Lieutenant Mansfield," Theresa replied. "It is a treat to see you again; you must visit us more often," Theresa got in the last word.

Chase entered to find Moscowitz, Packard, Whitten, and Barney aligned around the conference table.

Moscowitz, who was speaking when Chase entered, reacted first. "So good of you to join us lieutenant. We weren't sure you were still in town, or not."

"We were just discussing your investigation," Barney greeted him.

"Without much to discuss," Moscowitz said.

"This is an interesting case," Chase said as he joined the others at the table.

"How would you know? Moscowitz asked.

"The floor is all yours, Chase," Barney politely tried to warn Moscowitz to shut up.

"Things are about to get worse," Chase said.

"What have you done now?" Moscowitz asked, pushing her luck. Moscowitz was one of those people who did not know when to keep her mouth shut.

Chase again ignored her. "Professor Jesperson's new book is going to rattle a lot of cages. I haven't read it yet, but I'm told that somehow Jesperson acquired a source who passed along reliable information that indicates the Iranians have a nuclear bomb and are about to use it."

"There will be some red faces out at Langley," Moscowitz referred to the CIA.

"Embarrassment will be the least of their problems if the Iranians drop a bomb on Washington," Chase said.

"Christ, you're kidding," Barney said.

"That explains what Townsend was doing on campus last night," observed Detective Packard who along with his partner Whitten had handled the initial 911 call.

"Do you have a copy of the book?" Barney asked. "Is all this going to fall on our heads?"

The others, including a now silent Moscowitz, stared at Chase, waiting for him to elaborate. "I talked with Jesperson's agent who says the book's release is scheduled for next Wednesday. I suspect that that Jesperson's demise may have changed that plan."

"Who gave you the book?" Moscowitz demanded.

"I don't have it," Chase said. "Jesperson's father in Cambridge had the printer's proof copy. As soon as he told me what I just shared, I arranged with Special Agent Cotton to have someone from the local Bureau office retrieve it and hand-carry it to Washington."

"Not to you, I hope," Barney relaxed in his chair.

"I assume that Cotton is reading it as we speak and that early this evening Cotton and his director will be meeting urgently at the White House with the CIA director, the Department of Homeland Security, and President Featherstone."

"I'm glad we're not involved in that meeting," Barney said. "We're not, are we?" He stared at Chase.

Chase laughed. "I've got other plans."

"I'll bet you do," Moscowitz said. "What's her name?"

Chase ignored Moscowitz and spoke to Barney. "Fortunately, national security isn't our business."

"I'm not so sure of that," Packard said. "An atomic bomb hitting the White House or the Pentagon would take out most of Fairfax County."

"If not all of it," Whitten, his partner, corrected.

"We better brief the chief," Barney stood up. He started for the door but hesitated when he saw that Chase was not following.

"Don't you want to discuss the Jesperson investigation?" Chase, who remained seated, asked.

Barney stared at Chase, thought a few seconds before turning and opening the door. "Theresa, call upstairs and tell the chief I'll be up in ten minutes with important information."

"Yes sir." Theresa, always curious, asked, "The Jesperson investigation?"

Barney closed the door without elaborating and returned to the table. "Please make it brief before we all go up in smoke."

"That's out of our hands, now," Chase said.

"I hope," Barney said. "Talk, please."

"Professor Jesperson was an odd fellow," he began.

"He isn't the only odd fellow around here," Moscowitz couldn't resist.

"...quite introverted," Chase continued, again ignoring Moscowitz. "Jesperson spent his days on campus preoccupied with his research and his evenings locked up in his condominium with his three computers."

"You did his apartment without the techs?" Moscowitz blurted.

"I gave it a look-over and chatted with a resident," Chase said.

"I hope you didn't find any atomic bombs," Barney said, only half joking.

"It was quite austere. No bombs, everything in its assigned place." Chase turned to Moscowitz. "Sergeant," he said as he slid Jesperson's key case across the table towards her. "You might want to take some techs and thoroughly take the place apart. I checked the computers, two desktops and a laptop, but they were all password locked. You might find a draft or two of the book on the computers if you can find a tech who can get around the password."

"I'll do it right now," Moscowitz said as she snatched the keys and stood up.

"Wait," Barney ordered. "Do we really want to find the damned draft? The Bureau already has the book."

"We can't leak anything about the bomb business whether we have the manuscript or not," Chase said, not quite addressing Barney's question. "The media will panic the nation."

"Damned right, we can't, and they would," Barney agreed. "Who else knows about what's in the book?"

"The agent, the publisher, the printers, Jesperson's research assistant, his parents, his source or sources, and by now half the FBI, the DHS, the president and most of the White House staff," Chase smiled.

"I hope somebody alerts the Department of Defense," Moscowitz said. "They're the ones with the steel balls."

"It's already on the media wires," Barney said. "We've got to tell the chief." He rose from his chair.

"Wait," Chase held up his right hand. "One more thing. Jesperson had a flat mate, a young man in his twenties, about five nine or ten, black hair, with a good tan, possibly a Hispanic or maybe Middle Easterner."

"An Iranian," Moscowitz declared.

"Jesperson was gay," Packard said.

"I don't know if the houseguest was Iranian or not, and I don't know if Jesperson was gay. The old lady down the hall thinks so, but she has no pictures."

"How in the hell could she?" Moscowitz asked.

"My very point, sergeant," Chase said. "I suggest that you and the techs do what you can to identify Jesperson's guest who has been with him since August."

"And bring him in for questioning," Barney ordered.

"By me," Chase said.

Barney started for the door. When he realized, again, that Chase was still sitting, he turned. "Let's go."

"Would you object to handling the chief's briefing yourself?" Chase asked. "I've got a few things I need to work on." He did not admit it was to take clothes to the cleaners, pick up some groceries, and arrange his date with Barbara, in reverse order.

"He'll want to talk to you," Barney pressed.

"Just tell him…" Chase hesitated as he tried to think of an excuse. "… that I've got to talk with Cotton," Chase improvised. He could place a call to Cotton's cell phone on the way to the cleaners. He really didn't want to talk with Cotton about the book or what was happening, but he was confident that Cotton would be so busy that he would ignore any call from Chase.

"Keep me informed," Barney said, his tone that of an order, but his expression clearly indicating that he doubted his current assistant and former superior would do anything but what he wanted.

An amused Packard and Whitten smiled, and Moscowitz frowned. All three knew that Mansfield was assigned to CIB for rations and quarters, as the military like to say, and that Mansfield reported to no one but the chief, and then only irregularly when the whim struck him.

****

Chase arrived at Barbara's Fairfax City townhouse at exactly seven-thirty, only a half an hour late, and rang the bell. Chase had once had a door key, but after the appearance of Jacky in his life, Barbara had insisted on its return. After a lengthy wait that Chase assumed was deliberate, a form of punishment, Barbara opened the door and smiled sweetly.

"Nothing has changed, I see. Clocks mean nothing to our overworked men in blue, not even those who dress in multi-colors," she referred to his mismatched slacks and shirt.

"Good evening, professor," Chase ignored the challenge in her greeting. "I apologize profusely for my tardy arrival."

"Do we have plans?" Barbara asked. "Or do you have a late date with Wacky Jacky?"

"I haven't been to the peanut place in ages," Chase, still standing on the front stoop, said. The restaurant whose name Chase could never remember had been one of their favorite places. The filet mignon ranked with that of the Outback, and it was located in a shopping center near Fair Oaks Mall, a short drive from Barbara's townhouse. The name Chase used referred to the restaurant's quaint practice of providing gratis bowls of peanuts which patrons consumed at their pleasure while they casually tossed the shells on the floor.

Barbara nodded and shut the door in Chase's face. He wasn't sure that she had taken offense at his selection, his late arrival, or was simply taunting him. He waited patiently knowing she would join him, or not, depending on her mood. At times Chase had difficulty determining whether

Barbara was angry or fencing with him. After a quiet three minutes, the door opened, and Barbara exited.

"It's a beautiful October evening," Chase said glancing at the brilliant foliage. "I don't think it will snow tonight," he referred to Barbara's compulsive fear of the white stuff.

Barbara frowned as she ignored both of his comments, the evasive reference to the fall colors, and the feeble effort at a disarming, familiar taunt.

Ten minutes later, after a quiet ride, they were seated at what used to be their favorite table sipping from frosted mugs of Budweiser and cracking peanut shells. Chase was silently searching for a non-provocative way to broach the subject of Doctor Thomas Jesperson and his campus reputation—he assumed that Barbara knew the man better than she had admitted earlier in the day—when Barbara surprised him.

"Do you think that Townsend shot Jes?" She asked.

"Where did you hear about Townsend's involvement?" Chase asked.

Barbara laughed. "You're absolutely ridiculous. Jes hosts the congenitally secretive Secretary of Homeland Security at a public event, announces that he is an old personal friend, and presides while the secretary and the liberal academic community clash. Then, the two retreat to Jesperson's office where they share a convivial drink, or three, while the audience disperses. For a grand finale, the speaker guest vanishes; the host is found slaughtered in his chair, and you think no one is going to notice."

"Oh shit," Chase said. "How do you know all that?"

"Would it surprise you to learn I was a member of the audience?"

"What were you doing there? National security and foreign affairs aren't your things."

"I know. I'm just a simple English teacher, and such matters are far beyond my comprehension."

Chase could not come up with a non-provocative response so said nothing.

"I accompanied a friend, a congenial, reliable, attentive, gentleman friend, to a campus event," Barbara said.

"Where did you hear about Townsend's disappearance?"

"Why? Is it a big secret?"

Chase shook his head. "The FBI thinks so."

"Our government likes to keep the most absurd secrets," Barbara agreed. "Unfortunately for them, and you apparently, they know nothing about university campuses. I doubt there's a single soul within miles of George Mason who didn't hear the news by noon, but that's a minor issue. You may not have noticed those little satellite trucks parked in front of Robinson Hall, but they picked up the scuttlebutt, too."

"How do you know that?"

"I, along with the rest of the world, have been listening to the breaking news reports all day long. If you could find someone to show you how to turn on a television set or your radio, you too could share, but not to worry. You can read it in your *Post* over your burned toast and bitter coffee at breakfast. Now, are you going to answer my question? Did Townsend actually shoot Jes and go on the lamb or not?"

"I don't know," Chase answered honestly. "But please don't quote me."

"Why would I want to do that?" Barbara asked. "I would rather that my friends and colleagues not know that I am acquainted with the likes of you."

"Why do you keep calling Jesperson, Jes? Were the two of you close?"

"The identity of my friends is none of your business, Mr. Policeman."

"Barbara, please. This is very important. I haven't been able to identify a single person who knew a thing about Jesperson, the man."

"That's the reason for this?" Barbara waved her hand to signify the restaurant. "And naïve me thought we were having a date." She picked up a peanut shell and threw it at Chase's head.

Chase, recognizing that indifference was his best defense, ignored the gesture. To retaliate in kind would only invite another attack.

The waitress appeared with their meals. After she departed, Barbara cut a thin slice of the bright red meat dripping with juice and took her first bite. Chase did not even reach for his fork and knife. He soberly watched Barbara and waited. Barbara ignored him, continuing to eat, pretending to enjoy her beef and Chase's ostensible discomfort.

"Barbara, this is really important," Chase counter-attacked in his own way. "I'm in charge of the Jesperson investigation, and the Bureau and DHS are worrying about Townsend's disappearance."

"Again I ask, do you actually think he killed Jes?" Barbara asked between mouthfuls.

Chase stalled by cutting up his steak and starting on his food without actually tasting it.

Barbara pretended to ignore him until he capitulated.

"I don't know who shot Jesperson. I'm still on square one trying to learn as much about him as I can,"

"And you brought me here to interrogate me," Barbara smiled.

"Interrogate, no. It just shows how desperate I am."

"Desperate is good. Some honesty at last," Barbara said, not realizing that Chase considered her response a tactical victory. "I told you the truth when I said I only knew Jesperson casually. I simply wasn't completely candid."

Chase did not point out the fallacy inherent in her reasoning.

"A friend of mine once dated him," Barbara continued.

Chase concluded he was a subtle interrogator.

"She hasn't seen him in over a year, not since he took off on his sabbatical and didn't trouble to call on his return."

"You said 'she."

"Of course. Were you expecting a he?"

Chase shrugged.

Barbara laughed. "Sorry to disappoint you, but according to my friend Jes was at least half straight."

"Half straight?"

"She was quite impressed with his performance. It took a little while to get him started, but she attributed that to his bookish demeanor."

"You women," Chase shook his head. "Isn't there anything that you keep private?"

Barbara smiled and resumed her attack on her meat.

"What else did this friend have to say about him?" Chase asked.

Barbara ignored him.

"Please," Chase said, recognizing his tactical error.

"Sorry, I cannot divulge a friend's confidences" Barbara said.

For the rest of the evening, Chase asked his questions and Barbara refused to answer. Finally, Chase paid the bill and experienced a silent ride back to Barbara's townhouse where she thanked him for a delightful dinner and retreated inside, alone.

****

Although it was ten o'clock in the evening, every light in the anteroom outside the Oval Office was burning brightly. A curious Secret Service agent sat at Heather James' desk watching the assembled group of senior officials who were aligned in a perfect triangle as they waited for President Arthur C. Featherstone to make his appearance.

Special Agent Tracey Cotton and his boss, FBI Director Philip D'Antonio, stood with their backs to the corridor door. To Cotton's right, Claris Gore, a senior investigator with the Department of Homeland Security, and Patricia Marshall, the DHS Acting Secretary, formed the second leg of the triangle. Flanking them were two spooks, the Director of the Central Intelligence Agency, William H. Pace, and his Deputy Director for Intelligence, Adam Schultz. They stood in silence, all with worried expressions on their faces. The late night meeting was unusual but not unprecedented; the fact that the subordinate officials present kept their mouths shut was standard operating procedure; the absence of provocative banter among the seniors was precedent setting, and almost as noteworthy as a meeting of the top tier of the government's security and intelligence establishment without the presence of the Secretary of State, the Secretary of Defense, or the National Security Advisor.

The intercom buzzed, warning all that the president had entered the Oval Office from his private study. The Secret Service agent reacted, "Yes. Mr. President."

"Send our visitors in," President Arthur C. Featherstone ordered gruffly.

"Yes sir," the agent responded. He nodded to his fellow agent guarding the entrance to the Oval Office. "You may go in gentlemen and ladies," he spoke to the assembled group.

The agent blocking the door opened it and stepped back. The director of the CIA who stood nearest the door hesitated and deferred to the director of the FBI. This amused the Secret Service agents. Normally, the senior officials present jostled each other in their haste to lead the way into their master's presence. The FBI director in turn pretended to be a gentleman and gestured for the Acting Secretary of the Department of Homeland Security to accept the honor.

Patricia Marshall frowned. "You first, Mr. Director," she spoke to D'Antonio. "It's your show."

"And it's your boss who's missing," the FBI director smiled.

"But that is not what this meeting is about," Patricia Marshall held her ground with a stubbornness that the others expected from the opposing gender.

"Come in," Featherstone called, obviously not amused by the delay. They were working on his private time now. "I hope you are assembled to give me good news about my Homeland Security secretary," Featherstone said while the group aligned themselves around him. He glanced at the CIA director and then focused on the FBI director. "Tell me I'm correct because the presence of some of your associates worries me."

"Sir, we do not have good news," D'Antonio said. "We are not here about Secretary Townsend."

"I thought I made it perfectly clear that finding James was our number one priority," Featherstone frowned. "I'm not interested in another routine national security screw-up."

While the president and the director were fencing, Special Agent Cotton who sat to D'Antonio's right, opened his briefcase, and took out a sheath of papers and a book, an action that caught the president's attention.

"Special Agent Cotton, you can put that stuff right back where you found it," Featherstone ordered. "I don't have time for this."

"Please Mr. President, we apologize for intruding on your private time, but we have no choice. You must hear us out," Pace, the CIA director intervened.

Featherstone glared at him but settled back in his chair and waited.

"Special Agent Cotton," D'Antonio nodded.

Cotton handed several sets of stapled papers to Patricia Marshall and indicated with a wave of his hand that she should pass them on to the others. She quickly did so.

"I think everyone present is aware of the contents of the documents I am passing about except..." Cotton hesitated.

"Except me," Featherstone finished Cotton's sentence for him.

Cotton stood up and handed the president a set of papers.

"And I have no intention of reading another word tonight, Special Agent Cotton," the president grumbled while graciously accepted his package. "Brief me in ten words or less."

"The Iranians have a nuclear bomb, and they plan to use it," Cotton said grimly.

Nobody present counted the words. All stared at the president, waiting for the reaction.

The color drained from Featherstone's face, and he grasped the arms of his chair as he silently stared at Cotton. Up to that point, Featherstone, who shared a few less than admirable personality traits with one of his predecessors, Lyndon Baines Johnson, had been enjoying himself while berating his senior appointees. All now sat in silence, waiting for the president to speak.

"Where and when?" Featherstone's voice, to his credit, did not break.

"Soon," Cotton answered, bemused and irritated by the fact that all the brass in the room deferred to him. "We don't know precisely when."

"Sir," Adam Schultz, the CIA's Deputy Director for Intelligence spoke up. "We learned of this development only two hours ago, and our analysts have not had the opportunity to study it. We do know, however, how unpredictable the Iranians are."

"Unpredictable," Featherstone reacted. "Ahmadnutjob is a madman."

The president referred to Iranian President Ahmadinejad using the derogatory version of his name first employed by Jay Leno and co-opted by several peers who posed as late night talk show hosts.

"If they've got the damned bomb, they'll use it on us or the Israelis as soon as they can. How reliable is your information?" Featherstone focused his laser-like gaze on Special Agent Cotton.

"We fear it might be most reliable," CIA Director Pace answered before Cotton could respond.

"I didn't ask you, Director Pace," Featherstone snarled. "You damned spooks are always hedging. You fear it might be," he quoted Pace's words back at him. "What in the hell does that mean? We're talking Pearl Harbor, here. You remember Pearl Harbor, don't you?"

Pace, who obviously regretted intervening, flushed red, took a deep breath, and did not address the president's angry questions. It was safer to treat them as rhetorical.

Featherstone glared at Pace for a few seconds and then turned his attention back to Cotton, waiting for him to answer his question, "How reliable is your information?"

"Sir, have you heard of Professor Thomas Jesperson? He …" Cotton said.

"I read the damned newspapers Special Agent Cotton," Featherstone interrupted. "He's the George Mason professor who was killed the night James Townsend disappeared." Featherstone hesitated. "Christ, are you telling me that James' disappearance and this bomb business are related somehow?" Featherstone turned towards his Acting Secretary of Homeland Security. That's why you're here, Patricia."

"I'm afraid so, sir," Patricia Marshall answered.

Featherstone nodded and abruptly turned on the CIA duo. Catching subordinates when they thought he was focusing on others was a common Featherstone tactic.

"Alright, Schultz," he addressed the CIA's Director of Intelligence. "What did Jesperson know that you spooks don't?"

"I have only scanned these two chapters, Mr. President," Schultz held up his copy of Cotton's handout.

Featherstone did not react.

"We have all heard the famous quote of a former British ambassador to Iran. 'The Iranians are a people who say the opposite of what they think, and do the opposite of what they say.'" Schultz, a former academic, always tried to relax the president with a clever comment before he delivered his bad news. Unfortunately for him, this time Featherstone did not react as he intended.

Featherstone glowered as he waited for Schultz to continue.

"It's a form of what they call tagiya, a derivative of the Arab word waqa which means to shield or guard. To the Iranians it in essence means deception."

"Stop the bullshit, director," Featherstone erupted. "I know how intelligent you are. Now, just tell me about the damned bomb. Do the bastards have it, and where and when will they use it?"

"Sir, in the past we have discussed our fear that the Iranians were on the verge of producing a workable fission bomb despite their repeated allegations to the contrary." Schultz, who was working with a formidable handicap, tried to dissemble. No one in the room had sufficient, reliable, confirmed information to give the president the precise answer he demanded.

"Sir," William Pace, the CIA director and Schultz's boss, tried to intercede.

Featherstone silenced him with a sharp glare. Pace wisely retreated into silence, and the president turned back to Schultz who bravely soldiered on.

"Professor Jesperson, whose mother is a native Iranian married to an American citizen, recently returned from a year's sabbatical in Iran where he presumably used family contacts to develop the information that enabled him to draft a book, an advance copy of which Special Agent Cotton has acquired," Schultz said. "Those contacts apparently included sources deep within the Iranian nuclear establishment. The two chapters in question cite reliable but unidentified sources who allege the Iranians have the material to construct more than one nuclear bomb and intend to use them."

"Is Jesperson simply a sensation monger or is he a serious reporter? Can we believe what he says, or is he simply trying to sell books?" Featherstone demanded.

"I know, I knew, Doctor Jesperson personally," Schultz answered. "He was highly respected by his peers. He specialized in the Near East in general and Iran in particular. He held a Top Secret clearance and in the past has been employed as a contract consultant by my agency as well as the Congress and the National Security Council."

"Why didn't he share this information with his government?"

"I don't know, sir. Jesperson terminated his contractual relationship with the agency one year ago, just before he departed for Iran on his sabbatical. I understand that he feared a relationship with our government during the period he was visiting Iran would place him in personal jeopardy. He did not want to end up in an Iranian prison facing espionage charges. I also assume he cherished his academic independence and did not want his research to be discounted by jealous peers who could accuse him of subjectivity because of an ongoing governmental relationship."

"A wise man," Featherstone declared. "What does he say about the bomb?"

"As you know, sir, from your past briefings," Schultz tried again. "The Iranians have constructed two centrifuge enrichment plants at Natanz, and they have a heavy water production plant and reactor at Arak. By reprocessing its spent fuel, Iran can produce plutonium. Plutonium and uranium-235 are essential elements of a bomb. Uranium consists of three isotopes, uranium-234, uranium-235 and uranium-238. When extracted…"

"Stop," Featherstone shouted angrily. ""I don't want another one of your damned lectures. I didn't understand the first dozen times you delivered this lecture in this office, and I don't have the time now to try again." Featherstone, flushed, took a deep breath.

"I understand, sir," Schultz tried to placate the irate chief executive. Not knowing how to answer the president's questions simplistically, not given the complicated and highly important nature of the subject at hand, Schultz needed to cite details to make sure he was communicating fully. "Please forgive me and let me try again."

Featherstone, struggling to control his temper, nodded, apparently not willing to trust himself to speak.

"Sir, we calculate that Iran has the capability to produce a single atomic bomb with about 700 kilograms of low-enriched uranium. After further processing this would give them twenty kilograms of high-enriched uranium, the amount needed for their weapon. Three thousand centrifuges working for thirty days can produce twenty kilograms of high-enriched uranium."

"How many centrifuges do the Iranians have now?" Featherstone demanded.

"We do not know. Jesperson reports," Schultz waved his sheath of papers, "that in 2006 President Ahmadinejad authorized the construction of 56,000 centrifuges."

"And?" Featherstone interrupted.

"And Jesperson's source confides that they have a potential for reaching 30,000 in the not distant future."

"Oh shit, so they will soon have more than one bomb."

"With delivery platforms capable of carrying them," CIA Director Pace again tried to relieve his harried Deputy Director for Intelligence.

Featherstone glared once again at Pace, this time waiting for him to elaborate.

Pace spoke quickly. "Since the early1990's Iran has actively scoured the black market for Soviet multistage rocket propulsion systems. In 1997 the Iranian military successfully test-fired rocket engines. In late 2005 the Israelis learned Iran had acquired twelve former Soviet cruise missiles. Subsequently, the Israelis reported that the Iranians had purchased BM-25 surface to surface missiles with a 2,500 mile range from the North Koreans."

"So they now have the bomb and the means to deliver it," Featherstone groaned.

"And that is not the worst," Schultz reentered the briefing. "Jesperson also reports that the Iranians have developed a tactical nuclear weapon, a suitcase device weighing about sixty pounds. He alleges they copied a Soviet model, and we know they can be detonated by one man in ten minutes."

"And the target will be?" A shocked Featherstone leaned back in his chair and closed his eyes as he waited for his answer.

"A missile for Israel and a suitcase device for Washington, D.C.," Schultz said.

"When?"

"Jesperson quotes his source as saying the target date is tentatively set for November lst."

"And this alleged American citizen has been sitting on this information since August?"

"No sir. Not exactly," Schultz said.

"What in the hell does that mean?" Featherstone again lost his temper.

"Jesperson apparently had the basic information about Iran's nuclear program when he returned last summer. He notes that he lacked key details which he acquired only recently. He alleges he feared that we, the United States Government, would try to prevent the publication of the information in his book and, therefore, believing in the American people's right to know, insisted that it be released on October 15, next Wednesday, giving us time to react."

"That's stupid," Featherstone said. "Christ, as soon as we share with the Israelis, or they read that damned book, they'll launch their own preemptive attack."

"Yes, sir," CIA Director Pace and Schultz answered in unison.

"And this book is in the public domain?"

"It's already printed, but Jesperson refused to give his publisher and agent permission for an advance release. He insisted on an October 15 publication date," Cotton said.

"Then do whatever we can to put a lid on it," Featherstone ordered.

"We acquired the book six hours ago and have shared the contents with those in this room," FBI Director D'Antonio said.

"You've got to buy us as much time as you can before the story hits the media," Featherstone growled. "We've got to..." Featherstone stopped in mid-sentence and looked about the room. "Where in the hell is my Secretary of State, Secretary of Defense, National Security Advisor? We need their input. I can't do everything myself. And Defense has to put the damned country on alert."

"We were afraid to bring everybody on board until we discussed how you wanted to handle this, sir. We were fearful of leaks with even this many people involved," D'Antonio looked around the room.

"Oh shit," Featherstone said. He focused on what D'Antonio had not said. Both the Secretary of State and Secretary of Defense were political figures in their own right, each with their own tame media chorus.

"We've got to give the Israelis a heads-up," CIA Director Pace said. "I could have our station alert Mossad."

After a few seconds of thought, Featherstone shook his head negatively. "No, keep this completely within this room. I'll talk with State, Defense, and my people. We'll all meet here later. I'll let you know when. Between now and then, I want…" Featherstone looked directly at Cotton and his boss, "…you to shut down the publisher and the agent. Buy us some time."

"Should I raise the alert signal?" Acting Secretary of the Department of Homeland Security Patricia Marshall asked.

"No, except for what I just said, none of you should take any action whatsoever," Featherstone ordered.

"Sir, I should put my worldwide stations on alert," CIA Director Pace declared.

"For what? To look for a missile launch on Israel or a single terrorist with a suitcase?" Featherstone growled.

"Sir, we are obligated to alert our people overseas, and NSA, and NRO," Pace insisted, referring to the National Security Agency and National Reconnaissance Office. "It would be criminal..."

"And the DIA, Army, Navy, Air Force, Marines, D.C. cops, the Park Service, the paramedics, and, for Christ sake, NATO, and the whole damned world. We'll create an international panic and the Iranians will be just delighted with all the attention, as happy as pigs wallowing in shit," Featherstone blurted.

No one spoke; all shared the president's concerns, and not one wanted to take the responsibility for coping with the potential calamity that hung over them. Finally, Featherstone shook his head as if trying to clear it. "Alright. CIA should alert their stations, NSA and NRO. I will worry about Defense, State and everyone else. When we meet again, come with good news."

The visitors stood up; Featherstone remained seated. They all studied him with worried expressions on their faces, assessing him, wondering if he was up to the job ahead, even his protégé and intimate, Patricia Marshall. She was a close friend who he had stashed for personal convenience at DHS, not expecting her to be involved in this kind of mess.

"Secretary Marshall," Featherstone spoke to her directly. "Please stay. I have a few questions."

Marshall, who was leading the rush to the door, stepped to one side and let the others pass. After the Secret Service watchdogs discreetly closed the door, she circled the presidential desk and took up position behind Featherstone, who leaned back in his chair and began turning his head side to side in an exaggerated effort to expel the tension. A concerned Marshall placed long fingers on each side of the presidential neck and began massaging it.

"What a terrible day," the Acting Secretary of the Department of Homeland Affairs commiserated.

"Patricia, do you have any idea what happened to James? Is it possible that he actually shot this professor?" Featherstone asked.

"Arthur, I don't know. We haven't a clue where James is or what if anything happened to him," Marshall said. "I'm not qualified to deal with these kinds of things."

"I know," Featherstone said. "And I apologize for putting you in this terrible position. I'm not sure that anybody is prepared to cope with this kind of pressure. A damned atomic bomb, for Christ sake."

"What are we going to do?" Marshall stopped stroking the presidential neck, more worried about her own problems than the president's. He had asked for his job; she hadn't. The position at DHS had been his idea not hers. Living at the White House was more her style, but the president already had a spouse and was not prepared to abandon her.

"Don't stop," Featherstone ordered just as someone tapped lightly on the door that connected the study to the Oval Office and opened it without presidential invitation.

Both the president and his Acting Secretary of the Department of Homeland Affairs looked up with a start. They relaxed when they saw that the intruder was the president's chief of staff, Theodore "Ted" Bertram, who had started serving Featherstone as an intern in the Congress and had followed his master every step of the way to the White House. Bertram had been the one to introduce Marshall to the president some eight years previously at a fundraiser in the then congressman's home district, the 22d in upstate New York, and had served as a confidential go-between in the years since. In fact about once every two months Bertram loyally made his Northern Virginia condominium available for a relaxing presidential rendezvous whenever time and circumstances allowed, a situation usually created by the First Lady's contrived, official travel.

"Who called you?" Featherstone greeted his friend and aide in his usual abrupt manner.

Bertram, who treated the president as an equal in private, smiled but did not answer. Instead, he nodded at Marshall. "Patricia, how are you holding up under the pressure?" Bertram asked.

"I'm glad you're here," Featherstone, who expected to be the center of attention, spoke before Marshall could start whining. "We've got a crisis on our hands, and I need your help."

Bertram winked at Marshall who had dropped her hands to her side. "Don't stop on my behalf," he encouraged her to continue with her massage of the presidential neck. Bertram sat down in his usual chair facing the desk, opened his notebook, and looked at the president. "Please don't tell me that Townsend actually shot that professor. What on the earth for?"

"It's got nothing to do with Townsend," the president said. "At least I don't think it does. The damned Iranians have the bomb, and they are getting ready to use it."

"Yes sir," Bertram sat up stiffly in his chair. "I wondered why you had all the spooks in here without calling me."

"I didn't call the meeting, they did. They didn't tell me in advance what it was about, so I didn't call you."

"Is the information reliable?" Bertram asked.

"Probably," Featherstone said. "I don't have time to brief you. Patricia was here. I'll let her fill you in. Now," Featherstone dismissed them both.

Marshall obediently stopped massaging, and Bertram folded his notebook and stood up. He had long before learned that it was a waste of time trying to talk with Featherstone when he was in his autocratic gear, as he obviously was now. Marshall and Bertram started for the door.

"I have to call Harrison and Connors," Featherstone said.

"Do you want me to do it?" Bertram asked.

"No, I have to do it, personally. Both should have been here, and both are going to be pissed that they weren't invited."

"Why weren't they?"

"How the hell do I know? Ask the spooks. They set up the meeting."

"They were probably afraid of a leak," Bertram said.

All three knew that the Secretary of State and the Secretary of Defense were significant political actors in their own right. Both had been candidates for the presidential nomination, and both were biding their time to compete when Featherstone left office, either after a defeat in the next election or as a consequence of a natural or imposed incident. Featherstone had appointed Harrison and Connors to their current high positions because he wanted them where he could keep an eye on them while exercising a modicum of control over their political and media maneuvering.

"I'll give them their marching orders and include them in our yet to be scheduled crisis meeting," Featherstone continued. "Of course, I expect both of you to attend. Meanwhile, Patricia, brief Ted, and then get to work on your plan to shut down our borders. Ted, you give me a half an hour, and then you call Harrison and Connors and discuss what they have to be doing. Me, I'll be upstairs, and I don't want to be bothered again tonight. If any of the spooks come back and try to get in, Ted, you handle them."

"What do you mean shut down the borders?" Patricia asked.

"Discuss what I mean with Ted," Featherstone dismissed them by turning to his phone. As Marshall and Bertram started for the door, Featherstone called after them. "Damn it Patricia, you should learn what agencies work for you. They include Customs and the Border Guard, Transportation Security, Immigration, and the Coast Guard among others. I want every damned container and suitcase that comes into this country, whether by land, sea, or air examined."

Featherstone pretended not to see Marshall's shocked reaction or the fact that Bertram grabbed her arm and guided her out of the Oval Office as the agent closed the door behind them.

Chapter 5

Chase sat at his breakfast table leisurely sipping bitter coffee, nibbling at his blackened bagel, and scanning the *Post* when his cell phone chimed.

"What?" Chase greeted the caller, assuming it was Theresa. No one else troubled him at home this early.

"Mansfield?" A gruff male voice demanded.

"Who's this?" Chase countered, buying time. He thought he recognized the voice.

"Cotton," Special Agent Tracey Cotton identified himself. After his late night which included the extended White House meeting, Cotton had gotten only four hours sleep and was in no mood to play games with a Fairfax police lieutenant. However, Mansfield was the one who had put him onto the damned Jesperson book, and Cotton was now under pressure to make sure that no leaks about the frigging Iranian bomb came from Mansfield's end. Jesperson's father had provided the printer's proof copy of the book. Mansfield hadn't had an opportunity to read the book, but the father had alerted him to the passages citing the Iranian possession of the bomb and intent to use it.

"Hope I didn't wake you," Cotton said, not meaning it.

Chase glanced at the clock. Eight o'clock. Cotton was trying to be humorous, and Chase wondered what game he was playing. "No problem," Chase answered. "I'm always up by nine on Mondays."

"Good. I called to thank you for the heads up on that Jesperson book," Cotton said. "One of our boys retrieved it, and I had it in my hands by five. It makes real interested reading."

"I thought it might," Chase said as he visualized the frantic alarms that had sounded throughout Washington if the book contained information about Iranian plans for the bomb as Jesperson Senior had noted.

"I briefed the director and others. You can imagine the reaction."

"I sure can," Chase went along with Cotton's routine. "I would like to get a chance to take a look at the book, if I could, to see if there is anything in it that might provide a motive to Jesperson's shooting."

"No problem, but our analysts are studying it now. As soon as they are finished, I'll get it to you forthwith."

"Sounds good," Chase said, assuming he would be able to buy it in the bookstores before the Feds let it out of their hands. "Glad to have been of assistance," he reminded Cotton that he owed Chase.

"There is one little thing," Cotton continued.

"There always is," Chase waited for Cotton to table the real reason he had called.

"There's a little concern here and at the other end of Pennsylvania Avenue," he referred to the White House. "That this allegation about the Iranians and their bomb might leak prematurely to the media before the powers that be decide how to handle it to avoid a mass panic."

"I assumed that someone would have to address that little problem," Chase said.

"To tell the truth…" Cotton spoke softly as if he were afraid he might be overheard.

He's going to lie to me, Chase thought.

"It was suggested that I give you a call and ask that you not discuss this bomb business with anyone else. You haven't have you?"

"Haven't had a chance," Chase lied. "I planned to brief Barney and the chief and the rest of my investigative team in detail this morning. First thing."

"It would be appreciated by all concerned if you kept that little matter to yourself, for now," Cotton said quickly. "Just to keep it out of the hands of the media."

Chase pressured Cotton by not responding.

"For your information only, Chase," Cotton filled the silence. "As we speak our lawyers are pressuring the publisher to postpone releasing the damned book."

"Lots of luck. They've got a sure best seller on their hands, and Jesperson's murder will add to the public interest," Chase provoked Cotton by suggesting that his lawyers might find delaying the book release difficult. "If I were the publisher, I would move the release date forward rather than back."

"I know. Please promise me you'll help me keep this bomb business from leaking to the media. At least give us a chance to check things out," Cotton pressed.

"Of course, I'll do what I can to assist," Chase replied without promising anything specific.

While Cotton was digesting that comment, Chase continued. "There is one thing you can do for me in return," Chase took advantage of the situation.

"Of course," Cotton answered, his tone telling Chase that just uttering the words hurt.

"I would like a chance to go over Townsend's car," Chase said.

"Why would you want to do that?" Cotton reverted to his natural arrogance. "I thought we agreed that you would work the Jesperson thing and leave the Townsend disappearance to us."

"Of course. I just want to touch all the bases, cover my backside with the chief, to be honest." The transparency of that lie made even Chase smile at himself.

"I understand that," Cotton stalled. "But how does a look at Townsend's car help you?" Implicit was the reminder that the two cases were coincidental but unrelated.

"I just want to appear thorough," Chase said. "I don't expect to find a.22 caliber with smoke leaking out of its silencer under the front seat."

"I can assure you that you won't. Our techs have already been all over the vehicle."

"Nonetheless," Chase persisted. Chase's interest in the car was marginal. He really wanted to chat with Mrs. Townsend about her husband's relationship with Jesperson.

"Fine, go ahead. I don't have any objections," Cotton assumed he gave Chase nothing.

"As you know," Chase did not let Cotton wiggle off the hook with a pleasantry, "DHS security towed the car back to Townsend's place. I assume that's where your techs got a look at it."

Cotton grunted, neither confirming nor denying Chase's comment.

"I would appreciate it if you would have someone phone Townsend's DHS security detail and tell them I'll be dropping by first thing this morning."

Cotton greeted that request with silence, so Chase continued. "At least if I am not in the office, the temptation to gossip about the bomb thing won't come up," Chase hinted at a quid pro quo.

"We have a deal," Cotton said curtly and hung up before Chase fished for more.

****

An hour later Chase arrived at the office; Theresa greeted him with a smile, glanced meaningfully at the clock, presumably to remind Chase he was late, and said, "Barney wants to see you, and you have company waiting in your office."

"Good morning, Theresa," Chase said cheerfully and waited for her to identify the visitors.

"Good morning, lieutenant," Theresa nodded and turned her attention to her computer monitor, pretending to be oblivious to Chase's unspoken question.

Chase entered his office and was surprised to find a grim-faced, elderly couple waiting. Theresa had added a second chair to supplement Chase's one visitor complement.

"Good morning, I'm Lieutenant Mansfield," Chase said as he squeezed between the old woman and the wall, bumping her chair in the process.

"Excuse me," Chase smiled. "Tight quarters."

The old lady grimaced but did not did not yield an inch.

"Is the Fairfax Police Department short of funds?" The old lady asked as she turned her head from left to right, clearly denigrating Chase's cramped quarters.

"I apologize if you find it uncomfortable," Chase chuckled as he focused on the odd foreign accent. "Police department offices are always sparse. In this instance, however, I'm to blame not the department. I prefer a compact environment."

"What was it before? A broom closet? It's not big enough to have been a store room," the old lady said. "You should complain."

"I find it efficient and..." Chase began.

"And it discourages unwanted visitors," the old man chuckled, a bemused expression on his face.

"Present company excepted, of course," Chase said politely as he sat down. The voice and accent struck Chase as familiar. "I usually prefer to spend my time elsewhere."

"Eating doughnuts someplace, I assume," the old lady said.

"Investigating, dear," the old man spoke before Chase did. He turned to Chase. "Please excuse us for imposing on you without an appointment.

We know, lieutenant, that you are quite busy with our son's investigation."

"Doctor and Mrs. Jesperson," Chase reacted. "Please accept my condolences for your loss. Coping with a sudden death is always difficult, particularly when it strikes down a son in the prime of his life."

"Thank you, lieutenant," Jesperson said. He stood up and reached across the desk to shake Chase's extended hand.

The old man's firm grip surprised Chase. He glanced at Mrs. Jesperson who acknowledged him with a quick nod.

"We arrived in town late last night and felt we should inform you of our whereabouts first thing," the old man turned immediately to business as he sat back down.

"Have you identified our son's…killer?" The old lady asked, speaking over her husband's explanation for their presence.

"We are staying in our son's condominium," Doctor Jesperson ignored his wife's interruption before Chase could answer. "Is there any way we can help?"

"When can we see Hamid? Where is he?" Mrs. Jesperson continued.

Chase looked from one to the other, not sure which question to answer first.

"May I offer your guests some coffee?" Theresa spoke from the door before Chase could decide.

Chase deferred to the visitors with a look.

"Yes, please," Doctor Jesperson responded.

"What kind of coffee?" Mrs. Jesperson asked.

"Freshly percolated," Theresa answered with a smile. "How do you take it?"

"Hot and black," Doctor Jesperson said.

"Cream and sugar, real cream and real sugar," Mrs. Jesperson ordered.

Theresa looked at Chase, who nodded affirmatively, surprised because Theresa usually declined to serve him coffee.

After Theresa departed, Chase tried to control the discussion. "Doctor, Mrs. Jesperson, let me assure you that we are doing everything we can to identify your son's killer. To be honest, right now, our investigation is still in the early stages."

"That's to be expected, lieutenant. Could you brief us on the circumstances of Thomas' death?" Doctor Jesperson said.

"Why haven't you…" Mrs. Jesperson, whose dark black hair and clothing style made her appear at least ten years younger than her husband, interrupted.

Doctor Jesperson surprised Chase by reaching towards his wife and grasping her wrist. The gesture silenced Mrs. Jesperson in mid-question.

"Manujeh, let the lieutenant answer my questions, please," Doctor Jesperson ordered.

To Chase's surprise Mrs. Jesperson reacted with relative calm. She glared at her husband but said nothing more. Doctor Jesperson nodded and released her wrist.

"Your son hosted a meeting at Henderson Hall of George Mason University that began about seven. The guest speaker was a friend of his, the Secretary of the Department of Homeland Security..." Chase began his truncated report.

"Jimmy Townsend," Mrs. Jesperson blurted.

The old man silenced his wife with a look.

Theresa appeared and served the coffee before departing.

During the brief hiatus, Chase assumed that being eighty years old--at least that was what he estimated-- and having been married for almost fifty years, gave a husband some latitude. Chase doubted that he could get away with such controlling behavior with any of his female acquaintances; certainly Barbara and Jacky would react, physically if necessary.

"Yes," Chase said. "Secretary Townsend arrived on campus about seven. Doctor Jesperson escorted him to the auditorium where some two hundred students and faculty were assembled; Townsend addressed them for two hours, and Doctor Jesperson and Secretary Townsend returned to your son's office for a quick drink while they waited for the audience to depart."

"I'm surprised that even Thomas could persuade James to address a group on campus," Doctor Jesperson said.

"They've been friends since college days at Cornell," Mrs. Jesperson said.

"I know that, Manujeh, but I doubt that James can find a friendly audience on any campus today," Doctor Jesperson frowned as he addressed his wife. He turned back to Chase. "Lieutenant, you should know that Thomas and James were close friends in college, as my wife noted, but they drifted apart over the years. James followed a political career, and Thomas turned out to be surprisingly apolitical. I'm sure, also, that Thomas was a little envious of James' remarkable success."

"You are always belittling Thomas just because he didn't teach in an Ivy League school," Mrs. Jesperson challenged her husband.

Chase patiently watched the two spar. He rather liked the old man's directness, but Mrs. Jesperson was something else. She was still a handsome woman, and he assumed she must have been a beauty in her youth, but now she was clearly a handful. In public she appeared to bend reluctantly to her husband's admonitions, but Chase suspected that in private she more than held her own. He almost laughed as he visualized the less than harmonious domestic environment.

"Just because he's been at MIT for fifty years," Mrs. Jesperson spoke to Chase before glaring at her husband. "He has always belittled Thomas and his many achievements. You know you have," she frowned at the old man. "Thomas used to tell me you made him feel like he was a second class citizen."

Chase waited in silence for the old man to defend himself.

Instead, Doctor Jesperson ignored his wife and looked at Chase, waiting for him to continue his report. A sympathetic Chase nodded as he speculated that Mrs. Jesperson suffered from some kind of second-class resentment syndrome of her own caused by her immigrant status.

"I'm told that Secretary Townsend accepted the invitation only because of his personal relationship with your son," Chase said.

"You were saying that Thomas and James had a drink together after the meeting," Doctor Jesperson encouraged Chase to stop the extraneous chatter and continue his report.

"I'll bet it was Araq," Mrs. Jesperson interrupted again. "It was one of Hamid's favorites, his Persian genes talking," she smiled at Chase.

"Hamid was your son's middle name?" Chase asked, responding politely to her irritating interjections.

"I prefer to use Thomas," Doctor Jesperson tried to put an end to the diverting discussion of names.

Mrs. Jesperson smiled and nodded her head to answer Chase's polite question.

"I think it was Araq," Chase said.

"How long after James left did Thomas live before he was shot?" Doctor Jesperson pressed.

"We don't know, exactly," Chase said. "I am waiting for the coroner's report. Can either of you tell me the name of your son's house guest?" Chase asked, trying to cut short any discussion of Townsend. Thus far the media hadn't learned of the DHS secretary's unexplained disappearance.

Chase deliberately directed his question at both elderly Jespersons even though it was Mrs. Jesperson who had hung up on him when he had previously asked her the identity of the visitor.

"Mansour Taheri is one of my wife's numerous Iranian relatives," Doctor Jesperson answered.

"My nephew knows nothing about what happened to his cousin," Mrs. Jesperson said.

"Grandnephew," her husband corrected.

"My sister's grandson," Mrs. Jesperson snapped back. "Mansour has been in this country only a couple of days."

"At least two weeks," Doctor Jesperson said.

"Where is Mansour now?" Chase asked. "I would like to chat with him."

"What about?" Mrs. Jesperson challenged. "I told you he knows nothing."

"Did he tell you where he's staying, Mrs. Jesperson?" Chase pressed.

"She hasn't talked with him, lieutenant," Doctor Jesperson said. "Some of his things are in the apartment, but we don't know where he is."

"Does Mansour have friends in the Washington area?" Chase asked.

"No," Mrs. Jesperson answered.

"We don't know," Doctor Jesperson said. "As soon as he appears, we will give you a call."

"Thank you sir. I would appreciate that," Chase said. "And if any of your son's friends should contact you, I would appreciate knowing that also."

"Why?" Mrs. Jesperson demanded.

"Of course," Doctor Jesperson agreed, ignoring his wife. "Do you have any idea when we might have our son? We plan to bury him in a family plot in Cambridge and will return home as soon as we can. There is nothing for us to do here."

"That depends on the coroner's office," Chase answered. "I will inform the coroner of your desires."

"I want to see him," Mrs. Jesperson said.

"And I will arrange that also. As soon as we are finished here. Could you tell me a little more about Mansour? Will he be staying long?"

"No," Mrs. Jesperson answered quickly.

"Thomas was arranging for him to attend university here," Doctor Jesperson said. "Starting next semester."

"At George Mason?"

Jesperson nodded affirmatively.

"Of course," Mrs. Jesperson said. "The family wants him someplace where we can help him adjust. They're afraid that Mansour will find life here overwhelming."

"He's a naïve boy," Doctor Jesperson said. "I don't know what will happen to him now that Thomas isn't available to help him."

"We can't send him back to Iran now," Mrs. Jesperson spoke to her husband who tried to reassure her by patting her on the knee.

Chase waited for one of his visitors to explain.

"Mansour's mother, like all of us, is worried about how the publication of Thomas' book will impact on the family, particularly Mansour," Doctor Chase said.

Chase resisted the urge to ask why.

"Must we really go into all that now," Mrs. Jesperson glared at her husband.

"Yes, dear, I think so. If Lieutenant Mansfield is going to find who killed Thomas, he needs our help." Doctor Jesperson turned to Chase. "We've already discussed certain chapters in the book," Jesperson said. "Mansour's mother's brother was the source of much of Thomas' sensitive information. He is a nuclear scientist who was educated at MIT."

"My nephew Mehtab, Mansour's father, stayed with us in Cambridge, and my husband arranged for his scholarship," Mrs. Jesperson said. "That is what families do."

"I'm getting confused," Chase said.

Doctor Jesperson laughed wryly. "You're not alone. I have trouble keeping my wife's relatives straight. Mehtab Taheri, the son of my wife's sister, attended MIT. When he returned home, he married Anahi Baghai and had a son, Mansour. Anahi's brother," Doctor Jesperson paused and lowered his voice, acting as if he were afraid they might be overheard. "Anahi's brother," he repeated softly, "Obediah Baghai, attended MIT at the same time that Mansour's father Mehtab did. Obediah did not stay with us, thank God because two Iranians in the house at one time were almost too much for one person to stand," Doctor Jesperson smiled at his wife who frowned. "Obediah visited us often because the two boys were close friends, two strangers in a foreign environment. To be frank, Obediah was by far the most intelligent of the two."

"That's your opinion," Mrs. Jesperson interrupted, her tone unforgiving.

"It is," Doctor Jesperson nodded seriously. "An informed opinion if I must say so myself. Mehtab teaches physics in a local secondary school, and Obediah is a nuclear scientist. I would say their subsequent careers substantiates my professional opinion."

"Let me see if I have this straight," Chase said. "Mehtab Taheri is the son of Mrs. Jesperson's sister and attended MIT at the same time as a fellow countryman, Obediah Baghai. After graduation, the boys returned to Iran where Mehtab married Obediah's sister."

"That is correct, lieutenant," Mrs. Jesperson said with some asperity. "Obediah's sister's name is Anahi. That is not so difficult to understand, is it?"

"Not when you express it so clearly, Mrs. Jesperson. You must forgive me. I have not had much experience dealing with Persian names," Chase ignored her tone.

"What foreign languages do you speak, lieutenant?" Mrs. Jesperson asked abruptly.

"None, I regret to say," Chase answered with a forced smile before continuing. "Let me see if I have the relationships straight. Subsequently, Anahi and Mehtab had a son, Mansour. When your son Thomas, Doctor Jesperson, visited Iran he…"

"Lieutenant, we are speaking frankly with you about intimate and sensitive family details, and we must insist that everything we now tell you be treated with the utmost confidence," Doctor Jesperson said softly. "Otherwise, our lips are sealed. If any word gets back to Iran, many in the family will suffer."

"They'll kill everyone ," Mrs. Jesperson blurted as her eyes filled with tears. "My sister, my nephew…"

Doctor Jesperson stopped his wife's lament with another pat and a consoling, "Yes dear, we know." He then looked at Chase and continued. "I'm sure Mansour is in a quandary and doesn't know what to do. Are you familiar with the visa problem that Iranian students who want to study in the States face?"

"No," Chase answered honestly. The subject had never come to his attention, and he usually avoided any media articles on foreign affairs. He assumed that any bad news arriving from that direction would come to his attention too soon, and he accomplished nothing by wringing his hands with needless worry stimulated by foreign news reporters padding their bylines.

"We have a very strange policy. You know that we do not have formal diplomatic relations with Iran and have not had representation in Teheran since the mobs seized our embassy and held our diplomats hostage."

"Yes," Chase said, wondering where this was heading.

"Don't worry," the perceptive Doctor Jesperson read his reaction. "I'm not going to lecture you. I'm about talked out, anyway. Succinctly, our government issues student visas to Iranian students, one time visas."

"I don't know what that means," Chase said.

'It means that Iranians can apply for a student visa at our Embassy in Ankara or at another place where we maintain an Iranian Immigrant Processing Post, places like Vienna, Abu Dhabi, Frankfurt and Naples. After a lengthy process that can take several months, qualified applicants are issued a one-time student visa." Doctor Jesperson glanced at the look on Chase's face and laughed.

"Please bear with me. This is important to Mansour," Jesperson said. "A one-time visa means exactly what it says. The holder can enter the US just one time. If he leaves for any reason, a family emergency, a holiday visit home, whatever, he cannot return to the States to continue his study until he goes through the entire long applicant process again."

"That hardly seems fair," Chase said.

"It isn't," Mrs. Jesperson declared.

"But in this day of terrorism and given the current Iranian government's not very veiled support of our terrorist enemies, our government believes it has no choice but to closely monitor and control Iranian access to our country," Doctor Jesperson said.

"But it is terribly unfair to students like Mansour who are not terrorists," Mrs. Jesperson said. "I do not agree."

"Yes dear," Doctor Jesperson said, turning his attention back to Chase. "I'm sure that Mansour is in a panic. Someone murdered his American relative, his sponsor, and he must feel terribly alone."

"But he knows I am family, his grandmother's sister," Mrs. Jesperson protested.

"Yes, but I doubt he even remembers you. You only met him once, and at the time he was just a baby. Besides, to him, you are just an old lady."

Mrs. Jesperson glared at her husband giving Chase the impression that she did not appreciate her husband's description of her.

"In any case, I'm sure Mansour is worried out of his mind. He's in a strange country, and his American relative has just been murdered. He also knows the circumstances surrounding his presence here, the fact that his uncle secretly collaborated with Thomas to expose his government's nuclear machinations and that he has been sent to America to protect him and to guarantee his family's continued survival."

"The young man must be very worried and unsure what to do," Chase said.

"We're here to recover our son and to take him home and to do what we can for poor Mansour," Mrs. Jesperson restated the obvious.

"Lieutenant, we are speaking very frankly. Can we rely on you to protect our family confidences? We don't want to endanger anyone in Iran, and we refuse to become a public spectacle at this very difficult time for us," Doctor Jesperson said.

"I understand and sympathize," Chase said. "I will honor your trust. My duty is to bring your son's murderer to justice. The federal government will have to deal with national security and those other issues."

"I'll take you at your word, lieutenant," Doctor Jesperson said. "Obediah, Mansour's uncle, loves Iran and the United States. He is a talented scientist who began his career helping Iran develop its nuclear energy program. Iran's oil reserves are a blessing, but Obediah, like many of his educated peers, realizes that oil is a finite resource, and he has dedicated his life to helping prepare his country and its impoverished people for the future. Unfortunately, Obediah and his fellow scientists have been forced by misguided, evil leaders to assist in the development of a concentrated secret program to provide Iran with a nuclear arsenal. Thomas told me that Obediah over time realized that he has a moral obligation to let the world know that Iran's leaders have lied when they insist that their government's nuclear effort has only peaceful objectives. Obediah, of course, being an intelligent man, realized that such a course of action would endanger not only himself but his entire family. Thomas' arrival to research his book, which he told the government would focus on historical Iran, gave Obediah the opportunity for which he had been searching. Although Obediah is older than Thomas, the two developed a fraternal relationship during the period Obediah attended MIT. For obvious reasons, Obediah avoided public contact with Thomas in Iran but privately met with him in the homes of relatives. While they renewed their earlier intimacy, Obediah assessed his American relative. Finally Obediah decided he could trust Thomas with his life and confided in him. Realizing the importance of Obediah's disclosures, Thomas continued to research his historical tome while acquiring the information that he needed to draft the book that he eventually wrote."

Jesperson paused and took a deep breath. "Now, you know our problem.

We have to bury our son, assist Mansour, protect the family, and help you find our son's killer. We don't know for sure if the Iranians killed our son or not. I don't know what he confided to James, his friend, or what James is doing about the threat because I haven't been able to contact James. Somebody at his home refuses to let me talk with James, just tells me that Secretary Townsend is not available. What should I do?"

Chase hesitated before responding. The Jesperson story gave Chase much to think about; certainly, it could explain Townsend's strange disappearance. Somebody acting on behalf of the Iranian Government could be holding Townsend as some sort of hostage. Chase immediately began wondering what else Cotton and the Feds were not telling him. Chase glanced at Doctor Jesperson and noted that the old man and his wife were waiting for him to answer the question.

"Doctor Jesperson, Mrs. Jesperson," Chase said. "What you just told me is news to me, and it certainly must worry you as much if not more than it does me. I can't tell you what to do, of course, but I suggest that you concentrate on your son and family. I'll arrange to have you taken to the coroner's office where you can view your son, and I'll authorize them to release him to you. I also suggest that you not discuss what you just told me with another person, particularly not with the media. I will make sure that the federal government is appropriately aware of the situation and the need to keep that knowledge secret. As a matter of fact, as soon as you and I part, I will go directly to Secretary Townsend's home and office and will not rest until I meet with him and learn what he can do to assist us."

"Good," Doctor Jesperson said. He turned to his wife. "I told you this was the best place for us to start."

The old lady nodded, but the expression on her face did not tell Chase that she was convinced.

"I also need to talk with Mansour," Chase spoke to Mrs. Jesperson.

"As soon as Mansour appears, we'll contact you, lieutenant," Doctor Jesperson said, "and we will keep Mansour available until the two of you meet."

Mrs. Jesperson again frowned but did not object. Chase was not sure how she would handle his request if it were left to her.

"And please caution Mansour to talk with no one about this matter until we meet," Chase said. "Any public comment on the subject could be disastrous for the family as well as the country."

"You refer to the nuclear threat," Doctor Jesperson said.

Chase nodded.

"I want to go home, now," Mrs. Jesperson declared.

"Yes dear," her husband said. "As soon as we make arrangements for Thomas to accompany us, and we find Mansour in order to put him into good hands," Jesperson looked meaningfully at Chase.

****

FBI Director Philip D'Antonio, Acting Secretary of DHS Patricia Marshall, CIA Director William H. Pace, Assistant to the President for National Security Affairs Doctor Barbara Luce, Secretary of State Harriet Francis Connors, and Secretary of Defense Denver A. Harrison sat in their customary chairs around the cramped crisis center conference table. Special Agent Tracey Cotton occupied a wall chair behind his boss, the FBI director, and Theodore "Ted" Bertram, the president's chief of staff, stood near the door. All wore worried expressions as they waited for President Arthur C. Featherstone to make his appearance. Suddenly the door opened, and all turned with forced smiles, which changed into frowns, as soon as they saw Heather, the president's secretary, and not the man himself.

"Special Agent Cotton," Heather pointed a finger and indicated he should follow her.

All of the waiting senior officials glared at Cotton's back as he obediently followed Heather out the door.

"What is that about?" Secretary of State Connors demanded of FBI Director D'Antonio.

D'Antonio shrugged. Although he shared a mutual dislike with the secretary of state, he, too, resented the fact that the president chose to meet privately with the most junior official present prior to condescending to confer with his senior appointees.

"I fail to understand why I was not included in your meeting last night when you discussed this," the secretary of state waved a copy of the offending chapters from Jesperson's book.

"Madam Secretary, ask the president, not me," D'Antonio replied, glancing at the CIA director as he spoke.

Pace reacted with a smile before glancing at Acting DHS Secretary Marshall who ignored the exchange. The three of them, Marshall, Pace, and D'Antonio had agreed in a conference call prior to the previous meeting to restrict the participants in an effort to minimize the possibility of unwanted leaks.

As soon as she closed the door, Heather turned to Cotton. "Sorry if I embarrassed you," Heather said as she smiled at the room behind her. "You have a priority call from your ops center."

Cotton chuckled. "They think you have me is conferring with the president."

"You can take it over there," Heather pointed at a phone on the desk opposite her usual post in the crisis center. "You better hurry because the man is on his way."

Cotton picked up the phone. "Cotton."

"Special Agent Cotton, this is the duty officer. I have an urgent call for you from the New York office. Shall I put it through?"

"Make it fast," Cotton said.

"Tracey, I hope I'm not interrupting, but this is something you need to know. I'm calling from the publishers," the Special Agent in Charge of the New York Field Office, a peer and friend of Cotton, said without preliminaries.

"What's happening?" Cotton asked. He anticipated the news was bad because he had asked the New York office to lean on Jesperson's publisher in an attempt to get him to postpone the planned release date.

"We were too late. Upon hearing of Jesperson's murder, the agent and publisher conferred and agreed the opportunity presented by the author's death was too good to pass up. After conferring with their lawyers, they decided that Jesperson's death released them from the obligation to abide by his release date. A copy of the book was hand-carried to the *New York Times* this morning."

"Shit," Cotton swore.

"I assume the news is not good, Special Agent Cotton," President Arthur C. Featherstone announced his presence.

"The publisher is meeting with a group of network reporters as we speak," the New York SAC said. "And that's not all. The greedy bastards shipped some two hundred thousand copies to booksellers throughout the United States, and they have already authorized the printing of another five hundred thousand copies."

"Did they understand the full implications of their decisions?" Cotton asked.

"They said they considered what might happen and decided the people have a right to know."

"Thanks for nothing," Cotton said as he hung up.

"It's worse than bad news, Mr. President. That was our New York Office. The publishers have released the book, and the media has it."

The color drained from Featherstone's face. He frowned, nodded to acknowledge Cotton's words, and led the way past the Secret Service agents guarding the entrance to the crisis center conference room.

When the door burst open and the agitated president followed by Cotton entered, everyone turned. The expression on Featherstone's face told the senior officials everything they needed to know. Only Secretary of State Harriet Connors, who made no secret of the fact that she felt Featherstone was occupying an office that was rightfully hers, spoke. "Good Morning, Mr. President," Connors said.

Featherstone who normally treated his defeated rival with exaggerated courtesy frowned. "There's nothing good about it, Madam Secretary."

The rebuke hit Connors like a slap in the face. She flushed, took a deep breath, and glared at the president. Featherstone's tone was so sharp and frosty that none of the others spoke. Cotton's boss, Director D'Antonio, looked at his subordinate, but Cotton did not dare react with a whispered alert as he took his place behind him.

Featherstone dropped heavily into his chair and silently surveyed the room. Before he could speak, the door opened and Vice President Charles Z. Hampton burst into the room.

"Sorry sir, but I came directly from Andrews," Hampton greeted his superior. Unbeknownst to the others, Featherstone had ordered Hampton to cut short a political trip that featured a series of speeches across the south.

Featherstone nodded to acknowledge Hampton's arrival. Featherstone knew that the vice president's abrupt return to Washington would further agitate the media, but Featherstone considered Hampton a reliable friend who could be counted on to provide carefully measured and selfless advice in a time of crisis.

"We have a real emergency on our hands, Charles, and I'm afraid our options are being rapidly curtailed. If you forgive me, I will brief you more fully after we hear what our assembled experts have to recommend," Featherstone said.

"Certainly, Mr. President," Hampton said as he took his normal position at the table opposite the president.

"I believe everyone but the vice president is aware of our problem," Featherstone said as he turned to look at Cotton who sat along the wall to the president's right. "Special Agent Cotton, please brief us on your most recent conversation."

The sudden deferral surprised everyone, including Cotton, but he reacted with poise.

"Yes, Mr. President. "I just got off the phone with our New York Office. At the president's orders..." Cotton paused to defer to his director who had turned and was listening with the same intensity as the others. D'Antonio nodded, and Cotton continued. "...Director D'Antonio ordered our New York Office to contact the publishers of Doctor Jesperson's book "Nuclear Terrorism, the Iranian Challenge" with an urgent request. In the interest of national security, we asked that Regency Books temporarily postpone the book's release date, previously set for next Wednesday, in order to give the government time to assess the sensational information that Doctor Jesperson had collected during his most recent sabbatical in Iran. Unfortunately, Regency Books and Doctor Jesperson's agent had conferred and had decided they had an obligation to release the book immediately because the American people have a right to know. Some two hundred thousand copies of the book are now in the hands of the bookstores and the media."

"Thank you Special Agent Cotton," the president took charge before the others could start chattering about the implications of that development. "Before we begin a general discussion, I have several questions I will address to those of you who have specific responsibilities. I ask that you respond with precise answers devoid of opinion which we can address later."

"Mr. President, may I ask a question before we begin," Secretary of State Connors interrupted.

"I would prefer that you hold any questions until after I have asked mine," the president said.

"But…" Connors started to debate the response.

"Director D'Antonio," Featherstone ignored Connors. "My first question for you is, who killed Doctor Jesperson and why?"

"The Fairfax County Police have assumed responsibility for investigating Doctor Jesperson's death," D'Antonio answered before turning to Cotton.

"We are in close touch with Lieutenant Chase Mansfield, a senior and experienced investigator, who is directing the investigation," Cotton said. "As of eight o'clock this morning, Lieutenant Mansfield had yet to identify the perpetrator or his motive." Although he was tempted to speculate, particularly about potential Iranian involvement, Cotton knew better than say too much at this stage of an investigation, particularly in this politically sensitive milieu.

Although his expression indicated he was not pleased with the answer, Featherstone continued. "Thank you for the precise response." Featherstone turned to Acting Secretary of the Department of Homeland Security Patricia Marshall. "Secretary Marshall, where is Secretary Townsend?"

"I don't know sir," Marshall replied quickly. "The Bureau has assumed responsibility for locating James…Secretary Townsend."

"Director?" Featherstone looked again at D'Antonio.

"Sir, as part of our agreement with the Fairfax Police, the Bureau is investigating Secretary Townsend's apparent disappearance," D'Antonio said as he turned again to Cotton.

"Sir," Cotton said. "I am responsible for coordinating the investigation of the secretary's disappearance. At the secretary's insistence, his security detail did not accompany the secretary to George Mason University. We know that the secretary drove himself in his own car, was met by Doctor Jesperson, an old friend, and spoke to a large group of faculty and students, no media, in the Center for the Arts. After a spirited two-hour discussion, about nine PM. Secretary Townsend retreated to Doctor Jesperson's office on the second floor of Henderson Hall. There, the two of them chatted over a drink, presumably giving the audience an opportunity to disperse. We do not know what time the two men parted. At twelve thirty-five AM a campus guard phoned the Fairfax police to report a homicide. Subsequent investigation disclosed that a cleaning lady had found Doctor Jesperson alone in his office with two bullet wounds a few minutes prior to the twelve-thirty call to the Fairfax police. Secretary Townsend's personal car was subsequently found in a nearby campus lot. We have no indication how, when, or with whom Secretary Townsend departed the campus, and we do not know his current status or whereabouts. His spouse and his security detail cannot explain his sudden disappearance.

Featherstone turned to CIA Director William H. Pace. "Director, now that your staff has had an opportunity to review the information in the pertinent chapters from Doctor Jesperson's book, do you find the allegations that the Iranians have an atomic bomb and plan to use it reliable?"

"Mr. President I cannot give you the categorical answer that you desire," Pace answered.

"That I need from my intelligence chief," Featherstone corrected him. "What is your best guess?"

"My experts tell me that it is possible," Pace equivocated.

"What does that mean?"

"Sir, we do not know the identity of Doctor Jesperson's source. If the source was an Iranian nuclear physicist working in the Natanz complex in a position that gave him access to the information we are discussing and if we knew why he was motivated to confide in Jesperson, we could assess the reliability of the information he was providing. We cannot do that based solely on the data contained in the three chapters that we have reviewed thus far."

"How can a simple university professor acquire information that your organization cannot?" Featherstone asked.

Pace did not attempt to answer the question which he assumed was rhetorical. Featherstone frowned, and asked another.

"Director Pace, assuming the Iranians have the bomb, will they use it as Doctor Jesperson alleges in his book?"

"Mr. President, I cannot answer that question with certainty," Pace said. He glanced at the Secretary of State, silently appealing for support, but Secretary Harriet Connors wisely said nothing.

"Give me your best estimate," Featherstone pressed. "Your agency is in the business of publishing national estimates, are they not?"

"Sir, we do not have sufficient information to support an estimate on such a critical issue," Pace said. "As my Deputy Director for Intelligence, Dr Schultz, previously noted, predicting what the Iranians will or will not do is very difficult. Deception is a way of life for them, and they are not inhibited by the need to be consistent. What they say they are going to do today could change tomorrow. They clearly agree with Henry David Thoreau that foolish consistencies are the hobgoblins of foolish minds."

"So it is your position that Doctor Jesperson's source's allegation that the Iranians plan to use a nuclear weapon against us in the very near future is just speculation." Featherstone demanded.

Pace shook his head negatively, trying to convey the notion he did not know, but he did not speak.

Featherstone stared his disapproval and turned away from the embattled CIA director.

"Very well," Featherstone said. "Let me summarize the situation. A respected professor has been found murdered in his office on the eve of the publication of a book that quotes Iranian sources as reporting that the Iranians have a nuclear bomb and intend to use it in the near future. The billion-dollar United States Government intelligence community cannot confirm or deny those allegations and can only advise their president who is charged with protecting the American people that the Iranians are practitioners of deception, cannot be believed when they speak, and are inconsistent in their policies. Special Agent Cotton," the president surprised everyone in the room by interrupting his harangue and addressing the most junior official in the room. "Special Agent Cotton when can we expect Doctor Jesperson's predictions to appear in the media?"

Cotton, who had been slouching in his chair against the wall comfortably out of the angry president's line of fire, jerked erect.

"Sir, our New York Office reports that the book was delivered by messenger to the *New York Times* this morning. The publisher is briefing the networks and wire service as we speak, and some two hundred thousand copies of the book have been sent to bookstores throughout the United States. Also, the publisher has ordered a second printing of five hundred thousand books."

"Thank you Special Agent Cotton," Featherstone said. "That is the kind of precise and informed report that I expect from everyone in this room." Featherstone glared at his CIA director before continuing. "Now that we know that the American people are being bombarded with breaking news reports alleging that they are about to nuked, what do you recommend that this government do about it?"

A heavy silence filled the room as each and every member of the nation's national security leadership abided by the same commonsense adage. "It's better to be criticized for saying nothing than to try to justify offering bad advice."

"Mr. President," Doctor Barbara Luce, the National Security Advisor, an academic from USC, finally spoke. "I suggest we elevate the alert level."

"That's very helpful, Doctor," Featherstone said, his voice heavy with sarcasm. He looked about the room, but no one spoke. "The people are being told by the media to expect to be nuked, and their president announces he is changing the color of Homeland Security alert from green to red. That should relax them."

"Sir, I'm not sure it's possible to do that right now," Patricia Marshall, the Acting Secretary of Homeland Security said.

Everyone sitting around the table, including the president stared at her, waiting for her to explain.

"You may recall that last month everyone agreed that our five color code system wasn't working. Secretary Townsend charged me with managing its change. On Monday, I put out a memo announcing a changeover to a new Homeland Security Advisory System with the codes that the media had ridiculed immediately replaced with a new system. Now, our new alerts are only two tiered, either 'imminent' or 'elevated' with each announcement containing a concise summary of the potential threat, information about actions being taken to ensure public safety, and recommended steps that individuals and communities can take."

"Oh shit, Patricia," Featherstone blurted. "You're saying that I am supposed to tell the nation the Iranians are nuking us; all school children should hide under their desks, and everyone at home should take refuge in the bathtub or under the dining room table?"

"This was agreed to by everyone, sir," the Acting Secretary of Homeland Security tried to share her master's ire.

"I suggest that DHS immediately tighten security at ports, airports, all points of entry to the United States," Doctor Luce, the National Security Advisor, tried to support the Acting DHS Secretary.

"We are doing that, ma'am," Patricia Marshall said.

"And what does Defense have to say about all of this," Featherstone turned to Denver Harrison, the Secretary of Defense, a former congressman who specialized in budget management and public relations not armed forces deployment.

"Sir we should immediately alert our forces around the world," Harrison said.

Featherstone glanced at his old congressional friend, a political ally he had appointed to his present position with instructions to get a restraining hand on defense expenditures. "Saying what, specifically, Mr. Secretary?" Featherstone asked as worried about what Harrison might say.

"Implement a stage one alert, a nuclear attack is imminent," Harrison answered.

Featherstone grimaced; those were the very words that every president feared most. Harrison had misread him.

Privately, Featherstone acknowledged that Harrison was in a position far beyond his abilities, and Featherstone himself was directly responsible. He had appointed Harrison to the damned job simply because he wanted someone at the Pentagon he could control. Featherstone firmly believed that most defense secretaries, regardless of their individual competence, background, and qualifications, were quickly subsumed by the joint chiefs who were primarily interested in getting the largest share of defense monies for their respective service's latest toys.

"Let's not get too far in front of the situation," Secretary of State Harriet Francis Connors finally tossed her two cents into the pot.

A relieved Featherstone looked at Connors and nodded for her to speak.

"The Iranians are all bluster. We don't know for sure they have a bomb, and we certainly don't know that they are going to use it against us if they have one," Connors said. "All we have to go on is some damned professor's musings based on something that an Iranian source may or may not have said. For all we know, this professor may have made the whole story up just to sell some books. It has happened before."

"What do our foreign service experts have to say about all this?" Featherstone tried to encourage his political rival to turn from opinion to facts.

"Mr. President, you know we don't have an embassy in Iran, haven't had for over thirty-one years. We're completely dependent on diplomatic chitchat and the Agency," she glared at the CIA director who ignored her. "And you know my views about the latter."

Featherstone assumed Connors referred to the Agency's limited reporting, not diplomatic chitchat. Connors, who represented the party's left wing, had always been a knee- jerk critic of the Agency. "Have your analysts taken a look at Jesperson 's information? What do they say about it?"

"Mr. President, your security and intelligence directors did not see fit to share this information with State until this morning. My analysts haven't had a chance to study it." Connors frowned at the CIA and FBI directors before glancing at the National Security Advisor who in her opinion thought she should be managing foreign affairs instead of the Secretary of State and the Foreign Service cookie pushers.

"I would like CIA, Defense, and State to take a close look at the information available and tell me whether the Iranians have a bomb or not," Featherstone ordered.

"Do you want me to chair a working group?" Barbara Luce, the NSC Advisor asked.

"I think we should address the issues separately," Harriet Connors said. "Speaking for State, I suggest these damned working groups are a waste of time. They always end up as a cluster fuck," she hesitated. "A futile endeavor that never reaches any conclusions."

"Whatever," Featherstone said. He was tempted to ask what conclusion a cluster fuck was designed to attain, but he did not. He had problems to deal with that were bigger than debating bureaucratic turf issues. He turned to his NSC Advisor. "You sort it out and give me each agency's position by close of business today."

"I still think we should announce an elevation of the alert codes, sir," Patricia Marshall, Acting DHS Secretary said.

"Handle it," Featherstone said. "Just make sure that terrorists don't get any nuclear bombs into the country."

"And try not to shut down our ports or airports in the process," Ted Bertram, the president's chief of staff, spoke for the first time.

"Christ, no," Featherstone said. "The media and the public are going to be frantic as it is without our actions feeding the fire."

"But..." Marshall started to protest.

"Madame Secretary, you are the boss at DHS. Just take care of the problems without making more," Featherstone ordered.

"And I think we should put the Armed Forces on maximum alert," Denver Harrison, Defense Secretary, said.

Featherstone glanced at his chief of staff before replying.

"I don't think we have a choice," Bertram said.

"Do it," Featherstone ordered. He considered Bertram the only person in the room with an ounce of common sense untainted by a personal agenda.

Featherstone stood up and started for the door, then halted. "I want everyone to keep in close contact with Ted on this situation, and we'll meet here again at eight to go over what we have learned."

"Eight? Tomorrow morning?" Connors asked, her tone making it clear she thought that too early.

"Tonight, twenty hundred hours, eight PM," Featherstone said as he slammed the door behind him.

Chapter 6

After Chase briefed Barney and Sergeant Moscowitz, he introduced Moscowitz to the Jespersons and then accompanied the Jespersons to the County Coroner's Office where the old couple tearfully reunited with their son. Chase negotiated the release of Doctor Thomas Jespersons's body to his parents and departed, leaving an unhappy Moscowitz to escort the Jespersons through their ordeal.

After checking with Detective Whitten to learn that the Townsend residence was located in McLean off Route123, just east of the CIA headquarters building, Chase, driving his Prius, followed George Washington Memorial Parkway to Route 123. He took 123 west, missed his turn, continued on to the CIA entrance, made a U-turn, and finally located his intersection. He then traveled three blocks to the Townsend mansion. A uniformed security guard stopped him at the driveway entrance; Chase lowered his window and waved his credentials.

"Are you expected?" The unimpressed guard demanded.

"Yes," Chase smiled.

"Wait here," the guard ordered as he turned his back on Chase and retreated to the guard shack.

Chase stared at the lowered gate and ignored the officious man as he consulted a superior on his cell phone.

"Tell your story to security," the guard said when he returned and handed his cell to Chase.

"Hello," Chase said.

"Who the hell are you and what do you want?" A surly male demanded.

"I could be your worst nightmare," Chase said brightly. "My name is Mansfield, and I am in charge of the Fairfax County police investigation into the murder of Doctor Thomas Jesperson. Raise the damned gate, or I'll ram it."

"I'm impressed," the gruff voice said. "Now turn around and leave, or I'll have the guard take out his weapon and deflate all four of your tires."

"Do that and I'll charge him and you with attacking a Fairfax County police officer in the performance of his duty," Chase tired of the debate.

"You didn't answer my question," the unimpressed voice demanded.

"As I said if you listened instead of braying, my name is Mansfield. Special Agent Cotton of the Federal Bureau of Investigation cleared my visit," Chase said. "Now raise the damned gate."

"Just a minute," the voice ordered.

Several minutes passed. Just as Chase was trying to assess how much damage the wood gate would do to the front of his Prius, the man came back on line.

"Give the phone to the guard," the man ordered.

"He wants to talk to you," Chase handed the phone to the waiting guard.

The guard listened, nodded, turned his back on Chase, and retreated to his booth.

The gate rose.

"Park in front of the garage and knock on the front door," the guard ordered.

Chase waved and followed the paved driveway through a stand of trees and the curve to the front of a large, brick, one storey, California style mansion whose worth Chase estimated at two million. He immediately assumed that Secretary Townsend came from what the public called a good family because he knew that even cabinet members did not earn that kind of money. All Chase really knew about Townsend's background was that he had been a staffer favored by then Congressman Arthur Featherstone and had followed his mentor up the ladder until selected by President Featherstone to serve as Secretary of the Department of Homeland Security. The modern brick and glass palace told Chase that it had been a rewarding career despite the modest salaries paid government workers.

Chase parked in front of the closed, three-car garage as directed and strolled to the front door where he found a husky, short male with long hair and a wrinkled, ill-fitting suit waiting.

"Good morning," Chase said pleasantly.

The man grunted and held out his hand. Chase waved his credentials and patiently let the security guard scan them.

"There's nothing for you here," the man spoke for the first time.

"I know, but before I leave I'm going to inspect the secretary's car, and then I will chat with Mrs. Townsend about her missing husband who I need to interview as a part of a murder investigation," Chase smiled.

"And if she is not available?"

"Then I will have to chat with the media about my inability to interview the last person to see my victim alive."

"The next to the last person," the security officer growled.

"So we both hope," Chase said, implying he still considered Townsend a suspect.

"Wait here," the security officer ordered as he turned and entered the house.

Ignoring the curt instructions, Chase followed the man into the front hall.

"I told you to wait outside," the man turned on Chase.

"I'll wait here," Chase stopped smiling. "For a very brief period, and then I will start calling the networks."

The security officer glared at Chase, obviously considered physically escorting Chase back to the porch, but changed his mind and started down the hall. Chase, not really interested in scuffling, waited and watched as the DHS guerilla tapped on a closed door. After a few seconds, the door opened and an attractive girl in her twenties appeared. They exchanged a few words that Chase could not hear; the girl turned and spoke to another person; she relayed the message; the guard nodded and returned to confront Chase.

"Wait in there," the guard pointed to a large room on Chase's right. "I don't know why, but Mrs. Townsend will be with you when it suits her. Keep it short because the lady has things on her mind that are of no concern of yours."

"Mind sharing your insights?" Chase called after him.

The guard greeted Chase's query with a sarcastic grin and a raised middle finger.

Chase entered the room which was decorated tastefully with matching Danish modern, all dressed in muted colors. Although attractive, it was too sterile to be a family room, no books, magazines, photographs; it resembled an upscale doctor's reception room devoid of reading material. The security guard assumed a position near the door and silently watched Chase as he nonchalantly circled the room, pretending to study the framed reproductions that passed as artwork.

Five minutes passed, and Chase finally sat down in a stiff chair in one of the several conversational groupings that dominated the austere room. No sooner had his backside touched the cushion than a middle-aged woman appeared in the doorway. Chase, who had been expecting a young trophy wife, was surprised by the slender, fashionably dressed, fiftyish, but well preserved woman with short hair and wrinkle free face who smiled at him before addressing the guard. Chase immediately suspected face-lift.

"Thank you, Richard, you can return to your post," she dismissed the surly security officer.

"My orders were to …" the man started to protest.

Mrs. Townsend smiled and responded by pointing her finger towards the door. The security officer shrugged, and Mrs. Townsend closed the door behind him before turning to acknowledge her visitor.

"I am Nancy Townsend, lieutenant. How can I help you?" She said as she approached the now standing Chase.

Her commanding demeanor and her appearance impressed Chase. He had expected to confront a grieving, red-eyed woman whose husband was missing. Instead, Mrs. Townsend's blue eyes were clear, her posture confident, and she treated him like an unexpected, casual, social visitor, an inferior to be dealt with politely, and quickly dismissed.

"I am Lieutenant Mansfield of the Fairfax Police and…" Chase began his spiel.

"And you are in charge of the Jesperson investigation," Townsend completed Chase's sentence for him. "Sit it down, lieutenant. Thomas Jesperson was an old friend."

"I heard that your husband and Doctor Jesperson were friends from their college days," Chase tried to get control of the conversation. "But I didn't…"

Townsend laughed. "Thomas and I were once an item," Townsend again did not let Chase finish his thought. "Back in the dark ages, probably when you were still in kindergarten, Thomas introduced me to James," she referred to her husband.

"Then, the fact that Doctor Jesperson was murdered and your husband is missing must make the situation doubly difficult for you, Mrs. Townsend," Chase spoke bluntly as he wondered if her odd demeanor was caused by some kind of medication.

"Yes," Townsend frowned. "Lieutenant, I'm a very private person, and I work hard to control my emotions. Your presence here embarrasses me. I assure you I am going to miss Thomas very much, and I want his killer apprehended. I am not worried about my husband. The poor over worked man has been under considerable pressure for the past year, and he obviously needed some time alone to regroup. I am confident he will reappear soon with an embarrassed smile on his face. Now, how can I help you?"

Chase hesitated. He didn't believe her; she was too confident and too much under control; he wondered what she was concealing.

"Did he discuss his plans with you?" Chase asked.

"Of course not. Do you think I would let the government rush about searching for him if I knew where he was?"

"Where do you think your husband might be?"

"Believe me lieutenant, I do not know. I would not be sitting here having this uncomfortable chat with you if I did."

"Why did your husband not take his security detail with him? Certainly, he must have anticipated that a college campus presented a potentially hostile environment for someone in his sensitive position."

"You've never met my husband, have you?"

"No ma'am."

"Don't call me ma'am. I'm only a few years older than you. How old are you lieutenant?"

"Forty-five," Chase said.

"I'm fifty-five."

Chase hesitated and wondered if she were fishing for compliments or expecting him to say something superficial and stupid.

"Relax, lieutenant, I'm a happily married woman," She leaned forward and reached across the coffee table to pat his knee.

"Would you say your husband was worried about addressing a hostile audience at George Mason?" Chase asked, trying to control the interview.

"The very opposite," Townsend smiled. "James enjoyed challenges and was looking forward to carrying his message to a group of intelligent but naïve and uninformed people. Besides, he and Thomas were close friends who had drifted apart, and James wanted to rectify the situation." She hesitated before continuing. "Can you respect a state secret?"

"Mrs. Townsend, anything you tell me will be held in strict confidence. I am interested in only one thing, apprehending Doctor Townsend's killer," Chase said.

"And helping find my husband," Townsend suggested.

Chase thought about telling Townsend about his informal agreement on the division of investigative responsibilities with Cotton and the Feds but decided against it.

"Of course," Chase dissembled.

"Then I can tell you something that must be considered Top Secret," Townsend said.

Chase waited.

"James was worried about his meeting with Thomas and looking forward to it at the same time." Townsend hesitated again, giving Chase the impression she was trying to have him drag the story out of her.

"What was he worried about?" Chase asked, playing the game.

"James suspected that Thomas during his stay in Iran learned something of vital importance to national security that he was not sharing with the government as he should. Thomas worked on contract as a consultant to the government before his sabbatical and James felt he had an obligation to share as a citizen and as a former contractor."

"Why did your husband think Doctor Jesperson might…" Chase started to ask why Townsend thought Jesperson might withhold vital information but changed his mind. "May I ask a personal question?"

"If it's not too personal."

"Was Doctor Jesperson gay?"

The question surprised Townsend; her eyes widened, and she laughed. "Of course not. Take my word for it; I told you we once dated. Thomas was shy, a very private person, just like me, but he definitely was not gay. Why do you ask?"

"I haven't been able to identify any close friends of either sex," Chase said.

"That's not true, lieutenant. Both my husband and myself considered Thomas a good friend, and I assure you we represent both sexes." Townsend smiled at Chase as if she had made a joke.

"But…" Chase started to ask why the friends had drifted apart.

"But we haven't seen much of each other over the years," Townsend said. "What does that have to do with anything? Friends are friends. If Thomas needed something from either my husband or myself, all he would have to do is ask for it, and he knew that."

"And the reverse was true?"

"Of course. I just told you my husband intended to ask Thomas what he learned in Iran."

"And your husband assumed that if he asked his friend directly he would answer?"

Before Mrs. Townsend could respond, the door opened and the attractive young girl in her twenties with a worried expression on her face and a sheet of paper in her hand burst into the room.

"I'm sorry Mrs. Townsend but this just came in, and I think you should see it immediately," the girl said as she continued across the room.

"Mary," a relaxed Mrs. Townsend smiled. "This is Lieutenant Mansfield of the Fairfax County Police. He is investigating the Jesperson murder. Lieutenant, this is Mary, my secretary."

"Pleased to meet you, Mary," Chase said as he watched the girl ignore him and hand the paper to Mrs. Townsend.

Townsend, still unconcerned, frowned at her secretary, took the paper, and placed it on the small table beside her chair.

"I think you should read that right now, Mrs. Townsend," Mary said.

Townsend looked sharply at the girl and then retrieved the paper and glanced at it. Suddenly, she sat up straight and took a deep breath. She stared at the waiting Mary and then reread the message.

"It just came in. Shall I call security?" Mary asked.

Townsend shook her head. "I'll handle this, Mary," Townsend said. "Please do not discuss this with anyone," Townsend dismissed her.

Townsend waited until Mary left the room and closed the door behind her. Townsend reread the message a third time before raising her eyes and staring at Chase. She held the paper in one hand and clasped the other over her mouth. Although Townsend had Chase's full attention, something about her demeanor struck Chase as being overdone. As he waited for Townsend to explain, he had the uneasy feeling that there was something contrived about Townsend's reactions.

"Lieutenant, please read this and tell me what to do," Townsend said as she held the paper out to Chase.

Chase stood up and reached for the paper. One glance told him that it was the printout of an e-mail.

> From: Anony100@yahoo.com.fr
> Date: 10/17/10 09:30:43
> To: NTown1@gmail.com
> Subject: Yr Spouse
>
> Relax. Yr spouse is uncomfortable but alive. Whether he remains this way or not depend on you and his employer.

> If one word about the situation appears in the media, James's quality of life will change, drastically. Amerika must pay for her crimes against humanity. The world demands retribution. One hundred million dollars is fare. Tell Featherstone our price. We will not negotiate. Instruction will follow.
>
> The Suffering People

As soon as he finished scanning the missive, Chase looked at Townsend who was staring at him.

"What should I do, lieutenant?" Mrs. Townsend asked. Her eyes were wide but clear, and her hands grasped the arms of her chair.

Chase hesitated. He was tempted to analyze the message for her. He re-read it more slowly. He still could not tell if it were a sick hoax or not. It could have been drafted by a foreigner, a not very bright teenager, a poorly educated adult, or a bonafide kidnapper trying to masquerade as one of the foregoing. The awkward wording, poor grammar, and spelling troubled him. If the author truly had the Secretary of Homeland Security in his control, the fact that he was still alive was good news indeed, but Chase was reluctant to speculate.

"Mrs. Townsend, you should immediately inform the FBI about this. The Bureau has considerable experience dealing with this kind of investigation and negotiation," Chase said.

Townsend did not immediately react to Chase's words. She squeezed her eyes shut and covered them with her hands. She appeared to tremble, twice. Chase waited silently. Finally, Townsend took a deep breath, removed her hands from her still clear eyes, and held out one palm. Chase handed her the message.

"Can you do that for me?" Townsend asked softly.

"Yes," Chase said.

Chase took out his cell phone and poked in Special Agent Cotton's number.

"What?" Cotton answered gruffly. At the time he and his director were in a limousine traversing Pennsylvania Avenue on their way back to FBI headquarters from their tense White House meeting.

"Mansfield here," Chase said. "I'm at the Townsend house."

"Can I talk with you later, lieutenant? I'm rather occupied with something important at the moment," Cotton said. "It's the Fairfax cop," he told his director as he waited for Mansfield's reaction.

"You better get your ass out here, now," Chase said.

"What's happened?" Cotton sat up straight.

"Mrs. Townsend has just received an e-mail about her husband and needs advice and help immediately."

"Someone wants ransom?"

"It looks that way."

"Townsend is alive?"

"That is the implication."

"Who else is there?"

"DHS Security, a secretary, Mrs. Townsend, and myself," Chase said.

"What are you doing there?"

"Just what I told you this morning."

"Do they all know about the message?"

"No. Only Mrs. Townsend, myself, and the secretary who opened the e-mail."

"Don't tell another soul and don't give anybody any gratuitous advice. This is a federal matter, and I'm on the way," Cotton said.

Cotton turned to the director. "Somebody sent Mrs. Townsend a ransom request."

"And Townsend is alive?"

"Maybe," Cotton said, turning to the limo driver. "Get me to the parking garage," he ordered.

"I'll send out a support team," the director said. "And I'll alert the White House."

Cotton hesitated before speaking. "Sir, is that wise?"

"I tell only the president and suggest that any leak would be fatal."

"And I'll call Gore," Cotton said.

"Who in the hell is Gore?" The director asked.

"Agent Claris Gore. She's in charge of the DHS group assisting in the investigation," Cotton said. "We can't have DHS tramping about and inadvertently sabotaging any negotiations."

"I didn't even know DHS was investigating anything," Director D'Antonio said.

"Townsend is their damned secretary, sir, and their security detail let him go wandering about on his own."

D'Antonio frowned his displeasure but said nothing more.

At the Townsend house, Chase tried to re-assure the increasingly nervous Mrs. Townsend who slowly appeared to be adapting her reactions to that of a person adjusting to the realization that her husband was in serious difficulty. Finally, she excused herself, and Chase, who was not particularly adept at dealing with family members under stress, left the house to visit the garage and inspect Townsend's personal car that had been towed to McLean by the security detail. Although the car had been his ostensible reason for visiting the Townsend home, Chase did not expect to find any helpful clues, and he did not. He was preparing to depart when Cotton arrived in a five-car caravan that did not surprise Chase. Having worked with the Bureau in the past, Chase knew they always conducted their investigations by the numbers, meaning overwhelming force.

"Do you have the ransom note?" Cotton demanded as he confronted Chase in front of the garage.

"It's inside. Talk with Mrs. Townsend," Chase said. He thought about mentioning the wife's odd, understated demeanor but did not. Cotton's attitude irritated him.

Cotton started for the front door where his entourage waited, then stopped.

"What in the hell were you doing interviewing Mrs. Townsend?" Cotton demanded. "I thought we had an agreement."

"Common courtesy," Chase tried to ignore Cotton's tone. "Don't you think she deserved to be told what a Fairfax cop was doing in her garage?"

"What were you doing?"

Chase finessed the question. "As it turned out, Mrs. Townsend and Jesperson are old friends. She wanted to know how the investigation was going, and I was interested in what she could tell me about the victim."

"What did you learn?"

"Not much. The ransom note arrived before we got into it."

"Keep away from the Townsends," Cotton ordered as continued up the walk to the front door.

"We're going to have to insist on having an observer on your negotiating team," Chase called after him.

Cotton ignored him.

****

Forty-five minutes later, Chase arrived at the CIB offices where he found Barney and Theresa chatting.

"Good," Barney greeted him. "The chief's waiting. You can bring me up to date on the way." Barney pointed at the door, indicating that Chase should turn and go out the way he had entered.

"Doctor Jesperson has called three times," Theresa waved at Chase from her desk. "He said it was urgent."

"Why didn't you alert me?" Barney frowned.

"I was going to, but things have been hectic around here," Theresa winked at Chase as Barney turned back to confront him.

"Why am I the last one to know what's going on?" Barney complained.

"Where is he?" Chase asked, referring to Doctor Jesperson. Chase, like Theresa, treated Barney's question as rhetorical.

"At his son's apartment. Need the number?" Theresa asked.

"Got it," Chase said as he started for his office.

Barney watched Chase disappear into his closet office before turning on Theresa who shrugged her shoulders and pretended to study her monitor. Barney thought about quibbling with Theresa, decided that would be a waste of time, and followed Chase into his office where he found him poking a number into his cell phone.

Barney pointed his index finger at the ceiling, his way of indicating the chief was waiting.

"I have to find out what Doctor Jesperson wants," Chase said as the call was going through.

"The coroner released his son's body," Barney said. "Moscowitz has already told him."

"Hello," Jesperson answered.

"Doctor Jesperson, Chase Mansfield," Chase said.

"Lieutenant, good. I've been trying to reach you," Jesperson said.

"Theresa just told me," Chase said. "I've been out."

"Mansour's here. He appeared about an hour ago, and his aunt is serving him breakfast as we speak."

"Good. I need to talk with him. Could I come over now?"

"The sooner the better. He's worried about what it all means to him and would rather not get involved, but I told him he has no choice. He has to help you catch Thomas's killer. He claims he knows nothing."

"Please keep him there, Doctor Jesperson. It's imperative that I talk with him."

"I know. Come now."

"I have one little thing I have to do. I'll be there within a half an hour."

"The chief may want a little more of your time than that," Barney said.

Chase nodded as he listened to Doctor Jesperson say, "I'll keep him here, lieutenant."

"Thank you, Doctor," Chase said and hung up.

"Doctor Jesperson has the victim's third cousin at the apartment. The cousin arrived from Iran about two weeks ago and has been living with the professor. He may be the only person who knows what Jesperson has been up to recently."

"We still have to brief the chief," Barney said. "The President of George Mason called the chief several times wanting to know what is going on with the investigation. He claims the campus is in an uproar. All the faculty and students are in a panic, worried that they have a killer in their midst. When he didn't get a response that satisfied him, he mobilized several members of his Board of Directors, all big shots in the area, and they have been calling all morning. The chief wants to know where the investigation stands and what he can tell the callers and the media."

"OK," Chase said, sliding his cell phone back in his suit pocket as he stood. "Let's get it over, quick."

"You haven't kept us briefed," Barney complained as he walked with Chase towards the elevator.

"I apologize," Chase said, not meaning it.

"And the mouths," Barney referred to the Office of Public Information, "are…"

"...complaining," Chase completed Barney's sentence for him.

"…are being besieged by the media." Barney corrected Chase.

"We never comment on an ongoing investigation," Chase said.

"That's what we say, but we always do," Barney smiled.

"Somebody always leaks when we don't want to leak," Chase said.

"Sometimes we do," Barney said. "And usually the person who leaks is you."

"If I don't brief anybody on my lack of progress, the leakers can only speculate," Chase ignored Barney's allegation because it was true. "Do you want me to tell you what I have been doing?"

"Why not?"

"Searching for all the usual suspects," Chase smiled.

"That's it?" Barney asked as they stepped on the elevator.

"That's it."

"It's all I need to know," Barney glanced at the others on the elevator. "I'm really going to enjoy this briefing," Barney smiled.

They proceeded in silence to Chief Raymond Arthur's office. Barney opened the door and let Chase enter first.

"Good morning, gentlemen. Go right in, he's waiting for you. A word of warning," the chief's secretary said as Chase started for the open door to her right. "We're not in a very good mood this morning."

Chase turned the knob and stepped back, politely letting Barney enter and take the first salvo. Chase followed behind and was surprised to find the chief sitting stiffly behind his desk with a deep scowl on his face, an unusual development because the experienced and savvy Arthur usually was relaxed, primarily because he had early in his career learned how to delegate, an action that let subordinates carry the burdens of his office while he concentrated on what interested him, public relations.

The chief waved a hand in the direction of the two chairs facing his desk and waited sullenly until Barney and Chase were seated before speaking directly to Chase.

"Lieutenant, who killed Doctor Jesperson?"

"Sir, I do not know, and I do not have a single suspect," Chase answered honestly.

Chief Arthur leaned back in his chair and stared at his favorite investigator. He let a deep, heavy silence convey his negative reaction to those words. Finally, the chief took a noisy breath and said, "Do you mind telling me what you have been doing since no one else in the chain of command seems to know?" The chief glared at Barney.

"Chief, this is a very complicated case," Chase decided to be a little more forthcoming, but not a lot.

"Unlike most murders?"

"Professor Jesperson recently returned from Iran and at the time of his shooting was in the process of publishing a book," Chase began.

"The media tells me that it has been published," Arthur interrupted," and that it contains some relatively sensational information."

"Yes sir," Chase said.

"Attention catching stuff about nuclear bombs and planned attacks on our nation's capitol, that little city just across the river from where we sit."

"I suppose you have also heard that the last person to be seen in Doctor Jesperson's company was..."

"...Secretary Townsend of the Department of Homeland Security," Arthur finished Chase's sentence.

"I've just come from Townsend's home," Chase said.

"What were you doing there? Do you suspect he killed Doctor Jesperson?" Arthur asked.

"Not now, sir. Probably not now," Chase amended his statement.

"And may I ask why not?"

"While I was chatting with Mrs. Townsend, an e-mail ransom note arrived from the secretary's ostensible kidnapper."

Both Barney and the chief reacted with surprise to that revelation, pleasing Chase who was beginning to resent his superior's attitude. Chief Arthur for some reason was reacting to the pressure, something that he usually dealt with every day.

"I don't have all day to sit here and play word games with you, lieutenant," the chief snapped. "Just tell me what the note said and where your investigation stands."

"Yes sir, but I must stress the possible kidnapping and the murder present two separate avenues of investigation. We are working the Jesperson murder, and the Bureau is dealing with the Townsend inquiry. The e-mail apparently originated in France, and I assume you don't want me to drop the Jesperson case and fly off to Paris. Of course, I wouldn't object if you ordered me to do so, good soldier that I am."

"France?" The chief reacted, ignoring Chase's misdirected humor.

"Yes sir. It was sent from..." Chase consulted his notebook. "...from Anon100@yahoo.com.fr."

"Lieutenant, don't even try to make jokes about going to France," Chief Arthur frowned. "Major," Arthur turned to Barney. "I expect you to confiscate Lieutenant Mansfield's passport the moment you leave this room."

"Yes sir," Barney said. "This is the first I've heard about France."

"I'm not surprised. I expect you to closely monitor every detail of this investigation," the chief ordered.

"I should stress, sir," Chase smiled briefly, "our investigation is concentrating on the murder. Special Agent Cotton is assembling a Bureau team at the Townsend home as we speak, preparing the response to the kidnapper's note."

'Who is this Anon100 and what does he want?" Arthur demanded.

"Mrs. Townsend, of course, did not recognize the sender. I suspect that Anon is simply the ostensible kidnappers attempt to be clever by using Anon as a short form for Anonymous which of course is no help whatsoever. The note alleged that Townsend was uncomfortable but alive. It cautioned against informing the media of the situation, noting that Townsend's quality of life will change drastically if word of the demand should leak. It warned America, spelled with a k not a c, must pay for its crimes against humanity and demanded one hundred million dollars."

"How much?" Barney asked with raised eyebrows.

"Only a hundred million," Chase said. "The message ended with the phrase 'Instructions will follow.' It was signed, 'The Suffering People.'"

"Christ, if the government pays a hundred million a lot of the Suffering People will take early retirement," the chief leaned back in his chair, relaxing a little. He looked at Chase. "You did say that the Bureau is handling all this."

"Yes sir," Chase said brightly. "As soon as I read the note, with Mrs. Townsend's permission, I called Special Agent Cotton and alerted him. I waited at the Townsend home until Cotton and his army arrived, and then I came directly here to brief you."

Arthur's look told Chase that he did not buy the 'to brief you' throw-in, but Chase shrugged that off. Given Arthur's prickly attitude, it had been worth the effort, and it did open the door for another maneuver.

"I suggest that Major Hopkins may want to join the Feds at the Townsend house as an observer," Chase said, paying Barney back for whining about Chase's failure to keep him briefed. "While I continue to concentrate on the Jesperson investigation." Chase smiled at a frowning Barney.

"Agreed," Chief Arthur said. He looked at Barney. "Make sure the Feds don't try to put any of that hundred million on our backs."

"Yes, sir," a grim-faced Barney said.

"Where do you stand on the murder investigation?" Arthur turned his attention back to Chase.

"I'm not making much progress, but I've conducted initial interviews on campus." Chase did not admit that those interviews focused mainly on Jesperson's graduate assistant and an unproductive chat with Chase's girl friend, Barbara. "They indicate that Jesperson was an introvert, a loner, with few social relationships. He recently spent considerable time in Iran where he acquired the sources that provided the sensational information that he included in the book. I've talked with his parents—his mother is a native Iranian—and they confide her family facilitated Jesperson's research. One of the quid pro quos for family assistance in Iran was the victim's promise to protect a nephew's son by facilitating his movement to the States and sponsoring his matriculation at George Mason. The boy arrived here two weeks ago and has been living with Doctor Jesperson. As soon as we are finished here, I plan to visit with the boy at Jesperson's apartment."

"Why haven't you talked with him before this?" Chief Arthur asked.

"I was on my way to do that very thing when I was summoned to this meeting," Chase smiled at the chief, only partially concealing the fact he was offended by Arthur's uncharacteristic but surly attitude.

Arthur ignored that comment and waited for Chase to continue.

"Also, I was somewhat inhibited because I didn't know he existed until I phoned the victim's parents to inform them of the untimely death of their son. The father, also Doctor Jesperson, is a MIT retired professor; the elder Jespersons reside in Cambridge. They are now in town to retrieve their son. Doctor Jesperson called just minutes before this unscheduled session suddenly appeared on my schedule," Chase again fired back at the chief, "and reported that he had found his third-generation nephew and was keeping him at the victim's apartment until I could get there to debrief him. I really should get there soonest," Chase said, standing up.

"Wait, what should I tell the George Mason president and his friends who are hounding me for results?" Chief Raymond demanded, finally tabling the reason for his bristling attitude.

"All you can say is that the investigation is proceeding," Chase said. "We don't know who shot Jesperson or why. Since it is highly possible that Iran and its damned nuclear weapons are involved somehow, either the government directly or through a terrorist group, we can't risk any media exposure of our murder investigation or the Townsend disappearance."

Chief Raymond Arthur, who obviously did not like that answer, again glared at Chase. "Are you saying the Iranians killed Jesperson because of that damned book?"

"I don't know," Chase said.

"But you are saying that the Townsend.." Arthur hesitated. "I think you used the words 'ostensible kidnapping'...the Townsend thing and the book and the Iranians and the murder are all related."

"Certainly they are related somehow. I just cannot say if they are causal or coincidental or a little of both or neither."

"And what does that nonsense mean?"

"I can only promise to try to sort it all out," Chase smiled.

"And what should I say to those pressuring me?"

"That it is a very complicated situation that it is too sensitive and delicate for public speculation despite the curiosity of influential persons tangentially interested. You can assure the George Mason president and his friends that off the record he and they can assure the faculty and students that they need not worry that someone is targeting them. And, if they don't like that assurance, tell them to go piss up a rope."

"At least they should not worry until another one of their number is murdered," the chief backed off. "I'll have to think about that. For now, I'll simply tell them that the investigation is progressing normally, that we have no information to indicate that another of their number is being targeted, and that they should remain alert but continue their normal lives and programs, and you, lieutenant, should start worrying about how much you have invested in this career."

"Good reasoning, chief," Chase said, turning his back on his mentor as he started for the door with Barney close behind.

When they were back in the hall, Barney grabbed Chase by the arm. "You are pushing your luck. Thanks a lot for that kidnapping thing."

"I just did you a favor. You need to get out of that damned office of yours more often; there's a real world out there," Chase said angrily. "Now, I have to get over to the Jesperson apartment."

"Keep me in the loop," Barney said as he watched his friend head for the parking lot.

"Like always," Chase said.

Barney shrugged and turned for his office.

Chapter 7

Chase rapped on the door of Jesperson's Waples Mill condominium and waited. Down the hall, another door cracked open, and Marsha Hillencotter peeked out. She smiled when she saw Chase, waved, raised a thumb in approval, and shut her door softly. Suddenly, the door in front of Chase opened.

"Come in, lieutenant," a sober-faced Doctor Terrence Jesperson greeted Chase. Jesperson stepped back.

"I'm glad you're here," Jesperson said. "Mansour is a callow youth who is frightened out of his skin. He wants to return home immediately before American gangsters kill him like they did his cousin."

"American gangsters?" Chase raised his eyebrows.

"Yes, He's seen too many movies, and my wife is not helping. She's only been in this country for sixty years." Jesperson shook his head in disgust. "They're hiding in my son's study behind a closed door. Please have a seat, and I'll drag them out."

Chase waited until Jesperson started down the hall before turning and staring out the window. Chase heard a door open, and Jesperson say, "Lieutenant Mansfield's here."

Almost immediately, Mrs. Jesperson, followed by a short, slender, dark-skinned young man with black hair, a prominent nose, thin lips, an anxious expression, and brown eyes that glanced first at Chase and then the door. Chase had the impression that the frightened Iranian was actually considering flight. Chase, who had been expecting Mansour to be younger, estimated that he was in his mid-twenties.

Chase took two steps towards the young man and held out his hand. "Mr. Tahe...Tahe..." Chase hesitated having difficulty remembering how to pronounce Mansour's last name.

"Taheri, lieutenant, Mansour Taheri, with the accent on her," Mrs. Jesperson spoke sharply.

"Taheri," Chase repeated, keeping his attention on Mansour. "I'm pleased to meet you."

The boy/man shrugged his shoulders but did not speak as he held out a small, limp hand. He barely touched Chase's palm before pulling away.

"Have you captured the villain who killed my son, lieutenant?" Mrs. Jesperson tried to take charge.

"No ma'am," Chase answered politely. "I was hoping that Mr. Taheri might assist me. I'm having difficulty..."

"Nemidunam hichi," Mansour muttered softly as he retreated several steps back to a position behind Mrs. Jesperson.

"Speak English, Mansour," Doctor Jesperson ordered.

"He doesn't know anything," Mrs. Jesperson said as she glared at her husband.

Chase waited.

"Mansur said, he knows nothing," Mrs. Jesperson frowned at Chase.

"Let him speak for himself," Doctor Jesperson declared.

"I know nothing," Mansour said before Mrs. Jesperson could reply to her husband.

"Sit down and let Lieutenant Chase ask his questions," Doctor Jesperson ordered.

After a brief moment of indecision, Mrs. Jesperson chose the center of the couch and patted a spot next to her. Mansour obediently took his place while Chase and Doctor Jesperson selected flanking chairs.

"Have you been living here with your cousin since your arrival?" Chase asked, starting with an easy question in an attempt to establish some rapport with the anxious, young man.

Before answering, Mansour turned his head towards Mrs. Jesperson. She nodded affirmatively.

"Yes," Mansour answered the question.

"When did you get here?" Chase asked.

Again, Mansour glanced at Mrs. Jesperson, and again she nodded.

"Oh stop that nonsense or we will be here all day," Doctor Jesperson said.

Mrs. Jesperson frowned but did not argue.

"Ten days," Mansour answered.

"A week ago last Saturday," Mrs. Jesperson elaborated.

Chase took out his notebook and jotted down the answer.

"I don't understand why that is important," Mrs. Jesperson said.

Doctor Jesperson stood up. "That's enough. Manujeh, come with me. We will wait in the den while the lieutenant asks Mansour his questions."

"I don't think…." Mrs. Jesperson started to argue.

Doctor Jesperson leaned over, grasped his wife by the arm, and pulled her erect. Mrs. Jesperson jerked free and turned to Mansour. "We will be in the other room. Answer the questions truthfully, but if you have any difficulty, call me. The lieutenant does not have the right to force you to say anything you don't want to."

Mansour nodded.

Mrs. Jesperson glared at Chase. "Be careful. I'll call a lawyer if I must."

"Mrs. Jesperson, I'm not accusing your nephew of anything. I'm only trying to identify the murderer of your son," Chase said.

"Mansur did not do it," she replied.

"Come," Doctor Jesperson again firmly grasped his wife's arm. "Let Lieutenant Chase do his duty."

Chase waited for the door to the den to close behind the elderly couple. He smiled at the tense Mansour. "I understand that you intend to enroll at George Mason. It's a good school."

Mansour nodded but did not speak.

"Do you have to wait for the next semester to start your courses?"

Mansour shook his head negatively.

"Speak to me Mansour," Chase, who was beginning to lose his patience with the young Iranian, decided to let him know that he had to answer his questions.

"I already have degree from Teheran University. I have tutor who is improving me English so I begin graduate course soon, maybe."

"Maybe? What do you mean by maybe?"

"Maybe I no stay this dangerous country. Too many bad people."

Chase looked at Mansour skeptically, not sure if Mansour was bluffing or truly afraid."

"That certainly is your choice if you had nothing to do with your cousin's death," Chase decided to press him.

Mansour, clearly angry, stared at Chase. "I not kill Thomas. He helps me," Mansour declared.

"He was assisting you and your family," Chase said. "Don't you want to help me find out who killed him?"

"I know nothing. My family help Thomas, and now I afraid."

"You should know that Doctor Jesperson's book about Iran's nuclear bomb has been published. Every newspaper and television newscast is now talking about it. The Iranian government should be very angry to be so exposed. If you return home now, you will face the very problem that your family tried to protect you from when your parents sent you here."

"And you think I safe here? Bad people killed Thomas."

"What bad people?" Chase pressed.

Mansour leaped off the couch and began to pace. Suddenly, he stopped and faced the still seated Chase. "You," Mansour shouted.

Chase laughed. "Me?"

The door down the hall opened, and Doctor Jesperson looked out. Chase turned, waved a hand to reassure him. Jesperson nodded and shut the door, but Chase heard Jesperson and his wife arguing loudly.

"Sit down, Mansour, and don't shout," Chase ordered. You are upsetting the old couple."

Mansour stared angrily at Chase, glanced in the direction of the raised voices, and then surprised Chase by sitting as ordered.

"Why do you think I killed your cousin?" Chase asked.

"Not you. Your government," Mansour answered.

"Why would my government kill Doctor Jesperson?"

Mansour shrugged. "Not know. Americans hate Iran people. Maybe someone, maybe a hostage did." Mansour referred to the Americans that had been held hostage by the alleged Iranian students, one of whom was the current Iranian president.

"You're talking nonsense, Mansour," Chase said.

"Then I no talk with you," Mansour folded his arms and crossed his legs, a classic defensive posture.

"If you help me, I can help you," Chase said.

"No can help. Me stay here, learn English, see nobody, or maybe go home."

"Where did you stay last night?" Chase asked.

Mansour looked sharply at Chase but did not reply.

"The old couple said they slept here last night. Are you saying they lied to me?" Chase pressed.

Mansour turned his head from side to side, his thick lips clenched tightly.

"Did Doctor Jesperson introduce you to any of his friends?" Chase decided to focus on specific questions.

"No."

"Where did the two of you eat?"

Mansour pointed at the dining room table.

"Did Doctor Jesperson take you to the university?"

Mansour nodded affirmatively.

"What did you do there?"

"Write papers."

"What kind of papers?"

"So I can study there."

"Did you meet any students?"

"Two."

"What were their names?"

Mansour shrugged.

Chase stared hard at the young man.

"Nick," Mansour relented.

"Nicholas Dizekes, your cousin's graduate assistant?"

Mansour nodded.

"What did you and Nick talk about?" Chase asked.

"Not much."

"Why?"

"Nick did not like me."

"Why not?"

"Not know. Maybe because I Iranian."

"Did the professor leave the two of you alone?"

"Nick take me to lunch."

"How did that go?"

"Bad."

"What was bad?"

"Food. No like American food. Too greasy."

"Did you try a cheeseburger?" Chase smiled.

Mansour nodded. "Too greasy."

"Why do you think that Nick doesn't like Iranians?"

"The book."

"Why do you say that?"

"Nick say book say Iranian people very bad."

"Do you know what Doctor Jesperson say…said in the book." Chase decided he was wasting too much time with Mansour who had him talking in broken English.

Mansour's eyes focused sharply on Chase, giving him the impression that he knew exactly what Chase wanted him to say. After a few seconds, Mansour turned his attention to his shoes. "Know nothing about bomb. Me just student," Mansour muttered.

"What was the name of the second person you met?" Chase asked, abruptly changing the subject back to his original inquiry.

Again, Mansour hesitated.

"Mansour, answer my questions honestly, and I will leave," Chase said, letting his irritation show.

"At lunch Nick introduce me to another Iranian," Mansour said.

"What's his name?"

"No remember? English not good,"

"Your English is good enough to tell me the name of the Iranian student you met," Chase insisted.

Again, Mansour looked at the door, giving Chase the impression the anxious young man was contemplating flight.

Chase stood up and positioned himself between Mansour and the door. "What was the student's name?" Chase insisted.

"He belong to Foreign Students," Mansour stalled.

"Don't make me take the time to ask Nick for the name," Chase said, wondering why Mansour was being so evasive.

"Jamshid."

"Jamshid what?"

"Afgar. Jamshid Afgar."

"You were with Jamshid last night, weren't you?" Chase smiled as returned to the chair facing Mansour.

Mansour nodded.

"Where?"

"His house."

"Do you know the address?"

"No," Mansour shook his head negatively.

"No problem," Chase said. "I can easily get it from the school registrar."

"Jamshid is friend. No shoot Thomas," Mansour reacted. "He good Iranian."

"Does Jamshid know about Doctor Jesperson's book?"

"Know what?"

"About the Iranian bomb."

"Everybody know, now," Mansour glanced at the television.

"Did he know before the book was published?"

The infuriating Mansour reacted with a shrug.

"Did Jamshid know Doctor Jesperson was writing a book about Iran?"

"All students in seminar know," Mansour said.

"Was Jamshid Afgar a member of Doctor Jesperson's graduate seminar?" Chase asked.

Mansour nodded affirmatively.

"Did Doctor Jesperson have any visitors while you were here?" Chase tried coming at Mansour from another direction.

Before Mansour could respond, the door down the hall opened, and Mrs. Jesperson stepped out. "Lieutenant, you should be finished soon. My nephew knows nothing that can possibly help you," she said as she glared at Chase. "We have much to do."

"A few more minutes, Mrs. Jesperson," Chase answered evenly. "If we are inconveniencing you, I could take Mansour down to the station and finish our conversation there."

Mrs. Jesperson glared at Chase before stepping back into the room and slamming the door. Chase turned back to Mansour and found the young man watching him with a worried expression on his face.

"Did Doctor Jesperson have any visitors while you were here?" Chase patiently repeated his question.

"No," Mansour smiled for the first time.

"What did you and Doctor Jesperson do every night?"

"Thomas work in his office," Mansour glanced down the hall, "and I watch television."

"Didn't you get bored?"

"I like television," Mansour said.

"What are you going to do now?"

"Watch television," Mansour said.

"Mansour, stop playing games with me. I am only trying to find out who killed your relative who was so kind to you," Chase said. "What are you going to do now?"

"No know."

"When I leave, what are you going to do?"

Mansour looked down the hall, acting as if that gesture answered Chase's question.

"What are you going to do after Doctor and Mrs. Jesperson return to Cambridge to bury their son? Will you go with them?"

"Maybe."

And after the funeral, where will you live?"

Mansour shrugged.

"Answer me."

Mansour moved his shoulders again. Chase stood up and stared at the insolent young man.

"Maybe go home."

"Is that wise? Do your family and relatives agree?" Chase asked. "Didn't they send you here to keep you safe?"

"Like Thomas?

Chase felt like observing that an inherent advantage arrived with death--no one could again threaten you--but he did not. Mansour clearly lacked a sense of humor. "You would be safer as a student at George Mason than you will be in Iran."

"Like Thomas?" The stubborn Mansour repeated.

"If you cooperate with me, help me, we can arrest Thomas's murderer, and you can stop worrying," Chase said.

Mansour shrugged. "Like Thomas."

An irritated Chase relented, a little, but he did not back off completely. "Very well," Chase said. "Discuss your future with your relatives but do not leave Fairfax County without my express permission. At the very least, Mansour Taheri, I consider you an uncooperative material witness. This is an official warning. Do you understand?"

Mansour smiled thinly as he nodded once. His body language told Chase that the spoiled young man still intended do whatever he pleased.

"You may travel with Doctor and Mrs. Jesperson to Cambridge to attend their son's funeral, but then you must return to Fairfax. I will have someone watching you." Chase did not admit that the someone would most likely be himself plus, maybe, one other, a neighbor.

Mansour stopped smiling.

Chase turned his back on Mansour, went down the hall, and tapped on the study door. It opened quickly, and Mrs. Jesperson pushed past him without a word.

"How did it go, lieutenant? Find out anything helpful?" Doctor Jesperson asked.

"Frankly, not much. I'll have a talk with his friend Afgar." Chase shook his head and frowned, indicating his frustration. "I thank you for your help, sir. Mansour is a very difficult young man."

"It runs in the family," Jesperson agreed, giving Chase the very clear impression that he was talking specifically about his spouse. "Obstinacy is one of their dominant genes."

"Doctor Jesperson, do you plan to take Mansour with you when you return to Cambridge?" Chase asked.

"I'm going home this afternoon. I don't know what those two are planning," Jesperson glanced in the direction of the living room.

"I'm sure I will have more questions for Mansour," Chase said.

"Do you want me to make sure Mansour stays here?" Jesperson asked.

Chase's initial impression was that the idea of leaving Mansour behind appealed to the old man.

"I can't deny him the opportunity to attend your son's funeral," Chase said. "I'm sure your wife would appreciate having him there, but I would appreciate it if you keep me informed of his plans. If he decides to return to Iran, which he apparently is considering, I would like one more chat with him before he leaves the country."

"He would have to be very stupid to return to Iran at this unpropitious time," Jesperson said.

Chase almost replied that an independent observer might quickly assign Mansour to that category, but he restrained himself.

"Mansour is old enough, at least in years if not maturity, to make his own decisions," Jesperson said, hinting that he shared Chase's unstated opinion. "I will keep you informed lieutenant. I want to see the killer of my son brought to justice."

Doctor Jesperson accompanied Chase as he made his way to the door where Chase hesitated long enough to thank him again for his assistance and to speak to Mrs. Jesperson and Mansour who sat side by side on the couch watching television.

"Mrs. Jesperson, I thank you for your hospitality, and, Mansour, please remember my formal caution," Chase said.

Mrs. Jesperson and her nephew reacted as one; both continued to stare at the television while they pretended that they had not heard Chase.

"Lieutenant, I apologize for my wife and her relative's rudeness," Doctor Jesperson said as he closed the door.

Chase hesitated outside as he wondered how the two would react to that harsh criticism. He heard nothing, shrugged, and then made his way to the Prius.

Chapter 8

At the White House CIA Director Pace and FBI Director Philip D'Antonio waited outside the Oval Office door. A relaxed Pace, not quite sure about the purpose of the pending meeting, sat in the chair nearest Heather James' desk and chatted with the president's secretary while an anxious D'Antonio paced. Pace was already in the West Wing conferring with the National Security Advisor when Heather had summoned him. D'Antonio, on the other hand, had been sitting behind his Pennsylvania Avenue desk when Special Agent Cotton had called him from the Townsend home to announce the contents of the kidnapper's message; D'Antonio reacted to the shocking news of a missive from the kidnappers demanding a preposterous ransom for the missing DHS secretary by ordering his assistant to get him on the president's calendar. To his surprise, Heather had moved with alacrity, giving him thirty minutes to get to the White House. Normally, this would have been no problem; the White House was located only minutes from his headquarters. Unfortunately for D'Antonio, Special Agent Cotton, who had all the information, was in Mclean, a half an hour drive under the most ideal traffic conditions. Cotton, who was busy setting us his task force to handle the next message from the kidnappers, had appealed his superior's summons, but D'Antonio had ordered him to meet him at the White House forthwith. Now, the hapless D'Antonio was fretfully counting the seconds while he waited for Cotton to arrive.

Suddenly, the door to the Oval Office opened, and Ted Bertram, the president's chief of staff, pointed a finger at D'Antonio and then Pace, indicating the two directors should join them. CIA Director Pace, always an eager beaver in situations involving the president, leaped to his feet and was the first to cross the threshold when the smiling Secret Service agent who guarded the door stepped back. D'Antonio did not move. He looked at Heather as he was desperately searching his mind for an excuse when abruptly the door to the hall opened, and a puffing Special Agent Cotton materialized.

"About time," D'Antonio muttered as he pivoted and hurried to catch up with the fast moving Pace.

Special Agent Cotton reluctantly followed his superior into the Oval Office where he found the president sitting behind his massive desk, a gift in 1880 from Queen Victoria to then President Rutherford B Hayes. Using timber recovered from the British Arctic Exploration ship *HMS Resolute,* the Queen's artisans had crafted the magnificent piece which was subsequently used by presidents in a variety of White House locations; Jackie Kennedy installed it into the Oval Office in 1961 for her husband Jack, but Bill Clinton, however, was the president who found the most imaginative and practical use for the magnificent, historic gift.

Chief of Staff Ted Bertram sat closest to the president, and Vice President Charles Hampton was on the sofa. The CIA director commandeered the chair on the vice president's right, and D'Antonio grabbed the chair on the left. This confronted Cotton with a difficult decision; should he join the vice president on the couch or take a chair along the far wall? Cotton opted for the latter, but the vice president overruled him by sliding to his right as he patted the cushion on his left. Cotton surrendered and reluctantly joined the vice president on the couch directly in the president's clear line of fire.

Just as Cotton's backside touched the cushion, the president spoke as he glared at D'Antonio.

"What in the hell has happened now?"

"Sir," D'Antonio took a deep breath before continuing. "We've had a message from the…from the kidnappers who are holding Secretary Townsend. I'll let Special Agent Cotton who has just come from the Townsend home explain."

"Shit," the president swore as he turned his glare from D'Antonio to Cotton.

Cotton hesitated as the words 'thanks a lot' flashed through his mind.

"Who the hell has him? The fucking Iranians?" The president demanded before Cotton could catch his breath and decide how to begin. Cotton had jogged from the parking lot to the Secret Service checkpoints to the Oval Office and was having difficulty breathing.

"The ostensible kidnappers sent an e-mail to Mrs. Townsend at her home e-mail address. They signed it 'The Suffering People," Cotton gasped.

"The Suffering People?" The president looked at the CIA director and raised his voice. "Who in the hell are the goddamned suffering people?"

Pace shrugged. "This is the first I've heard of them. This is all news to me, sir."

The president looked at D'Antonio.

"Sorry, sir," D'Antonio said.

"Special Agent, you said ostensible kidnappers," the president turned back to Cotton.

"Yes sir. The e-mail is all we have to go on for now. It could be a terrible hoax or a message from someone holding the secretary. I have the message if you want to read it." Cotton took a folded sheet of paper from his inside suit coat pocket.

The president held out his hand, and Cotton jumped up from the couch and handed it to the president who scanned it quickly.

> From: Anony100@yahoo.com.fr
> Date: 10/17/10 09:30:43
> To: NTown1@gmail.com
> Subject: Yr Spouse
>
> Relax. Yr spouse is uncomfortable but alive. Whether he remains this way or not depend on you and his employer. If one word about the situation appears in the media, James quality of life will change, drastically. Amerika must pay for her crimes against humanity. The world demands retribution. One hundred million dollars is fare. Tell Featherstone our price. We will not negotiate. Instruction will follow.
>
> The Suffering People

When he finished reading, Featherstone dropped it on the *Resolute* desk and stared at Cotton who was now standing in front of him. To Cotton's immense relief, the angry president turned to his FBI director, obviously expecting informed comment.

"I haven't read it, yet, sir," D'Antonio said.

"Nor I," Pace said.

The president picked up the message, handed it to Cotton, who immediately delivered it to his superior.

““What are your views, Special Agent Cotton?” The president asked as Cotton was settling back on the sofa beside the vice president.

Cotton who had been hoping to get out of the president's sights answered quickly. “I fear it's genuine.”

“And why do you think that?”

“Although some of the faculty and students at George Mason University know that Secretary Townsend was on campus last night, the audience, the media, and the public have not been informed that Secretary Townsend is missing. We have deliberately withheld that information. Presumably, only ourselves and the person or persons who sent that message are aware of his status.”

The president leaned back in his chair and stared at Cotton. “Then should I conclude that message is from those who have Secretary Townsend or is a member of your investigating team playing games with us?”

“Certainly, not the latter, sir.”

“Then you are telling me that somebody is going to kill Secretary Townsend if I don't give them a hundred million dollars? Are they out of their goddamned minds?”

Cotton did not respond to what he assumed were rhetorical questions.

“Sir,” D'Antonio said. “We cannot pay a ransom. Our policy is clear. We do not negotiate with terrorists.”

The president glared at D'Antonio. “Mr. Director. I know what our policy is. That was not my question. I asked if somebody is going to kill Secretary Townsend if I don't give them a hundred million dollars.”

“The secretary may already be dead, sir,” D'Antonio did not back down.

“We don't know that terrorists are involved, sir,” William H. Pace, the CIA director said.

“You're splitting hairs,” D'Antonio turned on his rival.

Everybody in the room knew that the CIA director and the FBI director, reflecting the sometimes conflicting interests and responsibilities of their competing agencies, did not like each other.

D'Antonio continued. “If we meet the demands of whoever has the secretary, we will put other Americans at risk. It would only encourage the terrorists to take other American officials, innocent businessmen, and tourists hostage.”

“As I said, we do not know that a terrorist organization is behind this,”

Pace waved the e-mail in the air before handing it to the vice president. "I've never heard of an organization called 'The Suffering People.' It sounds patently phony to me."

The president nodded and looked at D'Angelo. "You're not going to try to tell me that the FBI has never sanctioned the payment of ransom to kidnappers are you?"

"Sir, you're absolutely correct," D'Antonio answered. "Ransom has been paid to homegrown American kidnappers. The Bureau always recommends against such a response but defers to the family of the victims and supports them if they insist. In this instance involving a ranking American official, I strongly advise that we not give in to the demands."

"What do you recommend, Mr. Director?" The president frowned at D'Antonio.

"Sir," Vice President Charles Z. Hampton spoke for the first time. "Would you like me to canvas our confidential fund raisers?"

"Hold off on that Mr. Vice President," the president answered.

"May I just make one point," Hampton, a strong man who did not hesitate when a situation required hard advice, appealed.

"Yes, Charles," the president said. "I need someone to do just that." He glared at his FBI and CIA directors.

"Sir, I'm no expert in these matters, but the threat in this," the vice president waved the e-mail in the air for emphasis, "is quite clear. If we don't pay the ransom, Secretary Townsend is a dead man, if he is not already."

"Thank you for stating the obvious, Charles," the president said. "Director," the president looked at Pace. "If terrorists have Secretary Townsend, will they release him if we pay the ransom?"

"I can't answer that question, sir," Pace held his ground. "If it is a terrorist organization, and I repeat we do not know that, they might release him, and they might kill him anyway. It depends on which terrorist organization has him."

"Sir," D'Antonio rejoined the discussion. "If a terrorist organization is involved, I suggest that it is one with Iranian connections. If the information in Doctor Jesperson's book is accurate, and given the allegation that the Iranians have the bomb and are planning on using it, I suggest that the Iranian Government or one of the terrorist organizations they support is involved."

"Let's be realistic," Pace said, his words and demeanor implied that D'Antonio was not. "Everything involved in this operation is too sensational, murder, abduction of a senior official, stratospheric ransom demands, nuclear bombs, terrorists. It's all designed to intimidate us into handing over a hundred million dollars. It is all connected. We cannot deal with each element separately."

That hard analysis gave everyone in the room pause.

"Fine, what do you suggest we do?" President Arthur C. Featherstone stared balefully at his CIA director.

"We have to let it play out," Pace said.

"Do we give them the hundred million?"

"No," the FBI Director answered first.

"Yes," the CIA Director said after a slight pause.

"If we don't, we are signing Secretary Townsend's death warrant," the vice president declared. "The money should not be a consideration; I'll take responsibility for raising it, and it won't cost the man on the street a penny."

Featherstone nodded and turned to Cotton. "What do you say, Special Agent Cotton? You are the man dealing with the kidnappers."

Cotton glanced at D'Antonio, his boss. The FBI director who had already expressed his opinion waited with a blank expression on his stony face. Cotton swallowed hard, took a deep breath, and then punted.

"Maybe," Cotton said.

"Maybe?" The president erupted. "What the hell does that mean? "You're the alleged expert. What should I do?"

"Sir, the negotiations have just begun. We need time to see if we can track this e-mail to its source. We do not know if Secretary Townsend is alive or not. We can insist on proof that he is alive. We can try to determine if he is still in this country or not."

"And how do you track it?" Featherstone focused on the e-mail.

"We will have agents contact Yahoo here and in France. We will have our Legal Attaché in Paris request the help of their French liaison contacts. We've only received one message. We are in the process of drafting a reply to the address of the originator of that one," Cotton glanced at the message still being held by the vice president.

"Do you think it will get through? Featherstone demanded.

"We can only try."

"I know that. What do you think?"

"We're working on it. I worry that it was sent from France."

"Why?" Featherstone asked.

"I fear any attempt to negotiate will bounce back on us because the sender of the first message, if he knows what he is doing, will have used a common on-line public facility and will have already closed the Yahoo account which was opened with phony information. A professional would know we would immediately backcheck the originator."

"How do you know it was sent from France?" Featherstone demanded.

Cotton retrieved the e-mail from the vice president and handed it to the president. "Please note the first line, sir," Cotton said.

The president did as he was told. He read, " From: Anony100@yahoo.com.fr"

"The 'fr' at the end of the From line indicates the place of origin, France."

"And?" Featherstone stared at Cotton.

"We surmise that 'Anony' is short for Anonymous," Cotton said. "We are checking with Yahoo to see what we can learn about the person who signed up for that identity, but as I noted I doubt it will lead us to the sender. These addresses are easily acquired, and I fear that the requester submitted bogus background information. A professional will have signed up using an internet connection in a commercial establishment of some kind, probably a Parisian coffee house. The next message will come from another location, even another country, if an experienced terrorist organization is involved. It would have been easier if they had used the telephone."

"Then how in the hell are we going to negotiate with the bastards?" The president demanded.

"I don't know yet, sir," Cotton backed away from the presidential desk, hoping to get the directors back in the discussion. "We can only try to take advantage of what the kidnappers give us."

"Sir," D'Antonio spoke up. "Right now the kidnappers, if there are kidnappers, hold all the advantages. They will send instructions to us. If we do what they say and hand over the hundred million dollars, the negotiations are over."

"And then what will happen?" The president asked.

"If Secretary Townsend is alive, which I doubt, they might release him," D'Antonio shrugged. "They might tell the world who they are and what they have accomplished. They might make a mistake."

"And if it is the Iranian government behind this, they might take our money and use it to finance their nuclear weapons program," Featherstone declared, his voice heavy with sarcasm. "And they might nuke us, just for the fun of it." His voice stressed the word "might" as he threw it back at his FBI director.

A heavy silence settled on the room. Cotton returned to the sofa and waited for his masters to sort things out.

"I again ask, what do we do?" The president glared at his security team.

"I suggest that I see what I can do about collecting some money," the vice president said.

"Does anyone object to that?" Featherstone challenged.

"No sir," the CIA director answered first. "I suggest, however, that any inquiries be handled with the utmost discretion.

"I wasn't thinking about placing an advertisement in the *New York Times,* for Christ sake," the vice president glared at Pace.

"We should continue with our investigation," D'Antonio said, ignoring the developing confrontation.

"And I will task all our stations," Pace said, deliberately keeping pace with his rival.

"Great! The terrorists are planning on killing our Secretary of Homeland Security and the damned Iranians are getting ready to nuke us, and it's business as usual on the home front," a frustrated president declared.

"You and the First Lady might consider moving to a secure location," Ted Bertram, the president's chief of staff suggested.

Featherstone glanced at Bertram, but he did not bother to comment. The president leaned back in his chair, took a deep breath, obviously attempting to reign in his dynamic temper, and finally spoke. "Fine. All of you get the hell out of here and do whatever you have to do. I'll expect you back here by four with some damned good news."

Special Agent Cotton leaped to his feet and led the silent, sober faced, senior officials towards the door. Cotton's hand touched the knob, and Featherstone broke the silence. "Special Agent Cotton, stop! I want a word with you."

The others turned their heads and looked at the president, but not one of them, not even Cotton's boss D'Antonio, offered to join Cotton and the president. A worried Cotton returned to the president's historic desk, but he did not sit down. He remained standing, facing the president, until the Secret Service agents closed the door with a soft snick.

"Sit down and relax. I'm not going to fire you," Featherstone said.

Cotton did as he was told, taking the chair previously occupied by his boss.

"Now give me straight answers, no hedging, Special Agent Cotton," Featherstone spoke softly, forcing Cotton to lean forward to hear him. "Do you think Secretary Townsend is alive or dead?"

"I have no evidence to indicate either way," Cotton answered.

"Do you have a chance of identifying the kidnappers and freeing Townsend?"

"If the e-mail is from kidnappers and Secretary Townsend is alive, the odds are on the kidnappers' side, if they are professionals. Amateurs always make mistakes. If you pay the ransom, and if the secretary survives, he may be able to assist us in identifying his captors."

"Who killed the professor?"

"The Fairfax Police are leading that investigation. We are coordinating closely, but they have yet to identify the shooter or his motive."

"Was Secretary Townsend involved in any way with the professor's murder?"

"I cannot believe he was the shooter; we have nothing to indicate that. If you are asking was he a witness? I don't know. Jesperson and Townsend were friends. Doctor Jesperson hosted the secretary's talk, and the two shared a drink afterward in the professor's office. We do not know when or how the secretary departed. Since the secretary's car was left on campus, it's possible the kidnappers seized him there."

"What are you going to do now?"

"Return to the Townsend home, coordinate our investigations, and wait for the kidnapper's next message. We will try to devise some way to entice the kidnappers, if that is what they are, to enter into a negotiation. Given the fact that the conversation is one way, I'm not confident we will succeed. I suspect that the next message will tell us where to send the money."

"How can we be sure that the sender of this," Featherstone picked up the e-mail message and waved it, "is bonafide?"

"As of now, we cannot."

"You realize Special Agent Cotton that you are not giving me sufficient information to make a decision."

"I realize that, sir, but you know what I know."

"Christ," the president shook his head in dismay. "If I give the writer of this message a hundred million dollars, and an exhausted Townsend suddenly reappears after having spent a quiet few days with a girl friend after a fight with his wife, I'm a fool. And, if I don't authorize the money, and the kidnappers dump a dead Secretary Townsend along the road somewhere with a note pinned to his shirt, I am responsible for a good man's death. And what about this bomb business? Do you think the professor knew what he was writing?"

"Sir, that is not my area of expertise."

"So who can tell me if the Iranians are getting ready to nuke this damned building?" Featherstone looked at the walls of the Oval Office.

""If the CIA doesn't know, and I suspect they would have said something if they did, then only Doctor Jesperson can tell you how good his sources were, and he's dead."

"This isn't something to joke about, Special Agent Cotton," the president glared at the FBI investigator.

"I know sir. I'm not joking. We can only hope that the investigation of the professor's death identifies the shooter. It's possible that the professor's murder was connected with the pending publication of his book."

The president sat up straight as a sudden realization struck him. "The only thing we really have to investigate at this moment is the professor's death and his damned book, and you say that is all in the hands of the Fairfax Police. Why the hell isn't the FBI handling that investigation?"

Cotton hesitated. That question was one that Cotton feared might come up because the answer was simple and complicated. At the time, the compromise had seemed like a logical one, letting the Fairfax cops investigate their murder while he concentrated on finding the missing Secretary Townsend. Now, however, it appeared as if he had made a big mistake.

"Lieutenant Chase Mansfield of the Fairfax Police is leading the investigation into the Jesperson murder," Cotton tried to cover his backside. "He has a reputation as a skilled, intuitive investigator who specializes in difficult murder investigations. We are coordinating closely. In fact, Mansfield was interviewing Mrs. Townsend when the e-mail arrived. He immediately alerted me."

Cotton did not admit that Mansfield's reputation also indicated he was a lone wolf investigator who marched to his own drummer, sharing only when he needed something.

"Special Agent," the president, who had been around long enough to know when he was not getting the whole story, asked, "Can you assure me that this Mansfield is the best person to handle the Jesperson investigation, and he will coordinate his progress in detail with you?"

Cotton swallowed hard before answering, "Yes sir."

Featherstone stared dubiously at him but did not comment.

"I best get to the Townsend residence, sir," Cotton said as he stood up.

The president dismissed him with a nod and a curt "Keep me informed, Special Agent Cotton."

Chapter 9

Chase visited the George Mason campus long enough to obtain the home address for Jamshid Afgar, which predictably was located in nearby Fairfax City. He had no difficulty locating the 1950-vintage rambler situated on a small lot marked by four cars parked on the grass perpendicular to the crumbling cement driveway.

Chase left his Prius in front of an adjacent rambler with a fading roof and peeling paint, a mirror image of its neighbor. Chase mounted the cracked concrete steps and pressed the button. He heard a buzzer sound in a distant room, probably the kitchen. Despite the cars crowding the driveway, nobody responded. Chase, who feared he was wasting his time, pushed the button and held it. Inside, the old buzzer responded, intermittently.

"Will sumeboddy answer de damned door?" An accented male voice finally reacted from a distant room, probably upstairs.

Suddenly, the door opened, and a scrawny, young man in Nikes, faded jeans, and a wrinkled George Mason sweatshirt confronted Chase.

"Whatever you're selling, man, we don't want any," the young man declared before attempting to close the door.

Chase caught the door with his left hand and shoved it open, surprising the young man who needed a haircut. He stepped back and stared.

"Fairfax Police Department," Chase waved his credentials as he stepped into the space just vacated by the obvious student.

"Where do they want us to park?" The young man asked.

"Are the neighbors complaining about your cars?" Chase smiled.

"One party a week doesn't hurt anyone," the young man tried again. "I can't help it if somebody's girl friend keeps turning up the volume on the CD player."

"Are you Jamshid Afgar?" Chase tired of the game.

Instead of answering, the young man turned and shouted down the stairs. "Afgar, the cops want to talk with you."

Without another word, the young man continued down a short hallway and disappeared in a room at the back of the house. He slammed the door behind him. Chase waited. At the base of the stairs, a door opened on the first room to the right, and a heavily muscled man with long black hair, a sharp protruding nose, and a scraggly beard appeared. He hesitated at the first stair step, pulled a sports shirt over his head, and silently made his way up the staircase. Chase noticed that he had particularly large feet that were stuffed into a pair of worn slippers that he wore with the backs folded under his heels.

"What?" The older man demanded.

Chase, resenting the hostile arrogance in the man's voice and demeanor, did not immediately identify himself. Instead, he coldly studied him. He appeared to be closer to thirty than twenty, far more mature than the average American student.

"I don't have all day," the man said, not the least bit intimidated by Chase's hard scrutiny.

"You have as long as I say you have," Chase said.

"Just because you're a cop you can't come busting in here and order me around," the man reacted. "This is Am…er...ika." He drew the word out into three long syllables with a sarcastic intonation obviously intended to denigrate the expression.

"Are you Jamshid Afgar?" Chase asked. "Show me some identification."

The man focused his large brown eyes on Chase, obviously trying to decide how to respond to that order. Chase waited. Finally, the man nodded, took a billfold from the rear pocket of his jeans, extracted a card from it, and silently handed it to Chase.

It was a George Mason University student card identifying the holder as Jamshid A. Afgar. Chase studied the picture of a clean-shaven man several years younger than the person with the beard standing in front of him.

"This doesn't look like you," Chase challenged.

"I was younger when the picture was taken," Afgar said.

"How old are you now?"

"What do you care?"

"You can answer my questions here or at headquarters," Chase said evenly.

"Show me some identification," Afgar insisted. "What are you, INS or a Homeland Security Gestapo of some kind?"

Chase held up the credentials that identified him as a Fairfax Police Department Criminal Investigation Officer. Afgar held out his hand expecting Chase to give him the credentials case. Chase folded the case and put it back into his coat pocket.

"How old are you?" Chase repeated his question.

"Thirty-two," Afgar answered, watching Chase's reaction closely.

"A little old to be a student aren't you?"

"I didn't know that there was an age limit for students," Afgar smiled, amused by his own cleverness.

"What year?" Chase asked, ignoring Afgar's response. The man's age and attitude was beginning to interest him.

"I'm a graduate student working on my doctorate," Afgar said. "You know what a doctorate is, don't you?"

"How long have you been here?" Chase asked.

"Are you INS working undercover?" Afgar countered.

"I asked how long have you been here?"

"In this room? About three minutes. You saw me come up the stairs from the dungeon, Lieutenant Mansfield."

Chase assumed that the surly young man used his name and rank to demonstrate how clever he was. "Let's go," Chase grabbed Afgar's arm firmly.

"Ten years," Afgar said, trying to pull free from Chase's grip.

Chase did not release him. "Where are you from?" Chase asked.

"I'm Iranian. Does that bother you? Do you hate Moslems?"

Chase released Afgar's arm. "Sit down there," Chase pointed at a worn sofa.

Afgar rubbed his arm as he turned toward the sofa. "And I'm a Shiite Moslem, too. Are you some kind of religious cop?"

"I don't care about your religion, your nationality, or your residency status," Chase said, not quite telling the truth. At least he didn't care for the reasons Afgar might suspect.

"Then why are you hassling me?"

"Because your deportment is not that of a law abiding, respectable visitor to this country, and I wonder why?" Chase said.

"Maybe I don't like Americans," Afgar said, clearly feeling more confident now that he had some space between him and his interrogator who was now sitting in a chair facing him across a scratched coffee table littered with empty beer bottles and filled ashtrays.

"That's your privilege," Chase said." I don't like some Americans either, particularly those who do not respect the law."

Afgar did not respond.

"How long did it take you to earn your bachelor's degree?" Chase asked.

"Five years. I wasted time improving my English. Then, I got my Masters in two years, and I have been working on my doctorate for three years. Add them up, that makes ten years."

"What is your major?"

"History, Near Eastern History."

"What's the title of your doctorate?"

"American and English Imperialistic Exploitation of Iran," Afgar smiled.

"Sounds interesting," Chase did not react as Afgar expected.

"Doesn't my choice bother you?" Afgar asked.

"Your subject doesn't. Your attitude does."

"I was naïve when I arrived in this country. Your fellow countrymen's attitude towards foreigners forced me to learn to defend myself."

"I can understand that," Chase said. "Who is your faculty advisor?"

"The better question is who was my faculty advisor? Is that why you are here? Do you think that a dirty Iranian murdered Doctor Jesperson?"

"Was Doctor Jesperson your faculty advisor?" Chase persisted.

Afgar nodded affirmatively. "I did not knock off Doctor Jesperson if that is what you think."

"I didn't accuse you."

"But that is why you are here, checking on the foreign students. If that's the case, you better talk with my housemates, too. The kid who opened the door for you," Afgar glanced down the hall towards the room that the first student had retreated to, "is an Iraqi, and he really doesn't like Americans. For some incomprehensible reason, he resents the fact that you invaded his country and are killing his people."

"Every one living here is a foreign student?" Chase said, ignoring Afgar's attempt to provoke him.

"Of course, all ten of us. And we are all members of the Foreign Student's Association."

"That Dr Jesperson advised," Chase said.

"You didn't answer my question," Afgar said. "Are you investigating Doctor Jesperson's murder?"

"I am in charge of the investigation," Chase admitted.

"I didn't kill him. I liked Doctor Jesperson. He encouraged my research for my dissertation. He's half Iranian, you know."

"I know. I've talked with his mother," Chase said, trying to build some rapport.

"I'm sure she's heartbroken. Her husband has a stick up his ass and really doesn't like Iranians."

"When did you meet the elder Jespersons?"

"Several years ago. Doctor Jesperson took me to Cambridge."

"Why did he do that?"

"Because I was new here and was having difficulty adapting. He wanted to show me what he called the 'real America' and to let me talk with his mother, a fellow Iranian."

"Did it help?"

"The talk with his mother? What do you think? She doesn't like Americans either. Real Americans look down on foreigners."

"But Doctor Jesperson was different," Chase said. Chase didn't admit it, but he agreed with Afgar's appraisal of the elder Jespersons.

"He was half Iranian and understood us. I suspect that's why he worked with the foreign students and helped us. Everyone in this house pretended to be his friend."

"Pretended?"

Afgar shrugged.

"Have you met Mansour?" Chase tested him.

"Taheri?" Afgar stared at Chase, his eyelids narrowing. He crossed his arms and legs and waited for Chase's answer.

"Yes, Doctor Jesperson's relative," Chase smiled. "Is Mansour here now?" Chase guessed that Mansour had spent at least one night in the house.

"I'm not sure," Afgar smiled. "I'll have to ask him.

"Invite him to come and join us," Chase said, assuming that Mansour's participation might encourage Afgar to speak more openly.

The alacrity with which Afgar descended the stairs made Chase wonder if he had made a mistake. A ten-minute wait persuaded him that he had, but finally a smirking Afgar ascended the stairs followed by an obviously reluctant Mansour. After they were seated on the stained sofa with the torn fabric, Chase smiled at Mansour.

"If you had told me that you were coming to visit Afgar, Mansour, I would have given you a ride. It would have saved me having to get the address from the Registrar," Chase said.

Mansour grinned but did not comment.

"Afgar and I were discussing foreign student life in the States and your relative Doctor Jesperson," Chase said.

Neither Afgar nor Mansour reacted.

"I think I might attend Doctor Jesperson's funeral," Chase, now irritated, decided to press the rude young man. "Would either of you like to come with me?"

Afgar chuckled as if the invitation were funny. Mansour simply shook his head negatively.

"I'm sure your aunt would appreciate the gesture, Mansour," Chase said.

"No," Mansour said.

"No what?"

"I not come with you," Mansour said.

"I think that's clear enough," Afgar smiled.

"Do you know if any of Doctor Jesperson's friends might attend?" Chase looked at Afgar.

"Friends?"

"From the Foreign Student Association, for example," Chase said.

"Jesperson was our advisor, not our friend," Afgar said without elaboration.

"Can either of you name a person who disliked Doctor Jesperson?" Chase tried again to ignore the fact that even he was getting tired of the same question in one form or another.

Mansour shook his head, and Afgar smiled.

"Did I say something funny?" Chase demanded.

"Somebody obviously had a problem with Doctor Jesperson," Afgar said, referring to the shooting.

"Are there any other students living here that I should talk to about Doctor Jesperson?" Chase persisted.

"None that I know of," Afgar answered. "Only foreigners like me live here."

"Then I thank you for the time," Chase stood up, dismissing the two young men, not hiding his irritation. At the door he turned back, surprising them. "It's too bad that the two of you aren't interested in assisting me find Doctor Jesperson's killer. If the positions were reversed, I'm sure that Doctor Jesperson would have gladly done what he could to help."

"I wonder," Afgar said. "Doctor Jesperson has already made his feelings for the Iranian people clear."

"What does that mean?" Chase asked.

"His scurrilous book," Afgar said.

Chase stared at Afgar and then departed without another word.

****

After two days of fruitless investigation, days that were highlighted mainly by constant harassment by the media, Chase caught a late flight to Boston, made his way to Cambridge where he spent the night before catching a taxi to Christ Church Cambridge on Harvard Square. Neither a churchgoer nor believer, and despite the fact that he had never met Doctor Thomas Hamid Jesperson, Chase was looking forward to seeing the church if not the funeral services. When he had called to inquire about the timing of the funeral service, Jesperson's father had confided that neither he nor his wife were church members, but Mrs. Jesperson, who followed the social conventions of her peers, had insisted on Christ Church primarily because she believed its aristocratic reputation was appropriate for her son.

Jesperson chuckled when he explained that Christ Church Cambridge had been founded by Church of England settlers in 1759; the same individuals who had abandoned it a short twenty years later when they joined an exodus of loyalist citizens who fled their homes for mother England when frightened by the dark storm clouds created by the rebelling New Englanders. The church was used as a barracks by Continental troops and was the site of a service in 1775 requested by Martha Washington. It had subsequently remained shuttered until 1790 but existed without a rector until 1820. Doctor Jesperson also noted that a Revered Spalding distinguished himself in 1879 when he dismissed a Harvard student who was teaching Sunday school at the church because he refused to convert to Episcopalian from his family acquired Dutch Reform beliefs. The fact that the student was Theodore Roosevelt who later attained prominence in politics continued to amuse less religious members of the local community including Doctor Jesperson. Chase assumed that Jacky Rossi, his lawyer friend, would appreciate his stress on these historical incidents more than a description of Jesperson's funeral service.

When Chase climbed out of the taxi, he found himself in a media maelstrom that included several satellite trucks, their cameramen, blow-dried men and women talkers, and a mass of reporters with and without cameras and microphones. Obviously, they had little to report because the mass turned to focus on Chase and his taxi. Chase ignored the question that the media almost as one asked rhetorically, "Who the hell is that?"

Chase slowly made his way past them and finally reached the thin line of police guarding the entrance.

"A friend of the family," Chase softly identified himself to a red-faced, blue uniform with sergeant stripes on his sleeves.

"Some people have no consideration for others," the sergeant said as he stared at the noisy media mob.

"Animals," Chase agreed as the officer opened the door to let him enter.

Once inside, Chase hesitated. He was impressed. The church was lighter, brighter, and more friendly than he had anticipated. The preacher was already in the pulpit, and he hesitated when Chase appeared in the doorway. Embarrassed, Chase quickly sat in the last pew before any of the handful of mourners turned to see who or what had caused the interruption. The preacher resumed his presentation, and Chase relaxed. He noted that Doctor and Mrs. Jesperson and Mansour sat in the first pew. Mansour's presence surprised Chase, but not as much as the fourth person in the family group. Jamshid Afgar sat to Mansour's immediate right. In addition to the Jesperson four, Chase counted only twenty additional mourners sitting as couples or individuals, no groups, all elderly. Chase immediately assumed they were friends, colleagues, and neighbors of the parents. Chase had hoped to identify a peer, a friend of the deceased loner who might assist Chase in profiling him. At least twenty vacant pews separated Chase from the mourners.

Chase, disappointed, folded his hands, and impassively tried to project a sad profile as inside he churned. He had only himself to blame for the wasted trip. Unable to identify a single person who could discuss Thomas Jesperson, the man, Chase out of desperation had decided to attend the funeral, and one quick survey of the pathetically restricted group of mourners told him he had misallocated his time. Chase closed his eyes as he tried to will the passage of time. Now that he was here, he had to stay long enough to convey his condolences to the elderly Jesperson couple. Although they really had been of little assistance to his investigation, they had tried; at least the old man had. He had put Chase in contact with the uncooperative Mansour. While Chase ignored the droning preacher who was lauding a man he and most of his audience had never met, Chase pondered how he might persuade the young cousin to trust him enough to speak frankly and to stop taking refuge in what Chase suspected was an exaggerated limit on his ability to communicate in English.

A slight movement to Chase's right intruded on his frustrated musings. He canted his head and discovered a woman in a black pants suit sitting alone some thirty feet away at the far edge of his pew row. He caught her looking at him, a curious expression on her face, and he nodded to establish some kind of rapport, but by the time he did so she had turned her attention back to the tedious preacher. Chase stared and his sense of frustration lifted. The Lady in Black was quite attractive with short blond hair, flawless facial features, and trim figure. He estimated that she was almost his age, early forties, which made her almost a contemporary of the deceased Doctor Jesperson, and she sat alone, apart from the family and the other mourners. Chase immediately decided that the trip was not a failure after all. Suddenly, apparently sensing Chase's scrutiny, the woman turned her head and caught Chase staring.

This time Chase established eye contact and nodded, twice. She reciprocated, once, and Chase turned away first, trying to present a non-intrusive image. Chase forced himself to stare at the preacher who had moved the focus of his oration from the deceased he did not know to the family, non-members of his flock who sat directly in front of him. Chase had the ungracious premonition that the preacher would now assiduously work the old couple who would be slipping him a gratuity for his labors; Chase prayed--something he did not indulge in often--that the effort would be a short one. Chase crossed and uncrossed his legs trying to will the tedious ceremony to an end. It was difficult ignoring his pew mate. She had caught him staring once, and he did not want to convey the wrong impression.

Fifteen long minutes later, the tedious preacher summarized his feeble oratorical effort with a curt prayer that ended with a loud amen. The small audience reacted with a silent, collective sigh of relief. On cue, four men in wrinkled suits, obviously employees from the undertaker's establishment, entered from the right and quickly shuttled the closed coffin through a side door. The Jesperson entourage stood up and followed the preacher up the aisle, Doctor Jesperson and his wife in the lead, Mansour and Jamshid right behind. Doctor Jesperson spotted Chase and stopped at Chase's pew.

"Thank you for coming, lieutenant. I fear it has been a wasted trip,"

Jesperson glanced at the sparse collection of mourners, conveying his understanding of Chase's presence.

"Please accept my condolences for your loss," Chase said, regretting the inadequacy of his words.

Mrs. Jesperson ignored Chase and tugged at her husband's arm.

"I'm not coming to the cemetery," Chase whispered. "I will call later."

Doctor Jesperson nodded and turned. With a frowning spouse on his arm, Doctor Jesperson stoically continued toward the door and the waiting preacher. Next came Mansour who ignored Chase by staring at the worn aisle floor. Jamshid followed and he irritated Chase with a sarcastic smile. Chase made a mental note to discuss this visit with the two who had told him they did not plan to attend the funeral.

After a slight pause, the older mourners began to depart, two by two. Most of the men appeared to be relieved that the tedious ceremony was over; the women to a person continued to play their assigned roles. Several glanced at Chase, obviously wondering who he might be. Chase waited and hoped that the Lady in Black would do the same.

After the last of the mourners passed, Chase sensed movement to his right. He turned and feigned surprise at discovering the Lady-in-Black side-stepping along the pew towards him

“"I don't believe I know you," the woman spoke first. "Were you a friend of Thomas?"

Chase hesitated, not sure how to respond.

"No, my name is Chase Mansfield," Chase answered succinctly but honestly. "Were you a friend?"

The woman stared at Chase with clear, bright-blue eyes and did not try to hide her surprise. "Then what are you doing here?"

"I'm from Fairfax, Virginia," Chase said, still stalling, trying to find a non-intrusive way of learning her identity.

"What newspaper?" The woman shook her head. "Some people have no consideration for the feelings of others. Please let me past."

"Ma'am, could I just have a few minutes of your time?"

"No. Let me pass."

Chase detected irritation but no panic in her voice. He reached into his coat pocket and took out his credential case. "I am Lieutenant Chase Mansfield, and I am in charge of the investigation into Doctor Mansfield's death."

The tear-free, blue eyes focused on the credentials before looking directly at Chase. "Lieutenant, please catch the bastard who shot Thomas."

"May I ask your name?" Chase said.

"Kendrick. Sally Ann Kendrick."

"Do you live in Cambridge?"

"No, lieutenant, now please let me out of this damned place," Kendrick frowned.

"Do you have time to answer a few questions? Please, I'm having difficulty locating anyone who knew Doctor Jesperson well."

"I'm not surprised. I doubt that anyone knew the real Thomas. Now move. I assure you, I swing a heavy purse," she said as she swiped her shoulder bag a couple of times in Chase's direction.

"Yes ma'am," Chase said, retreating into the now empty aisle.

"Thank you," Kendrick said as she gave Chase a firm push.

She walked quickly to the front door, and Chase followed, admiring the swing of her hips, regretting she was wearing pants not a mini skirt.

They found the preacher waiting patiently near the open door with a practiced, benevolent, but insincere smile.

"We thank you for joining us in saying goodbye to Thomas," the preacher said.

Kendrick nodded and continued past the preacher.

"Thank you, reverend," Chase said, not certain what Episcopalians called their preachers.

The man glanced curiously at Chase but said nothing as Chase hurried to follow Kendrick who appeared to be heading around the back of the building.

"Ms. Kendrick, may I ask where you are going?" Chase asked.

"You're full of questions, lieutenant," Kendrick said, not answering the query.

"I'm not going to the cemetery. I arrived in a taxi and need a ride," Chase said, trying to sound plaintive.

"Where are you going?" Kendrick asked.

"To my hotel to collect my bag and then to Boston to catch a shuttle, if I can, back to D.C."

"Which hotel?"

"Hyatt." Chase said.

Kendrick responded with a silent look that told Chase she didn't believe him.

"Honest Indian," Chase said.

"Alright, come on," Kendrick relented, a little ungraciously in Chase's opinion.

She led Chase to a small red Ford with Massachusetts plates. Nearing the car, Chase spoke first. "Nice car."

Kendrick laughed. "Not mine. It's a rental."

Chase nodded, wanting to know why she was driving a rental, not sure how to ask without irritating her. Kendrick unlocked the driver's door and climbed inside. Chase hurried around the car and joined her. Kendrick started the engine and drove out of the church lot.

"I'm staying at the Hyatt, too," Kendrick surprised Chase with her comment. "I have to pick up my bag, and you can relax, lieutenant. There is a shuttle to National. We'll be shuttle mates."

"You're from D.C.?"

"Reston, not D.C."

"You knew Doctor Jesperson in D.C.?"

"Do me a favor, lieutenant. Save your questions until we get on the shuttle. Until then, I want to concentrate on getting out of here."

"Yes, ma'am," Chase said.

"And please stop calling me ma'am. I'm getting along in years, but I'm not your mother's age. Or all those geriatrics at the church either. Who were those two boys? Iranian relatives?"

"The younger boy is Mrs. Jesperson's nephew who just arrived in this country. The other is the nephew's friend. How should I address you?"

"Sally will do."

"So will Chase. I am having a very difficult time identifying any of Doctor Jesperson's friends. May I just ask a few questions to make sure I am not wasting your or my time? It's very important."

"How many questions?" Kendrick frowned. "I'm really not interested in getting involved in your investigation, and I doubt that anything I might say is of any interest to Thomas now."

"Three," Chase answered, ignoring her last comment.

"Alright, three."

"How well did you know Doctor Jesperson?" Chase assumed that the answer to this question would determine those to follow.

Kendrick glanced at Chase before answering. "This is all off the record, right lieutenant."

"Yes ma'am." Chase acknowledged the strong-minded woman's use of his title was an attempt to put the conversation on a formal level despite her previous suggestion that he use her first name.

"Intimately," Kendrick surprised Chase with her answer. "That is one question. You have two remaining."

"Sally, you are the first person I have talked to with the exception of Doctor Jesperson's parents to acknowledge anything more than a casual acquaintance."

"Chase," Kendrick picked up on the name game, "that doesn't surprise me. At one time I might have challenged that statement, but after the events of the past year, I understand."

Chase glanced at Kendrick and wondered what she was telling him. Had something happened during the past year that had changed Jesperson. "What kind of person was Doctor Jesperson?" Chase asked.

"Lieutenant, that's your second question but it is not a fair or valid one. An honest answer would require more time than we have."

"A succinct response would suffice," Chase smiled. He felt like asking Kendrick if she were a lawyer, but he did not do so because she would immediately count it as his third question, and he had another in mind.

"My response will of necessity require me to summarize my reactions to Thomas, and I fear they may be emotionally subjective," Kendrick said.

"Anything you can tell me would be duly appreciated," Chase said.

"Very well. Thomas was a very private man, as I am sure you have learned. I am now confident the same was true when he was younger. He grew up in a strange family. His father lived for his work, his research. I doubt that Doctor Jesperson Senior enjoyed much of a relationship with his students or his associates at the university, and Thomas' mother was completely self-centered; I suppose that resulted from the fact she was a stranger in a culture that did not accept her and from her own Iranian upbringing. I wouldn't describe either Thomas or his father as introverted. A stranger might, but I would argue that both were strong, intelligent men completely preoccupied with their own interests. Other human beings and their petty concerns did not interest them; Thomas was a loner who simply did not need interaction with others to sustain his emotional well-being. He had no difficulty coping with social situations; he could be a perfect gentleman when the occasion required, but that did not mean he enjoyed doing so. Most of his acquaintances probably considered him cold, conceited, something like that. I didn't. That's not true. At first I did, but after I got to know him, I enjoyed his company. Individuals interested him, groups did not. On more than one occasion he remarked that personalities changed in social situations, and he did not enjoy conversations where people merely said what they thought others wanted to hear. He found women, including me, particularly prone to behave artificially that way."

Chase was tempted to note that he doubted that Kendrick fell into that category. She struck him as a tough, self-confident person who did not hesitate to say what she was thinking. He did not interrupt her train of thought, however, more interested in hearing what she had to say about Jesperson than he was in flattering her.

Kendrick suddenly stopped her monologue and glanced at Chase, giving him the impression that somehow she had sensed his reaction.

"Wh…" Chase started to ask 'What?' but caught himself as he realized Kendrick would count his blurted inquiry as his third question.

"Yes?" Kendrick smiled.

"That wasn't my third question," Chase smiled back. "Please go on, I find your comments very informative."

"A woman scorned, huh?" Kendrick did not accommodate him.

Chase did not reply.

Kendrick stubbornly said nothing more.

"Very well," Chase capitulated. "What happened during the past year that disrupted your relationship?"

"That's your third question," Kendrick said as she guided the Ford into a space in the Hyatt parking lot. "You're clever, lieutenant. I'll give you that. No one word answers for you. Get the witness talking about herself. That's what women like to do."

Kendrick turned off the engine and opened her car door. As she was turning to climb out, Chase protested.

"You promised to answer three questions," Chase said.

Kendrick stopped, turned back, and closed the door. "Alright, and then we'll chat about the weather or some other impersonal nonsense all the way to Reagan National," she said.

"Agreed," Chase said, not telling the truth. He intended to keep her talking about Thomas Jesperson.

Kendrick looked at Chase, not hiding her disbelief, and brushed one hand through her short blond hair. "Alright," she agreed. "We have a bargain.

Kendrick placed both hands on the steering wheel and stared straight ahead at a SUV that was parked facing them, blocking their view of a solid wall.

"Iran happened," Kendrick announced, smiled, turned, opened the door, and climbed out.

"Two words are not an answer," Chase protested as he hurried to join her.

"I didn't promise long answers," Kendrick said as she started for the Hyatt entrance.

"Then we don't have a bargain," Chase said as he rushed to walk at her side.

Kendrick shrugged. "You weren't sincere when you agreed," she said. She waved at the smiling doorman and turned to the elevator. "I checked out this morning. I'll see you on the next shuttle to National if you make it."

"You have to turn in your rental car," Chase said.

"At the airport."

"Give me a ride," Chase asked.

"If you are at the car when I leave," Kendrick said.

Chase punched the button for the third floor and Kendrick the sixth.

"I'll be there," Chase said when he exited at the third.

Kendrick waved an indifferent hand.

"Shit," Chase complained as he rushed towards his room.

Five minutes later Kendrick was not in sight when Chase, his carry-on in hand, entered the empty elevator. Back in the lobby, he hurried to the checkout counter which was fortunately empty. Chase handed his key and his American Express to the smiling clerk.

"Did you enjoy your stay, sir? Was the room to your satisfaction?" The clerk asked.

"Everything was fine. I apologize for my haste but I'm running late and have to hurry to catch my flight," Chase said.

The clerk nodded, grabbed Chase's key and card, played with her computer, nodded, ran the card through the little machine, and handed the card, a copy of his bill, and a slip to sign without another comment. Chase grabbed the card, signed the receipt, thanked the clerk, and hurried to the door. Outside, he relaxed when he saw the Ford parked near the door in a space reserved for taxis. A smiling Kendrick sat behind the wheel chatting with the doorman who stood by her door. She waved; Chase waved, hurried to the car and tossed his bag on the back seat before climbing in beside Kendrick.

"Have a safe journey," the doorman smiled as he deposited the tip Kendrick had handed him into a side pocket. "Come back and see us," he said.

Kendrick nodded, and Chase said, "We will."

"We will?" Kendrick parroted his words, placing particular stress on the "We."

"Just a polite expression," Chase smiled, not sure he would or would want to see the attractive, but overly confident Lady in Black, after the next leg of their journey ended.

"That's too bad," Kendrick said.

Chase could not tell whether the enigmatic comment was sincere or simple sarcasm. Today's professional women always puzzled Chase who had trouble determining if they were behaving the way they thought men did or if they had simply forgotten how to act and flirt like women, at least the way men of Chase's age had grown up expecting them to behave.

The drive to the airport, the car turn-in, and the check-in was filled with long silences marked by casual comment unrelated to the Jespersons.

As soon as they were seated in the shuttle departure lounge, Chase turned to Kendrick. "Sally..."

Kendrick's throaty laugh interrupted, "Lieutenant, again, the interrogation continues. You've already exceeded your three questions."

"That limitation applied only to the ride in the Ford," Chase protested. "We're back on neutral turf now."

"I know, for at least another hour. So, ask your questions. I assure you all of my answers will apply to a previous era."

"Previous era?"

"Yes, a pre-Iran sabbatical era."

"If I understood you correctly, you were once quite ... "Chase almost used the word 'intimate,' but caught himself, "...close, but something happened to interrupt your relationship."

"I said we were intimate. By that I mean, we spent the occasional night in each other's company. You do understand what that means?"

"Yes," Chase said, not sure what she wanted him to say or to not say.

"We were engaged, and we shared alternate weekends in each other's beds," Kendrick said.

"Yes," Chase said, not really interested in discussing those events in detail.

"I should explain," Kendrick said.

Chase nodded, somewhat embarrassed by this turn in the conversation.

"Oh I'm not going to discuss Thomas' performance in bed," Kendrick laughed, amused by the expression on her interrogator's face.

"Good."

"As I told you, I live in Reston in a condominium, twenty minutes in non-rush hour traffic from Thomas's Fairfax apartment. I assume you've been there."

Chase nodded. He said nothing, preferring to keep Kendrick talking.

"Thomas' place is rather nondescript. I'm sure you noticed."

"It's much like my own townhouse," Chase said, not prepared to criticize a murder victim's choice of homes.

"I tried to encourage him to raise his standard of living a few degrees, but that sort of thing did not interest him. He could have afforded better. His last couple of books sold pretty well." She hesitated as an obvious thought struck her. "He certainly could now. This last bombshell is going to be a big best seller. That's ironic. I'm sure all this money is going to make his father very wealthy, and money doesn't mean anything to him either. Like son, like father, the old saw in reverse."

Chase nodded. Now that Kendrick seemed to relax, she was almost chatty. Chase rather hoped she was becoming comfortable with his presence.

"Are you a lawyer?" Chase asked. Kendrick was beginning to remind him of Jacky Rossi, his current, occasional female intimate. Jacky was one of the toughest defense lawyers in Fairfax County. She specialized in criminal case and was universally despised by members of the Fairfax Police establishment.

"What in the world makes you think that?" Kendrick asked, a look of amazement on her face that surprised Chase.

"Something about your rather aggressive demeanor," Chase said, grinning to lessen the impact of his words.

"Are you one of those pseudo macho men who are intimidated by professional women?"

"I rather like some kinds of professional women," Chase tried to make a joke of her question. "It's lawyers that give me a pain in…the neck."

"If you mean to say pain in the ass, say it. Don't play games with me, lieutenant."

"It's that kind of comment that made me wonder if you were a lawyer," Chase said.

"Why is my speaking style of importance to you?" Kendrick demanded.

Chase shrugged. Answering that kind of question was counter-productive in any kind of discussion with a woman. He knew from past experience that any response would be challenged and categorized as critical.

"If you are not a lawyer, what do you do?" Chase tried to change the subject.

"I'm a working woman," Kendrick smiled. "Does that trouble you?"

"You're an educated, mature woman free to do what you choose," Chase's tone revealed his disappointment despite his best effort. He had no interest in getting involved with a high-class call girl. Given his dual incomes from his job and his books, he assumed he could afford her, but the thought of sharing with others did not appeal to him.

"I am educated and quite mature, if forty-three is mature, but I'm sorry I am going to have to disappoint you. I'm not a working girl in the sense that you seem to assume. I'm a techie. I own an interesting software business in Reston. Have you heard of Starpower Software?"

"I'm computer literate, sort of, but I'm no technophile," Chase smiled disparagingly. "I'm afraid the proper answer is no."

"You can use a computer but not repair it, and you look down on those that can," Kendrick said.

"Please don't misunderstand," Chase tried to recoup. "I intended nothing critical. I was merely explaining my ignorance."

"That's not necessary, lieutenant," Kendrick said coldly. "Besides, I wasn't always a techie. Once, I was even a junior diplomat."

"Really," Chase said, allowing himself to be drawn off topic. Kendrick's odd background interested him. Her style was anything but diplomatic.

"Yes, I graduated from college with a major in foreign affairs and a minor in computer science. Being headstrong, I ignored my parents's advice and joined the Foreign Service. After surviving the written and oral test ordeal that all Foreign Service Officer applicants have to endure, I did well enough in my training to be sent to the Foreign Service Institute where they tried to teach me French. Somehow, I completed the course and went off to the Paris Embassy where they assumed I knew nothing and gave me lots of scut work. As the junior man, so to speak, in the political section, the counselor assigned me responsibility for keeping track of the third country refugees hiding out in France. That's where I met my first Iranian, and that's an interesting story we don't have time for today. I soon tired of the shallow, meaningless diplomatic swirl, and after my first two-year tour

I resigned from the State Department and returned home to admit to my parents they had been right all along and I had made a terrible mistake. I found a job with AOL in Ashburn. That was great for a while but eventually, as all good things do, AOL got too big and crumpled under its own weight. That's when I took my preposterous bonuses and started my own business in Reston. How does that bittersweet tale strike you so far?"

Kendrick's abrupt question surprised Chase. "I think it is a fascinating story," Chase improvised.

"Fascinating my ass," Kendrick laughed. "Now you are saying to yourself 'I bet she is one of those people who goes through life jumping from one self-produced emotional crisis to another.'"

"Nothing I say pleases you," Chase responded weakly. "When did you meet Doctor Jesperson?"

"Now we get back to what really interests you," Kendrick said, implying that Chase was indifferent to her trials and tribulations.

Chase let that pass.

After a brief pause, Kendrick surprised him by continuing. "A year and a half ago, six months before the shit decided to take a year's sabbatical in Iran, we were introduced by a mutual friend on the George Mason faculty. After only three months, we started sharing each other's beds; after five months we were engaged, and after one month of bliss, that I mistakenly assumed was mutual, Doctor Jesperson got cold feet and took off for Iran alone. We had a great six months and then nothing."

"Did he explain why?" Chase asked, amazed that anyone could walk away abruptly from this attractive and complicated woman.

"He tried to hide behind the excuse of his important research. I didn't buy his crap about 'this is the most important book of my life.' I accused him of wanting to dump me, and he tried to hide behind some nonsense. He said things were moving too fast between us, and we both needed some time to think. I said, 'think, bullshit, you're just an emotional coward afraid to let anyone inside that protective shell of yours.' I called him a damned human terrapin, waved goodbye, and walked out of his life. Best thing I ever did. I never talked with him again."

"How did he take being called a turtle?" Chase smiled at the one-sided description of the confrontation.

"He didn't argue."

"When did this conversation take place?" Chase asked, concealing his sympathy for the apparently over-matched Jesperson.

"In May a year ago, three weeks before he took off for Iran. He didn't even call to say goodbye."

Not sure what he should say about the breakup, Chase decided to concentrate, if he could, on Jesperson and his plans. "What did he say he was going to research in Iran that made this book so important?"

"I think that is rather obvious," Kendrick snapped. When Chase did not comment, Kendrick continued. "A two week visit, I could understand. A full year told me where I stood on his list of priorities. There is a difference between being a private person and a selfish person."

Chase suppressed the impulse to observe that the media and the public's sensational reaction to the book's publication tended to substantiate Jesperson's expectations.

"Do you think I was unfair?" Kendrick demanded.

Chase laughed. "I don't know about unfair, but I have no doubt that you are a tough handful for most men."

Kendrick's eyes narrowed. She clenched her long slender fingers into tight fists, and Chase was sure she was thinking about slugging him. Before he could decide whether to apologize or at least step back, she surprised him a second time. Her eyes widened' she unclenched her fists, and she smiled. "Do you think you could handle me, lieutenant?" She asked playfully.

"It would be a challenge, but it might be fun to try," Chase answered honestly. Wacky Jacky was as tough as Kendrick but far more predictable.

Kendrick smiled. "Enough about me. Now that I've told you that Thomas was a turtle when it came to dealing with other humans, what other questions do you have?"

Chase laughed, amused by Kendrick's kaleidoscopic ability to switch moods in an instant. Before he could ask another question, the loudspeaker announced that the shuttle was boarding.

After they were seated and the plane was in the air, Chase returned the conversation to Jesperson.

"Turtle or not, I find it difficult to believe that Doctor Jesperson had no close friends or associates other than yourself," Chase said, deliberately risking another explosion. He knew, of course, that Townsend had been a friend.

"Do you think I am lying?" Kendrick asked.

"Of course not," Chase said quickly. "He had to have someone that he ate lunch with in the cafeteria. Didn't he ever go to a ball game or movie?"

"Not to my knowledge. Thomas spent his days alone in his office, the library, or in his apartment. He watched basketball and football and an occasional movie on the TV. He ate breakfast and dinner at home and usually carried a sandwich that he prepared at home for lunch at his desk."

"I've checked the numbers in his little black book," Chase said. "All he had listed were the electric company, the local Ford and Honda dealers, Verizon, and Cox television. He had his mother and father's number, but not yours, or anyone in his department at George Mason."

"Thomas had a very good memory. I'm sure that the numbers he called often he had no need to list anywhere. That is one of the things I liked about him, his phenomenal mind. You never had to tell him anything twice," Kendrick said.

"I assume he was highly introverted," Chase said.

"He wasn't afraid of people. He wasn't an absent-minded professor dominated by his subject. Thomas could deal with others when he chose to; he just didn't choose to, not often."

"But you and he got along fine, for six months," Chase said.

"That's right. With me, he was perfectly natural. He was a good conversationalist, aware of the world, and things going on around him. He followed international affairs, American politics, read four newspapers, ignored television news because he found it too shallow, but he didn't take the trouble to denigrate the chattering newsreaders. He simply ignored them."

"Did you ever go to parties, visit your friends' homes, share nights out on the town with other human beings of like minds?" Chase asked.

"No," Kendrick answered firmly. "In the early months I suggested it, but Thomas declined. I soon learned that Thomas had no interest in normal socializing, and to be frank, I was rather flattered. He enjoyed my company exclusively. Living in Reston, I always had time for my friends. Thomas simply was not involved."

"Who do you think killed Thomas?" Chase asked abruptly.

"It wasn't me, if that is what you are asking," Kendrick responded immediately. "As I said, I haven't seen or talked with him for over a year."

Kendrick turned away from Chase and looked out the window, clearly indicating that the question had irritated her.

"I apologize," Chase said. "I didn't mean to imply that you might know who shot Doctor Jesperson."

"Then why did you ask?" Kendrick demanded.

"Because you are the only person I have found who knew Doctor Thomas Jesperson, the man. I have the impression that not even his mother or father understood their son."

"That's right. Once we had a conversation about his relationships with others and Thomas explained that he had always been a loner, even as a youth. He claimed that for good or bad he didn't need other people and was simply more comfortable living with his own thoughts; he said he had no compulsion to share with others, at least not orally."

"Not orally?"

"Yes, Thomas said that he enjoyed research and writing, hence his chosen profession, and that seemed to provide him all the social interaction he needed. He said then that I was the exception. I accused him of being anti-social, and he denied it, claiming that he was speaking only for himself. He said he read a lot of Emerson and Thoreau in grade school and assumed they had infected him with their diatribes about the importance of the individual. You know, society is always pawing the individual with its filthy institutions and all that nonsense."

"You aren't a devotee of Emerson and Thoreau?" Chase smiled.

"I outgrew it. I guess Thomas never did. I'm only trying to explain Thomas to you, so don't try to psychoanalyze me," Kendrick frowned.

Chase raised his hands in surrender.

"Thomas once said his family life wasn't of the Father Knows Best variety."

"The television show or literally?"

"The distorted, idyllic view of family life presented by the television show, all bliss and happiness with the parents interested only in their children. Thomas said his mother and father each were self-preoccupied. Do you understand what I'm trying to say?"

"I do," Chase replied. "I've met them both. Dad is focused on MIT and his professorship and mother on family and things Iranian."

"Exactly."

"And I am at a loss in trying to identify the motive behind Doctor Jesperson's killing. Means, motive and opportunity is a detective story cliché, but all three considerations are usually involved in any murder investigation. In this instance, I'm stuck on the publication of Doctor Jesperson's book as the motivating factor. You served abroad. How do I, a simple Fairfax County cop, investigate the Iranian Government? The Iranian Government is the institution that has to be offended by Doctor

Jesperson's research. Its secrets have been revealed. And what did shooting Doctor Jesperson accomplish for them? That act did not prevent the book's publication, and now how do they learn where he acquired his information? Who leaked it? Jesperson can't tell anyone now?"

"And you need to find someone closer at hand to blame?" Kendrick laughed, irritating Chase, who expected her to sympathize with, not ridicule, his candor.

Chase frowned.

"Don't glower at me, lieutenant," Kendrick said. "I didn't create your dilemma, and I have made it perfectly clear I don't even like discussing it. You are the one who has been pressing me."

"I told you why I had to ask you my questions," Chase replied.

"You're just doing your job," Kendrick said.

Kendrick's light-hearted comment and the way she said it irritated Chase even more. He leaned back and stared at the front of the plane.

"And you wish this damned flight would end," Kendrick, now clearly enjoying herself, said. "On that I agree with you."

Chase did not bother to reply. Silently, he chastised himself for admitting to the frustration this damned investigation was causing. Normally, he kept his own counsel. Unfortunately, Kendrick's apparent sincerity in discussing her past involvement with Jesperson had beguiled him and led to the unprofessional admission. Chase's preoccupation with his own foolishness was interrupted by a soft pat. Chase turned and found Kendrick's long fingers with the red nails resting on his wrist.

"To answer your question, lieutenant, you can't," Kendrick smiled.

"I can't what, Ms. Kendrick?" Chase asked, more harshly than he intended.

"Can't investigate the Iranian Government," Kendrick said. "I know from my State Department days that is a job for the federal government, the FBI or the CIA."

"No way," Chase said. "Solving murders is my job."

"Spoken like a good county cop," Kendrick said before turning away while getting in the last word. "Lots of luck."

Chapter 10

President Mahmoud Ahmadinejad leaned back in his chair and glared at his Minister of Intelligence and Security Naveed Behbehani. The fact that Behbehani, a hulk of a man, was clearly not intimidated did not help the president's mood. Behbehani, who owed his appointment to his mentor, Supreme Leader Ayatollah Ali Khamenei, was the one independent member of Ahmadinejad's cabinet who responded to the president's frequent emotional tantrums with bemused tolerance not fear. Ahmadinejad, who on occasion had been criticized by Khamenei, considered Ayatollah Mohammad Yazdi, a Qom cleric, his mentor.

"Please tell me, Mr. Minister," Ahmadinejad demanded. "Who in VEVAK (the Vezerat-e Ettela'at va Amniat-e Keshvar, the Ministry of Intelligence and Security) authorized this American's extended stay in our blessed country? Was it you?"

Behbehani smiled but did not respond. The braying donkey sitting behind the big desk knew the answer to his question as well as Behbehani did. After a lengthy application process, Americans planning to visit Iran were issued two-week visas only. Jesperson had stayed for almost a full year, and this exception had been granted on the explicit orders of Ahmadinejad himself. In this very office, Behbehani had objected, and the president had over-ruled him. One of Ahmadinejad's mullah friends had appealed to the little man and arranged a meeting between the American and the president. Jesperson had somehow conned the president into believing that he was a prominent American academic who was going to write a definitive and very flattering history of the ancient city of Persepolis, a project that appealed to the diminutive Ahmadinejad's oversized ego. In 1971 the Shah had hosted an extraordinary extravaganza attended by world leaders and celebrities for the express purpose of celebrating the 2,500th anniversary of Cyrus the Great's founding of the Persian Empire while simultaneously glorifying the Shah and his contemporary achievements. Obviously, Ahmadinejad assumed that this minor American professor would use his little book to praise himself and not the Shah, taking a page from the Shah's book, so to speak. Given the fact that Jesperson had lied and used Ahmadinejad for his own purposes, the little man now was trying to conceal his role in facilitating the miserable spectacle that now preoccupied the world's media.

"And please summarize for me VEVAK's analysis of Jesperson's extended stay in Iran. I am particularly interested in knowing who you think provided that miserable person with detailed information about my nuclear development program."

Behbehani nodded and sipped from his teacup, deliberately giving Ahmadinejad the opportunity to continue with his tirade. In private Ahmadinejad claimed that the atomic bomb project was his while in public he denied its very existence, alleging that his Iran did not need an atomic weapon to defend itself. Behbehani knew the truth. The Supreme National Security Council, which reported directly to Khamenei, set Iran's nuclear policy. The council included two representatives appointed by Khamenei, insuring that the Supreme Leader controlled its decisions. Khamenei had publicly criticized Ahmadinejad for trying to personalize the nuclear issue. Behbehani found the little man's feeble effort to cover his mistakes in dealing with Jesperson ridiculous. Ahmadinejad had ordered Behbehani to keep his VEVAK goons off the professor's back. Behbehani considered Ahmadinejad an embarrassment, a weak idiot who actually believed the nonsense he spouted. After he calmly deposited his teacup on the president's desk, Behbehani glanced at the country's frantic leader and was surprised to find him red-faced but silently staring at him, actually expecting a response to his self-serving questions.

"Have you had the opportunity to read the professor's book?" Behbehani asked calmly, ignoring the president's posturing.

"Of course I have," Ahmadinejad raised his voice. "No thanks to VEVAK."

"Our representatives have provided more volumes than we require," Behbehani ignored the president's lie. "If you wish, I could courier you a copy immediately."

Ahmadinejad hesitated. All he really knew about the book was what his personal assistant quoting from the media had told him. "Very well, we could use another," Ahmadinejad said. "You should have alerted me when it first appeared."

"Would you like a signed edition?" Behbehani bluffed as he sipped his tea.

Ahmadinejad hesitated, giving Behbehani the impression that he was actually considering the offer, not realizing that Jesperson had died before the book was made available to the public. "You did not answer my question," Ahmadinejad, sensing a trap, ignored the offer.

"What question was that, Mr. President?" Behbehani asked.

"Where did Jesperson get his information?"

"It's a big book. I'm sure he had manifold sources," Behbehani replied. "A year is a long time, and the professor traveled extensively. Certainly he talked to hundreds, maybe thousands, of our citizens."

"And you should know their names," Ahmadinejad declared as he leaped from his chair, stumbled off the platform, caught himself, and began to pace. "Surely VEVAK carefully monitored this spy's contacts. VEVAK should have arrested him when it had the opportunity."

"Yes, Mr. President. Since the professor had presidential..." Behbehani deliberately paused, letting the little man worry about what he was going to say next. Ahmadinejad stared at Behbehani but said nothing. Behbehani nodded and rephrased his comment. "...Since the professor had the confidence and support of ranking governmental personages, VEVAK refrained from inconveniencing his research. We had been advised," Behbehani waited until Ahmadinejad stopped pacing and turned to face him, "that his research was of a historical nature. The professor spent most of his time in Kashan, Isfahan, Shiraz, and, of course, Persepolis."

"Kashan!" Ahmadinejad erupted as Behbehani anticipated he might.

Behbehani would not have been surprised if the excited president starting hopping up and down. He waited for the obvious question.

"Did it not occur to VEVAK that Kashan is only seventy kilometers from Natanz?" Ahmadinejad did not disappoint him.

Ahmadinejad tripped on the platform that held his desk and chair a good six inches higher than the chairs of his visitors, an ego prop that compensated for his diminutive stature.

Behbehani resisted the urge to smile or comment as the little president returned to his self-manufactured throne. Once seated, Ahmadinejad glared at the Minister of Intelligence and Security. "Do I need remind you what is located at Natanz?"

"A nuclear research center and two centrifuge enrichment plants," Behbehani said.

"Be careful what you say, Mr. Minister," Ahmadinejad warned coldly.

"I understand," Behbehani said. "Even these walls have ears. However, as you obviously are aware from your reading of the professor's book, the world now knows what is located at Natanz."

"Are you trying to be humorous?" Ahmadinejad asked.

"No, Mr. President, I am just stating the obvious." Behbehani finally lost his temper. Usually, the arrogant president amused him with his posturing, but today his performance had become too personal. "As you know from your perusal of the professor's book, he has reported that we have 4,000 centrifuges in operation with another 1,600 about to come on line. This American spy wrote that Iran has close to 3,000 pounds of low-enriched uranium which has no civilian use."

This revelation, of course, had surprised even Behbehani.

Ahmadinejad's wide eyes told Behbehani that this was the first time he had learned of the extent of Jesperson's disclosures. The irritated Behbehani decided to add to the little man's concern.

"He also noted that 3,000 centrifuges can produce twenty kilograms of high-enriched uranium in thirty days, an amount sufficient to make one atomic bomb. He further reported the obvious; 6,000 centrifuges can produce enough weapons grade fuel to make a bomb every sixteen days."

"Who told him this?"

"He also wrote that converting the weapons-grade uranium into uranium metal and producing a warhead would take another six months, giving us a nuclear tipped missile. I assume you are aware how the Israelis will react to this information."

The color left Ahmadinejad's face, and his bloodless hands clenched the edge of his desk.

Behbehani, a practical, hard-headed man, silently hoped that the emotional, fiery Ahmadinejad was reviewing in his mind some of the many injudicious public statements he had made including phrases like, "we will wipe Israel off the face of the earth," "we will obliterate the Anglo-Saxon world," and his frequent reference to the imminent return of the Twelfth, the Hidden Imam. The later reference particularly amused Behbehani who publicly was a devout Shiite, a practical necessity for an ambitious official in Iran's dictatorship of the mullahs, but who privately was not a religious man, not a believer, true or otherwise. Ahmadinejad had apparently swallowed the whole Twelfth Imam fable.

Muhammad ibn Hassan, the twelfth descendent of the Prophet

Muhammad's son-in-law, Ali, was born in 868. At the age of six, he disappeared mysteriously. Believers of the tradition were taught to expect that the boy would one day reappear in the company of Jesus and reveal himself as the Hidden Mahdi (the Rightly Guided One) just before the Day of Judgment when a new era of divine justice would prevail with Shiite Islam recognized as the true world faith. Unfortunately for the Twelvers, the Believers, the return would be preceded by cosmic mayhem, war, and bloody devastation after which the Hidden Mahdi would lead the world to a Shiite dominated era of peace. Ahmadinejad had publicly stated on more than one occasion that the day of Armageddon was nigh; this would be the day of a decisive battle between the forces of good and evil and would be followed by the Day of Judgment when Shiite Islam would be acknowledged as the true global faith.

In Behbehani's opinion, Ahmadinejad's Mahdi beliefs and his position as commander of Iran's nuclear forces made him a very dangerous person, certainly not one to be dismissed as a mere borderline lunatic.

"I suggest, Mr. President," Behbehani said, "that you pay particular attention to the professor's allegation that Iran is on the threshold of mounting a nuclear attack on somebody."

"That's nonsense," Ahmadinejad blurted.

"You would know that better than I," Behbehani said. "It's very dangerous, nonsense or not. One never knows what the Israelis or the Americans might do in the name of peemptive self-defense. In this nuclear age, they seem to think that is their very necessary prerogative."

"That professor was a madman for saying such things," Ahmadinejad declared.

Behbehani did not quite dare voice his thoughts on the matter, particularly pointing at the real madman involved in the equation. However, he felt it his obligation as a loyal Iranian to at least discuss the dangers inherent in the current situation despite his doubt that Ahmadinejad had enough connection with reality to realize what he must do, to wit, defuse the situation immediately before death rained on them all from the sky, a mighty scourge from the west that would have nothing to do with the return of the Mahdi, whatever his number, or a Shiite takeover of the world.

"Mr. Minister, I want you to concentrate on identifying the professor's sources. Find everyone he talked to and arrest them," Ahmadinejad ordered.

Behbehani responded with an indifferent nod.

"When you have the person who shared our top secret nuclear information, bring him to Teheran. I want to interview him personally," Ahmadinejad continued.

"And the source who disclosed our military plans?" Behbehani asked without revealing he assumed that individual was the president himself. Ahmadinejad was well known for his end of the world bluster and Mahdi nonsense.

"Of course." Ahmadinejad's eyes narrowed as he tried to intimidate Behbehani with a frown, and Behbehani again resisted the urge to smile. He realized that the fiery president grasped what he was not saying.

After a few tense moments, Ahmadinejad relaxed and dismissed Behbehani. "Very well. Keep me informed."

Neither man was pleased with the outcome of that tense meeting.

Chapter 11

On the day following her son's funeral, Manujeh Tabatabai Jesperson waited in their Cambridge home until her husband departed on his morning walk before calling her sister Mahube Tabatabai Taheri in Teheran. Manujeh's long international conversations with her Iranian relatives never failed to agitate her husband.

"Kojas?" Mahube picked up the phone.

That familiar one word greeting made Manujeh Jesperson smile. It made her feel at home while it always irritated her husband. The colloquial "Kojas" when translated into English literally came out as "Where are you?" Manujeh's husband, the stiff MIT professor, insisted that the Iranian way of answering the phone was rude. "They could at least say hello," Doctor Terrence Jesperson would frown.

"Mahube, it's me," Manujeh Jesperson said.

"Oh, Manujeh, I've been so worried for you," Mahube Taheri said.

"We buried Thomas yesterday," Manujeh said. "It's done."

Mahube greeted those words with sobs.

"I've cried for the past week, and now I'm trying to adjust to a life without my son," Manujeh said.

"Oh poor Manujeh," Mahube commiserated. "Is there anything we can do for you? Do you want to come and visit with us? Stay as long as you want."

"I miss my friends and family," Manujeh said, meaning it even though she had not visited Iran in ten years. "Oh my poor country."

"Then come home," Mahube said.

"I can't. I would be too afraid. Particularly now."

"Because of Thomas's..."

"Yes," Manujeh said. "It's...it's...been done. Have you heard?"

Mahube greeted that question with silence.

"It created a big sensation here. Have you heard?" Manujeh repeated her question.

"We read about it on the Internet. Everybody's talking, but we are afraid to say anything, particularly on the telephone," Mahube warned. After another pause, she spoke softly. "I'm so afraid. How is…"

"He was here for the funeral but returned to Fairfax with a friend right after the service. It was so nice of him to come." Manujeh realized that Mahube was referring to her grandson Mansour but was afraid to mention his name. Everybody in Iran knew that their phones were always monitored. At least that was what they assumed.

"We all worry about him every day. Please tell him we are thinking of him. I haven't talked with Mehtab for days," Mahube referred to her son, Mansour's father," not since the news of…you know…reached Iran. Everybody is afraid of what might happen."

"What are they afraid of?" Manujeh asked.

"That the Americans might drop all their bombs on us. "Arman and me," she referred to her husband, "we're thinking about going to Isfahan or someplace where we might be safe."

"Why is everyone afraid the Americans might drop their bombs?" Manujeh asked.

"Because of what…what that...you know...said…that the Iranians are planning on dropping an atomic bomb on America," Mahube blurted. "That's why I'm not talking with Mehtab. He said they're arresting lots of people looking for the ones who told...all those secrets."

"Even…?" Manujeh did not dare mention Mehtab's brother-in-law, Obediah Baghai.

Manujeh knew from previous conversations with Mahube that Thomas had discreetly visited with Obediah who was employed as a nuclear physicist at the Iranian secret installation in Natanz. Manujeh remembered Obediah from the time he had attended MIT at the same time that Mehtab had. Obediah had even introduced Mehtab to his sister Anahi. Mehtab and Anahi had married and settled in Kashan where Mehtab taught physics in a local secondary school, something that irritated Manujeh's husband. The MIT professor always complained that Mehtab had wasted a good education by settling on a career in secondary education. Although she refused to discuss it, Manujeh believed her husband was aggravated by the fact that he had wasted his time counseling her nephew, and this bothered him more than Mehtab's career choice. On the other hand, her husband was proud of the fact that Obediah was a working physicist even if it was for a second class country like Iran.

"We don't discuss things like that," Mahube said quickly.

Mahube knew that Mehtab had facilitated Thomas' meetings with Obediah. She didn't know what they talked about, but what little she did know frightened her. That is why she had insisted that Thomas sponsor her grandson Mansour's education in the States.

"What is he going to do now?" Mahube asked.

"What is who going to do now?" Manujeh asked. All this double talk confused her.

"You know. After he attended the funeral," Mahube referred to her grandson Mansour.

"Oh, I think he still plans to go to college here. Don't concern yourself for him. I will take care of him." Manujeh finally realized that Mahube was worried about Mansour, and that irritated her. Manujeh's son had been murdered, and her sister fretted about her grandson more than she worried about her sister, Manujeh.

"Tell him to call me or his mother. We haven't heard from him since… you know happened." Mahube hesitated, waiting for Manujeh to say something, but she did not. Manujeh was insulted by her sister's off hand reference to her son's murder. Finally, Mahube broke the silence by asking, "Where is he living now?"

"I'm not sure," Manujeh said irritably. "I've been too busy with Thomas' funeral to worry about anything else. Now we have all this nonsense in the media."

"You don't know? Is he a kuche person?

In Teheran, the kuche is a street gutter that serves as a source of drinking water and as an impromptu toilet for the poor. Most believe that running water has to traverse only ten meters to cleanse itself.

"No, he's staying in a house with other students. Thomas…had…it all arranged. I'll have Doctor Jesperson," Manujeh referred to her husband by his title, "tell him to call home."

"Please, Manujeh, I'm so worried. Should I come and check on him?" Mahube asked.

"Will they let you travel?" Manujeh asked. She was in no mood to have her sister come for an extended visit. She knew that just discussing that possibility with her husband would send him through the roof.

"I don't know," Mahube answered weakly.

"You stay there and look after your family. This is no time for you to be going abroad," Manujeh said firmly. "Besides, I'm so upset. I've just lost my only son, and I'm in no condition to give you the attention you deserve."

"I know, Manujeh, and I worry about you. I'm sorry, but all this has my nerves burning. Arman says all I do is sit about the house crying."

"Well..." Manujeh, realizing that she had gotten all the sympathy that she was going to get from her sister when she was in this mood, decided to hang up. "Oh, I'm sorry, Mahube, I have to go. The Doctor just returned from his walk and needs me."

****

At the Teheran phone company a VEVAK clerk charged with monitoring international calls noted that the parties had hung up. He had dozed through most of the conversation between the two sisters who were preoccupied with family matters, and he had heard nothing of security significance. Since neither of the participants were on his watch list, he switched to another call and did not bother to make an entry in his log.

****

After hanging up, Mahube called her son Mehtab in Kashan.

"Kojas," Anahi, her daughter-in-law answered after several rings.

"Oh, Anahi, I was calling Mehtab, I'm sorry," Mahube said.

"He's at school where he usually is at this time," Anahi said.

Mahube, although irritated by Anahi's words and attitude, ignored both as she usually did. "I was just talking with my sister Manujeh." Mahube did not elaborate, knowing that her comment would command the rude girl's attention.

"Ohh," Anahi reacted. "Did she say how...he...likes it there?" She spoke her son's name softly, "Poor Mansour." After a pause, she continued, "We haven't heard from him since...." She did not finish her sentence.

Mahube assumed she was referring to Thomas's murder, the publication of his book, and the international media frenzy that followed. Mahube hesitated, making Anahi, her son's wife, Mansour's mother, wait for her response.

"You know what I'm talking about?" Anahi filled the silence.

"Yes. Manujeh was quite upset," Mahube said. "She buried her only son yesterday, and I had to spend most of our conversation consoling her."

"But what about...?"

"She said he was at the funeral, like the good boy he is, but returned to university right after the service."

"Then…he has everything arranged, enough money, someplace to live now that…is gone?"

"Manujeh will take care of everything. Don't worry, and have Mehtab call me as soon as he can," Mahube ordered and hung up before Anahi could ask another question.

"But we are all so worried," Anahi spoke into the empty phone before she realized what had happened. Anahi angrily slammed the phone back into its cradle. All of her problems were her mother in law's nephew's fault.

****

Following his meeting with the president, Naveed Behbehani returned to his ministry, told his secretary to summon General Nasiri, ignored the reception room filled with citizens waiting to discuss their petty problems with him, and slammed his office door shut behind him.

Behbehani was sitting with his feet on the sill relaxing while he watched the struggling traffic joust on the street below when a tap alerted him that his VEVAK commander had arrived.

"Enter," Behbehani ordered without turning.

The door opened and the portly general dressed in ill-fitting civilian clothes entered. "How did the meeting with our illustrious leader go?" Nasiri asked as he settled into the chair facing Behbehani's desk.

"The little donkey brayed exactly as you predicted," Behbehani said as he turned to face his trusted associate. The two friends had joined the ranks of the 1979 Revolution together and had rode Ayatollah Khamenei's robe-tails over the years until they had reached their current exalted pinnacle.

"Everything is our fault," Nasiri smiled. "He never met the American professor, did not order us to facilitate his extended stay, and now wants us to find out who revealed government secrets to this CIA spy who has written a book telling all."

"Old friend, you truly are omniscient," Behbehani chuckled.

"Don't wish that on anyone," Nasiri said.

"Well, you are going to have to keep pretending that you are," Behbehani said. "Are we making any progress?"

"Nothing that we haven't already discussed."

"There has to be somebody we can blame."

"You have been spending too much time with our president," Nasiri said.

"I know. However, finding scapegoats is what we do."

"Scapegoats are easy. All of our nuclear scientists are worried stiff. To a man they are already pointing fingers at their colleagues. I'm afraid, however, that the American covered his tracks pretty well. He spent most of his time in the south, but nobody we've interrogated actually saw him talking with anyone from Natanz."

"But we know he talked with one of those intellectual bastards," Behbehani frowned.

"We're working on it. We assume that his source had to one of our experts who was educated in the United States and that is where the American met him."

"That's reasonable, but since most of them were educated there how do we flush him out?"

"As you know we've narrowed our suspect list down to ten scientists who have access to the information cited in the book and who were educated in America. We are looking at each one in detail. Somewhere there exists someone who can connect Jesperson to one of the suspects. We'll find him."

"I know," Behbehani agreed. "We always do. Unfortunately, we face a potential deadline."

"Deadline, a good choice of words," Nasiri smiled.

"You always did have a morbid sense of humor," Behbehani chuckled.

"That's right. But this time I'm not joking. We have to find the source, neutralize him, put the blame on your braying donkey friend, and remove him before the Americans and Israelis obliterate us with their missiles."

"I don't know what the hell our president was thinking when he decided to build an Iranian atomic bomb and publicly threaten to demolish Israel and the Americans when any reasonable person would know we could never create enough bombs to win a war with the Americans." Behbehani shook his head in dismay.

"Our president thinks with his mouth," Nasiri said.

"Unfortunately," Behbehani agreed. "We don't have the time to find the professor's real source. The Americans will watch us closely, but they don't act precipitously."

"And they know we don't have the capability of obliterating their country in a first strike," Nasiri opined. "They'll debate the situation until something forces their hand. That should give us some time."

"You're right, but don't forget the Israelis. They are not a patient people. They've learned not to wait for disaster to strike first, and they have the bomb too. They could mount strikes against our facilities this afternoon."

"They have the will, the bombs, and the fear to respond. We can survive if they only attack Natanz and one or two other places."

"We could, but we can't take that chance. We must do something to give them a reason for hesitating."

"The Americans will pressure them to wait," Nasiri said.

"I'm sure they have already. The Israelis listen politely, agree to disagree, and then do whatever their self-interest requires."

"What can we do?"

"Arrest the ten suspects. Persuade whoever talked with the Americans to confess."

"That won't stop the Israelis," Nasiri said.

"I will talk with our military colleagues. If they agree, we can jointly approach the mullahs and frankly tell them that the regime, the people, the country's very future depends on our removing the donkey from office and shutting down our nuclear program in a very public way."

"You mean invite the UN inspectors back."

"Exactly put everything on the donkey's back and demonstrate to the world that we are a peace loving nation," Behbehani said.

****

After his unsatisfactory session with Behbahani, his Minister of Intelligence and Security, President Ahmadinejad conferred with one of his most loyal supporters, Commander Yahya Saidi of the Revolutionary Guards.

The Sepah-e Pasdaran-e Enqqelab-e Eslami, The Army of the Guardians of the Islamic Revolution, was founded in the aftermath of the 1979 Revolution by Ayatollah Ruhollah Khomeini to safeguard the regime against internal and external opposition forces. Although its commander reports directly to Supreme Leader Ayatollah Khamenei, Khomeini's successor, Commander Yahya Saidi considered himself one with President Ahmadinejad with whom he had served in the desert during the Iran/Iraq war. In fact, Ahmadinejad since his 2005 election had greatly expanded the Guards' role to include virtually every facet of Iranian life, social, political, military and economic. In the post 2009 election period the Guard had led the suppression of opposition protests. Under Ahmadinejad the Guard's internal affairs tasking grew to include internal and border security, law enforcement and control of the nation's missile forces. To facilitate this mission the Guards, operating independently, maintains its own army, navy, air force, intelligence, and special force units. Additionally, the Guards control the Basij militia's some 90,000 troops.

"One of these days, old friend, we are going to have to do something about that padar-e sag (son of a dog) Behbehani," Ahmadinejad shook his head in disgust as he referred to his Minister of Intelligence and Security.

"Haven't I always said that," Commander Yahya Saidi said. "You should have let me do it before the Supreme Leader insisted that you make him a minister."

"I know. I made a mistake. I can't do everything myself," Ahmadinejad complained.

Saidi was the one man with whom he could speak frankly; they had served together as young officers in the Guards' intelligence and security apparatus during the war; they had jointly dispatched tens of thousands of Iranian youth to die as they marched in human waves, clearing minefields with their bodies, so that more experienced soldiers could advance against the enemy. That had been a bonding experience. Now, they both served at the Supreme Leader's command, and, unfortunately, so did Behbehani.

"Maybe we can manage this current atomic bomb mess so that the Americans, Jew dogs, and Behbehani get the future they so rightly deserve," Ahmadinejad said.

Yahya Saidi smiled as he nodded agreement. "How can I help?"

Silently, Saidi added a fourth name to the list, that of the president himself. The bombastic little man had been a useful friend, but of late Ahmadinejad had displayed signs of believing his Hidden Mahdi nonsense. Saidi frankly admitted to himself that he was more a selfish opportunist than a true believer. Saidi knew that the president's father, a poor village barber, had changed his name from Saborjhian to Ahmadinejad when he had moved the family to Teheran in search of a better life. The father had reasoned that the new name sounded better than the old which in Farsi meant "thread painter," a most humble occupation usually performed by children. Saidi on occasion amused himself by speculating that the father should have selected the name given to the president by late night American humorists, AhmadNutJob.

"I need to know which of our expert scientists in Natanz leaked information about our nuclear program to the American Jesperson," Ahmadinejad slapped his desk for emphasis. "And I need to know who in the military revealed our plans for using our bombs to wipe the Jews and Americans off the face of the earth."

"I understand," Saidi said, not committing himself to anything. Firstly, he would relay the president's concerns to Ayatollah Khamenei, and then do what the Supreme Leader ordered. Saidi assumed that the Supreme Leader would place the president's name at the top of the list of those who were responsible for the current stupid crisis, and Saidi would then deal with them all in a way that would benefit Saidi personally.

Ahmadinejad stared at his old colleague and friend, immediately reading the ambiguity in his reply. That subterfuge angered Ahmadinejad who often used the same tactic; he immediately realized that Saidi assumed that he was not intelligent enough to comprehend what the unsatisfactory response meant. The big bastard was going to consult with Khamenei before doing anything. Ahmadinejad impulsively decided to show Saidi who the people had elected president.

"You are aware of the American's book and the way it is being treated in the world media?" Ahmadinejad asked coldly.

"I am. I have read a copy of the book," Saidi answered.

Ahmadinejad knew this was a lie. Saidi, unlike the university educated Ahmadinejad, had a very limited knowledge of English.

"Good," Ahmadinejad pretended that he did not notice the falsehood. "The dog Behbehani promised that he would have VEVAK arrest those who met with this Jesperson during his visit here and interrogate them appropriately until they identify the American spy. I want you to arrest them first. Only you know how to get the information we require."

Saidi answered with an affirmative nod.

Although he recognized that this response was just another ambiguous artifice, Ahmadinejad continued. "And, as I noted, we must also determine who in the military was talking about our plans for the bombs. This is something that I am sure you can handle since the Guards are responsible for our missile systems," Ahmadinejad watched Saidi closely, expecting a stronger reaction to his not so veiled threat.

This time Saidi blinked before nodding, telling the alert Ahmadinejad that he got the message.

"Do think you can handle this little assignment in a timely manner before Behbehani wakes up from his siesta?" Ahmadinejad asked.

"I will get right on it, Mr. President," Saidi leaped to his feet.

"Good. I suggest you start in Natanz, Kashan, and Isfahan where Jesperson spent most of his time," Ahmadinejad said.

Saidi restrained the impulse to ask, "Not Qom?"

"Given our current state of relations with the Americans, I assume it will not be difficult to track the presence of an American professor in those cities over an extended period," Ahmadinejad observed.

"I'll keep you informed," Saidi said as he paused at the door.

"At least twice a day," Ahmadinejad smiled. "And if you don't mind," he continued. "I'm going to have a brief conversation with our Basij friends."

Ahmadinejad referred to the Nirou-ye Moqavemat-e Basij, the Mobilization Resistance Force, a paramilitary organization of volunteer militia also founded by Khomeini. Although loosely associated with the Revolutionary Guards, the Basij consists of a loose group of allied organizations, many controlled by individual clerics. The Basij on its own initiative involves itself in internal security and local law enforcement, including morals policing, suppression of dissident meetings, and organizing counter demonstrations.

The calculating Ahmadinejad deliberately referred to the Basij, alerting Saidi to the fact that he would have lots of competition in this investigation; the Basij has a well-deserved reputation as an organization that conducts its own investigations in its own uninhibited, informal style. By deploying the Ministry of Security, the Guardians, and the Basij, the president was insuring that at least one of the three competing organization would develop the information he thought he needed.

As Ahmadinejad watched the door close behind Saidi, he smiled as he visualized the commander's next telephone call, an urgent report to his master in Qom.

Chapter 12

Three phone messages were waiting for Chase when he arrived at his office; two were surprises, and one was not. They were from: Special Agent Cotton, Doctor Jesperson, and the Lady in Black. Two requested that he contact them urgently. Chase selected the third message, the when you get a chance please call from Sally Kendrick, the Lady in Black who he had met at the Jesperson funeral service in Cambridge. Chase regretted the way they had parted with Chase irritated with himself, and Kendrick apparently amused.

"Kendrick," Sally answered on the first ring.

"Ms. Kendrick. This is Chase Mansfield," Chase identified himself.

"Mansfield, Mansfield? May I ask who you represent, Mr. Mansfield?"

"I believe you called me, Ms. Kendrick," Chase said, assuming that the Lady in Black was playing a game.

"Is this Lieutenant Mansfield, Fairfax's Mr. Moto, who is matching wits with the Iranian irredentists?"

Chase laughed. "I don't even know what an irredentist is."

"Then you had better be careful. They might work on your head but certainly don't consult one if you have a toothache."

"I've been thinking about you," Chase said.

"Poor baby. Why don't we have lunch one day and discuss your problem?"

"I'm free at noon," Chase reacted.

"We'll meet halfway, Paolo's in the Reston Town Center," Kendrick said and hung up, surprising Chase who was prepared to chat.

He shrugged and dialed the number listed in Special Agent Cotton's message.

"Cotton," the FBI man answered promptly, gruffly, but softly.

"Mansfield, you called," Chase identified himself.

"Good. Working half days?" Cotton asked.

Chase glanced at his watch. Ten o'clock. "No, just getting an early start. What do you want?" Chase asked, not interested in fencing with the FBI so early in his workday.

"We need to talk," Cotton said.

"Fine. So talk."

"In person."

"I'm in my office," Chase said. "How are your negotiations coming?" Chase chuckled as he thought of the e-mail demanding one hundred million dollars for Secretary Townsend's return.

"I'm rather tied down at the moment," Cotton said. "I would appreciate it if you could inconvenience yourself by coming to me."

"So get a local boy scout to untie you. I understand they are good with knots," Chase smiled.

"Forget the Bob Hope routine," Cotton growled. "You know I can't leave here until we get the next message."

"You still haven't heard from your correspondent?" Chase asked, amused by the frustration in Cotton's voice.

Communication with the kidnappers was one way, and all Cotton could do was wait for another e-mail. "I assume you have your bags packed and your French visa in hand," Chase said, referring to the fact that the first message had originated in Paris. When Cotton did not react, Chase continued. "I really envy you federal civil servants with your overseas travel at taxpayer expense. The best I could manage was a paid trip to Cambridge for a funeral."

"We have to talk about that, too," Cotton said. "Can you come now?"

"Come where?"

"You know where. I've been here in McLean since our last chat."

"I'm sure the lady of the house is delighted to have all the company," Chase referred to Mrs. Townsend.

"Just get your ass out here," Cotton growled.

"As it turns out, I have a luncheon date in Reston," Chase smiled. "I could drop by for a few minutes on my way."

"You heard me," Cotton reacted. "If you aren't here within the hour, your chief will be getting a call from the director or maybe the president."

"Don't we have a liaison officer present to help you pass your lonely hours?" Chase referred to the fact that Barney had agreed to serve as an observer for the negotiations with the kidnapper.

"Major Hopkins appeared, briefly. Don't you guys communicate with each other?"

"You're right. I've been derelict in my responsibilities, Special Agent Cotton. I certainly will have to coordinate with Major Hopkins before I can confer with you," Chase said and hung up. As he was terminating the conversation, he heard Cotton swearing in the background. "God-damn-it, Mansfield..."

Chase looked up in time to see Major Barney Hopkins, the CIB Commander materialize in the doorway.

"Theresa told me you were here," Barney greeted him.

"Good for Theresa," Chase said as the CIB secretary gave Chase the finger from her position behind Barney. "Special Agent Cotton, who just got off the phone, told me that you weren't there. I thought you were observing..."

"The Feds are still waiting for the other shoe to drop. They don't know if that first e-mail was a hoax or the real thing. If the former they could be in McLean until they retire," Barney said as he lowered himself into Chase's solitary visitor's chair. Theresa assumed her usual post in the doorway.

"Did they actually collect a hundred million dollars? How big a package does that make? Bigger than a shoe box? Smaller than a freight car?" Chase smiled. "The last time I saw a million dollars..."

"The last time you saw a twenty dollar bill," Theresa laughed as she corrected him. "It was covered with cobwebs."

"The president was still considering the demand the last I heard," Barney said. "CIA and the FBI have conflicting positions. We don't negotiate with terrorists, but we don't know if the kidnappers are terrorists. Sometimes somebody pays the ransom, and sometimes nobody does. I understand the vice president is collecting the cash to use if Featherstone caves, and the CIA and the Bureau are chasing their tails looking for clues. What have you been doing?"

"I attended the professor's funeral in Cambridge," Chase said.

"And?"

"And I met the only non-Jesperson who admits to having anything more than a casual relationship with the victim."

"And?"

"And we are having lunch today at Paolo's."

"Certainly you have already had a chat with this unusual person."

"I have. We had a nice talk all the way back to D.C. from Cambridge."

"Did he have any ideas about who might have put two slugs into the professor as he sat behind his desk at Robinson Hall?"

"Did she..." Chase corrected. "The Lady in Black is a she."

Theresa clapped. "Oh goody, we have a mystery. Please, please, lieutenant tell us more."

"Lady in Black?" Barney said.

"Yes, she wore a lovely black pants suit to the church," Chase smiled.

"And all the way home, I hope," Theresa said.

"I assume so," Chase smiled, enjoying himself. "But I don't know. We parted at the airport."

"But not forever," Theresa said.

"Please don't encourage him, Theresa," Barney said.

"No, you will be pleased to hear that I have just got off the phone with the Lady in Black and that is when we scheduled our debriefing."

"At Paolo's Ristorante," Theresa said. "Can I come along to take notes?"

"No, I fear that would not be appropriate. First, I have to establish the requisite rapport."

"Of course," Theresa smiled. "Always the lieutenant first has to lay..."

"Theresa," Barney said.

"I was just going to say that the lieutenant always takes pains to lay out the ground rules for every interrogation," Theresa said. "Is the Lady in Black attractive?" Theresa smiled at Chase.

"She was once engaged to Professor Jesperson," Chase said.

"But she isn't now."

"Certainly not. The professor is dead," Barney said. "What did she say?" Barney spoke to Chase.

"We worked on our rapport," Chase said. "I did learn the professor effectively terminated the engagement by going off to Iran for a year, but I assume Sally, Ms. Kendrick, who owns a computer company in Reston and resides in Reston, will prove to be a veritable fount of needed background information."

"After sufficient development by the renowned investigator Lieutenant Chase Mansfield," Theresa said, "who is particularly skilled at laying..."

"Theresa," Barney cautioned.

"...at laying a foundation for a successful interaction with attractive witnesses of a particular age group," Theresa completed her sentence.

"Who else did you meet at the funeral?" Barney asked.

"Only the parents of the victim," Chase said. "Jesperson's cousin, Mansour Taheri, and his friend Jamshid Afgar were also present, but I did not talk with them. I intend to deal with them here. The Lady in Black and I sat in the back, and about twenty friends of the two older Jespersons were present. Outside, there was a media circus, but of course I evaded them."

"Of course," Theresa said. "Because you were intent on laying your groundwork."

"You seem particularly obsessed with that one word," Chase finally reacted.

"What word is that, sir?" Theresa played the innocent.

"Laying," Chase said. "Are you trying to imply something?"

"Me? Imply something? What is there about the verb 'to lay' that troubles you?"

"Nothing about the verb 'to lay' troubles me," Chase smiled. "You are the one that seems to have the hang up. To me 'to lay' refers to a very normal human activity."

"Stop it," Barney pleaded. "Please stop all this 'to lay' nonsense."

"Very well, Chase said. "But I reserve the right to address the 'to lay' issue at a later time. Now that I have briefed you two, I must consult with Special Agent Cotton at the Townsend household," Chase stood up. "Would you like to accompany me?" Chase asked Barney. "Given your observer status."

"No thank you," Barney smiled. "After Special Agent Cotton briefs you that he has not heard from the kidnappers and is not sure now if the original message was from a hoaxer or the real thing, please offer him my regards and ask him to give me a heads up if they should receive a second e-mail."

"Now, I must point out that 'heads up' is another interesting expression worth discussing," Theresa said. "Particularly in its singular form."

"You really should consult a therapist specializing in female problems," Chase spoke to Theresa. He started for the door, nodded at Barney, and said. "I will convey your words to Special Agent Cotton."

"When you set up another debriefing with the Lady in Black," Barney said. "I would like to sit in on that."

"Me too," Theresa said. "I could always sit in the background and take notes."

"I'll keep you both in mind," Chase smiled.

"And what should I tell the chief?" Barney called after Chase.

"Give him my regards," Chase answered from the outer door.

Forty minutes later Chase cleared security at the gate to the Townsend mansion, parked near the open garage, and made his way to the front door which was opened by a member of the Townsend Department of Homeland Security team.

"Special Agent Cotton is expecting me," Chase said as he waved his credentials case.

"Good luck," the DHS man said. "I assume you know where the study is."

Chase nodded. "Is Mrs. Townsend home?"

"Upstairs."

"How is she holding up?"

"Surprisingly well for someone whose husband has been kidnapped," the DHS agent whispered.

"Does she spend all of her time in her room?" Chase asked.

"Not at all. She's planning on joining a couple of her friends for lunch at the country club, and she has made it perfectly clear she will drive there herself."

"Without any security?"

"That's right. If it weren't for Cotton and his friends, life here would be perfectly normal. Yesterday, she spent the day at Tyson's shopping, without security. She insists no one cares what she does, she's just a housewife. Her only problem is the media but as you may have noticed they gave up on us three days ago."

"The place was a circus the last time I was here," Chase said.

"We had a little trouble at first, but after we moved them out beyond the perimeter, they hung around for a couple of days then left."

"It's about time," Cotton, who had appeared suddenly, called from the other end of the hallway.

"Our master's voice," Chase said as he winked at the DHS security agent.

"Traffic was a bear," Chase said as he offered his hand to Cotton.

Cotton took Chase's hand, squeezed it hard showing who was the strongest, looked skeptically at Chase, and turned, leading him into the study. As Chase expected, FBI agents in shirtsleeves had made themselves at home. Three sat on a sofa near the window, while two others relaxed on side-by-side recliners facing a muted television. Chase nodded at Mrs. Townsend's secretary, the efficient Mary, who Chase had met on his previous visit. She sat behind her desk with a silent computer, monitor, keyboard, modem, and printer on a credenza to her left.

"Good morning, lieutenant," Mary greeted him with a smile.

"Good morning, Mary," Chase said. Mary had been the one to first view the e-mail from the kidnappers. "How are you faring?" Chase glanced at the FBI agents who were silently watching his every move.

"I'll be glad when all of this is over," Mary answered honestly. "I can't get a single thing done with all this help," she said with a shrug. "And, of course, we are all still very worried about Secretary Townsend. Have you learned anything? I understand that you attended Doctor Jesperson's funeral."

Those words told Chase that the Bureau team had been discussing him. He nodded his appreciation for Mary's warning as he answered. "It was a very sad occasion. Just the parents, their friends, and one relative and friend. Of course the media were there in force."

"As they were here, but as you noticed, they have finally left us in peace," Mary said.

"How is Mrs. Townsend?"

"She's doing fine," an impatient Cotton interrupted. "Let's you and I go down to the sitting room where we can have our chat in private."

Chase nodded but politely waited for Mary to answer his question.

"She's a strong woman," Mary said. "She's upstairs now, but I am sure she will want to say hello. If I were in Mrs. Townsend's position, I would be going out of my mind."

"Please give Mrs. Townsend's my best," Chase said.

"We both appreciate your kind and considerate assistance," Mary said, referring to Chase's presence in the home when the first e-mail arrived and to his professional help in alerting the Bureau.

Chase winked at Mary and turned to follow Cotton who had already left the room. He assumed that Mary and Mrs. Townsend particularly appreciated the fact that he had not moved in with them as the Bureau and DHS security team had.

"And please give my regards to Barney. He and I had several nice chats during the time he was with us," Mary said, ignoring the listening FBI agents.

Chase followed Cotton to the front sitting room. He shut the door softly behind him and joined Cotton on a pair of facing love seats. Cotton's suit was wrinkled, and he wore his tie with his top shirt button open. His face was puffy, and his entire demeanor radiated weariness.

"I imagine everyone is getting tired sitting here waiting for something to happen," Chase feigned sympathy.

"It goes with the territory," Cotton growled, making it perfectly clear that he wasn't interested in Chase's contrived empathy. "Have you identified the shooter yet? Or are you still running in circles."

Cotton's demeanor and phrasing irritated Chase; both were contrived to put him on the defensive.

"The fact that you are still camped out here tells me you haven't found Secretary Townsend, yet," Chase replied.

Cotton glared at Chase. "You didn't answer my question."

"And you didn't answer mine."

"I didn't hear you ask one."

"I apologize if I wasn't blunt enough for you. Are you going to pay the hundred million?"

"That's none of your business."

Chase laughed and stood up.

"Sit down," Cotton ordered.

Chase responded by walking to the door.

"We're waiting for the second e-mail," Cotton relented, a little.

Chase turned the knob and opened the door.

"Before making a decision about the money," Cotton added.

Chase turned, looked at Cotton, and waited for more.

"The vice president is raising the money," Cotton said.

"That's better," Chase said, closing the door. "But the decision to pay hasn't been made yet."

"The White House is still debating the issue. Sit down," Cotton pointed at the love seat Chase had vacated. "Do you have any leads?"

Chase returned to his chair but stubbornly did not sit down as Cotton ordered. "No. I need to talk to Townsend for obvious reasons."

Cotton laughed. "Lots of luck. What makes you think he's still alive?"

"What makes you think he isn't?"

"A professional guess. If you were the kidnapper, would you go to the trouble of keeping Townsend alive. That's a lot of bother."

"At least until I get the money. If you started to stall, I would begin returning body parts by parcel post."

"You don't need a live body to do that. Terrorists are not your run-of-the-mill kidnappers. All we can do is wait and see what develops. What did you learn in Cambridge? Did any suspects appear?"

"You know as well as I do what happened in Cambridge," Chase smiled.

"Who was the Lady in Black that you picked up at the church?" Cotton confirmed he had officers at the funeral.

"Didn't the clerk at the airport give you her name?"

"Ms. Sally Kendrick, a resident of Reston, Virginia," Cotton smiled. "We haven't interviewed her, yet. Was she a good friend of Professor Jesperson?"

"Not recently," Chase smiled back.

Cotton waited for Chase to elaborate. He did not.

"I think I'll have someone from our Reston office visit Ms. Kendrick," Cotton said.

"Do you think Ms. Kendrick was acquainted with Secretary Townsend?" Chase reminded Cotton of their turf agreement. He handled the Jesperson investigation while the Feds managed the Townsend disappearance.

"You are a pain in the ass, Mansfield," Cotton reacted.

"Thank you," Chase said. "Coming from a Special Agent of the Federal Bureau of Investigation, that is a real compliment."

"What do you mean 'not recently?'" Cotton returned to his interest in Kendrick.

"Professor Jesperson and Ms. Kendrick were engaged to be married. Jesperson effectively terminated the engagement when he departed for his rather lengthy sabbatical in Iran."

"Was it a mutually agreeable separation?"

"Ms. Kendrick seemed to take it rather personal."

"And?"

"We didn't go into any details."

"But I am confident you will do so in the near future, given the fact she was the only mourner present at the funeral who was from the professor's age group," Cotton said.

"That's true. I happen to have an appointment with Ms. Kendrick pending."

"Really? Soon, I hope."

Chase checked his watch. "As a matter of fact, very soon. We are scheduled to meet in Reston at noon."

"For lunch of course."

"What else? Coincidentally, we both tend to take a few minutes at the height of our mutually busy days to take in a little sustenance."

"Will this taking of sustenance with Ms. Kendrick be an exclusively social occasion? I ask only because the pictures I have seen of Ms. Kendrick indicate she is a most attractive young lady."

"Young is a relative term. I would say she is closer to my age than yours, fortunately. I would describe this session as more business than social, although I must confess that it comes about at Ms. Kendrick's initiative not my own."

"How lucky for you," Cotton observed.

Before Cotton could continue the door to the hall burst open and two FBI agents entered, followed by Mary, Mrs. Townsend's secretary, and Mrs. Townsend herself.

The lead agent held a piece of copy paper in his hand. He held it up for Cotton to see while he stared meaningfully at Chase.

"He's OK," Cotton said. "Is that what we have been waiting for?"

"He won't let me read it," Mrs. Townsend declared. "This is my house. That is my e-mail, and I insist!"

Everybody in the room with the exception of the lead agent who had the e-mail stared at Mrs. Townsend. Chase was surprised by Mrs. Townsend's appearance. Her hair and make-up was immaculate, and she looked like she was dressed for lunch at the club with friends or a day of shopping at the high-end stores of Tyson's Corner Galleria Mall. Her eyes were clear, not filled with tears that one would expect to find in the wife of a kidnapping victim being held by terrorists threatening to kill if their demands were not met.

When Cotton reacted to Townsend's loud demands by silently holding out his hand to receive the e-mail from his subordinate, Townsend turned from Cotton to Chase.

"Lieutenant, please help me," she said.

Chase, who had established a degree of trust with Mrs. Townsend by assisting when the first e-mail had arrived, nodded. "I'm sure that Special Agent Cotton will share the message with all of us as soon as he reads it," Chase said as he watched Cotton quickly scan the message. When he finished, Cotton frowned and silently handed the message to Chase. Chase stood up and beckoned Mrs. Townsend to share it with him. The two stood side by side as they read.

From: Anony100@yahoo.com.mt
Date: 10/18/10 09:00:43
To: NTown1@gmail.com
Subject: Yr Spouse

Relax. Yr spouse is still alive because you and his employer have behaved appropriately. You must now forward the requested sum immediately to the following account:

Acct. No. 746822910
Cayman Freeman Bank
North Street
George Town
Grand Cayman, Cayman Islands
Fax 949 9999

This is our final communication on this subject. If the designated sum does not reach this account by 1400 hours today, if your investigators interfere in any way before the sum is processed, the individual in question will expire. Pay or pray.

The Suffering People

When he finished reading, Chase looked at Cotton, waiting for the Special Agent to take charge. Before Cotton could speak, Mrs. Townsend snatched the e-mail from Chase's hands and surprised everyone in the room by turning and starting for the door.

"Mrs. Townsend, wait," Cotton reacted first.

The grim-faced spouse stopped and turned. She did not speak.

"May I have that message, please," Cotton said.

"Why? Do you want it for your scrapbook?" Mrs. Townsend demanded.

"No ma'am, but I need to consult with my superiors, immediately," Cotton answered, surprising Chase with the soft compassion evident in his tone.

"I should not have listened to you," Mrs. Townsend reacted angrily.

"Please," Cotton said.

"Are you going to send the hundred million dollars?" Mrs. Townsend demanded.

"That is not for me to decide," Cotton said.

"You don't expect me to, do you?" Mrs. Townsend asked. "I'm afraid my checking account cannot cover it."

Cotton did not answer.

Mrs. Townsend started for the door but stopped abruptly. "This is my e-mail, and this is my home. I want everyone but Lieutenant Chase to leave. Now."

"But I need the e-mail," Cotton said.

"This is my copy. I'm sure that your agents have already printed out several others." Mrs. Townsend stared at her secretary who nodded her head.

"So leave," Mrs. Townsend ordered. "I have to count the minutes until my husband's death."

Townsend looked at Chase, who did not react, and then at the agent who had delivered the message. The agent nodded, presumably indicating he had other copies. Cotton turned back to Mrs. Townsend, who was clutching her e-mail defiantly, daring anyone to take it away from her.

"Mrs. Townsend, I understand your concern." Cotton spoke with sincere compassion. "I must now, for your husband's sake, consult my superiors. I promise I will personally advise you of their decision."

Townsend did not react.

"I must tell you that you cannot take anything the kidnappers say at face value" Cotton continued. "We may very well receive subsequent messages. A hundred million dollars is a lot of money, and they certainly know that problems could arise beyond our control. With your permission, I would like to leave our team in place to assist in any way that they can."

To Chase's surprise, Mrs. Townsend looked at him, apparently asking him if he she should accept Cotton at his word.

"Special Agent Cotton is correct," Chase said.

Mrs. Townsend nodded, apparently giving her permission for the team to remain in place.

Cotton glanced at Chase and then at the sheet of paper that Mrs. Townsend was now clutching to her chest.

"This is my e-mail," Mrs. Townsend declared, easily reading Cotton's unspoken appeal.

"Mrs. Townsend," Cotton said, his voice almost a whisper. "I concede that is your e-mail. I must point out, however, the kidnappers have warned us that if the media should learn of our negotiations you will never see your husband again."

"I'm not stupid," Mrs. Townsend reacted.

"Very well, I must immediately inform the president of the kidnapper's ultimatum," Cotton said as he started for the door.

Cotton led his team into the hallway. Mary, Mrs. Townsend's secretary, hesitated.

"Please excuse us, Mary. I need to talk with the lieutenant in private," Mrs. Townsend said.

Mary nodded and was closing the door behind her when Cotton reappeared.

"Mansfield, may I have a quick word with you?"

Chase looked at Mrs. Townsend who did not react. Chase took the non-response as approval and joined Cotton in the hall.

"Don't let her do anything stupid," Cotton growled.

"She's just distraught," Chase replied.

"Of course she is," Cotton reacted. "I would be too. Nobody is going to hand over a hundred million dollars to terrorists or con men. We don't know who is sending these messages. They may or may not have Townsend."

"Not many people know Townsend is missing," Chase said, referring to the fact that Townsend's disappearance had yet to hit the media, a situation that surprised them all.

"Why in the hell does she trust you so much?" Cotton demanded. "What have you been telling her?"

"I haven't talked with the lady since the first day," Chase said, referring to his presence in the Townsend household when the first message arrived.

"We had a deal. You handle the murder, and I'll take care of the alleged kidnapping."

"I know," Chase said, understanding but not appreciating Cotton's attitude.

"What in the hell are you doing here anyway?" Cotton demanded.

"I'm here because you invited me," Chase said.

Cotton glared at Chase. "Alright," he conceded. "But watch out what you say to that woman. She's keeping a journal. I'm told that the secretary has seen her doing it. She's sitting in her bedroom writing down everything we say and do."

"Why..." Chase started to ask and then laughed. "She's writing a book?" He said softly.

Cotton nodded.

“Thanks for the warning,” Chase said as he turned back to the room.

“What did he want?” Mrs. Townsend asked as soon as Chase closed the door behind him.

“Don’t be too hard on him,” Chase said. “Like you, he’s under a lot of pressure.”

“Not like me,” Mrs. Townsend turned her defiance on Chase. “It’s my husband that those bastards are going to kill.”

“I know, but we can’t give up hope. The longer we can string out the negotiations, the better chance we have of catching the perpetrators.” The words sounded trite and bureaucratic, even to Chase who spoke them, but he didn’t know what else to say.

“They don’t know where to look.”

“Do you know what ‘mt’ signifies?”

Mrs. Townsend stared at Chase, not understanding what he was talking about.

“On the e-mail,” Chase said. “The ‘fr’ in the addressee line on the first message indicated it was sent from France. There is a ‘mt’ on that one.”

Mrs. Townsend immediately studied the e-mail.

“From: Anony100@yahoo.com.mt”

“You’re right, lieutenant. I missed that,” Mrs. Townsend said.

“You were focused on the text,” Chase said. “Do you want me to ask one of the agents where the e-mail originated?”

“I’ll ask Mary,” Mrs. Townsend said as she grabbed the phone from the table next to her chair.

After a brief conversation, a slight hesitation, she looked at Chase. “Mary says the ‘mt’ indicates the e-mail was sent from Malta. What does that mean?”

Chase shook his head as he considered the question. After a brief pause, he answered honestly, “I’m not sure. I’m not an expert on e-mails, kidnapping, or terrorists, and I don’t know what the Bureau’s relations are with Malta’s police or security service, if they have one. Obviously, whoever is sending the messages is trying to confuse us and slow down our efforts to backtrack the e-mails. Moving from country to country might do that.”

“I’m not sure where Malta is. Do you think that is where they are holding my husband? How did they get him there?”

"I can't speculate on that, Mrs. Townsend," Chase said, recalling Cotton's warning about Mrs. Townsend's journal.

"Oh please call me Nancy Lou, lieutenant."

"Yes ma'am. And I'm Chase."

"I said Nancy Lou, not ma'am," Mrs. Townsend said.

"Yes, Nancy Lou," Chase said, uncomfortable at addressing the suffering spouse with such a cutesy name.

"Where's Malta?"

"In the Mediterranean between Italy and Africa, someplace," Chase answered.

"Does the FBI have an office there too?"

"I assume we have an embassy. I doubt the Bureau has an office there."

"So Cotton has to send an investigator from somewhere to investigate," Mrs. Townsend said.

"Yes, probably from Rome. I read somewhere they have an office in Rome."

"You don't know these things?"

"No ma'am, I'm a simple Fairfax police officer."

"Then why are you involved?"

"I'm not involved in your husband's kidnapping."

"Why are you here?"

"I'm involved only tangentially. I'm in charge of investigating Professor Jesperson's murder."

"Oh, I'm sorry, Chase," Mrs. Townsend said as she patted Chase's arm. "I knew that. I'm so concerned about James that I forgot."

"That's understandable," Chase said as he pondered Townsend's strange demeanor. She seemed angrier with the Bureau's response to her husband's disappearance/kidnapping than she was emotionally distraught.

"I still don't understand sending the e-mail from Malta." Mrs. Townsend said. "Are there many terrorists there?"

"I'm sorry. I don't know," Chase replied honestly. "I doubt that anything connected with Malta will actually impede Special Agent Cotton's investigation," Chase tried to divert her.

"Why?"

"If I were investigating, I would concentrate on this Cayman bank. I'm sure the Bureau has officers who are quite familiar with the offshore banking thing."

"Money laundering and all that," Mrs. Townsend agreed. "That sounds like a good lead. Do you think I should give this back to the agents?" She held up the e-mail.

"I'm confident they have other copies, like you said," Chase resisted the urge to smile.

"Maybe, I should point out to them that they have to get busy investigating this bank," she said, rising to her feet.

"I'm sure they are already working on it," Chase said. "But it wouldn't hurt suggesting it. They could certainly tell you more about what is happening than I can. Is there anything I can help you with?"

Chase glanced at his watch. He still had time before he was due to meet Sally Kendrick in Reston for lunch, but he had little interest in chatting with Mrs. Townsend, particularly since he had learned she was keeping a journal.

"I appreciate your taking your time to chat with me. I feel isolated here in my own home without James, particularly since I'm surrounded by these strangers watching me all the time."

"I understand."

"I feel like a stranger in my own home."

Chase did not comment.

"You know, I visit friends, go shopping, anything to make time pass while I wait for something to happen."

Chase nodded, trying to look sympathetic.

Mrs. Townsend patted Chase on the arm. "Really, Chase, I find talking with you reassuring. Please come back when you can."

Chase didn't know what to say to that. He almost felt that the suffering spouse was making a move on him.

"You explain things that are happening in a way that I can understand," Mrs. Townsend said, giving Chase the impression that she was reading his thoughts or reactions.

"Anything I can do to help you professionally, I will," Chase said.

Mrs. Townsend blinked once at his use of the word professionally, but she withdrew her hand from his arm.

"I best talk with someone about this Malta thing," Mrs. Townsend turned and led the way to the door.

Chapter 13

Chase parked the Prius in the lot behind Paolo's. He had ten minutes to spare, so he paused to study the crowds in the square that faced the Reston Town Center Fountain. He was studying the legs of a particularly attractive, mini-skirted shopper when a voice behind him declared.

"She's about twenty-years too young for you, lieutenant. Someone in your position should know there are laws against what you're thinking."

Chase turned and was feeling a little guilty at being caught staring when he spotted a smiling Sally Kendrick. The Lady in Black was now wearing a red suit, remarkable for the amount of bare skin displayed below the short skirt.

"May I ask your age, young lady?" Chase smiled.

"I'm old enough to know better," Sally said.

"Good. I need someone your age to teach me the things I should know."

"Men don't think about such things. They just react."

"Why do women always ask each other, what do you feel?"

"And what do men ask?"

"What do you think? Men always use their brains not their emotions."

"Give me a break."

"Would you please join me," Chase nodded in the directions of Paolo's, "and share one of my favorite lunches?"

"Need I wear handcuffs?" She held out her wrists.

"Not for lunch," Chase said.

There was something about Kendrick's demeanor and style that reminded Chase of Mrs. Townsend when she was playing Nancy Lou. Of course, there was a considerable age difference—Townsend once could have worn a dress like that of the Lady in Black, but time had taken its toll—still, each clearly made Chase feel that every gesture and comment was directed by a previously devised agenda.

After they were seated in a booth, neither looked at the menu.

"I know what I want," Kendrick smiled.

"So do I," Chase said and smiled back.

"Do you come here often?" Kendrick asked.

"Not really," Chase answered. "This feels uncomfortably like a first date."

"It's not. It's a business meeting," Kendrick said as she kicked him in the shins with one of her pointed pumps.

Before Chase could respond to either the kick or the statement, a male server appeared. Chase assumed he was a college student.

"Would someone like something to drink before you order?" The server asked.

Chase waited for Kendrick to respond first.

"I do. At business meetings," she said, "I always have a dry, double vodka martini on the rocks to get me through the dull spots."

"I'm still on duty," Chase hesitated.

"Lieutenant, don't make me drink alone," Kendrick ordered.

"Give me a draft," Chase relented without admitting that he always had a draft beer with his pizza.

"Do you have a preference?" The waiter smiled. "We have..."

"Bass ale," Chase interrupted. He knew the routine.

"We can order now," Kendrick said.

Chase nodded, acknowledging he had lost control.

"I want calamari and a house salad with blue cheese dressing," Kendrick said.

"And I'll have the Pizza Bolognese," Chase said.

****

In the Oval Office Special Agent Cotton once again found himself the junior man present. President Arthur C. Featherstone, obviously not in a congenial mood, sat behind his desk. Cotton was trapped on the couch between the two adversaries, the portly FBI Director Philip D'Antonio, and the slender, almost emaciated, CIA Director William H Pace. Vice President Charles Z. Hampton occupied an armchair facing Patricia Marshall, the Acting Secretary of Homeland Security. On the right of the president's massive desk NSC Advisor Doctor Barbara Luce, and Chief of Staff Theodore "Ted" Bertram sat side by side in stiff wood armchairs with leather seats.

Featherstone silently glared at the assembled group, moving his hard eyes from one to the other, beginning with those on the couch. When his attention finally settled on the chief of staff, Featherstone spoke. "I assume there is a reason why we are meeting without the Secretary of Defense and the Secretary of State."

Before Ted Bertram could answer, FBI Director D'Antonio spoke, "Sir, that's my fault. I suggested that we limit the attendees. We've received another e-mail from the kidnappers."

"I'm not sure I want to know what it says," Featherstone grumbled. "Have we identified the bastards yet?" He looked first at D'Antonio and then at CIA Director Pace.

Pace shook his head negatively. "No sir," he said as he turned towards D'Antonio, ignoring Cotton.

"No sir," D'Antonio echoed Pace.

Featherstone frowned. "Don't just sit there. Give me the damned message."

Cotton leaped to his feet and quickly handed the president a single sheet of paper before turning and handing out duplicates to the others.

Featherstone adjusted his glasses and began reading.

From: Anony100@yahoo.com.mt
Date: 10/18/10 09:00:43
To: NTown1@gmail.com
Subject: Yr Spouse

Relax. Yr spouse is still alive because you and his employer have behaved appropriately. You must now forward the requested sum immediately to the following account:

Acct. No. 746822910
Cayman Freeman Bank
North Street
George Town
Grand Cayman, Cayman Islands
Fax 949 9999

> This is our final communication. If the designated sum does not reach this account by 1400 hours today, if your investigators interfere in any way before the sum is processed, the individual in question will expire. Pay or pray.
>
> The Suffering People

Featherstone scanned the message, started to place the paper on his desk, paused, and re-read it. Finally, he leaned back in his chair, took a deep breath, removed his glasses, and stared at the group. No one reacted. All sat stiffly waiting for the tirade to begin.

"Will someone please tell me what this means and what you suggest we do about it?" Featherstone surprised them all by speaking calmly.

After a brief but thick silence, D'Antonio turned to his left and looked at Cotton while addressing the president. "Sir, Special Agent Cotton leads our response team."

"Tell me something I don't know," Featherstone said, his voice still moderated, lacking its using bite.

Cotton did not react.

"Special Agent Cotton you are the expert in these matters. Please share your views with us," Featherstone ordered.

"Sir," Cotton said from his position on the couch. "I fear this is the last message we will receive from those holding Secretary Townsend." He hesitated, waiting for someone else to comment. No one did, not even the president. "That leaves us with no way to negotiate with the senders. They have been very clever. They give us but one option, send the hundred million dollars by fourteen hundred hours or they will kill Secretary Townsend."

"We could find the bastards," Featherstone interrupted.

"Yes sir, but we have failed to do that," Cotton said as he turned to his right in an obvious appeal to Director D'Antonio.

"That is correct, sir," D'Antonio spoke up, taking the heat as he must. "Despite the Bureau's best efforts, here and overseas, we have failed to identify the kidnappers. None of our experts or sources have heard of an organization calling itself "The Suffering People."

"And neither has the Agency," Director Pace said.

"And our analysts have not been able to help," NSC Director Doctor Barbara Luce joined the chorus. "We have discreetly polled all of our confidential academic contacts without result."

Featherstone grimaced and nodded at Cotton. "Please continue Agent Cotton."

"We have backtracked the first message to its place of origin, but that told us little. It was sent from an on line computer connection in a modest cafe on the left bank frequented by tourists and students. Neither our agents on the ground nor our French liaison contacts can identify the originator. We assume the sender has left France. The From line in the second message indicates it was sent from Malta."

"Malta? Why in the hell Malta?" Featherstone dropped his calm pose.

"They are telling us that we cannot identify or find them by backtracking the messages," Cotton said. "They also warn us in the second paragraph of this new message that they will be watching to see if we attempt to reach them by tracking the ransom payment and threaten that if we do so they will kill Secretary Townsend."

"So we're supposed to send them one hundred million dollars and stand back while they retrieve and hide it and accept their implicit promise to release Secretary Townsend if we do so?"

"Yes sir," Cotton said.

"And what do you recommend we do?" Featherstone demanded.

"As a matter of principle I agree with the premise that the United States Government cannot give in to terrorist demands. To do so would place American citizens around the world in jeopardy."

"And if these are simple kidnappers not terrorists?" Featherstone did not let Cotton evade his question with generalities.

Cotton again turned to his director.

"As a matter of policy," D'Antonio accepted the hand off. "The Bureau opposes the payment of ransom to kidnappers. However, in domestic cases, the final decision rests with the family. If they refuse to accept our recommendations, we always do everything we can to use the transfer of funds to identify and apprehend the perpetrators."

"And you cannot guarantee success?"

"No sir."

"And you expect Nancy Lou Townsend to come up with a hundred million dollars?"

"No sir."

"Are you saying, director, that since Secretary Townsend is a government official and not the possessor of a hundred million dollars, that the government in this instance must place itself in the position of the family in a common kidnapping situation and decide whether to pay the ransom?"

"When you put it that way, sir, I am," D'Antonio answered.

"I suggest," Pace joined the discussion. "We must assume from the phrase, "The Suffering People," that we are dealing with an organization, a terrorist organization, and with that given I oppose paying a ransom. Clearly, if the United States Government pays one hundred million dollars to free Secretary Townsend we would be placing every prominent official and wealthy citizen at risk, here and abroad."

Featherstone glared at Pace and shook his head. "That is apparent to all of us, director. Please stop spouting clichés and tell me what I should do. Don't we owe James Townsend something? If one of you were in his position, and what makes you think there is a good chance you will never be, what would you want me to do for you and your family? Just relax and mouth nice sounding clichés? What will the people of the United States say if we lean back in our comfortable chairs and let James Townsend be killed?"

The room remained silent. Nobody, of course, had an answer.

Featherstone waited.

"We could pay the hundred million," Vice President Charles Z. Hampton said what they were all thinking.

Featherstone looked at his vice president. "Mr. Vice President," Featherstone said. "Let me honestly say that at this moment I do not know why either one of us, or for that matter any sane person, should want to sit in this chair in this magnificent office and be forced to make this kind of decision."

Hampton, assuming that Featherstone was not finished with his lament, nodded agreement but did not speak.

"James Townsend is a loyal friend, a hardworking senior official, not a murderous felon who I can pardon or send to the gallows. I cannot sign Secretary Townsend's death warrant."

President Featherstone turned and stared out the window with unseeing eyes.

After several minutes of uneasy silence, FBI Director Antonio spoke. "Sir, we're working against a deadline." As soon as the words were out of his mouth, D'Antonio regretted them. "Deadline" was a most inappropriate word.

Featherstone turned, glanced at D'Antonio, ignored the offending word, and addressed his vice president. "Charles can you raise the full hundred million dollars?"

"By mixing private funds offered by patriotic supporters and contributions from independent agencies with contingency funds," Hampton glanced at Pace and D'Antonio, "Maybe."

"By two o'clock? Meet the deadline?" Featherstone asked.

"Maybe, sir."

"What do you mean, maybe?" Featherstone asked.

"If not all of it, certainly some of it," Hampton answered firmly. "Maybe some of it would satisfy them."

"Without first consulting Congress?"

"Yes sir," Hampton said. "We must anticipate that eventually everything will come out. Someone will leak to the media, and then Congress will start screaming and investigating."

"That's a given. If we consult Congress now, one of them, maybe all of them, will run from the conference table to their favorite reporter, and the bastards holding James will know what we are going to do before we have a chance to do it."

After another heavy pause, Featherstone spoke directly to Hampton again. "Collect the money." He turned his attention to D'Antonio. "Do your people know how to send a money transfer to the Cayman Islands?"

D'Antonio glanced at Cotton who swallowed hard and nodded affirmatively. "Yes, sir."

"Good," Featherstone said. "Get ready to meet the deadline, Agent Cotton. Coordinate with the vice president directly."

"Sir, I must continue to object," CIA Director Pace said.

"That's your right. Go back to your office, draft your resignation, and prepare to write your memoirs, if you must," Featherstone spoke coldly.

Pace did not reply. The vice president leaped out of his chair. "I've work to do," he announced.

The others stood up, the Acting DHS Secretary smiled, and the rest appeared worried.

"I want some quiet time, alone, Ted," Featherstone spoke to his chief of staff, "while I make my decision."

The last comment stopped everybody. They turned as one and stared at the president.

"Prepare to do what the bastards want. I reserve the option of giving the go or no go command."

"Sir, we're going to need time," D'Antonio said, "if we're going to meet the deadline."

"You'll have my decision by one o'clock. Will an hour be enough?"

"We'll be ready, sir," Vice President Hampton said. "Director D'Antonio and I will coordinate everything."

"Thank you, Mr. Vice President," Featherstone said.

As the group hurried as one towards the door, Featherstone called after them. "Special Agent Cotton!"

Cotton turned to see the president wave a finger calling him back. The others looked at the president, and he indicated they should continue onward. After the door closed behind them, Featherstone said, "I want one additional bit of information from you."

"Yes sir," Cotton said, worried about what was coming next.

"What was the name of that Fairfax officer you said was handling the investigation of Professor Jesperson?"

"Lieutenant Mansfield," Cotton replied.

"Can you contact him directly?"

"Yes sir."

"Please do so and order him to get his ass to the White House forthwith. I have a question I must ask him before I make my decision."

"Sir, I've kept close contact with Mansfield. In fact, we were conferring at the Townsend home about our respective investigation when the new e-mail arrived," Cotton said.

"He knows about this message?" Featherstone picked up the e-mail and waved it.

"Yes sir," Cotton said and immediately started worrying about Mansfield's coincidental involvement.

"Good, then I can talk frankly with him?" Featherstone again surprised Cotton.

"Yes sir. Mansfield was also meeting with Mrs. Townsend discussing his investigation when the first e-mail arrived."

"And he has kept his mouth shut, didn't leak to the media?"

"No sir. He is an experienced officer with a solid reputation. He knows how to deal with the media." Cotton worried that he was overstating his regard for Mansfield but felt he had no alternative. "If you would like me to participate in your meeting with him..."

"That will not be necessary. Just get him here before one o'clock and on your way out tell Heather to expect him and to see that she gets him to me forthwith."

****

Chase was munching on a breadstick dipped in some kind of olive paste, half way through his first beer, and Kendrick had her second double vodka martini on the rocks in front of her, yet untouched, when the waiter appeared with his pizza and her calamari and salad.

"We're going to share," Kendrick announced, pointing at the pizza, calamari, and salad.

"Agreed," Chase said as Kendrick's cell phone chimed.

"Hello," Kendrick smiled at Chase as she answered. "What? When?" She sat up straight.

Chase helped himself to one of the calamari. He was dipping it in the spicy red sauce when Kendrick said, "Sorry."

A surprised Chase watched as she slid out of the booth and grabbed her purse.

"Sorry," she repeated. "I'll have to take a rain check. Crisis at the office." She patted Chase on the cheek, gulped half of her martini, and turned. "Give me a tinkle, lover," she called over her shoulder.

"Anything I can do?" Chase called after her.

"Computer stuff. Way over your little pointy head," she smiled and hurried away.

Chase was studying the table and the three huge portions of food and trying to decide how much of it he could consume and how much he would have to box up and take with him when his cell phone chimed.

"What?" He said when he realized that Kendrick had stuck him with the bill.

"Mansfield?" The thick male voice asked.

"Yes," Chase said, recognizing Cotton's voice. "What can I do for you Special Agent Cotton?"

"Where are you?"

"Where are you?" Chase grabbed another calamari as he fenced with Cotton. "How long will it take you to get to Reston?" Chase wondered if he could stick Cotton with all or at least half of the bill? One of them could probably write it off their expense sheet.

"Please answer my question," Cotton ordered gruffly.

"Only if you answer mine," Chase said as he washed the spicy calamari down with a sip of beer." He hailed the passing server getting ready to order another draft.

"This is important."

"So is this," Chase glanced at the food. Cotton's share was going to be a little cold, but Chase dismissed that thought as Cotton's worry.

"Can you get to the White House in thirty minutes?" Cotton asked, catching Chase's attention.

"The White House? That's out of my jurisdiction."

"The president wants to meet with you forthwith, and he's working on a deadline," Cotton said.

"The e-mail?" Chase asked, recalling the kidnapper's demands.

"Yes, now stop chattering and start moving."

"The bill and several boxes," Chase said to the server, wondering if the president liked pizza, calamari, and salad.

"The two o'clock deadline?" Chase asked.

"Be there in half an hour. I'm working on the package."

"Why me? I don't know anything?" Chase protested.

"I know that, but the president doesn't," Cotton laughed. "I lied and told him you're competent."

"Oh shit," Chase said. "How do I get in the place?"

"Try the entrance behind the Executive Office Building. If you can't find that, climb the fence," Cotton chuckled.

"Thanks a lot," Chase said.

"Use your siren and lights," Cotton ordered.

"But..."Chase found himself talking into a dead phone as the waiter approached with the bill and the boxes.

Chase handed the waiter his credit card and said, "Emergency, process this fast while I pack up the stuff."

Chapter 14

Five minutes after her hasty departure from Paolo's Kendrick was back in her car. Just as she shut the door, her cell phone chimed. "Hello," Kendrick answered. "Sorry about that, but I was having lunch with the Fairfax detective who is investigating Jesperson's murder. He's a nosy fellow, and I couldn't talk in front of him. How are things going? I've been worried stiff about you?"

"Nothing to worry about," a male voice answered. "I've been flying all over the world setting things up."

"No problems?" Kendrick asked.

"None. Just a lot of details to take care of."

"Make sure you don't make any mistakes," Kendrick said.

"If things go the way they should, it'll all be done in three or four hours."

"Good. I miss you," Kendrick said.

"I've been too busy to miss you. If I never see another airplane or airport when this is over, I'll be a happy man."

"You will be. I promise," Kendrick said as she started her car. "I've got to get out of here. The detective just rounded the corner and is heading this way."

"Why are you bothering with him? You're asking for trouble."

"I picked him up at the funeral. When he started asking a lot of questions about my relationship with Jesperson, I decided to feed him enough to get him interested."

"And why did you do that?"

"Because I've been sitting here not knowing what was going on, and decided I could at least learn how his investigation is progressing. Don't worry, I know what I'm doing. He's just a local cop." Kendrick turned in the direction of Reston Avenue.

"Don't underestimate him."

"You worry about your end, and I'll worry about me."

"I have to. We're almost there. We've worked too hard and risked too much to let one silly misstep screw things up now."

"OK," Kendrick laughed.

"Do you mean it?"

"I mean it."

"Good. I miss you."

"Me too."

"We've talked long enough. I won't call again until all of this is over."

"Be careful," Kendrick cautioned.

"And you stop your silly games," the man said and hung up.

****

A uniformed guard stopped Chase at the entrance to the Executive Office building parking lot.

"I've got an appointment," Chase said as he reached for his credential case.

"Name?" The guard demanded.

"Mansfield," Chase said. "I was told to..."

"Good," the guard interrupted. "We've been waiting for you. You're late."

Chase checked his watch. It said twelve-fifty. He had made better time than he had anticipated.

"Park over there," the guard pointed at a vacant VIP slot near the entrance. "And turn off that damned light."

Chase had switched off his siren a block from the White House complex but had inadvertently neglected the flashing light on the roof. Chase parked in the designated slot, pulled the light from the roof, tossed it onto the passenger seat, and hurried into the security entrance.

"My name's Mansfield. I have an appointment..." Chase started to explain to the guard behind the desk.

"You're late, lieutenant," the guard interrupted. "Give me your weapon. You can pick it up on the way out. Get through the metal detector."

Chase handed his weapon to the guard and turned towards the security screening cage. A second uniformed guard thrust a plastic basket at him.

"Keys, badge, change, all metal," the guard ordered.

Chase tossed his credentials case and keys into the basket, cleared the metal detector, and retrieved his possessions.

"Follow me and hurry before someone over there has a heart attack," a civilian male who Chase assumed was Secret Service took charge.

"What have you done?" The Secret Service agent said as they hurried along the walk behind the Executive Office Building.

"Nothing that I know of," Chase shrugged as he jogged along behind.

"Maybe that's the problem," the Secret Service agent said. "Brace yourself, then. I think the president is about to fire you. He's had a bad morning."

"Who hasn't?" Chase complained. "I didn't get a chance to eat my lunch."

The Secret Service agent ignored him.

A minute later they entered the White House and fast walked down the corridors.

"Been here before?" The agent asked.

"First time," Chase answered.

"This is the West Wing. I'll turn you over to the president's secretary. She's a nice lady, but watch out for the old man. "I don't know what's going on, but I'm told he's breathing fire. Are you sure it isn't your fault."

"Don't have a clue."

"Then someone is feeding him stories about you. He called us personally and threatened to fire us all if we didn't get you to his office before one o'clock."

Chase checked us watch. "I think you're safe. We've got two minutes to spare."

"It's not funny," the agent said as he opened a door and announced. "He's here."

The agent stepped aside, gave Chase a push from behind, and closed the door.

"You cut it short, lieutenant," a grinning lady with white hair greeted him. She hit a button on her intercom and announced, "He's here."

Chase did not hear what the person, presumably the president, at the other end said, but the matronly secretary turned to the two agents guarding the door behind her and said, "Shove him in."

She turned to Chase and smiled. "Just agree with him no matter what he says. He's never in a good mood, but today he's downright vicious. Believe me, I've got the scars to prove it."

Chase did not know how to respond; he couldn't tell if she were joking or not.

One of the agents quickly opened the door, and Chase reluctantly entered to find the president, who in person looked much older than his pictures, sitting in a chair looking out the window at the Potomac River in the distance. President Featherstone inclined his head in Chase's direction, pointed at a chair to his right, and said, "Lieutenant, I apologize for the rush, but I'm working on a deadline. Special Agent Cotton tells me you've read this," he waved a sheet of paper in the air.

"The e-mail message, sir?" Chase said.

"That's right."

"I understand the tight deadline, sir, but I'm not sure there's anything I can say or do about it," Chase said honestly.

"Relax, I'm not going to try to borrow one hundred million dollars from you," Featherstone smiled.

The door behind Chase opened. He turned to see Vice President Hampton standing in the doorway. The absurdity of the situation made Chase smile; he was in the presence of the two most powerful men in the world, and he hadn't voted for either one of them.

"Please give us a minute, Charles," Featherstone said.

"Yes sir," Hampton said. "I thought you should know that it's now one o'clock, and I have some commitments for the money. I may not have the full hundred million, not even half, but..."

"Thank you, keep working on it," Featherstone interrupted, and Hampton withdrew closing the door behind him.

Chase shook his head in amazement. Here he was, standing in the Oval Office watching the president tell his vice president to wait outside while he chatted with Chase, and Chase had no idea why.

"Lieutenant, Special Agent Cotton tells me that you are in charge of the investigation into Professor Jesperson's murder. Since I'm an old man and not always sure I understand what I'm being told, I must ask, is that correct?"

"Yes, sir."

"I realize you may not consider me authorized to ask you questions about your investigation, but this," he waved the e-mail, "forces me to do so."

"Yes, sir."

"I have two simple questions. Please answer them frankly. Have you identified the shooter?"

"No, sir."

"Do you have any reason to suspect Secretary Townsend was the shooter?"

That was the last question Chase expected the president to ask, and he hesitated before answering. If it were not for the two e-mails from Townsend's ostensible kidnappers, Chase would rank Townsend high on his list of suspects. His unexplained absence and the fact that he was presumably one of the last if not the last person to see Jesperson alive made him a logical suspect. Because Jesperson was not available for Chase to question, and because he had deferred the investigation of Townsend's disappearance to Cotton and the Bureau, Chase had not been able to probe the Secretary/Jesperson relationship for a possible motive. Chase had not pressed as he would normally because the e-mails, which the Feds appeared to accept as bonafide, indicated that Townsend, too, was a victim. Chase was not sure how to respond. His first impulse was to ask the president why he asked the question, did he know something that Chase did not that indicated Townsend had a motive for shooting his ostensible friend, or did the Bureau have information they shared with the president that led them to conclude the ransom demands were not what they appeared to be, the result of terrorist or common extortionist machinations.

"Lieutenant, I need a frank and honest answer to that question, now," Featherstone pressed. "The minute has arrived when I must decide whether to send one hundred million dollars, or a good part of it, to someone who calls themselves 'The Suffering People' or risk signing a good man's death warrant."

Chase took a deep breath and answered. "Secretary Townsend's absence, those e-mails, and the Bureau's assumption of responsibility for investigating Townsend's disappearance have precluded me from investigating the possibility that he was the shooter as thoroughly as I might have desired. Under normal circumstances, the secretary would have been my primary suspect. I can only say I do not know."

"Thank you, lieutenant. That was what I was afraid you might say."

Although he recognized that he had been dismissed, Chase asked the obvious question. "Sir, do you think it is possible that Secretary Townsend was the shooter?" Chase did not ask the corollary question, "Do you think the kidnapping has been staged?"

"Lieutenant, I recognize that I owe you a response. You have been candid with me, so I will be with you. I, like you, do not know. Between you and me, I have been worried about James Howard Townsend, the man, for the past few months. Many of these jobs are man killers. James has been under considerable strain, and frankly he has shown it. Several incidents, which I am neither inclined nor free to discuss, have made me realize that the job was getting to my old friend. That is all I can or will say. Thank you, and please ask the vice president to join me."

Chase exited the Oval Office and found himself the unwelcome target of several sets of hostile eyes. He nodded at Special Agent Cotton, shrugged, and spoke to the vice president, "The president will see you now." Chase tried to act as if the situation were commonplace for him.

The vice president nodded his appreciation and entered the still open door. The Director of the CIA, William H Pace, bumped Chase's shoulder as he hurried after the vice president, clearly interpreting Chase's announcement as including him. Chase knew that it did not, but decided to leave it to the president to clarify the situation. The Director of the FBI Phillip D'Antonio, apparently unwilling to let a competing peer gain an advantage, followed on Pace's heels. At the door, D'Antonio paused and ordered Cotton to follow with a nod of his head. Chase winked at the frowning Cotton. After the Secret Service closed the door softly behind the invading group, Chase whispered to the president's secretary, "He's a pussy cat."

"I know," Heather James laughed. "I'm glad to make your acquaintance, lieutenant. You're welcome to drop back anytime. Nobody else around here believes me."

"He may be a pussy cat, but watch out for those great big teeth, lieutenant," one of the Secret Service agents guarding the door said. "They go gnash, gnash, gnash."

"The better to eat you with," the second Secret Service agent laughed.

Chase waved and made his way back to his car where he sat behind the steering wheel and thought about his brief conversation with the President of the United States. Featherstone had asked, "Do you have any reason to suspect Secretary Townsend was the shooter?"

Chase assumed that there was far more behind that question than the president had admitted. Pressure in high office came with the job. Chase immediately wondered why the idea that the Secretary of Homeland Security might have murdered a relatively insignificant college professor had occurred to Featherstone. It had to be something important because it had forced the president to ask the question of a mere detective lieutenant working for a county police force. Chase shook his head while he reacted with a strong sense of dismay mixed with amazement. Now, he had real problem on his hands. He had to ignore an agreement with the FBI that had let him ignore the apparent kidnapping of a senior government official and concentrate on a relatively minor murder case that had a potential for exploding in his face. As soon as word of Townsend's odd disappearance leaked, and Chase knew it would, probably sooner rather than later, the media would immediately link the two cases and all hell would break loose.

Chase started his Prius and turned west, heading for Memorial Bridge and I-66.

****

In the West Wing of the White House behind him, Vice President Hampton spoke first. "Sir, I apologize for interrupting your meeting, but, as I reported, I have commitments for the money..."

"Thank you, Mr. Vice President," Featherstone interrupted.

Discussing the intricacies of off the record fund raising always irritated him. It was a dirty process, quite politically sensitive, and sometimes legally borderline; it was a political necessity, a feature of public life, but Featherstone tried to stand as far from the grubby process as he could. One old politician had summed it all up nicely, "Keep your hands clean; at least don't let anyone see the dirt."

"We are all in your debt," Featherstone said.

Recognizing that the president did not want to discuss the money details in front of the others, Hampton backed off. The fact that he had only thirty million in hand worried him, but he had alerted the president to his problem. Obediently, he said, "Not to me sir. To a considerable number of our loyal supporters."

"Are we going to have to explain to disbelieving oversight committee members why the CIA and FBI do not have a single penny left in their contingency funds to assist with pet congressional projects?" CIA Director Pace asked, sourly reminding the president that the ransom came not only from loyal supporters.

FBI Director D'Antonio said nothing, but he waited for the president's response with a concerned expression on his face.

"I'll rely on you gentlemen to handle the petty problems when the occasion requires," Featherstone said coldly. The president looked at the FBI director. "Can I assume that you are prepared to securely send the money transfer without alerting the world?"

Like a good bureaucrat, D'Antonio shared the responsibility by looking at Special Agent Cotton. Cotton noticeably stiffened as he figuratively fell on the offered sword.

"Yes sir." Cotton answered. "Hopefully, Secretary Townsend will be released when the money reaches its destination."

"The Cayman Freeman Bank in the Cayman Islands," Featherstone held up his copy of the e-mail.

"I doubt that the Cayman Islands will be the final destination. We assume that will be a first stop. Professionals will have instructed the bank to forward the transfer to one or more subsequent accounts elsewhere."

"Can you track it?" Featherstone persisted.

"Unfortunately, the Freeman Bank is one of those that hide behind the excuse that the privacy of their clients is paramount," D'Antonio risked his career by supporting his subordinate.

"I thought we had sources in these money laundering enterprises," Featherstone looked first at D'Antonio and then CIA Director Pace.

"In some of them sir," Pace said. "The Freeman Bank is a relatively small activity. We've targeted it, but penetrating the higher priority banks has consumed most of our attention to date."

"I assume you have raised the Freeman Bank higher on your priority list," Featherstone said.

"To the very top," Pace said.

"Then can I also assume that we may soon acquire the information we need?"

"Yes, sir, but I must stress that there are no certainties in the intelligence business," Pace said.

"Then I can't assume anything," Featherstone growled.

No one spoke.

"Where will the money go when it leaves the Cayman Islands?" Featherstone looked at Cotton, the junior man present, whose expression indicated that he was wishing at the moment that he was anyplace but standing at attention before an angry president.

"Worldwide," D'Antonio bravely answered for Cotton. "There are numerous banking centers that would be more than happy to process transactions of this magnitude. The Caymans and Switzerland are preferred by many who strive to conduct their money transactions in secret. Of late, as you know, the Swiss have been more responsive, but most of their institutions do so most reluctantly. In addition, we must consider Antigua, Belize, the Cook Islands, Cyprus, Hong Kong, Liechtenstein, Malta, Mauritius, Monaco, Nauru, the Seychelles, to name a few."

"And don't forget Panama, one of our major uncooperative centers," Pace surprised even himself with his support for D'Antonio.

The president frowned. He stressed his dissatisfaction with the answers by again addressing Cotton by name. "We don't have all day. Special Agent Cotton, if you were the damned kidnapper, how would you handle the money?"

"This is not my area of expertise, sir," Cotton answered. "But if it were me, I would have instructed the Freeman Bank in advance to break up on receipt the hundred million into... say five transfers and to immediately send them to designated accounts in five different countries around the world leaving...say a million dollars behind in the Freeman Bank to keep it silent and happy. And if I were being particularly careful, as I suspect the people we are dealing with are, I would have each of the five subsequent institutions again separate the transfers into smaller amounts of say five to ten million each and forward these deposits to additional worldwide accounts, all open and waiting."

"Sounds to me like setting up that number of accounts would require considerable planning and advance work," Featherstone said.

"Yes sir," Cotton said, "but a hundred million dollars is worth a little extra effort."

"I agree with Special Agent Cotton," D'Antonio said. "It sounds like a lot of cash moving around the world, but today's computers render it relatively easy. I should note that transferring this much cash involves more people and institutions in the laundering process."

"Are you saying the more people and institutions involved, the better are our chances of finding and tracking one of the transactions which will let us identify the perpetrators?" The president said.

"Yes, sir," D'Antonio and Pace answered, almost simultaneously.

Cotton, who was tempted to point out that Panama had a canal that buttressed it against outside pressures, did not speak.

"And there is one additional complication to be considered," Vice President Charles Z. Hampton announced.

Hampton had tried to discuss the money raising with the president, but Featherstone had held him off. Telling himself it would be a non-issue if the president decided not to pay the ransom, and wondering if Featherstone had already made a negative decision, he was not ready to share with others; Hampton had waited. Unfortunately, Hampton now sensed that Featherstone was about to decide to send the money on its way. The problem was that despite his best efforts and the raid on the FBI and CIA contingency funds, Hampton had only assembled a meager thirty million. He had commitments for the full amount but needed more time to collect it, and time was something he did not have.

Featherstone took a deep breath and waited for his vice president to explain.

"We have only thirty million in hand," Hampton declared.

"Only thirty million?" Featherstone leaned back in his chair, feigning surprise he did not feel. Hampton had tried to discuss the subject with him, and Featherstone had fended him off.

"Yes sir," Hampton said. "I have commitments from our friends for the whole hundred million, but most of them need more time to come up with the cash."

"Something we do not have," Featherstone said, his tone wry, not condemning.

Unfortunately, Featherstone understood the problem, one that could not be overcome with a simple temper tantrum. Hampton had been lucky to assemble thirty million in such a short period. Few people, certainly not their wealthy friends who knew better, kept millions hidden under their mattresses. That kind of money was always working, in stocks, bonds, real estate, tax shelters, and the like, and it required time to free it from the tentacles that bound it.

"Only you could have come up with thirty million in such a short time frame," Featherstone lifted the worry from the shoulders of his vice president and placed it where it belonged, squarely on his own.

President Featherstone checked his watch, stood up, walked to the window, and stared at the Potomac with his back to the others. Several long minutes crept past. The others exchanged worried glances; not one of them was sure what the president would decide. Even thirty million dollars was a lot of money. Uncertainties abounded; they did not know if they were dealing with terrorists, run-of-the-mill kidnappers, or a con man simply seizing an opportunity. The one certainty was that Secretary Townsend was missing, and the person or persons sending the e-mails from France and Malta knew it; news of Townsend's disappearance had miraculously not leaked. In most cases of this nature, someone, the spouse, one of the investigators, a staff member would not have been able to resist the opportunity to leak, complain, seek solace, attention, or relief from frustration in the silence of the aftermath.

Suddenly, President Featherstone turned and spoke four words: "Send the thirty million."

Pace, D'Antonio, Cotton, and Vice President Hampton stared. Not one of them spoke. The president ignored them and returned to his desk. Cotton turned and hurried towards the door with the other three trailing in his wake.

Chapter 15

In Teheran President Mahmud Ahmadinejad sat erect in his padded chair, a gift from the President of Syria, and tapped his fingers on the desk as he tried to intimidate his Minister of Intelligence.

"Do you not recall, Mr. Minister, that in this very office I asked you to report to me twice daily on the progress of your investigation?" Ahmadinejad raised his voice for emphasis.

"Yes, sir, I do," Naveed Behbehani smiled when he replied.

"How many days have passed since we had that discussion?"

Behbehani casually studied his watch, pretending that empty gesture would help him formulate his answer more precisely. Several seconds of silence passed before Behbehani deigned to answer the question. "Exactly seven."

"And how many times did you report as ordered?"

"Mr. President, I cannot answer that question," Behbehani replied with a straight face. He shifted in his chair and casually locked eyes with the president. It amused Behbehani when he did that because it obviously discomforted Ahmadinejad. Despite the platform under the president's chair, Behbehani's bulk still enabled him to avoid having to look up to his ostensible superior.

"And why, Mr. Minister, can you not answer that simple question?" Ahmadinejad slapped his desk for emphasis, intimidating no one.

"To answer accurately, I must consult General Nasiri," Behbehani referred to the commander of VEVAK, his security and intelligence organization.

"I gave the order to you."

"And in the interest of efficiency I transmitted it to General Nasiri."

"I have heard nothing from either of you," Ahmadinejad complained.

"I don't understand; I will have to investigate; General Nasiri has briefed me regularly."

Bring me up to date."

"Of course, sir. Would you like to schedule a briefing?"

"Now."

"Now, sir?"

"Tell me where your investigation stands. Have you identified this American's sources?"

"No, sir."

Ahmadinejad waited for his Minister of Intelligence and Security to elaborate, but he said nothing.

"I need details. How can I make correct decisions without reliable, timely information?" Ahmadinejad controlled his temper with difficulty.

"You cannot, sir."

"So tell me what you know?"

"Yes, your excellency," Behbehani said. "VEVAK has proceeded with circumspection as you ordered."

Ahmadinejad did not recall having used the word circumspection when he ordered the investigation. He remembered telling this fool to find everyone the American had talked to and arrest them, but he did not allow Behbehani to divert him by debating the subject. He waited for the idiot to continue.

"General Nasiri reports that VEVAK is conducting a very thorough investigation," Behbehani said.

"And how are they doing that?"

"By carefully rechecking the backgrounds of every scientist working at Natanz."

"And?"

"And the investigations are underway as we speak," Behbehani smiled.

"Where are the scientists now?"

"General Nasiri has arrested ten of them."

"Only ten?"

"Yes, sir."

"And the others? Where are they? Why haven't you arrested all of them?"

"General Nasiri reports that is not possible."

"Why is it not possible?"

"I was hoping you could tell me," Behbehani said.

"Me?" Ahmadinejad leaped from his chair, tripped when he stepped off his platform, caught himself, and in his irritation began to pace.

"Yes, sir. The Basij-e Mostaz'afin (the Basij, Mobilization of the Oppressed) arrested some of the scientists, and the Guardians (the Revolutionary Guards) have the rest. Neither will discuss the issue with General Nasiri. They claim you authorized their investigations and tell Nasiri to mind his own business."

"The Basij and Guardians have the other fifty scientists and refuse to coordinate their investigations with VEVAK?" The little president shouted, acting as if the confusion was the Minister of Intelligence and Security's fault.

"Yes, sir. As a Basij officer, you know firsthand how independent they are." Behbehani ignored the spurious accusation.

Ahmadinejad paced as he concealed his reaction to that comment. He had asked the Revolutionary Guards, a branch of the military who now involved themselves in civilian matters, and the Basij, a paramilitary volunteer force composed of enthusiastic young men, to also investigate. Without thinking the matter through, he had impulsively assumed that competition between the Guards, VEVAK, and the Basij would be helpful. He had not, however, anticipated that all three would immediately begin to arrest his nuclear scientists in some kind of mad competition. This morning his Minister of Defense and the Vice President and Head of the Atomic Energy Organization had complained. The arrests had shut down their Natanz operation, and Ahmadinejad had assured the Supreme Leader Ayatollah Khamenei, Khomeini's successor, that he considered Natanz his most important priority. Of course, Ahmadinejad could not discuss this with Behbehani.

"Arresting our scientists was a major mistake," Ahmadinejad turned on his Minister of Intelligence and Security and pointed a finger directly at him. "What were you possibly thinking?"

Behbehani did not bother reminding the blustering little man that he had just admitted he had ordered the arrests. Fortunately, VEVAK had not actually taken the ten scientists into custody. They had interviewed them politely and placed them and their families under "protective" surveillance. Behbehani had merely exaggerated slightly when he described the surveillances as arrests. He resisted the temptation to smile at the thought that the amateurs who led the barely controlled Guardians and Basij were going to have to now explain why they were holding the scientists in isolation and aggressively interrogating them. Nasiri had reported that very morning that at least two scientists had succumbed to the interrogation procedures.

"Release the scientists immediately," Ahmadinejad ordered. "I want them back at work in Natanz, now. Didn't it occur to you that arresting these men would threaten our most vital defense program?"

"I will so instruct General Nasiri," Behbehani said, ignoring the president's question. If Ahmadinejad were a sane man, he would have explained that he always operated on the theory that it is wiser to explain why one did nothing rather than having done something foolish.

Ahmadinejad continued to pace, acting like he had dismissed Behbehani.

Behbehani rose from his chair. Now standing, he towered over the little president. "About the scientists now being interrogated by the Guards and the Basij, do you want Nasiri to liberate them?"

Ahmadinejad stopped, turned, and looked up at his minister whose height now intimidated him.

"This might require the use of force," Behbehani pressed, curious about how Ahmadinejad would handle that problem.

The president retreated quickly toward his desk, stumbled as he climbed up on his platform, and glared at his minister. With his confidence apparently restored somewhat by the diminishment of Behbehani's height advantage, Ahmadinejad made a decision. "No," he ordered. "You have already created too many problems. I will deal with the Guards and the Basij."

"Yes, sir," Behbehani turned for the door, hiding his amusement at the presidential posturing. The man was still a dangerous and unpredictable enemy. "I will issue General Nasiri his orders immediately," Behbehani said and departed before Ahmadinejad could respond.

As soon as the door closed behind his minister, Ahmadinejad poked at his intercom and ordered his secretary to get Commander Saidi on the phone.

"Yes Mr. President."

Saidi came on line.

"Release all the scientists and get them back to work at Natanz immediately."

"But..."Saidi tried to explain the extenuating circumstances. Not all of the scientists were in a condition to return to work immediately. To send them back without proper treatment would be bad for morale.

Unfortunately, Ahmadinejad had hung up on him.

Next, Ahmadinejad contacted the Basij commander.

"Release all the scientists and get them back to work at Natanz immediately."

He then called the Minister of Defense and the Vice President who served as head of the Atomic Energy Commission and directed both to come to his office forthwith. No more than thirty minutes later, they arrived almost simultaneously, and Ahmadinejad curtly greeted them from behind his desk.

"I have ordered VEVAK and those other security fools who thoughtlessly arrested our Natanz scientists and almost destroyed our atomic project in the process to release them immediately. How could the two of you allow this to happen?" He demanded as soon as they were seated.

Houshang Soltani, the Minister of Defense, and Akbar Mahsuli, the Director of the Atomic Energy Organization, exchanged worried glances, but neither spoke. Each had been separately briefed by staff; they knew that the president himself had ordered the arrests. It was typical of Ahmadinejad to impulsively shout orders without giving a single thought to likely repercussions.

"I directed VEVAK to identify the foreign agent who betrayed the nation by disclosing state secrets to that American professor," Ahmadinejad continued. "I did not instruct them to destroy our most sensitive project. Director Mahsuli, how much harm have they done? When can I expect our first product?"

"That is difficult to say, Mr. President. With your permission, I will leave immediately for Natanz and assess the situation."

"I don't want another assessment. I want to know when I will have our first bomb...product," Ahmadinejad shouted as he leaped from his chair and stumbled off his platform.

While the angry president was recovering his balance, the two visitors again stared at each other. The Minister of Defense smiled as he shrugged his shoulders trying to pretend indifference. The Atomic Energy Director, who was the one bearing the brunt of the excitable president's tantrum, shook his head.

"I'm sorry, sir, but I fear no one can provide you with a definitive date," Director Mahsuli said.

"I insist," Ahmadinejad, still pacing, demanded as he approached the worried director's chair.

"I'm sorry, Mr. President," Mahsuli added the ridiculous little man's title when he repeated his answer.

"Sorry? I'm not interested in sorry," Ahmadinejad grumbled as he turned abruptly to confront the Minister of Defense. "Mr. Minister. What do your sources tell you? Certainly you are monitoring your ministry's coordination with Natanz."

"If Director Mahsuli cannot answer your questions, Mr. President, no one can," Soltani tried to keep Ahmadinejad focused on Mahsuli.

Ahmadinejad pivoted and resumed his pacing. "What do you say to that, director?" Ahmadinejad asked with his back to Mahsuli.

"As you know, sir, Natanz was struggling to recover from the CIA's insidious virus attack when the effort was disrupted by the arrests of the scientists, the only experts in Iran capable of negating our enemies mean effort."

"I thought we had resolved that problem," Ahmadinejad stopped in mid-stride and turned to face Mahsuli from five meters away. "Didn't you tell me..." Ahmadinejad hesitated as he tried to remember when the conversation had taken place. Unable to recall the date, Ahmadinejad finessed it, "...recently...when we last met...that you had devised a solution?"

Ahmadinejad referred to the sudden appearance of a virus in the Natanz computers that managed the vital centrifuge programs that produced the weapons-grade fuel essential for his atomic bomb. Although a non-practicing engineer, Ahmadinejad had only a limited understanding of computers and viruses. As a student Ahmadinejad had majored in political protest not academics.

"It is imperative that we teach the Americans and their CIA spies a lesson. We must demonstrate that my Iran, my Persia, is now a world power and will not tolerate such provocations," Ahmadinejad continued.

"We all support you, Mr. President," Minister of Defense Soltani flattered the little man. "Just give the order and your armed forces will lead the way."

Ahmadinejad nodded at Soltani who was reacting as his president expected him to behave. When Ahmadinejad had selected Soltani for his current job, he had known that the man was a sycophant who took no chances. The last person Ahmadinejad wanted at the top of the Defense Ministry was a strong, independent man with his own ambitions and agenda.

"Yes, sir, I agree," Director Mahsuli declared, confusing both Ahmadinejad and Soltani. Neither understood what Mahsuli was a agreeing to, and both stared, waiting for him to continue.

Mahsuli said nothing more.

Out of frustration, Ahmadinejad asked, "What about this virus?"

Mahsuli reacted with a blank stare, tempted to answer an odd question with a question, "What about it?"

Ahmadinejad waited for a response. Mahsuli looked at Soltani, silently begging for help. The Minister of Defense offered none.

Finally, Mahsuli improvised. "When we last met, sir, I assured you that we were on the threshold of defeating the American CIA's feeble efforts. Unfortunately, replacing all of our computers at Natanz is an expensive and time-consuming effort. I assure you that when we have our scientists back in place and when the ordered replacement computers arrive and are properly programmed, the project will move forward at an accelerated pace."

"What assurance do we have that the Americans will not sabotage the new computers?" Ahmadinejad asked.

"Our experts are now on the alert. All programs assigned to the new and vastly more powerful computers will be fully screened."

"Why were our experts not on the alert before the virus attack?" Ahmadinejad demanded.

"We are urgently addressing that question, sir," Mahsuli said, "and I assure you I will fully brief you when the results are known."

Ahmadinejad stared at his Director of Atomic Energy. "For your sake, Mr. Director, I sincerely hope so," the president muttered as he climbed back on his platform and sat down behind his desk. Once settled in his chair, he again focused on Mahsuli. "Director, I want you personally to visit Natanz and to do whatever is necessary to make sure the virus is defeated; the scientists are at work, all of them; the processors are spinning and do not come back until you can tell me when I will have my first bomb."

"Yes sir," Mahsuli said.

"Leave now," Ahmadinejad ordered.

Mahsuli leaped from his chair and hurried to the door.

When Soltani stood up, Ahmadinejad stopped him with a wave of his hand. "Mr. Minister, please stay. We also have some matters to discuss."

Soltani, who had been delighted at the opportunity to escape the madman's office, obediently sat back down while masking his disappointment and worry behind a false mask.

"After that incompetent produces my first bomb, how long will it take you to send it on its way?" Ahmadinejad asked softly.

"We must first test it to make sure it works," the Minister of Defense said. Soltani was no atomic expert, but past experience with less complicated weaponry had taught him his troops would require considerable training before he could dispatch them on missions with confidence.

"No," Ahmadinejad surprised Soltani.

"Sir?"

"No," Ahmadinejad repeated. "We cannot test an atomic bomb; we cannot alert the world that we have the bomb before we use it. Even a donkey would know that; as soon as the Israelis and Americans detect our test they will react, not with words, but with their planes and missiles."

"But sir, we have constructed our installations in the south to withstand such an attack," Soltani blurted.

"I know that Mr. Minister. I am the one who insisted on it. One must think strategically. If the Americans or Jews attack us without provocation, they will limit their strikes to our suspected research sites. This, the world will not tolerate. They will condemn our enemies for attacking us first. That would be good, but it is not enough. We must surprise them, frighten them, inhibit the lambs, and the rest of the world. One good bomb exploding in Washington, killing all their leaders, destroying their buildings and infrastructure, making them fearful where we will strike next, will paralyze the Americans. We will negotiate the new peace and emerge from the chaos with the assistance of the Mahdi as the new superpower."

"I agree totally, Mr. President. Our day will come," Soltani said, not believing a single word that he or the madman uttered.

"Good, Mr. Minister," Ahmadinejad said. "Now answer my question. How long will it take you to send it on its way?"

"Mr. President," Soltani stalled. "My experts tell me that our recent setbacks in Natanz will delay the production of our bomb indefinitely."

"What? You dare to disagree with Director Mahsuli?"

"That is not my place, sir. I am a military man, not an atomic expert. Speaking as the former, I must assure you that it will be sometime before we have our own weapon."

"Why did you not share this opinion before this?"

"It was not my place," Soltani said softly, fearful of being recorded. "And the setbacks occurred recently, sir."

"I am not pleased with you," Ahmadinejad frowned.

Soltani, now worried for his own safety, feared what the angry president might say next. "We don't have to use our own bomb," Soltani blurted.

"What are you saying? Do you think the Americans might sell us one of their old ones?"

"The Americans? No, sir, but the Russians already have," Soltani said, revealing something he knew should remain hidden from the madman sitting in front of him. "We have two, sir."

"Where are they now? When did we acquire them?" Ahmadinejad demanded, sitting straight, hands braced on his desk, dark eyes flashing.

"Ahvaz, sir, outside of Ahvaz, sir," Soltani referred to a southern Iranian city near the Iraqi border.

"Tell me more," Ahmadinejad ordered.

"We purchased them from secret funds in 1997. I understand that it was all handled by two officers acting with funds authorized by the Supreme Leader himself. They purchased them for one million dollars each from a dissident ex-Soviet officer."

"But how did they move them, hide them?"

"They are small bombs, one kiloton devices the size of a suitcase. We never learned how to use them. I'm told the Russian provided a manual. I've never seen it but..."

"One kiloton, the size of a suitcase?" Ahmadinejad could almost visualize the device. It was exactly what he needed. "And we have two?"

"Yes, sir," Soltani admitted reluctantly, privately cursing his own weakness. The little president's intense interest frightened Soltani, who too late realized he should have kept his mouth shut.

"And we have a manual that tells us how to detonate the suitcases?" Ahmadinejad pressed.

"Yes, sir."

"Can one person make this bomb work?"

"Presumably. I understand the Americans have such devices that can be carried on a soldier's back."

"Good," Ahmadinejad smiled. "We can always claim the CIA bungled again and exploded their own device."

Soltani, fearing he had already said too much, said nothing.

"Bring one to me," Ahmadinejad ordered.

"Here?" Soltani turned his head from side to side, staring wide-eyed at the office walls. "I don't know what condition the devices are in after all these years," Soltani admitted, his voice wavering.

"Not here, stupid. To Teheran, to a safe place, where I can examine it personally."

"Yes, sir," Soltani said. "But I will need assistance," he said. "It is stored in a bunker at an airfield in Ahvaz,"

"I don't care about all that," Ahmadinejad reacted. "I want to see this device tomorrow. Arrange it," he dismissed the shaken Minister.

****

Lila Baghai, who spent most of her days peeking out the window at the surveillants parked in front of their modest Natanz home, turned to her husband.

"They're not there now," she declared. "What does it mean?"

Obediah Baghai shrugged. "How do I know? They were there ten minutes ago." Obediah, a fatalist, had made peace with his fears; he was prepared to take whatever fate had in store for him. He had not anticipated that his revelations about his work to the visiting professor would have such sensational impact; however, despite his initial anxious reaction, he was privately proud that he had succeeded in changing the course of history, maybe. At least, he had tried. He was confident that the government, if they identified him as Thomas's source, would not harm Lila, and he was not afraid, now, to die for his actions, for doing what he thought right.

"I am so frightened," Lila said from her post at the window.

"I know."

"I wish..."

"Please," Obediah said as he stood up and joined his wife, placing a gentle hand over her mouth. "We discussed this," he whispered. "You know we cannot speak openly in this house. The walls have ears."

Lila nodded. Obediah withdrew his hand.

"Can we take a walk outside?" She asked softly.

"If they are not there," Obediah nodded in the direction of the road. "Who's to object."

As they started for the door, the phone rang. Lila turned to her husband, her face distorted by alarm. "Who is it?"

The phone had been silent for almost a week; it had not rung since their ordeal had begun.

"There is only one way to find out," Obediah shrugged.

"Kojas," Obediah picked up the phone.

"Obediah," Mehdi, his closest friend at the installation that they called "the laboratory" in public, surprised him. "We have received orders to report to work immediately."

"Everybody?"

"That's what I'm told."

"Who told you?"

"Sardar." Mehdi used the Persian word for 'Leader," a semi-code word they all used when talking about their supervisor in public. Even the names of their coworkers were classified, not to be used on the phone or when others might overhear.

"Sardar?" Obediah repeated.

"Yes."

"Really? Everybody? You and me?"

"Yes. Sardar ordered me to call everybody and pass the word."

"That's good news," Obediah said, then hesitated. "Tell me specifically what Sardar said. Did he actually say 'report to work?'"

"That's what he said," Mehdi confirmed.

"I hope he meant what he said," Obediah observed as an image of all the scientists standing side-by-side in the desolate desert with armed men pointing rifles at them flashed through his mind.

"Do you want to ride with me?" Mehdi asked, deliberately trying to keep his friend from making another injudicious comment on the phone.

"Yes," Obediah picked up on the unspoken warning. Friends facing danger did so silently but together.

"I'll pick you up in fifteen minutes," Mehdi said.

"I'll be ready," Obediah said.

As soon as her husband left the house, a very nervous Lila dialed her brother in Kashan.

"Kojas," her sister-in-law Anahi, answered the phone.

"Anahi, I am so worried," Lila said. "Can I speak with Mehtab?"

"He's at school, Lila," Anahi said. "Is there something I can help you with?"

"Obediah just left. They've ordered him back to work," Lila said.

Those words shocked Anahi, and she did not immediately respond. They could signify very good news or very bad.

"They just called him and ordered him to report to the laboratory immediately. I don't know what it means," Lila said, fighting back the tears.

"I'm sure it is good news, Lila," Anahi tried to reassure her sister-in-law while fearful thoughts raced through her mind as she tried to assess what the news meant to her and Mehtab. Mehtab was a simple physics teacher, but he had facilitated forbidden meetings between his American relative and Anahi's brother, Obediah. "Was Obediah pleased with the news?" Anahi asked, undermining the reassurance she had tried to project.

"He was pleased to get back to his important work," Lila said. "But...," she sobbed and did not finish her sentence.

"I know," Anahi said as she brushed back her own tears. She feared for her brother and at the same time worried about her own family. They had all been so stupid to take such chances. The regime's plans, no matter how terrible, were none of their business. "I'll call Mahube," Anahi referred to her mother-in-law in Teheran, "and see what she has heard."

"Please have Mehtab give me a call as soon as he can," Lila said. "I'm so alone."

"I'm sure that Obediah will come home after a busy day with good news," Anahi tried to convey an optimism she did not feel."

"Thank you," Lila blurted and hung up.

Anahi did not try to reach her husband. She knew he was in class and beyond the reach of the phone. Instead, she dialed the number of Mehtab's mother, Mahube, in Teheran.

"Kojas," Mahube answered.

"It's me," Anahi said. "I just talked with Lila. She says they have ordered Obediah back to work."

"That's good news," Mahube said.

"We hope so," Anahi said. "Lila did not seem sure what it all meant. Have you heard anything?"

"I have no news. The papers are filled with nonsense, and all the people are talking about is that atomic bomb business," Mahube said.

"What are they saying? Do they know where...the American got his information?"

"Nobody knows. They just listen to CNN and play on the Internet. I don't do either."

"Have you talked with Manujeh lately?" Anahi was desperate so she pressed.

"No, I told you about our last conversation. Have you talked with Mansour? How is he doing?"

"He hasn't called me. All I know is what Manujeh told you, and I'm worried about him, all alone in that strange country."

"I'm sure he is doing fine. Both Mehtab and Obediah loved it, and so will Mansour after he learns their strange customs."

"You're probably right, Mahube. Could you please call Manujeh and see what she has heard. You know why we are so worried," Anahi said, her voice breaking as she spoke.

"I know. Both you and Lila need to get out of the house."

"Please," Anahi asked.

"I will call Manujeh and let you know what she says," Mahube said. "She wasn't very happy with me last time. She's still suffering from the loss of her only child," Mahube said. "But I will do it. The family must stay together during these trying times."

"Thank you so much," Anahi said and hung up.

Chapter 16

Chase drove directly from the White House to his office. Theresa's chair was vacant, and Chase joined Barney in his office.

"Welcome home, detective," Barney greeted him with a smile. "The chief's been calling."

"Chief? Chief? Have I met this fellow?" Chase smiled as he collapsed in the softest chair in the room.

"He remembers you. I'm not sure how fondly," Barney left his desk and took the chair opposite Chase.

"You won't believe where I've been," Chase said.

"Try me."

"I've just had a little chat with the president."

"And did the president of George Mason ask you the same question that the chief asked me?" Barney played the game. "Have you identified our murderer yet?"

"That is not the question that the other president asked me in his little odd shaped office," Chase said.

"You're referring to that office in that white building across the river?"

"That's the one," Chase smiled. "Some call it the White House."

"Was that gentleman's name Feathersomething?"

"Featherstone. That's the guy."

"And you had a chat with him? Don't tell me he's on your suspect list," Barney said. "The chief's not going to believe this."

"Who's going to tell him?"

"You are," Barney said, rising from his chair.

"Don't you want to know what this Featherstone guy wanted to discuss?" Chase asked.

"I don't want to waste your time," Barney said. "By making you tell the story twice."

"Are you sure the chief will want to see us?"

"I'm sure. I suspect he will insist on it as soon as we tell him where you have been spending your mornings."

"It wasn't a long conversation," Chase said as he followed Barney out the door.

They took the elevator to the 7th floor and were quickly admitted to the inner office where they found the chief sitting at his desk intently studying the *Post* sports section.

"I don't know who is in bigger trouble," Chief Raymond Arthur greeted them. "The Redskins or the *Post.* I can remember when the Redskins could actually win a ball game, and the *Post* could afford a six page sports section."

"As bad as the Redskins, Wizards, and Nationals are, three pages are two too many," Chase said as he and Barney took the chairs facing the chief's desk.

"You're going to have to give up newspapers, chief," Barney said.

"I already have," Arthur said. "I keep the *Post* around to amuse my occasional visitors. It's good seeing you again, lieutenant," Arthur looked at Chase. "I can't remember when you last visited. Have you been keeping busy?"

"I don't like to waste your time when I have nothing to report," Chase smiled.

"And your unscheduled appearance means you have identified the murderer? Or is that too much to hope for?"

"There have been developments on the Townsend side of the investigation," Chase said.

"Since you did not answer my question, lieutenant, I assume your response is a negative."

"I'm still trying to find a useful witness," Chase admitted honestly. "I just came from the White House where I had a meeting with President Featherstone."

Chief Arthur leaned back in his chair and stared at Chase before turning to Barney. "Major, please tell me my ears are malfunctioning. I swear Lieutenant Mansfield just said he visited with President Featherstone."

Before Barney could think of a proper response, Chase continued. "Special Agent Cotton and I were comparing notes on our respective investigations this morning at the Townsend house when coincidentally an e-mail arrived from the kidnappers."

Chief Arthur sat up straight and waited for Chase to continue.

"It was a short one. The kidnappers, whoever they might be, directed that one hundred million dollars be wired to an account in an offshore bank in the Cayman Islands."

"One hundred million dollars," the chief repeated.

"Yes, a nice tidy sum," Chase confirmed.

"And since the United States Government doesn't negotiate with terrorists, what is the FBI going to do?"

"Responsibility for that decision was kicked up to the White House," Chase said.

"Please tell me, lieutenant, that you did not meet with the president to help him decide what to do," Arthur said. "I thought it was agreed that the FBI is handling the Townsend disappearance, and you are investigating the Jesperson murder."

"That's correct sir. I met with Cotton at the Townsend house only to compare notes on our investigations. Secretary Townsend was one of the last persons to meet with Professor Jesperson, and it is imperative that I interview him in depth as soon as possible."

"And you find it inconvenient that Secretary Townsend has been kidnapped," Chief Arthur pretended to find that amusing.

"Yes sir."

"And you accompanied Special Agent Cotton to the White House to advise the president what to do?" Arthur asked.

"No sir. Special Agent Cotton met his director at the White House, and I assume they met with the president."

"And why does that concern you, lieutenant?"

"I had an appointment in Reston with another witness," Chase said. He deliberately did not admit that his appointment consisted of lunch at Paolo's with the very attractive Lady in Black.

"And how in the hell did you get involved with the president?"

"That happened later. While I was meeting with the witness, Special Agent Cotton called and ordered me to report forthwith to the White House."

"And you always do what the FBI orders you to do?" Arthur stared at his often insubordinate subordinate.

"I told Special Agent Cotton that the White House was out of my jurisdiction, and Cotton replied that the president wanted to meet with me forthwith. He said the president was working on a deadline."

"And?"

"And I did what I was told. I parked behind the Executive Office Building and was rushed into the president's office," Chase said.

"I'm sure that your Prius enjoyed its space, and the president, who apparently had nothing better to do, was delighted to meet you, an old friend."

"Sir, I've never before been to the White House or met this president or any other," Chase said.

"I'm relieved to hear that. What did this president say? Did he congratulate you for your failure to identify Professor Jesperson's killer?"

"The president told me he was working on a deadline and showed me the e-mail message from the Townsend kidnappers. I assured him I had read the message, understood the deadline, but also stressed that there was nothing I could do or say about it."

"And that is what he wanted to hear?"

"He told me to relax, that he wasn't trying to borrow one hundred million dollars from me."

"Very funny."

"That's what he said, sir. He then asked me to confirm that I was in charge of the Jesperson investigation." Chase waited for Chief Arthur to react, but he said nothing, so Chase continued. "He said he had two questions he needed to ask me about my investigation. The first was, 'have you identified the shooter?' I answered in the negative. The second question was, 'Do you have any reason to suspect Secretary Townsend was the shooter?'"

"And what did you say? God, I hope you didn't say Townsend was a suspect."

"I hesitated. Obviously, if it wasn't for the two e-mails, I would consider Townsend a suspect. His unexplained absence, combined with the fact he was one of the last persons to see Jesperson alive, would rank him high on any investigator's list. Also, because I had agreed to let the FBI deal with his disappearance, I haven't been able to probe the Jesperson/Townsend relationship for a possible motive."

"Did you tell the president this?"

"I told him 'Secretary Townsend's absence, those e-mails, and the Bureau's assumption of responsibility for investigating Townsend's disappearance, have precluded me from investigating the possibility that he was the shooter. Under normal circumstances, the secretary would have been my primary suspect. I can only say I do not know.'"

"I guess your answer could have been worse," Arthur admitted, reluctantly.

"It was the truth sir."

"I know. Was that all you said?"

Chase smiled. "I asked the president if he thought it possible that Secretary Townsend was the shooter."

"Oh shit," Arthur frowned.

"The president handled my question with aplomb," Chase said.

"With aplomb?" the chief erupted. "What in the hell does that mean, lieutenant? Aplomb, for Christ sake," Arthur glanced at Barney, expecting agreement.

Barney shrugged.

"The president was quite reasonable," Chase answered. "He said he knew he owed me a response. He said that just between the two of us he had been worried about Townsend for the past two months. He said their jobs were man killers, and that Townsend has been under considerable strain. At that point me thanked me and sent me on my way."

Chief Arthur thought for a few seconds and then asked, "Does the president really think that Townsend was the shooter?"

"I don't know, but I suspect he might."

"A hundred million dollars is a lot of money," the chief changed the subject. "Where are they going to get it?"

Chase raised both hands upwards, indicating he had no idea. "I hope they find it, and Townsend eventually reappears because I have a few questions I want to ask him," Chase said.

"I'm sure you do," Arthur said, abruptly dismissing them.

As Chase approached the door, Arthur called after him, "Lieutenant, the next time the president needs your advice, let me know, in advance."

When Chase and Barney were back in the elevator, Barney turned to him.

"Chase, what are you going to do now?"

"If I don't get another summons from the president, I think I'll visit a couple of foreign students out at George Mason to see how they are adjusting to life on campus," Chase smiled.

****

"Lieutenant," Theresa greeted Chase when they reached the CIB reception room. "Check your phone messages."

"Good day, Ms. D'Angelo," Chase smiled. "How was your morning?"

"Great, until you walked in," Theresa smiled back.

Chase turned to Barney. "I do believe the staff is a wee bit stressed, today," Chase said.

"I suggest it might be best if we let them work it out for themselves," Barney said. "And I think I will pay a visit to the Townsend home to see what is happening."

"Please give me a heads up if Secretary Townsend reappears," Chase said.

"Do you think the Townsend family financial situation may have improved dramatically recently?" Barney asked.

Teresa stared at the two, obviously interested in the cryptic exchange, but she asked no questions until Chase disappeared into his office. Then, Teresa followed Barney and asked, "Have they heard from the kidnappers?"

Barney responded with a wink that irritated Teresa more than it satisfied her curiosity.

"I've have a few errands to run," Barney said as he started for the door. "You can reach me on my cell."

"You're getting more like him every day," Teresa called as the door closed behind Barney.

In his small office, Chase found his inbox filled with paper and several phone messages scattered about the desktop. He ignored the inbox and leafed through the messages until he found three that interested him, all from Professor Jesperson in Cambridge. They had a common theme, please call.

Chase sat down in his chair and retrieved his cell phone from his suit coat pocket. He checked his notebook, found the elder Professor Jesperson's number, and poked it into his cell phone. To his surprise, Professor Jesperson answered on the third ring.

"Jesperson," the deep male voice identified itself.

"Professor, Chase Mansfield," Chase said as he pondered the oddity that it was most difficult to identify a person's age by the sound of his telephone voice. The senior Jesperson was in his eighties but his telephone voice could be that of a thirty year old.

"Lieutenant, finally," Jesperson let his exasperation show.

"I know," Chase said. "I apologize for not returning your calls sooner, but I spend as little time in the office as possible, and I just found the messages on my desk. How can I help you?"

"I just wanted to find out how your investigation is proceeding. My son may be in the ground, but I'm still interested in seeing that his killer is apprehended."

"I understand, sir. I'm working the case full time, but I regret to say I have yet to identify the shooter. I'm having a very difficult time identifying your son's friends, those who can assist in helping me track down Doctor Jesperson's movements during the period since his return from Iran."

"Thomas was something of a loner, lieutenant, but that's not a crime, is it?"

"No sir, I was merely expressing my frustration. Have you by chance thought of anyone I might contact here who might help?"

"Academics live in an intellectual world, just like writers, lieutenant. Given your other career, I assumed you of all people would understand that."

"Yes..."

"The more senior those of us in the teaching profession become," Jesperson spoke over Chase, "and the less time we spend in class talking to disinterested students, the more we focus on our own thoughts while researching our subjects. During the past year, Thomas concentrated exclusively on Iran and his book."

"Yes, sir," Chase said, giving the old man time to talk himself out.

"I noticed you met that Kendrick girl at the funeral," Jesperson said, changing his focus slightly. "I never liked her. I always felt she was more interested in using Thomas than she was in him as a person."

"Really?"

"Yes. I don't know what she was doing at the funeral. Manujeh did not appreciate her temerity. She and Thomas parted, thank God, a year ago before he went to Iran."

"I think she just wanted to say goodbye to your son, professor," Chase said.

"I doubt it. Kendrick is a user. I'm sure she had something else in mind. Did you have a useful conversation?" Jesperson asked.

"We happened to take the same flight back to D.C.," Chase said, not replying to the professor's question. He had nothing to share.

"You didn't answer my question."

"I do not believe she saw your son recently," Chase said. "As best as I can tell the decision to go their separate ways was a mutual decision."

"He dumped her," Jesperson insisted. "Can you make the media go away?"

"Have they been bothering you?"

"The phone never stops ringing. At least, they've stopped knocking on the door," Jesperson said. "And my wife complains about them constantly. For some reason she thinks it is my fault."

"It's the book," Chase said. "I'm sure your son's agent and publisher are encouraging them."

"I don't understand the damned media. They're nothing but a bunch of bubble headed kids," Jesperson said.

"At least they're promoting book sales," Chase said, thinking of the more modest reception of his puny efforts.

"Fat lot money means to Thomas now," Jesperson said. "At least Thomas would have appreciated the sales figures, but I'm not sure he would have liked the reviews, particularly the *Times*."

At least he's getting reviews, Chase thought. He was tempted to ask how Jesperson's son's estate would be handled; he was particularly interested in knowing who would benefit from the best seller profits, but he decided common courtesy and continued rapport with the parents required a deferral of those questions to a later date.

"Do you by chance know where Mansour is now?" Chase changed the subject.

"The little jerk attended the funeral and then took off with his Iranian friend. He's more interested in himself than the feelings of others."

"He's still young," Chase defended the boy with contrived compassion.

"He's old enough to have some manners," Jesperson said. "My wife is constantly in tears, but she still worries about her poor relative. She's driving me crazy. Mansour's the spoiled son of her nephew; that makes him a goddamned grandnephew, nothing more. They share a handful of genes, not very impressive genes at that. He's a zero to me, and my wife insists on using Thomas' new but hard earned wealth to support the delinquent. I'm tempted to tell the media the kid was Thomas' source."

"I'm afraid that would cause serious problems for your wife's Iranian relatives," Chase said.

"Oh don't worry. I'll keep my mouth shut. The old lady would make my life more miserable than she usually does if I offered an opinion."

"Do you know where Mansour is living?" Chase persisted.

"I'm sure he's camping out in Thomas's apartment," Jesperson said. "My wife insisted on it. She's also paying all his expenses and giving him an allowance. Since he's too dumb to get a scholarship, I don't understand why he can't get a job flipping burgers and work his way through college like most American kids do."

"Have you remembered anything more about Thomas's lifestyle since his return from Iran?" Chase again changed the subject. "I still need to talk with anybody who can help me track his recent movements."

"Can't help you there. Thomas never discussed his friends and social life with me. Neither of us was big on small talk; it's too bad he never asked me my opinion of that Kendrick person. I could have saved him a lot of heartburn."

"Maybe, Mrs. Jesperson could help me," Chase suggested, also not interested in discussing the Lady in Black with the old man.

Jesperson answered with a laugh. "She doesn't talk with anyone but her relatives in Iran. Now that's a chatty family. You should see our phone bill. Our primary topic of conversation is her poor me syndrome."

"I hope they don't discuss anything sensitive," Chase said. "I'm sure the Iranian authorities are working hard to identify your son's sources."

"You mean watch out for phone taps and that kind of stuff," Jesperson chuckled.

"We live in a highly technological age," Chase said.

"I don't listen to her conversations. She talks with her sister, and they both worry a lot, but I don't think they use names."

"You might suggest to her that conversations today require considerable discretion. One never knows who might be listening."

"Good thought, lieutenant. I'll tell her, but she won't listen. She'll just accuse me of trying to keep her from talking with her family. She knows my views about her relatives."

"If anything comes to your attention that you think might help my investigation," Chase said. "I would appreciate you giving me a call."

"I doubt that I'll come across anything useful," Jesperson said. "I don't talk with many people these days, never with anyone from your area."

"And if your wife should learn anything..." Chase said.

"Of course, and when you finally identify the shooter, please let us know," Jesperson said. "Have you learned what happened to James?"

"Townsend? He's still missing," Chase said, deliberately not discussing the messages from the kidnappers.

"I haven't seen anything in the media about his disappearance," Jesperson said.

"The Bureau is trying to keep it that way," Chase cautioned.

"Don't worry. They won't hear it from me."

"Well if there is nothing else, professor," Chase tried to terminate the conversation.

"There is one more thing," Jesperson said after a brief pause.

"Yes?" Chase reacted, now alert.

"If you could find some reason to arrest my wife's kin, that Mansour, you won't hear any objections from me," Jesperson chuckled.

Chase politely laughed. "I'll keep that in mind, professor, but I'm not sure Mrs. Jesperson would approve."

"Not to worry. Inquisitive she isn't. Her focus is quite narrow; in fact, I'm no longer surprised at how much she doesn't know; haven't been for years, make that decades," Jesperson said and hung up.

****

After his conversation with Jesperson, Chase decided it was time to visit Mansour Taheri at Doctor Jesperson's Waples Mill condominium off Route 50 in Fairfax, a short ten minute drive from his office. He parked the Prius in an empty space in the adjacent lot and took the elevator to the condominium, not fully confident he would find Mansour there. Not wanting to alert the youth that he was coming, he had not called. Chase tapped on the door and waited. When no one responded, he knocked harder. He was about to give up when the door opened suddenly, and a frowning Jamshid Afgar glared at him.

"What now, lieutenant?" The surly Iranian graduate student greeted him.

"Where's Mansour?" Chase answered with a question.

"Do you have a warrant?" Afgar demanded.

"What business is that of yours?" Chase asked.

"I live here now," Afgar replied.

Chase pushed past Afgar and headed for the living room, leaving Afgar standing near the still open door.

"Do you pay rent?" Chase asked as he settled on the soft sofa.

"That is none of your business," Afgar said as he slammed the door shut.

"Yes it is. You don't have a very good grasp of American law, do you?" Chase bluffed.

Afgar did not answer.

"This is still a crime scene," Chase said.

"No it isn't, lieutenant," Afgar smiled. "Professor Jesperson was murdered in his office. That's the crime scene."

"And this is his residence," Chase said, pretending that it mattered. "How do you know where he was murdered Mr. Afgar? Were you there?"

"Don't try to be clever with me, lieutenant."

"I won't. I'm confident you wouldn't understand if I did. Tell Mansour to come out. I have questions for both of you, and I'm not leaving until you answer them."

"And if we don't?"

"Then, I'll simply arrest the two of you and take you in handcuffs to headquarters where I will lock you up until you answer my questions," Chase smiled.

"On what charge?"

"You've been watching too many television shows, Jamshid," Chase said. "Material witness will do just fine until I charge you with something more serious."

Afgar did not react.

"Tell Mansour to get his ass out here. I'm tired of playing games," Chase ordered.

Afgar glared at Chase but finally closed the hall door. Chase wondered if Marsha Hillencotter, the observant neighbor, had listened to that exchange. Afgar did not speak, but it did not matter. Mansour who had been listening from a nearby bedroom materialized.

"Good morning, Mansour," Chase smiled. "Please sit there," he pointed at the chair to his immediate right. "And you," Chase looked at Afgar. "Land there," Chase indicated a chair to his left.

"You can't tell me what to do in my own apartment," Mansour said.

Chase laughed. "Mansour, you and Jamshid have much to learn about what I can and cannot do. Your English has certainly improved since our last conversation. I congratulate you."

"I am a good learner," Mansour said.

"Why did you pretend you had difficulty understanding and answering my simple questions?" Chase asked, not admitting that the young

Iranian had succeeded in making him believe he could not speak very good English.

Mansour shrugged.

"Did you know it is against the law to lie to a police officer?" Chase asked.

"That's bullshit," Afgar laughed. "Don't believe a word he says, Mansour. You don't have to say anything without a lawyer present."

"Do you think you need a lawyer Mansour?" Chase asked.

"Just leave," Afgar said.

"I want to know what you two are doing in this apartment," Chase said.

"It is my apartment," Mansour said sullenly.

"Do you own it?" Chase asked.

Mansour shook his head.

"Is your name on the lease?"

"No, but I have my relative's permission to live here. You can ask her," Mansour said.

"You are speaking about Mrs. Manujeh Jesperson?"

"Yes. Ask her. She said I could stay here as long as I want," Mansour said.

"Are you here on a student visa?" Chase asked.

"He is. And he is now enrolled for next semester at George Mason," Afgar said.

"When was the last time you saw Doctor Jesperson?" Chase asked Mansour, ignoring Afgar.

Mansour shrugged.

"And when did you?" Chase turned on Afgar.

Afgar, mimicking Mansour, shrugged.

Irritated by Afgar's belligerent attitude, Chase pressed. "How long have you been in this country on your student visa?"

"Ten years."

"And how long do you plan to stay?"

"As long as it takes."

"Who pays your expenses?" Chase asked.

"My family," Afgar smiled.

"Don't you think it is about time that you thought about a job?"

"Not on a student visa. That would be illegal."

"In your own country."

"I will when the time comes."

"Who is your dissertation advisor?"

"Doctor Jesperson."

"Have you consulted with him recently?"

"I haven't felt the need."

"When you do, you might have difficulty locating him."

"I'm sure the History Department will suggest another."

"Where in Iran does your family live?"

"Why do you ask? Are you thinking of visiting them?"

"Just answer my question," Chase said, now irritated by the arrogant Iranian.

"Teheran," Afgar said. "Have you ever visited there?"

Chase did not answer.

"Have you ever been outside of this country?" Afgar asked.

Mansour smiled, encouraging his friend.

Afgar suddenly stood up and nodded at Mansour while speaking to Chase. "And now, lieutenant, you are going to have to forgive me and my friend."

Chase remained seated and waited for Afgar to elaborate, anticipating the brash Iranian would say something he shouldn't.

"I have work to do in the library, and Mansour has a class," Afgar said.

"I thought you were enrolled for classes beginning next semester," Chase ignored Afgar and addressed Mansour.

"He's auditing English as a second language," Afgar answered for Mansour.

"Does Afgar always speak for you?" Chase tried again with Mansour.

"He's my friend," Mansour smiled at Afgar.

"How do you get from here to the campus?" Chase asked, abruptly changing the topic, trying to keep Mansour off guard. He recalled Mrs. Hillencotter's complaints about the ancient Beetle with a dented fender.

"I have a car, Mansour said.

"A Beetle?" Chase let Mansour know he had been checking on him.

Mansour shook his head negatively. "The Beetle is broke."

"A Lexus," Afgar laughed.

"Is that true?" Chase asked Mansour. Chase recalled his inspection of Doctor Thomas Jesperson's vehicle in the George Mason lot, a late model Lexus.

Mansur answered with a nod.

"A nice car," Chase said. "Did you buy it?"

"Mansour has rich American relatives," Afgar again answered for his friend.

"What relatives?" Chase continued to address Mansour.

"The Jespersons," Afgar said. "Book sales are very good."

"If I'm not mistaken," Chase said. "Doctor Jesperson had a Lexus. Are you driving his car?"

Mansour nodded again.

"Do you have the Jespersons permission, or did you just find the key and start driving?"

"Of course he has permission," Afgar declared.

Chase made a mental note to ask Doctor Jesperson about the car business. He suspected Mrs. Jesperson had authorized Mansour to drive the Lexus without discussing it with Doctor Jesperson. Otherwise, he assumed Jesperson would have mentioned it.

"I'm sure Doctor Jesperson will be very pleased to learn that you two are enjoying this apartment and his son's Lexus," Chase said as he stood up.

"Does it bother you, lieutenant, that two poor Iranian boys are benefitting from the sales of a book that maligns the Iranian government?" Afgar asked.

That aggressive question surprised Chase, but he decided not to debate the issue for now. He recalled the advice of his training partner at Chase's first crime scene; "always look carefully at those who gained from the crime." Chase had other calls to make and opted to defer his remaining questions to another time when he could confront the more pliable Mansour without the arrogant Afgar standing by as a defensive crutch.

"Not at all," Chase dismissed Afgar's interesting question and started for the door where he paused to say, "I look forward to discussing with both of you Doctor Jesperson's book and the fact you feel it maligns the current government."

"I suggest you read it first, lieutenant," Afgar said rudely.

"I will, and I advise the two of you not to leave Fairfax County without my permission," Chase said. "That is an official order, not a suggestion."

"Do you also work for INS and the State Department, lieutenant?" Afgar asked.

"I'm speaking for the Fairfax County Police Department," Chase said. "If you don't want an introductory tour of our local correctional system, you had best listen to what I say."

Chase turned and departed, irritated that the boys had gotten the best of him. They had forced him to fall back on trite threats.

Frustrated by his failure to make progress in his investigation, Chase drove directly to the George Mason campus in a very determined mood. As he entered Robinson Hall, he acknowledged that he had allowed himself to be distracted by peripheral issues and had not paid sufficient attention to the crime scene and Doctor Thomas Jesperson's campus associates. George Mason University was where the professor spent most of his days, and it was where he died. Although the victim obviously was a self-contained man, a loner, logic told Chase that at least one, maybe more than one, of Jesperson's associates knew more about the man than anyone had admitted to date, and of course that person had not shared that information because Chase had not made himself available to hear it. He had chatted with Nicholas Dizekes, Jesperson's graduate assistant, and then had gone charging off chasing leads that conversation had developed. He had left the rest of the initial interviews with Jesperson's Robinson Hall associates to Detective Jane Moscowitz and her crime scene crew. Chase now intended to correct his initial oversights. Chase privately acknowledged that he had a tendency to over rely on his intuition and shortchanged the plodding but tried and proven professional approach. When that happened, he forced himself to retrace his steps, and that is what he now intended to do.

He started with Jesperson's office. He removed the crime scene tape and entered the dark room. He turned on the light and sat down behind Jesperson's desk. Little appeared to have changed since his initial visit. Even the bottle of Araq, the odd absinthe that Jesperson had shared with his friend Secretary Townsend, stood forlornly in the center of the desk. The techs had bagged the glasses and carried them off to their lab for further study. Bloodstains under the chair still marked where Jesperson had died. Powder residue on the door, the desk, the bookcases, the chairs, and file cabinets testified to the crime scene techs due diligence. Chase flipped through the papers and books on the professor's desktop and opened the desk drawers one by one. Nothing caught his attention; not a single oddity collided with any of the details he had gathered elsewhere. Chase leaned back and stared at the ceiling as he reviewed the case. He was missing something and sensed it, a not uncommon occurrence.

Suddenly, someone tapped on the door. Chase stifled his irritation at the interruption and forced himself to call, "Come in."

The door opened and Nicholas Dizekes, Jesperson's graduate assistant, cautiously poked his head into the room.

"I noticed the torn tape," Dizekes referred to police scene marker, "and hoped it might be you, lieutenant," Dizekes said.

"Have a seat," Chase invited. "Have you thought of anything we should have discussed and didn't?"

"No sir. How is the investigating progressing?" Dizekes asked as he took a chair facing the desk.

"Slowly. I'm having great difficulty identifying anyone who knew the professor as well as you did," Chase said, flattering the graduate student before probing deeper into the young man's assessment of his reticent advisor.

"I've been thinking a lot about Doctor Jesperson," Dizekes said. "Frankly, I miss him more than I thought I would. It's a shame he didn't get a chance to enjoy his book's success. It's already a worldwide best seller. Life's unfair."

"I suspect he anticipated the book would have an impact," Chase said. "And I hope you're getting credit for all you did to assist him."

"Nobody knows about me; Doctor Jesperson deserves all the credit," Dizekes said, not doing a very good job of concealing his disappointment. "I just helped with the grunt work."

"I'm sure that the rest of the faculty knows better than that," Chase said. "Has Doctor Adams congratulated you?" Chase referred to the department chairman.

Dizekes forced a laugh and shook his head. "Doctor Adams and the faculty are too busy trying to capture some of the limelight for themselves to worry about me," Dizekes said sourly.

Chase let that slide. He knew how self-centered some professors could be, and he did not criticize them for that. In the bigger universities they lived in a publish or perish environment and depended on their own output for advancement. It really wasn't a team effort.

"Doctor Adams is going to appear on Gordon Peterson's talk show this weekend. The focus is going to be on Iran, The Nuclear Threat. I doubt that Adams even knows where Iran is. His specialty is the Arab world, and Iranians are Moslems but not Arabs."

"If they are going to discuss Doctor Jesperson's book, they should have invited you to participate," Chase suggested. He hoped he had not overdone it, come across as too patronizing.

"I could only tell them about how Doctor Jesperson put the book together, the mechanics, that sort of thing," Dizekes said, apparently taking Chase's overdone flattery in stride. "They should have Doctor Jalili on the program if they really want someone who knows Iran. She was born there."

"Doctor Jalili?" This was the first time Chase had heard the name mentioned.

"Didn't I tell you about her?"

"I don't believe so," Chase said, wondering what else Dizekes had failed to tell him.

"Doctor Jalili is one of my favorites," Dizekes smiled. "She's just an instructor, but everyone says that she is going to get this office." Dizekes looked around the room to stress his point. "I hope so. She's now serving as my faculty advisor, and I'm grading papers for her survey courses."

"Tell me a little about her," Chase said. "How did she and Doctor Jesperson get along?"

"I don't think they knew each other very well. Doctor Jalili arrived after Jesperson left for his sabbatical. She sort of filled in for him while he was in Iran, so she's a natural to replace him. She's much younger than Doctor Jesperson, so I guess that works against her, but all the students like her, and she's a good looker too. At least all the males think so. I suspect the girls are just jealous."

"She sounds a natural. Where did she get her doctorate?" Chase asked.

"That's impressive too. She speaks four languages, and she has her PhD from the University of Paris."

"University of Paris? Is she French?"

"Oh no. She's a native Iranian. She graduated from the University of Teheran and then went to Paris for graduate school."

"Did Doctor Jesperson discuss his book with her?" Chase asked.

"I doubt it," Dizekes answered immediately. "I'm the only one who had access to Doctor Jesperson's book."

"I'm surprised that Doctor Jesperson didn't discussed things Iranian with Doctor Jalili," Chase said.

"I never saw the two of them chatting, not ever," Dizekes said.

"Not in the halls or over lunch? They had a common interest, Iran. You don't think Doctor Jesperson, a bachelor, found her attractive?"

"He was almost fifty," Dizekes smiled.

"Too old to think about girls," Chase laughed. "I'm almost forty-five, and I still notice nice figures."

"You're different, lieutenant, not bookish like Doctor Jesperson," Dizekes shrugged. "Doctor Jalili is probably thirty, at most, but she doesn't look that old."

"You make her sound interesting," Chase said, ignoring, the implication that thirty was over the hill. "Where's her office?"

"At the end of the hall. Last door on the right," Dizekes said. "She's built like a brick shithouse, but hippy, like most Iranian girls."

Chase had the impression that the young man was trying to discourage him with his last comment; besides, any shithouses, brick or not, that Chase had seen were all quite rectangular. He wondered how many Iranian girls Dizekes had met in his short lifetime but changed the subject.

"The last time we talked," Chase said, "I asked if Doctor Jesperson had any close friends on the faculty that you knew of, and you answered in the negative. Now that you've had time to think about it, is there anybody on campus who was close to Doctor Jesperson? I'm having great difficulty finding anybody who knew him more than casually. I find that very unusual. Everybody seemed to like him."

Dizekes answered with a shake of his head. "Doctor Jesperson was very reserved. He treated everyone alike, even me. He was friendly, but he never asked about your private life, and he never discussed anything about his."

"What did he do for recreation?"

"I don't think he did anything."

"Never watched movies, never mentioned the Redskins or Wizards, played tennis or golf?"

"He discussed class work, books about the Middle East, Iran, things like that. He didn't talk about his own research with anybody."

"Not even you?"

"He gave me assignments, but we never had any intellectual discussions. He kept his opinions to himself."

"Very strange."

"All professors are strange," Dizekes laughed. "Here, he was pretty much like everyone else. Very self-centered and focused, but not absent minded like some."

"And you want to be a professor?"

"Why not? They have an easy life. All they have to do is teach a couple of classes a week and write a book every couple of years. It's a good deal, unlike ours. Nobody's taking pot shots at them all the time."

Chase smiled and waited for Dizekes to realize what he had said.

"Oh shit," Dizekes focused. "Except for Jesperson. Somebody shot him."

"I wonder why anyone would want to shoot someone like Doctor Jesperson." Chase said. "It doesn't appear to me that he bothered anyone."

"Just those Iranians," Dizekes said seriously. "I'm sure they're not happy with that book of his."

"Have you heard any of the foreign students discussing the book?"

"No, they keep pretty much to themselves. I've tried talking with some, but they don't seem to like Americans very much. At least none of the Near Eastern types do."

"Why do you think that is?"

"Jealous, I guess." Dizekes thought briefly. "Doctor Jalili isn't that way. She has a green card and plans on becoming an American citizen."

Chase nodded. "Dizekes," he said. "Dizekes, your name sounds Greek."

Dizekes laughed. "It sure is. My parents were born here, but my grandparents on both sides were immigrants. Greeks aren't anything like the Arabs. We like life, people, girls, particularly girls."

"I've noticed that," Chase said. "Obviously, you're an extrovert. Are you sure you want to spend your life buried in books like Doctor Jesperson did?"

"Life is what you make of it," Dizekes grinned. "I think I'll be able to handle all of it. I suppose you've noticed there are lots of good looking girls on campus."

"I've noticed, but don't forget it won't be long before you are too old for the undergraduates."

"Maybe," Dizekes smiled. "Depends on the person."

"You're right," Chase said. "Doctor Jesperson obviously was preoccupied with affairs of the mind, books, not people."

"That was him," Dizekes said.

"Well, I've enjoyed our chat, Nicholas. If anything else occurs to you that you think might help me with my investigation, please give me a call," Chase said as he handed a card to the confident young man. "Now, I'll see if I can have a little chat with Doctor Jalili."

"I'm sure she's in her office," Dizekes said. "In fact, I'm sure she is. I just came from there. She's got forty-five minutes before her next lecture."

Dizekes followed Chase out of Jesperson's office and watched as Chase restored the police scene tape. When finished, Chase smiled at Dizekes and said, "last door on the right?"

"I can come with you if you want, lieutenant," Dizekes eagerly volunteered.

"That won't be necessary, Nicholas. I find it best if I conduct my interviews one on one. People react differently if there is a third person present."

"Right," Dizekes said, not hiding his disappointment as he turned to his left. "I'll be in my little cubby hole if you need me."

Chase checked the signs on the doors as he made his way to Jalili's office. The last door on the right had a stenciled sign, "Doctor Jalili." Chase tapped on the door, and a husky feminine voice answered, "Come in."

Chase opened the door and found himself in an office that was half the size of the one he had just left. Windows on two sides greatly reduced the wall space, limiting the number of bookcases that could be accommodated. Books dominated the room on two sides, but the windows with a clear view of the campus provided a sense of openness. An attractive Doctor Jalili sat behind the desk with half-lens reading glasses perched on her nose. She had short, dark hair, a pleasant smile, and prominent breasts displayed in a bright red sweater set. Chase could not see her skirt, legs, or backside; Dizekes had described her as hippy.

"Yes?" Jalili peered at Chase over the top of her glasses.

"I apologize for the interruption," Chase offered his most disarming smile. "I am Lieutenant Mansfield, and I am in charge of the Doctor Jesperson investigation." He waved his credential case.

"Oh," was all Jalali said.

"I am in the process of consulting Doctor Jesperson's faculty colleagues and would appreciate the chance to ask you a few questions," Chase said.

"I certainly welcome the opportunity to assist as I can," Jalili smiled as she placed her reading glasses on the desk next to a small vase of dried flowers. "But I must warn you that my acquaintance with Doctor Jesperson was quite limited. He was on sabbatical when I arrived, and we have been faculty mates for only a brief period. I'm sure that there are others who knew him far better than I."

"I understand, Doctor Jalali, and I will be quite brief. I rather hoped that your background had given you unique insights."

"Nicely put, lieutenant," Jalili laughed. "You refer, of course, to my nationality."

"That and the subject matter of Doctor Jesperson's research," Chase said.

"I'm a historian not a physicist," Jalili smiled. "Let me assure you I was not Doctor Jesperson's confidential source. I do not know the source's identity, and I have had no contact with officials or agents of the current Iranian Government. I was born and attended primary and secondary schools in Teheran. I graduated from Teheran University five years ago. Although many Iranian students were and still are politically active, I was not. My father owned a small carpet factory which he sold after my graduation; he and my mother now reside in Paris. Although my mother like most Iranian women of her generation is apolitical, my father does not approve what the mullah's and their theocracy have done to his beloved country, and, as an impressionable young lady, I tend to agree with him; his one act of protest was to leave, and after graduation I followed my parents to Paris, an act that proved quite fortuitous. I love the French and spent some of the most enjoyable years of my life in Paris. I fear, therefore, that I cannot assist your investigation if things Iranian are your concern."

"That is very interesting, doctor," Chase said. "May I sit down?" Chase asked as he did so.

"Please do. However, I must say that I have a class that is due to start soon and still must work on my lecture."

"Yes, and, again, I apologize for imposing on your valuable time. I promise that my simple questions of necessity focus on Doctor Jesperson, the man, not your background. I apologize if my thoughtless reference to your citizenship offended you. I assure you, doctor, that, like your colleagues, I am awed by your academic credentials. Like most Americans, I am quite impressed with individuals like yourself who have mastered multiple languages. I cannot cope with a simple French menu, much to my regret."

"Lieutenant, as you Americans say, let's stop the bullshit," Jalili smiled. "I will gladly answer any of your questions to the best of my limited ability. I liked Thomas as a person and will assist you if I can. Right now, however, I just do not have the time. University students can be very cruel if they suspect their lecturer is unprepared or posing with false credentials. I'm still new here; I'm untenured, and I do not want to be laughed out of my classroom. I suspect you attended university somewhere. Did you graduate from George Mason?"

"William and Mary," Chase smiled, still working on rapport. He had noted Jalili's casual use of Jesperson's first name. She was the second person outside of Jesperson's parents to do so, and the first person had once been Jesperson's fiancée.

"What major?"

"Philosophy," Chase said. "Please don't laugh.

Jalili laughed. "I always thought philosophy majors were a bit out of touch with reality. What made you become a cop?"

"I believed in the Socratic approach?"

"You like to ask questions," Jalili pointed an accusatory finger at Chase.

"Guilty."

"Now leave," Jalili ordered. "We can arrange to meet later."

"What about over lunch?" Chase asked.

"Don't have time for lunch. And I have appointments and graduate seminars this afternoon."

"I didn't think professors carried such a busy schedule," Chase said.

"They don't. I'm a lecturer, not a tenured professor, and I am now doing Doctor Jesperson's work as well as my own."

"I'm impressed."

"Don't be. I'm in over my head."

"Do you eat dinner?" Chase took a chance.

"Business or pleasure?"

"Just a little bit of business."

"OK, I can handle that. I assume you won't go away until I agree to something."

Chase smiled as he nodded his answer.

Jalili jotted something on a small yellow pad. "Pick me up at seven," Jalili ordered as she handed the note to Chase.

He glanced at slip of paper. It contained a Fairfax City address. "I can handle that," Chase mimicked her. At the door, he paused. "Do you eat seafood?"

Jalili dismissed him with a wave.

"See you at seven, doctor," Chase said.

"OK, lieutenant. After seven you can call me Lyla."

"Lyla Jalili," Chase said, struggling with both names.

"I know, too many 'l's', Jalili laughed.

"I'm, Chase," Chase said.

Jalili smiled as she retrieved her reading glasses, and Chase departed, quite pleased with the outcome of his non-interview.

Chapter 17

Chase parked his Prius directly in front of the Fairfax City townhouse which was located in the same complex as another acquaintance, Doctor Barbara Jordan, a professor in the GMU English Department. Since his relationship with Barbara was now strained, primarily because Chase had taken up with Jacky Rossi, a lawyer known as Wacky Jacky to fellow Fairfax cops, Chase rather hoped that Barbara planned a quiet evening at home because Chase intended taking Doctor Lyla Jalili to one of his favorite restaurants, the Crab Shack in Fair Oaks. Barbara had a tendency to be abusive when crossed, and Chase wanted to have a chance to check out Lyla's hippyness before having to cope with any female generated controversy.

Chase rattled the doorknocker and waited. Behind him, a portly, middle-aged woman walking a yapping, ill-mannered terrier stared at him, but Chase pretended not to notice. He was reaching for the knocker again when suddenly the door opened and a smiling Lyla Jalili, wearing tight-fitting yellow slacks and a Redskins sweatshirt, greeted him.

"Good evening, lieutenant, please come in."

"Good evening to you, doctor," Chase replied.

Jalili waved at the still staring neighbor with the rude dog before stepping back, allowing Chase to enter as she said. "My observant neighbor. Do you think she's working for the FBI? Please call me Lyla."

"And I am Chase," Chase smiled. "No, she's just curious. Do you have many visitors to amuse your neighbors? I like your shirt."

"Not really," Lyla said. "I just blend in, act like a real American. All I know about the Redskins is that they are some kind of team. Is the shirt too much?"

"On you it looks good," Chase stared. "I don't like your choice off teams. The Skins are a real disaster."

"I don't understand American football. Should I have chosen the Cowboys? Thomas once told me the Cowboys are America's team."

Jalili's sudden quoting of Jesperson, a man with whom she claimed only limited contact, surprised Chase. He wondered if it were a slip or an intentional disclosure. In the interest of establishing some kind of rapport, Chase decided to let it pass, for now.

"You are doing just fine with the Redskins," Chase said. "I'm sure most of your neighbors, particularly the males, support the Redskins, but I have difficulty understanding why."

Jalili led Chase into a small sitting room. The furnishings were functional, looked new, sexually neutral, solid colors, not frilly with lots of flowers and bright colors, the kind usually found in homes decorated by women living alone without masculine advice. A large oil painting hanging above the mantle over a small fireplace and a worn Persian prayer rug were the only signs of Iran that Chase detected. Jalili assumed a standing position near the fireplace and waited for Chase to select a chair.

"I like your rug and your painting," Chase said as he moved closer to the fireplace and studied the painting which featured stark mountains capped by white snow.

"That's home," Lyla said. "I woke every morning and stared at those lovely mountains. I found them comforting because I felt they were mine. Americans consider them ugly, I know. No trees, but my father used to say the mountains represented Iran's timeless strength. They remind you to persevere; your petty difficulties will pass. We were surrounded by instability in my youth, and the unchanging mountains assured me that the world would survive."

"Teheran is on a mountain?" Chase asked.

"Our home was in Shemiran, a suburb of Teheran. Shemiran is at the base of the mountains and has trees and lovely old homes in big green compounds. Teheran is dirty, flat, crowded, noisy, and busy."

"And your mountain was not."

"At least not from my window. My mother painted that picture."

"She was very good."

"Did you study art as well as philosophy?" Lyla asked.

"Are you making fun of me?" Chase asked.

"No, but you are not the typical policeman."

"Do you know many policemen?"

"Not really. But I read books and watch television."

"What kind of books?"

"All kinds. I even like mysteries. I'm not really an intellectual," Lyla said. "You would know that if you asked any of my faculty colleagues."

"I suspect they're just jealous. You are young and quite attractive with an impressive resume. I'll bet you are the only member of the faculty with a PhD from the University of Paris."

"Do you read mysteries?" Lyla smiled as she tried to shift the conversation away from herself.

"Sometimes. I prefer to write them," Chase surprised himself with his candor. Normally, he refused to discuss his second career which he considered a hobby.

"Really? Now, lieutenant, you truly mystify me. I don't believe I've read many books by Lieutenant Chase Mansfield."

"I haven't either."

"You haven't published? Neither have I, but my department head told me last week I have to get busy."

"You will, I'm sure. What about your dissertation?"

"I've submitted it, but I haven't found an agent or publisher who is interested in a monograph on the women of Persepolis. They tell me I'm forty years too late. An adequate supply of Persepolis books were written when the Shah hosted the 2,500 year celebration of the Persian Empire. The market reached its saturation point in 1971 and has yet to recover. Can I offer you a drink?"

"Why don't we wait and have a couple at the restaurant?" Chase suggested.

"We're not going to a restaurant," Lyla said. "That's why I'm dressed so informally. As a detective, you are not very observant. What do you drink?"

"Could I have a beer?" Chase said. Lyla had surprised him again, and he was hungry.

"Abejou," Lyla said as she turned for the kitchen.

Chase, who wasn't even sure which of her four languages the remarkable young woman was using, was analyzing the fact that intellectually he was playing far out of his league when she reappeared with two bottles of Budweiser in one hand and two frosted glasses in the other.

"My favorite. How did you know?" Chase asked, trying to act suave, a pose he seldom tried.

"Barbara warned me," Lyla smiled as she handed Chase a glass and a bottle.

Chase retreated to a chair, not sure what to say next.

"You are acquainted with Doctor Jordan?" Chase asked with forced indifference as he wondered what his volatile former companion might have said about him. Barbara was still bitter about nothing, only his occasional social outings with Jacky Rossi.

"Oh yes," Lyla chuckled. "Even though we serve different muses, Clio for me and Calliope for Barbara, we sometimes lunch together in the cafeteria and compare notes on the students and our respective male bigots. We met by accident today in the cafeteria, and I happened to mention that a Lieutenant Mansfield had scheduled me for interrogation."

"Oh," Chase hesitated. "Please don't take what Professor Jordan had to say literally. She has a very odd sense of humor."

"Not about you, she doesn't. Professor Jordan doesn't think you are very funny at all."

"We once had a modest social relationship," Chase said.

"So she said. Can I confess something? When we were discussing writing mysteries earlier, I was testing you. Barbara told me that you spend your evenings as Travis Crittenden writing prolifically. She also told me you were a very good writer who refused to discuss it, and she was right. She predicted you would obfuscate."

"That sounds like Barbara," Chase said wryly as he raised his glass in toast.

"And she also predicted you would try to take me to the Crab House which she hates."

"She always told me she loved it," Chase said.

"I'm sure that was early days in your relationship," Lyla said.

"Are you telling me our dinner date is off?" Chase asked.

"Why? Are you hungry?"

"I'm starved."

"How are you with Iranian food?"

"I don't know."

"Good, tonight I'm going to introduce you to my favorite meal."

"I accept with a caveat."

"Which is?" Lyla asked. "But be careful what you ask for."

"Please don't mention Professor Jordan again tonight."

"Agreed. How are you with the barbecue?"

Chase liked the sound of that. "I'm very good with the barbecue."

"Then let's get busy," Lyla said as she sipped beer directly from the bottle.

"First, I've got a question for you," Chase said, holding up one finger.

"I'll answer one question after you make me one promise," Lyla said.

"Do you always negotiate all your conversations?" Chase asked.

"Was that your question?"

"No," Chase said. "That was merely a rhetorical query not a question."

"Ari."

"What do abejou and ari mean?"

"That's two questions."

"It's one question with multiple facets."

"Beer and yeah."

"Yeah?"

"Yeah, OK, slang for yes. Now let's get to work."

Chase followed Lyla into the kitchen. Noticing the swing of her hips in the tight-fitting yellow slacks, Chase decided Dizekes had been correct. She was a little hippy, but he liked it.

While he was staring, Lyla turned abruptly. "Don't say it. I know. I'm hippy, like most Iranian girls."

Under orders to not comment, Chase simply watched as Lyla opened the refrigerator and took out a large yellow bowl covered with plastic. She sat it on the table and turned back to the fridge. She took out another, smaller bowl and deposited it near the first. She patted the fridge's dull aluminum finish and declared, "I love American appliances. Your women are so lucky."

Before Chase could come up with a snappy response, she opened a cupboard drawer and pulled out four skewers. She dropped them on the table next to the covered bowl.

"Wash your hands and skewer the meat," she ordered.

As Chase was washing his hands, Lyla continued.

"I hope you like lamb, marinated lamb, chellokebab, because that is what you're getting. The onion is in the smaller bowl. The charcoal is already lit, so get busy."

"Yes ma'am," Chase said.

Lila turned to the stove where a large pot with a lid with a thin towel draped under and folded over it, simmered.

"And Persian long grain rice," Lyla said. "It's not really Persian rice because we import it from Bangladesh, but it is long grain and very tasty."

"Sounds good,' Chase agreed.

"And you have to eat the rice with ghee and raw egg yolks."

"I suspect that isn't very sanitary," Chase said.

"Don't be a pussy," Lyla surprised him with her choice of words.

"Where did you learn your English?" Chase asked.

Lyla laughed. "Here and there, but mostly in Iran and Paris where I had some very interesting teachers."

"I'll bet," Chase said. "The lamb's skewered."

"Then barbecue it, but don't overcook it. I like a little red in my lamb."

"Me too," Chase said, although lamb was not his favorite dish. "I've never had anything but chops and roast lamb," Chase admitted as he started for the door.

"Not to worry," Lyla said as she took a bowl of salad from the refrigerator.

"Is that Persian too?" Chase asked, wondering what the unpredictable girl would be adding to the salad.

"Nope, Greek. Lots of feta. No lettuce."

"Feta and what?" Chase paused.

"Barbara said you were a finicky eater," Lyla laughed.

"Barbara should keep her big mouth shut," Chase said as he went out the kitchen door with his skewered lamb and onions.

Lyla followed him to the door and handled him two large shakers. "Liberal doses of salt and garlic salt, please," she ordered.

"Now you're speaking my language," Chase smiled. "You didn't say what the Greeks put in their salad."

"Tomatoes, cucumbers, feta, and chunks of onion, heavy with olive oil, virgin vintage."

"No vinegar?"

"Vinegar is for tourists. Ten minutes at the outside," Lyla said as she closed the door.

Ten minutes later Chase opened the door and entered to find his hostess depositing a large platter filled with steaming rice on the table. Next to it she set a half dozen egg yolks in half shells propped on flour on a saucer. Chase placed the plate with his lamb, still on the skewers, next to the rice. As he turned, Lyla handed him a wine bottle.

"Open it," she ordered as she sat down at the kitchen table.

Chase first studied the label. "Retsina." Chase shuddered. He had tried the vile stuff once. One swallow of the vinegary liquid had been enough.

"What's wrong? Don't like retsina?" Lyla challenged.

"Love it," Chase bluffed. He assumed he could fake a swallow and quickly follow with some of the rice.

Chase popped the cork, sat down opposite Lyla, and watched as she used a serving spoon to heap a large mound of rice on a square of strange white substance that he assumed was ghee.

Lyla glanced at him as she reached for the eggs. "You don't know what ghee is, do you?"

"No ma'am."

"Relax, it's just goat butter," she smiled.

"That's what I thought," Chase bluffed.

"Sometimes," Lyla added enigmatically.

Before Chase could protest, Lyla dumped two egg yolks on his steaming rice.

"Don't worry," Lyla said. "The heat of the rice cooks the yolk."

"Sometimes," Chase said.

"Somewhat," Lyla said, speaking simultaneously.

They laughed.

Lyla then handed him a cereal bowl containing chopped onion. "Now add onion, liberally," she ordered.

Chase did as he was told, hoping the onion would mask the yolk and ghee whatever.

Chase passed the onion bowl to Lyla. "Now, take your fork and stir all these wonderful ingredients together," she ordered.

Chase tried and was embarrassed when he spilled rice from his overloaded plate on to the white tablecloth.

"Not to worry," Lyla said as she mixed her rice.

Chase retrieved his spilled rice with his fork and forefinger and casually dumped it back on his plate. He stirred some more and was surprised to see the yoke absorbed by the rice. He dipped his fork into the mass and was preparing to try it when Lyla raised a hand.

"Wait, add salt, liberally," she said. She dumped salt on her rice and passed the shaker to Chase.

"With all this butter, egg yolks, and salt, this is not a very healthy meal," Chase observed as he salted his rice.

"Who cares? Wait until you get to the tadiq," Lyla smiled.

Chase didn't bother to ask what the tadiq might be. He liberally loaded his fork with the treated rice and raised it to his lips, not sure what to expect. To his surprise, it was delicious. He quickly tried a second forkful.

"I don't have room on my plate for the lamb," Chase said when he found Lyla watching.

"Just eat some more rice and make room," Lyla ordered.

Chase quickly did as he was told. Anxious to try the glistening lamb which was covered with what he assumed was a tasty juice, he grabbed a skewer and dropped three chunks of lamb and one of onion on the cleared space. He was reaching for his knife when Lyla spoke.

"Stop," she ordered. "Philosophy majors have no manners," she said. "Now is the time for a toast."

She grabbed the retsina bottle and liberally filled both glasses. Chase regretted she had gotten to the wine bottle first. He had intended to err on the side of caution when addressing his own glass.

Lyla raised her glass first. "To new friends," she said.

"To new friends," Chase repeated, hoping she meant what she said when she described him as a friend. "May this be the first of many such meals," Chase added.

"Don't forget you owe me a seafood dinner," Lyla said. "Unlike Barbara, I like the Crab House."

She sipped from her glass, and Chase in his enthusiasm for the moment did likewise. To his great surprise, the vinegary, medicinally flavored wine blended with the tasty rice and was only half-bad.

Chase was cutting his first bite of the lamb when Lyla hopped up. "I forgot the sanyak."

Chase watched apprehensively as she retrieved the sanyak from the oven. The sight relaxed him. He had not known what to expect. Sanyak appeared to be just round, flat bread that had been warmed in the oven.

"Sanyak is Iranian bread," Lyla said as she dropped the bread on the table. She tore a piece and handed it to Chase. "In Iran, you have to be careful with sanyak. We bake it in outdoor ovens, and it frequently comes with large, embedded pebbles that can break a tooth. We have it delivered to our homes on the back of an ass."

Not knowing how to respond to that comment, Chase sipped his retsina.

After sitting back down, Lyla lifted her wine glass towards Chase and held a piece of sanyak in the other as she quoted:

> "A jug of wine, a loaf of bread and thou beside me singing
> in the wilderness—and the wilderness is paradise enow."

"Omar Khayam," Chase said.

Lyla waited with raised glass, and Chase, ignoring the fact that he had just sipped the nasty retsina, enthusiastically responded.

"Do you know what Khayam means in Persian?" Lyla asked demurely after they had set their glasses back on the table.

"No, what?" Chase responded.

"My testicles," Lyla smiled.

Chase stared at her in disbelief before he started laughing. "You're kidding," he finally said when he regained control.

"Nope," Lyla confirmed.

"You don't have any testicles," Chase said.

"I know that. I was merely translating."

"I'll have to use that in my next book," Chase said, still chuckling as he attacked his lamb.

After a magnificent dinner and a quick cleanup, Lyla led Chase back to the small living room. She adroitly directed him to the most comfortable chair before excusing herself. A few minutes later she re-appeared carrying two wine glasses and another bottle of the retsina.

"I really do not need any more of that," Chase pointed at the malicious wine.

Lyla smiled and filled his glass. Chase showed his manners by sipping it, gracefully. It still tasted like vinegar to him, but to his surprise his palate seemed to be adjusting.

Lyla sat down opposite him, folded her hands in her lap, crossed her legs, and smiled. "I am ready for my interrogation, lieutenant. Do your best because I have some questions of my own."

Chase for some reason, probably the wine, felt a little giddy, lightheaded. The last thing he was prepared to do at this moment was question this lovely Iranian girl about Doctor Thomas Jesperson. Stalling for time, he took another sip of wine, drinking more deeply this time. He cleared his throat, opened his mouth, but no words came out.

Lyla patiently waited with her brown eyes watching him closely.

Chase's mind was a blank.

"I'm waiting, lieutenant," Lyla smiled.

Chase tried again. He felt like he was standing outside his own body watching when he heard himself say, "Who would you say...Ahh...who in your lovely opinion knows Doctor...Ahh...Jesperson best?" Chase detected a slight slur in his voice.

"His mother," Lyla laughed, apparently ignoring Chase's difficulty enunciating his words.

Chase laughed at the answer. "I must confess...Ahh...Lyla I think I may have had a little too much of your lovely wine."

"Not to worry, lieutenant," Lyla smiled. "Please ask your questions. I promise you I have other things in mind." She reached across the coffee table and topped off his wine glass without touching her own.

"Would you say...that..that you were close friends? I'm sure that Doctor ...err...Jesperson found you most attractive," Chase heard himself say.

"As I told you, lieutenant, Doctor Jesperson and I were colleagues for only a few short weeks. During that time, Thomas was preoccupied with the publication of his book."

"But given...but because of..." Chase had trouble remembering what he was going to say.

"Because I am an Iranian," Lyla completed his thought for him.

"Yes," Chase said. "For that reason, he must have been interested in discussing his visit...his research with you."

"We never discussed his research," Lyla said firmly.

Chase sipped his wine trying to clear the sudden dryness he felt in his mouth. He leaned back in his chair.

"Are you alright lieutenant?" Lyla asked as she took the glass from his hand.

"I'm just feeling a little dizzy," Chase said. "This is so...embarrassing."

"Just close your eyes and relax. You've had too much to eat and drink," she said. "While you're resting, I'll ask the questions for you."

Chase closed his eyes. Lyla set the glass on the coffee table, moved to the couch beside Chase, and waited. After a few minutes, Lyla stood up, took the wine and the two glasses to the kitchen where she dumped the residue down the sink, put the empty bottle in the trash, and washed out the glasses. Afterwards, she returned to the living room, sat down on the couch, placed a hand on Chase's knee, and asked, "Chase are you alright?"

"Ahh...m... fine," Chase mumbled without opening his eyes.

"Tell me, Chase," Lyla whispered into his ear. "Do you know who shot Doctor Jesperson?"

Chase turned his head back and forth in a negative motion.

"Do you think the terrible Iranians shot him because of what he said in his book?" Lyla asked.

"Don't...don't...can't discuss," Chase answered with difficulty.

"Not even with me?" Lyla caressed his thigh.

"Ex...cuse me. Got...seep...sleep," Chase mumbled.

"Lieutenant, listen to me," Lyla said. "It is very important that we discuss your investigation because I may be able to help you."

"Good...need help," Chase said.

"Just relax and answer my questions," Lyla spoke firmly.

Chase nodded once. "Need sleep few minutes."

"First," Lyla said, as she grabbed his arm. "Tell me who shot Doctor Jesperson."

"Need talk...with...friends," Chase said.

"Why do you need to talk with his friends?" Lyla insisted.

"No friends. You friend."

"I told you I didn't know Doctor Jesperson very well," Lyla said. "Don't make me angry."

"No," Chase said. "No angry."

"Padar-e sag (son of a dog)," Lyla swore.

Chase did not react.

"Who in Iran was Doctor Jesperson's source?" Lyla pressed.

Chase turned his head from side to side but did not speak.

"Who told him about the Iranian bomb?"

Chase's head fell back.

Lyla stood up, lifted his legs, dropped them on the sofa, and turned the comatose Chase so that his head rested on the seat cushion.

"Who told Thomas that the Iranians planned to detonate a bomb here?" Lyla's voice rose.

Chase did not react. Lyla irritably grabbed his shoulders and shook him. "Listen to me! I know you talked with his parents and met his fiancée at the funeral. Who did they say was Thomas' source?"

Chase groaned but did not react. Lyla slapped his face, but Chase's eyes remained closed. Lyla swore in English. "Shit, shit, shit."

She stood up, removed the comatose Chase's shoes, and vented her anger by throwing them at the chair on the other side of the coffee table. One shoe bounced off the chair back and landed on the floor under the table. The other stayed in the chair. Lyla loosened Chase's belt, unzipped his fly, and pulled the trousers down over his stocking feet. Chase groaned, but he did not move. Lyla threw the trousers behind the couch and irritably grabbed Chase's crotch. She squeezed hard, but the comatose Chase did not move. She squeezed harder and pulled, Chase moaned again, but he did not speak or open his eyes.

Lyla released her grip, opened his suit jacket, and pulled his notebook from the inside pocket. She scanned the several pages of scribbled notes but had difficulty deciphering them. The handwriting was cramped, filled with abbreviations, with names indicated by single letters. Chase obviously had his own shorthand system. Deciding it would take some time to decipher, Lyla took the notebook into her study and scanned it into her laptop. Returning to the living room, she put the notebook back into Chase's jacket pocket. She again grabbed Chase's crotch, squeezed hard, and spoke sharply, "Chase, Chase, wake up."

When he did not respond, Lyla irritably turned off the lights and stamped up the stairs to her bedroom. Angry with herself for having overdosed her visitor with the Rohypnol-laden wine, she had to content herself with the notebook and Chase's few almost incoherent answers.

The next morning Lyla returned downstairs to find the drugged American still slumbering. She checked to make sure he was breathing; he was. She went into the kitchen and scribbled a brief note:

> "Chase, I'm sorry but the retsina was obviously too much.
> Please excuse but I have an eight o'clock class. We can try
> again another time,
>
> Lyla

She re-read the note, decided that the last line was a wee bit much, but did not re-write it. The American could make whatever he wanted out of it. She dropped the note on his chest and quietly shut the door behind her as she hoped that he would wake up soon and leave too embarrassed by his crude behavior to return.

Two hours later Chase woke with a dry throat, a horrendous headache, and unprecedented pain in his groin. It took him several minutes to get his eyes open. They felt like they were glued shut. He had trouble focusing, unsure just where he was. Finally, he forced himself into a sitting position with his stocking feet on the floor. He was surprised to discover he was dressed in his shirt, tie, suit jacket, and underwear but wore no pants. He couldn't remember having taken them off or where they now were. He recognized Lyla Jalili's living room and wondered what happened to her.

"Lyla?" He called softly.

"Receiving no response, he tried again, louder, "Lyla?"

He noticed a sunbeam glancing off the coffee table and checked his watch. "Ten o'clock." He slowly comprehended that he had spent the entire night comatose on Lyla's couch. He worried about what might have happened. He could not believe he had drunk himself unconscious; that was not his style. He remembered a bottle of beer and a couple of glasses of wine, maybe more than a couple. The simple Iranian meal of lamb and rice had been delicious, but now his stomach was protesting. Despite the dizziness, Chase realized he had to find his pants and get the hell out of here. He was too embarrassed to lie back down and risk being found here despite the fact that his body argued against movement. Facing Lyla in this condition, or her cleaning lady if she had one, was not an option.

Chase noticed one shoe lying in the chair on the other side of the coffee table. He could not believe he had crudely thrown it there. His missing trousers and the pain in his groin made him worry what worse things he might have done. Chase pushed off the couch, stumbled around the coffee table, and tripped over his second shoe, as he was reaching for the first in the chair. Assuming that his pants had to be nearby, he ignored the shoes as he began his search in his stocking feet. Finally, he located his pants behind the couch. With difficulty he pulled his trousers on, fighting the pain in his extremities. His head throbbed excruciatingly, but his groin hurt worse. He tucked in his shirt, buckled his belt, and carefully, very carefully, zipped his fly. Then, he slipped his feet into his shoes, expended considerable effort tying the laces. Next, he stopped in the guest bathroom where he used the toilet with difficulty and then splashed water on his face. He stared at his image in the mirror. He looked terrible. He had seen less ravaged faces on dead men lying in coffins.

Chase thought about checking the kitchen for coffee but decided against it. He also passed up the chance to see if he could find some kind of clues to what happened last night after he and Lyla had moved to the little living room. He remembered the meal and getting ready to ask his questions about the Iranian relationship with Jesperson but that is all. He checked his jacket pocket, hoping that he had taken notes. To his surprise, the notebook was in the wrong pocket. He always carried it on the right because normally he wore his weapon on the left. Fortunately, tonight he had left the weapon in the Prius, but, still, the notebook was in the wrong pocket.

Chase glanced at the living room as he headed for the front door and that was when he noticed a piece of paper lying on the floor near the couch. Hoping to find notes that might jog his memory about the interrogation, he retrieved the note. He read:

> Chase, I'm sorry but the retsina was obviously too much. Please excuse but I have an eight o'clock class. We can try again another time.
>
> Lyla

Deciding that the note did not explain much, Chase shoved it into his pants pocket and slowly made his way to the Prius. As Chase opened the door, he saw a sight that made a terrible day worse. Halfway down the block, the door to Professor Barbara Jordan's townhouse opened. Barbara appeared and unfortunately glanced in Chase's direction before he could take refuge in his car. The smile on her face evaporated, and a serious frown appeared. Chase softly closed the door and watched as Barbara's eyes moved from the Prius to the front door of Lyla Jalili's apartment. Barbara glanced at her watch and marched to her car with a stiff back and angry stride.

Chapter 18

Still perplexed about the previous evening's debacle, Chase arrived at his office shortly after noon, freshly shaved, showered, and in clean clothes. His head still hurt; he was troubled by a lingering slight dizziness and a protesting groin.

"You look like hell, lieutenant," Theresa greeted him with a bright smile and an offensively loud voice that made his head ache worse.

"I had a late night," Chase said.

"That is still lingering," Theresa laughed. "You've got an urgent message," Theresa said as she waved a little yellow post-it in the air.

"Urgent?"

"That's what Special Agent Cotton said."

"Cotton?"

"Yes."

"When did he call?"

"He just hung up."

Chase turned and moved as fast as his bruised condition allowed towards his office. He assumed that the Bureau had found Townsend or his body or the kidnappers had demanded more money. "What did he say?" Chase hesitated at the door to his closet.

"What I told you. It was urgent."

"Nothing else?"

"He asked to speak urgently with either you or Barney."

"What did Barney say?"

"He's not here."

"Where is he?" Chase let his irritation show. His head was throbbing, and he was having difficulty focusing, and Theresa's banter was not funny.

Theresa shrugged, and Chase surrendered. He slammed the door behind him, sat down at his desk, and poked Cotton's number on his cell phone.

"Where in the hell have you been?" Cotton demanded when he picked up on the second ring.

"Good morning, Special Agent Cotton," Chase ignored the man's tone as he rested the back of his head against the chair and closed his eyes.

"He's appeared," Cotton said, surprising Chase who sat up straight.

"Townsend? Dead or alive."

"Apparently alive. He just phoned his wife and told her to come and pick him up."

"Where is he? Where has he been?"

"How the hell do I know?" Cotton answered with his own question. "I didn't talk with him."

"So he's alive?"

"His wife claims that is all he said."

"What did he say?"

"I told you. He said come and pick me up."

"Did he say where?"

"On the farm."

"What farm?"

"Mrs. Townsend said they have a small place on the eastern shore."

"Has he been there all this time?" Chase ignored his throbbing head.

"She claims he told her to pick him up at the farm and hung up."

"And that's it?"

"That's it. Look, I'm busy. I gave you a heads up. I've got to go."

"Wait, damn it," Chase refused to let Cotton brush him off. Silence greeted Chase, and he feared that Cotton had hung up on him.

"Look, I've got ten people asking me questions at once. When I learn something, Mansfield, I'll call. You know what I know."

"I'm coming with you," Chase said, talking as he pushed out of his chair.

"Don't bother. We won't be here."

"You're picking him up," Chase said.

"Damned right. He's not going to say a word to anybody that I don't hear."

"Or me," Chase said starting out the door.

"Don't push your luck. You deal with your investigation, and I'll handle mine."

"Townsend belongs to me, too," Chase said. "Ask the big man in the White House if you don't believe me."

"What does that mean?"

"Exactly what it says," Chase said.

"You think that Townsend was your shooter?" Cotton growled.

Chase did not answer.

"Goodbye," Cotton said.

Chase smiled. Cotton did not hang up and was waiting for Chase's response. Chase had him, so he pressed. "If you don't involve me in the pickup, you'll get the answer to your question in the media."

"You're a shit, Mansfield. We had a deal," Cotton complained.

Chase smiled. His headache had disappeared. "Where are we meeting?"

"Andrews," Cotton said. "I'm leaving now. If you miss the copter, tough shit," Cotton said and hung up.

"I'm on my way to Andrews," Chase told a wide-eyed and surprisingly silent Theresa who had listened to Chase's half of the conversation.

"Did Secretary Townsend shoot the professor?" Theresa asked.

"I'll be in touch," Chase said as he opened the outer door.

"And you talked with the president about this?" Theresa asked.

Chase waved.

"What should I tell Barney? The chief?" Theresa called after him.

Chase did not answer as the door closed behind him. Chase hurried past two detectives who stared. Chase was smiling, pleased with Theresa's puzzled reaction. She really thought she knew everything that was happening in the CIB.

With lights flashing Chase covered the some twenty miles to Andrews Air Base in less than thirty minutes, a record time he was sure. He used his credentials to clear the military check point, parked the Prius in a reserved slot a short distance from the VIP terminal, and trotted to the gate guarding the access to the copter pads. He spotted two large, unmarked silver copters with slowly turning blades and worried that he was too late. He was waving his credentials and negotiating with a beefy air force military policeman guarding the gate when Cotton and Mrs. Townsend exited the terminal surrounded by a bevy of male civilians in dark suits.

"Cotton!" Chase called loudly.

Cotton frowned when he saw Chase, waved one hand in a come-on motion, and turned back towards the copters.

The MP stepped back; Chase pushed past and hurried to join the departing group. Chase saw Cotton help Mrs. Townsend into the first chopper, and Chase jogged to join the group as the last person to board. Once on the plane, Chase hesitated. Cotton and his party appeared to fill every seat' Cotton smiled when he saw Chase's dilemma. He ignored Chase and fastened his seatbelt. Then, Chase saw Mrs. Townsend wave. She had her hand on an empty seat cushion to her immediate right. Chase joined her.

"Good news, Mrs. Townsend," Chase greeted her.

"I hope, Chase," Mrs. Townsend smiled at him.

"Did your husband tell you where the kidnappers released him when he called?" Chase asked as he fastened his seat belt.

"No, we didn't have time to discuss anything. He just said, 'Nancy, I'm at the farm. Please come and pick me up.' He sounded tired, and I don't think he wanted to go into any detail over the phone. I am too happy that he's alive and well to be angry with him. I'll chastise him for his behavior, if necessary, after I see what kind of condition he's in."

"I'm happy for the two of you," Chase said.

Suddenly, the roar of the blades interrupted before Chase could continue. The copter lifted into the air and tilted forward as the pilot turned the craft towards the east. Chase did not even try to look out the small window. The noise and motion caused Chase's headache to return, and he clenched his seatbelt with both hands.

"I hate copters," Mrs. Townsend shouted in his ear.

"This is my first time," Chase shouted back.

"Wait till it starts bouncing. That's always worse," Townsend said.

Chase closed his eyes. "We should have driven," Chase muttered.

"This is faster," Townsend said. "I'm still worried for my poor husband."

"Did Cotton have the locals send help to your farm?" Chase asked.

"No, and I refused to tell him where it is, exactly," Townsend answered.

Chase glanced at her but did not ask the obvious question.

"The farm is our secret place. James insisted we not tell anyone we owned it," Townsend said. "Our life is so public, we need a refuge someplace."

"May I ask where?"

Townsend grinned. "Since you will be landing there soon, I think

James will forgive me for telling you. The Eastern Shore, two miles east of Ocean Pines off Route 90. Do you know the area?"

"I'm familiar with Ocean City and Route 90. Do you think Secretary Townsend has been there the whole time?" Chase asked.

"No, I checked the first day."

Chase did not ask how. Bureau agents on each side of them were listening to their every word.

"When he called, he didn't ask that I send help. He just said come and get me," Townsend said.

Mrs. Townsend's words and an accompanying stare told Chase she didn't want him to ask any more questions, not with so many others listening.

Chase nodded and sat silently, fighting his misery, until a firm hand grasped his shoulder from behind.

Chase turned, and found a stern faced Bureau agent staring straight ahead past Chase. Chase looked and saw Cotton standing in the front of the copter. Cotton glared at Chase, aimed his index finger at him, and pointed over his shoulder, indicating, Chase assumed, that Cotton was ordering him to join him. Chase thought about ignoring Cotton but changed his mind, deciding that maybe Cotton had something more he was willing to share.

"Did she tell you where we're going?" Cotton asked, his voice gruff.

"Just now."

"Then, you didn't know about this farm?"

"You were the one covering Townsend's disappearance, not me," Chase's tone let Cotton know he did not like his attitude.

"That's right. Why were you so pushy on the phone? I don't like anyone threatening to talk with the media about one of my cases."

"Neither do I, but this is no longer just your investigation. I hereby cancel our agreement effective immediately, and nobody tells me who I can or cannot interview."

"There is a first time for everything," Cotton responded. "Townsend's disappearance is a federal investigation, and I'll decide who interrogates him, and who doesn't. The latter category includes you."

Chase glanced at Mrs. Townsend, who was watching them closely. "We'll see about that. Secretary Townsend may have something to say about your little list."

"Why are you being so difficult, Mansfield?"

"That's my nature."

"What's with you and Mrs. Townsend? Have you been meeting with her behind my back?"

Chase smiled.

"And why do you want to meet with Townsend?"

"The president and I discussed that little issue. I suggest you ask him, and maybe, if he thinks you have a need to know, he'll tell you."

"You think Townsend shot Jesperson, don't you?" Cotton challenged.

Chase did not answer.

An angry Cotton turned towards the cockpit, and Chase returned to his seat.

"I don't think he likes you very much," Mrs. Townsend smiled. She leaned towards Chase as she spoke, presumably to make it harder for the nearby members of Cotton's team to hear what she said. As she did so, her shoulder and thigh touched Chase. The cramped space prevented Chase from pulling away, and Townsend pretended she did not notice the intimacy.

"He's just doing his job, and he doesn't like other investigators working his turf," Chase said.

"I don't like his attitude," Mrs. Townsend persisted. "I would rather have you talk with James about his experience." She patted Chase on the knee.

"I need to talk with your husband about his visit to George Mason and his private meeting with Doctor Jesperson after his public appearance, but details about his kidnapping take priority, and that is a federal issue," Chase said.

"On the other hand, James is now safe. Thomas was James' friend, and he may not know that Thomas is dead. He will want to help you." She patted Chase's knee a second time and then withdrew her hand.

"And he will also want to help Special Agent Cotton track down his kidnappers," Chase said.

"Nonetheless, I will make sure James knows that he must talk with you," Mrs. Townsend said as she straightened in her seat.

"Did you husband's voice tell you anything about his physical condition?" Chase asked, referring to the phone call asking her to come to the farm.

"No, he sounded perfectly normal," Mrs. Townsend said.

Chase nodded, pretending that her answer satisfied him. Privately, he found Mrs. Townsend's behavior quite abnormal. She was acting like they were chatting at a cocktail party with her showing none of the signs of strain that one might expect from a woman whose husband had been held by kidnappers for a stressful two weeks, no tears, no hysterics, no frantic questions, and in Townsend's case she was handling the entire affair completely without the support of family or friends.

Chase looked up and caught Cotton staring at them from his seat near the cockpit door. The expression on his face told Chase that the same questions about Mrs. Townsend were also coursing through Cotton's mind, and in this instance they were undoubtedly accompanied by others about Chase and his relationship with the emotionally grounded spouse of the victim.

After a noisy and uncomfortable forty-five minutes, Cotton made his way down the short aisle.

"Mrs. Townsend," Cotton said, ignoring Chase, "the pilot sends his apologies for disturbing you but asks if you would kindly come forward and help him locate your farm. We are approaching Route 90."

"Of course," Townsend said. She unfastened her seat belt and followed Cotton to the front of the copter.

"That's one tough lady," the agent sitting behind Chase leaned forward and spoke into his ear.

Chase turned and recognized one of agents who had staffed the detail assigned to the Townsend house waiting for the kidnappers to establish contact.

"She's a piece of work," the agent said.

"Did she ever show any sign of emotion?" Chase asked.

"Not a single tear. I don't think she missed her husband very much."

"Any long conversations on the phone with friends?" Chase asked.

"None. She spent most of her days shopping, visiting friends, or lunching at the country club."

"I guess she is a very strong person," Chase said, not believing a word he said.

"Under similar circumstances my wife would be a basket case," the agent said. "And if she wasn't I would hope she would miss me a little bit."

Abruptly the copter took a turn to the left, and Chase and the agent broke off their little chat. For a long ten minutes the copter maneuvered as the pilot and Mrs. Townsend apparently tried to locate their destination.

Chase's headache returned, and he leaned back in his hard seat. Finally, Mrs. Townsend returned to her seat.

"We found it," she announced, and Chase opened his eyes.

"I've decided that this is going to be my last copter ride," Chase said.

"Chase, you obviously don't travel well," Townsend laughed. "You look like you have a hangover. Were you out late last night? With a lady friend?" She asked as she again patted his knee and pushed a firm thigh against his.

Chase shook his head in reply.

"She must have been something to wear out a virile young man like yourself."

Chase forced a smile as the copter dropped heavily toward the earth. Two hard bounces and they were down. Chase took a deep breath and forced himself to relax. Mrs. Townsend removed her hand from his knee and her thigh from his. Someone opened the door, and the reception team eagerly jumped out. When Chase and Mrs. Townsend reached the door, they found Cotton waiting for them. He assisted Mrs. Townsend and let Chase stumble down on his own.

Chase watched the first two agents enter the front door of the nearby farmhouse with weapons drawn. Assuming the Feds would resent any attempt on his part to assist, Chase stood back and studied the setting. The copter had landed on the overgrown lawn in front of the house. The structure itself was a two-storey frame square with a roofed porch that stretched completely across the front. Although Chase was no expert in the field of architecture, if asked, he would describe the house as late Victorian probably built in the late 1890's or early 1900's. Not a mansion, it looked like the working home of a hardworking, successful eastern shore farmer who owned several hundred acres and was assisted by several tenant farmers or handymen. The Townsends obviously kept their ocean retreat in excellent condition. Someone had added two large picture windows on the first floor; the wood frame had been painted recently, and the brick on the two chimneys was solid and in good repair. The large, faded, red barn on the left was not in as good condition as the house; the corrosive salt air of the ocean had obviously been busy on the paint. The barn doors were closed, and Chase could not tell if the Townsends used it as a garage or not. There were no cars in evidence; Chase wondered how Secretary Townsend had made his way. Chase turned. A rutted dirt road led from the house to somewhere; Chase could neither see nor hear any traffic. Also, the retreat was well chosen because overgrown fields stretched in all four directions without a single neighbor to be seen. Chase could not even tell which way was east.

An agent appeared in the doorway and waved what Chase assumed to be an all clear signal; immediately, Cotton and an impatient Mrs. Townsend moved forward, and Chase followed along close behind. By the time they reached the front steps that led to the porch, Mrs. Townsend was several steps ahead. Chase paused at the base of the wood steps, grasped the rail, and glanced at Cotton on his left as he started to climb to the porch.

Cotton nodded, acknowledging Chase's silent question. He, too, had noticed that Mrs. Townsend appeared to be emotionally involved in the situation for the first time.

"James?" She called as she disappeared inside.

Cotton crowded in front of Chase and followed the anxious spouse, clearly wanting to monitor the reunion. Chase, who was one-step behind Cotton, entered to find himself in a large living room filled with worn Sears and Roebuck furniture that the inexperienced might label antiques. Members of the Bureau team were deployed throughout the room, all with holstered weapons. Mrs. Townsend was kneeling before a man in a chair that faced the smoke stained, fieldstone fireplace that dominated the room from the right wall. Chase had seen pictures of Secretary Townsend, even carried one now in his jacket pocket, but he did not recognize the man in the chair. His white hair was overlong and uncombed; the stubble on his face was dark. Chase estimated he had not shaved for at least two weeks. He wore a dirty dress shirt, open at the collar with the second and third buttons missing, no necktie. The shirttail on the right hung over the dirty and wrinkled suit pants. He wore no shoes, just dirty socks with a big toe peeking out on his right foot.

Mrs. Townsend stood directly in front of the man who watched her with wide, red-rimmed eyes.

"James, I'm sorry, I didn't think to bring you any clothes," Mrs. Townsend said, her voice breaking. "You look awful."

Chase, like Cotton and his men, was watching the scene closely. Chase immediately decided that if either of the Townsends were acting for effect, they were doing it like professionals.

Mrs. Townsend dropped to her knees, leaned forward, and laid her head on her husband's knees. He put one hand with dirty fingernails on top of her head. He bent back.

"I'm so tired," he sighed.

"I know," Mrs. Townsend raised her head and studied her husband. "Did they hurt you? Do you need a doctor?"

Townsend shook his head negatively, giving Chase the impression that he was too tired to talk, either that or he was acting as if that was the way he should behave.

Mrs. Townsend pushed herself erect and took charge. "Everybody out. Give us some time."

Everybody, including Chase, looked at Cotton who was staring at the now composed Mrs. Townsend.

"Except you, doctor," Mrs. Townsend spoke to a member of the team carrying a black satchel that Chase, who had been focusing on the Townsends, had not noticed.

Cotton turned and silently led his team toward the door. The doctor moved in the opposite direction approaching Townsend for the first time. Chase hesitated, anxious to observe every minute detail of Townsend's return, but finally he retreated.

"No, Chase, you stay. I want an independent witness," Mrs. Townsend ordered.

Chase stopped, and so did Cotton, who had reached the front door. He turned to protest.

"Not you. Out of my house, now," Mrs. Townsend ordered, pointing directly at Cotton.

Cotton took a deep breath, obviously preparing to argue, and then, to Chase's surprise, glared at Chase, obviously blaming him for the preposterous order, and departed.

"Close that door and lock it," Mrs. Townsend insisted.

"I don't think that will be necessary, Mrs. Townsend," Chase said.

"Chase, I told you to call me Nancy," Mrs. Townsend smiled as if that social nicety was more important than what Chase had just suggested.

Chase hesitated again. Mrs. Townsend looked at her husband who to Chase's surprise nodded his head once, apparently agreeing with Chase.

"Water," Townsend croaked, his voice sounding dry and raspy.

"Yes, dear," Mrs. Townsend said and turned toward a back doorway that Chase assumed led to the kitchen.

"May I please check your vitals?" The doctor asked as he pulled a stethoscope from his bag. "Are you injured anywhere? Just point, don't try to talk."

Townsend shook his head negatively. While the doctor was listening to Townsend's heart, Mrs. Townsend returned. She pressed a tall glass of water into her husband's hand. He held it and waited for the doctor to remove his stethoscope.

"Strong but rapid," the doctor announced. "Are you taking your blood pressure medication? Any medication?"

Townsend shook his head negatively and then raised the glass to his lips using both shaking hands. After sipping, he looked at the doctor. "Can't talk. Mouth too dry."

"I understand," the doctor said sympathetically. "Don't try."

The doctor took a blood pressure band from his bag and wrapped it around Townsend's arm. Townsend sipped again, this time using one hand wrapped around the glass. The doctor pressed the little ball and watched the pressure gauge. Nobody said a word. Finally, the doctor released the pressure and put the band back in his bag before commenting.

"Slightly elevated but not surprising for what you have been through," the doctor pronounced. "I think it would be best if you checked into the hospital and let us run a few more tests."

"No," Townsend said, his voice firm and clear this time.

"Strictly precautionary, Mr. Secretary," the doctor smiled.

"No," Townsend repeated.

"I don't think he wants to go to the hospital for tests," Mrs. Townsend declared.

"But..." The doctor started to protest but stopped when he looked at Townsend who was sitting with one hand shaking while holding the glass and the other hand bloodless white clenching the arm of his chair. "Later, then, when you are ready," the doctor surrendered.

"Please leave me alone with my husband," Mrs. Townsend ordered.

The doctor looked at Chase, apparently expecting him to comment. Chase said nothing. The doctor packed his bag and started for the door. With his hand on the knob, he tried again. "Mr. Secretary, I strongly recommend..."

"No," Townsend said.

The doctor shrugged and departed. Townsend turned his head and stared at Chase. Before Chase could respond, Mrs. Townsend spoke, "James, this is Lieutenant Mansfield of the Fairfax County Police. Please listen to what he has to say. It is important."

Townsend surprised Chase by nodding.

"I know this is a very stressful time for you, Mr. Secretary," Chase said. "But I have some very distressing news for you. I don't know who was with your friend Doctor Jesperson when you departed, or what happened when you left his office, but a party or parties unknown shot Doctor Jesperson."

Townsend's eyes widened, but he did not speak. Mrs. Townsend, who was now standing beside his chair, placed a consoling hand on his shoulder. Townsend ignored the gesture and sipped from his glass before handing it to his wife. "More," he said.

Mrs. Townsend took the glass but did not leave the secretary's side.

"Please," Townsend said softly.

Mrs. Townsend obediently left the room.

"And?" Townsend said.

Chase, who was having difficulty reading the Townsends, hesitated. He could not tell if Townsend was showing the effects of bad treatment at the hands of kidnappers or simply was doing a good acting job. For her part, Mrs. Townsend did not seem to be particularly stressed by her husband's appearance or apparently weakened condition.

"Doctor Jesperson was found a little after midnight by a cleaning lady. He had been shot twice and death was instantaneous."

Townsend's only reaction was to stare at Chase.

"Was anyone else present when you left?"

Townsend shook his head negatively. Before Chase could ask another question, Mrs. Townsend returned and handed her husband the refilled glass. "I'm so sorry, James," Mrs. Townsend said. "I thought you should know." Mrs. Townsend turned to Chase. "James and Thomas have been friends for thirty years."

"May I ask you a couple more questions, Mr. Secretary. Except for the killer, you are the only person to have talked with Doctor Jesperson after your lecture."

"I...know...nothing," Townsend said.

Mrs. Jesperson sat in the chair opposite her husband, but she did not attempt to limit Chase's questioning. Chase, who assumed that time was short, knew that Cotton would be outside the door fuming.

"I am only interested in apprehending Doctor Jesperson's killer," Chase said. "The Bureau," Chase glanced towards the door, "will want to discuss the details of...of your experience," Chase said.

Townsend nodded.

"What time did you leave Doctor Jesperson's office?" Chase asked.

"Nine-thirty," Townsend said without hesitation. "Alone. I left Thomas alone."

"You left Doctor Jesperson alone in his office at nine-thirty," Chase repeated, wanting to be sure he understood Townsend's response correctly.

Townsend nodded affirmatively.

"Do you know if he was expecting another visitor?"

Townsend shrugged.

"That's a negative, sir?"

"Yes. I do not know. Obviously, he had one."

"Chase," Mrs. Townsend said.

Assuming she was trying to end the questioning, Chase nodded but held up one finger. "Did Doctor Jesperson seem worried to you? Did he share any concerns?" Chase spoke quickly.

"No. Thomas was looking forward to publication of his book," Townsend started to use complete sentences.

Before Chase could ask another question, the front door opened and a frowning Special Agent Cotton pointed a finger at Chase and indicated with a wave that he should join him.

"Please excuse me," Chase said as he turned for the door.

"Come back, Chase," Mrs. Townsend said, once again surprising him. "We want you here."

Chase nodded and joined Cotton on the front porch. Other sober faced members of the Bureau team were deployed between the porch and the now silent, looming copters. Chase could see the pilots sitting at the controls.

"What in the hell is going on in there Mansfield?" An angry Cotton demanded.

"I don't know," Chase answered honestly.

"What did he say about his kidnappers?" Cotton asked.

"Nothing. I told him that you would address that issue. I informed him of Jesperson's murder, explained I was handling the Jesperson investigation, and asked him a couple of questions."

"Did he do it?" Cotton asked.

"I don't know. I can't even tell if he is playacting or actually suffering from his hostage experience. He appears to be recovering quickly."

"What did he say?"

"An unworried Jesperson was alone in the office when Townsend left at nine-thirty, and he did not mention another visitor to Townsend. Jesperson was in a good mood looking forward to the publication of his book."

"And?"

"And that's all he said. Mrs. Townsend refilled his water glass and patted him on the shoulder."

"She's taking all this pretty calmly, don't you think?" Cotton watched Chase closely.

"She's a tough lady who doesn't wear her emotions on her sleeve," Chase said.

"And what's going on between you and her? She calls you Chase and treats you like an old friend."

"Nothing's going on between Mrs. Townsend and me. I've only seen her at her house or out here, and you and your team have always been around."

Cotton stared at Chase, clearly not believing him. "You're quite the charmer, Mansfield. Are you a lover boy too?"

"Back off, Cotton," Chase let Cotton know he wasn't intimidated.

"Don't push your luck, Mansfield," Cotton blustered.

"Don't push yours, Cotton," Chase replied before smiling. "We sound like a couple of schoolyard kids. What now?" Chase asked. "You heard Mrs. Townsend tell me to come back. I think she wants me as a witness."

"The doctor says Townsend is in pretty good shape for a hostage. If there were kidnappers, they didn't treat him badly." Cotton ignored Chase's what now question.

"He told the doctor he wasn't interested in going to a hospital for tests," Chase said.

"You were in there. How should I handle this?"

Cotton's uncharacteristic request for advice made Chase laugh. "Since he's a member of the president's cabinet and one his buddy's, I don't recommend that you haul him in and give him the rubber hose treatment."

"That's exactly what I had in mind," Cotton returned to form. "There are a lot of important people in D.C. waiting to hear from me."

"It's going to leak."

"Screw the damned media."

"Let's you and I go back in. I'll keep my mouth shut and let you ask him as many questions as he is willing to answer."

"Why you?" Cotton glanced at his waiting team.

"I was invited."

"This is some deal," Cotton complained. "That guy cost a lot of people thirty million dollars, and I have to play by his rules."

"Thirty million?" Chase said. "Don't you mean a hundred million?"

Cotton glared at Chase. "Forget I said that."

Chase studied Cotton and then began to chuckle. "You and the president shortchanged the kidnappers. Did you give them a promissory note for the rest?"

"That's all the vice president was able to raise in a short period of time. They decided to give them what they had."

"That was taking a big chance."

"Which was better, to give them nothing, or give them chump change? They didn't give us a chance to discuss things. The e-mails were all one way."

"Whether the secretary is a victim or a blackmailer, he's not going to be very happy with you. You gambled with his life by going cheap."

Cotton shrugged.

"The media are going to go bananas with this story," Chase grinned. "I think I got the best part of our deal."

"Don't be a wiseass. I've got enough problems to deal with without advice from a local cop who thinks he's Jay Leno."

"Look at the positive side. You got the president's buddy back and saved him seventy million in the process."

"Yeah."

"And I've still got a dead body on my hands," Chase said. "At least your victim is still walking."

"Wait here," Cotton growled at his team before leading Chase back into the farmhouse.

Inside, they found the limp secretary sipping water and chatting with his wife who sat opposite with her hands calmly folded in her lap, looking every bit like a society wife having tea with a friend.

"The doctor really thinks you should check into a hospital for a couple of days, Mr. Secretary," Cotton said.

"No," Townsend answered.

"But I told him the decision was yours, sir. You know how you feel."

"Thank you Agent Cotton," Townsend said with a voice that clearly was recovering quickly.

Water sometimes works miracles, Chase thought to himself as he quietly took a chair near the front door.

"I know this is a burden," Cotton said, sitting opposite Townsend and his wife, "but I must ask about your ordeal. The president is sitting anxiously in the Oval Office waiting to hear."

"I understand," Townsend said as he set his water glass on the table beside his chair. "But I insist that none of what I say be released to the media."

"The story will leak," Cotton said. "The president will have to brief the Congress and inform the American people about your kidnapping."

"I know," Townsend said. "I will personally discuss the matter with the president and handle all media releases through my people at Homeland Security."

Chase resisted the urge to smile. Despite his apparently weakened condition, the presidential friend and cabinet secretary was taking charge. He did not envy Cotton and the Bureau.

"Did the kidnappers tell you that the president authorized the ransom payment?" Cotton asked.

Chase gave Cotton credit. He did not begin with the obvious questions but started with the finale, something that the kidnappers had no way of knowing.

"No, but I assumed someone did," Townsend hedged.

"They demanded a hundred million dollars," Mrs. Townsend blurted.

"The United States Government paid a hundred million dollars for me?" Townsend showed surprise.

"They demanded one hundred million dollars. All we had time to collect was thirty million," Cotton said. "We had no way to communicate with the terrorists, and the president decided personally to send what we had."

Chase was looking at Mrs. Townsend while Cotton was talking. An odd expression crossed her face when the figure thirty million was cited. He wasn't sure if it was surprise or disappointment, and, if the latter, he asked himself why? Chase considered thirty million to be a preposterous amount, but maybe Mrs. Townsend thought it undervalued her spouse.

"I would have opposed giving them anything. It is our policy not to negotiate with terrorists," Townsend said.

"Do you have any idea who the terrorists represented?" Cotton asked.

Townsend shook his head.

"May I quickly walk you through your experience?" Cotton asked. "We need somewhere to start our investigation."

"I'll hold you to your word, quickly," Townsend said. "We can go into detail later, but frankly I don't know much."

"Please tell me in your own words what happened," Cotton said as he took a small recorder from his pocket and placed it on the table pointed at Townsend.

Townsend frowned but nodded permission. "I assume you know I gave a short talk on homeland security to a small audience at George Mason," he began.

Cotton nodded encouragement.

"I told them that, James," Mrs. Townsend said tartly.

Chase noted she had not smiled since the figure thirty million had been mentioned.

"It was arranged by Thomas, who I had known since Cornell. Normally, I avoid such public appearances, but Thomas was a friend who had recently returned from Iran. I admit I selfishly wanted to hear of his experiences there and discuss his book." Townsend looked at his wife. "Has Thomas' book been released yet?" He turned back to Cotton. "We discussed the book, but Thomas refused to share any details not even when I mentioned the president's interest."

"It's been released dear, and is an international best seller," Mrs. Townsend said.

"Good, Thomas would be proud. Did it mention the Iranians having the bomb?"

"Yes, and he claimed they intend to use it against us." Mrs. Townsend said.

"You understand, therefore, why it's imperative that we get as much information about your experience as possible, sir," Cotton tried to get control of the interview. "It's possible your seizure, the Jesperson killing, and the book are all linked."

"That's obvious," Townsend said. "So that's why you're here," Townsend looked at Chase, who nodded.

"Lieutenant Mansfield is handling the Jesperson investigation, and we are dealing with everything else," Cotton said. "What happened after your lecture at George Mason?" Cotton asked.

"We returned to Thomas' office and had a glass of some awful Iranian drink while we waited for the audience to clear the building. We chatted briefly, as I told Mansfield, about the book, but Thomas was not forthcoming, and then I left at nine-thirty." Townsend glanced at Chase who acknowledged the reference to his previous question.

"You left alone, and Doctor Jesperson was alone. Was he expecting another visitor?" Cotton asked.

"We both were alone, and I doubt that Thomas was expecting another visitor. We didn't discuss his plans," Townsend said.

"Then what happened?"

"I returned to my car, which was parked in a nearby lot. I passed a few students on the way," Townsend hesitated after hinting at witnesses who could possibly substantiate part of his story, and both Chase and Cotton sat erect. Townsend was approaching the heart of his story.

"Just as I was unlocking my car—I unwisely drove myself leaving my protective detail at home—I was struck from behind." To emphasize his point, Townsend rubbed the back of his head. "I had a huge knot for several days, but it is gone now. Still sore to pressure, though."

Cotton nodded and waited.

"The next thing I know is that I woke with a gag, a blindfold, and my hands and feet tied. I was lying in the back of what I assume was a van or a small truck. There was someone with me. I only know that because a foot prodded me periodically. The person never spoke. We drove for what seemed like several hours."

"How many do you think?" Cotton asked.

"I don't know," Townsend said irritably. "I don't know how long I was unconscious, and I couldn't see my watch with my hands tied behind me."

"Did you hear any sounds?"

"I've thought about that and have tried to remember everything. I, of course, knew you would ask these questions. I heard traffic. I think we drove for a long time on a major highway. There were cars and trucks, but I have no way of knowing which direction we were traveling."

"Take a guess," Cotton said.

"I don't think we crossed any bridges. We could have done that while I was unconscious, so my guess could be wrong. We could have gone south on I-95, or maybe east, or even north."

"Why not west?"

"Because I didn't sense that we climbed any mountains."

"Can you estimate the passage of time?"

"I would say six or seven hours, maybe less or more. I was quite disoriented. Must we go into this detail now? Let me just stress, I do not believe anything I can tell you will be of much assistance."

"I understand, Mr. Secretary," Cotton said. "When you reached your destination what happened?"

"They locked me in a small room where I remained for the entire time. I don't know how many days. I lost count."

"Describe the room for me, please."

"Four walls, ceiling and floor. There was a mattress on the floor. No chair. No windows. Nothing else."

"Describe your captors if you can."

"Two males, average height, one taller and larger than the other. White males. They always wore ski masks so all I could see were their eyes. One had hazel eyes and the other, I'm not sure, blue green. Neither wore glasses."

"Skin color?"

"White hands."

"Feet?"

"Average size. They both wore athletic shoes. Old ones, dirty, I don't know what kind."

"And you only dealt with two men?"

"Yes."

"Can you estimate their ages?"

"No. Probably young, maybe twenties or thirties, but I could be wrong. They could have been older or younger."

"Voices?"

"They didn't chat with me, if that is what you mean."

"Accents?"

"Maybe one of them, I'm not sure. They both spoke good English."

"Must we go through all this now?" Mrs. Townsend asked irritably. "Can't you see my husband is exhausted?"

"We really want to catch these people," Cotton answered.

"They are nowhere around here now," Townsend said. "They dropped me off hours ago."

"Dropped you off?" Cotton asked.

"Yes, you don't think I would know my own house if they had held me here, do you?" Townsend asked irritably.

"How did you get here?"

"By limousine," Townsend said, his voice reeking with sarcasm.

Cotton waited.

"They came into my cell, tied my hands, taped my mouth, and blindfolded me. They walked me outside and put me in the back of the van or truck, tied my feet, and drove for about three hours."

"Three hours?"

"I didn't have a chance to check my watch," Townsend snapped. "They took it the first day, and my eyes were covered anyway. They bounced me around for a long time. It could have been three hours, six hours, I don't know. It certainly wasn't ten minutes."

"And they brought you here?"

"I'm here, aren't I?"

"Did they just let you out at the front door?" Cotton asked.

"No, they dragged me inside, threw me on the floor, and one of them said if I worked at it I might find a knife on one of the chairs."

Cotton waited.

"I heard the truck drive away. I waited, afraid they might come back, and after a while got to my feet. I couldn't walk. I had to hop. With difficulty I made my way around the room. It took me a while, and I finally found the knife. I eventually cut myself loose. It's not easy with your hands tied behind you. Look," Townsend said as he held out his wrists. "I cut myself several times in the process."

Cotton checked several shallow slashes on Townsend's wrists. "We better have the doctor come back and check those out."

"No," Townsend frowned. "I'm fine. I'll check with my own doctor."

"Yes sir," Cotton said. "How did they know to bring you here?"

"I don't know. When I got free and discovered where I was, I thought about that myself. I don't know. Maybe they had me under surveillance sometime."

"We spent at least one weekend a month here," Mrs. Townsend said.

"At any time did you or your protective detail notice any surveillance?" Cotton persisted.

"We always left the detail at home," Mrs. Townsend said.

"We would have reported anything suspicious if we had seen it," Townsend said. "We're not stupid."

"Is there anything about your kidnappers that made you think they might be terrorists? Did they say anything?" Cotton asked.

"No, now please leave us alone. If I think of anything, I'll get in touch. I need some time to rest and recover. I haven't been on a luxury cruise, you know."

"We've got two copters, and it's a short flight back to D.C.," Cotton said.

"I'm staying here," Townsend said.

"We're staying here," Mrs. Townsend left her chair and moved to her husband's side where they presented a united front.

"There is still much we have to cover, Mr. Secretary," Cotton persisted.

"And we can do it Monday when I get back in Washington," Townsend said.

"You should really check into a hospital like the doctor recommended for a few tests," Cotton said.

Townsend answered by clamping his lips shut and moving his head from side to side. Mrs. Townsend pressed a hand on her husband's shoulder.

Cotton looked at Chase, who did not respond. "Very well," Cotton said, picking up his recorder. "I'll leave a guard detail."

"No," Townsend said.

"I forbid it," Mrs. Townsend spoke at the same time as her husband.

"As soon as the media pick up the story..." Cotton began.

"They don't know about this place," Mrs. Townsend declared. "If you don't tell them." She glared at Cotton as if he were responsible for their problems.

"I will deal with all that on Monday," Townsend insisted. "First, I am going to get two days of peace and quiet. Please go."

"Sir..." Cotton persisted.

"Do I have to call the president personally?" Townsend threatened.

"I am only doing my duty and trying to look after your best interests, sir," Cotton tried again.

"Then do what I ask, Agent Cotton," Townsend sighed. "I've had a bad experience and need some rest before coping with the aftermath. I apologize if I appear uncooperative but..."

"Leave," Mrs. Townsend ordered. "I assume full responsibility for my husband's welfare."

"How will you get back to DC?" Cotton signaled his capitulation. "Do you want me to have your security detail join you here?"

Townsend looked at his wife, and she answered. "No, I will get us back home."

"May I ask..." Cotton began the obvious question.

"We have a car in the barn. It's old but reliable," Mrs. Townsend said. "I am a perfectly competent driver."

Cotton, with Chase following, started for the front door. "I will inform your security detail that you are here."

"Don't," Mrs. Townsend, who now appeared to be in charge, ordered. "I will call them myself and give them their instructions."

"Very well," Cotton said as he glanced at Chase who had witnessed the entire exchange.

Chase who had contributed nothing to the debriefing felt like a material witness. He turned to speak to Mrs. Townsend.

"Thank you Chase for all your support," Mrs. Townsend said as she moved towards the door.

"We are all pleased that your husband survived his ordeal," Chase said.

Mrs. Townsend nodded but did not respond, giving Chase the impression he had just been dismissed along with Cotton.

Mrs. Townsend followed Cotton and Chase to the door and firmly closed it behind them. Chase heard the deadbolt slide shut.

Cotton glared at Chase and turned towards his waiting team. Cotton pointed at the copters with the forefinger of each hand and said, "Let's get out of here?"

"We haven't had a chance to check out the place," Cotton's second-in-command protested.

Cotton ignored him and headed for the copters.

"What's going on?" The second-in-command asked Chase.

"The secretary wants some time to unwind," Chase shrugged.

When they reached the copter, Chase climbed in behind a now irate Cotton. The second-in-command did not join them. Instead he blocked the door and declared, "Sir, we should at least keep a protective detail here."

"The secretary ordered us to leave," an angry Cotton snapped. "And I have to report to the director and the president."

"Then, I will stay here with the detail and the second copter," the second-in-command insisted.

"I know it's none of my business, but he's right," Chase said.

Cotton glared at Chase and then his stubborn deputy. He took a deep breath and forced himself to relax. The pilot and co-pilot watched from the cockpit. "You're right, of course," Cotton finally growled. "They are going to complain," he glanced at the closed door of the farmhouse. "But ignore them. Tell them you are only following my orders. She alleges they have a car in the barn. You won't be able to follow them in the copter if they leave."

"What should I do if they try?" The deputy asked.

"Just take a couple of men and climb in the back seat. Let the witch drive. She claims she can. If they protest, say you are following orders."

"Yes, sir."

"And I will alert their security detail and have our local office here get you a couple of cars," Cotton said.

"Get me back to Andrews," Cotton ordered the pilot.

"Something tells me the Townsends are not going to be very pleased with you," Chase tried to make light of the situation.

"I'll discuss it with your friend, the president," Cotton said sourly as the pilot started his engines.

When they were back in the air, Chase ignored Cotton's mood and asked, "What did you think of Townsend's story?"

"Do you think Townsend shot Jesperson before taking off with his kidnappers?" Cotton answered with a question.

"Did you notice Mrs. Townsend's face when you admitted you only paid thirty million for her husband?" Chase did the same.

"No." Cotton looked at Chase waiting for him to elaborate.

"I got the impression she was disappointed," Chase smiled.

"Why in the hell should she be disappointed?" Cotton demanded.

"Maybe she fears her friends will consider a mere thirty million ransom demeaning. Weren't you taking a big risk shortchanging the kidnappers? Wouldn't terrorists just take the thirty million and shoot their hostage, particularly a VIP like Townsend?"

"Thirty million was all the vice president could dig up on short notice," Cotton said. "And the president was the person who made the decision to send the money, not me. He figured he could at least buy some time. You may have noticed we had no way to bargain with the bastards."

"Why pay anything then? I thought you guys didn't negotiate with terrorists?"

"Who the shit negotiated with anyone? I told you it wasn't my decision. Featherstone is your asshole buddy. Didn't he discuss it with you?"

"Hey, I met the man once. He summoned me."

"And why did he do that? Did he think the Bureau needed your damned advice?"

Chase did not react. The president had ordered him not to discuss their conversation with anyone, and Chase assumed that particularly meant Special Agent Cotton.

Cotton waited.

"It really bothers you doesn't it?" Chase stalled.

"Damned right it does. Don't you know that you can't trust those lousy politicians? You can't be that naive. They'll squeeze little guys like you and me dry and toss us out with the garbage without giving it a second thought."

"Well," Chase admitted. "It bothers me too. He just wanted to ask me a question about my investigation. We didn't discuss yours."

"And the question had nothing to do with that shit Townsend? He's a politician too, you know. I don't trust him either."

"If I repeat the question, will it remain between the two of us?" Chase asked.

"Of course," Cotton answered, his response dripping with sarcasm.

"Oh shit," Chase said.

"I give you my word as a fellow police professional I will not share your confidence with another person," Cotton said.

Chase still hesitated.

"And I also promise you if you do not confide in me I will make sure that the Bureau will not acknowledge any future request for assistance from the entire Fairfax Police Department, and we will let it be known that Lieutenant Chase Mansfield is responsible for that situation."

"Not everyone will consider that a bad deal," Chase smiled. "Particularly not me."

"But your chief likes to send his bright young officers off to Quantico for career enhancing training," Cotton smiled back.

"I'm neither bright nor young," Chase countered.

"I'm not disputing that," Cotton said.

After that exchange several silent minutes passed as the copter droned its way towards D.C.

"I gave you my word that I will not share your confidence," Cotton broke the tension by retreating from his threat.

"And I gave my word to the president," Chase said.

"And no politician really expects you to do what you promise."

"Because they don't?"

"That's right. More lies have been told in the Oval Office than any other place in the world," Cotton laughed.

"You really don't trust politicians, do you?" Chase laughed.

"Tell me one reason I should," Cotton challenged.

"They are at least consistent," Chase said.

"Consistent liars and moneygrubbers."

"OK, he asked me if I had any reason to suspect that Townsend was the shooter," Chase said.

"A fair question," Cotton said. "And what did you say?"

"I answered honestly. I pointed out that our agreement kept me from investigating Townsend's disappearance and that precluded me from exploring the possibility that he was the shooter. I noted that under normal circumstances the secretary would have been a suspect."

"And?"

"And I honestly admitted that I did not know if Townsend was the shooter."

Cotton smiled. "That's what I suspected, but your conversation did not end there."

"What makes you say that?"

"I know you. You are a persistent and devious fellow. You asked him if he knew something that made him suspect Townsend was the shooter."

"Something like that," Chase admitted.

"Well, what did he say?"

"You never give up, do you?"

"And never do you, Mansfield. That's why I like you so much," Cotton chuckled.

Chase laughed.

"What did he say then?"

"He told me that jobs like Secretary of Homeland Security are man killers and Townsend had been showing the stress."

"That's it?"

"That's it."

"And that is why you have been sniffing after Mrs. Townsend."

"Not at all. She and her husband have known my victim for a long time and I was legitimately trying to identify any mutual friends."

"Alright. Now answer my question that you avoided by asking about the ransom," Cotton said.

"And that question was?"

"Do you think Townsend shot Jesperson before taking off with his kidnappers?"

"I'll tell you the same thing I told the president. I don't know."

"But now you have some questions for Secretary Townsend that they did not give you a chance to ask at that little rural retreat of theirs."

"You were doing all the asking," Chase said.

"Alright, your turn will come," Cotton said.

"What about our separate investigations?"

"They will continue. My job is to identify the kidnappers, terrorists, or whatever, and your job is to find Jesperson's killer."

"And you won't object if I ask the Townsends a few questions?"

"I suspect you already have during that little time out you spent with the Townsends after they locked me out," Cotton said.

"I tried but you interrupted as I was just getting started," Chase said.

"What did he tell you?"

"That he had a drink with Jesperson waiting for the lecture crowd to disperse and the professor was alive when he left at nine-thirty."

"How much nicer it is when we share," Cotton said.

"Were you taken in by his little act back there?" Chase asked.

"No, were you?"

"He looked in bad shape when we arrived, like a man who had been held under trying circumstances for two weeks," Chase said.

"But he recovered damned fast."

Chase nodded. "Is that how kidnap victims behave?"

"Maybe. Everyone's different, and it depends on how they've been treated. Some even start to empathize with their kidnappers. It's also not unusual for a released victim to experience a high followed by depression and a physical reaction later."

"We'll have to keep an eye on Secretary Townsend," Chase said.

"But discreetly. He has friends in high places," Cotton said.

"I guess," Chase said.

Cotton stared at him. "What does that mean?"

"I agree with you," Chase smiled.

"Shit. That's means I'm in trouble."

Chapter 19

A Bureau car transported Cotton from Andrews to headquarters where he briefed Director D'Antonio who immediately alerted the president and was told to report to the Oval Office forthwith.

Special Agent Cotton and D'Antonio were quickly ushered inside where they found President Arthur C Featherstone, Vice President Charles Hampton, and Chief of Staff Ted Bertram waiting.

"Where is he?" Featherstone demanded, apparently expecting his FBI director to have Secretary Townsend with him.

"With your permission, sir, I will let Special Agent Cotton brief you and answer your questions," D'Antonio reacted like an experienced bureaucrat facing a hostile superior. He delegated.

Featherstone abandoned his position on the couch and retreated behind his massive desk, a gesture that made it perfectly clear this was neither a celebratory nor social occasion. Once seated, Featherstone nodded at Cotton.

"Sir, the secretary is now resting at his retreat on the eastern shore," Cotton addressed the president's question.

"What is he doing there? Why isn't he in the hospital for a checkup?" Featherstone demanded.

"His captors released him there and..." Cotton started to explain.

"I know that," Featherstone rudely interrupted. "Director D'Antonio briefed me on the phone call to Mrs. Townsend. Why did you leave him in Ocean City?" The president's tone and body language signaled that he thought Cotton had acted unprofessionally.

Cotton bristled at the president's unfair attitude, but after a slight hesitation, during which he fought to keep his volatile Irish temper under control, he responded curtly but evenly.

"The secretary refused to accompany us back to D.C. Our doctor gave him a cursory examination and recommended that he check in a hospital for follow up tests, but the secretary refused."

"Did the poor man know what he was doing? What kind of shape is he in? Did they mistreat him?" The president continued to fire from the hip.

Cotton opted to answer the president's questions seriatim. "He initially appeared to be slightly confused, but he quickly improved. Secretary Townsend lucidly described the events leading to his abduction. They grabbed him as he was about to enter his car, rendered him unconscious, tied his arms and legs, gagged, and blindfolded him. He woke on the floor of a van or small truck—he was not sure—and was driven for several hours until his captors locked him up in a windowless room where he was kept for the entire time. He has no idea where that was, and he could not identify or describe his captors who always wore ski masks."

"Poor James," Featherstone said, demonstrating compassion for the first time. The president leaned back in his chair and stared silently at the ceiling.

Cotton relaxed slightly, but his posture, tight facial features, and clenched fists indicated he was still fighting his anger. "The secretary describes his treatment as uncomfortable; he suffered considerable emotional distress, but he was not physically abused."

"Good. What is his current condition?"

"Mentally, stable. Physically, he needs rest. That is why we acquiesced when he insisted on staying at his farm, his retreat, he called it."

"You didn't leave him alone?" The president frowned, his words more an accusation than a question.

"I did not. Mrs. Townsend is with him, and I assigned members of our team to provide security."

"The doctor is not with him?"

"No, sir. The secretary insisted that he and his wife be left undisturbed. I assigned the security over his objections."

Featherstone nodded approval but did not speak.

"The secretary said he would remain at the shore until Monday when he would return to Washington and report to you directly."

"And you are certain he cannot identify his abductors?" The president asked.

"He claimed he could not, but my debriefing was quite limited."

"Because?"

"Because the secretary refused to answer any more questions until he had met with you."

"How is Mrs. Townsend handling all this?" Featherstone asked.

"Very well. She seemed to be in complete control of her emotions," Cotton said.

"She's a tough woman," Featherstone said. "She will take care of her man. Were you able to draw any conclusions from what the secretary told you?"

"No, sir."

"Were his captors terrorists?"

"We do not know. They spoke with American accents," Cotton answered, his responses to the president's questions still clipped.

"I'm not sure that is definitive, sir," D'Antonio said, joining the exchange because he feared that Cotton might lose his volatile temper, an indiscretion that could have dire consequences with this president.

For some reason, D'Antonio's comment seemed to irritate the already agitated Featherstone. "Have we been able to track the money?" Featherstone turned on his FBI director.

"We have teams working on it," D'Antonio said. "This is a slow process. As you know these offshore bankers resist sharing information. Their businesses and reputations depend on their ability to safeguard their clients' confidentiality."

"I know that." Featherstone's tone indicated that he was in no mood to accept any excuses. "This isn't a simple tax case."

D'Antonio nodded but did not comment.

"Where do we stand with our inquiry?" Featherstone pushed.

"We have a team in the Caymans meeting with officials of the Freeman Bank, and they are still stalling," D'Antonio said.

"How long are we going to put up with that?" Featherstone asked.

"It is a long standing issue, sir," D'Antonio said. "We're working with CIA and the State Department on the problem."

"Is there someone I should call?"

"We've got a couple of potential leads, and State is of the opinion that political pressure would be counter-productive."

"State always thinks pressure will be counter-productive. The cookie pushers prefer to just talk," Featherstone said.

"Sir, if you agree, I will join the director's discussions with State on the issue," Vice President Hampton volunteered. The implication that he would lean on the Secretary of State was clear.

Featherstone did not immediately respond. After a few seconds of uneasy silence, Featherstone nodded. "Thank you, Charles, that might prove helpful. However, I am determined that we track that money one way or another. Do what you can, but please keep me informed."

Featherstone turned his attention back to D'Antonio. "Do what you have to do but follow that money and identify the perpetrators. Now that Secretary Townsend has been released, I'm confident the full story will leak to the media, and we all know what that means. The combining of the killing of Doctor Jesperson with an atomic threat and the kidnap of our Homeland Security Secretary will drive the media into a frenzy. We cannot be seen sitting here twiddling our thumbs. I will deal with Iran, but I want the killer of Doctor Jesperson and the kidnappers of Secretary Townsend brought to justice. Do you understand?"

"Yes, sir," D'Antonio said.

"This is our number one priority. If we don't succeed, not a single one of us will be sitting in this room much longer," Featherstone said before turning his back and staring out the window, rudely dismissing them. Not one of the others missed the menace in his voice.

Cotton, who had been sitting closest to the door, had his hand on the knob when Featherstone, twisted in his chair and spoke in a still angry voice, "Special Agent Cotton, I expect to see Secretary Townsend in this office Monday if you have to handcuff him and deliver him on a stretcher."

"Yes, sir," Cotton said as he opened the door and hurried through the outer office followed by a shaken D'Antonio.

****

Chase retrieved his Prius and drove directly from Andrews to his headquarters where he briefed Barney and the chief on the recent developments. When Chase finished, Chief Raymond Arthur leaned back in his chair and thoughtfully studied his lead detective, Chase, and CIB commander, Major Barney Hopkins.

"Do you really think the Secretary of Homeland Security is our shooter?" Arthur asked.

"I frankly do not know," Chase answered honestly.

"Who are your other suspects?" Arthur asked calmly.

"May I be honest, chief?" Chase asked.

"I would have it no other way, detective."

Chase noticed that the chief did not refer to him by his rank. When talking officially, Arthur always addressed him as lieutenant. Informally, Arthur called him Chase. The use of the simple title detective was not a pejorative, but it was a new approach, and it worried Chase. Chase wondered if it meant that the chief was not angry but not relaxed either, probably feeling political pressure from somewhere.

"Secretary Townsend claims he left Doctor Jesperson's office at nine-thirty and his long time friend was alive then. I cannot identify a single person who saw Doctor Jesperson between nine-thirty and twelve-thirty when a cleaning lady found his body." Chase hesitated.

"And that means?" The chief asked.

Chase shrugged. "Either the secretary shot him and is lying about it or a person or persons unknown did."

"Who had a motive?" Arthur, an old homicide detective, asked.

"Certainly, the Iranians," Chase said.

"On what do you base that theory?"

"The furor created by the publication of the professor's book. Doctor Jesperson cited what some consider reliable information that indicates the Iranian Government in defiance of the United States, the United Nations, and much of the world, has created an atomic bomb which the professor alleges the Iranians plan to use."

"I've read the news stories," Arthur said. "If the Iranians killed Doctor Jesperson to prevent the publication of his book, they failed miserably. Why would the Iranians think killing the professor would stop its publication?"

"I don't know," Chase said. "Obviously, I'm not an expert on Iran, but it is my impression that their government does not always anticipate the consequences of their actions correctly."

Arthur nodded, his expression skeptical, but he did not dispute the point. Instead, he asked, "Have you identified any potential Iranian agents who might have acted on behalf of their government? I'm talking about suspects who might have killed Jesperson."

"Identifying Iranian spies is difficult to do, sir, because as you know relations between our two governments have been disrupted for a number of years," Chase said.

"Something like thirty years, since the hostile takeover of our embassy in Teheran and the reprehensible holding of American citizens as hostages by alleged students," Arthur said.

"That's right, sir. There are no Iranian diplomats in Washington and no American diplomats in Teheran."

"But there are Iranian citizens in this country."

"Yes, sir. There are many Iranian refugees, pro-Shah types, residing here. I'm told that most love their country but despise its current government."

"Have you identified any Iranians residing in our area who are not refugees, who are loyal citizens here for other purposes, bonafide businessmen for example?"

"Yes sir, we have Iranian students who plan to complete their education and then return home."

"Are there any at George Mason?"

"Yes sir."

"Have you talked with any of them?"

"Yes, sir," Chase answered, thinking of the Foreign Students Association in general and Mansour Taheri, the victim's mother's relative, and his friend Jamshid Afgar, particularly the latter who was in his thirties and had resided in the States for ten years.

"Do you think any of them could be an agent of the Iranian Government?"

"Yes, sir, that's possible. Of course identifying foreign spies is not my area of expertise."

"I know that, lieutenant. Sometimes I wonder just what is your area of expertise, as you put it. I'm simply trying to find out what you have been up to. Have you coordinated this possibility with Special Agent Cotton?"

"I have not reached that point yet, sir, and Special Agent Cotton has been preoccupied with the Townsend case."

"When do you believe you will reach the point?"

"When I develop evidence that supports the hypothesis," Chase smiled, liking his choice of words.

"Please explain that to me, lieutenant. I am not as much a wordsmith as you seem to think you are."

"Two Iranian students were close to Doctor Jesperson. One in fact lived with him, a Mansour Taheri, who is a grandson of the victim's mother's sister. That makes him a distant relative."

"I know what a relative is," Arthur interrupted. "Please continue without trying to amuse Major Hopkins or myself."

"Mansour arrived in this country only two weeks before the doctor's death."

"Do you find that coincidental?"

"Yes, sir, but it is one of the reasons I carry Mansour on my list. The

Iranian Government could have dispatched him to kill his distant cousin, but I tend to doubt it."

Arthur waited for Chase to explain.

"Mansour strikes me as an insecure, young man quite overwhelmed by his new country. He was living with Doctor Jesperson at the time of his murder, dependent upon his distant relative who acted as his sponsor."

"And now?"

"Mansour appears to have attached himself to the other Iranian student, Jamshid Afgar. He is the one that interests me. Afgar came to the States on a student visa and has never left. He appears to have slipped under the INS radar."

"Is he still a student?"

"In a manner of speaking. He has completed all his coursework on his PhD and claims to be now writing his doctorate."

"Claims to be?"

"He doesn't appear to be working very hard at it. He attended Doctor Jesperson's funeral in Cambridge with young Mansour."

"That's interesting."

"Maybe. Jesperson was the faculty advisor overseeing Afgar's dissertation."

"Where does Afgar get his money?"

"Presumably from his family in Iran. I was planning on pursuing that when I was distracted by the Townsend connection."

"Tell me more," Arthur ordered.

"I am only involved on the periphery of the investigation into Townsend's disappearance, as you know. Mrs. Townsend, for some reason, doesn't particularly like the Bureau in general and Special Agent Cotton in particular. I suspect it is because they have invaded her home. As a part of my investigation—Secretary Townsend was the last known visitor to have seen Doctor Jesperson prior to his murder and is one of the few friends I have been able to identify—I have to keep the secretary on my list of suspects."

"Not at the top, I hope," Arthur smiled.

"No sir, but I have interviewed Mrs. Townsend on a couple of occasions, and she seems to appreciate my concern."

"Not too much, I hope," Arthur cautioned. He was aware of his subordinate's bachelor status and reputation for having a roaming inclination, even his tendency to be distracted by attractive young women on the periphery of his investigations.

"No sir," Chase said. "She's a little old for me."

"How old?"

"Past her prime."

"How far past?"

"She's a well preserved fifty something."

Chief Raymond Arthur, who was in his mid-fifties, reacted. "Lieutenant, let me give you a little advice. Many of these well-preserved ladies in their fifties have wandering eyes. Be careful with your attempt to cultivate a source because if misunderstandings of your intentions develop, they could be quite counter-productive, especially when the wife of a cabinet secretary is involved."

"Counter-productive, chief?" Chase asked.

"Yes. There is another thing you should understand about women of that age."

Chase glanced at Barney and grinned, which was a mistake because the chief was frowning when Chase turned his attention back to him.

"I'm speaking seriously, lieutenant," Arthur said.

"Yes, sir," Chase said, not quite succeeding in his attempt to hide his amusement.

"Women when they turn forty begin to sour," the chief said.

"Sour, sir?"

"Yes, sour. Every single one of them," Arthur glared at Chase. "And by the time they reach fifty, they have completely soured. Some of them hide that simple fact, presumably like your Mrs. Townsend, and most do not. Souring changes their personalities. When younger, they act as if a man is the focal point of their lives. They pretend their man can do no wrong. After the souring process completes, they drop the pretense; from that point on, man, their man, any man, can do no right. If this Mrs. Townsend is acting as if she is relying on you in reaction to Special Agent Cotton and the Bureau, beware. This soured woman is merely acting, using you, for her own purposes."

"I'm sure that's where the phrase sourpuss came from, chief," Chase humored his superior, not daring to look at Barney this time.

"Don't be cocky, lieutenant. Beware, I am quite serious. What does Mrs. Townsend stand to gain by using you?"

Given the context of their discussion, the chief's choice of words amused Chase even more. Chase had to force himself to think seriously about Arthur's question. Not having given the subject any thought, Chase hesitated before answering. After a pause, he said, "She may be protecting her husband."

"From what? I thought he was the victim."

"Maybe she is trying to keep me from investigating her husband as a suspect in my murder case," Chase said, simply trying to get the chief off his back.

"And that takes me back to my original question which you tried to finesse; do you really think the Secretary of Homeland Security is our shooter?"

"I answered honestly when I responded that I do not know," Chase said.

"Then I suggest you work on the answer to that question," Arthur ordered.

"The secretary's kidnapping was a real impediment," Chase said, regretting the words as soon as he spoke them. Excuses always irritated the chief, just like they did Chase. "I unwisely accepted the Bureau's suggestion that I investigate the Jesperson murder and leave the secretary's disappearance to them," Chase tried to dig himself out of the self-created hole.

Arthur smiled at Chase's discomfort when he turned to Barney, his CIB commander. "I thought that an unwise compromise at the time, major, but I said nothing when I saw that you agreed with the lieutenant."

"Yes, sir," Barney said the only thing he could. He rather enjoyed watching Chase's suffering, but not when the chief unfairly included him as part of the problem.

"I assume, lieutenant," Arthur turned back to Chase, "the secretary's return removes that little impediment from your path."

"Virtually," Chase said.

"What does that mean?"

"On the flight back from the shore, Cotton and I discussed the issue of separate investigations."

"And?"

"I told him quite forcefully that I had to ask Townsend some questions."

"Did he object?"

"Initially, of course, but after I confided that the president and I had discussed the fact I had to consider Townsend a possible suspect in my investigation, Cotton acknowledged my position."

"You revealed the substance of your conversation with the president?" Arthur asked.

"Yes sir."

Arthur shook his head in disapproval. "You said Cotton acknowledged your position. What does that mean?"

"He insisted that the separate investigations continue. He said his job now is to identify the kidnappers, and my job is to find Jesperson's killer. I frankly told him my investigation required me to interview the Townsends, and he did not object."

"I assume no objection represents progress," the chief smiled wryly. "Now that you have the Bureau's and the president's authorizations to proceed, I expect you will be moving ahead at top speed."

"Tacit authorizations, sir. I will still have to move with circumspection."

"Please don't start the word games again with me, lieutenant," Arthur said. "Can I assume that your use of the word 'tacit' was simply an inadvertent reaction and not an attempt to qualify your authorizations?"

"Yes, sir," Chase said. He did not state that his agreement connoted only acknowledgement that the chief could assume anything he wanted.

"Good. Do what you have to do, but don't overlook Townsend or the Iranian connection. You haven't come across any Iranians except for the two you cited?"

Chase hesitated before answering. Normally, the chief deferred completely to him on his investigations, but given the involvement of the Bureau, a cabinet secretary, the president, a foreign government, allegations of a possible atomic attack on the United States, and the world media, Chase understood Arthur's interest, particularly the president's involvement. He really did not want to mention Doctor Lyla Jalili, however.

"There is one other Iranian person of interest," Chase finally admitted.

"I assume there are many others that we do not know of," the chief said. "Tell me about this third person."

"There is a young instructor at George Mason who has taken over Doctor Jesperson's academic responsibilities for the remainder of the school year," Chase said.

"A person who gained from Doctor Jesperson's demise," Arthur observed. "That's interesting. Tell me more."

"Doctor Jalili is a young Iranian who recently graduated from the University of Paris. GMU hired her as an instructor, and she arrived in the States just before Doctor Townsend departed on his sabbatical. She filled in for him during his absence. Although the Near East and Iran are her subjects, she had only limited contact with him since his return because he was preoccupied with his book and resuming his classes."

"The fact that she is female does not rule her out as the shooter," Arthur said.

"No, sir. I've interviewed her twice." Chase did not admit that she had served him an excellent dinner in her home and had filled him with enough wine to cause him to pass out and spend an unconscious night. "I plan to continue the interview again as soon as I can schedule it."

"You say young. How old is she?" Arthur asked.

"She hasn't begun to sour," Chase smiled.

The chief frowned.

"Late twenties, early thirties, sir."

"Attractive?"

"Some men would think so," Chase equivocated.

"And you?"

"Yes, sir. She's no...she's no...." Chase tried to think of a movie star with dark hair whose name the chief would recognize. "...Ava Gardner," Chase said.

"Oh shit," Arthur reacted. "Where did these interviews take place?"

"In her GMU office and at her Fairfax townhouse," Chase answered reluctantly.

"Her townhouse?"

"Yes sir. Doctor Jalili has a very busy schedule," Chase smiled. "So I tried to accommodate her."

"I'll bet you did. Over dinner?"

"Yes sir."

"Where?"

"At the townhouse. The doctor was quite rushed."

"Make sure your next interview takes place in a public venue."

"I'm not sure that is advisable, sir," Chase said.

"Why is that?"

"Because of the media sir. I don't want the media to conclude we are focusing on Doctor Jalili."

"And why is that?"

"That's all this investigation needs, the involvement of a Mata Hari."

The chief thought about that for a few seconds and then turned to his CIB commander. "What do you think, major?"

"I defer to Chase's judgment," Barney said.

"I expect you to monitor this little side issue," Arthur said.

"There's another attractive female in the equation," Chase tried to distract the chief.

"And that is?"

"The Lady in Black, sir."

"The Lady in Black?"

"Yes sir, Ms. Kendrick, Doctor Jesperson's former fiancée. I met her in Cambridge at Doctor Jesperson's funeral. I had scheduled an interview with her but it was interrupted by the president's summons."

"Don't let this president thing distract you, lieutenant," Arthur ordered. "This fiancée, is she the one that Jesperson dropped a year ago?"

"Yes sir, prior to the sabbatical. She hasn't seen Doctor Jesperson since."

"So why is she important?"

"Because she is the only person I have been able to identify who had anything more than a casual relationship with Doctor Jesperson. I need to identify others who can tell me about the victim's lifestyle."

"Don't forget Secretary Townsend and his wife," Arthur ordered. "I hope you are not allowing all these side issues to distract you."

"No sir. Apprehend the killer. I'm quite focused."

"Good," Arthur said before waving his hand in the air and casually dismissing them.

"Somebody's gnawing on his backside," Barney said when they were back in the hall.

"Better his than mine," Chase laughed.

"Speaking of backsides, you better watch yours with all these unsoured women in this case," Barney laughed.

"Only two unsoured and one concealing it," Chase referred to Mrs. Townsend.

"I know, but I've got explicit orders to keep an eye on you," Barney said.

"Have fun," Chase laughed.

Chapter 20

After briefing a shocked cabinet on the Townsend kidnapping and release without mentioning the thirty million dollar ransom payment, Featherstone took refuge behind the walls of the Oval Office where he found his Secretary of Homeland Security patiently waiting.

"James," Featherstone clutched Townsend with both arms.

"Mr. President," Townsend replied formally.

Featherstone stepped back and studied Townsend. He was clean shaven, pale, needed a haircut, and he looked like he had lost weight; he appeared almost normal, nothing like the person that Cotton had described when he had reported on the scene at Townsend's eastern shore retreat.

"I apologize, Mr. President, for not properly scheduling this visit or attending your cabinet meeting," Townsend said.

"James, don't talk nonsense," Featherstone said, taking Townsend by the arm and guiding him to the couch. James allowed the president to lead him, but he did not sit down. He waited politely for the president to seat himself first.

"Sit down, James," Featherstone ordered.

"I'm not an invalid, Mr. President," Townsend said.

Featherstone pressed Townsend on the shoulder until he lowered himself onto the couch. Featherstone then seated himself opposite. The two men stared in silence at each other until the president finally spoke, "We were very worried about you, James."

"I know and I apologize for all the problems I caused," Townsend said.

"Nonsense. James you were a victim. Was it bad? I feared they had killed you."

"I was uncomfortable and frankly bored," Townsend said. "At no time did they threaten me directly."

"Do you have any idea who they were?"

Townsend shook his head negatively. "I wish I did. I suspect you know more about them than I do."

"Tell me what happened, chronologically," Featherstone said.

"This won't take long. First," Townsend said. "I must thank you for saving my miserable life."

"I was afraid I might have caused your death."

"How in the world could anyone accuse you of doing that?" Townsend asked.

"I don't know. How much do you know," Featherstone asked.

"Only what Nancy Lou told me," Townsend referred to his wife.

"Nancy probably knows more than I do." Featherstone hesitated, waiting for Townsend to comment. When he did not, Featherstone continued. "They sent two e-mails, one from Paris, and one from Malta. They signed themselves "The Suffering People."

"Never heard of them," Townsend said.

"No one else has either. The communications were only one way. We couldn't negotiate with them. They demanded a hundred million dollars. In the second message they set a deadline and ordered us to wire the money to the Cayman Freeman Bank in the Cayman Islands."

"I don't know the bank," Townsend said, "but I'm sure the Bureau does."

"They're working on it," Featherstone said. "They also told us to pay or pray because if we didn't respond you were dead."

"So you paid," Townsend said. "If I had been advising you, I would have argued against sending the money. The United States Government cannot give in to terrorist demands."

"I know, James," Featherstone said. "We were only able to raise thirty million in the short time allotted to us. We must thank Charles," he referred to the vice president, "for that."

"I will. You and he saved my miserable life. I'm glad you did, but I think it was the wrong thing to do. We've placed Americans around the world at risk."

"I was hoping that they would accept the thirty million and demand the rest, giving us time to collect it while continuing our search for you and them. Why do you think they took the money and released you?"

"I don't know, Mr. President. I didn't have a single conversation with them. They grabbed me in the parking lot following my talk at George Mason, tied me up, covered my eyes, gagged me, and drove me around for several hours. After what seemed an eternity, they locked me up in a windowless room, gave me a pot to piss in, fed me two meals a day, told me nothing, asked me nothing. I didn't know if it was day or night or how much time passed. They took my watch along with my wallet, suit coat, belt, and shoes. It seemed like an eternity to me. I assumed they were holding me for a reason, demanding something. I didn't know who they were or what they wanted, money, prisoner release, I just didn't know."

"It must have been terrible."

"It was. And now we all have to face the media onslaught."

"I know," Featherstone said. "We should keep private the fact they did not interrogate you."

"Real terrorists would have seized the opportunity," Townsend agreed.

"Somehow we kept everything out of the media," Featherstone continued without noting that the failure to interrogate the Secretary of Homeland Security about ongoing American operations truly puzzled him. "The media focused on your friend Doctor Jesperson's murder and the publication of his book. Those two things were sensational enough, particularly the allegations about the Iranian bomb and all that. Do you think there is a connection?"

"There has to be. I was taken shortly after I left Thomas's office, and someone killed him. Do you think the kidnappers murdered Thomas to cover my kidnapping? Christ, I hope not. I couldn't bear carrying that responsibility on my back for the rest of my life. And how could they have known where I was going to be and that I would arrogantly leave my security detail at home? I just wanted to talk with Thomas about that book. We had heard rumors about what was in it, and I needed to learn about his sources, find out if they were reliable or not."

"Did you?"

"No, sir. My friend refused to tell me a thing."

"The Bureau and the Agency will eventually break it all down; they always do."

"I know, but I'm afraid it might all be my fault," Townsend said.

"I doubt it," Featherstone disagreed. "Everything points at the Iranians. If they had someone close to Doctor Jesperson, they would have known about your visit. Not the fact that you were leaving your protective detail behind, but they could have learned about your lecture, and they could have decided to kill two birds with one act, so to speak-- eliminate Jesperson and his book, and pay their expenses by kidnapping you. I'm surprised they released you. Killing you was something I'm sure they might think was something worth doing all by itself."

"I don't know," Townsend said. "I still feel like it was all my fault."

"Then stop feeling that way," Featherstone ordered. "Did Doctor Jesperson discuss his sources, tell you that the Iranians really have the bomb and are getting ready to nuke us?"

"He declined to discuss his book with me, told me I would have to wait and buy a copy." Townsend shook his head in dismay. I've known Thomas for over thirty years—we were at Cornell together—and he refused to answer my questions or discuss his sources."

"Then our troubles have just begun," Featherstone said, watching Townsend closely. "Do you know what your friend said in his book?"

"I haven't read it, but Nancy Lou gisted it for me. The Iranians have the bomb and plan to use it." Townsend shook his head in dismay.

"I'm sure the media are clamoring out there as we speak," Featherstone glanced at the door to his office. "I just briefed the cabinet on your kidnapping and release."

Townsend grimaced.

"I know, but I had to James. I'm sure half the cabinet is standing in front of microphones and television cameras by now."

"You had best put out a public announcement, sir. You can connect it with the release about my resignation," Townsend said as he pulled an envelope from his pocket.

"No, put that away," Featherstone pointed at the envelope.

"I'm sorry, sir, but this is not negotiable. I've compromised myself. The hundred million dollar man," Townsend shook his head in disgust. "Because of me, my friend is dead. You and the country are facing an atomic threat, and the United States Government has surrendered to terrorist demands, paid a ridiculous ransom."

"I need your sage advice now more than ever," Featherstone said.

"Not really sir. Please excuse me, but this is the time for frank honesty. The truth be known I never was up to the job you entrusted to me."

"That's not true," Featherstone said.

"I appreciate your support, but I know what I can and cannot do, could and could not do. I am now convinced that the Department of Homeland Security was a bad solution to an almost unmanageable problem. I'm not sure that any one man can take all those competing different organizations and make them function as a compatible unit."

Featherstone surprised Townsend by laughing. "James," he smiled wryly, "you are looking at the man the Congress and the American people have charged with doing just that. You are my solution to the impossible problem."

"Then I have let you down, Mr. President. The job is beyond me. We were better off when all those agencies reported to different people. At least then they were working on the tasks assigned to them. Now, they are too busy fighting their bureaucratic wars to do even that."

"You've got to bang heads, James. I told you that when I gave you the job. I'll support you. Replace them all if you have to."

"Sir, I can't do it," Townsend said as he placed his envelope on the table between them. "I tried and failed. Now, I'm compromised."

"Compromised? Stop talking nonsense. If anyone is compromised, it's me," Featherstone tapped his chest with a forefinger. "You know what Harry Truman said, the buck stops right here, right at that desk." He turned and pointed at the Resolute desk behind him.

"I've lost the will to fight, sir," Townsend stood up.

"Nonsense, Secretary Townsend," Featherstone deliberately used the shaken man's title as he remained seated. "You're just feeling the impact of your recent experience. Take some time off. Talk with a shrink. You and Nancy Lou regroup at your place on the shore."

"We're selling the farm; Nancy Lou and I are getting a divorce," Townsend said.

"Good God, man, don't start making decisions you are in no condition to make. You'll regret every one. You need medical help."

"Maybe I do, sir," Townsend said as he started for the door. "My resignation is effective immediately."

"What are you going to do? You're too young to just lie down and die."

"Maybe I'll write a book. They say that can be therapeutic."

"The media will beat you to it. By the time they finish with this story, there will not be anything left for you to write about. You know as well as I do the public has a very short attention span."

"I thank you for everything, Mr. President."

"I didn't give you anything you didn't earn, James," Featherstone said as he realized that he had lost the poor, broken man.

"Thank you for giving me a job that I could not handle, for saving my miserable life which was not worth saving," Townsend said and departed.

Featherstone sat in his chair and reviewed the conversation that had just ended until the door opened and his secretary entered, closing the door behind her.

"Mr. President, I'm very sorry to bother you, but we have a crisis on our hands," Heather said.

Featherstone who had been deep in thought looked up with a start, nodded at Heather, and then started laughing, surprising Heather who had feared that her interruption was going to precipitate an angry eruption. Heather waited patiently until Featherstone smiled at her.

"Sorry about that, Heather? Sometimes this place functions more like a loony bin than the office of the most powerful man in the world. I often wonder what in the hell I'm doing here, trying to act like a sane man."

"Without you sir, the world is in serious trouble," Heather said the first thing that came to her mind.

"You don't really mean that, do you?" Featherstone started laughing again. "You just can't be serious."

Heather did not respond; she just stared at her boss, the President of the United States.

Finally, Featherstone stood up, picked up the envelope from the table in front of him, and returned to his desk. After sitting down behind it, Featherstone nonchalantly tossed the envelope on the worn Resolute timbers and spoke to his secretary.

"Heather, you are really going to have to work on your sense of humor."

Privately, Featherstone appreciated his hard working, efficient assistant but doubted that she had any sense of humor whatsoever, a failing common in most women, including his spouse, who actually took her responsibilities as First Lady seriously, particularly the nonsense that the media wrote about her.

"Yes, sir, I will," Heather said. "We really do have a crisis. Ms. Turner and Mr. Bertram are in my office waiting to speak with you urgently." Heather referred to Patty Turner, the White House Press Secretary, and Theodore Bertram, Featherstone's Chief of Staff.

"Please show Patty and Ted in," Featherstone said.

"Yes , sir," Heather said as she turned for the door.

"Wait," Featherstone stopped her. "Tell me one thing. Did Secretary Townsend make it out of your office without falling over a chair or getting lost?"

"Yes, sir," Heather answered seriously as she wondered what the president was talking about. Sometimes he said the dumbest things.

"One thing, Heather," the president said.

"Yes sir."

"Please invite that Lieutenant Mansfield of the Fairfax Police to come and see me at his earliest convenience."

"Yes, sir," Heather made a note on her pad.

"And, after you have him scheduled, arrange for D'Antonio and Special Agent Cotton to meet with me right after Mansfield."

"Yes, sir."

"But not before Mansfield."

Heather waited for the president to continue, but he did not. Heather opened the door and nodded to the waiting chief of staff and press secretary. The pacing Patty Turner was the first into the Oval Office.

"Sir, the media have picked up on the Townsend story," Patty announced.

"It was inevitable," Ted said as he carefully closed the door behind him.

"Did you see Secretary Townsend when he left here?" Featherstone greeted his two aides with a question.

"Yes, sir," Turner and Bertram answered, simultaneously.

"He looks like hell warmed over," Turner added.

"He's going to look worse after the media get a hold of him," Bertram said.

"He's had a very bad experience, and he didn't come out of it in as good condition as I hoped he might," Featherstone said. "Please sit down, both of you," Featherstone indicated the two chairs facing his desk. "We've got a lot to discuss."

After his two assistants were seated, Featherstone looked directly at his press secretary. "Patty, I assume the mob is clamoring for some kind of announcement."

"Yes sir," Turner said. "They've got the story of Townsend's kidnapping. All the networks are treating it as breaking news and Fox and CNN are already alleging cover-up."

"That's nonsense," Featherstone fumed. "When you leave here, I want you to conduct a formal briefing in the press room."

"The story's really big sir. It might be best if you handled it yourself," Turner suggested.

"No, I'm not going to appear defensive about the way we handled the

Townsend thing," Featherstone glared at his press secretary. "If you can't deal with the media, we can find someone who can."

"I can handle it, sir," Turner retreated. "But I will need someone to brief me on the details. I haven't been involved..."

"I know that. Ted can brief you. I've got more important things to worry about."

"We could defer to the Bureau," Ted suggested cautiously.

"No, I want it handled here and now. Nip this nonsense about cover-up in the bud." Featherstone glared at his chief of staff before turning back to Turner. "The kidnappers grabbed Secretary Townsend following his appearance at George Mason the night that professor, his friend, was murdered. Townsend just told me the story. They tied him up and blindfolded him, drove him around for several hours, and then held him captive in a windowless room. They sent us two e-mails threatening to kill the secretary if we did not pay a ransom. After an urgent attempt to track them down failed, we decided to pay the ransom. We did so, and the kidnappers released the secretary. That's the story you should tell. Stress there was no cover-up as some of the misguided and misinformed members of the media allege. We did not announce Secretary' Townsend's disappearance because to do so would have resulted in his immediate execution. Don't take any follow-up questions. Let the Bureau and DHS manage any subsequent announcements."

"That will work sir," Turner stood up.

"Wait, I'm not finished," Featherstone ordered.

"Since I have to do all the work around here," Featherstone paused long enough to glare at his two silent assistants, "I will tell you what to do first. Start with an announcement. Secretary Townsend submitted his resignation this morning."

"Did he give a reason, sir? The media will want to know," Turner said.

"Damned fools," Featherstone declared.

Neither Turner nor Bertram could tell if the president was talking about them or the media, and neither asked.

"The poor man has just undergone a very trying experience and needs time to recuperate. You may say I accepted the resignation with great reluctance and expressed my appreciation for his outstanding service in a most demanding job. I wish him well in his future activities."

"Do we know what he plans to do next?" Turner asked.

"How the hell do I know?" Featherstone reacted. "Probably write a damned book."

"Tell them that is a question that Secretary Townsend himself should address," Bertram suggested.

Featherstone nodded. "Can you do your jobs now?"

"Yes, sir," Turner leaped to her feet and started for the door, now more anxious to deal with the media than continue with the president in this mood.

Bertram remained seated.

Featherstone turned his chair and faced out the window.

Bertram immediately got the message. "If there is nothing else, sir..." Bertram stood up.

Featherstone did not bother to reply, and Bertram retreated, following the rapidly moving Turner out the door. After it closed behind him, Bertram glanced at a worried Heather.

"Christ, he's in a terrible mood," Bertram forced a smile.

Heather shrugged and turned to her monitor. The two Secret Service agents guarding the door exchanged smiles.

****

After a brief appearance at his office, Chase headed for George Mason University where he intended to visit the elusive Doctor Lyla Jalili in her office, elusive because he had tried to phone her several times over the weekend, and she had not answered the calls nor responded to his messages. The last he could remember about their evening together was that they were getting along just fine. They had had a delicious meal and were sharing a glass of postprandial wine when everything went blank until he woke in his underwear on the couch in an empty house. Suddenly, his cell phone paged, and Chase answered, hoping Lyla had finally discovered his calls.

"Mansfield," Chase said.

"Hang on, lieutenant," Theresa said. "You've got a call."

"Who is it?" Chase asked.

"You'll never guess," Theresa laughed before Chase's cell phone started to click, indicating she was transferring the call.

"Lieutenant Mansfield?" An unfamiliar female voice greeted him.

"Yes," a disappointed Chase answered. Lyla was still ignoring him.

"This is Heather James, President Featherstone's assistant."

"Good morning, Heather," Chase answered neutrally, hiding his concern that she was the bearer of tidings he did not want to receive.

"Good morning, lieutenant," Heather matched his tone. "May I ask where you are right now?"

Oh shit, Chase thought. *Not again.*

"I need to know how long it will take you to get to the White House," Heather did not wait for him to answer her question. "The president would like to speak with you forthwith."

"I'm in Fairfax on Route 50 on my way to George Mason University where I have an important interview scheduled."

"You can be here in forty minutes, right?" Heather ignored his reference to an important interview.

Chase said nothing.

"Good, I'll schedule you to see the president at eleven thirty-five," Heather said. "If you can, you might want to listen to a news station as you make your way." Heather terminated the call before Chase could make another excuse.

Chase briefly thought about ignoring the summons but quickly decided that would not be politic. He doubted that the president wanted to give him a medal, but he had few options. Besides, when the president called upon a loyal citizen etc, etc, etc. Chase, not wanting to risk an arbitrary draft, flicked on his flasher and made a U-turn, inadvertently cutting in front of a speeding semi coming from the west. The trucker immediately hit his brakes, slowed to thirty-five miles an hour, the posted speed limit, and pulled to the right lane, now a law abiding driver. Chase frowned and waved a cautionary forefinger at the trucker as he sped past at fifty miles an hour. Chase glanced in his mirror and caught the trucker giving him a middle finger.

Chase turned on the Prius's radio, which he kept set to 103.5, a local twenty-four hour news station.

"Minutes ago, amidst a breaking news story reporting that the administration has negotiated with terrorists to secure the release of Secretary of Homeland Security James Townsend who was seized over two weeks ago following an appearance at George Mason University, the administration announced that Secretary Townsend has just met with President Featherstone in the Oval Office and submitted his resignation. Neither Secretary Townsend nor President Featherstone has made himself available for comment, but a White House spokesperson confirmed that the administration paid a sizeable ransom to secure the release. This of course is counter to established policy which states the United States Government does not negotiate with terrorists and certainly does not pay a ransom to secure the release of hostages. Already, senior members of Congress have publicly questioned the wisdom of this deviation from established policy. The influential Chairman of the Senate Intelligence Committee has noted that this questionable action by President Featherstone has placed all Americans living or traveling overseas, officials and private citizens alike, in harm's way."

Chase turned off the radio in order to consider what the news report meant to him and his investigation. Of course, the coverage contained little substance, and, except for the report of Townsend's resignation, nothing therein was news to him. Chase assumed the president simply wanted a progress report from him on his Jesperson investigation, given the linkage with the Townsend seizure, but, unfortunately, progress was one thing that Chase did not have. As he forced his way through traffic, Chase decided to revise his tentative schedule. He now needed a candid discussion with Townsend, who presumably had a restful weekend. Chase assumed that he could find Townsend under siege at his McLean residence; the clamoring media might prove an obstacle, but it might also increase the pressure on Townsend.

Chase arrived at the Old State parking lot with seven minutes to spare. Once again, the uniformed Secret Service agents were expecting him. Chase parked in the same VIP space, locked his weapon in the Prius, was rushed through the security procedures, and escorted into the White House. Pretending to be a regular visitor, Chase followed his silent escort through the halls of the West Wing, misbehaving only once when he winked at a pretty secretary in a short mini, and entered the reception room dominated by the president's assistant whose name Chase now knew.

"Good morning, Heather," Chase greeted her before he saw the two frowning gentlemen sitting along the wall to his right.

"What in the hell are you doing here Mansfield?" Special Agent Cotton demanded.

FBI Director Philip D'Antonio, who sat to Cotton's left, said nothing. His irritated frown was sufficient.

"Very good, Lieutenant Mansfield," Heather greeted him after glancing at the wall clock in front of her. "You are two minutes early."

Heather held up one finger, entered the Oval Office, and closed the door behind her.

"We don't need him in our meeting," Cotton spoke to D'Antonio.

Before the FBI director could respond, the door to the Oval Office opened, and Heather reappeared.

"The president will see you now," she smiled.

Cotton and D'Antonio promptly stood up. Chase was already standing.

"You may enter, lieutenant," Heather spoke to Chase.

She glanced at Cotton and the FBI Director and shook her head negatively. "I apologize, director, but you will have to wait a few more minutes."

Cotton and D'Antonio sat back down. Both frowning men ignored the fleeting smiles that crossed the faces of the two burly Secret Service agents who stood shoulder to shoulder in a human barricade before the Oval Office door.

Inside, Chase found the president seated behind his historic Resolute desk. He hesitated.

"Have a seat, lieutenant," President Featherstone smiled as he studied a document labeled Top Secret.

After a few seconds, Featherstone grabbed his gold pen and scribbled his name on the bottom before casually tossing the document towards the right corner of his desk. Chase rather liked the bare desk approach, no inboxes, just the gold pen set and one lonely document. He made a mental note to institute the same procedure in his little cubby hole. Just seeing Theresa's reaction would be worth the effort.

"I assume you've heard the news," Featherstone said. "Secretary Townsend has resigned. Now, brief me on your investigation."

"I assume you're asking about my investigation of Secretary Townsend as a suspect in the Jesperson murder," Chase said.

The president did not react, forcing Chase to proceed as if his assumption were correct.

"I talked briefly with the secretary at the shore," Chase said. "He appeared to have been surprised when I told him that someone shot Doctor Jesperson the night of his appearance at George Mason."

"Appeared to have been?" Featherstone quoted Chase's exact words back to him in the form of a question.

"Yes, sir," Chase said. "Only the secretary, Mrs. Townsend, and myself were present at the time. I honestly could not tell if the secretary was genuinely surprised or not. He did not react strongly, or ask many questions, but of course he was still acting like a man trying to recover from a difficult experience."

"Acting like?" Featherstone glared at Chase. "Do you or you don't you know if Townsend was faking it or not?" Featherstone demanded.

"I do not, sir," Chase replied, carefully limiting his response this time. He was already tired of having his words quoted back to him as a question.

"Do you suspect that he staged his own kidnapping? To cover up the fact he murdered his friend?"

"I cannot answer that question," Chase said.

"But he could be an innocent man answering your questions to the best of his ability?" Featherstone pressed.

"Yes, sir. He could be telling the truth or perpetrating a masterful hoax."

"And why would a successful man like Secretary Townsend with an unblemished career of service do that?"

"You suggested one possible answer, Mr. President. To cover up a murder."

"And can you think of another motive, lieutenant?"

"Thirty million dollars," Chase answered. "Usually, it's the money."

Featherstone clearly did not like Chase's answers. He glowered at Chase who shared Featherstone's distaste for the discussion. The two stubborn men exchanged stares until the president broke the silence by asking, "What else did the secretary tell you?"

"The secretary said he left Professor Jesperson alone in his office at nine-thirty. He did not know if Jesperson was expecting another visitor or not. I asked if Doctor Jesperson appeared worried or shared any concerns with him, and the secretary replied negatively with the observation that his friend was looking forward to the publication of his book."

Featherstone nodded and encouraged Chase to continue by asking, "And?"

"And at that point we were joined by Special Agent Cotton who quite correctly turned the discussion to the secretary's experiences with the kidnappers."

"Is Secretary Townsend your only suspect in the shooting of Doctor Jesperson?" Featherstone asked coldly.

"No sir," Chase said. "Given the revelations contained in Doctor Jesperson's book, we must also consider the Iranians."

"Why?"

"Also, motive," Chase answered. "The Iranians may have learned of the contents of Professor Jesperson's book and could have acted to prevent its publication."

"May have learned and could have acted," Featherstone played the word quoting game again. "Where may they have learned that information, and what makes you think they could have acted?"

"We're now talking motive and opportunity," Chase replied. Suddenly, the president no longer intimidated him. "There are Iranian students at George Mason, and Doctor Jesperson was the faculty advisor to the foreign student association. I don't know how much Doctor Jesperson shared with the foreign students. Certainly, his graduate assistant who assisted with the book's formatting was aware of its content. Also, a young Iranian, a distant relative who was preparing with the Doctor's assistance to matriculate at GMU, was living temporarily with Jesperson at the time of his death. There is an older Iranian graduate student who particularly interests me. Additionally, an Iranian national has held an instructorship in the GMU foreign studies program for the past year. Any one of these individuals may have learned about Doctor Jesperson's planned revelations and reported same to Iranian contacts."

Featherstone surprised Chase by laughing. "Christ, lieutenant, your investigation is more complicated than I thought. Now you are telling me that Iranian agents, spies, could be involved. What does the Bureau have to say about that possibility?"

"I haven't discussed it with them, yet. The Bureau has concentrated on the kidnapping while I worked the murder investigation," Chase said.

"All by yourself?"

"I have the full resources of the Fairfax Police Department available as needed," Chase said. He did not admit that he had not called upon them. "I have kept Chief Arthur briefed as needed."

"You may or you may have not," Featherstone chuckled. "Now please speak frankly. For my ears only. Who do you think was the shooter, Secretary Townsend or one of these crazy Iranians?"

"From a means, motive, and opportunity standpoint, Mr. President," Chase said. "I'm keeping an open mind."

Featherstone frowned.

Chase, now enjoying himself—playing with words was his game--smiled as he continued.

"We always consider motivation, opportunity, and means. Re motivation, the Iranians had a strong motivation given the revelations in Doctor Jesperson's book; re opportunity: several Iranians had access to the GMU campus; re means: it should not have been difficult for the Iranian Government to provide the weapon. On the other hand, Secretary Townsend is the only person I can place in Doctor Jesperson's office at the crucial time; opportunity points at him. I'm sure he would have had no difficulty acquiring a .22 caliber weapon; hence, he had the means. Motivation, however, remains a mystery. There is always money; thirty million dollars would motivate me; clearly, I've got more work to do now that I have access to the secretary."

"And I'm sure you know how to proceed, lieutenant," Featherstone smiled. "Let me know if I can be of any assistance," Featherstone dismissed Chase catching him by surprise.

"Yes, sir," Chase said as he eagerly rose from his chair, intent on making his escape. Just sitting in this damned office made him nervous. Besides, he retrospectively worried that he had let his enthusiasm get out of hand.

In the reception room Director D'Antonio and Special Agent Cotton greeted Chase with angry stares. Cotton deliberately raised his wrist and studied his watch. Chase grinned, shrugged, winked at Heather, and departed.

"I can find my own way out," Chase waved to the watching Secret Service agents.

A light on Heather's intercom blinked; she picked up the phone, listened, smiled, and said, "Yes, sir." She turned to the grim faced visitors, "He will see you now, gentlemen."

"Good riddance," Heather muttered softly as the door closed behind Cotton and D'Antonio. The two antsy bureaucrats had gotten on Heather' nerves with their twitching impatience. She didn't set the priorities around here, the president did.

Inside the Oval Office, Featherstone greeted his visitors with a casual wave, indicating the two chairs facing his desk.

"That was interesting," Featherstone smiled but did not elaborate.

"Now what does the Federal Bureau of Investigation's finest have to report? I hope it is something good because I warn you I am in a lousy mood. This has been a terrible day, so far."

"Sir," D'Antonio said, and then hesitated, not sure what the president wanted him to say. He had summoned them. He and Cotton had been discussing the media's report that Townsend had submitted his resignation when Heather had called ordering them to report to the White House forthwith.

"I assume you've heard the news," Featherstone said, tacitly acknowledging that he had merely been playing the provocateur. "Secretary Townsend appeared without an appointment one hour ago and submitted his resignation." Featherstone waved the envelope in the air.

"I'm sorry about that," D'Antonio said.

"What in the hell do you have to apologize for?" Featherstone snapped.

"We should have had men with him; he's been through a terrible experience," D'Antonio turned and frowned at Cotton.

"I assumed you were debriefing him," Featherstone said coldly.

"We were planning on doing just that, starting this morning," Cotton said. "As we discussed, Secretary Townsend needed the weekend to recover. We left a detail with him at the shore and accepted his insistence that the full debriefing be conducted here after his meeting with you."

"When did he return to D.C.?"

"He got up at three this morning, and he and his wife drove themselves back."

"Alone?"

"He tried. I guess that's why he left so early, trying to surprise us, but he didn't succeed. We had two cars with him the whole way."

"And where is he now?"

"In McLean. In the family residence. I'll join him there as soon as we're finished here," Cotton said.

"Did you know he's getting a divorce?"

"No sir," Cotton answered, figuratively throwing himself to the floor before the angry president, hoping D'Antonio appreciated the effort.

"I told him he wasn't thinking straight, that as a consequence of his experience this was no time to make important decisions, but he wouldn't listen."

"I'll get the shrinks to talk with him as a part of his debriefing," Cotton said.

"I don't think it will do any good. James has made up his mind, and he's a stubborn man. That's why I appointed him to that impossible job."

Neither Cotton nor D'Antonio knew what to say to that so they kept their mouths shut.

"Do you think he shot Doctor Jesperson?" Featherstone surprised them with the abrupt question.

D'Antonio again looked at Cotton. "Is that what Mansfield told you?" Cotton unwisely responded with a question.

"I asked what you thought." Featherstone glared.

"We have left the details of that investigation to Mansfield and the Fairfax Police," D'Antonio tried to cover for Cotton.

Featherstone ignored his FBI director as he waited for a response from Cotton.

Cotton hesitated as he tried to devise an answer that wouldn't further provoke the president. "I have no knowledge of any evidence that enables me to say yes or no," Cotton finally answered honestly. "I'm troubled by the secretary's appearance and demeanor since his return."

Featherstone, who knew when to be quiet and when to bluster, waited for Cotton to continue.

"He looked like a man who had just spent several weeks locked up in a room not knowing what the future held for him. His face appeared drawn; he hadn't shaved, and his clothing was dirty and wrinkled. At first he had trouble communicating, but after a glass of water and a few minutes he seemed to recover quickly, almost too quickly. The doctor gave him a cursory examination; his blood pressure was slightly elevated, and his heart normal, despite the fact he had not taken his medications for two weeks. The doctor wanted him to go to the hospital for a few tests, but the secretary declined and his spouse did not press. Maybe I'm being unfair, but I must say I had the uneasy feeling that the entire affair was staged." Cotton paused to catch his breath before continuing, heard D'Antonio cough, glanced at his boss, and found him frowning.

D'Antonio said nothing but turned his head slightly from side to side trying to warn Cotton that he was repeating himself. Cotton had already covered that ground in his previous briefing.

Cotton immediately read the message. Featherstone was many things, but patient he wasn't. Cotton kept his mouth shut and looked at the president.

"Are you saying you don't think he was kidnapped by terrorists?" Featherstone frowned.

Cotton relaxed slightly. Featherstone had apparently not noticed Cotton's transgression. "I don't want to be unfair to the man," Cotton answered quickly. "I must say that I don't know. The secretary just might be the rare man who can undergo the experiences he appears to have undergone and be strong enough to recover quickly and deal with them."

"You are accusing the Secretary of Homeland Security of having stage-managed his own abduction and extorting thirty million dollars from the United States Government, from me?" Featherstone's voice rose.

"No sir. It's just a possibility that must be considered. I frankly don't know. I've just got this terrible feeling," Cotton said.

"What do you think, Mr. Director? Do you share Special Agent Cotton's terrible feeling?" Featherstone glared at D'Angelo who until that moment had succeeded in staying out of the president's direct line of fire.

"I respect Special Agent Cotton's instincts," D'Angelo replied calmly. "But the Bureau cannot make such a horrendous accusation without more evidence than we now have."

"From where I sit, I don't see any evidence whatsoever," the president challenged his director.

Neither Cotton nor his superior commented on that presidential edict.

"You didn't really answer my original question, Special Agent Cotton," the president turned back on the subordinate. "Do you think he shot Doctor Jesperson?"

"He could have," Cotton replied firmly. "But Mansfield cannot prove it." Cotton assumed that the president had asked Mansfield that question. After a slight hesitation, he put his career on the line by challenging the president. "What did the lieutenant say?"

Featherstone flashed a quick angry glare and then surprised both Cotton and D'Antonio with a thin smile. "Yes, Special Agent Cotton, Lieutenant Mansfield answered just as you did. He doesn't know but considers former Secretary Townsend a prime suspect for the same reasons. I must, therefore, ignore my own instincts and support the conclusions of my professional investigators. We consider Secretary Townsend a suspect, a possible extortionist who rigged his own kidnapping, and a killer who murdered a close friend. Investigate, we will, but we will not ignore other suspects and other potential scenarios which vindicate Secretary Townsend as an innocent man."

"Yes, sir," Cotton and D'Antonio answered in unison.

"Good, and I suggest, Special Agent Cotton, that you coordinate more closely with Lieutenant Mansfield and the Fairfax Police Department. Mansfield has other suspects, you know, suspects operating under a very dark national security cloud. I assume that you will also more aggressively investigate Doctor Jesperson's allegations about a pending atomic attack on the United States, on Washington, D.C., on this very office where we are now so comfortably sitting."

"Sir," D'Antonio said. "The Bureau is aggressively investigating the possibility of an Iranian attack as alleged in Doctor Jesperson's book."

"Are you investigating any Iranians connected with the George Mason University campus?" Featherstone demanded, his voice rising again.

D'Antonio looked at Cotton who did not dare reply that he had deferred that investigation to Lieutenant Mansfield.

After a few seconds of silence, a now passive Featherstone again smiled thinly. "Lieutenant Mansfield is. I repeat my suggestion that you assist the lieutenant and follow his lead to the best of your limited abilities."

The president, using one of his favorite dismissal techniques, then pivoted in his chair, and pretended to study the Potomac River's rushing polluted waters.

The FBI Director and Special Agent Cotton hurriedly evacuated the Oval Office. They silently passed Heather and did not speak until they were safely harbored in the back of the director's limousine.

"I'm going to debrief that son-of-a-bitch ex-Secretary of Homeland Affairs and coordinate a murder investigation with that damned homicide lieutenant," Cotton muttered through clenched lips.

"I'm afraid we may have delegated too much to the Fairfax Police," Director D'Antonio said softly.

"I assure you, sir, that little oversight will be duly corrected."

"Good," D'Antonio, who regretted having put his subordinate directly in the presidential line of fire, said as he patted Cotton's knee. "Just remember the president used the words 'assist the lieutenant and follow his lead to the best of your abilities.'"

"Yes, sir," Cotton muttered, resisting the urge to point out that the president had said 'to the best of your limited abilities." Silently, he vowed to prove who had abilities and who had the goddamned limited abilities.

Chapter 21

Chase followed the George Washington Parkway to Route 123 and McLean. Outside the Townsend home, he sat in the Prius and dialed Sally Kendrick's cell, hoping to set up another lunch at Paolo's in Reston. He still had questions to ask the Lady in Black that he had not been able to ask at their previous lunch, the one aborted by Chase's summons for his first White House visit and Kendrick's office emergency. He had tried several times to reach her since then, but she had proved elusive. When Kendrick again failed to respond to his call, Chase irritably tossed his cell phone on the seat beside him, climbed out of the Prius, and made his way up the brick walk leading to the Townsend mansion.

To his surprise, Chase made it all the way to the front door without encountering a single member of the DHS security detail. He rattled the brass doorknocker and stepped back and waited. After thirty odd seconds marked by the absence of sound from within, Chase impatiently rapped again with the knocker.

"I'm coming," a female voice dripping with irritation called.

Chase waited, and the door opened suddenly. A frowning Mrs. Townsend glared at Chase, but quickly broke into a broad smile when she recognized her visitor.

"I apologize for not calling first," Chase smiled. "But I was in the neighborhood and impulsively decided to stop by, Mrs. Townsend. I would appreciate it if your husband could spare me a few minutes." Chase tried to sugarcoat his need to ask Secretary Townsend more questions. "If it isn't convenient, I can come back another time."

"It's more than convenient for me, Chase," Mrs. Townsend laughed. "I always have time for a handsome gentleman like yourself."

Chase smiled but let that comment slide. Mrs. Townsend stepped back, and Chase obediently entered the dark hallway.

"Your security detail must be on a break," Chase said. "You shouldn't have to answer the door yourself," Chase made small talk. He really didn't care who answered the door.

"There's no one here but little old me," Mrs. Townsend laughed.

Chase smiled as he followed Mrs. Townsend into the living room. He admired her figure from behind. She was dressed to go out, probably to a lunch with the girls. She obviously had good taste, wore expensive clothes, and exercised strenuously because she was in good shape for a woman of her advanced age, at least fifty plus. That thought brought to mind the chief's warning about soured women. Chase admonished himself to keep that thought in mind; the chief was not frequently wrong.

"I assume you've heard the news," Mrs. Townsend announced as soon as they were seated. "The security detail disappeared the moment my ex-husband resigned. Good riddance to all of them."

A puzzled Chase nodded. He knew about the resignation and should have expected them to have withdrawn, but the comment about an ex-husband caught him by surprise.

"The bastard moved out this morning." Mrs. Townsend flashed a bright smile at Chase. "So, we have the house all to ourselves, Chase. Of course, Mary is still here," she referred to her secretary, "but she is discreet and stays in her little office unless needed elsewhere."

Chase wondered if Mrs. Townsend was flirting with him. At the least, she was telling him things he did not need to know.

"I'm not sure I understood you, Mrs. Townsend. Did you say ex-husband?" Chase asked.

"Please call me Nancy Lou, Chase. It's awkward when friends keep addressing each other by titles."

Chase nodded.

"You heard correctly. The weasel is now my ex. Of course, we are still married in the eyes of the law, at least until the divorce goes through, but in this house I'm free. No man enters unless I invite him. Present company excepted, of course."

Mrs. Townsend uncrossed and re-crossed her legs with a swish and flash of nylon, clearly catching Chase's attention. Chase looked up and found Mrs. Townsend studying him with an amused expression on her face.

"I'm very sorry to hear that," Chase said. "About the divorce, not the status of the house," Chase corrected himself, fearing that he was getting himself into another hole, or something like that.

"There's nothing to be sorry about, Chase," Townsend said. "One man's loss is another's gain."

"Do you know where I might reach Mr. Townsend?" Chase tried to get the conversation back on a formal level devoid of nuances.

"I don't know, and I don't care," Mrs. Townsend said firmly. "Further communication between the weasel and me will be through our respective lawyers."

"Do you think someone at his office will know how I may communicate with him?" Chase persisted.

"Oh shit, Chase, he has no office. I'm sure that everyone at DHS feels the same as I do, glad the weasel is gone."

"But..."

"I can ask Mary," Townsend smiled, "if that will help you. I'm sure she knows where to send the bills."

"That would be very helpful," Chase said as he leaned back in his chair and relaxed.

Mrs. Townsend stood up, and Chase assumed she was going to consult her secretary. Instead, she slid around the coffee table that had separated them and sat on the sofa in a position where she could reach him, if she wanted. Chase, uneasy about the close proximity, thought about moving to the chair she had just vacated, thus putting some space back between them. He did not because he was not sure how she would interpret his retreat.

"Now, Chase," Mrs. Townsend said. "Is there anything else I can do for you? Anything at all?" She patted him gently on the knee.

The patting did not bother Chase, but the fact that she left her palm resting on his knee did. He wasn't quite sure how to handle that. He feared she might take offense if he reached down and gently removed it, and he had some more questions he wanted answered, so he ignored the intrusion.

"Did the kidnapping somehow contribute to the divorce?" Chase asked, trying to divert Mrs. Townsend with conversation.

"Of course not," Mrs. Townsend laughed. "What kind of woman do you think I am? This has been coming on for some time. The weasel has been going through some kind of belated mid-life crisis. The girl friend is not new business."

"Oh," Chase said.

"I imagine that is where he is right now, unpacking his bags."

The thought appeared to amuse rather than irritate her.

"We had a silent but entertaining ride in from the shore this morning.

As soon as we arrived, he informed the detail that he was resigning and that they should get the hell off his property. He went upstairs, packed his clothes in four bags, and loaded them in the car. He's in such poor shape it took him four trips to get his stuff out of the house. I just watched. Then, he drove to the White House to submit his resignation to the president. He probably didn't even know where to park."

Chase shook his head with what he hoped was a sympathetic expression on his face.

"I haven't seen him since. Now, Chase, ask your questions. I'll probably be more honest than the weasel. You can't believe a word he says, believe me. Let's you and I get the nonsense out of the way, so we can get down to the important stuff." She playfully squeezed his thigh.

"First," Chase stalled as he took his notebook from his suit coat inner pocket. "Would you kindly ask Mary where I might find Secretary Townsend?" Chase asked. "Even a phone number would be useful."

"Alright," Townsend withdrew her hand and stood up, a false pout on her face. "I won't ask her. I don't want to clutter my mind with unimportant details, but you can ask her yourself."

Mrs. Townsend moved to the hall door swinging her hips deliberately as she went. At the door, she paused and looked over her shoulder with a smile on her face. She winked and continued on her way.

Thirty seconds later, Mary appeared. "Good morning, lieutenant. Mrs. Townsend tells me that you have a question you want to ask me."

"Yes, Mary, if you can share me a few minutes of your time," Chase said.

Mary entered and stood behind the chair on the opposite side of the coffee table from Chase.

Chase waited for Mrs. Townsend to reappear. When she did not, Chase asked Mary, "Will Mrs. Townsend be joining us?"

"I don't think so," Mary said. "She says she knows what questions you are going to ask and that she doesn't want to hear my answers."

"I hope I didn't offend her," Chase said, privately not caring if he had.

"Oh no, lieutenant, I frankly think Mrs. Townsend likes you," she said softly. "A lot."

Chase let that pass. "I assume you've heard the news," he said.

"That the secretary presented his resignation to the president this morning?"

"Yes."

"I was so sorry to hear that," Mary said. "I assume the president was surprised. The rest of us were, particularly given everything that has happened recently."

"Yes," Chase repeated. "I'm sure that Secretary Townsend had a very stressful experience, but at least he survived. Not everyone does."

"I know," Mary said as she sat down in the chair opposite Chase. "Do you think the stress was responsible for the other developments?"

"You mean the resignation?"

"That and the divorce, everything," Mary said softly, glancing at the door to make sure she was not overheard. "I assume that Mrs. Townsend told you that the secretary moved out this morning."

"She did. That must have come as a shock," Chase said.

"Not really," Mary's answer surprised Chase. "Things here," she glanced at the walls of the room, "have been...uneasy...for over a year."

"Can you tell me why?" Chase asked.

"It's not really my place to discuss...to discuss things domestic," Mary said. "I am Mrs. Townsend's secretary, but Secretary Townsend paid my wages. So, I guess I worked for both of them."

"And now?"

"Mrs. Townsend assures me that nothing will change. She still needs me even though the social burden on her will lessen."

"I guess the same thing happened to the Townsends that happens to many married couples these days," Chase pressed.

"Probably," Mary said. "Mr. Townsend has a girl friend," Mary whispered.

"Do you know her name?"

Mary shook her head negatively.

"Mrs. Townsend said he is probably moving in with her as we speak."

"I don't know. Secretary Townsend never discussed such intimate matters with me. Our relationship was quite formal."

Chase concealed his doubts about her last comment. Mary was an attractive young lady, certainly a household distraction if not something more

"And you don't know how I can reach him?" Chase pressed. "Mrs. Townsend seemed to think that you might be able to help me."

"You could call him on his personal cell," Mary said. "I'm sure he won't change that. He used it strictly for personal matters. Not the office. He had another cell for that."

Chase handed his notebook and pen to Mary, and she wrote down the number for him.

"Thank you, Mary," Chase said as she returned the notebook and pen.

"Is there anything else?" Mary asked.

"How is Secretary Townsend recovering from his experience?" Chase asked. "I saw him Friday at the shore, and he appeared quite...weary, worn down by the ordeal."

"It must have been just awful," Mary said. "We didn't discuss it. I only saw him for a few minutes this morning. Frankly, I was surprised how good he looked, almost normal."

"Really?"

"Normal for him doesn't mean good," Mary said quickly. "His job was very difficult. You can imagine, fifteen-hour days and under constant pressure, threats from terrorists and all that. He's lost a lot weight, at least twenty pounds, over the past year. Frankly, he's been very haggard looking for months. I'm not surprised he resigned from that horrible job."

"And now he's got the divorce on his back," Chase said.

"I'm not sure that's a bad development. Both Mrs. Townsend and Mr. Townsend seem relaxed about it. I would be devastated, but they frankly appear relieved, almost happy. If there was ever a cordial, a mutually acceptable parting, this has to be it. I think they are still friends."

"We are," Mrs. Townsend announced as she reentered the room.

"I hope I didn't say anything that offended you, Mrs. Townsend," Mary said as she leaped from her chair.

"Mary, I wasn't eavesdropping. I'm sure Chase," Mrs. Townsend smiled at him, "would arrest me for interfering in an official investigation if I did. I only heard you say the Mr. Townsend and myself are still friends. That's true, we are, even if I consider him a weasel. He looks like one, don't you think."

"A friendly weasel?" Chase chuckled.

"Exactly," Mrs. Townsend smiled.

"Will that be all, lieutenant?" Mary asked as she moved towards the door.

"Thank you, Mary. You have been very helpful," Chase said.

After Mary departed, Mrs. Townsend sat down on the sofa and looked at Chase. "Was I right? Did Mary know the weasel's girl friend's name?"

"No, but she suggested that I call the secretary on his personal cell," Chase said.

"Why didn't I think of that?" Mrs. Townsend said.

Mrs. Townsend's tone led Chase to assume that she had thought of the cell phone but had deferred to Mary for reasons of her own. Mrs. Townsend was on her way to becoming a gay divorcee; and she probably would have enjoyed life as a merry widow if things hadn't turned out as they had. Chase decided that Townsend was a very lucky man despite the fact he was facing a divorce that would render him much less wealthy. At least he was still alive.

"And I want to thank you for your time on this trying morning," Chase said as he pushed himself out of the chair.

"Don't leave, yet, Chase. We have much to...to discuss," Mrs. Townsend winked.

Before Chase could devise an answer that would cover his escape, someone rattled the brass doorknocker.

"Oh shit," Mrs. Townsend frowned. She did not move. "Wait, maybe they'll go away."

Chase hesitated.

Fortunately for him, the visitor was not as patient as Chase had been. He attacked the knocker with renewed vigor after only a few seconds.

"Stay," Mrs. Townsend pointed a forefinger at Chase as she irritably hurried to the front door.

Chase disobediently followed along behind.

"What?" Mrs. Townsend demanded harshly as she opened the door and confronted a frowning Special Agent Cotton.

Chase smiled. Relief was at hand.

"Go away," Mrs. Townsend ordered as she started to close the door.

Cotton caught it with a large, beefy hand. "Mrs. Townsend, I have a few questions I must ask your husband."

"Good morning, Special Agent Cotton," Chase said before Mrs. Townsend could go on the attack.

"What in the hell are you doing here?" Cotton glared at Chase.

"Are you following me?" Chase asked before turning to Mrs. Townsend. "Thank you for your time on this trying morning," he repeated. Chase positioned himself in the doorway between Mrs. Townsend and Cotton.

"My pleasure," Mrs. Townsend responded. "Please call. I so enjoy our chats." She frowned at Cotton. "Regrettably, I can't say the same for all my visitors."

"You are quite the charmer," Cotton surprised Chase by attacking him while ignoring Mrs. Townsend. "Does the president buy your little act?"

"Don't worry about the president, Chase," Mrs. Townsend intervened with saccharine smile. "Arthur is an old, old friend."

"We've got to talk," Cotton growled at Chase.

"About what?"

"About coordinating your White House visits if nothing else," Cotton said.

"Certainly," Chase grinned. "It would be best if you scheduled the timing with my secretary," Chase said as he turned and headed for his Prius. The thought of the surly Cotton negotiating with Theresa amused him. As the door closed behind him, Chase heard Cotton say, "Is Secretary Townsend home? I have some questions I must ask him."

"I'm sure he's home by now, wherever that might be," Mrs. Townsend answered.

Chase did not hear Cotton's response, but he smiled anyway. He knew how that conversation would go.

Back in his Prius, Chase retrieved his cell and poked in the number that Mary had given him. He listened as it rang several times on the other end. Suddenly, it shut off without giving Chase a chance to leave a message. He tried a second time with the same result. He assumed Townsend was busy moving in with his girl friend as Mrs. Townsend suggested and was not interested in chatting with others. Not knowing the girl friend's identity, Chase did not have the option of an unannounced visit. He thought about visiting Townsend's old office at the Department of Homeland Security but decided against it. Even if Townsend's former secretary knew the identity of her ex-boss's current paramour, he doubted she would share it. Temporarily blocked, Chase tried a second number, that of Sally Kendrick, the Lady in Black, Jesperson's former fiancée he had met at the funeral. Mclean was only a few miles from Reston where Kendrick had her computer office, and Chase was in the mood for resuming their aborted lunch at Paolo's.

The phone pealed several times, and to Chase's surprise Kendrick picked up.

"Lieutenant," she greeted him. "I feared you had forgotten about me."

"No chance, Ms. Kendrick. You still owe me a lunch." Chase referred to her premature departure that terminated their last meeting.

"Call me sometime when you're free," Kendrick said.

"I'm free right now," Chase said.

"Too bad. I'm rather busy," Kendrick replied quickly.

"To be truthful, I am too, but I can still make time for you," Chase appealed. "I've learned some interesting things about your ex-fiancé."

"So tell me," Kendrick said.

"Only in person over calamari and Pizza Bolognese."

Kendrick hesitated. "Just a minute," she finally said.

Chase waited with his cell phone against his ear. He could hear Kendrick talking to someone, but he could not make out what she was saying. She obviously had her hand over the phone. After a full two minutes of frustrated waiting, Chase's irritation level began to rise. He thought about terminating the call, but he could still hear Kendrick.

"Shit," Chase complained as he slapped the steering wheel with his free hand.

"Great," Kendrick said as she came back on line.

Chase wondered if she was addressing his vocal complaint or responding to his persistence.

"Are you still there?" Kendrick asked.

"Yes, ma'am," Chase replied, assuming she had not heard him.

"Sorry about that. I've got a small problem here at the office."

"Oh," Chase tried to sound disappointed, which wasn't difficult because he was looking forward to chatting with the attractive Kendrick as much as he was interested in asking more questions about Jesperson.

"But I've got it under control. Can you meet me at Paolo's? Say in half an hour or a little more."

"I'm on my way," Chase said.

"I warn you. I could be a little late."

"No problem. I'll just start without you."

"And I can order seconds if I need them," Kendrick laughed.

"We've got a date, " Chase said.

"An appointment, not a date," Kendrick corrected him.

"Right. I'll see you," Chase said as he hung up. Chase wondered where her office was located; he knew it was in Reston, so she should be able to get the Town Center far faster than he could.

Chase had just hit the start button on the Prius when the front door of the Townsend house opened and a flushed Cotton emerged. He slammed the door behind him, making it obvious that the session with Mrs. Townsend had not ended well.

"Hey, wait!" Cotton called as Chased moved the lever into drive.

Chase, not interested in an extended debate with the federal agent, thought about ignoring Cotton but did not, assuming he would find amusing Cotton's account of his brief discussion with the recently separated Mrs. Townsend.

Cotton surprised Chase when he opened the Prius door and climbed into the passenger seat.

"Don't make yourself comfortable," Chase said. "I have a luncheon appointment."

"With the First Lady?" Cotton growled.

"What makes you ask that?" Chase laughed.

"You're the lover boy. At least that is what all these old ladies seem to think. There must be some kind of highly disabling mental virus that targets old women going around."

"Just doing my job," Chase laughed. "I assure you Special Agent Cotton that I'm no microbe."

"Did she tell you that her husband walked out on her?" Cotton asked, glancing at the Townsend house.

"The subject came up," Chase admitted.

"What do you think that's all about?"

"I don't know. I thought separation was supposed to make the heart grow fonder," Chase referred to the kidnapping.

"I guess it's your warped sense of humor that the old ladies like," Cotton grumbled. "Where is Townsend camping out?"

"I don't know. Mrs. Townsend suggested that he moved in with his girl friend, but she claimed not to know her name or where she lived."

"That's what she told me. I don't believe her. Something strange is going on here."

"Agreed."

"Is that what you're going to tell your buddy the president the next time you see him?" Cotton challenged.

"I'll leave that up to you," Chase said, assuming that his visit to the White House is what had Cotton so agitated. "Understand one thing. I was only there because I was summoned. It is not something I care to repeat."

"I don't believe you."

"Believe what you want."

"I will." Cotton took a deep breath as he fought to control his temper. "There's something you should know. I've been ordered to take a look at your murder investigation."

"We had an agreement. Separate investigations."

"That was before you told the president that you were looking at some Iranians as the shooter," Cotton flashed an insincere grin. "Foreign agents operating on American soil are the Bureau's responsibility. Unless invited, local cops are required by law to mind their own business."

"I only mentioned that I was looking at more than one suspect," Chase said as he privately realized he should have been more circumspect in discussing his investigation, even if he was talking with the President of the United States.

"And a ranking senior United States Government official is another of your so-called suspects. That's also a federal matter."

"A former senior official," Chase said.

"Now, but not at the time of the shooting."

"We had an agreement," Chase repeated, hating the fact that he was beginning to sound wimpy.

"Our agreement is off," Cotton declared as he climbed out of the car.

"Fine," Chase said.

"Good. Stay away from the Townsends and every damned Iranian in town. The professionals are now in charge."

"The Jesperson murder is my investigation. Keep away from my suspects," Chase said angrily. "And I will talk with anyone I damned choose to talk with."

Cotton smiled, pleased he now had Mansfield agitated. "Who are you having lunch with?"

"None of your business."

"We'll see whose business it is," Cotton said.

"I'll arrest every damned federal agent who gets in my way," Chase blustered.

"And I'll arrest you and every damned Fairfax cop who hinders my federal investigation," Cotton said as he slammed the door.

Chase flipped the gear lever back into drive and tramped hard on the accelerator as he tried to leave Cotton behind in a cloud of dust. Unfortunately, the Prius is not a muscle car; the driveway was paved, and Chase's departure was more sedate than he intended.

Chase followed Route 123 to the beltway where he turned and headed for the Dulles Access Road and Reston. Unfortunately, traffic around Tyson's Corners was heavy, backed up by the work on the Metro Extension, and the trip consumed more time than Chase anticipated. Finally, about forty minutes late, he arrived at the Reston Town Center where he left the Prius in the lot and hurried into Paolo's. To his surprise, relief, and dismay, the Lady in Black was not there. Chase followed the hostess to a back booth and ordered a draft Bass Ale.

He was hungry, on his second draft, and considering placing his order for his calamari when Kendrick surprised him.

"Sorry I'm late," Kendrick said, as she slid in the booth opposite. Chase admired the tight fitting bright purple sweater but said nothing.

"Still fighting the problem at the office?" Chase asked.

Kendrick glanced at Chase with an expression that told him she didn't understand the question.

"On the phone you said you had a little problem at the office," Chase explained.

"Oh," Kendrick laughed politely. "I've forgotten about it."

Chase noted she did not elaborate on the reason for her late arrival.

A server materialized.

"Would you like something to drink?"

"I'll have the usual, a double vodka martini on the rocks, very dry, no olive; I'm on a diet," Kendrick answered first.

"And you sir?"

"I'll stick with this," Chase indicated his half-empty glass.

"Bring him another," Kendrick ordered. "I'm not going to drink alone."

"But..." Chase started to protest but caught himself. To point out that he was already on his second draft would highlight how long he had been waiting. He did not want to start this return engagement with a self-defeating complaint. This was a working lunch for him, but he decided to accept the third drink, anyway. He fallaciously reasoned he would not have to consume it; he knew he would.

"What?" Kendrick smiled her challenge.

"What, what?" Chase smiled back.

Kendrick reached across the table and patted Chase's hand.

"Don't worry, lieutenant. I'll get the check. It's my turn." Kendrick referred to the fact she had aborted their last meeting and had rushed off sticking Chase with the bill for their untouched meals.

"I'm going to order calamari," Chase declared.

"The pizza for me," Kendrick said.

Last time Chase had ordered pizza and Kendrick calamari.

"But we'll still share," Kendrick said.

"But we didn't share. Neither of us got a bite," Chase smiled.

"Really?" Kendrick didn't believe him.

"Scout's honor," Chase raised his left hand in an awkward salute.

"Then we'll have to correct that," Kendrick laughed. "Now, tell me. How is your investigation going? Have you arrested the perpetrator, my hero, yet?"

Chase shook his head, not quite sure how to respond to a question phrased like that. He had no intention of discussing the investigation, but to simply reply that he could not comment at this point might be misinterpreted. He wanted frank answers to his own questions, and he had to keep the ambiance of the lunch friendly. He rather liked the attractive, self-confident ex-fiancée of his victim. If one ignored how it ended, she was the only person he had found who had any kind of open relationship with Jesperson.

Kendrick chuckled at Chase's hesitation. "Don't fret, detective, I'm not going to publish your response. Remember? I'm an interested party. The law doesn't require an ex-fiancée to be bitter and hate her almost spouse."

"I know, but this isn't your everyday murder case," Chase said

"It isn't my everyday anything," Kendrick volleyed his inadequate words back at him.

Before Chase could reply, the server rescued him by arriving with their drinks. They ordered their calamari and Pizza Bolognese.

"Good choice," the server announced and departed.

Chase and Kendrick raised their glasses in an obligatory toast.

"I hope the food arrives before our phones start to ring," Kendrick said.

"I'll turn mine off if you will," Chase said. Even he thought the effort at humor trite.

"You're on." Kendrick graciously played along by reaching into her purse. "I'm off."

"You're damned right," Chase said, taking out his cell and punching a button. "It's off, and I'm on."

"This should prove interesting," Kendrick rotated her head back and forth in a motion that denied her words. "Now, Mr. On," she said. "Tell me about your investigation and turn me on, too."

"I'm still working it," Chase stalled again, rather pleased with the coincidental ambiguity of the exchange.

"Did the Iranians really kill Thomas?" Kendrick pressed.

"Frankly, I don't know who shot Doctor Jesperson," Chase answered.

"The things Thomas wrote in his book certainly could not have pleased them. I've just finished reading it. I'm not surprised it's a best seller, but I don't know if it is truth or fiction."

"I haven't figured out how the Iranians knew in advance what Doctor Jesperson intended to write," Chase said. "And even if they did know, they acted too late. The book was at the printers. They couldn't have believed that killing him would prevent the book's publication. The murder only gives the publisher a lever to spur sales."

"Maybe one of their agents confronted Thomas' agent and reacted out of desperation when he refused to edit the book or halt sales."

Chase smiled at the Lady in Black's adroit use of the word "agent." She gave the word two separate meanings in one sentence; one agent connoted spy and the other business representative. Her only mistake was to assume her ex-fiancée's agent was a male. Before he could compliment and correct her, she continued.

"I don't know how much you know about Iranians, but as an ex-Foreign Service officer let me assure you they do not have a reputation for rational or logical behavior. Look how they behaved towards their own people during the Iran and Iraq war. They used children to clear minefields ahead of their army."

"I need evidence to charge anyone," Chase retreated.

"I know there were Iranian students attending George Mason a year ago when Thomas and I were engaged. I can assure you he did not have a high opinion of their scholarship."

"Can you give me a name?"

"Sorry," Kendrick shrugged. "But I would take a close look at all of them if I were you."

Chase nodded but did not comment. He wondered why Kendrick was pushing so hard on the Iranian button.

The server arrived with their food. Chase helped himself to a bite of calamari and reached across and grabbed the piece of pizza that Kendrick had cut for herself. She retaliated by sticking a fork into a large calamari and dipping it into the red sauce before lifting it to her mouth.

"Delicious," Kendrick declared.

Kendrick watched as Chase lifted her pizza to his mouth and then asked her next question as he relaxed, trying to enjoy the food.

"I heard on the radio that Secretary Townsend was released by the kidnappers and that he surprised everyone by immediately submitting his resignation to the president. What's happening with James? Did his experience cause him to go off the deep end?"

Chase stopped chewing and stared at the persistent Kendrick. He was the one who wanted to ask the questions. "James? Do you know Secretary Townsend?"

"Of course I know James. He was my fiancé's oldest friend. Since he was one of the last persons to see Thomas, do you think James shot him?"

"I haven't had a chance to debrief Secretary Townsend," Chase said. "I talked with him briefly after his return, and he said that Doctor Jesperson was alive and well when they parted."

"Good, because I would be very sad to learn that James had killed Thomas. Why would anyone consider him a suspect?"

Chase shrugged. "Can you think of any reason?" He struck back by answering a question with a question.

"Of course not. Do you expect to arrest the real killer anytime soon?" Kendrick asked.

"I'm sorry, Ms. Kendrick," Chase said. "I really can't discuss the details of an ongoing investigation."

"Bullshit, lieutenant. You don't trust me, do you? You can't think I shot Thomas. I haven't seen him for over a year. What possible motive could I have?"

"A jilted lover?" Chase smiled.

"Right, and I waited a year to do the deed." She helped herself to more calamari. "I'll let you in on a secret. I dumped Thomas. He told me about his sabbatical, and I told him, buster, shove off and enjoy yourself. Just don't expect me to be waiting for you when you return."

Chase did not comment.

"Now that we've clarified that little matter, lieutenant, stop stalling and tell me one thing," Kendrick said.

Chase calmly chewed on the pizza as he waited. He decided to give Kendrick her one question and then he would start asking his own.

"How much money do you think that book is going to make for someone? It's number one on the *Times* best seller list."

"A lot. Do you think you have a chance to get your hands on any of it?"

Kendrick laughed. "Me? Ex-fiancée's are the last to be included in any will."

"All that money makes a good motive," Chase said.

"That's true. What do you think mommy and daddy are going to do with it? Do you really think dear old dad knocked off his son for the money? Is this some kind of Oedipus thing?"

Before Chase could answer even one of the questions, Kendrick continued.

"Don't you think it would be ironic if mommy packed up all the money and sent it back to Iran?"

"I doubt the Iranian Government would let Mrs. Jesperson create a Doctor Thomas Jesperson Foundation in Teheran," Chase said.

"Particularly one devoted to end nuclear proliferation," Kendrick laughed.

"Ms. Kendrick," Chase said as he prepared to take advantage of the light-hearted moment with his own questions.

"Sally, please," Kendrick interrupted.

"OK, Sally. I'm Chase," Chase again tried to ask his question but the quick-witted Kendrick again edged him out.

"Chase? Why don't you use Travis?" Kendrick surprised Chase by referring to his pseudo.

Chase usually tried to keep references to his avocation out of his conversations because they always led to discussions of a frivolous subject, mystery writing. Chase smiled and ignored the question.

"I'm sure, Sally, that Doctor Jesperson introduced you to friends and acquaintances other than the Townsends. I really need to identify them. As it stands, you and Townsend are the only Jesperson friends I have been able to identify, and I can't locate him."

Kendrick drained her martini glass and waved to the passing server for another. The server looked at Chase who glanced at his still full third glass and shook his head negatively.

After the server departed, Kendrick looked at Chase, smiled thinly, shook her head, and said, "It's very sad. I honestly don't know of any others. Thomas was a very nice, attractive and intelligent man who strangely was quite reserved. I wouldn't say he was shy; he could relate to others without difficulty when the situation demanded. He was an unusually quiet man content to live within himself. He didn't need social contacts; he was the most self-reliant man I ever met. He used to joke that his father introduced him to Emerson and Thoreau when he was in the first grade and he never outgrew them."

"But..." Chase tried to press.

"Not another question, lieutenant," Kendrick smiled. "Now, I'm going to concentrate on the delicious food and refuse to discuss anything related to sad subjects."

"But..." Chase tried to start again.

"And that includes any sentences beginning with the word 'but,'" Kendrick said.

"But..."

"One more 'but' from you and I'm getting my butt out of here," Kendrick said as she put her hands on the seat, pretending to prepare to slide out of the booth. "If you make me leave, the check's yours."

"I surrender, for now," Chase announced quickly.

"Now tell me, Chase," Kendrick smiled. "Setting all the dead guys and kidnappings aside, how was your week? Entertaining?"

Chase thought about Doctor Jalili but wisely did not mention her. "Nothing extraordinary," Chase said. "I really like this calamari."

"Did you know that in Greece this dish is called kalamarakia?" Kendrick asked.

Chase shook his head and waited for another boring lecture on foreign cuisine.

Chapter 22

Following his unproductive luncheon with the Lady in Black, a distracted Chase, disturbed by the fact he had let Kendrick dominate him, was approaching his office when at the last minute he changed his mind and detoured to Robinson Hall. Having made no progress in his belated investigation of Secretary Townsend, who he could not get to answer his cell, he impulsively opted to refocus on the Iranians. While Doctor Lyla Jalili did not rank very high on his suspect inventory, she was the only Persian on his list that he had any interest meeting, and that was because he owed her an apology for his inexplicable behavior following their delicious meal. Having struck out with Mrs. Townsend and Kendrick, adding Jalili to his list of consecutive interviews made sense; anticipating another frustration, Chase decided to deal with them all in one futile lump.

Chase knocked on the door to Jalili's office and was surprised to hear her respond, "Please come in."

Chase entered to found her staring at her monitor.

"I'll be right with you," she greeted him without glancing in his direction.

Chase stood near the door and waited, admiring the very attractive, dark haired academic.

She typed a few words, turned off her monitor, and smiled, looking up for the first time.

"Oh excuse me, lieutenant. I assumed you were one of my students."

"I should have phoned first, but when you didn't return my calls I thought it best if I didn't give you fair warning." Chase hesitated, not sure what to say next.

"Oh, I know, Chase; I'm so sorry I didn't return your calls. I wanted to, but I couldn't find your card and didn't want to bother you at the office. I know how busy you are," Lyla smiled. "I apologize profusely."

"I'm the one who needs to apologize," Chase said. "I don't normally drink that much wine."

Lyla laughed and waved one hand dismissively. "I drank as much as you did. You obviously were exhausted. Please sit down."

Chase lowered himself into the solitary chair facing Lyla's desk. Now that he had Lyla's attention, he was not sure how to begin. He realized that to ask, "When did I take off my pants?" was an attention grabber but not the best opening line.

Jalili waited.

Finally, Chase leaned forward and said, "I'm embarrassed. That is the first time that ever happened to me," Chase said, referring to the fact he had passed out and spent the night on the couch half-undressed. "I don't even remember what happened. I hope I didn't behave inappropriately."

"Inappropriately? Not that I remember. You were sleeping so soundly I didn't want to wake you. I apologize for not serving you breakfast."

"That delightful meal was more than enough," Chase said. "I'm sorry I was a boor."

"You weren't. We are going to have to do it again."

Chase smiled, relieved to be past the delicate problem. "I really wanted to ask you some questions about Doctor Jesperson."

"I've already told you everything I know," Lila said. "Now, I must excuse myself. I have a class waiting."

"I don't even remember asking any questions," Chase admitted.

"No problem," Lila said standing up. "I told you I only knew Doctor Jesperson as a colleague for a couple of weeks, and we didn't discuss Iran. He was too busy polishing his manuscript, and I now understand why. I've read his book and it is quite sensational. Have you been able to identify any of his sources?"

Chase laughed. "I haven't been able to identify anyone who knew him very well except for his parents, who live in another state, Secretary Townsend, who says they had drifted apart, and one ex-fiancée, who he hasn't seen for a year," Chase deliberately answered a different question.

"Poor boy," Lila patted Chase on the shoulder as she paused in front of his chair. "I didn't know about the ex-fiancée. You must tell me about her when I have more time. Were you also involved in the investigation of Secretary Townsend's kidnapping?"

"Only on the periphery. As the media reports. Secretary Townsend, an old friend of Doctor Jesperson's, was one of the last persons to see him that night."

"It all sounds terribly exciting," Lyla said as she opened the door. "We'll have to discuss it."

"When?" Chase asked.

"Leave your card on my desk, and I'll give you a ring," Lyla said. "I'm sorry, Chase, but I really have to run. My students only wait for ten minutes and then leave. If that happens, I'll be in serious trouble with my department head."

"Let me..." Chase tried to offer to walk her to class, but the closing door cut him off.

Chase dropped his card on the desk and hurried after her. Lyla waved from the end of the hall before disappearing into a classroom. Chase hesitated at the door, glanced at Lyla's desk, thought about looking around a little, dismissed that as impolite, changed his mind, and decided to start doing his job. He closed the door softly and sat down in Lyla's chair. He turned on her computer but was immediately thwarted by a demand for a password. He switched the computer off and scanned the desktop. It was completely bare with the exception of a single envelope postmarked Teheran. It was addressed to Doctor Lyla Jalili in care of the Department of Foreign Studies at GMU. That told him nothing. He assumed it was from a personal friend or relative of some kind; Lyla had told him her parents now resided in Paris. The return address did not identify the sender; at least not for Chase. It was written in Arabic script. Chase opened the letter and was dismayed to find it too in Farsi or Arabic.

Chase glanced around the office. Lyla did not rate a copy machine. Chase, assuming any letter left carelessly on the desktop had to be from a Persian friend, decided it was not worth the trouble of searching for a copy machine and risking being seen reproducing someone else's mail. Besides, Chase reasoned, if Lyla was an Iranian agent, which Chase doubted, she would know better than to leave secret messages untended on her desk, particularly with a police investigator in the room. Chase refolded the letter, put it back in the envelope, and returned it to the desk in the same approximate location he had found it.

He then quickly searched the desk drawers but found nothing interesting. He was about to leave when he noted a worn briefcase standing erect on the right side of the desk kneehole. Chase grabbed it and leaned over to open it below the level of the desktop. He didn't want to be seen by an unexpected visitor, a student, or another faculty member, rifling her briefcase.

The briefcase appeared well worn; it looked like one that Lyla might have carried for years as a student. Fortunately, it was not the kind with a lock, just a zipper to protect the contents. Chase quickly unzipped it and opened it on his lap, careful not to spill or disturb any contents. A quick examination showed that it contained only two files and two paperback books. One of the books was an English/Persian dictionary, well worn. The second book was brand new, and the picture on the back made him smile. The author's picture was his own, a not very good likeness, a copy of a ten year old passport picture that Chase had submitted rather than bother with visiting a professional photographer. The author's name was Travis Crittenden, his pseudo, and the title was that of last year's mystery. The book's presence could mean that Lyla had been telling the truth when she said she was a reader of mysteries, or it could indicate that she was engaging in a little, worthless, background research, probably the latter.

Chase opened the first file. It was labeled 'Near East Survey" and appeared to contain the text of research in support of class lectures. The first section dealt with Beirut, 1983. Not interested in that subject matter, Chase checked the second file. The subject line described it as "Notes for Modern Iran, The Rise and Fall of the Shah." The first page, labeled "Iran's Tragedy Begins," described the CIA's role in the 1953 ouster of Mossadeq and the restoration of the Shah to his throne.

Lacking the time to wade through that boring stuff, Chase shoved the books and files back into the briefcase, restored it to its place under the desk, and slipped out of the room. He paused at the doorway that led to Lyla's classroom, watched her speaking energetically to an apparently interested class from the rostrum in the front, stayed long enough for her to glance in his direction, and wave.

Chase returned to his office where he found the usual scene, Theresa sitting behind her desk staring at her computer screen. She smiled at Chase, glanced at the wall clock, and asked, "Have an interesting lunch?"

"I hate working lunches," Chase smiled back. "I never get a chance to enjoy my food."

"I know. You have such a trying life," Theresa commiserated. "What was her name?"

"You know me, Theresa," Chase answered. "I have a terrible time remembering names."

"I'm sure you'll recognize her next time you see her," Theresa nodded agreement. "You are renowned for your ability to recall faces and figures."

Chase surrendered and turned towards his closet office.

"Even after a brief introduction," Theresa called after him as she stood up.

Chase entered to find his desk blanketed with little yellow post-its.

"Particularly if the introduction is at close quarters and intimate," Theresa continued her verbal assault from the open doorway.

"Please close the door behind you, Theresa," Chase said as he settled into his chair. "I have some details to work out."

"I'm sure you need rest after all that heavy lifting at lunch. You have a few messages; Special Agent Cotton was particularly persistent," Theresa said as she closed the door. "I had the impression that something was bothering him. Could it have been you?"

Chase studied the messages and noted that all of them were from Cotton. Three in the center had times listed. The rest cited Cotton as the caller, but Chase assumed they were manufactured by Theresa to emphasize her point, a tactic that she on occasion employed to harass Chase. Theresa refused to recognize that investigation involved field work, and Chase declined to humor her by even pretending to keep regular office hours.

Chase, deciding to ignore Cotton and his message importuning, turned in his chair, placed his feet on his credenza, inadvertently bumped his monitor with his right shoe, and studied a passing cloud. This damned case was proving much more difficult to resolve than he had initially thought. Run of the mill murders that did not include theft inevitably involved a relative, close friend, or acquaintance of the victim. Chase had learned early in his detecting career to focus on personal relationships and identify motive; killers usually were driven by emotion and made mistakes. An experienced investigator with a modicum of effort could detect the clues and unravel the mystery.

Chase's intercom buzzed as he ruminated on the clues in the Townsend case.

"Sir, an irate Special Agent Cotton is on line one," Theresa announced and clicked off before Chase could respond.

Chase glared at the phone with the blinking light. Assuming that Theresa had already informed Cotton that he was in, he could hardly pick of the phone and claim he was out of the office. Chase was not skilled at using false voices, and certainly Cotton would recognize his voice anyway.

Chase irritably grabbed the phone. "Special Agent Cotton," he greeted the caller.

"Asshole," Cotton greeted him back. "You've got your cell turned off, and you don't answer your messages."

"Sorry about that," Chase said, putting as much insincerity into the three words that he could muster.

"What did you learn from that Iranian sweetheart and that broad at lunch?" Cotton demanded. "Why haven't you mentioned the Iranian suspect before this, and who the hell is the broad? You tend to work the girls, don't you?"

"You bastard," Chase reacted. "You're having me surveilled."

"I told you the Bureau is taking over both investigations. Didn't you hear me when I ordered you to keep away from every Iranian in town?"

"And you unilaterally and arbitrarily cancelled our agreement," Chase said. "The Jesperson investigation is mine. Keep away from my suspects."

"And who was the broad at lunch? You didn't answer my questions," Cotton said.

"Her name is none of your business. She was once Jesperson's fiancée."

"I've got her license plate," Cotton laughed. I'll identify her, and then I'll have a chat with her. Do you think she's the shooter?"

"Be my guest. Chat with her and waste your time. They broke up a year ago."

"Sometimes these broads carry grudges for a very long time, particularly ex-fiancées," Cotton hesitated before continuing. "Jesperson's fiancée, huh? Did she ever meet Townsend?"

Chase did not answer.

"Sure she did," Cotton laughed. "That makes her part of my investigation. Did she like Paolo's, or should I take her to a better class restaurant?"

"Chase your tail if you want," Chase said, immediately regretting his choice of words. "Have you found out where Townsend is living? I want to talk with him."

"Given the way you are cooperating? Sure, I'll fax it right over. You just sit there, think about your girl friends, and wait for Townsend's current address to arrive," Cotton chuckled. "I'd concentrate on Mrs. Townsend if I were you. Given her age, the old girl is half preserved. Just your type."

"If you dare put surveillance on me again, I'll arrest them and charge them with interfering with an ongoing murder investigation," Chase said.

"You keep looking over your shoulder," Cotton said. "The next person you see will be me, and I'll arrest you for withholding information vital to a federal investigation."

Chase said nothing.

"You really need a refresher on how to spot surveillance. Ask your chief to send you to Quantico for some training by the experts," Cotton chuckled. "I would be happy to pass along a good word for you. We could tailor make some tails for you."

"Very funny. For an alleged professional, you have a half developed sense of humor," Chase said.

"Do you think Professor Jalili will be in her office this afternoon?" Cotton asked. "I've some free time, so I think I will drop in for tea. I hear foreigners are big on tea. Do you mind if I use your name as a reference?"

"You will be wasting your time," Chase said.

"Then I'll be in good company, won't I?" Cotton laughed and hung up, obviously feeling he had bested Chase in the exchange.

Chase slammed down the receiver and waited for Theresa to appear. She did not disappoint him. She entered without knocking and sat down in Chase's visitor's chair.

"That went rather well, didn't it, lieutenant?" She smiled.

"Cotton is an asshole," Chase said. "Please get me a cup of coffee."

"I thought he was the bastard, and you were the asshole," Theresa said.

Chase smiled. Thinking back on it, he realized the conversation had been rather silly and childish. "I guess neither of us handled it very well," he said.

"I thought you lost," Theresa said.

"Thank you for your support," Chase said.

"If you are going to start on me, get your own coffee, and give me time to get my recorder. A good recording will support my harassment charges," Theresa smiled as she stood up.

"I'm not going to harass you, Theresa, I'd lose. Please do me a favor this once and bring me a coffee. I've had a bad day."

"OK, this once," Theresa said. "Just listening to that conversation made my day. Imagine the fun I'll have putting a description of that on the vine." Theresa referred to the interoffice senior secretary solidarity network.

"Please don't. I'll get my own coffee."

"I'll get your coffee, lieutenant, but just remember the next time you harass me, I really have a great story to tell."

"OK, but remember harassment charges can cut both ways," Chase said. "Please go light on the sugar, sugar. I'm on a diet."

"That must have been a great lunch. Who was the broad?"

"And do me a favor, please," Chase ignored the jab. "I need the office phone number of the Secretary of Homeland Security."

"I thought he resigned," Chase's request caught Theresa by surprise.

"I just want to talk with the secretary's secretary," Chase smiled. His conversation with Cotton and Theresa's monitoring of same sparked an idea. If anyone knew the identity of Townsend's girl friend, his secretary would.

Five minutes later, Chase was sipping his excessively sweet coffee—Theresa had ignored his request, as he knew she would—the coffee was just the way he needed it as he dialed the private line of the Secretary of Homeland Security.

"Homeland Security," an efficient female voice answered.

"This is Lieutenant Mansfield of the Fairfax County Police," Chase identified himself. "I'm trying to reach the office of the secretary."

"Congratulations, you've succeeded, lieutenant," the voice answered.

"May I ask who I am talking with?" Chase asked.

"What office are you in, lieutenant?" the voice asked.

"I am a senior investigator assigned to the Criminal Investigation Bureau."

"Are you in the office now?"

"Yes," Chase grinned as he realized that the efficient senior secretary was going to double check him.

"Let me call you right back, lieutenant," the secretary said and hung up.

Chase leaned back and called to Theresa. "The lady is going to call right back. You can confirm my identity and put her through.

"Are you sure you want me to break precedence and do that?" Theresa challenged.

"Theresa, please," Chase said as he heard Theresa's phone ring.

"CIB," Theresa answered.

Chase listened as Theresa said, "Yes, yes, that is correct. Lieutenant Mansfield is in his office now, would you like me to put you through."

"Lieutenant, sir," Theresa called. "The Office of the Secretary of Homeland Security would like to speak with you."

"Congratulations, you've succeeded," Chase repeated the secretary's words.

"Do I sound that snotty?" The female voice asked. "Standby, the secretary is coming on line.

"Wait!" Chase reacted. "That will not be necessary; you sound sweet, not snotty."

"I'm glad you think so, lieutenant," a different female voice declared. "This is Patricia Marshall. We haven't met, but I am the acting secretary filling in since...since Secretary Townsend's unfortunate experience and his premature resignation. I have heard your name mentioned several times as lead investigator in the Jesperson murder. I understand you called our private line. How can I assist you?"

"I apologize for bothering you, Madam Secretary," a surprised Chase reacted. I need a small piece of information and was trying to reach Secretary Townsend's assistant."

"I've been that, lieutenant. Maybe I can help you. Please call me Patricia. Madam Secretary is still a bit overwhelming and really quite inaccurate. I am neither a madam nor the secretary; I'm merely an acting. Is your request official? A part of your investigation?"

"Yes, ma'am. As you may recall, Secretary Townsend was one of the last persons to see Doctor Jesperson."

"Yes. As a favor to Doctor Jesperson, a long time friend, Secretary Townsend met with a group of academics at George Mason that unfortunate night."

"And I have some very important questions about that evening that I must ask Secretary Townsend."

"I'm sorry, but Secretary Townsend has not returned to the office. We are trying to negotiate a visit so his many friends here can wish him well on his future endeavors. You will have to contact him directly."

"That's exactly what I am trying to do," Chase said, "but I am having difficulty reaching him."

"I can understand that," Marshall said. "I'm certain he is not trying to avoid you. However, the media is a problem at the moment."

"I've talked with Mrs. Townsend, and I know that there has been a change in their relationship."

"Yes."

"And she does not know Secretary Townsend's current address."

"Yes."

"If your office is currently working with Secretary Townsend or one of his representatives to arrange an office event, I assume someone knows where I can reach him," Chase pressed.

"Lieutenant, I am the person who has been in contact with Secretary Townsend, and I am not sure I can violate his confidence by disclosing his whereabouts," Marshall said stiffly.

"I fully understand, but as I noted I am working on official police business. I could always resort to a warrant demanding the information, but I would really prefer to handle this discreetly. My need is quite urgent."

Marshall laughed. "Surely, lieutenant, you are not threatening to serve a warrant on the Acting Secretary of the Department of Homeland Security."

Chase resisted the urge to chuckle as the thought crossed his mind that they should consider renaming the Department of Homeland Security; Department of Homeland Affairs would be more appropriate.

"That is the last thing I want to do," Chase replied. "President Featherstone is aware of my investigation and considers it a number one priority. If you wish, and it is not my business to suggest such a thing, you could obviously consult with him on my request."

Marshall did not immediately react.

"And as I said this is quite urgent," Chase overstated his need. "I am worried that if the media picked up on the situation..." Chase tried to understate his threat but was confident that Marshall would pick up on his message. "...I'm sure it would needlessly embarrass everybody concerned. I'm just a police officer doing his duty."

"Don't overdo it, lieutenant," Marshall reacted. "You're standing right on the threshold of a crossing a line you might regret crossing."

Chase waited.

"I'll give you Secretary Townsend's cell number. I can't guarantee that he will answer it."

"Thank you," Chase said, not admitting he already had the cell number. "You are most kind."

"And don't overdo the humble bullshit, lieutenant," Marshall said. "I may be acting and a woman, but I'm not in this job because I'm a pushover."

"I must see him, and if you think he won't answer the cell..." Chase pushed his luck.

"So you want his current address."

"Yes."

"Alright," Marshall said after a slight pause. "I've visited Secretary Townsend at his current lodging. I don't remember the exact address, but I can tell you how to find it."

Chase did not believe her but assumed that by making him work to find Townsend she could cover herself a little.

"Do you know Reston?" Marshall asked.

"Of course."

"Lake Anne?"

"Yes." Chase did not comment, not wanting to say anything that would lead Marshall to change her mind.

"North Shore Drive?"

"Yes."

"From the Plaza, third building on the right, top floor apartment. Lieutenant, I don't care how you think you acquired this information, but it was not from me."

"Agreed," Chase said.

"We have never met nor talked," Marshall declared. "But you owe me a big one."

"Agreed," Chase.

Chase heard Marshall mutter, "Shit, I'm stupid," before she terminated the conversation.

Chase leaped up from his chair and hurried through Theresa's office.

"Don't say a word," Chase ordered as he passed her desk.

"Jesus, you're devious," Theresa reacted with wide eyes and an open mouth.

"Don't overdo it, Theresa. I may be a man but I'm not a pushover," Chase paraphrased Acting Secretary Marshall.

"Can't blame a girl for trying," Theresa laughed.

Chase winked and closed the door softly behind him.

Forty-five minutes later and after carefully making sure he had no FBI surveillants behind him, Chase parked his Prius in the Lake Anne Plaza lot and approached the third building on the right from behind on foot. He didn't know what questions he was going to so urgently ask Secretary Townsend, but he was looking forward to the challenge.

There was no name on the apartment door identifying the occupant, but Chase knocked anyway, prepared to brazen his way inside. He doubted that the name of Townsend's new girl friend would mean anything to him anyway. It was Townsend he needed to question, though he was interested in getting a look at the new paramour to see if Townsend had upgraded in the process.

Chase heard voices in the apartment react to his knock, but he could not make out what was said. One was female and one male; he could not identify the latter as Townsend, but the female voice struck Chase as being oddly familiar. Everything went quiet, and Chase assumed it was possible the occupants were waiting for the unannounced visitor to go away. Chase was raising his hand to knock again, determined to get an answer, when the door opened suddenly. Chase and the woman who stood before him stared at each other, equally astonished.

"What are you doing here?" Sally Kendrick blurted. "I told you everything I had to say at lunch."

Chase had planned to follow-up the lunch with the Lady in Black, but not quite so quickly; he was too surprised to immediately answer her question. He simply stared.

"How did you find me? I never gave you my address?" Kendrick asked as she stared at Chase from her defensive position behind the partially open door.

"May I come in?" Chase asked, ignoring the questions.

"That would not be convenient," Kendrick said.

"It's important," Chase persisted.

"I have company," Kendrick said.

"I won't stay long," Chase said.

"No," Kendrick said as she started to close the door.

Chase stepped forward and stopped the door with his foot as he took his cell phone from his suit coat pocket. "Please don't make me do something I don't want to do," he said.

"I'll call the cops," Kendrick said.

"Good," Chase smiled. "And I'll ask them to bring along a warrant. I'll stand right here until they arrive." Chase stepped back and withdrew his foot.

An angry Kendrick glared at him, but she did not close the door. Behind her a male voice spoke. "Please let him in, Sally. We don't need a scene."

Kendrick hesitated, and Chase waited, not sure what his no longer charming luncheon partner was going to do next. After a few tense seconds, Kendrick stepped back. Chase pushed against the door and stepped into the apartment. Kendrick with clenched fists still confronted him. Not interested in a fistfight, Chase watched her closely.

"I congratulate you on your tenacity, lieutenant," Secretary James Howard Townsend greeted him.

"I apologize for the intrusion," Chase said, not meaning it.

"I answered all the questions that I am going to answer at lunch," Kendrick said, still blocking him.

"But there is so much you didn't tell me," Chase smiled.

"Don't hold your breath," Kendrick muttered. "Did you follow me here?"

Chase laughed but did not explain that he was the one who was surveilled after their lunch.

Chase's amusement only irritated the agitated Kendrick more.

"It's alright, Sally, I assume I am the one who the lieutenant wishes to interrogate now," Townsend said. "Let's just let him ask his questions and leave."

Again, Kendrick, who demonstrably was not one who took orders gracefully, hesitated before relenting. Obviously fighting the urge to continue her challenge, she turned reluctantly and stomped into a large kitchen on her right. Chase read her defiant body language: talk with him if you must, but without me.

"Would you like a cup of coffee, dear?" Kendrick asked with a low, saccharine intonation.

Since she obviously was not speaking to him, Chase resisted the urge to respond.

"Yes, please," Townsend answered. "And bring one for our unexpected visitor."

"Thank you," Chase said as he joined Townsend in a spacious sitting room that was decorated more like a family room than a formal parlor.

Townsend sat in a recliner positioned near a large floor to ceiling wall of glass that looked out over Lake Anne. To Townsend's left set a matching recliner. Both faced an internal corner dominated by a large, high definition television; a single upholstered chair set in the corner next to the television. A fireplace, surrounded by bookcases and three sectional couches completed the arrangement. Although a decorator with limp wrists would undoubtedly disapprove, Chase rated the decor as comfortable, a man's room.

"Take your choice," Townsend waved at the second recliner on his left and the chair opposite. Chase took the chair.

Before Chase could speak, the still glowering Kendrick rejoined them, carrying only two coffee cups that she set on the table between the two recliners. Chase decided that anger did not flatter his luncheon companion; the frown considerably aged her. Townsend caught her eye, glanced at the two cups and then Chase, asking the obvious silent question. Kendrick stubbornly shook her head negatively as she sat down in the second recliner. That little exchange made Chase speculate that Townsend's divorce would simply mean that he was exchanging one problem for another, possibly a much more difficult one.

"Nancy Lou reported that you were looking for me," Townsend smiled at Chase, referring to his spouse.

"She said she did not know the name of your new..." Chase hesitated. He was going to say girl friend but that did not seem appropriate. "...interest," he improvised.

Townsend nodded and glanced at Kendrick who did not react. Undismayed, Townsend turned his attention back to Chase.

"She also said she did not know your current address," Chase said.

"You followed me, you bastard," Kendrick assigned Chase a common title.

"What made you suspect that Sally had given me a refuge, a sanctuary from unwanted media and official intrusions?" Townsend asked.

"I apologize for my imposition, but I cannot answer that question," Chase grinned. "I'm not sure that you now hold the proper clearances."

"Thank God," Townsend smiled back, equally insincere. "Sally tells me that you know that she was once my good friend Thomas's fiancée," Townsend continued. "That makes my new interest," as you so politely describe her, "an old and dear friend."

"A friend of a friend is a friend," Chase said.

"Something like that," Townsend agreed.

"Mansfield, just ask your damned questions and leave," Kendrick ordered.

"You were the last person to see Doctor Jesperson alive," Chase said as he got down to business.

Townsend and Kendrick exchanged smiles as they sipped from their coffee cups. That curious exchange intrigued Chase. They knew something he did not and clearly did not intend to share it. Their arrogant confidence irritated him, but he concealed it.

"Not quite," Townsend answered, not the least offended by the implications of Chase's opening statement. "The shooter must have looked at Thomas before he fired."

"That's true," Chase said. "Who do you think hated Doctor Jesperson so much that he or she," Chase stressed the she, "felt compelled to murder him?"

"I don't know," Townsend replied evenly. "Thomas had been out of the country for the past year and since his return both of us have been quite busy, Thomas with his writing and settling back into his teaching, and me, of course, with the drudgery of a demanding office."

Chase glanced at Kendrick and caught her glaring at him, her eyes filled with anger.

"How often did you meet him following his return?" Chase asked.

"In person, just once, the night of my talk at George Mason. We also chatted one time on the phone. You can check with my secretary and my protective detail if you haven't done so already. My movements and phone conversations were fully logged."

"You left your security detail behind on the night of your visit to GMU. Was that a common practice for you?"

"Of course not. That was an exception as my detail will confirm."

"Were your discreet visits to Ms. Kendrick also exceptions?"

"That's none of your business," Kendrick interrupted.

"That's not true, Ms. Kendrick. It is very much my business."

"Are you accusing James of murdering his best friend?" Kendrick demanded.

"Of course he is," Townsend calmly set the coffee cup on the table between them and patted Kendrick on the knee. "And the lieutenant thinks that you are my motive. I killed Thomas in order to steal his fiancée."

"That's bullshit," Kendrick exploded. She turned on Chase. "Get out of my apartment right now."

Chase, waiting for the temperate Townsend to calm his paramour, did not move. He found their interaction interesting, particularly since he now assumed that Kendrick had been playing a role, performing, during all their previous contacts beginning with the chance meeting at Jesperson's funeral, and he also realized that the Lady in Black was not the only one manipulating her relationship with him. Clearly, Mrs. Nancy Lou Townsend had been using him also. She had taken in both Special Agent Cotton and Chase; they both had assumed, apparently mistakenly, that Nancy Lou had been attracted by Chase's scintillating personality. Given Cotton's somewhat intemperate demeanor, Chase assumed the Cotton's reaction when he learned of this interpretation would not be as moderated as Chase's.

"I share your indignation, Sally, but I understand," Townsend said evenly. "The lieutenant is just doing his job. The simple fact that I was one of the last persons to see Thomas—it makes the lieutenant's job more manageable to consider me the very last—raises me to the top of his list of suspects."

"But his obstinate refusal to believe me when I say my relationship ended with Thomas a year ago before he went to Iran when combined with our current association even adds to his suspicions, and I personally find that insulting even if you do not," Kendrick glared at Chase as she spoke.

"The lieutenant is obviously a skilled investigator, dear," Townsend again patted Kendrick's knee. "And I am sure that he will eventually learn that we are speaking honestly. Simply antagonizing him by venting our emotions is self-defeating. We should help him find the truth."

Disbelief and disagreement were still evident on Kendrick's face but she surprised Chase by not debating the issue. She simply turned and stared a silent challenge at Chase.

"I've already told you, lieutenant, what Thomas and I discussed and what happened when I tried to return to my car," Townsend calmly spoke to Chase. "I don't know what else I can tell you."

"Did Doctor Jesperson know about your relationship with Ms. Kendrick?" Chase asked, waiting for another eruption from Kendrick.

Kendrick did not speak; Townsend answered. "He did not. One of my reasons for deviating from my usual practice of avoiding public engagements was to discuss the situation with Thomas like two mature adults. We had drinks together after the public session, but unfortunately I was not able to raise the subject in a manner that felt comfortable to me. We digressed on the subject of his book, and that was clearly his primary preoccupation. I am not the kind of man who enjoys discussing personal matters, not even with friends." Townsend reached towards Kendrick and took her hand. "I simply was not able to table the issue of my relationship with Sally in a manner that was not awkward, and I know she would have been angry with me if I had been able to inform her of that failing following my session with Thomas. Unfortunately, my rude treatment at the hands of others prevented me from acting like a gentleman."

"I understand," Kendrick said, patting the back of Townsend's hand.

"What did Mrs. Townsend think about all this?" Chase asked.

"Pose that question to Mrs. Townsend at your own risk, lieutenant," Townsend said, standing up. "Sally Lou has a strong temper, believe me, I know. Now, it's time for us to end this unwarranted intrusion of yours. I've said the last that I will about this unpleasant subject. Please leave."

Those words made Kendrick smile.

Chase calmly nodded his acquiescence; two could play the gentleman game. Although he was not as satisfied with Townsend's answers as his two antagonists might think, he was patient enough to wait for another day. The simple revelation of the Townsend/Kendrick relationship gave him much to consider. He had hoped to learn more about the victim, his personality, and the identities of his current friends from the former fiancée and ostensible best friend, but their apparent uniting greatly complicated that approach. Chase doubted that he could place much reliance on any information about Jesperson that he obtained from them now; they had their own interests to protect.

Chapter 23

President Ahmadinejad twitched nervously as he watched Nevad Behbehani, the Minister of Intelligence and Security, and General Obadias Nasiri, Behbehani's VEVAK commander, settle into the chairs facing him. It always irritated Ahmadinejad when he had to meet with the two oversized men whose bulk compensated for the platform under his chair. He much preferred to have his subordinates looking up at him rather than face him with eyes on the same level. Psychologically, it negated a useful tool, and with these two the president needed all the advantages he could muster. The fact that they had double-teamed him did not help; if the arrogant Behbehani had asked for permission to bring Nasiri to this meeting, Ahmadinejad would have denied it. Ahmadinejad made a mental note to remind his mentor Ayatollah Yazdi that they had to manipulate the early replacement of the two Ayatollah Khamenei henchmen soon.

"Do you have any news for me?" Ahmadinejad asked rudely, dispensing with the normal polite preliminaries. No Salom Aleikoms or Hal-e Shoma Chitor-es.

"Yes." Behbehani responded curtly, mimicking the president's lack of courtesy.

Behbehani turned to General Nasiri. "With your permission, general," Behbehani pretended to ask his subordinate's acquiescence.

"Of course, sir," Nasiri played the minister's game.

"Everything is in motion," Behbehani spoke to Ahmadinejad.

"What in the hell does that mean?" Ahmadinejad reacted.

"General Nasiri's agents are preparing to implement your plan, Mr. President."

Behbehani's deft assignment of responsibility for the action under discussion was clearly recognized by Nasiri and Ahmadinejad for what it was, a clear denial of culpability by Behbehani. Nasiri had no recourse other than to accept his superior's ploy, but not the president.

"Are your people in place or not, Mr. Minister?" Ahmadinejad deliberately stressed the phrase "your people."

"They are, sir," Behbehani countered the little man's word games by giving the "sir" a slightly sarcastic emphasis.

"Good," Ahmadinejad declared. "Sometimes the efficiency of VEVAK surprises me." Ahmadinejad deliberately did not explain whether that surprise was for the good or the bad. "When should we mount Phase Two?"

"That is your decision, sir," Behbehani said.

Ahmadinejad frowned and turned to the VEVAK commander. "General?" Ahmadinejad demanded an answer.

"We will soon be ready to implement," Nasiri answered.

"Can we rely on your operatives?" Ahmadinejad pressed.

"Even though we plan for every contingency, we do not control the operational environment," Nasiri hedged.

"What does that mean?"

"We must rely on our agents' skill and professionalism," Nasiri smiled. "The man on the point frequently must make critical decisions. We can only select the best people for the job, give them the resources they need, and support them as we can, but we must recognize in an operation of this kind we must rely on the field agent to make tactical decisions."

"Tell me about the agents you have dispatched," Ahmadinejad countered the general's attempt to shift ultimate responsibility elsewhere.

"There are only two," Nasiri said. "I of course have not met them personally, but I am assured they are the best we have."

"What are their names?"

Nasiri hesitated.

"Operational security requires that their true names be divulged on a strictly need to know basis," Behbehani supported Nasiri. "I commend the general's professionalism," Behbehani smiled at his colleague.

Ahmadinejad, who knew better than to trust these two, considered insisting on an answer but decided not to press the issue. If he did not know the names, he would be blameless if they should leak as often happened when something went wrong, a not infrequent development.

"You say they are the best," Ahmadinejad hedged. "Why?"

Nasiri was tempted to reply with the truth, but he did not. "Because they are the best agents we have in America," Nasiri looked at Behbehani, who nodded, deferring to his subordinate.

Nasiri swallowed. "Our primary is a male who has been in place for almost ten years. He knows America so well that he could pass as a native, if necessary. This is important because the man at the point frequently has to improvise. We of course have no previous experience in this kind of operation. No one does. It will be a first."

"Are you saying that you expect the operation to fail?" Ahmadinejad demanded.

"No, sir," Nasiri answered. "But I stress there can be no guarantees. We are mounting a unique operation in a hostile environment facing highly professional security services who have been alerted."

"Alerted? Has the operation been compromised?"

"General Nasiri refers to the Jesperson book and its sensational allegations," Behbehani said.

"It is a bunch of lies," Ahmadinejad declared.

"But..."

"No buts. We will negate the lies with Phase Two."

"The timing..." Behbehani started to respond.

"No," Ahmadinejad interrupted. He leaped from his chair, stumbled off his platform, and began to pace.

Neither Behbehani nor Nasiri spoke. When the moving Ahmadinejad turned his back on them, they exchanged smiles.

"The timing will never be ripe for this kind of operation," Ahmadinejad declared as he turned to face them. "I will start Phase Two personally. Immediately."

"If you think that is wise," Behbehani seized the opportunity.

"Thank you Mr. Minister for your permission," Ahmadinejad snapped.

"Have you cleared the operation with Qom?" Nasiri asked, referring to the ayatollahs.

"I will deal with policy," Ahmadinejad said as he returned to his chair. "You, general, concern yourself with the implementation. Now, tell me more about these agents of yours."

Nasiri looked at Behbehani who nodded, a silent request for permission and an approval; both irritated Ahmadinejad. He did not speak, however, but waited.

"He is an experienced agent who is what we call a sleeper," Nasiri began.

"A sleeper! What does that mean? You've assigned an agent who does nothing but sleep?" Ahmadinejad erupted.

"A sleeper is an agent who is buried deep in the target society. He waits to perform a task commensurate with his talents. In other words, he has done nothing that would pose a security threat to a highly important operation," Nasiri paused, not wanting to say too much. He feared that Ahmadinejad was too impulsive, too unpredictable to be trusted with not jeopardizing a sensitive operation. The president's career record was riddled with counter-productive, injudicious, and often incorrect media allegations.

"And does this sleeper have the technical background to detonate our... our...suitcase?"

"No," Nasiri answered. "Agent Number one will provide the necessary support, something he is highly qualified to do. Technical details will be the prerogative of Agent Number Two."

"Also a sleeper?" Ahmadinejad asked, his question laden with heavy sarcasm.

"No, sir. We consider Agent Number Two a penetration agent."

"And what has Agent Number Two penetrated that makes him technically qualified. The American nuclear energy program, I hope."

"That was our long range objective, sir. Agent number two is a highly qualified female who has been in place only a relatively short time. Agent Number Two, like Agent Number One, is an Iranian citizen."

"Don't tell me that both of these so-called agents are former officials of the corrupt regime," Ahmadinejad referred to the Shah and his despicable establishment of criminals, exploiters, and thieves.

"No sir, both are devout, loyal citizens we have dispatched to America under appropriate covers."

"Such as?"

"Sir, do you really want the responsibility for this kind of detail? We hold these agents' lives in our hands," Nasiri said.

"Answer my questions. I will decide when you have told me enough to justify proceeding with the mission."

"Agent Number One is a thirty-two year old male in America with a valid student visa."

"He's been a student for ten years?"

"Yes sir."

"At our expense?"

"Yes sir."

"And all he's done is sleep?"

"Believe me sir, he's earned his salary, living in a hostile environment, separate from his family, performing low profile tasks such as spotting, and the like."

Ahmadinejad shook his head in disbelief. "And Agent Two?"

"A female graduate of Teheran University with two degrees, a BS in Physics, and n MS in Nuclear Physics. She spent the past five years in Paris earning her doctorate in Nuclear Physics."

Ahmadinejad, a engineering graduate of Teheran University, nodded approval. "And she is now a student in the States?"

"No sir, she has a working visa."

"Tell me she now works for the American Government."

"No sir, but that is the plan. Now, she is an instructor at a university in the District of Columbia Metropolitan area."

"But she is trying to get a job in the American nuclear energy program?"

"That is the plan?"

"And she is qualified to work with the suitcase?"

"Yes sir, with the help of Agent Number One."

"What does he do?"

He assists in the transport of the suitcase."

"And Number Two has been trained in handling the suitcase? She knows how to...how to make it detonate? Why is this the first time I have heard of her?"

"She is one of our most sensitive and highly trained assets."

"Who trained her to use the suitcase?"

Nasiri glanced at Behbehani who nodded.

"No one sir. But clear written instructions have been dispatched to her along with the suitcase, and she is more than competent to implement them," Nasiri said.

Ahmadinejad waited for more.

Nasiri looked at Behbehani who answered the unspoken question. "She is," Behbehani said. Before Ahmadinejad could ask another question, Behbehani attempted to divert him. "Remind me again, Mr. President, what Phase Two entails," Behbehani said.

Ahmadinejad glared at the minister but caught himself before he declared that Phase Two was none of Behbehani's business. It occurred to him that Behbehani was once again trying to assign responsibility.

"Of course," Ahmadinejad smiled as he folded his hands on the desk in front of him. "Please tell me if you approve."

Behbehani, recognizing he had misspoken, nodded.

"As you are both aware, the Americans have launched a sneak attack on our nuclear research program. Their CIA has arrogantly infected our computers that manage the centrifuges producing our weapons grade fuel."

"As you directed, we released the scientists with access to the Natanz program," Nasiri said, trying to negate another Ahmadinejad complaint before it got started.

"I must note that the release has greatly impeded our attempt to identify the traitor responsible," Behbehani supported Nasiri.

"I am not surprised," Ahmadinejad declared. "We can resume our investigation in due course. Now, we must turn this alleged CIA success back on them. I have directed our Ambassador to the United Nations to register a formal complaint protesting this despicable American attack on our sovereignty."

"The Americans will deny the charge," Behbehani said. "And the world media will ridicule us. We know who is responsible for the virus, but we have no proof."

"Proof," Ahmadinejad laughed. "We are talking diplomacy. We can worry about proof later. We are just firing a verbal warning shot, telling the world that we have been wronged. We can invite the UN to investigate our peaceful nuclear energy program."

"But they will insist on visiting Natanz," Behbehani smiled at Ahmadinejad's naiveté. "They know we will refuse and use that against us. This is an old battle that we always lose."

"Why are you debating with me? I know all that. The situation will never go that far. Phase 3 will make them all forget the details. The world will only remember that we were the first harmed. I personally guarantee that."

"What is Phase Three exactly?" Behbehani did something that he seldom did. He admitted ignorance.

"General Nasiri will mount Phase Three on my command," Ahmadinejad smiled as he waited for one of his visitors to ask him to elaborate.

"And how do I do that?" Nasiri complied.

"You will arrange a massive explosion at Natanz," Ahmadinejad said. "Something impressive, but not too damaging to our infrastructure. Blow up an annex containing our infected centrifuges. Make sure that it appears to be the result of a foreigner's bomb, not an accident."

"But we need every centrifuge we can get in operation," Behbehani protested.

"I know that," Ahmadinejad glowered. "Be ingenious. Must I handle every little detail myself?"

"An act of sabotage," Nasiri appeared to seriously consider the plan.

"A follow-up act of sabotage," Ahmadinejad encouraged the VEVAK chief. "Make it loud with lots of flames and smoke. Throw in a couple of the scientists, those we suspect of being the CIA spies. A few bodies are always useful."

"And you can invite the UN lackeys to inspect the damage," Nasiri opined.

"That's correct," Ahmadinejad said. "I will escort the inspectors and the foreign media myself."

"Do you think that wise?" Behbehani said, masking his surprise and the fact he was impressed with the plan. "Aren't you afraid that they will insist on visiting the other buildings?"

"No problem. We will declare the other building unsafe for humans."

"The media will allege radiation and panic the world," Behbehani said.

"Good, and our suitcase, Phase Four, the continuation of Phase Two will focus their concern on Washington."

"But they will then blame us, accuse us of retaliating for the attack on Natanz," Behbehani cautioned.

"Is this my Minister of Intelligence and Security talking?" Ahmadinejad asked sarcastically. "Aren't you the man in charge of our black operations?"

"But..." Behbehani, now on the defensive, prepared to defend himself.

"But nothing," Ahmadinejad interrupted. "Use your imagination. Do what the people pay you to do or resign."

Behbehani did not reply.

"We will deny any allegations and suggest that the explosion in Washington was caused by CIA ineptitude. The bunglers mishandled their own equipment as they prepared to launch another attack on us."

"But the Americans will know better," Nasiri said.

"Who will believe them?"

"There is always the information in the Jesperson book that allegedly came from Iranian sources."

"More CIA disinformation. It proves that Jesperson was just another CIA provocateur."

"And the objective of your imaginative program?" Behbehani asked.

"We prove to the world that the Americans are desperately trying to halt their rapid decline while denying Iran its rightful place as a superpower. Remember the 12th Mahdi."

Behbehani glanced at Nasiri. The two had previously discussed Ahmadinejad's preposterous belief in the Hidden Mahdi fable. He frequently referred to the return of the Mahdi in his public speeches and private conversations. He truly appeared to believe that the Twelfth Imam, the twelfth descendent of the Prophet Muhammad's son in law, who had disappeared at the age of six in 874, would return soon, an event that would mark the Day of Judgment when Shiism would assume its rightful place as the true faith. Behbehani and Nasiri jointly believed that Ahmadinejad expected that event would also mark Iran's replacement of America as the world's preeminent superpower with Ahmadinejad, of course, its paramount leader.

Behbehani turned his attention back to the little man sitting on his platform behind the oversized desk and found him staring at him. Unable to respond as Ahmadinejad obviously expected, Behbehani said nothing.

The two men, the president and the minister of information and security, exchanged hostile stares for almost thirty seconds until Behbehani tried to extricate himself from the tension with a comment that committed him to nothing.

"A remarkable plan," Behbehani declared.

Ahmadinejad turned to Nasiri.

"And what do you think, general? Can you manage Phase Three?"

"Yes sir," Nasiri answered promptly. He could think of no counterargument or any way to extricate himself from the madman's delusive scheme.

"Good, make your preparations and stand-by to implement on my direct order," Ahmadinejad said.

Ahmadinejad stared at the silent Behbehani.

"Minister, I want to be informed immediately when your American agents are prepared to implement."

"Yes Mr. President," Behbehani capitulated.

"The man is mad," Behbehani declared as soon as the two had cleared security. "He thinks he is the Hidden Mahdi who has returned to rule the world."

"What options do I have?" General Nasiri shrugged.

"What do you think he would have said if I had told him that our highly qualified agent has never fired an explosive device in her young life?" Behbehani smiled.

"What do you think he would have said if you had admitted she is teaching history not physics at Doctor Jesperson's university?" Nasiri asked.

"And that she is now responsible for the late Doctor Jesperson's very own classes," Behbehani added.

"I'm sure he would assume that she is a CIA spy, just like Doctor Jesperson," Nasiri said.

"That would certainly give the president a little heartburn," Behbehani said as they parted. "Do you think we should revisit our leader?"

"No," Nasiri said firmly.

"Neither do I," Behbehani waved. "All of this intelligence scheming makes this an interesting but complicated career."

Chapter 24

Special Agent Cotton parked his black Chevy in the lot and joined the stream of students making their way towards Robinson Hall. Although the campus was the scene of the murder and the kidnapping, it was not familiar turf for him. Now, however, Cotton considered it his, even though he belatedly followed in Chase Mansfield's footsteps. Despite the fact that he had initially delegated the investigation of the Iranian connection to Mansfield's murder investigation, Cotton now needed to unilaterally negate their agreement, and he intended to start with Doctor Lyla Jalili. A phone tap was in place, and routine background checks from overseas were starting to come in. The Bureau's Legal Attaché in Paris had yet to identify the sender of the first e-mail message, but the attaché's French liaison contacts had passed along interesting data on Jalili. She had earned a doctorate in nuclear physics but was lecturing on area studies at George Mason, a little item that Cotton had not shared with Mansfield. Cotton also wondered if Jalili had discussed her politics with Mansfield, particularly the fact that in Paris she had been an active supporter of the mullah's revolution. Cotton had let Mansfield think he had just learned of Jalili's presence at GMU, but her name had come to his attention when one of his officers had compiled a list of all Iranians on campus, and Cotton had requested routine name checks. He was most interested in seeing what kind of tales Jalili would spin for him about her background.

Cotton tapped on the door and entered to find Doctor Jalili worrying her computer.

"I'm busy, come back later," Jalili said, not looking up.

"Doctor Jalili?" An amused Cotton asked, closing the door behind him.

Jalili turned and greeted the intruder with a frown. "Do I know you?"

"I doubt it," Cotton smiled. "But I suspect we'll soon correct that little oversight."

"You are too old to be a student; you are not a faculty member, and I don't meet with anyone else without an appointment. If you are a cop, you are wasting your time," Jalili declared as she turned back to her computer. "I have already answered all of Lieutenant Mansfield's questions."

"I am none of the above, and believe me, Doctor Jalili, you will interrupt your busy schedule to talk with me," Cotton replied as he studied her profile. She was an attractive young lady; at least as much of her as he could see from the waist up.

Still frowning, Jalili flipped off her monitor, presumably so that her visitor could not read what she had been writing. She pivoted her chair. "If you are INS, you can check your records. I have a valid work visa."

"As I said, doctor, you will talk with me, now, either here or at my headquarters," Cotton let a little menace color his tone.

"Show me your credentials," Jalili countered, not the least intimidated.

Cotton, unbidden, sat down in the chair facing Jalili's desk.

They exchanged silent stares.

"You are truly a rude man," Jalili bent first.

Cotton extracted his credentials case and held it up for Jalili to see.

She reached out her hand, expecting Cotton to surrender the folder to her.

Cotton closed the case and put it back in his pocket.

"FBI," Jalili said with evident disapproval. "I want to see the picture. How do I know you aren't an imposter?"

"How well did you know Doctor Jesperson?" Cotton asked, ignoring the young Iranian's posturing.

"By reputation? Well enough," Jalili answered.

"Personally," Cotton said. "You had much in common."

"Personally?" Jalili laughed. "He was old enough to be my father."

"How old are you?" Cotton asked, resisting the temptation to reply that age surely would not be an impediment to someone like Jalili.

"That's none of your business."

Cotton moved with deliberate slowness as he took his small notebook from his pocket. He opened it, pretended to read, and announced, "Date of birth, July 5, 1981. That makes you twenty-nine."

Jalili did not comment, but Cotton noticed that her eyes were focused on the notebook. He folded it shut but placed it on the desk between them, using it as a threatening lever.

"Were the two of you intimate?" Cotton asked.

"Intimate?" Jalili glared at her interrogator.

"Yes, you know, friends," Cotton said. "The kind that share garments." Cotton deliberately threw in the word "garments." In his experience with people who were speaking English as a second or third language, Cotton had found that most were not sure what words like garments meant, and he was trying to unsettle Jalili's confidence by making her worry about his questions. He assumed she was too arrogant to ask him to explain.

"Doctor Jesperson was on sabbatical when I arrived. He returned only a few weeks ago. I certainly knew him by reputation, but never, I repeat never, shared a private conversation with him. He was our department's luminary and preoccupied with his book, too busy to share time with an unpublished foreign nobody like me."

Cotton liked the answer particularly the sensitivity indicated by the use of the word "foreign" and the reference to the book.

"Have you read Doctor Jesperson's book?" Cotton glanced at a copy prominently displayed on the left corner of Jalili's desk.

"What if I have? Is that against the law?" Jalili challenged.

"No. I'm interested in what you think of it," Cotton said.

"Why should it matter what I think of it?" Jalili asked.

"It is about your country and your government," Cotton smiled. "Should I buy a copy?"

"I would assume that a senior FBI officer like yourself would have already read the book since you seem to be involved in investigating the author's murder," Jalili smiled back.

"What makes you think I am a senior officer?" Cotton asked, not interested in the answer but determined to keep Jalili talking.

"Your age," Jalili chuckled.

"I have read the book," Cotton gave that round to Jalili.

"And?"

"And it worries me," Cotton said.

"Why is that? "

"Because of the assertions that it makes. I'm in the security business, and talk about pending nuclear attacks worries me. You're here in the target zone. Does that trouble you?"

"Not at all Special Agent Cotton," Jalili said.

The use of his name and title surprised Cotton, not the negative answer to his question. Jalili had good eyesight in addition to a sharp tongue. He had merely flashed his credentials at her, and he had not mentioned his name or title.

"Don't you believe Doctor Jesperson? He just spent a year in your country," Cotton stressed the "your."

"I am a simple instructor without tenure on a two year contract in the foreign studies department," Jalili said. "Who am I to doubt a bestselling author like Doctor Jesperson?"

"I assume you are also a loyal Iranian citizen," Cotton said. "If Doctor Jesperson published untruths about your country, shouldn't you as a member of the educated elite point that out?"

"The sensational elements of Doctor Jesperson's book deal with subjects beyond my expertise," Jalili said.

"Really?" Cotton said, most interested in Jalili's answer to his next question. "What is your area of expertise?"

Jalili hesitated. She glared at Cotton, presumably assessing him and his intent, before answering.

"I lecture on current and political trends and developments in the Middle East," Jalili responded.

"I'm impressed. Was that your major at university?"

"Of course."

"Congratulations." Cotton nodded.

Jalili had just lied to him. He knew from the information provided by the FBI's embassy based Legal Attaché that Jalili had studied Nuclear Physics at the University of Paris. "I guess that explains why you were so politically active during your university days."

"Who told you that?" Jalili demanded.

"No one. I just assumed that someone of your background and interests would naturally get involved in student politics."

"Special Agent Cotton, go away. I'm busy," Jalili said as she turned back to her monitor.

Cotton noticed that she stared at a dark screen. She was bluffing.

"I will if you will just answer a few more of my questions."

"Promise?" Jalili spun back to face her interrogator. "How many?"

"Until I finish," Cotton said.

Jalili took a deep breath and frowned. She glared at Cotton with flashing dark brown eyes.

"Were you politically active at Teheran University?" Cotton asked.

"No. I am apolitical."

"What about the University of Paris?"

"What about the University of Paris?" Jalili fired back.

Cotton relaxed in his chair and stared at Jalili. She was a challenging protagonist, and Cotton was beginning to enjoy himself. After all, he held all the cards, and Jalili held none. She was on his turf, subject to his law, and most importantly she did not know what he knew.

"Were you politically active in Paris?" Cotton asked bluntly.

"Of course not."

Again, Jalili lied.

"Did you ever discuss Doctor Jesperson's sources with him?" Cotton changed the subject abruptly.

"No. I told you I never had a direct conversation with him."

That was not completely accurate, but Cotton did not challenge her directly.

"As an intelligent Iranian citizen, please tell me what you think of Doctor Jesperson's allegations about your government's nuclear program?"

"I am confident Doctor Jesperson was misled by an unreliable informant with questionable motives."

"Why are you so confident?"

"Because I trust my government."

"Really?"

"Really."

"Why are you living here in the United States? To say that our two countries have serious disagreements is an understatement. We don't even have diplomatic relations."

"The disagreements are between our governments, not the American and Iranian peoples. Most Iranians love and respect Americans."

"Really?" Cotton shook his head, indicating disbelief.

"Really!"

"Then you don't fear the Iranian government is preparing to mount an atomic attack on the United States?"

"I do not."

"But Doctor Jesperson and his source or sources thought so. Most Americans who buy and read his book share his concern," Cotton pressed.

"I can't help that."

"So you don't think I should build a bomb shelter in my back yard to protect my family?"

"You can do what you want, but I doubt a bomb shelter would be sufficient to protect you from a nuclear attack."

"Really?"

"Yes, really."

"Why?"

"Radiation."

"Explain it for me."

"I'm not a nuclear expert. I told you that."

Jalili lied again, delighting Cotton. The lies told him he was on the correct tack.

"Do you think your government killed Doctor Jesperson because of what he had written?" Cotton asked, feigning indifference.

"No."

"Think about your answer. Are you telling me the truth?"

"Do you think I killed Doctor Jesperson?" Jalili laughed. "Just because I am an Iranian citizen?"

"We always look at individuals close to the victim with a strong motive for killing him," Cotton spoke evenly.

"I guess that leaves me out. You are going to have to look elsewhere," Jalili chuckled.

"Why do you say that?" Cotton asked.

"I wasn't close to Doctor Jesperson. I barely knew him and certainly had no motive, as you say."

"Political motives have been responsible for many assassinations," Cotton said.

"I have a political motive because I am a loyal citizen who loves her country?" Jalili shook her head in disbelief.

"Stranger things have happened."

"Not involving me. You are insulting. Now leave before I call security," Jalili stood up.

"I think you will find that security will ask if there is anything I need. The FBI is well respected, and Jesperson was highly regarded. How do you relate to your students and fellow faculty members?"

Jalili sighed as she sat back down. "Sometimes life as a visitor to a foreign country can be quite trying."

"Good. Please answer my question."

"My relations with fellow faculty members are normal. That means some like me, some tolerate me, and some are jealous of me. I get along just fine with my students."

"Does that last comment apply to Doctor Jesperson's students as well? I understand you now handle many of his courses."

"Many of his courses?" Jalili laughed. "Both of them. Seminars, a total of twelve students. Do you want to take a poll? I have a seminar starting in ten minutes. We are going to discuss American policy in Iraq."

"No thank you. I am sure that it will be on a plain far above my humble head," Cotton smiled. He noted, however, that Jalili had spoke disparagingly of Jesperson for the first time.

"Do you have anything to do with the foreign students attending GMU?" Cotton again changed the subject.

"Foreign students? Are you trying to insult me because I am a guest in this country?"

"Sorry. I did not mean to insult you. Associating with fellow visitors seems like a natural thing to do."

"Doctor Jesperson advised the Foreign Student Association. I do not," Jalili spoke with some heat.

"No contact with fellow Iranian citizens?"

Jalili hesitated before answering. "I've talked with one or two if by contact you mean polite conversation."

"What are their names?" Cotton picked up his notebook.

"I'm not sure I remember."

"Let me try to refresh your memory. Does the name Mansour Taheri mean anything to you?" Cotton pretended to consult his notes.

Jalili, again on her feet, stared at Cotton as she hesitated. "Taheri. That's familiar. Are you referring to Doctor Jesperson's young relative?" Jalili gave stress to the "young" "Who recently arrived in this country as a guest?"

"I am."

"I've met the young man once or twice in the halls. I don't think he's enrolled at George Mason, however."

"These were just brief contacts?"

"Yes, very brief. If I remember correctly, Doctor Jesperson introduced us as fellow countrymen."

Cotton wrote the last comment into his notebook, not particularly interested in the statement, just posing to pressure Jalili. "Who were the others?"

"Fellow countrymen at GMU?"

"Yes."

"I've met some of the other students, but I don't recall their names. As

I told you, I have nothing to do with them, and there are no other Iranian nationals in my classes or the seminars."

"Who is advising the doctoral candidates who were working with Doctor Jesperson?" Cotton again pretended to consult his notebook.

"Oh, I know who you are talking about." Jalili acted as if she had just remembered. "There is an older student here, also Iranian, who is working on his dissertation. I am not his faculty advisor, but I met him once or twice in the cafeteria. If I recall correctly, Doctor Jesperson's relative introduced us."

"Oh, you met Taheri more often than just once or twice in the hallway," Cotton smiled and made an entry in his open notebook.

"So arrest me," Jalili reacted. "I forgot a chance meeting in the cafeteria."

"This fellow countryman's name was Jamshid Afgar," Cotton read from his notes.

"If you say so. I don't remember," Jalili snapped.

"I say so. Do you know where Doctor Jesperson's relative is now living?" Cotton asked.

"No. How can you expect me to know that?"

"Because Taheri and Afgar are living together in Doctor Jesperson's condominium apartment," Cotton smiled.

"Why are they doing that?"

"Because they are fellow countrymen, I guess," Cotton said.

"And I am supposed to know where every Iranian visiting the United States is living?"

Cotton shrugged and stood up as Jalili collected her class notes.

"I acknowledge it is presumptuous of me to inquire, but would you by chance know where I can find Doctor Adams office?" Cotton asked with a smile.

"Special Agent Cotton," Jalili blurted. "You are not only presumptuous but quite insulting."

"I work at it," Cotton said as he studied Jalili from behind as she hurried towards the door. His initial impression had been accurate and quite correctly circumspect. Jalili was most attractive from the waist up, but quite hippy. The surveillance reports had been spot on as usual.

Cotton glanced at the computer and desk, thought about taking a look-see, but decided to leave that to the tech team that would be visiting the office that night. He doubted someone as sharp as Jalili would have left him in her office if there was anything in it she did not want him to see.

Just as he stepped into the hall, he spotted Jalili, who was entering a far classroom, glance in his direction. He waved, and she ignored him as she escaped from his line of sight.

Although Jalili had not answered his question about the location of the department chairman's office, Cotton had not pressed. He knew exactly where it was, in the center of the building a short distance from the stairs and the elevator. Cotton knocked, entered, and identified himself to the young secretary manning the outer office.

"I have an appointment with Doctor Adams," Cotton said as he waved his credentials at the girl.

"Please have a seat, sir, and I will inform Doctor Adams you are here." She glanced at the clock, a silent reminder that Cotton was half an hour late. His tardiness did not worry Cotton who assumed that all professors, including department heads, were absent-minded and accustomed to flexible appointments. Cotton had enjoyed his exchange with Jalili and had found it too useful to break off for a simple protocol visit.

Cotton had barely sat down when the secretary reappeared. "Doctor Adams will see you now," she announced.

Cotton entered the inner office to find an older man with a thick crop of long white hair that reached almost to his shoulders sitting behind a desk littered with stacks of blue covered examination booklets.

"I just hate exam periods," he greeted Cotton.

"I can imagine, Doctor Adams," Cotton said as he reached across the desk, offering his hand in greeting.

"I always have and always will," the old man smiled as he casually brushed palms with Cotton. "Examinations are one of the necessary evils of the classroom; it's not well known, but they're harder on the professor than the students. Some employ graduate students as graders, but I don't. It's a matter of principle. If you don't read the papers, you don't know what the students don't know."

Cotton wasn't certain what to say to that, so he said nothing, just nodded.

"I'm still teaching, Adams said. "Two courses, just to remind myself what this business is all about." Adams glanced meaningfully at a wall clock.

Cotton read the message. "I apologize for my tardiness, but I had an interesting discussion with one of your professors."

"Doctor Jalili is an instructor not a professor," Adams corrected him.

"She must be very bright to have earned your trust," Cotton launched his inquiry.

Adams leaned back in his chair and studied Cotton over the top of his reading glasses. "I sense a question of some kind in that comment," he smiled.

"I understand that Doctor Jalili holds impressive degrees from Teheran University and the University of Paris," Cotton said.

"That's correct. I hired her myself. What would a self-respecting area studies department be if it did not have a bright foreign lecturer on its faculty?"

Cotton did not comment.

"Doctor Jalili is a pretty little thing, but she has a BA and MA from Teheran University and a PhD from the prestigious University of Paris. The fact that she chose to accept an instructorship from little George Mason was quite a coup for our modest department."

"I'm obviously not an academic, professor," Cotton said. "But I think you undervalue George Mason's reputation."

"I just love flattery, Agent Cotton," Adams replied, not the least impressed by his visitor's obvious attempt to curry favor. Adams had students who were far more adept at cultivating their betters, and Adams had considerable experience in managing their puny efforts to hustle their professor in order to improve grades or explain repeated classroom absences.

"How were Doctor Jalili's grades?" Cotton asked.

"Straight A's."

"In Paris too?"

"Yes, Doctor Jalili speaks four languages that I know of," Adams said. "English, French, Arabic and, of course, Farsi."

"What was her major?"

"Area studies with a focus on political developments in the Middle East."

The answer surprised Cotton. He was particularly interested in learning why George Mason had hired a young Iranian with a PhD in Nuclear Physics as an instructor in its area studies department.

"That's interesting. Does Doctor Jalili have any kind of background in the physical sciences?"

"Why would you ask such a question, Special Agent Cotton?"

"One of our sources reported she studied physics at the University of Teheran," Cotton answered.

"Nonsense. As I said, Doctor Jalili's primary interest is the study of political and economic currents at work in the undeveloped world, particularly the oil rich Near East, an area of primary interest to our government. We hired Doctor Jalali because of her intention to publish, knowing that would make her a natural to complement Doctor Jesperson. I had hoped that development would give our little department two best selling authors, one male and one female, whose views would impact on world events. The fact that we share Metropolitan Washington with the world's pre-eminent policy makers, leaders, and thinkers did not escape our humble notice. I suggest you take a closer look at that informant of yours."

"Doctor Jesperson's latest book certainly is having the impact that you desired," Cotton said.

"I did not anticipate his unfortunate demise," Adams said.

"We are working closely with the Fairfax Police Department in a combined effort to identify and apprehend his killer," Cotton said.

"Lieutenant Mansfield," Adams said.

"Who had a reason for killing Doctor Jesperson?" Cotton asked, ignoring the pointed reference to Mansfield.

"Certainly not Doctor Jalili."

"Did the two work closely together?"

"What gave you that idea?"

"I understand that Doctor Jalili is now handling Doctor Jesperson's seminars," Cotton said.

"And you think that gave Doctor Jalili a reason for killing Doctor Jesperson," Adams laughed. "Course work is a distraction for researchers like Doctor Jalili and Doctor Jesperson."

"Publish or perish," Cotton smiled.

"That's a cliché." When Cotton did not react, Adams continued. "It may be true for some departments, but not mine. Talented researchers like Doctor Jalili and Doctor Jesperson live to write their books; they do not need bureaucratic pressure from martinets occupying positions like mine to induce them to produce. They have rare talent that lesser academics like me can only envy."

"The Iranian government does not share your appreciation of Doctor Jesperson's efforts," Cotton came at Adams from a different angle. "I understand they take exception to some of Doctor Jesperson's revelations."

Adams smiled and pointed a forefinger at Cotton. "You are indeed devious, Special Agent Cotton. You asked if Doctor Jalili had studied Physics. You think that Doctor Jalili was dispatched by the Iranian Government to infiltrate my little department. I assure you that is nonsense of the first order."

"Doctor Adams," Cotton demonstrated that two could play the name game. "Doctor Jalili is an Iranian national."

"So are eighty million other individuals."

"Given the fact that Doctor Jesperson's mother was born in Iran to Iranian parents, Doctor Jesperson can be considered half Iranian. I assume that this gave Doctor Jesperson and Doctor Jalili something in common. Did..."

"I can see where you are going, Special Agent Cotton." Adams interrupted. "Let me make one thing perfectly clear to you. Doctor Jesperson had nothing to do with Doctor Jalili's employment by GMU. I hired her for the reason I stated. Doctor Jalili arrived here after Doctor Jesperson departed on his sabbatical. I personally introduced them in this very office when Doctor Jesperson returned. I explained what I wanted from the two of them, and they both seemed quite receptive. I did not encourage them to work together. I knew that Doctor Jalili was just starting her career, and that Doctor Jesperson was fully preoccupied with preparing his book for publication. They spent a few weeks together on our faculty here, and I question the allegation that they developed a personal relationship. In any case, I doubt that one existed; the age difference militated against that. I saw them together only once during the time in question; they were having coffee together in the cafeteria, a not very exceptional development. If Doctor Jalili was dispatched by the Iranian Government to pursue Doctor Jesperson in an illicit way for a malevolent purpose, I doubt that she succeeded. Why would she wait for Doctor Jesperson to turn his book over to his publisher if her objective was to prevent its publication? Logically, Special Agent Cotton, your hypothesis is fallacious. If you are serious about identifying Doctor Jesperson's killer, I suggest you refocus. If I were grading your test paper, I would give you a large F with this red pencil." Adams pointed a red pencil at Cotton.

"Doctor Adams," Cotton stood up and offered his hand again. "I thank you for sharing your valuable time with me, and I promise I will give your comments the consideration they deserve."

"Well said, Special Agent Cotton," Adams laughed. "Particularly your use of the phrase 'the consideration they deserve.' If you need further advice from me, please do not hesitate to call and schedule an appointment when I can reciprocate by giving you the time you deserve."

Chapter 25

Chase parked the Prius in the lot outside Jesperson's Waples Mill apartment and took the elevator to the sixth floor. He deliberately bypassed Doctor Jesperson's apartment where he planned to re-interview Mansour Taheri and continued on to an adjacent door. Chase gently rattled the brass knocker and waited. Getting no response, he was raising his hand to try again when the door opened suddenly. A smiling Mrs. Marsha Hillencotter, the kindly old lady who had been so helpful previously, appeared; she was the one who had told him about Mansour sharing Doctor Jesperson's apartment.

"Good morning, lieutenant," Hillencotter greeted him. "Please come in and tell me what is happening. Have you arrested the scoundrel who murdered poor Doctor Jesperson?"

"Good morning, Mrs. Hillencotter," Chase replied. "Regretably, the answer to your question is no. I hope I'm not interrupting something important."

"No problem," Hillencotter said. "I'm having another day, just like all the rest. How do you want your coffee? Black, as usual?"

"That would be very nice," Chase said.

Hillencotter escorted Chase into her small, formal parlor before scurrying off to the kitchen. Chase relaxed and waited, hoping that the observant, old lady would have news to share. Chase heard the sound of rattling porcelain.

"Please, don't go to any trouble on my behalf," Chase called, assuming that his hostess was preparing to honor him with the good china.

"I'll be right with you," Hillencotter answered. "Make yourself at home."

Again, Chase heard the clatter of a delicate cup against saucer.

"Can I help?" He asked.

"I can manage," Hillencotter called back. "It's these damned old hands; they won't stop shaking."

Chase picked up a dated issue of the *Ladies Home Journal* from the coffee table. He flipped through the pages, amused at the nonsense that apparently targeted teenagers and the young married set.

"My niece left that here; it's not mine," Hillencotter nodded at the *Journal* as she crossed the room carrying a small silver tray holding two fragile cups and saucers.

"You didn't have to risk the good stuff," Chase smiled as he dropped the magazine back on the coffee table where he had found it. "I have clumsy thumbs." Chase rubbed a thumb against forefinger, ostensibly proving his point.

"It's for me not you," Hillencotter said, glancing at the tray. "You're just the excuse."

Hillencotter deposited the tray on the coffee table and then sat down in a chair opposite. She took a deep breath, making a show of recovering from her exertions; she then looked at Chase and waited. Chase obediently picked up a delicate saucer and cup; he studied the little red roses and fragile china and nodded his head in what he hoped would be interpreted as rapt admiration.

"It belonged to my grandmother. She brought it with her from Germany," Hillencotter said.

"Very pretty," Chase said. The words sounded inadequate, but his hostess smiled.

"You're my very first guest in months," Hillencotter said, apparently not noticing the deficiencies in Chase's tea talk vocabulary.

Not knowing what to say to that sad comment, Chase lifted the cup to his lips. The coffee was a too weak, but he complimented it. "Perfect. We must have similar taste buds."

Hillencotter smiled and left her cup and saucer on the tray, the coffee untasted. "Now, lieutenant, tell me how I can help you."

"I'm still trying to identify Doctor Jesperson's killer," Chase admitted with a negative shake of his head. "And out of desperation I'm retracing my steps in case I missed something important."

"On television the little clues are the ones that solve the crime," Hillencotter agreed seriously. "The detectives overlook them at first, but in the end they always get their man. I'm sure you will do the same."

Chase laughed. "Not always, I'm afraid, but I'm not going to stop until I do, this time."

"Good. I told you Doctor Jesperson was a good man. I've read his book. Have you?" Hillencotter asked.

"Yes. Doctor Jesperson was a skilled researcher and writer," Chase said.

"Just like Travis Crittenden," Hillencotter surprised Chase by referring to his pseudonym.

Chase looked up from his coffee cup and found the old lady smiling at him.

"I like Travis best," she continued. "Doctor Jesperson's book is a little deep for the likes of me."

Chase laughed. "And Travis Crittenden's detectives always get their man."

"He has to work at it, but that's fine with me," she said. "I like his sense of humor, too."

"We have that in common then," Chase laughed. "Have you noticed anything happening in your neighbor's apartment?"

"You know that young man is still living there?"

"Yes, he has Doctor Jesperson's parent's permission to do so," Chase said.

"And he has a friend living with him. Did you know that?"

"Is the friend Iranian and older, in his thirties?"

"Yes."

"That's Jamshid Afgar, another student."

Hillencotter nodded.

"Did you know he's started driving Doctor Jesperson's Lexus?"

"What about the Beetle?"

"It's in the parking lot collecting dust."

Hillencotter grinned, enjoying Chase's reaction. "Do you think the boy has Doctor Jesperson's parent's permission?"

"I don't know," Chase said. "Maybe one but not the other.

"Mrs. Jesperson said yes and Doctor Jesperson had other ideas."

"Probably. What have the boys been up to lately?" Chase changed the subject.

"I really don't like either one of them," Hillencotter said.

Chase waited for her to explain.

"Neither one appears to be very interested in school," Hillencotter said. "I understand that Mansour will not start classes until the next semester, but I haven't seen either one of them with a book in his hands, not coming, not going, and the older one should be attending class or studying in the library if he's a student. At least there have been no loud parties."

"Afgar has finished his class work and is now researching his dissertation," Chase said.

"In the apartment?" Hillencotter asked, clearly skeptical.

Chase shrugged, not interested in defending either of the two young men.

"You said no loud parties. Do they ever have any visitors?"

The old lady smiled. "Now you are asking the right questions."

Chase again waited.

"One, a very attractive young lady about the same age as the older one, maybe a little younger."

"Can you describe her?"

"Excuse me for saying it, lieutenant, but she looked like a prostitute. The only thing is she didn't dress like it."

"How did she dress?"

Hillencotter leaned forward and whispered, acting as if she were afraid she might be overheard. "She wasn't wearing one of those little skirts that don't hide anything. I understand young ladies dressing to attract men's attention, but I think those mini things are scandalous."

"Are you telling me, Mrs. Hillencotter, that you would never wear a mini?" Chase mimicked her confiding tone.

"At my age?" Hillencotter asked, clearly taking the question seriously.

"When you were three or four years younger."

"It depends on the situation," Hillencotter laughed. "Don't get me wrong, this girl was trying to make the best of what she had. She wore a nice pants suit, but it couldn't hide the fact that she was a bit big in the hips."

"What color was her hair?"

"She was a brunette on both occasions."

"She visited the boys twice?"

"Yes, and she stayed an hour each time."

"Morning or afternoon?"

"Seven in the evening. It looked like a social visit to me. She stayed two hours, both times. Do you think she was a prostitute?"

"Maybe she was just a friend. Do you think she was an American?"

"I don't know. I wondered about that since both of the boys are Iranian. I tried to hear her voice. You know, to check on the accent, but she never said a word that I could hear. She just knocked on the door. One of the boys opened it quickly, like they were expecting her, and she just marched in like she owned the place."

"Did you see her car?"

"No, I didn't think of it, but I will see if I can get her license number next time."

"That would be helpful, but I don't want you to go to any trouble," Chase said.

"I won't take any chances, lieutenant. Who would want to hurt an old lady?" Hillencotter smiled. "I'm not sure she will be around for a while, though."

"Really?"

"Yes. The boys are on a driving trip."

"A trip?"

"Yes. I shared the elevator with them this morning. They each had a suitcase, and just to make conversation I asked Mansour if they were taking a trip. Mansour said yes, he and his friend were driving to New England. He said he wanted to try out his new car before he started classes, and his friend wanted to see the leaves and the countryside."

"It's a little late to see the leaves in New England," Chase said. "They're more likely to see snowflakes."

"I thought that too, but I didn't say anything. Would you think I'm being petty if I said good riddance. I really don't like those two. I'm sure Doctor Jesperson would be unhappy if he could see how they are using his apartment and car and wasting his money. The poor man worked so hard. He didn't get a chance to enjoy what he earned before someone killed him. Do you really think you will find the bad person?"

"I hope so. Did you say they were using Doctor Jesperson's car?"

"Yes the Lexus. Do you think they have permission?"

"I'll check on it," Chase said. Is there anything else you can tell me about the boys? Have there been any other visitors besides the woman?"

"Sorry."

Chase sipped the last of his coffee. "Then I better get to work if I am going to catch the bad person," Chase said.

"What are you going to do next?"

"Would you keep it a secret if I told you that I think I will take a chance and look around the boys' apartment while they're not home?" Chase confided, suspecting that the old lady would be watching him through the peephole in her apartment door anyway.

"Good idea. Can I come?"

"I don't think that is a good idea," Chase said.

"Do you have a warrant? How are you going to get in?" Hillencotter asked eagerly.

"I have Doctor Jesperson's keys and his father's permission to check out the apartment," Chase said. He told the truth about the keys but stretched it considerably when he claimed to have Jesperson Senior's permission.

Hillencotter nodded as if she believed him.

"And I thank you for sharing your thoughts and your coffee with me," Chase said as he stood up. "May I put the tray in the kitchen for you?" He offered.

"Of course not, lieutenant. You are my guest and always welcome," Hillencotter struggled out of her chair and followed Chase to the door. "And I will let you know if the mysterious lady visits again."

"Please don't do anything you would not normally do," Chase said.

"I'll act like a member of a neighborhood watch committee," Hillencotter smiled. "That's legal, isn't it?"

"Yes, but I don't want you to trouble yourself," Chase said.

"You don't want me to get into trouble," Hillencotter corrected.

"Just remember, a very bad person shot Doctor Jesperson," Chase cautioned.

"Oh, nobody's going to worry about a nosy old lady," Hillencotter said.

Chase hesitated and was thinking about challenging that statement when Hillencotter pushed past him and peered out the peephole in the door. She surprised Chase when she turned and said in a conspiratorial whisper, "It's OK, lieutenant, the coast's clear."

Chase was still chuckling when the door closed behind him. Assuming she was still watching him through her peephole, he waved his hand in acknowledgment as he walked the several paces to the Jesperson apartment.

Chase rapped on the door to apartment 604 and waited. There was no response. He rapped a second time with the same result and finally took Jesperson's keys from his pocket and entered. There was a strange odor of decay in the air, and the disorder surprised him. Chase was a bachelor who lived alone; he was no neat freak, and he practiced a relaxed housekeeping style. Everything had its place, but it did not always find it. On his first visit, Chase had been impressed by Jesperson's fastidiousness. This time the place was a mess. The polished dark wood table was littered with the debris of several meals. Dirty dishes covered with rotting food remnants were surrounded by empty milk cartons, beer cans, and cereal boxes. The crystal chandelier even sported a dirty T-shirt. Chase turned and studied the living room. A pair of worn Nikes set on the shiny wood coffee table right next to some dirty athletic socks. Old newspapers covered the print fabric at one end of the couch. Chase glanced into the kitchen, took in the littered cabinet counters and the sink filled with dirty dishes, and did not bother to enter. The sunroom with its recliner and high definition television set was in a similar condition. The lamp next to the recliner was still burning brightly, and the remote lay on the floor beside it. Chase turned off the lamp.

Chase remembered the smaller bedroom. On his previous visit its contrast to the rest of the house had alerted Chase to the fact that it had been occupied by a second person who turned out to be Mansour. Then, the bed had been carelessly made. This time it was just a jumble of tangled sheets, pillows, and a single blanket. The closet contained even fewer clothes. One pair of worn Nikes on the floor was partially covered by a pile of dirty clothes waiting for attention. The odor irritated Chase. The drawers of the small dresser were now empty. Previously they had contained a supply of underwear and socks, T-shirts, and jockey shorts; Chase assumed they were now divided between the closet floor and the suitcase in the trunk of the Lexus that was transporting Mansour and Jamshid through the sights of New England, if that is where they had actually gone.

Before Chase could continue on to the master bedroom and the third bedroom that had served as Doctor Jesperson's office, someone rapped on the apartment door. Assuming that a curious Marsha Hillencotter was checking on him, Chase turned and started for the front of the apartment. Before he reached the door, the visitor rapped again, harder this time with enough strength to make him doubt that it was the fragile hand of Marsha Hillencotter.

Without bothering to check the peephole, Chase opened the door and was surprised to find himself face to face with a scowling Special Agent Cotton.

"What in the hell are you doing here?" Cotton demanded.

"And what in the hell are you doing here?" Chase repeated the question with a similar edge in his voice.

"Where are those two Iranians?" Cotton asked as he pushed past Chase and entered the apartment.

"Christ what a mess," Cotton reacted to the disorder just as Chase had. "And what's that smell? Do you have another body stashed here?"

Chase laughed. "I don't think Doctor Jesperson would approve of his relative's housekeeping style."

Cotton marched directly to the couch, tossed the newspapers over the back, sat down, and then grabbed the sneakers from the coffee table. With Chase watching, Cotton irritably threw the Nikes across the room in the direction of the floor to ceiling windows.

"Those things stink," Cotton declared as he hurled the socks in the same direction.

"Open those doors and air this damned place out," Cotton ordered.

"Open them yourself," Chase said as he sat in the chair opposite the sofa.

Cotton stood up and opened the balcony doors before returning to the sofa.

"You didn't answer my question," Cotton glared at Chase.

"Which question was that?" Chase stared back. He was irritated by the fact that Cotton was following up on his threat to investigate every damned Iranian involved in Chase's murder case.

"Taheri and Afgar," Cotton smiled as he indicated he knew exactly who was living in Jesperson's apartment. "Where are you hiding them?"

"That's none of your business," Chase said. "We have an agreement. The murder investigation is mine. The kidnapping is yours."

"We had an agreement. The kidnapping investigation is over. Secretary Townsend is home."

"Not quite over," Chase said. "Have you apprehended the kidnappers? Recovered the ransom?"

"That's what I'm working on now," Cotton said as he relaxed, enjoying the conflict.

"You think these two students kidnapped a ranking United States Government official and extorted a hundred million dollars from the president?"

"Iranians are on my suspect list," Cotton said. "Somebody extorted thirty million from the president. I assume they aren't home. Did they hire you as a house sitter now that they are flush?"

"I'm investigating my murder," Chase said, stressing the "my." "Keep your big federal nose out of my business."

"Christ, you ought to clean this sty once in a while."

Chase did not react.

"Did someone invite you in, or do you have a warrant?"

"That is none of your business, Special Agent Cotton," Chase said.

Before Cotton could react, someone tapped lightly on the door. Chase glanced at the door but did not immediately react.

"That's someone at your door, detective," Cotton said. "Don't you think you had better answer it?"

Chase stood up, opened the door, and found Marsha Hillencotter waiting.

"Is everything alright, lieutenant?" Hillencotter asked as she tried to see past Chase who blocked her entrance. "I heard shouting."

"Everything is fine, Mrs. Hillencotter. Thank you for your concern," Chase answered.

Hillencotter did not move.

"Special Agent Cotton and I were having a little discussion."

"Special Agent? FBI?" Hillencotter asked.

"Yes."

"Is the FBI investigating Doctor Jesperson's murder too?"

"Not really," Chase smiled. "But they are conducting a parallel investigation."

"There were no federal laws broken," Hillencotter declared. "I don't understand."

"I don't either," Chase said. "I'll discuss this little transgression with Special Agent Cotton and brief you later."

"Good luck," Hillencotter said. "If you need my assistance, lieutenant, please let me know."

Chase closed the door and turned back to Cotton.

"Who the hell was that?" Cotton demanded.

"A good friend," Chase smiled. "Have you tracked the ransom payment?"

"We're working on it."

"What does that mean exactly?"

"It means that in the Caymans the money was divided into two batches of fifteen million each and forwarded to separate accounts in Hong Kong and Venezuela."

"And in whose names are these accounts?"

"They're numbered accounts, and we do not have access to the identity of the owners."

"Separate accounts in Hong Kong and Venezuela," Chase mused aloud. "Two kidnappers?"

"Or a very careful organization."

"Are you going to learn more about the accounts?"

"We're working on it," Cotton said.

"You and the CIA?" Chase asked.

Cotton nodded. "And NSA."

Chase laughed. "That's how you knew the money was transferred; you don't have human access."

"These banks are very sensitive about sharing information on their account holders," Cotton said. "Don't worry it. The ransom is none of your business anyway. Just concentrate on your murderer."

"Are you saying our separate investigation agreement is still valid?" Chase asked, not trusting Cotton or the Bureau.

"It always has been."

"Then what are you doing here?"

"My investigation has me pointed in the direction of all Iranians in the United States, and these two pigs qualify," Cotton smiled.

"You're treading on common ground," Chase insisted.

"Shit happens."

"Then quit complaining when I interview the Townsends."

"As I said, shit happens."

"Agreed," Chase nodded. "Shit happens."

"You will probably hear from your girl friend that I just visited Robinson Hall," Cotton admitted. "That Jalili babe is a good looker, from the waist up."

"Why have you been talking with Doctor Jalili? You think she kidnapped Townsend?"

"Do you think she murdered Jesperson?"

Neither answered the other's question. They sat in silence for a few seconds until Cotton asked another. "Did you know that Doctor Jalili, as you call her, lied to you and is defrauding the university?"

"Care to explain that?" Chase asked.

"Not particularly, but I will," Cotton smiled, pleased with the opportunity to embarrass the local law officer.

Cotton hesitated, letting Chase simmer as he searched his mind trying to anticipate what Cotton was about to tell him.

"Our Legal Attaché in Paris had The Deuxième Bureau do a little background check on Doctor Jalili. They report that she earned her degree in nuclear physics not political science or area studies."

Chase stared at Cotton.

"Her transcript from Teheran University shows that she majored in physics not liberal arts," Cotton continued. "She misrepresented her qualifications and submitted false transcripts to George Mason. Why do you think she did that?"

Chase did not immediately answer because the conclusion was too obvious. Jalili had been dispatched by the Iranians on some kind of mission under academic cover.

"Somebody had to create a whole new set of supporting documents for her. Changing all the course names in the transcripts would have been an impossible job easily detected," Chase said.

"Our techs are working on the transcripts as we speak," Cotton said.

"But she arrived in the States a year ago," Chase said. "Jesperson had just started his research for his book; the Iranian government couldn't have been worried about its content, the nuclear research report and the atomic bomb stuff."

"She could have been dispatched on a different mission and the Jesperson problem just fell into her lap," Cotton said. "Unless we can get her to talk, we may never know."

"I find it hard to believe," Chase said as he thought about his strange collapse following a couple of glasses of wine during his evening and night at Jalili's home. He was too embarrassed to admit that she might have drugged him.

"What?" Cotton asked.

"What what?"

"There's something about Jalili you're not telling me," Cotton accused.

Chase shook his head negatively. "I just find it difficult to believe," Chase said. "That's all," he lied. "You said you just talked with Jalili. Did you press her?"

"No, I was just sounding her out," Cotton smiled. "I asked her about the nuclear bomb stuff in Jesperson's book, and she lied to me. She claimed to be a political science type with no knowledge about nuclear physics."

Chase did not try to defend Jalili.

"And I asked her if she had been politically active as a student," Cotton said. "And she lied about that. She claimed to be apolitical."

"And?"

"And the French report that she was a very active, pro-mullah organizer during her time in Paris," Cotton said.

"That's very interesting," Chase said. "I'm going to have to take a closer look at her as a prime suspect in the Jesperson shooting."

"And she is high on my list, too, as an Iranian spy and a likely participant in the Jesperson kidnapping caper."

"If the Iranian government has your thirty million, why would they be moving it around the world?" Chase asked.

"To launder it, getting it ready for use in their espionage activities here?" Cotton shrugged.

Chase smiled as he considered the possibility that the United States Government was now funding Iranian intelligence activities in the States.

"What?" Cotton demanded.

"Nothing," Chase replied. "I was just trying to wrap my mind around the whole deal."

"Don't try," Cotton frowned. "You might break something."

"What is her relationship with the two boys?" Chase asked, indicating the apartment where they sat.

"She admitted that she knew Afgar and Taheri," Cotton said. "She claimed that Taheri introduced her to Afgar."

"That's probably a lie too. Afgar has been in this country for ten years and is a graduate student in Jalili's department. Certainly, she had to have met him before Taheri arrived recently."

"That's why I'm here," Cotton said. "The chances are that the three of them are a deep cover team."

"I doubt that Mansour Taheri is involved," Chase said. "The other two might be using him, but he doesn't strike me as the spy type. Too inexperienced and naive."

"Spies come in all types, and they have to start sometime," Cotton chuckled. "Where are the two boys now? Why are you just sitting here?"

"Mrs. Hillencotter, the neighbor who just visited us, tells me that they are on a sightseeing trip to New England to admire the trees."

"Your friend, Mrs. Hillencotter," Cotton laughed. "Is she keeping a good eye on your suspects for you?"

"She's an observant neighbor who liked Doctor Jesperson. She has her doubts about these two."

"Do you know where in New England the boys planned to visit?"

"No."

"Maybe somewhere close to the Canadian border?"

"I doubt they would leave the States. Both are on one-time student visas and would not be able to get back in the country if they left."

"Then they are meeting someone from Canada," Cotton said. "What kind of car are they driving?"

"Doctor Jesperson's Lexus."

Cotton stared at Chase with raised eyebrows. "A Lexus? Pretty fancy for two kids."

"Jesperson apparently purchased it before he took his sabbatical," Chase said.

"Think we ought to see if we can locate the boys with a spot and notify bulletin?"

"Agreed," Chase said. "While we're having this helpful little discussion, I suggest it might be worthwhile to table the Townsends."

"Table away," Cotton laughed. "I assume you have checked out this pig sty and found nothing useful."

"No, but feel free to have a look around for yourself," Chase said.

"I will. About the Townsends?"

"Have you visited them recently?" Chase asked.

"I've done all the talking with the Townsends that is necessary for identifying the kidnappers and tracking the president's money, for now," Cotton said. "I don't like either one of them."

"You might be interested to know that Secretary Townsend moved out of the mansion on the day he submitted his resignation," Chase said.

"So I hear. Think the secretary is trying to avoid the media?"

"The media and Mrs. Townsend," Chase said.

"Can't blame him for that," Cotton smiled.

"A divorce is in the works," Chase said.

" "You wouldn't happen to know where Secretary Townsend has taken up residence, a local hotel?" Cotton asked.

"He's moved into a condominium in Reston," Chase said. "It has a very nice view of Lake Anne, and Secretary Townsend should find it quit restful following his recent difficult experiences."

"And away from the media, I assume. Does Secretary Townsend have appropriate company to help him through his recovery period?"

"He does."

"And what is her name?"

Chase laughed. "She's quite a lovely young lady, at least fifteen years younger than the secretary. She owns and operates a thriving Reston tech company; her name, which might be familiar to you, is Sally Kendrick."

"And why should I...?" Cotton started to ask but stopped and stared at Chase.

"Ms. Kendrick was once Doctor Jesperson's fiancée," Chase smiled.

"Christ, she's the one you picked up at Jesperson's funeral?"

"Exactly."

"And Townsend has left his wife and moved in with her?"

"Yes. That rather complicates my investigation, doesn't it," Chase said.

"This investigation is getting all wrapped around itself," Cotton said.

"I'm beginning to suspect it was just one investigation from the very beginning," Chase agreed.

"The shooting and the kidnapping," Cotton said.

"I guess that means both investigations now belong to me," Chase said.

"Bullshit," Cotton erupted. "The damned Iranians belong to me."

"You can have them," Chase agreed. "But I will also continue to take a look at them."

"Particularly Doctor Jalili," Cotton laughed.

"Probably," Chase agreed. "And, of course, the Townsend threesome, if that is what develops."

"If it were up to me you could have the whole damned ball of wax, Iranians and all," Cotton declared. "But, unfortunately, it isn't up to me," Cotton added when Chase started to smile.

After Cotton departed, Chase took out his cell phone and poked Doctor Jesperson's number in Cambridge.

"Hello," the elder Jesperson picked up on the third ring.

"Doctor Jesperson?" Chase asked.

"Who is calling, please?" Jesperson answered with a question.

"This is Chase Mansfield," Chase replied.

"Lieutenant, I've been thinking about calling you. Are you making any progress in identifying my son's killer?"

"Things are moving along, but I am in no position to make any arrests, not yet."

"Can you tell me who you suspect?"

"No, sir, I cannot."

"I understand. How can I help?"

"Is Mansour on his way to visit you?" Chase asked.

"Why would he do that? He's supposed to be concentrating on his

English classes getting ready for next semester," Jesperson said, his tone clearly announcing that he was not pleased to hear that Mansour was travelling when he was supposed to be studying.

"I'm not sure," Chase answered. "I'm sitting in your son's apartment as we speak. One of the neighbors told me that Mansour and his housemate left this morning in your son's Lexus on a sightseeing trip to New England to see the leaves."

"That's damned foolishness," the elder Jesperson declared. "All the leaves here are on the ground." After a pause, he continued. "Did I hear you accurately? Did you say the Lexus?"

"Yes," Chase answered, interested in Jesperson's reaction.

"Shit," Jesperson swore. "My wife and I discussed that Lexus. She told me she was going to let Mansour drive it because that Beetle was a wreck waiting to happen. I opposed the idea, but we never discussed it again. Give me a minute."

Chase listened and heard Jesperson shout, "Manujeh, Manujeh, come here, right now."

After a pause, Chase heard Jesperson say, "I'm on the phone with Lieutenant Mansfield. He tells me Mansour is on a driving trip to New England to see the leaves in the Lexus. Did you give him permission to take it on the highway?"

Chase could not hear Mrs. Jesperson's reply but he had no difficulty with Jesperson's next comment. "You knew how I felt about letting Mansour drive that car!"

Again, Chase could not hear Mrs. Jesperson's response but it clearly agitated Jesperson.

"Manujeh, he's your relative, but I still don't approve."

Mrs. Jesperson again replied.

"Manujeh, let me finish with the lieutenant and then you and I are going to have a serious discussion," Jesperson declared.

"Lieutenant, excuse me," Jesperson came back on line. "Is there something I can do for you?"

Jesperson was clearly anxious to get off the line, but Chase continued. "Could you ask your wife if she knows Mansour's itinerary?"

"Manujeh, do you know where that young man is going on his trip? The lieutenant wants to know."

Chase did not hear Mrs. Jesperson's reply, but Jesperson relayed it. "She wants to know why you want to know," Jesperson said with evident exasperation in his tone.

"I have a few questions to ask him," Chase said.

Jesperson relayed Chase's comment.

"She says she does not know, lieutenant, if you can believe her; I don't. And I assure you, I don't know where the boy is," Jesperson spoke with considerable heat in his voice.

"That's alright," Chase said, trying to insert some calm into the discussion. He had not intended to create disharmony in the elder Jesperson household. "I apologize if..."

"You said that boy was travelling with his housemate," Jesperson interrupted. "Were you referring to Afgar?"

"Yes," Chase answered. "I understand he and Afgar are sharing your son's apartment. I assume they have your permission for that."

"My wife's relative, yes. I don't approve of that Afgar, but my wife obviously doesn't discuss everything with me."

"Do you plan visiting Washington any time soon?" Chase asked.

"We have to come sometime to clear up some of Thomas's affairs, including doing something about that Lexus," Jesperson said. "Why do you ask?"

"I think you might be interested in the condition of your son's apartment," Chase said. "And I have a delicate matter we should discuss."

"Does the apartment look like a pig sty?" Jesperson demanded.

"It looks different, lived in. Your son was a neat and fastidious person," Chase tried to finesse the question without getting into details involving Mrs. Jesperson's young relative.

"I knew it," Jesperson said. "Was that your delicate matter?"

"No," Chase said.

"Then broach it," Jesperson ordered.

Chase hesitated.

"Please, lieutenant, I have enough problems to worry about without having to try to guess what else that boy has done that you consider too delicate to discuss on the phone," Jesperson said. "You'll give me a heart attack."

Chase doubted that but decided to give Jesperson a hint even though he doubted that it would add to the older man's peace of mind.

"Mr. Jesperson, can I speak to you in absolute confidence?" Chase asked.

"Of course," Jesperson answered too quickly, but Chase decided to take him at his word.

"Once you confided to me that you and your wife are helping Mansour as a favor to Mrs. Jesperson's sister's family." Chase referred to the fact that they had also confided that Mrs. Jesperson's nephew's brother-in-law was an Iranian nuclear physicist working at Natanz. The nephew was Mansour's father, and Chase assumed that the Jesperson's were now helping Mansour as a favor, probably because the nephew had introduced Doctor Thomas Jesperson to his brother-in-law, his source.

"Yes?" Jesperson turned cautious, clearly recognizing what Chase was referring to.

"I worry that Afgar who is much older than Mansour might be a bad person for Mansour to associate with," Chase confided.

"May I ask why?"

"He may have an unhealthy connection with the Iranian government," Chase said. "I cannot prove anything right now, and my suspicions are quite sensitive. I must ask that you not repeat them to another person, not even, particularly not even, to your spouse."

"Oh Christ, I understand," Jesperson said. He immediately realized that Chase was warning him that if Afgar grew curious about Mansour's relationship with the Jespersons, a subsequent investigation might lead to the nephew's brother-in-law, and that could have deadly consequences for all involved.

"I think I had better visit Washington immediately to...to discuss this car business," Jesperson said.

"Remember," Chase cautioned, "you cannot discuss my suspicions with another person, particularly Mrs. Jesperson."

"And you say that Afgar and Mansour are on a car trip?" Jesperson asked.

"Yes."

"And you don't know where."

"No, but we are looking for them."

"I hope you find them before..." Jesperson caught himself because his wife was listening to his end of the conversation.

"We will," Chase spoke with more confidence than he felt. He didn't want to panic the elder Jesperson any more than he had.

"Is there anything else we should discuss?" Jesperson asked.

"No sir."

"I will contact you as soon as I reach Washington and sooner if I hear from Mansour," Jesperson said and hung up.

Chapter 26

Mansour, who was driving, turned to his companion, Jamshid Afgar, and said, "I'm tired."

Afgar looked at his young companion. "You've been driving since we left Washington."

"It's my car," Mansour whined. "I can do what I want. Let's stop at the next motel."

"We only have sixty miles to go," Afgar said. "I've got to get there. We should have left yesterday."

"I told you I had to get the car serviced."

"Why should you worry? It's not really your car."

"I'm responsible for it."

"Want me to drive?" Afgar asked.

"I'd rather stop."

"Damn it," Afgar said, losing his patience. "I told you I have an appointment tomorrow at eleven, and I can't miss it."

"Big deal," Mansour said, not wanting to let Afgar drive his car. If Afgar smashed it up, the Jespersons would hold him responsible. "I'm just doing this as a favor."

Lately, the older Afgar had been acting more like his father than his friend. Mansour regretted having invited him to share the apartment. The elder Jespersons, particularly his father's aunt, had been most considerate. First, she had offered to let Mansour live in Doctor Jesperson's apartment when he complained that he had no place to live, didn't like the States, was lonely, and wanted to return home. Mrs. Jesperson had argued against that, saying it was not possible. His parents had sent him to the States to be safe from the government, and he did not know why. After Doctor Jesperson's book had been published, Mansour had begun to suspect the answer. He knew his uncle worked on the Natanz nuclear project and had access to secrets like those revealed in Jesperson's book. Mansour didn't care; it wasn't his fault that his uncle had been indiscreet. He doubted that the government would blame him for his uncle's mistakes, and he wanted to go home. To calm him down, Mrs. Jesperson had let Mansour use her son's car. At first it had worked, but now the excitement was beginning to wear off. This damned trip had been a damned mistake.

"I won't wreck your damned car," Afgar lost his patience. "Just pull over and let me drive," Afgar ordered.

Mansour glanced at Afgar and then at the road ahead. Dusk was falling and he was having difficulty seeing the highway. He suspected he needed new glasses.

"There's a rest stop coming up, Taheri," Afgar used Mansour's surname. "Pull over, injas!" He used the Persian word for here.

Now intimidated, Mansour did what he was told. "I have to use the bathroom," Mansour whined, pretending he was not reacting to Afgar's rude order.

Afgar silently followed his sullen companion into the men's room. Afterward, they stopped for coffee, ignoring the ingratiating looks that a well-dressed, effeminate appearing man kept casting in their direction.

Finally, the man attempted to engage them in conversation. "Going far, boys?" He asked.

"We're not interested," Mansour said.

"That's a pretty car you're driving," the man persisted. "Where are you from?"

"Piss off," Afgar growled.

"Foreigners," the man sashayed away.

"He was trying to pick us up," Mansour said as they made their way back to the Lexus.

"You have to be careful in these rest stops," Afgar said. "They're meeting places for the queers."

"I don't like America," Mansour said.

"Who cares? Go home if you don't like it here. Give me your damned keys," Afgar ordered.

Mansour reluctantly gave Afgar the keys. "Drive carefully."

Afgar did not bother to respond as he climbed behind the wheel. He didn't care about the damned car or Mansour either. All he wanted was to reach Niagara Falls, find a motel, and get some sleep. He had a very important meeting tomorrow. He finally had a chance to prove himself to his superiors in Teheran, and he was determined not to fail.

Afgar did not own a car, had never owned one, and was not an experienced driver. In Teheran he had survived on a ten year old motor scooter. He had asked his superiors for a car to support his mission in America, but they had declined, insisting that he had to live his student cover. Afgar had argued that all American students had cars, but his controller had arrogantly told him to buy a bicycle.

Afgar had no trouble starting the Lexus. He had carefully watched the spoiled Taheri. He turned the key, flicked on the headlights, and backed carefully out of the space. He pressed the accelerator, and the tires screamed as they laid two trails of burnt rubber on the pavement behind them. Afgar kept his foot on the gas pedal and tightly grasped the steering wheel with both hands. The car swerved from side to side as it raced down the highway, and Afgar drew strength from the sense of power that being in control gave him.

"Slow down," Mansour pleaded.

"This baby is something else," Afgar exulted as they charged down the highway. He was beginning to feel like a race driver. The Lexus quickly reached eighty miles an hour, and Afgar pulled into the center lane passing every car that they overtook. Afgar glanced at Mansour and smiled. The boy sat with clenched fists and a worried expression of his face. He was terrified, and Afgar was enjoying every moment. After a good fifteen minutes of highway dominance, Afgar's world came crushing down on his shoulders when a siren screamed. He glanced in the rear view mirror, saw the flashing lights of a police car directly behind him. Afgar pulled into the right lane and deliberately lifted his foot from the accelerator until they slowed to the legal sixty-five. The police car pulled even with them. A brute of a state policeman pointed to their right, indicating that Afgar should pull on to the shoulder. Afgar did as he was told while a silent Mansour watched with wide, frightened eyes.

"Don't worry, he'll just give us a warning," Afgar said with more confidence than he actually felt.

Mansour fidgeted, and Afgar nervously tapped the steering wheel while they waited. Mansour turned and through the rear window saw the state trooper with a microphone raised to his mouth.

"He's reporting us," Mansour whispered. "I told you that you were going too fast. Now they'll arrest us."

"He's just checking our license plates."

Afgar laughed, trying to show more confidence than he felt. His contact in Niagara was too important to miss, his first real mission. He glanced in the mirror and saw that the trooper was still talking on his radio. After a five-minute delay that seemed much longer, the trooper got out of his car and approached. Afgar lowered his window and waited.

"Driver's license and registration," the trooper demanded from his position to the right of Afgar's window where Afgar had to turn his head to see him.

Afgar grabbed his wallet from his pocket and took out his International Driver's license.

"Don't you have an American license?" The trooper asked.

"No sir," Afgar answered. "Do you want to see my passport?"

The trooper answered by holding out a giant hand.

Afgar obediently gave him his passport. The trooper studied it. He compared the picture with Afgar, nodded, and turned to the visa. "You've been here ten years. Are you still a student?"

"I'm working on my dissertation," Afgar said.

"You're a slow worker, a little old to be a student. Thinking about getting a job?"

"Yes sir, as soon as I get my doctorate," Afgar said.

"You know you aren't authorized to work on a student visa," the trooper said.

"Yes sir. I plan on returning home."

"Good," the trooper smiled. "Registration, please."

Afgar turned to Mansour who had been watching the exchange between the cop and Afgar with wide eyes. This was his first contact with an American trooper, and he was quite anxious.

"Do you have your registration?" Afgar asked Mansour.

"This is my friend's car," he explained to the trooper.

"What's that?" Mansour asked.

"The form they gave you at the Department of Motor Vehicles that shows you own the car and purchased the license plates," the trooper said. The younger boy seemed frightened.

Mansour nodded and opened the dashboard compartment in front of him. He took out a large envelope and began leafing through the papers.

"Let me find it for you," Afgar said. Mansour handed him the envelope.

"Been here long, son?" The trooper asked.

"No sir, almost three weeks," Mansour said.

"Passport, please," the trooper spoke to Mansour as he took the registration card from Afgar.

The trooper glanced at the registration and then studied Mansour's passport. "You are a student too," he said.

"Yes sir," Mansour mumbled.

"Your parents buy this fine car?" The trooper asked.

"Yes sir," Mansour said.

"Why is your father's name Thomas Jesperson and yours Mansour Taheri?" The trooper asked.

Mansour stared at the trooper. He tried to speak, but no words came out of his mouth. His brain did not know what to say.

"Doctor Jesperson is Mansour's cousin," Afgar spoke for him. "His parents sent Doctor Jesperson the money to buy Mansour's car for him."

"Is that true, son?" The trooper asked Mansour.

The thoroughly intimidated Mansour nodded.

"You've been in the country only three weeks, but the registration is a year old," the trooper said. "How do you explain that?"

Mansour shook his head.

"His English is not very good, and he had trouble getting his student visa," Afgar again intervened.

"And you are helping him," the trooper said. "Where did you two meet?"

"At school," Afgar said.

"What school?"

"George Mason University."

"Never heard of it. Where is it?"

"Fairfax, Virginia."

"And what are you doing here?" The trooper asked.

"Mansour had read about Niagara Falls and wanted to see it. He loves everything American," Afgar said.

The trooper laughed. "That's such a dumb story, it must be true. "Do you know what a speed limit is?"

"Yes sir," Afgar answered.

"What is it on this road?"

"I'm not sure," Afgar replied, feigning ignorance.

"On the New York State Freeway it is sixty-five miles an hour. The speed limit is posted on those little signs, and we diligently enforce it. You know what diligent means, don't you?"

"No sir," Afgar said, still hiding behind his foreign status.

"I clocked you at seventy-five miles an hour," the trooper frowned.

He took a notebook and ballpoint pen from his pocket. He glared at the boys and tapped the pen on the notebook giving them the impression that he was thinking about writing a ticket.

"I'm not used to the car. It's new, and very powerful. I didn't realize I was going too fast. It was a big mistake, and I promise I won't do it again," Afgar pleaded.

The trooper appeared to consider Afgar's words. He frowned, watched the boys fidget, and then asked.

"What is your destination?" The trooper asked.

"Niagara Falls," Afgar replied. "We're just sightseeing. My friend is new and wanted to see some of this wonderful country before he begins classes."

"Where are you staying in Niagara Falls?"

"We don't have reservations," Afgar answered. "Do you think we will have trouble finding a place to stay?"

"At this time of year? No," the trooper laughed. He looked at Afgar sternly. "Since you are foreign visitors, I'll let you off with a warning this time. Don't let me catch you speeding again, or I'll throw the book at you."

"Yes, sir, I won't," Afgar responded, trying to sound as contrite and sincere as he could.

"Drive safely, and remember, we patrol the freeway constantly," The trooper said as he turned and returned to his patrol car.

Afgar raised his window. "That was close," he said as he started the engine.

"I told you not to speed," Mansour whined.

Back in his car, the trooper smiled as he watched the Lexus carefully reenter the highway and continue on its way. He picked up his radio and reported to his dispatcher.

"That was the two Iranians on the FBI watch list. I stopped them, checked their papers to make sure, gave them a warning, and sent them on their way. Spot and report, just like the watch list requests. They claim they are sightseeing and are heading for Niagara Falls. I hope they don't fall in. Those two come across as naive. What does the Bureau think they've done?"

"They don't say," control answered. "Where are they staying?"

"They don't have reservations," the trooper said.

"Good work. I'll alert the cars along the way to keep an eye out for them."

As soon as the Lexus had left the trooper behind, Afgar turned to Mansour and smiled, "Americans are so stupid."

"I told you not to speed," Mansour said.

"Don't be a baby," Afgar said as he placed the Lexus in cruise control, setting the speed at exactly sixty-five.

"They'll be watching for us now," Mansour cautioned, ignoring the insult.

"They're not smart enough to catch two Iranian boys," Afgar bragged as he checked his rear view mirror.

One hour later they reached the outskirts of Niagara Falls. Night had fallen and they had difficulty locating the town center.

"Do you know where you're going?" Mansour asked.

"No. Never been here before. I'll find a decent hotel near the falls, don't worry."

"Not too expensive," Mansour cautioned.

"It's my treat," Afgar said. He was confident this was one expense account VEVAK auditors would not question.

After forty-five minutes of circling, which included a drive-by of the awesome falls which caused Mansour to marvel at the fact that a man had been stupid enough to ride over them in a barrel, they found themselves on a wide avenue named Rainbow Boulevard.

"Enough," Mansour pleaded. "No more sightseeing. Find a hotel, any hotel. I'm hungry."

As chance would have it, Jamshid spotted a Holiday Inn before Mansour could recycle his complaint as he tended it do.

"This looks expensive," Mansour said.

"One thing about America that you are going to have to learn," Jamshid said. "Park a car like this near a cheap motel, and someone will steal it."

"Really?"

"Really," Jamshid assured him. "If they don't steal it, they'll strip it."

"Will it be safe here?" Mansour asked.

"Read my lips," Jamshid said.

"How do I do that?"

"Just listen to your big brother," Jamshid smiled, relieved that they had finally arrived in time to schedule his vital appointment. As soon as they checked in, he had to make a phone call that would trigger the rendezvous.

"Why are we parking so far from the building?" Mansour asked as Jamshid parked his Lexus at the end of the row.

"Because it is the safest," Jamshid said. "The thieves always work on cars in the center of the rows because they can work without being seen." Jamshid chuckled. Taheri was so naive he believed anything he was told.

Jamshid took the keys out of the ignition and dutifully handed them to Mansour. "I'll sign us in, and you lock up and bring in the suitcases," he said.

"Why can't I sign us in?" Mansour complained.

He didn't want to carry the heavy suitcases like a servant.

"Do you want to pay the bill or do you want to make sure your car is secure?"

"The car," Mansour said.

Jamshid Afgar smiled, strolled down the partially filled lot, and entered the lobby where he registered them as John and Charles Richards, two brothers from Richmond, Virginia. After learning that checkout was eleven AM, he paid cash in advance for a day, assuring the disinterested clerk that they would be checking out by noon. American hotels were a delight for foreign agents; visitors were not required to show their passports or other identity documents; a credit card or cash sufficed.

Afgar met Mansour at the front door, handed him a room key, and took his small suitcase from him. Declining assistance from the waiting bellboy, they took an elevator to a room on the seventh floor. Afgar unlocked the door and led their way into a large sitting room.

"Where are the beds?" Mansour asked. "I don't want to sleep on the floor."

"It's a suite," Afgar grinned. He pointed at a doorway to his right.

Mansour hurried into the next room but stopped suddenly. "This is a bathroom."

"Just kidding," Afgar laughed and led the way into a bedroom that was larger than the master bedroom in the Jesperson condominium.

"Those are huge," Mansour declared as he followed Afgar into the room which featured two Queen beds.

"Make yourself comfortable. I have to go to the lobby and call to set up my appointment," Afgar said.

"You can call from here," Mansour said as he stretched out on the nearest bed.

"All the phones in American hotels are tapped," Afgar said.

"What does it matter?" Mansour asked. "Your Canadian friend is just bringing you a box of new clothes and things from your parents," Mansour said.

Afgar smiled indulgently, pleased that Mansour had swallowed his cover story about an Iranian friend resident in Canada who had just returned from Iran bringing a suitcase filled with clothes and presents from Afgar's parents who had not forgotten their only son who they had not seen for over ten years.

"Relax, I'll be right back," Afgar said.

"But I'm hungry," Mansour said.

"You can order from room service if you want," Afgar said. "But I'm going to eat in the restaurant downstairs. Then, I'm going to take a walk. They say the falls are beautiful at night."

"How can you see them at night?"

"They're illuminated with colored lights, asshole," Afgar said as he started for the door.

"Hurry up. I'll wait and eat with you," Mansour said.

Mansour grabbed the remote and switched on the television. The trip was beginning to look better.

Afgar took the elevator to the lobby, selected a chair in a far corner, and pulled his cell phone from a pocket. He carefully poked in a number and waited.

"Hello," a deep male voice with an Iranian accent greeted him.

"Hi, I'm here," Afgar said.

"Who is this?"

"Sorry," Afgar said and continued with his parole. "I'm a visitor from Memphis, and I'm told the falls are illuminated at night with only red lights. Is that true?"

"No, they use multicolored lights on the American side," the deep voice responded.

"That should be very beautiful. Will they be still on at eleven tonight?" Afgar asked.

"Twenty-three hundred hours will be perfect."

"I'm driving a white Lexus with the license plate "JES 1," Afgar said. "I have it parked at the far end of the lot at the Holiday Inn-Niagara Falls. Do you think it will be safe there?"

"Do you?"

"Yes."

"You best keep the car locked. The papers say there's a gang targeting tourists in the area."

"I'm not sure I locked the trunk. I guess I had better check before I go for dinner and visit the falls."

"It wouldn't hurt. You can't be too careful," the deep voice said. "Enjoy your visit and have a safe trip back to Memphis."

"Thank you, I will," Afgar said.

"Make sure that you drive very, very carefully and don't have an accident," deep voice said and hung up.

Afgar put his phone back in his pocket and exited the front door. He slowly crossed the parking lot to the Lexus, ducking between the cars, making sure that he was alone. He unlocked the Lexus trunk using a set of keys he had made while running an errand the previous week for the lazy Mansour; he pretended to check the trunk for something, and then slowly closed the trunk without latching it.

Afgar returned to the hotel, collected Mansour, and then took the elevator back to the main floor. They followed the signs to the main dining room. A stern man in a dark pin striped suit watched as Mansour and Afgar crossed the lobby and disappeared into the dining room. He waited five minutes, stood up, folded his newspaper, went to the restaurant entrance, and peered inside. He noted the two Iranians sitting at a window table studying large menus. The man checked his watch, sighed, returned to his chair, took out a cell phone, whispered a few words, hung up, and unfolded his newspaper.

Outside, a black Ford with a whip antenna entered the parking lot, cruised through the lanes, and stopped in front of the Lexus. A man, wearing a wrinkled, dark suit that made him look like a travel-weary salesman, got out of the passenger side, leaving his door open wide. He circled to the trunk of the Ford; the driver popped the lid, and the businessman reached inside. He turned to the Lexus, ignored the unlatched trunk, stepped to a position near the right rear fender, and reached under it. A soft clunk indicated the magnets had grabbed hold. The man stood up, returned to the Ford, closed the trunk, and rejoined his companion. The driver slid the gearshift into drive, and the Ford moved slowly forward.

The beacon was in place and the entire operation had taken no more that forty seconds.

"The trunk lid was unlatched," the businessman said.

"They're either very careless or they're expecting a drop," the driver said.

The boys enjoyed their leisurely dinner. Afgar had the lamb chop with rice and Mansour a cheeseburger and fries. Afterwards, following the directions given by the friendly doorman, they walked the short block to the Horseshoe Falls. Although both were quite impressed by the lighted extravagance, Afgar hid his reaction behind a cynical facade. Mansour, however, who had prepared for the visit by scanning literature he had found in their room, gushed.

"It's the most powerful waterfall in America," he exclaimed. "Sometimes six million cubic feet of water cascade down in just one minute."

"So what?" Afgar asked.

"Thirty million people a year visit here," Mansour ignored him.

"What do you want me to do about it? Open a kebab stand?"

"We could get rich," Mansour said. "I know what I want to do tomorrow morning."

"I've got to meet my friend," Afgar said.

"I don't. I'm going to ride the Maid of the Mist," Mansour said.

Afgar laughed. "I hope she enjoys it."

"The Maid of the Mist is a boat."

"Too bad. Seen enough of the lights? I'm ready to go back to the motel," Afgar checked his watch.

"I want to stay here for a while," Mansour insisted. "Do what you want. What time is it?"

"Eleven o'clock. I need a beer before the bar closes."

"OK," Mansour relented. "But I don't want a beer. I want to try the Jacuzzi."

"Fine, you Jacuzzi, and I'll beer," Afgar laughed.

"And tomorrow, I'm taking the boat trip," Mansour said.

"Do what you want just as long as you are ready to leave after lunch.

Fifteen minutes later they reached the hotel.

"Think we should check the car?" Mansour asked.

"Why not?" Afgar responded indifferently.

They held hands as they strolled down the dimly lighted lane to the Lexus. Afgar watched as Mansour circled the car, checking for scratches, trying the doors. When he reached the trunk, Mansour pushed down on the lid. It was firmly locked. Afgar smiled.

So did the businessman sitting in the Black Ford several lanes away. He picked up his cell phone and whispered, "The boys have checked their car, even the trunk."

"Good," the man in the lobby answered. "The guy who made the drop is clearing customs as we speak. Headquarters has the Mounties checking the plates."

"Do they want us to retrieve the drop?"

"No, we're just supposed to track it."

"All the way to DC?"

"We'll have help."

"The boys are on their way back inside," The man in the Ford said.

"For the night, I hope. I'll wait until they settle down in their room and then join you."

The next morning Mansour and Afgar ate breakfast and then parted.

"We must be out of here by noon," Afgar said. "Don't be late or they will charge us for another day."

"It depends on the Maid of the Mist. If I'm a few minutes late, just wait for me in the lobby. My suitcase's packed."

"Don't be late," Afgar repeated.

"And don't you. It's my car. If you're not here, I'll leave without you," Mansour tossed his keys in the air.

"Don't worry. My friend is always reliable," Afgar smiled. All he had to do this morning was check the trunk to make sure his package was in place. He was worried about the drive home. His contact had stressed that he should drive very, very carefully and not to have any accidents. Now that he had the package in his possession, he was not as sure about this first important mission as he had been. Going active was fun, but he hadn't counted on it being dangerous as well. He was glad he had been smart enough to allow the damned thing time to settle down after its long trip from Iran to the States. He hoped the rest would do it good. Now, all he had to do was get it from Niagara Falls to Fairfax County without incident. His orders were to conceal the package in a secure storage locker using an alias and not to try to hide it anyplace else. He had protested that it would be safer if he kept it under his personal control, but now he was relieved he had been overruled by Teheran where presumably they knew what they were doing. Once he got it safely secured in Fairfax, his partner, who claimed to have the training to handle the package, could assume responsibility. Afgar, who had the storage facility already rented, only had to survive the next twelve hours.

Afgar gave Mansour time to board his boat before going to the parking lot. Again, he was oblivious to the man in the lobby and the watcher in the Ford. Afgar found the Lexus where they had left it, alone in a space at the far end of the parking lot. He checked the vicinity before placing the key in the trunk lock. Carefully, very carefully, he raised the lid. He studied the package without touching it while he worried about the possibility that it might now be radiating. His controller had described it as a suitcase; it was like no suitcase Afgar had ever seen. The size of a large box wrapped in green plastic and bound with four canvas straps, it had no discernible handles and no markings. He didn't know how his superiors had arranged to transport it from Iran to Canada, but obviously they had. He assumed it had come as diplomatic baggage, appropriately labeled and concealed. Afgar didn't know how his contact had managed to circumvent American customs, and he didn't care. His job was to get the damned thing to Fairfax.

Afgar leaned forward, not too close, and tried to hear if it were ticking. He heard nothing. Afgar, not knowing what else to do, stepped back, and carefully lowered the trunk lid until the lock clicked. Only then did he take a deep breath and exhale.

"He looks scared to death," the man sitting behind the wheel of the black Ford spoke to his companion.

"If that is what we think it is, I don't blame him," the man in the passenger seat said.

"Don't worry," the driver said with more assurance than he felt. "It had a quiet night," he laughed nervously. "Now, all we have to do is get it out of Niagara Falls; the highway teams can escort it to wherever it's going."

"I hope it has a careful driver," the passenger said.

"Have you ever tracked an Iranian driver before?"

"Yes, that is what has me worried."

"Relax, the desk clerk says they promised to check out by noon. We'll just sit here until that happens."

"And then?"

"Then, we'll follow from a distance until it gets on the New York State Freeway, and we wave goodbye."

"I'm worried about that damned beacon," the passenger said. "Do you think that was wise? Beacons emit radio signals."

"We were just following orders. That's what Washington told us to do."

"And you think they know what they're doing? We're the ones sitting here. The bureaucrats are sipping coffee at their desks on Pennsylvania Avenue. Want me to see if the beacon's still transmitting?"

"Shit no," the driver exclaimed. "Assume the damned thing's still transmitting. That's what it's supposed to do. If it isn't, that's fine by me."

"Checking the signal is passive. It shouldn't impact on what's happening on board that Lexus."

"Let's not disturb the status quo," the driver ordered. "If that damned package is happy listening to the beacon, don't worry it."

The passenger looked at the driver before commenting. "I suggest we watch from the far end of this lot."

"Good idea," the driver said as he started his engine. He glanced at his companion with a worried expression on his face. "Do you think moving will make a damned bit of difference if that sucker wakes up?"

"No, but every inch between me and it makes me feel better."

"We could stamp it 'Return to Sender' and drop it off at the post office."

"You can if you want," the passenger said. "Me, I'm not going near that thing."

Back in his room, Afgar started pacing. He thought about taking a walk and decided against it. He wanted to be ready to leave as soon as Mansour reappeared, and at the same time he was no longer convinced that this operation was a great idea.

At five minutes to twelve, an exhilarated Mansour opened the door and charged into the room.

"That was just great," he enthused.

"You're an hour late," Afgar griped as he stood up, ready to leave.

"Let's stay another day," Mansour said. "I want to see the Canadian side."

"You can't leave this wonderful, democratic country, remember," Afgar frowned. "The visa. If you leave, you won't be able to get back in."

"That wouldn't be all bad," Mansour pouted. "Besides, who would know if I cross the border for a few minutes of sightseeing?"

"Just Customs and the INS is all," Afgar said. He didn't really care if the kid got himself in trouble, but he had a schedule to keep. He had promised he would have the package in Washington today. Plans had been made, and it was up to him to deliver, literally, on this his first real assignment. Besides, he was looking forward to teaching the arrogant Americans a lesson they wouldn't ever forget.

"Damn," Mansour dropped heavily on his bed.

"Let's go. I've got to get back to school," Afgar, who stood by the door with his hand on the knob, said.

"It looks like rain," Mansour said.

"Tough shit. Cars have windshield wipers in America."

In Iran it was impossible to keep wipers on a car unless one went to the bazaar every day to buy a set on the black market, often the very wipers that had been stolen the night before.

"I don't like driving in the rain. It's dangerous," Mansour said.

"I'll meet you at the car," Afgar said, opening the door. He was really tired of listening to the crybaby.

The door closed behind Afgar, and Mansour surrendered. He really wanted to stay another day. He had nothing to do in Fairfax but to go to that damned remedial English class, and it bored him. Besides, he was quickly learning that mastering foreign languages was not something that appealed to him.

Mansour used the bathroom and then hurried after the older Afgar who was beginning to act like his father, always ordering him about.

"Here comes the older one," the driver of the black Ford said.

"Good, I want to get them out of town and far away before that damned thing wakes up," the passenger said.

"Don't worry," the driver said, glancing at his companion who was now hunched down in his seat with a New York Yankees cap pulled low over his brow. "Washington said the beacon shouldn't set it off."

"Just don't follow too close. Give them a mile or two. Shouldn't doesn't mean couldn't," the passenger grumbled. "The bureaucrats sitting on their fat asses aren't the ones chasing that damned thing around."

Afgar was standing next to the rear door of the Lexus with his suitcase resting beside him when Mansour caught up with him. Neither spoke until Mansour took his keys from his pocket and was reaching toward the trunk lock.

"Not there," Afgar ordered.

Mansour looked up irritably. "Why not? It's my car, and I'll put my suitcase in the trunk if I want."

"Because my suitcase that my friend gave me is an extra large one and fills the whole trunk," Afgar said. "We'll have to put our suitcases on the back seat."

"Put your crap on the back seat," Mansour said as he opened the trunk.

"Duck, the damned fools are going to set it off right here," the passenger in the Ford warned.

The driver reached for the ignition key but hesitated before turning it.

"Christ that's no suitcase," Mansour said as he stood with the trunk lid wide open while he stared at the green plastic covered box bound tight with straps.

"Yes it is," Afgar said as he joined Mansour at the rear of the car. Afgar peered around them to make sure no one was watching. He saw no one. "I told you it was extra large and they wrapped it and used those straps to make sure it would not break open in transit."

"What in the hell is in it?" Mansour demanded.

"It's just clothes and stuff from home," Afgar said as he gently closed the trunk. He pulled the keys from the lock and stared at Mansour. "We better get on the road and away from here before it starts raining."

"I don't like driving in the rain. It's dangerous. I told you that," Mansour complained.

"Then I'll drive," Afgar said as he unlocked the driver's door and opened the rear door. He tossed his suitcase inside and reached for Mansour's.

"Be careful," Mansour complained. "You'll tear the seat covers or something."

"Then put your own suitcase inside or leave it here. I don't care," Afgar said as he climbed behind the wheel.

As soon as Mansour joined him, Afgar started the engine.

"Good," the man in the passenger seat said as he grabbed the microphone to alert the surveillance net that the target was moving. When finished, he again cautioned the driver. "Give them a lot of room. We can track the beacon if we have to."

The driver smiled but waited until the Lexus had left the parking lot and turned left before moving. "If the damned thing blows, I hope it waits until they are out on the highway," he said, admitting that he was as worried about this surveillance as his partner.

"I've marked a new return route," Afgar told Mansour as they were leaving the town limits.

"Why?" Mansour demanded. "You should have asked. It's my car," he said.

Afgar smiled as he handed the kid a road map. "I marked the new route this morning while you were taking your boat ride. Check it out."

"I'm not good with maps," Mansour said as he studying the confusing lines.

"I didn't like that damned New York Freeway," Afgar finally admitted. "This route looks more direct, and it guarantees we'll not run into that same cop. He wouldn't let us go with just a warning this time."

"Then don't speed," Mansour said as Afgar pressed on the accelerator.

"Don't worry, I can go exactly six miles over the speed limit, and they won't stop us," Afgar said.

"How do you know that?"

"That's what everyone at school says. After you are here a while, you'll learn these things."

"I'm not sure I want to," Mansour said.

"Then go home."

"Think I could take the Lexus with me?"

"That's up to Jesperson's parents. They're the ones that own it."

"I don't think they'll let me take it home. Mrs. Jesperson said it was a loaner, whatever that means, but I really like it."

"Study the map," Afgar ordered, tired of the kid's naiveté. "I've got the route marked with red ink. Look for a town named Painted Post. That's where we link up with Route 15; that will take us all the way to Route 50 and home."

"What kind of name is Painted Post?" Mansour asked. "That's stupid."

"I don't know. I didn't name it," Afgar said.

"I can't find it," Mansour complained and tossed the map on the floor.

"That's OK, I can," Afgar said. "Just pick the map up and put it someplace where I can reach it."

Mansour did as he was told and glanced out the windshield. "Look," he said. "It's starting to rain. I told you it would."

"Not to worry. We can test the Lexus and see how it handles on a wet road," Afgar said.

"Don't get us in an accident," Mansour said.

"You have insurance, don't you?"

"I don't know," Mansour admitted. "I assume Doctor Jesperson did."

"Lucky you," Afgar said as he wondered why nitwits like Mansour were always the ones with rich relatives.

Behind them, the two men in the black Ford turned the surveillance over to two men in a Honda SUV and two others in a red pickup.

"Good luck," the relieved passenger in the Ford said as he waved goodbye to the back of the Lexus with his Yankee cap.

Mansour rode in worried silence until Afgar turned on to Route 90, the New York Freeway. "I thought you said we're not going to take the freeway," Mansour said.

"I didn't say never. I told you to read the map. We take the freeway to Henrietta, and there we'll get off the sucker. We'll go south on 390 until we get to Painted Post. You remember I told you that, I hope."

"All these different roads confuse me."

"Just remember Route 15. After we find that, you can drive for a while."

"Thanks, but I'll decide who drives and when," Mansour said petulantly. "It's my car."

Afgar glanced at his companion and shook his head. Replying to the kid wasn't worth the effort. He decided that when they got back to Fairfax he was moving back to the house. Living in the condominium had sounded like a good idea at the time, but putting up with Mansour wasn't worth it. Teheran had ordered him to check out Jesperson's apartment for information identifying his sources for his book, but Afgar had found nothing. Now, it was time to move on.

Traffic was heavy, and the rain had turned into a heavy downpour interlaced with snow showers in the mountains. Despite Mansour's litany of protests proclaiming he was hungry, Afgar, who was anxious to deliver his package, refused to stop. By the time they reached Williamsport, dusk had descended further impeding their progress. Between Williamsport and Lewisburg, they stopped at a roadhouse for dinner. There, Afgar made the mistake of drinking two beers, and when they came out, neither Iranian was in a mood to continue fighting the unfamiliar road.

"Let's find a motel and spend the night," Mansour suggested.

"It's too dangerous to continue in the dark and the rain," Afgar agreed without saying that he was more worried about his package than the weather. He, too, was very aware of the risk of an accident with that treacherous load in the trunk.

A few miles south of Lewisburg he spotted a motel and stopped.

Behind them, relieved surveillants reported. A FBI supervisor in Washington directed one team to check into the same motel and the other to position itself further down the highway.

The night passed without incident, and two fresh teams joined the positioned surveillants. When the boys resumed their journey, they were unknowingly part of a convoy with one FBI car in front and three tucked in behind them.

Chapter 27

Chase and the two older Jespersons were sitting in the Jesperson condominium in Fairfax surrounded by a work crew of maids and packers when the front door opened and Mansour entered.

"Where have you been, Mansour?" Mrs. Jesperson greeted her sister's grandson. Even she was beginning to lose patience with the naive Mansour. Like her husband, she recognized it was her duty to look after the nephew of Thomas's source, but she had not realized how trying it would be when she had too quickly assumed her dead son's obligation.

Mansour did not immediately reply. He had expected to find a familiar scene, his quiet sanctuary in a strange and complicated American world. Instead, he was greeted by chaos, his two distant relatives, a bunch of strangers who were dismantling his new home, and worst of all, Lieutenant Mansfield, the policeman who was investigating Doctor Jesperson's murder.

"Wh...Wh...What is happening?" Mansour stammered.

"Come and sit down," Doctor Jesperson ordered.

"You didn't answer my question," Mrs. Jesperson frowned.

Mansour found his great aunt's demeanor difficult to understand. Of all the people he had met in America, she had always been the most considerate. They shared family genes. She was the one who had approved his stay in her son's apartment, and she had insisted that he drive her son's Lexus. Without her support, Mansour did not know what he would do. She was his lifeline.

Mansour sat down on the couch, as far from the menacing Lieutenant Mansfield as he could get. Mrs. Jesperson sat on the chair to his right, and her husband, not a blood relative, sat facing him. Mansour turned to his protector.

"We were on a sightseeing trip," Mansour spoke to Mrs. Jesperson.

"Only two nights. We were on our way home last night and got stopped by a terrible rainstorm."

"Where did you go?" The grim faced Doctor Jesperson asked. The old man truly intimidated Mansour.

"Where is your friend, Jamshid?" Lieutenant Mansfield asked simultaneously.

The confused Mansour did not know who to answer first. He looked at Mrs. Jesperson, silently begging for help.

"Where did you go?" Mrs. Jesperson repeated her husband's question.

"Niagara Falls," Mansour answered, his voice almost a whisper.

"Niagara Falls," Doctor Jesperson laughed. "Were you on your honeymoon?"

"Terrence," Mrs. Jesperson cautioned her husband. "Behave yourself."

Doctor Jesperson glanced at his wife and then smiled at Chase. He shook his head in amazement, as he repeated, "Niagara Falls?"

"Where is Jamshid?" Mrs. Jesperson asked Mansour Chase's initial question, obviously trying to short-circuit another brash comment by her husband. He had little sympathy for any of today's youth with gay tendencies.

"Jamshid borrowed the Lexus so he could deliver his package," Mansour said.

"Borrowed the Lexus? What package?" Doctor Jesperson asked before Chase could.

"His suitcase from Iran," Mansour said.

"What suitcase from Iran?" Doctor Jesperson demanded.

"The one we picked up in Niagara Falls," Mansour said. "His friend who lives in Canada brought it from Jamshid's family in Iran for Jamshid. Things he needs."

That comment made the others pause.

"Nothing illegal," Mansour looked directly at Chase as he spoke into the silence.

"Where is he taking it, Mansour?" Chase asked.

"I don't know."

"Did you see what was in the package?" Chase asked.

"No, it was a big package wrapped in green plastic with straps."

"How did Jamshid describe it?" Chase pressed as he and Doctor Jesperson exchanged concerned glances. Both were quite aware that the Doctor's son had predicted in his book that the Iranian government planned an attack on the United States.

"He just said it was a suitcase of stuff sent by his parents. It was a very big suitcase."

"Did you help Jamshid move it?" Chase asked.

"No. Jamshid went off on his own to meet his friend from Canada and the package was in the trunk when he returned."

"Then you don't know if it was duly cleared through customs?" Chase asked.

"No. I was on a boat trip under the falls, the Maid of the Mist," Mansour said.

"Whose idea was the trip, Mansour," Mrs. Jesperson asked.

"Jamshid suggested it. He said we could get his stuff and see the country too," Mansour said.

"And you didn't think to tell us?" Doctor Jesperson said.

Mansour answered with a shake of his head.

"Is Jamshid coming back here?" Chase asked.

"He lives here," Mansour answered.

"Excuse me," Chase said standing up. "I have a phone call to make."

No one said anything until the door closed behind Chase.

"Mansour, you've disappointed me," Mrs. Jesperson said.

"What's happening here?" Mansour asked.

Mrs. Jesperson deferred to her husband with a nod.

"We've decided, Mansour, that this is not a very good place for you," Doctor Jesperson said sternly.

"Where am I going to live?" Mansour whined as he began to fidget in his seat. He addressed his question to Mrs. Jesperson.

"We've decided to sell this apartment," Doctor Jesperson said.

"But I like it here."

"We've discussed the matter with your family, Mansour," Mrs. Jesperson said as she patted the nervous boy's knee in a weak attempt to calm him.

"And they agree that it would be better if you attend college in Boston next semester," Doctor Jesperson said.

"But I know George Mason now," Mansour protested. "I want to stay here."

"Given all the media attention to our son's book, the fact he was murdered at George Mason and his killer is still at large, we all think it would be best if you left this unhealthy environment," Doctor Jesperson said.

"But my friend Jamshid is here," Mansour whined.

In hall, Chase, using his cell phone, quickly briefed Special Agent Cotton on developments.

"It's alright. We're on it," Cotton replied evenly.

"What does that mean?"

"It means that we have Jamshid under surveillance as we speak. He just deposited his package in a shed at the storage facility at 29/211 and Waples Mill and is on his way back to the apartment. I'll make arrangements to examine the package, carefully, and join you at the apartment when I can."

"What about Afgar?"

"Don't worry about him. We have him under surveillance."

"Keep me informed," Chase said.

"I'll be in touch," Cotton said and hung up.

Chase returned to the apartment to find Mansour and the Jespersons sitting exactly where he had left them. All three stared at Chase, waiting for him to explain. Chase sat down on the sofa with Mansour.

"We've just told Mansour that we're selling this apartment and moving him immediately to Boston," Doctor Jesperson explained.

"But I don't want to go to Boston," Mansour complained. "I don't know anybody there."

"You'll find Boston College a great school. All the students thrive there," Doctor Jesperson said. "And I have friends on the faculty who will look after you."

"I wanted you to come and live with us and go to MIT," Mrs. Jesperson said.

"But of course that is not possible," Doctor Jesperson declared. He looked at his wife. "We've already discussed that."

Mrs. Jesperson frowned but said nothing.

"I'm afraid that Mansour is not academically qualified to be admitted to MIT," Doctor Jesperson addressed Chase. "Maybe after a semester or two at BU, we can arrange something," he turned to Mansour.

Chase doubted Doctor Jesperson wanted Mansour living in his home.

"But all that depends on Mansour and how well he does at BU," Doctor Jesperson continued.

"Can I keep the Lexus?" Mansour asked.

"We can discuss that later," Doctor Jesperson said.

"I have to do something with the Beetle," Mansour whined.

Doctor Jesperson did not reply.

"Do we have to go soon?" Mansour asked.

"We have much to do to get you ready for next semester," Mrs. Jesperson said. "We have to find you a place to live and everything."

"And first of all we have to get you admitted," Doctor Jesperson said. "Do you have any objection to that, lieutenant?" Jesperson turned to Chase.

"I don't, but we're going to have to discuss it with Special Agent Cotton," Chase said.

"And when can we do that?" Doctor Jesperson asked, not pleased with Chase's qualified response.

Chase shrugged. "He's very busy at the moment, but I expect him to show up here soon." After a brief hesitation, Chase looked at Doctor Jesperson and said, "I suggest we raise that question you and I discussed on the phone with Mansour."

Doctor Jesperson appeared puzzled but not object.

"Mansour, I have an important subject to discuss with you, and I need you to answer my questions honestly," Chase said.

A look of worry crossed Mansour's face; Mrs. Jesperson frowned, and Doctor Jesperson silently stared at Mansour.

"Did you ever discuss your family relationship with Professor Jesperson with your friend Jamshid?" Chase asked.

Mansour stared at Chase, shrugged, and looked at Mrs. Jesperson, apparently waiting for her to intervene. For once, she did not speak. Mansour nervously scratched the back of his hand, shifted in his chair, and obviously was thinking about how to respond to the question.

"Just answer honestly, Mansour," Doctor Jesperson ordered.

"A couple of times Jamshid asked me how I got to live here," Mansour admitted.

"Did you tell him you were related to Mrs. Jesperson?" Chase pressed.

"Not everything," Mansour hedged.

"What did you tell him?" Doctor Jesperson insisted.

"I know why I'm here," Mansour still evaded a direct answer. "I know my family would be in danger if anyone learned too much," Mansour glanced at Mrs. Jesperson, "particularly if they knew where my uncle works. We agreed I should say my father is a schoolteacher who studied at

MIT where he met Professor Jesperson and Mrs. Jesperson who is some kind of distant relative. My father gave me a letter of introduction when I got my visa and admission to George Mason, and Doctor Jesperson took pity on me and let me stay here until I found my own room someplace. Then, Doctor Jesperson was killed and I have been sort of camping out here until Professor Jesperson and Mrs. Jesperson sell the place. That's all I told Jamshid, honest."

"And what did you tell Jamshid about the Lexus?" Chase said.

"I just told him I found the keys in Doctor Jesperson's desk and have been driving it without permission," Mansour said.

"Does he believe you?" Chase asked.

"I think so, particularly after I let him move in with me. We've been sneaking around so that people would not be asking us a lot of questions."

"And you don't think driving the Lexus attracted a lot of attention?" Doctor Jesperson said, frowning first at Mansour and then at his wife who pursed her lips in silent protest, but she did not argue.

"My Beetle won't start, and I need some way to get to school and back," Mansour whined.

Doctor Jesperson shook his head in disgust.

Before Chase could continue, a key turned in the lock and the apartment door opened to reveal Jamshid Afgar.

"I got rid of my stuff," Jamshid announced before he saw the visitors. The door closed behind him, and Jamshid stepped back against it.

"We've got to move. The Jespersons are selling the apartment," Mansour said.

Jamshid stared at Mansour but did not speak.

"They are not very happy that I've been living here," Mansour said.

"We don't appreciate the fact that the two of you have been living in my son's apartment without permission," Doctor Jesperson glared at Jamshid and then Mansour. "I've half a mind to press charges."

"This is very serious," Chase declared.

"I didn't know," Jamshid defended himself. "Mansour invited me to stay with him."

"I'm sorry. I thought it would be alright. Doctor Jesperson said I could stay here until I found a place of my own. I didn't break anything."

"Did you have the Doctor's permission to drive his car?" Chase asked sternly.

Mansour did not immediately reply.

"Did you?" Doctor Jesperson demanded.

"Terrence, don't be angry. Remember your heart," Mrs. Jesperson weakly tried to calm her husband. "I'm sure Thomas would not have minded."

"Look at this place," Doctor Jesperson glared at Mansour and Jamshid as he waved a hand in the air. "Pigs would take better care of a sty than this. Our son would be embarrassed, and the Lexus. He was proud of that car."

"If they didn't have your permission to drive the Lexus that could be construed as car theft," Chase announced.

"I'm an innocent guest," Jamshid said. He looked at Mansour. "You didn't tell me you were living here without permission."

"I didn't have any place else to go," Mansour whined.

"Tell them you lied to me," Jamshid insisted. "I'm innocent," Jamshid, regaining some of his usual arrogance, spoke to Chase. "Ask him," he pointed at Mansour.

"I want to go home," Mansour surprised them all. "I don't want to study here anymore."

His apparently sincere bleat surprised the Jespersons, Afgar, and Chase. They stared at him.

At that moment, one of the packers emerged from a rear bedroom. "Pardon me, but there are some things in here that we don't know what to do with," she announced.

"Let me handle it," Mrs. Jesperson leaped to her feet.

"Some of them are probably mine," Jamshid said. "I just came to retrieve them," he lied.

"Is all this your fault?" Chase turned on Mansour. "Is Afgar your guest or a co-conspirator?"

Mansour nodded affirmatively.

"What does that mean?" Doctor Jesperson asked before Chase could.

"It's all my fault," Mansour said as he shrank back into his chair.

"Do you accept that or do you want to press charges on the two of them?" Chase formally asked Doctor Jesperson.

"Let that one go," Doctor Jesperson pointed at Afgar. "I want to think about this wretched creature," he glared at Mansour. "He's the one who abused my son's hospitality."

"You are going to have to come to the station with me," Chase spoke to Mansour. "Stand up and put your hands behind your back."

"Can I get my things and get out of here?" Jamshid asked.

Chase nodded.

"Be quick about it before I change my mind," Doctor Jesperson ordered.

Jamshid quickly followed Mrs. Jesperson into the bedroom.

Chase winked at Mansour to calm him and loosely cuffed the youth's hands behind his back. Chase ordered Mansour to sit back down on the couch, took out his notebook, and was pretending to question Doctor Jesperson for details when Jamshid returned from the bedroom carrying a filled laundry bag.

"I'm very sorry for all this, sir. It was a huge misunderstanding," Jamshid spoke directly to Doctor Jesperson. "We all respected your son and regret very much what happened to him."

Jesperson nodded grimly but did not reply.

"I may want to talk with you again later," Chase spoke to Afgar.

"Yes sir," Afgar said. "You can always reach me at the foreign student house at GMU. I'm seldom anyplace else."

As soon as the door closed behind Afgar, Chase and Doctor Jesperson exchanged smiles. Mrs. Jesperson with a worried expression watched from the bedroom door as Chase unlocked the handcuffs.

"I don't know what your plans are, Mansour," Chase said. "But I recommend that you avoid further contact with Mr. Jamshid Afgar."

"Yes sir," a chastened Mansour replied as he rubbed his wrists. "I'm not going anywhere near George Mason ever again."

"You are leaving for Boston tomorrow with us," Doctor Jesperson declared with absolute certainty.

"I'll give Afgar time to clear the area, and then I'll leave you to your work," Chase spoke to the Jespersons.

****

President Mahmud Ahmadinejad sat at the head of the conference table and smiled at the three senior officials who had assembled in the underground room in Natanz to discuss Phase 3.

"Gentlemen, I thank you for taking time from your busy schedules to confer with me today," Ahmadinejad said. "Now that the time has come to implement Phase 3, I thought it imperative that we meet here to insure that we all understand what is about to take place. We can tolerate no mistakes. Am I correct in assuming that the decision to implement Phase

3 is unanimous?" Ahmadinejad paused to give the others an opportunity to express a view.

Ahmadinejad was the only person smiling. The other three, Naveed Behbehani, the Minister of Intelligence and Security, Akbar Mahsuli, the Director of the Atomic Energy Organization, and General Obadias Nasiri, the Commander of VEVAK, all sat with stoic expressions on their faces.

No one spoke.

"Very well, I accept your silence as enthusiastic concurrence."

Ahmadinejad did not doubt that to a man the others opposed his plan; he was in no mood to tolerate opposition, but he was amused to find that they did not dare object. He looked directly at Akbar Mahsuli.

"Are we prepared to implement?" Ahmadinejad asked.

"We have designated the target facility," Mahsuli answered. "General Nasiri's men have installed the explosives." Mahsuli glanced at Nasiri in a blatant attempt to shift the meeting's focus to him.

"And have you selected the victims?" Ahmadinejad asked Mahsuli before Nasiri could speak.

Ahmadinejad assumed the general would bombard them with irrelevant minutiae, a time wasting, stalling tactic that Ahmadinejad was determined to avoid. Ahmadinejad did not care about details; only results mattered.

"Yes sir. Three of them. I must say..." Mahsuli began.

"Please don't," Ahmadinejad interrupted. "I am not interested in petty details. Just assure me that they are mediocre scientists whose contributions are not essential to the continued success of our program."

"The three have evaluations that put them in the lowest percentiles when ranked against their peers. They are considered marginal, professionally."

"Excellent. We kill three birds with one shot," Ahmadinejad grinned.

No one else in the room smiled.

"They are family men who..." Mahsuli again tried to go on the record in front of his peers.

"Enough!" Ahmadinejad again silenced Mahsuli in mid-sentence. He turned to Behbahani. "Have you checked the names of these three scientists? Are they carried as suspects on your list of possible informants who talked with that American spy Jesperson?"

"I defer to General Nasiri," Behbahani replied, clearly wanting to have no responsibility for identifying the potential victims.

"I have nothing of substance to contribute, Mr. President," Nasiri said, deliberately not answering Ahmadinejad's question.

"Very well. I accept VEVAK's determination that the three scientists in question are traitors," Ahmadinejad declared.

Ahmadinejad paused, daring Nasiri to disagree. The mute Nasiri pretended to study his shoe tops.

Ahmadinejad waited. Mahsuli cleared his throat, but Ahmadinejad spoke first, "Are we prepared to implement Phase Three tomorrow?"

No one answered.

"Well?" Ahmadinejad demanded.

"On your command," Nasiri surrendered, ending his minute of silent protest.

"General, I'm delighted to see that you have recovered your ability to speak," Ahmadinejad stared briefly at Nasiri, again challenging him.

Nasiri said nothing, capitulating completely. Ahmadinejad glanced at Mahsuli and then spoke to Behbehani. "You have a fine team, minister, one of whom cannot speak and one of whom cannot keep his mouth shut."

Behbehani glanced at his two colleagues, giving them an opportunity to defend themselves. Neither Nasiri nor Mahsuli did.

Ahmadinejad smiled. "Very well. Your silence tells me that you all support the plan. I accept your proposal. Implement Phase 3 tomorrow morning. I will meet with the media and denounce the insidious American sneak attack as soon as I receive your report that the building has been destroyed."

Again, the three subordinates reacted with shocked silence.

Ahmadinejad turned to his Atomic Energy chief. "Have we identified the source of the infection?" He referred to the computer virus that had frozen the computers driving the centrifuges. The centrifuges were programmed to strengthen the spin cycle of the uranium gas in order to increase the level of enrichment by another twenty-five percent, the difference between producing nuclear fuel for a civilian reactor and creating enriched weapons-grade fuel for an atomic bomb.

"That is very difficult," Akbar Mahsuli said.

"I want to talk with the physicist engineer responsible," Ahmadinejad reacted.

"Very well," Mahsuli stalled.

"Now," Ahmadinejad declared.

A very nervous Mahsuli looked to Behbehani and Nasiri for assistance.

Each responded with a blank expression. Mahsuli went to the door and ordered the guard to summon Physicist Baghai. Mahsuli returned to his seat and waited. No one spoke until the door opened and a white coated, middle aged Iranian entered.

"Mr. President," Mahsuli announced. "Physicist Baghai as you ordered."

"Sir," Mansour's uncle, recently released from prison and reinstated, stood at attention before the tribunal, not one of whom he had ever previously met.

"Physicist Baghai," Ahmadinejad stared at slender scientist. "I understand that you are responsible for the virus."

"The virus, sir?" Baghai reacted, his left eye suddenly starting to twitch.

"Yes, the one that has attacked our centrifuges," Ahmadinejad said. "Have you identified the source?"

"We have isolated the affected centrifuges, sir," Baghai, still standing rigidly at attention, said.

"Relax man, we just need information," Ahmadinejad said, letting his irritation show.

"Yes sir," Baghai said.

"How many of our centrifuges has the virus infiltrated?" Ahmadinejad asked, hoping that he had phrased the question correctly. Computers and centrifuges were a complete mystery to him.

"Eight hundred and sixty-four," Baghai replied.

"And how many are now free of the virus?"

"Thirty-two," Baghai answered.

"Thirty-two," Ahmadinejad repeated, concealing the fact that the number was meaningless to him. He shook his head in dismay. "How many do we need to complete our project?"

"Three thousand centrifuges can produce twenty kilograms of weapons-grade uranium, enough for one bomb, in thirty days," Baghai replied.

Ahmadinejad slapped the table in disgust. "We need three thousand centrifuges working for thirty days to produce just one bomb?" He shouted.

Baghai nodded. Ahmadinejad turned on his Atomic Energy director. "We have only thirty-two operational centrifuges?"

"Yes sir, our weapons program has a difficulty, but we are working on a solution," Mahsuli answered quickly before looking at Baghai trying to focus the irate Ahmadinejad's attention back on the hapless physicist.

"Correct my math if I'm wrong," Ahmadinejad said. "We have thirty-two operational centrifuges out of a total of 896. Physicist Baghai now tells me we need three thousand centrifuges working for thirty days to produce one bomb. If all of our centrifuges were operating, it would have taken us..." Ahmadinejad hesitated, waiting for one of the others to finish his calculations for him.

"Another forty days, give or take five days, depending on the functioning centrifuges," Baghai said.

"But someone has damaged our centrifuges with this virus," Ahmadinejad declared. "Can someone tell me when I can have my first bomb?"

"We will be able to reprogram some of the centrifuges when we succeed in isolating the virus," Baghai said.

"Not all of them?"

"Sir, I cannot definitively answer the question until I am able to assess how much damage the virus has caused," Baghai said. "We may have to replace all of the infected computers and centrifuges."

"And how long will that take?"

Baghai looked at the Director of Atomic Energy, deferring the answer to him.

"Procuring advanced computers and centrifuges in quantity is a time consuming process," Mahsuli shrugged. "Everything depends on our sources of supply and how much pressure the Americans and the United Nations put on them.

Ahmadinejad glared at Mahsuli and then ignored him. He turned to his Minister of Intelligence and Security who had said little during the discussion. "Who is responsible for this virus?"

"I have no information that lets me definitively answer that question, Mr. President," Behbehani answered. "If pressed, I would say the American CIA. They are the only ones with the resources to mount such an attack, but I must caution, that is merely my hypothesis."

"And what do you say Mr. Engineer Physicist Baghai?" Ahmadinejad turned back to Mansour's uncle. "This American author has the ability to penetrate our nuclear research program and divine our plans and intentions, but our VEVAK can only provide me with an hypothesis."

"Sir, I am a simple scientist," Baghai shrugged. "I am confident we will be able to isolate the virus and develop an antivirus, but I am not sure we will ever be able to determine its source."

"Thank you, Scientist Baghai," Ahmadinejad abruptly dismissed the man. "I thank you for your honest contribution."

Ahmadinejad waited until the door closed behind Baghai before turning angrily on Behbehani, Nasiri, and Mahsuli.

"What else do you gentlemen not know?" He demanded.

"About Phase 4," Behbehani said.

"What about it?" Ahmadinejad asked.

"The timing," Behbehani said. "We should place our armed forces on full alert immediately after the device explodes in Washington. We can expect a harsh retaliation."

"Are you afraid our armed forces will not be able to defend the motherland?" Ahmadinejad laughed.

Behbehani glanced at his two colleagues who reacted with silent but strained expressions. Behbehani likewise did not comment. All three were aware that if the Americans and their Israeli allies reacted with nuclear weapons, they had the capability to obliterate Iran.

"Don't worry, I will personally alert the armed forces," Ahmadinejad filled the silence.

"I humbly suggest that nothing be said before the explosion," Behbehani said. "An early alert will only be interpreted by the world as indicating we knew the terrorist act was coming."

"Do you want to assume responsibility for the timing?" Ahmadinejad challenged.

Behbehani shook his head negatively but did not trust himself to speak.

"I suggest, Mr. Minister," Ahmadinejad smiled meanly. "That you remain in Natanz to insure that everything goes according to plan."

"Do you think that wise?" Behbehani reacted.

"Are you challenging my decisions?" Ahmadinejad glared at Behbehani.

"I was only suggesting, Mr. President, that the world will investigate us closely. If I were to be in Natanz when the explosion occurs, the media will immediately present that as evidence indicating that Phase 3 was staged."

Ahmadinejad did not immediately respond. After a few seconds of silence during which Behbehani, Nasiri, and Mahsuli waited anxiously, Ahmadinejad spoke. "I accept your point. We all should return to Teheran immediately. Make sure that no one on your staff is aware that we met here today."

Behbehani was tempted to point out that many people in Natanz already knew of their presence, including Air Force personnel on the planes that transported them, security in Natanz, Engineer Physicist Baghai, his fellow scientists, and only Allah knew who else. He said nothing, however.

Following their obvious dismissal, the three subordinates silently filed from the room. Not one of the three shaken men dared to comment on their president or the meeting that just concluded.

Before boarding the plane for their return flight, Behbehani turned to his two companions.

"The president's admonition about advising staff of this meeting is considerably belated. I'm sure most of my office is aware that I visited Natanz today." It was not necessary for him to add five words, "to meet with the president."

"I too have the same problem," Mahsuli agreed.

"We have a major problem, but it is not with our respective staffs," Nasiri said, referring to the president.

"I know," Behbehani immediately commented. "There are many people in Natanz who are aware of our visit." Behbehani realized what problem Nasiri referred to, but he spoke deliberately to cover himself first and Nasiri second.

****

At FBI Headquarters Special Agent Tracey Cotton left his assembling team and took the elevator to the director's office.

"I need to see the director urgently," Cotton announced as soon as he entered the outer office.

"He's in a meeting," the director's secretary tested the urgency behind Cotton's demand.

"Now," Cotton said as he started for the closed door to the inner office.

"Let me announce you," the secretary leaped to her feet and beat Cotton to the door.

Cotton hesitated; the secretary opened the door and said, "Excuse me sir, but Special Agent Cotton needs to see you, urgently."

Director Phillip D'Antonio looked up from his position at the head of the table. Despite the irritated expression on his face, he nodded.

"Please excuse me, gentlemen," D'Antonio dismissed the six senior officers, each of whom commanded a FBI field office, who had been summoned to Washington for this meeting with the director. "Please stand by while I deal with Special Agent Cotton's emergency."

Cotton circled the director's secretary and nodded to the frowning SAC's as they filed past him. Clearly all six were irritated by the interruption, and all six were senior in grade to Cotton who aspired to be selected to replace one of them.

Cotton waited until the door closed behind him before speaking.

"Just as we feared, the two Iranians had a rendezvous in Niagara Falls with a contact from Canada," Cotton reported.

D'Antonio nodded but did not speak. That news did not justify the interruption.

"They spent the night in Lewisburg and returned to D.C. this morning."

D'Antonio still waited.

"Afgar dropped off Taheri at the Jesperson apartment and drove immediately to a storage facility in Fairfax," Cotton continued. "Afgar loaded a large, heavy package that worries me considerably in a previously rented compartment and returned to the Jesperson apartment."

"Why does the package worry you?"

"I've had preliminary discussions with our explosive experts and scientists from AEC." Cotton referred to the Atomic Energy Commission. "Given the allegations in the Jesperson book about Iranian plans, the package worries them too."

"Why?"

"The package dimensions trouble them. It could be a Soviet suitcase bomb. I'm sure you recall that sensational CIA report that alleged the Iranians purchased several of them from dissident officers following the breakup of the Soviet Union."

"That report was never substantiated."

"I have a warrant authorizing a search at the storage facility."

"Do you think we should alert the president?" The director started to focus.

"I recommend it," Cotton replied.

D'Antonio reluctantly left the conference table and moved to his desk.

He punched the intercom and spoke to his secretary. "Please get Heather on the line," he ordered.

"The president is preparing to depart," D'Antonio said as he checked his watch, "in about twenty minutes for New York where he has a scheduled address to the UN. He plans to spend the night in New York City and return tomorrow morning."

"Shit," Cotton muttered as the intercom buzzed.

"Heather is on the green line," D'Antonio's secretary said.

D'Antonio poked the blinking light. "Heather, I'm sorry to bother you. I know things are busy over there right now, but I have an urgent matter I need to discuss with the president."

"He's in a meeting right now with Director Pace," Heather said. "And he must leave immediately after for New York."

"Could you please interrupt and inform the president that I and Special Agent Cotton have an urgent matter we need to discuss," D'Antonio pressed.

"I can't promise anything, but I'll try. He is not in a very good mood today," Heather whispered before placing D'Antonio on hold.

"He's meeting with Pace," D'Antonio repeated to the pacing Cotton.

"I should really get out to that storage depot. I have a team assembled," Cotton said. "We don't know what's in that package, but..."

"He says no," Heather came back on line. D'Antonio held up a finger to silence Cotton.

"But..." D'Antonio decided to press now that he had started.

"He says tell you to handle your emergency. That's what you're paid to do," Heather interrupted.

"But..." D'Antonio tried to explain.

"He says to tell you CIA has an urgent problem, too," Heather said. "I'll schedule you for first thing tomorrow morning. Will that do?"

D'Antonio hesitated. It occurred to him that there was nothing the president could do about the package in Fairfax other than to order them to do what Cotton and his team already planned. "Yes, thank you, Heather," D'Antonio said. "I'll handle our problem, but I must see the president tomorrow morning, first thing. I hope I didn't get you in trouble."

"No problem. That's what I'm here for," Heather said as she terminated the call.

D'Antonio shook his head as he frowned at Cotton. "The president is busy with Pace who has an urgent problem and doesn't have time for us.

He says we should handle our urgent situation, and he'll see us tomorrow morning."

"We tried. If the damned thing explodes tonight, at least he won't be in Washington," Cotton said.

"You take care of that damned package and leave politics and the White House to me," an irritated D'Antonio ordered.

Cotton shrugged and started for the door.

"And tell the barons to get their asses back in here," D'Antonio continued.

"Yes sir," Cotton said as he reached for the doorknob.

"And keep me informed," D'Antonio ordered. "I don't want to sit here listening to petty west coast problems while the damned city around me vaporizes."

Cotton nodded.

"Wait," D'Antonio said.

Cotton closed the door and waited.

"You said you've got the AEC involved. What about Defense?" D'Antonio referred to the Department of Defense.

"I didn't want to get Defense rolling until I found out what is in the damned package," Cotton said. "You know how that place leaks."

"Still, we've got to cover our asses. Get the AEC people to bring in their weapons contact at Defense," D'Antonio ordered. "Tell them to stress this is a highly sensitive, ongoing investigation, and we need someone who knows what a Russian suitcase atomic bomb looks like."

"Are you sure?" Cotton asked. "Talk like that could provoke Defense to raise Alert Status to Level One, a war is imminent. I'm certain they have all read that Jesperson book."

"Just do what I told you. Make sure they understand this is an ongoing investigation, and we need someone who can tell us what to look for."

"I could say it's a training exercise," Cotton said.

"Just do what I said," an irritated D'Antonio dismissed him. "And don't let Defense nuke Iran without the president's approval."

"If the damned thing goes off and destroys half of Washington they might."

"Then don't let it go off without checking with me first."

Cotton laughed, and D'Antonio frowned.

"I'm not kidding," D'Antonio muttered.

Cotton shrugged. There was nothing he could say to that. He opened the door a second time and waved the waiting barons back inside.

Five glowering SACs filed into the room, unanimously rewarding him with disapproving grimaces. The sixth, a former Cotton classmate who was now Special Agent in Charge of the Bureau's San Francisco office, greeted him with a sarcastic smile and a soft question, "What's happening?"

"Just the beginning of the end of the world," Cotton whispered as he passed.

"I'm supposed to keep the director informed," Cotton told the secretary after the door closed.

"I'm always here," the secretary shrugged, her indifference indicating she had seen it all before.

****

"Sorry about that," the president said as he turned from the intercom. His expression told CIA Director William H Pace that his words were not serious.

"Now what do you have to tell me that can't wait until tomorrow morning?" President Arthur C. Featherstone asked.

"I'm sorry sir," Pace said. "I know you have an important speech scheduled for later this evening."

"And that noise you hear behind you comes from the turning blades of a copter waiting impatiently to ferry me to Andrews," Featherstone said. "Do you know how much it costs a minute to run those things?"

Featherstone sat behind his massive desk, and the CIA Director stood in front of him expecting to be invited to sit down. Featherstone deliberately did not do so as he waited for Pace to share his urgent information.

Recognizing that a few seconds were all that he was going to get, Pace started his report. "Our most sensitive Iranian agent has just submitted an alarming report," Pace said.

"Wait," Featherstone interrupted. "Remind me, which most sensitive agent are we discussing?"

Featherstone sincerely believed the Agency always overvalued its sources; hence, source details were important to him. Featherstone was old school; he still read the *New York Times.* When pressed, he admitted that the *Times* had seriously deteriorated over the years, but he still dutifully compared their reporting with his daily intelligence summaries.

Pace took a deep breath. Featherstone pretended he was too rushed to deal with urgent security problems and in the next breath asked extraneous questions. During the past three weeks, Pace and the president had discussed APEX/1's reporting in detail. APEX/1 was the Agency's most reliable Iranian asset operating at the core of a threat situation. The president had repeatedly asked the Agency to share that information with the FBI, State, and Defense, and Pace had respectfully declined. APEX/1 was actually at the point of the threat and this presented the Agency with a monumental problem as well as the most unusual reward of being in a position to report authoritatively on the hostile machinations of a bandit nation like Iran led by a certifiable nutcase. While the Bureau was deeply involved in the investigation of an Iranian covert operation, the Agency controlled the Bureau's ostensible target. The Agency had much invested in the agent and high expectations for future production against a priority target; even the president understood the asset's potential value, but at the same time he had to manage a very real threat.

"APEX/l," Pace whispered, uncomfortable pronouncing even the cryptonym outside the Agency's protective security barriers. Pace was not confident that even the Oval Office was secure enough to peel back the Agency's protective veneers.

"What?" Featherstone asked. He now understood who Pace was referring to and why he was behaving so obstinately, but Featherstone was in no mood to make things easier for the cold and tightlipped Agency director.

"APEX/1," Pace capitulated, speaking a little louder. "APEX/1 reports that the Iranian package has arrived in Washington."

"What!" Featherstone repeated himself. This time his "What!" was a worried comment not a question. He stared at his CIA Director, an unbelieving expression on his face. He was a worried man no longer play-acting for an audience of one.

"Yes, sir," Pace said, now pleased that he had his master's attention. When that happened, Featherstone transformed himself from a politician into a leader. "I'm sure that is why Director D'Antonio so urgently needs to talk with you."

"You are telling me that the damned Iranians have successfully succeeded in placing a nuclear weapon in Washington, D.C., and that those madmen actually plan on detonating it?"

"Yes sir," Pace answered concisely.

"And you want me to do something about it?" Featherstone asked softly.

"No sir."

"I'm supposed to sit back and let the Iranians blow up half of

Washington, myself and my wife too, and do nothing any order to protect the security of your source?" Featherstone stared at his own madman.

"Sir, APEX/1 has been tasked to detonate the device, and we control APEX/1."

"Are you certain? Really certain?"

"Yes sir."

"How can you be so sure?" An appalled Featherstone demanded. "You've told me on more than one occasion that something can always go wrong in that dark world of yours, and it usually does. Everything is not always what it appears. Didn't one of your predecessors assure young Jack Kennedy that an invasion of Cuba would succeed?"

"I doubt that is what President Kennedy was told, sir, but the circumstances are completely different this time."

"And how is that?"

"I'm sure you do not have time to go into operational detail," Pace equivocated.

"Tell me anyway. The world won't end if I don't make a speech tonight. But if the Iranians set off a nuclear bomb in Washington, I don't know what might happen. You know we have many large missiles in place and targeted, primed to fire almost automatically if we are attacked with nuclear weapons."

"It won't get that far, sir," Pace said.

Featherstone waited.

"We control APEX/l."

Featherstone snorted.

"We have APEX/1 under twenty-four hour surveillance, physically and technically. We also have the package under control."

"Under control?"

"Under surveillance."

"Is this APEX/1 acting alone?" Featherstone scowled. He knew the answer to that question. Pace had already briefed him.

"No sir," Pace answered, forcing himself to keep his responses simple and as devoid of jargon as possible. "APEX/1 has one accomplice."

"APEX/2, a sleeper, I think was the word you used."

"Yes sir. APEX/2 has been in place for almost ten years. This is his first meaningful assignment."

"Meaningful assignment?" Featherstone glared at Pace. "You call exploding an atomic bomb a meaningful assignment? What do you call ten thousand dead American citizens? Corollary victims?"

"APEX/2 is not a skilled physicist. He needs APEX/1 to arm the device."

"Are you certain?"

Pace hesitated before responding. "APEX/2 does not have military service or training in his background. He is a simple academic."

"Simple but lethal," Featherstone declared. "Stop equivocating and give me direct yes or no answers I can understand."

Before Pace could think of a response, the president's intercom buzzed. He pushed a button and declared, "I know, I'm coming," not giving Heather a chance to deliver her message.

Featherstone stood up. "I'm leaving. I want you in my office tomorrow morning at opening of business, and I don't want either of these APEXes to do a single thing between now and then. "Don't let either one of them approach the device. Tomorrow, we're going to have a frank discussion with the Bureau, with State, with Defense, and with the Atomic Energy Commission and decide how to end this nonsense forthwith."

"But sir," Pace tried to protest.

"You heard me," Featherstone started for the door. "I hold you personally responsible for insuring that nothing happens between now and tomorrow morning, and if you don't heed my words you will be lucky to find a job as a dog catcher in Fiji, and in Fiji they don't have many dogs. They eat them for breakfast. Am I making myself perfectly clear?"

"Yes, sir," Pace said as the president slammed the door behind him leaving Pace alone in the Oval Office.

Chapter 28

Cotton and his team approached the Waples Mill storage unit in a ten-car cavalcade with Cotton and his warrant in the lead. He waved his credentials case at the overwhelmed teenaged attendant, displayed the warrant, and ordered his driver to proceed to unit ten. The following cars deployed, blocking all access. Cotton leisurely climbed out of his car, pointed at unit ten, and ordered the entry team to open the locked overhead door.

Ten minutes later a smiling tech stepped back holding the lock in one hand and the key he had obtained from the teenaged attendant in the other.

Cotton waited for the entry team leader to raise the door, turn on the light, and step back. Cotton frowned. The team leader, who took pride in the fact that he always was the first man through the door, deferred to Cotton. He too had been briefed on the locker's package. Alone, Cotton stepped inside to find the locker empty except for a solitary container in the center of the narrow room wrapped in green plastic and bound with canvas bands. Cotton studied it carefully with his hands at his sides for a full minute and then retreated. Whatever the plastic covered now belonged to him. Step by step process and extreme caution were now his guiding watchwords. Feeling like a symphony conductor, Cotton pointed at the second vehicle, a van, and signaled with two raised fingers. Two large gentlemen dressed in astronaut costumes climbed out of the back of the van with difficulty. Each was covered from head to foot in impressive gear with heavy containers containing pure oxygen strapped to their backs.

"Open that sucker carefully, very carefully, and preserve the plastic and straps for me," Cotton ordered. "I need the wrapping intact."

The lead human robot responded with a nod of his encased head. "Yes, sir," the electronically modulated voice rasped.

Cotton judiciously retreated to his vehicle and sat in the rear with tinted armored windows and heavy doors tightly closed.

"Keep the damned motor running," Cotton ordered the driver.

He knew that nothing could save them if the technicians in the costumes erred, and the package detonated, but he still felt better with the motor running.

He grabbed the microphone and reported to the anxious headquarters duty officer. "We've got it. We're waiting to see if the experts know as much as they pretend they do," Cotton said.

"Standing by," the duty officer reported, his voice filled with tension. "Should we be using the radio?" The duty office asked.

"Of course not," Cotton replied as he turned off his radio.

He watched as the AEC lead technician in his fancy garb circled the package.

"What are you looking for?" The nervous second technician standing near the storage container door asked.

"How the hell do I know?" The circling AEC lead replied. He carefully took a radiation detector from his shoulder bag and waved it over the package. The needle did not waver. "We've got to open it," he suggested, peering through his mask at his companion in the doorway.

"I was afraid you were going to say that," the second man said.

He turned and waved at the van. An identically garbed man struggled out of the rear of the van carrying a common black leather satchel with straps and no metal buckles. Unaccustomed to his gear, he waddled to join the man in the doorway.

"Open the sucker," the man in the doorway spoke into his microphone as he pointed a gloved finger at the package.

The team leader, still standing over the package, turned, "Carefully," he ordered. "They want to reuse the cover and straps."

"Shit, I know that," the third man said.

"And don't set the damned thing off. It's old and highly volatile," the team leader ordered as he retreated in the direction of the van.

The third man chuckled nervously as he opened his bag.

In the first car, Cotton's cell phone buzzed. "What?" Cotton answered quickly.

"What's happening?" D'Antonio demanded.

"We've got the device, and the techs are opening the package," Cotton answered and terminated the conversation. He turned off his cell phone which he had forgotten. They had come too far to let an ass kissing chat with the director cause an impulse that triggered the damned thing.

The driver who assumed the call was from someone important glanced at Cotton but said nothing. He, like Cotton, watched with twitching nerves as the AEC tech circled the device.

"Does he know what he's doing?" The nervous driver asked.

"I hope so," Cotton answered as he climbed out of the car. He swallowed hard as he ignored the white-faced agents who had formed in a semicircle about twenty feet from the wide-open storage compartment.

"Do you think that thing might go off?" A member of Cotton's team asked.

"If it does, you'll never know it, so stop worrying," Cotton replied with false bravado.

Cotton entered the compartment and silently watched the technician. Suddenly, the man who had been kneeling, studying, but carefully not touching the package, slid back, stood erect, and looked at Cotton.

"Is that what we think it is?" Cotton asked.

"How the hell would I know?" The AEC scientist/technician shrugged. "It's the right size, but all I see is a big something wrapped in green plastic and bound with straps."

"What about that?" Cotton pointed at the radiation detector the scientist held in his right hand.

"This?" The man waved his detector in the air. "All it tells me is that thing," he glanced at the package, "is not sterilizing us at the moment. If you are worried about creating a future generation, I suggest you leave."

"What are you going to do next?" Cotton asked.

"I don't know," the scientist/technician answered frankly. "I was thinking about discussing that question with some of the alleged experts from the Pentagon," he glanced at a group of men standing by a small bus some fifty yards away. "But I doubt they know any more about these things than I do."

"Then get busy," Cotton ordered. "We have to unwrap that thing, measure the suitcase, find another to replace it, and then use that green plastic and the bands to make it look just like the original, and we don't have all night."

"Lots of luck," the scientist/technician chuckled without humor.

"And we have to do it now. I don't know when the owner of that thing is returning to collect it, and that could be as soon as tomorrow morning," Cotton said.

"You're kidding me," the scientist/technician glared at Cotton. "I'm not going to try to disarm that thing here. It could go off and take out half the city. What do you think the president would say if we vaporized the White House?"

"The president is out of town," Cotton shrugged with an indifference he did not feel. "But I'm sure he would be really pissed when he gets the news."

"Are you going to assume responsibility for that, and will you guarantee to look after my family? I've a wife and two kids."

"Tell me about this thing," Cotton said.

"According to our best information, and only God knows how reliable that is, the Soviet Union at its height had a bunch of these things," the scientist/technician said.

"What's it called?" Cotton asked.

"If that," he pointed at the green plastic package, "is what somebody thinks it is, it's a one-kiloton Soviet suitcase nuclear device. Our army calls them tactical nuclear weapons. Our W-54 SADM weighs about sixty pounds and was designed to be parachuted behind enemy lines where our Special Forces would use it against enemy bridges, ports, command posts and the like. The Russian version was suitcase sized, just like that little fellow sitting there."

"Does it look like a real suitcase?" Cotton asked.

"So I'm told. I've never actually seen one."

"How many people would it take to carry one?" Cotton asked.

"One person if he were a big, strong fellow."

"And could one person fire the damned thing?"

"With the proper training," the scientist/technician answered.

"Could someone without training but with good written instructions detonate it?"

"Maybe. Depends on the person."

"Tell me what else you know about it," Cotton said, not admitting that he had run out of questions.

"I read a report that said the Russians had some 250 of the suckers, and that 150 could be accounted for. I assume that one, if that is what is inside that plastic, is one of the 100 missing. All the Russians will admit is that 100 are out of their control."

"Where did they go missing?" Cotton asked.

"Nobody knows; they just disappeared. Our intelligence people assume that dissident Russian military carried them off and sold them on the black market."

"They just took them to the local bazaar and sold them to the highest bidder?" Cotton asked.

"Probably something more complicated than that. We assume that black market arms merchants served as intermediaries between the ex-military and rogue states anxious to become nuclear powers the easy way."

"Like Iran, Libya, North Korea," Cotton said.

"Exactly."

"So this could really be a tactical nuclear weapon," Cotton glanced at the green package with heightened respect and discernible apprehension in his eyes.

"That's right, and who knows how stable it might be," the scientist/technician studied the package with the same anxious deference.

"You are saying I shouldn't pick it up and shake it," Cotton chuckled mirthlessly.

"You can if you want. Just give me enough warning to get out of here," the scientist/technician said.

"OK," Cotton said. "You say you want to take this someplace less populated to disarm it."

"I didn't say what I was going to do to it. I said I didn't want to open that package here," the scientist/technician said.

"Carefully take those bands and the plastic off the suitcase, and then you can do whatever you want with it," Cotton said.

"You want me to get on my knees, cut off the bands, and unwrap the plastic right here?" The man asked, staring at Cotton with disbelief etched on his face.

"That's right. Unwrap the damned thing, let me see what it looks like, measure it for me, and then it's all yours."

"Let me get two of my boys and some equipment while you back the rest of your army out of here," the man said as he started for the door.

"How far?" Cotton asked.

"That's up to you," the scientist/technician smiled. "Just remember that baby carries the kick of 100,000 sticks of dynamite."

Cotton retreated and ordered his team to withdraw to the deserted parking lot in the Fair Oaks Mall about a mile away. "I'll call you," Cotton waved his cell phone, "when I need you."

"How long should we wait?" His assistant team leader asked.

"Until I call or until you hear a big bang," Cotton said without a trace of a smile on his lips.

After the cavalcade had departed, Cotton joined the AEC scientist/technician and two others in the storage locker. The scientist/technician introduced his companions as weapons specialists from the Pentagon. One of the technicians opened a black bag and took out a simple cutting tool, the kind available in any hardware store. He kneeled in front of the package, glanced at his fellow specialist and the AEC scientist/technician, took a deep breath, and began to carefully cut the first band. He didn't just grab the band with one hand and start slicing; he carefully drew the tip of the razor point across the band cutting a thin line into the tough material. Nothing happened. The AEC technician waved his radiation detector over the package. The needle did not move. Growing more confident, the specialist with the blade cut the band repeatedly, slicing until the band snapped apart.

Cotton stepped outside and checked the road leading into the storage area. It was deadly silent. Cotton glanced at the sky, noted the full harvest moon and twinkling stars, and returned to the container where the specialist was now working steadily.

Ten minutes later all the bands were severed, leaving only the thick green plastic sheath between them and the suitcase. The specialist shifted his attention to one end of the package; working more quickly now, he sliced through the plastic in one motion, stood up, leaned over and cut across the top of the plastic. He peeled back the plastic and peered inside. He nodded, apparently satisfied with what he saw, and glanced at the AEC scientist/technician who studied the meter on his radiation detector. The scientist/technician smiled and nodded. The specialist moved to the other side of the package, slit the plastic and let it fall to the floor exposing the suitcase.

To Cotton's amazement, that's exactly what the damned thing looked like, an oversized brown suitcase made of dull plastic with a leather handle.

The AEC technician stared at Cotton. "Satisfied?" He asked in a flat voice.

"Just measure the thing and get it out of here," Cotton grumbled to conceal his relief.

The specialist with the cutting tool dropped it back into his leather satchel and took out a folded carpenters ruler made of wood. "The less I challenge this thing by waving metal at it the better," the man said.

He quickly measured the suitcase's length. "Fifty inches," he announced.

Cotton took out his notebook and pen and made a note.

The specialist measured the suitcase's width. "Thirty-eight inches," he said, as he checked the case's width. He measured the depth, "ten inches."

"That's a damned big suitcase," Cotton said as he again recorded the figures. Now check out its weight."

"I don't have a scale," the specialist laughed nervously.

"Step back," Cotton ordered.

Cotton leaned over, grasped the suitcase in the middle with two meaty hands and lifted.

"Christ, don't drop it," the scientist/technician ordered.

"I don't intend to," Cotton said. "That's a good hundred pounds if it is an ounce. Want to try it?"

"Hell no," the scientist/technician replied.

Cotton gently lowered the suitcase to the floor.

"Is there anything else you need? Want to peek inside?" The AEC scientist/technician smiled at Cotton.

"No thank you," Cotton smiled back. "If no one objects, I'll step outside and summon the caravan."

"Why don't we all step outside and let baby here nap," the AEC scientist/technician suggested.

The two specialists and the scientist/technician followed Cotton into the deserted parking lot.

"Look at that moon," the specialist who had cut into the package said.

Cotton and the other two stared into the night sky.

"I'm sure glad we have someone up there watching over us," the second specialist said. "I'm not sure what you needed me for tonight," he spoke to his companion.

"I just wanted to be sure we had someone available to fetch the coffee if we needed it," the first specialist smiled.

Cotton walked some twenty paces from the storage locker before he poked a button and summoned his team to return.

"That's something I should have cautioned you about," the AEC scientist/technician smiled at the two technicians as he spoke to Cotton. "Radio signals are a no, no around these babies," he said as he glanced at the inert suitcase inside the almost empty storage container.

Cotton smiled back but said nothing. He recognized relief talking.

"What do you think about the Redskins?" The first specialist asked the AEC scientist/technician.

"I try to ignore them," the scientist/technician answered. "We really need a completely new football team."

"We need help with our basketball and baseball too," the first specialist agreed.

"We need new owners and then new teams," Cotton joined conversation. "Where are you going to take that thing?" Cotton asked the AEC scientist/technician.

"Belvoir," the three experts answered in unison.

Five minutes later the cavalcade's first car turned into the storage facility's driveway. A Bureau crime scene investigator carefully entered the storage locker and photographed the menacing suitcase from several angles. Ten minutes later Cotton sighed with relief as half the cars departed with the suitcase loaded in the back of the heavily armored van.

"Now, we can get to work," Cotton announced.

After a quick review of what needed to be done to restore the package to a precise rendition of its previous condition including an estimated weight of one hundred pounds, Cotton departed leaving his assistant team leader in charge. Cotton drove directly to the Georgetown home of FBI Director D'Antonio.

"Why didn't you call to tell me what was happening," D'Antonio greeted Cotton at the front door.

"I thought it best if we kept the radio signals to a minimum, sir," Cotton said, knowing that was a position the director could not dispute.

D'Antonio nodded as he led Cotton through the house to his office.

After they were seated, D'Antonio looked at Cotton and asked, "Are we still going to have jobs in the morning?" He referred to their scheduled meeting with an angry President Featherstone.

"I think we've got it, sir," Cotton smiled, treating the director's question as rhetorical.

"The suitcase?"

"It's on its way to Fort Belvoir," Cotton said as he took out his cell phone. He turned it on and focused on a picture of the suitcase he took from the door to the container.

Cotton stood up, rounded the director's desk, and held out the cell phone for D'Antonio to view.

"It doesn't look like much," D'Antonio said.

"No sir, but it is a tactical nuclear weapon with the kick of 100,000 sticks of dynamite," Cotton said.

"You're kidding me," an appalled D'Antonio stared at Cotton as he returned to his chair.

"No sir, and I'm also told that some one hundred of these things are missing," Cotton said.

"Missing?"

"At least the Russians tell us they don't know where they are."

"And those bastards have sold them to Iranians and who knows who else?"

"That's right."

"Damned CIA better get busy. I'll have to remember to remind the president that the Bureau can't keep doing the Agency's job for them," D'Antonio smiled.

"Yes sir. It's their job to catch these things before they reach American soil," Cotton smiled back.

"Now what happens?"

"The experts will take this thing apart at Belvoir."

"And what about the Iranians who tried to use the damned thing?"

"The techs are preparing a dummy suitcase that will look just like the original. We've got the agent who picked up the damned thing from his Canadian contact under surveillance. The Mounties are working the contact from their end. We have the storage locker under control, and we'll track him when he retrieves it and delivers it to the person who the Iranians think will detonate it."

"That way we can wrap up the entire net," the director said. "Do we know any of the others?"

"They are concentrated at George Mason," Cotton said. "I've talked with the person I think is the brains behind it, probably the one supposed to detonate the damned thing."

"And that person is?"

"An Iranian national by the name of Lyla Jalili."

"A female? She's competent to detonate the thing?"

"She has a doctorate in nuclear physics from the University of Paris."

D'Antonio nodded. "Is she strong enough to handle the device?"

"It weighs in the neighborhood of a hundred pounds. One person can carry it, and she has help, the Iranian graduate student who transported it from Niagara Falls. He's a big fellow."

"Do you think one of the Iranians at GMU was Jesperson's source?"

"I doubt it. They wouldn't have leaked information about their own operation. It would be too risky to them."

"Then how did Jesperson get his information?"

"We're still working on that."

"When this story breaks, the Iranians are going to self destruct. We'll have caught them engaging in an act of war against us; they'll have lost valuable agents, and they'll have a major leak in their nuclear establishment."

"That's all good news for us," Cotton said. "Do you think Featherstone will respond by attacking Iran?"

"I never know what that man is going to do," D'Antonio said. "At least, thanks to you, we come out looking good."

Cotton tried to pretend he was impervious to flattery, but he failed. His broad smile gave him away.

"So what happens next on our side?" D'Antonio asked.

"We watch our two Iranians and the phony bomb. When they pick it up, we'll track them and apprehend them in the act. They'll have a hell of a time trying to detonate a box of bricks."

D'Antonio looked at Cotton with a broad smile on his face. "Between you and me, Special Agent Cotton, all this deserves a drink. I'm really looking forward to our meeting with the president tomorrow morning."

****

Chase sat in his office reviewing the status of his investigation into Jesperson's murder. Unfortunately, Iranians kept popping up and complicating things for him. He was pleased that the elder Jespersons were taking Mansour home with them. The boy struck Chase as a lost soul, in over his head here in the States, and he needed someone to guide him. The elder Jespersons would do what they could, he was sure, but Mansour should have stayed in Iran. Chase realized that was not wise, under the circumstances, but attending Boston College should keep Mansour out of the way. Jamshid Afgar and Doctor Lyla Jalili were another story. In the latter's case, Jalili remained a mystery, a riddle wrapped in an enigma, mainly because she seemed to be avoiding him while he still felt he owed her an explanation for his bizarre behavior at her apartment following the otherwise delightful meal.

For the second time that day, Chase picked up his cell phone and poked in Jalili's office number; again, it tolled without a response. Chase turned in his chair, stared out the window, and was just beginning to relax when his intercom buzzed. Irritably, Chase resented the disruption, assuming that Theresa was playing because she was bored.

"What?" Chase demanded.

"Sir," Theresa greeted him with exaggerated deference, thus warning Chase that she was preparing to provoke him with another of her games.

Chase waited without comment.

"If you are still there, sir, I suggest you pick up line one," Theresa said.

Chase glanced at the blinking button on his desk phone. No one he ever wanted to talk with called him on that line.

"You don't by chance know who is calling, do you?" Chase demanded.

"Yes, sir," Theresa replied. "It's one of your favorites," she said and hung up without identifying the caller.

Chase pushed the blinking button and greeted the caller with a simple, "Hello." One never knew with Theresa. It could be the IRS calling to fix an appointment to discuss a tax return adjustment or simply his dentist's assistant reminding him that he was late in scheduling a routine checkup.

"Hello stranger," a familiar voice greeted him. "What rock are you hiding under now?"

"Jacky, what an extraordinary coincidence. I've been sitting here thinking about you," Chase lied.

Jaclyn Rossi was a local attorney who had occupied much of Chase's casual time over the past year, a relationship that had evolved out of a murder investigation that had included her brother as one of Chase's prime suspects. Fortunately, the brother had turned out to be somewhat innocent, at least not guilty of the murder, and Jacky had emerged as less hostile towards Chase than her defense attorney occupation had made her appear. Nonetheless, Chase's department peers still referred to Ms. Jaclyn Rossi as Wacky Jacky, an attitude that Chase had studiously amended for himself. At least he dropped the Wacky as an appellation when discussing the aggressive lawyer. He had yet to devise a more appropriate substitute for the Wacky. Tackey, lackey, snackey, crackey just didn't have the right resonance.

"Good," Jacky said. "I'm not busy tonight. What about you?"

"Now I am," Chase replied. He needed a night off from tormenting himself about his investigation. There were too many people involved, too many Iranians, and too many complications for his peace of mind. "I'll pick you up at seven."

"You're on," Jacky responded and hung up.

Chase immediately decided to forget about the Jespersons, the Iranians, and all his convoluted theories. He abandoned his closet office, waved at a surprised Theresa, and departed, ignoring Theresa's parting shot.

"What should I tell the chief if he should call?" Theresa called after him.

"Make something up," Chase smiled as he transited Theresa's office.

"OK, I'll tell everyone you are in conference, with Wacky Jacky," Theresa giggled.

Chase waved as the door closed behind him.

He returned to his townhouse, showered, shaved, and doused his face with extra lotion. With Jacky, he knew how the evening would end, and he wanted to smell nice for the inevitable climax.

At exactly seven, he parked the Prius at the curb in front of her townhouse, beeped twice, and waited.

Jacky did not disappoint him. She immediately exited her front door, slammed and locked it behind her, and joined Chase in the front seat.

"The Crab House," she greeted him.

Chase grinned, hit the drive button, made a U-turn, and headed for his favorite restaurant. He felt better already.

"Is everything I hear about you true?" Jacky asked.

"Probably," Chase said as he patted her bare knee. Two things he liked about Jacky, her trim legs and mini-skirts. In court she dressed like a man, trousers and all. Chase considered that a terrible waste.

"They say you are in over your head on the Jesperson investigation and your incredible luck has deserted you," Jacky said in her perky way.

"Undeniably," Chase agreed. Early on in their relationship Chase had learned that Jacky was too smart and too adroit at cross-examination for his usual fencing.

"Think you could get away for the weekend?" Jacky asked. "My brother will be busy elsewhere."

Jacky hinted that her brother's incredibly scenic mansion overlooking his coal empire outside of Keyser, West Virginia was available.

"Oh God, I would like nothing better," Chase said.

"I take it that is a negative," Jacky said. "You're in trouble, aren't you?" She stared at Chase, expecting a straight answer.

Chase beeped at a Mercedes that cut him off. "I don't know." Chase answered with as much honesty as he could muster, which usually was not much.

"If they bring charges and you need an unscrupulous lawyer, I'm available," Jacky smiled.

"Are you sure you are in the mood for wobbly crab legs?" Chase asked.

"Why else would I call a wobbly like you?" Jacky asked.

"I'll demonstrate the answer to that question later," Chase grinned as he parked the Prius in the most convenient space, one with the blue handicapped sign prominently displayed.

"I've got wobbly moves the likes of which you have never seen."

Jacky laughed. "Shaky, I've really missed you."

She patted Chase on the cheek as he opened the dash and pulled out his "Official Police Business" placard.

Jacky, a lawyer who was known to bend the law in her defense of a client, did not bother to comment. She opened her door and climbed out. Chase followed her into the Crab House, waved at the hostess who was dealing with a line of patrons behind the "Wait to Be Seated" sign, and she responded with a wave of her hand, indicating he should bypass the line and proceed to his usual table in the back. Ignoring the hostile stares of the queued patrons, Chase grabbed two menus and led Jacky to the table.

As soon as they were seated, their regular waitress approached.

"The usual?" She asked.

Chase and Jacky nodded, and the waitress hurried away.

"I hear you have been busy," Jacky said.

Chase shrugged.

"Who shot Doctor Jesperson?" Jacky persisted.

"I wish I knew," Chase smiled. "How is your campaign to keep all criminals on the street?" Chase referred to her criminal defense business.

"Booming, but I can always use another high profile defendant," Jacky said. "Can you prove the Iranians did it to prevent the publication of that book?"

The way Jacky pronounced "that book" gave Chase pause. He bent his head to the right and flashed his most quizzical expression, which he hoped conveyed doubt, amusement, and interest all at once.

Jacky laughed. "No, I don't have any new clients who speak with an unusual Iranian accent, whatever that may sound like."

"Months go by without a single sighting of my best girl friend," Chase continued, "and then suddenly a phone call, an invitation to dine at my favorite restaurant, and a hint about the possibility of an amorous weekend in a mountain mansion. Either I've been living right or somebody wants something."

"The former is a physical impossibility," Jacky replied, "and the latter is an open question."

Before Chase could contrive a peppy response, he glanced over Jacky's shoulder and saw the hostess heading their way with two customers in tow.

"Oh, oh," he said.

"A problem?" Jacky asked. "An old girl friend on the horizon?"

"Some days nothing goes right," Chase lamented.

Jacky turned just as the hostess reached their table.

"Good evening, counselor," Barbara Jordan, Chase's alternate girl friend, greeted Jacky with an insincere smile on her face. She glanced at Chase and then ignored him.

"Good evening, Doctor Jordan," Jacky answered while Chase nodded as he stared at Barbara's companion, the elusive Doctor Lyla Jalili who had been avoiding him for days.

"This is a pleasant surprise, Chase," Lyla greeted him, pretending that he had not left a score of messages on her machine. Lyla glanced at Jacky but did not speak.

Neither Barbara nor Lyla paused to chat. The hostess politely continued on to a table located past the family grouping that sat to Chase's immediate right, and Barbara and Lyla followed. Neither Chase nor Jacky said another word until the new arrivals were seated.

"Where were we when your girl friend made her appearance?" Jacky asked with a smile. "Or should I have pluralized the active noun?"

"You know what they say about bad pennies," Chase said as he watched their waitress serve their clam chowder and two beers.

"What do they say about bad pennies?" Jacky asked as Chase poured his Budweiser into the frosted mug.

Chase silently raised his mug and toasted Jacky before she had a chance to fill her own. She raised her bottle, and Chase drained half his Budweiser.

"I keep asking questions that pass unanswered," Jacky noted as she filled her mug.

"I don't remember what we were discussing, something about physical impossibilities," Chase said. "They keep reappearing," he continued while Jacky sipped her beer.

"Old girl friends?" Jacky asked.

"Bad pennies," Chase said.

"You should know, lieutenant," Jacky smiled. "Who is the dark haired beauty who called you Chase?"

"She's a little hippy for my taste," Chase said.

"You should know. What's her name? She's foreign, isn't she?"

"Iranian."

"I thought I detected an accent. Is she one of your suspects?"

Chase did not respond.

"I take your silence as an affirmative response, lieutenant," Jacky smiled. "If we were in court, and I had you on the stand, I would now ask the judge for permission to treat you as a hostile."

"And without doubt, given your overwhelming charm, he would approve," Chase said.

"He? We have female judges too," Jacky said.

"He, she, I'm sure you would have your hypothetical way. You always do."

"I really like this chowder," Jacky said.

"Me too."

"Lieutenant, I'll repeat my question," Jacky resumed her interrogation. "If there is something about it that you do not understand, I'll restate. What is her name and why did she use the word pleasant to describe your chance encounter? I notice Doctor Jordan didn't speak to you. Was that because of something you've done?"

Chase drained his beer glass and waved at the waitress to bring him another. Chase smiled at Wacky Jacky and asked, "What?"

"What what?"

"You confuse me counselor. What question do you want me to answer when?"

"Set your own priorities."

"I don't think Doctor Jordan likes me," Chase said. Expecting his comment to divert Jacky's attack, Chase waited for a response. He didn't mind chatting about Barbara. Lyla was a different matter.

"I understand that," Jacky said. "Please continue."

"Doctor Lyla Jalili and Doctor Jordan are colleagues on the George Mason faculty," Chase said.

"Why did she use the word pleasant?"

"You will have to ask her."

The waitress delivered Chase's beer. He smiled at the waitress and asked, "Do you find me pleasant?"

"Of course, lieutenant," the waitress smiled.

"See," Chase grinned at Jacky. "You are in the minority."

The waitress looked at Jacky and winked before departing.

"I'm not so sure about that," Jacky laughed. "I think I would like to meet Doctor Jalili. I'm sure we could find many pleasant things to discuss," Jacky stressed the word 'pleasant.'

"I'm really looking forward to the crab legs," Chase said.

Jacky glanced at him before replying. "If there is a double entendre in that comment, forget it. I'm not impressed. For it to work you would have to use the possessive."

"Crab's legs," Chase repeated. "I'm going to have to work to remember that."

The waitress arrived with two plates and a heaping platter of Alaskan King Crab legs. Chase and Jacky attacked their meal and forgot their light banter about the two GMU professors sitting two tables to their right. They finished about the same time, and Chase capped the excellent meal by sitting back and announcing, "Those were the best crab's legs I have ever eaten. We're going to have to do this again, soon."

"I think I caught the check last time," Jacky said.

"Are you sure?" Chase asked, noting that she made no commitment.

"Positive," Jacky said. "You work on the check while I visit the lady's room."

Chase nodded and watched as Jacky backed away from the table. She stood up and immediately crossed the aisle and approached the table occupied by Lyla and Barbara.

The ladies room was located in the front of the restaurant, not two tables to Chase's left. He watched as Jacky said something to the two women, and they both turned to glance in his direction. Immediately, all three women laughed. He didn't know what Jacky had said that was so funny, but he was confident that it was something he would not appreciate. He wondered what Barbara and Jacky would say if Lyla confided that he had recently passed out and spent the night on the couch in her town house. He knew that both might laugh, but neither would actually find the incident amusing, particularly not Jacky.

Chase paid the check and turned in his chair, trying to convey the impression that he was totally disinterested in the three-way conversation two tables away. Unfortunately, he found the blank wall less than spell binding. After a few minutes of counting the cracks and food smears, Chase pushed back his chair and without a glance at the chatting women made his way to the bar located in the right front of the restaurant. There, he ordered his third beer. He was contemplating ordering a fourth when finally Jacky rejoined him.

She placed a hand on his shoulder and announced, "Thank you for waiting. That was really interesting."

Chase, resisting the urge to make a sarcastic comment about the strange location of the lady's room, tried to be funny. "When you have to go, you have to go."

Jacky flashed a smile and withdrew her hand from his shoulder. "Do you want me to drive?" She glanced meaningfully at his empty beer bottle.

"No problem," Chase said as he pivoted his stool and stood up.

They walked in silence to the Prius.

"I truly enjoyed the evening, Chase," Jacky said.

Chase noted he was Chase again, not lieutenant, and wondered what had caused the reversion. He did not ask, however, fearing that he might not like the response, and that would be bad news because he usually enjoyed Jacky's company. Despite her reputation as an aggressive and determined courtroom lawyer, who did not hesitate to forcefully attack police officers when testifying to the criminal transgressions of her clients, Jacky usually was a charming and flirtatious evening companion.

"I don't think Barbara likes you very much anymore," Jacky surprised Chase as he was backing the Prius out of the handicapped slot.

Chase did not know how to answer that comment without telling Jacky more than he wanted her to know, so he said nothing.

"Don't you care?" Jacky asked, reminding Chase that asking questions and getting answers was a skill required by her profession.

"Of course I care," Chase answered honestly. "But we were never more than casual friends."

"Casual friends?"

"I had a working lunch with her three weeks ago."

"And before that?"

"I hadn't seen Barbara for months," Chase said honestly. He did not add, "not since I started seeing you."

"She doesn't miss you," Jacky said. "In fact she implied she thought you were too self-preoccupied."

"And what does that mean?"

"That your vocation and your avocation took up too much of your time."

"Time that I should have devoted to her," Chase forced a laugh. He found the topic uncomfortable.

"Something like that."

"And how do you feel?"

"I like what I feel," Jacky laughed as she leaned towards him and patted his thigh.

Chase looked at her. "Is that an invitation?"

"Not tonight," Jacky pulled her hand away. "Like you, I have my job. Unlike you, I don't have time for an avocation."

"Implying what?"

"Maybe I can work you in on alternating weekends."

"Alternating with what? Chase asked.

Jacky smiled. "Please don't start interrogating me, lieutenant, or I might be tempted to counter with a cross examination. I don't think you would like that."

"Agreed," Chase said.

They rode in silence until they reached Jacky's townhouse. She opened the door and climbed out.

"Would you like me to come in?" Chase asked. He wasn't sure what he would do if she said yes, because he was suddenly tired of the bickering and looked forward to a full night's sleep.

"I'll give you a rain check," Jacky said. "Maybe Saturday, if you're not too busy. You might be interested in some of the funny things that Lyla had to say."

"Funny things?"

"About your lamb and rice dinner and your night on her sofa," Jacky said as she slammed the door and hurried into her townhouse.

"Shit," Chase swore as he pulled away from the curb. He had thought he had put that experience behind him. Now Barbara and Jacky had something amusing to pummel him with.

Chapter 29

Former Secretary of the Department of Homeland Security James Townsend sprawled comfortably in the recliner facing the television in the family room of his fiancée Sally Kendrick's Reston condominium watching a miserable Wizard game. Sally was in the kitchen dutifully cleaning up the debris from their Chinese carry-in meal that had been delivered by a local taxi service. The Chinese had been Sally's idea; she had come home from the office too tired to change and go out, as was their usual practice. Although they had yet to set a date for their marriage—his divorce from Nancy Lou was still pending—Townsend and Sally were gradually beginning to resemble an old married couple. Thus far, Sally didn't seem to mind the fact that Townsend spent his days diddling round the apartment while Sally, who was a good fifteen years his junior, put in long hours trying to grow her computer company.

Townsend did not need to work despite the fact that he had agreed to give Nancy Lou their mansion and all communal property as a part of their settlement. Money was no problem because they each now had a sizeable nest egg of mutual proportions, thirteen million dollars equally. Besides, Nancy Lou was as anxious to be free from him as he was from her. The divorce was something they had planned for over a year now, and neither anticipated encountering any blocks in their mutual escapes. All of the worry and manipulation was behind them.

"How can you sit there and watch that nonsense?" Sally said as she entered the room, pointing at the Wizard game.

Townsend answered by reaching for the remote.

"Watch if you want," Sally relented, surprising Townsend with her flexibility, a trait that Nancy Lou did not know existed. It had always been Nancy Lou's way or no way.

Sally sat down and began to watch with him. "I thought the new owner unloaded all the old players and was going to build this team from scratch," Sally said as the first quarter ended with the Wizards down thirty to ten.

'It takes money to make money," Townsend said.

"Tell me about it," Sally laughed.

"A terrible record lets you lose a lot of games and get a high draft pick."

"And with the high draft pick you get to chose an inexperienced player with superstar potential," Sally said.

"Teams like the Wizards overhype and underpay him for three years before trading him to a serious organization for a couple of big names, past their prime players who talk a good game and coast towards retirement on your money. Then you start the rebuilding process all over again."

"Think that would work for me?" Sally referred to her business.

Before Townsend could answer, the door buzzer sounded. Townsend glanced at Sally and asked, "Expecting visitors?"

"Not me," Sally smiled.

"Nobody knows I'm here," Townsend smiled back.

"Then answer the door and tell nobody you are not at home," Sally ordered.

"I guess I'm going to have to get used to this," Townsend said as he pushed out of the recliner.

Before he got to the door, the buzzer sound again, longer.

"I'm coming," Townsend groaned.

He opened the door, and Nancy Lou, his soon to be ex-wife, pushed into the apartment.

"It's nobody," Townsend called to her back and announced, "No one is at home."

"Children," Nancy Lou replied. "I hope I'm disturbing something important."

Sally greeted Nancy Lou with a half-hearted wave. Nancy Lou ignored the indifferent greeting and sat down in the recliner that Townsend had just vacated. Townsend joined his undeclared fiancée on the sofa.

"Turn that crap off," Nancy Lou pointed at the television.

Townsend, who was still humoring the former love of his life in the interest of a quick divorce, stood up, picked up the remote from the table at Nancy' Lou's elbow, and muted the sound.

"That's the first time he ever did a single thing that I asked," Nancy Lou laughed. "I'm beginning to enjoy this single life." She stared at Sally, inviting a rejoinder, but Sally ignored her and stared at the silent television.

"You might have called," Townsend complained.

"Afraid I might have caught you at an inappropriately intimate moment?" Nancy Lou asked. She looked at Sally. "Been there, done that," she said.

Sally did not react.

Nancy returned her attention to Townsend. "We have some things to discuss, old man."

"Talk to my lawyer," Townsend tired of the game.

"Shall I mention those two offshore accounts in Panama?" Nancy Lou asked.

Townsend glared at his wife. "Don't be stupid," he warned.

"Don't you be stupid, stupid," Nancy Lou threw his words back at him.

Townsend turned the sound back up on the television. "Walls have ears," he declared.

"I don't care who is listening," Nancy Lou responded. "I didn't break any laws."

"You might think differently when the Department of Justice charges you with extorting thirty million dollars from the United States Government," Townsend said.

"I'm not the one who should be worried. You two are the ones who faked the kidnapping and did all the extorting," Nancy Lou raised her voice for effect.

"This bickering is not doing anyone any good," Sally suggested.

"Mind your own business, you little tramp," Nancy Lou challenged her.

"You were a willing accessory," Sally fired back.

"Prove it. I didn't shoot poor Thomas either. You two owe me thirty-five million," Nancy Lou said. "Fifteen million plus thirty-five million makes fifty million, my promised share."

"We agreed we would ask for a hundred million, and we would split it fifty-fifty," Townsend said evenly, trying to head off a catfight.

"And you were the limp dick who folded and accepted thirty-million," Nancy Lou said.

"I took what I thought we could get," Townsend said. "Your share of thirty million is fifteen less expenses. Get used to it."

"And you are getting the house, cars, and everything else," Sally said.

"And look what you are getting, you little bitch," Nancy Lou said. She stared at Townsend and then at Sally. Nancy Lou surprised both Sally and Townsend by laughing. "Maybe I am the lucky one," she grinned. "Still, you shit," she turned back on Townsend. "You owe me another thirty-five million, and you can start by giving me the account number for the other fifteen."

"You'll play hell getting it," Townsend lost his temper. "We both knew that a hundred million was just an opening bid. I wasn't even sure we would get a cent. We have a firm policy for dealing with terrorists, no negotiations, and no ransom payments. We were lucky to get thirty million."

"That's bullshit!" Nancy Lou shouted. "I'm not the one who shot my ex-fiancée," she glared at Kendrick. "And I'm not the one who faked a kidnapping and extorted money from the president of the United States," she smiled at her husband.

"You are a co-conspirator. It's a simple fact. Stop being greedy," Townsend stood up and started pacing. "There's no way you can spend twenty million dollars in the few miserable years you have left."

"Fourteen million, after expenses," Nancy Lou said.

"Plus another five when you add the house, the cars, the farm, and all the rest of the crap I'm giving you," Townsend stopped pacing and sat down beside his fiancée.

"Please, let's stop this quibbling over money," Sally patted Townsend's knee while staring at Nancy Lou, making it perfectly clear who she thought was being petty.

Nancy Lou laughed, again surprising both Townsend and Sally. "Forgive me, you're right. I should be paying you," she spoke to Sally. "For taking this miserable bastard off my hands."

"Good, you've had your fun, now leave," Townsend, not amused, pointed at the door.

"I'm not going to be the one who leaves," Nancy Lou said as she opened her large shoulder bag and pulled out a weapon that Townsend had never seen before.

Nancy Lou cocked it and pointed it at her husband.

"Don't be foolish," Townsend, more amused than intimidated, spoke softly. He had never seen his wife with a gun in her hands. In fact she had complained bitterly when he had brought a revolver home from the office following his appointment as Secretary of Homeland Security.

Sally tensed but said nothing. She uncrossed her legs, raised one hand to cover her mouth, and stared at the gun. Handguns, per se, did not frighten her. A farm girl, she had grown up with weapons in the house. In fact, she had her own weapon in the top drawer of the small chest that stood next to her bed. A small caliber toy, it was a leftover from her days as a single woman living alone in a foreign city, Paris. Her father had given it to her as a precaution. "You can't go wrong being prepared," he had said.

"What do you think?" Nancy Lou asked her husband as she lowered the gun slightly. "Did I make the right choice. I bought it the day you moved out and our security detail abandoned me."

"It looks like a Glock," Townsend said, trying to distract Nancy Lou with small talk. "Can I see it?"

"You still think I'm stupid," Nancy Lou chuckled. She glanced at the rigid Sally. "He really doesn't like women, you know."

Sally did not respond.

Townsend shifted slightly, moving forward a fraction of an inch.

Nancy raised the barrel of her weapon. "I'm told it's called the Pocket Rocket, a perfect choice for women, small enough to fit into a woman's purse."

"I'm impressed," Townsend said. "Now put it away before it goes off and it hurts someone."

"Wouldn't that be a tragedy?" Nancy Lou smiled. "Let me show you something else."

An alert Townsend and a nervous Sally watched carefully as Nancy Lou reached into her purse. Neither knew what to expect next from the highly agitated woman.

"There's no need for these theatrics, Nancy Lou," Townsend said. "I thought we were all in total agreement," Townsend glanced at Sally trying to reassure her.

Sally did not even notice. She continued to stare as she watched Nancy Lou take out a silencer and screw it on to the barrel of her cocked weapon. Sally recognized the silencer because she had one for her own pistol.

"Christ, be careful," Townsend reacted. "That thing is cocked and could go off."

"If it does, I'm confident it won't disturb the neighbors," Nancy Lou said as she pointed her gun once again at her husband. "They won't hear a thing. It just makes a phishing sound. Want to hear it?"

"Don't provoke her. Give her whatever she wants," Sally spoke softly to her intended.

"That's right, dear. Give me whatever I want," Nancy Lou said.

"And what is that?" Townsend asked. This time he spoke with a slight tremor in his voice.

"My thirty-five million dollars, my promised share," Nancy Lou declared. "Where is it?"

"We've already discussed that," Townsend said, his firm voice tinged with irritation.

Nancy Lou smiled but said nothing.

"They only wired thirty million, and you already have your half."

"I want the rest. What do I have to do to make you understand? This?" She raised her weapon and fired once hitting a picture hanging on the wall behind the sofa.

The painting, Sally's favorite, was a depiction in oil of the family farm done by her mother, an amateur artist of considerable native ability. Sally did not turn. She continued to stare wide-eyed at Nancy Lou.

"Have you been drinking?" Townsend demanded. His wife's intemperate action transformed his irritation into anger.

"I'm cold sober and serious, dear," Nancy Lou said as she aimed directly at her spouse's forehead.

Nancy Lou glanced at Sally. "Please don't let this little family disagreement concern you, dear. Just watch the basketball game and enjoy it; your turn in the saddle will come." Nancy Lou nodded towards the muted television. "Want me to turn up the sound?"

Sally said nothing. She did not even shake her head, positively or negatively, fearing any movement might set off her fiancée's wife who was waving her lethal Glock about like a toy.

"I guess my little Pocket Rocket worries her," Nancy Lou returned her attention to her husband.

Townsend was busy calculating his chances of surviving a leap across the coffee table and a swipe at his wife's gun hand.

"Please don't dear. You are not as young as you used to be," Nancy Lou, who was obviously enjoying the situation, warned. She glanced again at Sally. "I feel sorry for you, dear. If you get a chance, you will learn that men do not age as gracefully as we women. Too many of them die prematurely."

Nancy Lou turned abruptly on her husband. "Where is the account information for my second fourteen million?" Her anger sharpened her tone, replacing the chatty, amused posturing.

"Forget it," Townsend answered quickly.

"I'll bet it is in your briefcase in that little secret compartment," Nancy Lou smiled.

Townsend raised his right hand and ran it through his hair and down the back of his neck.

Nancy Lou laughed. She looked at Sally. "Did you see that? He always does that when I'm right and he doesn't want to admit it."

Nancy Lou raised her Glock and pulled the trigger. The weapon phished, and a small, round spot appeared in the center of Townsend's forehead while bone, hair, tissue, and blood drenched the wall below the smashed oil painting of the Kendrick farm.

Sally, the enigma that Chase privately called the Lady in Black, turned and with an open mouth stared at her fiancé who had fallen back against the couch. Before she could scream, the Glock phished again, and the shot hit her in the temple. Sally fell across the stricken Townsend and her blood cascaded down his chest into his lap.

"I thank you both for your time if not your consideration," a smiling Nancy Lou said as she casually unscrewed the silencer from her Glock, while ignoring the mess on the couch across the coffee table from her.

Nancy Lou put the silencer and the Glock back in her purse and stood up. Always a fastidious and thoughtful person, she took the time to turn off the television before she entered the master bedroom. She admired the bedspread and the matching drapes before checking the walk-in closet. It was filled with her husband's fiancée's clothes. Nancy Lou moved a few hangers and approved of Sally's exquisite taste. Several cocktail dresses with Parisian labels caught her eye. She shook her head with disappointment as she acknowledged they were several sizes too small. She noted a small safe in the corner near the closet door. She tried the handle on the safe, but it did not move. She gave the dial a spin; nothing happened, and Nancy Lou, ever a realist, moved on. Nancy Lou had learned how to handle a gun, but she had not anticipated needing a safe cracker's skills.

Seeing none of her husband's possessions, she checked the jewelry box on the dressing table. Unfortunately, Sally's taste ran to costume jewelry. The cheap stuff did not interest her. She glanced with longing at the closet and its safe and decided she had to find her husband's briefcase that was now rightfully hers.

In the second bedroom, which Sally had decorated as an office, she ignored the desk which she assumed was filled with Sally's detritus. She opened the smaller closet and hit pay dirt. Four wrinkled suits, two dress shirts, and several sports shirts hung on hangers. Two pair of dress shoes and two Air Nikes, Townsend's favorites, stood on the floor next to the briefcase. Nancy Lou grabbed the briefcasecase and retreated to the desk. She shoved a couple of files to one side and opened the briefcase; as usual, it was unlocked. James always ignored the combination lock because he had trouble remembering the combination; for some reason Jame's acute mind had difficulty remember the digits, 1, 4, 3. This errant flaw had always amused Nancy Lou; James had considered her the bubblehead, while he could master whole pages of complicated issues, but could not master a simple 1, 4, 3 combination.

The briefcase was empty except for a cheap paperback with a half-naked girl on the cover and James' checkbook. Nancy Lou picked up the checkbook and studied the balance. She frowned when she saw it was a new account without her name listed. She still used their joint accounts with their automated bill payments. She smiled when she saw the balance, five hundred dollars. That made her wonder if he had yet touched his numbered account in Panama. She had not because James had cautioned that she should not withdraw any money for at least a year.

Nancy Lou tossed the checkbook into the briefcase. She ran her hand along the inside edge of the leather interior until she felt the slight indentation, just as James had taught her. She pressed on the indentation until she found the small button and pushed, twice, paused, and then again. James had laughed when she had had trouble mastering the pause, remembering to count to three before pressing the last time.

The released spring freed the latches that held the bottom of the suitcase in place. It popped up about an eighth of an inch. Nancy Lou grabbed the sides and lifted; the interior tray holding the checkbook easily came out. She set it on the desk and studied the hidden compartment. It held a single sheet of paper. Nancy Lou quickly scanned it and discovered that it contained everything that she needed. It listed two Panama banks, two numbered accounts, and the name and phone number of the responsible executive. The first account carried the identical number that James had claimed held Nancy Lou's fourteen million dollars. However, it listed only thirteen million five hundred dollars. She checked the second account and noted it had a different number and a different sum, fifteen million. The bastard had paid the account expenses out of Nancy Lou's share.

She shrugged off her initial irritation over James' perfidy. What's a million and a half dollars between friends, ex-friends, she asked herself with a smile. She folded the document and carefully placed it below her Glock and silencer in the bottom of her bag. She carefully returned the tray that covered the secret compartment to the briefcase. She pressed on both edges simultaneously, and it clicked once as it locked into place. Nancy Lou glanced at the checkbook, thought about taking it or at least one check, but decided against it. She could wait until probate to recover the five hundred.

Having completed her mission, Nancy Lou retreated to the front door. There, she paused and reviewed her actions. She thought about all the fingerprints she had left at the scene, but following her original scenario, she decided to ignore them. She rationalized she had nothing to explain. She could try to conceal the fact she had been in the apartment by wiping everything that she touched, as the criminals did on television, but had concluded that was too risky. It would be far easier to explain that her separation was amenable to two reasonable adults, and that she had visited her husband to discuss mutual concerns on more than one occasion as he had returned home to retrieve his clothes and other treasured possessions. Certainly, his fingerprints were all over her home, and hers had been placed naturally in his new abode.

Nancy Lou glanced at the intertwined bodies of James and Sally on the couch. Nancy smiled and said softly, "I hope you enjoy your new life, James, wherever it might be."

Neither Nancy Lou nor James believed in the hereafter, God, or all that other ritual nonsense. The James she had known was now dead. She planned, if and when given the opportunity, to have the body cremated. Just the thought of placing his ashes in a nondescript tin can and dumping it in the garbage for the usual collection gave her a warm feeling all through her body. Whoever could do whatever with dear Sally.

Nancy Lou softly closed the door behind her and made her way to her car which she had carefully parked in the nearby plaza lot.

Chapter 30

In Natanz, Obediah Baghai, Mansour's uncle, kissed his wife Lila and reluctantly started for the office, beginning what he feared would be the most difficult and personally threatening day of his life. His wife Lila, knowing what was at stake, put up a stout front. She kissed him at the door, waved when he backed out the drive, and retreated to the bedroom where she hid in the bed and cried herself to sleep.

Obediah parked in his usual space, but he did not go to the guarded mud building housing the elevators that provided access to the secure rooms thirty feet below the scalded desert sand. Instead, he went to the concrete structure that once housed the top-secret secure spaces. Obediah had started his career in that now obsolete structure. Normally, he took the elevator to the cavernous underground complex that now hid Iran's massive centrifuge installation. 896 of the centrifuges were now inoperative, thanks to the subversive invasion by the CIA's destructive virus. Obediah's reluctant efforts kept 32 centrifuges humming, working to produce the fuel for Iran's first nuclear bomb.

Obediah casually inspected the large empty building. The centrifuges and personnel had long ago moved underground. All that remained were crumbling cement walls and debris accumulated by two years of deliberate neglect.

"Har kas, enjas?" He called. (Anyone here?)

No one answered.

"Har Kas, enjas?" He repeated, louder.

Again, no one responded.

Obediah nodded, reassuring himself. He had done his best. He returned to the entrance, carefully closed the door, and hurried across the burning sand to the small structure housing the elevators.

"Stay alert and watch yourselves," Obediah spoke to the two indifferent guards protecting the elevators.

"Sob behar, aqa," the older guard greeted him. (Good Morning, sir.")

Obediah looked at the man who had always treated him with respect. Obediah knew he had a family while the second guard was a rude teenager.

"Pain amadan," Obediah ordered. (Come down.)

The older guard boarded the elevator with him.

Obediah said nothing. When they reached the subterranean passage that led to the underground administrative offices, Obediah led the way past a small waiting room. He pointed at a chair to the right of the corridor door that led to his own office. The older guard obediently sat down, assuming that the senior scientist had a chore for him to perform.

Obediah, one of the first to arrive, carefully shut the door behind him. He sat down behind his desk and dialed the four-digit extension of his superior, the senior administrator who reported to their head offices in the Atomic Energy Commission in Teheran.

"Kojas?" The senior administrator answered the phone on the first ring.

"Koll Hazer," Obediah said and hung up. (All ready.)

Obediah slipped out of his chair, knelt on his knees, bowed his head, closed his eyes, and appealed to Allah. He did not know if he was doing the right thing or not, but he was now committed. "Please Allah," Obediah, whispered, "Do not let anyone be hurt."

Obediah knew that his appeal was fraught with hypocrisy, but he hoped Allah would understand. The situation, concern for his family, particularly his sister's son Mansour, and the misguided administration in Teheran made him do it.

Obadiah's superior pushed four buttons and said two words, "Do it."

On the surface in a bunker located two hundred yards from the deserted cement building, a non-commissioned officer with a shaggy beard turned to a private and ordered, "Hala." (Now).

The private pushed a plunger. The sergeant and the private, who had his fingers crossed behind his back, waited. Three seconds later a tremendous explosion shook the ground. Sand rained down on them, and both men dropped in fear to the earth. All around them concrete rubble cascaded on the desert. The dust forced them to close their eyes and filled their lungs. The private feared that he was going to die.

"Alhamdollilah!" the private shouted. (Praise be to Allah.) The sergeant coughed but said nothing as he waited for his heavenly reward. He hoped the seventy virgins were not a false promise. One could never be sure with the mullahs.

Still seated at his desk, Obediah heard and felt the explosion. His chair shook slightly; a small cloud of dust fell from the ceiling; his phone rattled in its cradle, and Obediah grasped the edge of his desk with trembling fingers. He waited for the ceiling to crumble and the walls to collapse, but they held. He leaned back in his chair and looked upward as he thought about dropping to his knees and giving thanks to Allah for his forgiveness. He had survived. Three of his coworkers rushed into his room; one shouted, "What was that?"

Obediah shook his head, feigning ignorance. "Something above us," he said.

"The elevator?" The physicist, who had enough poise to ask the first question, shouted again.

The coworkers turned as one and raced down the hallway in the direction of the elevator with Obediah running behind them. At the elevator they encountered a mob of pushing and chattering scientists crowding the elevator entrance.

"It's alright, it's alright," a voice from inside the elevator shouted.

"That's easy for you to say," a man standing next to Obediah challenged.

"It's working. Just wait your turn," the man inside called back as the elevator door closed.

"We're trapped," a man in the center of the roiling mass of panicked workers screamed.

"No, we're safe," Obediah spoke with more certainty than he felt. He pointed at the light that indicated the elevator had reached the surface.

Several of those on the fringe of the pushing and shoving mass dropped to their knees, "Alhamdollahlah," they began shouting. (Praise be to Allah.)

Recognizing that the time for panic had passed, Obediah turned and jogged down the now deserted hallway to his superior's office where he found the Natanz chief administrator sitting calmly at his desk. Only the two of them among the agitated mass still underground knew what had happened on the surface.

"It's done," Obediah reported.

"Have you been to the surface?" The administrator asked.

"Naxeir. Qorban," (No, sir), Obediah replied. "But that explosion was so intense nothing can be left standing up there." Obediah stared at the ceiling to emphasize his point.

The supervisor grabbed his phone and dialed his Teheran superior's private number.

"Kojas?" Akbar Mahsuli, the Vice President and Director of the Atomic Energy Organization, answered on the first ring.

"It's done, sir," the administrator reported.

"Are you sure?" Mahsuli demanded.

"Yes sir," the administrator answered.

"Do you have pictures?"

"We have a plane standing by to bring them to Teheran as directed," the administrator said, finessing the question.

"Good," Mahsuli said as he terminated the conversation.

"He asked about the pictures," the administrator looked at Obediah holding him responsible.

"I will check and dispatch them immediately to Teheran," Obediah said as he turned and rushed from the room before his superior could ask another question that he was not prepared to answer.

In Teheran, Mahsuli phoned President Ahmadinejad who was sitting in his office on his elevated throne watching the hands of the wall clock opposite.

"It's done," Mahsuli reported.

"Alhamdolilah," Ahmadinejad reacted. "May Allah punish the CIA devils," he declared and hung up.

Ahmadinejad hit a button on his intercom. "I am ready for the ministers, General Nasiri, and the cursed media heathens," he announced.

He leaned back in his chair and smiled until he remembered he had not asked about the pictures. He frowned and reached for the phone to call Mahsuli, but was interrupted by the opening of the door.

Hushang Soltani, the Minister of Defense, and Naveed Behbehani, the Minister of Intelligence and Security, led the parade. Behind them came General Nasiri, the Chief of VEVAK, and Sadeq Golhak, the press secretary; the chattering media, Iranian and foreign, television and print, followed.

Ahmadinejad stood behind his desk and greeted them with hands locked behind his back and a solemn frown on his face.

Sadeq Golhak, his communications manager, started the proceedings as planned.

"The president has an important announcement for the world," Golhak said.

The foreign media representatives greeted that statement with chuckles and broad smiles.

Golhak ignored them and continued. "The president will take no questions. I give you His Excellency, the President of Iran."

"Thank you," Ahmadinejad nodded at his press secretary. "And I thank you ladies and gentlemen of the media for taking time from your busy schedules to accommodate this office on this day of infamy if I may quote the words of that famous American President Franklyn Delano Roosevelt." He paused and gave his audience time to exchange confused looks. Ahmadinejad knew most in the room did not respect him; some, particularly the foreigners, took particularly pleasure in ridiculing him, calling him names like Ahmadnutjob, but he now had their attention and intended to make the most of it.

"It is my sad duty to inform you that today the perfidious Americans declared war on Iran!" Ahmadinejad paused. Having caught them by surprise, he gave them the opportunity to react with their customary derision.

The Iran media representatives stared at him with wide eyes, but their cameras continued to roll. The foreign media shrugged and exchanged amused smiles. The CNN cameraman lowered his lens, but his correspondent twirled a finger ordering him to keep shooting. Ahmadinejad assumed the correspondent was already drafting a laconic report to accompany the pictures of another Iranian president who had lost contact with reality.

"I can tell from your reactions," Ahmadinejad frowned, "that once again, you, the elite of the media's elite, whose job it is to keep the people of the world informed, do not know what is happening around you."

Again, Ahmadinejad paused, as he watched his audience react to his hard words. This time anger and disbelief were mixed with the amusement on the faces of the foreign reporters. He had actually had the temerity to publicly criticize them. He assumed they were already formulating the phrases they would use to describe the humiliation of his self-crucifixion.

"At exactly eight minutes after nine o'clock this morning, Teheran time, a CIA drone attacked Iran's scientific research center at Natanz with a barrage of missiles that destroyed the installation and killed many of our most respected scientists. This was an unprovoked and despicable attack on the Iranian nation by gangster terrorists deployed by the world's hypocritical super power."

"Can you provide indisputable proof of this astonishing allegation?" The BBC correspondent, who was no friend of Iran, shouted first.

"As noted," Press Secretary Golhak bravely stepped forward. "The president will make a statement and accept no questions."

Ahmadinejad nodded at his aide.

"The world's media will have the opportunity to view the site, interview witnesses, and assess the damage," Ahmadinejad said. "In due course. I have been assured that proof in the form of pictures are being transported to Teheran as we speak. Before the media is given access to the site at Natanz, I insist that objective observers from the United Nations be given an opportunity to inspect the crime scene before others sully it."

"You consider this an act of war?" The CNN correspondent shouted.

"Don't you?" Ahmadinejad challenged.

Suddenly Ahmadinejad's audience erupted with shouted questions.

Ahmadinejad sat down and nodded at his press secretary.

"That concludes the president's statement," Golhak announced.

As planned, presidential security began herding the media towards the door. Ahmadinejad and his core ministers soberly waited until the protesting crowd was shoved out of the room, and the door closed behind them. Ahmadinejad waved a hand, indicating the ministers should take their normal seats. As soon as they all had done so, Ahmadinejad smiled and announced, "I think that went well, don't you?"

They dutifully applauded.

"I have only one more item on today's agenda," Ahmadinejad said as he sat back in his chair and enjoyed the puzzled expression that masked the assembled faces.

"For you, Minister Behbehani," he looked at the Minister of Intelligence and Security.

"Bali, Qorban," Behbehani replied. (Yes, sir.)

"A very simple one which will have drastic consequences," Ahmadinejad said.

"Bali, Qorban," Behbehani repeated.

"Inform your team in Washington to implement Phase Four immediately," Ahmadinejad ordered.

"In America?" Behbehani appeared staggered.

"Yes, that is where Washington was located the last time I checked," Ahmadinejad smiled at the others.

"Implement Phase Four immediately," Behbehani turned on General Nasiri.

"Fouran," Ahmadinejad said. (Immediately.)

"Fouran," A shaken Behbehani repeated.

"That will be all," Ahmadinejad dismissed them.

The ministers stood up and headed for the door. Behbehani paused one last time and stared at Ahmadinejad who dismissed him with a casual wave of the hand.

"He's devanegi," (a lunatic) Behbehani whispered to General Nasiri as they started for the elevator.

"What are you going to do?" Nasiri asked.

"What he ordered," Behbehani answered. "Would you like to debate the issue with him?"

General Nasiri shook his head and followed Behbehani down the hall.

Chapter 31

The morning after his trying evening at his favorite fish restaurant with Jacky, Chase sat at his dining table chewing his burnt bagel and sipping instant coffee. He indifferently scanned the *Post* while his television featuring CNN droned in the background. Chase had trouble focusing because the events of the previous evening continued to trouble him. He had really needed a relaxed evening out with the unpredictable but always entertaining Jacky, and fate had dealt him an undeserved bad hand. He now acknowledged that introducing all his female friends to Captain Crab had been a major mistake despite the quality of the food and how much Chase truly enjoyed it. He had no way of knowing that Barbara and Lyla would join forces and appear together on the very same evening that he and Jacky had decided to indulge themselves. Chase blamed himself for not anticipating what could happen if three strong minded, independent females chanced to congregate, particularly with Chase on the premises.

"We turn now to breaking news," the CNN newsreader's strident intonation caught Chase's attention, interrupting his pathetic musing.

Chase, weary of his abusive self-torment, turned and stared at the television, anticipating a report touting some politician's self-serving announcement. Instead, he saw a starting streamer cross the screen.

"IRANIAN PRESIDENT ACCUSES AMERICANS
OF DECLARING WAR ON IRAN!"

"Today, at a hastily called news conference in his Teheran office," the newsreader announced breathlessly, "President Ahmadinejad of Iran made the following sensational announcement."

A picture of Iran's president appeared. Chase laughed. The little man needed a shave and a haircut. Ahmadinejad started talking in Persian. Subtitles flowed cross the bottom of the television screen.

"It is my sad duty to inform you that today the perfidious Americans declared war on Iran!" The subtitles alleged.

The report abruptly shifted back to the studio after allotting the Iranian president only five seconds of valuable airtime. The transition caught the newsreader by surprise. She looked up and stared at the camera, giving Chase the impression that the attractive young lady was not quite sure what to say next. The headline and one sentence intrigued Chase; he had difficulty believing that his government would launch a sneak attack. Iran was a pesky little country, quite irritating, but still it was a sovereign nation entitled to allege anything it chose. In Chase's uninformed opinion, truth and foreign policy often made incompatible bedfellows.

Although far from being a foreign affairs aficionado—Chase usually focused on the local and domestic news—he did not ignore developments abroad, particularly those in the Near East because of their impact on the oil market which in turn could have a dire influence on the economy. Chase accepted the fact that news reports were frequently inflated, deceptively so, often designed to help the writer, newspaper, network, or newsreader attract the public's attention to themselves. It pleased sponsors and boosted individual egos.

Still, Ahmadinejad's words troubled Chase, particularly when viewed through a prism focused on Jesperson's book and his allegations about a pending Iranian nuclear attack.

The newsreader turned and consulted with someone off camera. After a few seconds, she resumed her breathless report. "The following was filmed by a CNN team in President Ahmadinejad's office."

A picture of Ahmadinejad standing behind his desk appeared on Chase's screen. Ahmadinejad looked directly at the camera and said:

"At exactly eight minutes after nine o'clock this morning, Teheran time, a CIA drone attacked Iran's scientific research center at Natanz with a barrage of missiles that destroyed the installation and killed many of our most respected scientists. This was an unprovoked and despicable attack on the Iranian nation by gangster terrorists deployed by the world's hypocritical super power."

Again, the camera focused on the newsreader. "We will return to our breaking news coverage immediately following the break," she announced.

CNN shifted to a commercial. Chase took a bite of his bagel and washed it down with a sip of coffee. Before he could begin to speculate about what this startling news allegation might mean to his investigation of Jesperson's death, particularly the fact that Iranians kept complicating things for him, Chase's cell phone chimed.

"Mansfield," Chase said.

"Detective, this is the ops center. At exactly 0817 we had a 911 call from an excited female who stated she was a maid who had just reported to work at her employer's home in Reston. She claimed her employer and a male friend were lying on the couch in a huge pool of blood. We immediately deployed a patrol who reported back at 0832. The patrol found a man and a woman on the couch as described by the maid, each with a single bullet hole in the head."

"Why are you calling me?" Chase asked. "Isn't there a duty team on call in CIB?"

"We followed normal procedure and a Detective Moscowitz suggested that we call you. She says the victims are part of one of your ongoing investigations."

Chase sat up straight, now fully alert. "Have you identified the victims?"

"A Sally Kendrick and a James Townsend," the duty officer said. "I understand that the victim recently retired as Secretary of the Department of Homeland Security."

"Were they found in Ms. Kendrick's Lake Anne condominium in Reston?" Chase asked brusquely.

"Yes, sir," the duty officer answered.

"I'm on the way. It's my case," Chase said.

Chase arrived at Kendrick's building exactly thirty-five minutes later. He parked in front of the building leaving the Prius behind three patrol cars that had effectively blocked the street. Chase hurriedly climbed the stairs to Kendrick's top floor condominium, greeted the uniform guarding the door, and entered to find a police sergeant, a second uniform, and Detective Jane Moscowitz chatting in the little hall. He stared at the crumpled bodies of Townsend and his new fiancée, Sally Kendrick, intertwined on the couch that Chase had sat upon during his visit.

"Why do I always have to cover for you, lieutenant?" Moscowitz complained, putting heavy emphasis on the "I." "Don't you ever answer the phone?"

"Probably because that's all that someone thinks you're good for," Chase replied irritably. Normally he ignored Moscowitz's aggressive hostility, but this morning he was in no mood to indulge her feminine complexes.

"You can add these two to your burgeoning list of unsolved murders, lieutenant," Moscowitz declared. "I'm out of here."

"No you aren't, detective," Chase said. "Call and get the crime scene squad here forthwith."

"They're on the way."

"Good, start canvassing the neighbors," Chase ordered.

Moscowitz frowned, and the sergeant and the uniform smiled.

"You two get canvassing," Moscowitz delegated. "I'll take this floor, you do the rest."

Chase turned his back before the bickering started. He noted the television was still playing with the sound muted. It was replaying last night's Wizard game.

"The Wizards lost that one, their sixteenth in a row. So much for rebuilding," the police sergeant was watching Chase from the door.

Chase waved acknowledgement. The subject didn't deserve comment. The sergeant smiled and departed.

Chase approached the couch and studied the couple who had recently surprised him with the announcement of their intention to marry as soon as Townsend managed his divorce. Chase shook his head. No more than a month ago he had spent time with the dead woman. He had met her at the Jesperson funeral, had flown back to Washington with her, and had even considered spending a few nights with her after debriefing her about her ex-fiancé Doctor Thomas Jesperson whose death Chase was still investigating. He had privately called her the Lady in Black because of the outfit she was wearing when he first met her at the funeral. In death she looked considerably older and less fetching, particularly with that hole in her temple and the opposite side of her head missing. Chase carefully studied both victims and concluded that the shooter had either changed weapons or was not the person who had killed Jesperson. That killer had used a silenced .22. Clearly, Townsend and Kendrick had encountered a larger caliber weapon, a .38 or 9mm.

Chase retreated around the coffee table and sat down in the upholstered chair that faced the sofa, assuming it had been occupied by the killer. With the victims still in place, Chase tried to visualize the scene as the killer had viewed it. The tableau was truly ugly. An odd thought struck him as he stared at the victims. Kendrick shared two things at least with her two ex-fiancés; all three had been friends, and all three had been murdered. He wondered if that would complicate things in heaven, if there was such a place. How would they share paradise? Would a threesome be acceptable there? And if a threesome was acceptable, which threesome would it be. Jesperson/Kendrick/Townsend or Townsend/Kendrick/Nancy Lou? Chase smiled at the thought then chastised himself for being frivolous. He now had a three-victim murder investigation to solve and no hot suspects. If the morning news was to be believed, the Iranians had more things on their minds to worry about than these two.

Chase sat on the sofa and quietly contemplated the two victims. While Chase was staring at the grisly sight, a conversation with his own well-meaning father for some reason intruded on Chase's thought process.

"Son," the senior Mansfield had counseled the eighteen-year-old Chase as he prepared to depart for Williamsburg and William and Mary, "I have only one piece of advice. Be careful what you ask for when it comes to women. Young men are always searching for the prettiest girl with a lively personality who treats them like a king; they marry their queen, and they always end life with a grumpy old lady who thinks their pants are shabby, their shirts out of style, and their sense of humor misunderstood."

Chase had not asked his father to explain what his advice meant; instead, in his immaturity he had nodded and concluded his father was well meaning but delusional. Looking at former Secretary Townsend with his new fiancée's blood staining his shirtfront, Chase was not longer sure. Chase wondered if some part of his brain was trying to suggest that Townsend ended up on that couch because he was trying to fight fate, leaving his aging queen for a new princess.

The front door burst open and the eager tech team interrupted Chase's reverie.

"Where do you want us to start, lieutenant?" The team leader asked.

"Right here," Chase said from his chair facing former Secretary Townsend and his fiancée.

The four members of the tech team stopped and waited for the lieutenant to move, but he did not. The team leader shrugged and approached the entwined corpses.

"Christ, this is weird," he declared as he looked over his shoulder at the lieutenant.

Chase did not respond. He was busy reviewing every step he had taken in his futile investigation.

"Do I know this guy?" The team leader asked.

"Former Secretary of DHS," Chase replied.

"The guy who was held hostage by the terrorists?" The team leader asked.

Chase nodded. "Just do your thing and forget the questions," Chase ordered.

"His wife?" The team leader glanced at the Lady in Black.

"No, his fiancée," Chase said.

"Christ, this is a mess," the team leader said as he turned his back on Chase.

The three members of his team exchanged glances and started to check the room.

****

At the White House, President Arthur C. Featherstone sat behind the desk and studied the impassive face of his CIA Director, William H Pace. At the moment, Featherstone was very angry with the man he had appointed with specific instructions, "Get those damned spooks under control. I want only one thing from you, no embarrassments." In his opinion, the Agency created more problems than it solved.

Pace, reading his master well, silently waited for the onslaught to begin. An experienced bureaucrat, he had long ago learned that it was easier to explain why you didn't do something than justify what you did.

"Have you seen the morning news reports?" Featherstone began his attack with his temper under control.

"Yes, sir," Pace answered.

"Did you declare war on Iran as that madman seems to believe?" Featherstone asked.

"No sir. Our satellites confirm that something happened at Natanz, but I assure you we had nothing to do with it," Pace said.

"Can you account for every single one of your drones?" Featherstone asked, his voice even and still under control. Three of Featherstone's predecessors, every single still surviving man who had sat in this very office, had advised him to be careful of the spooks. They were not to be trusted.

To a man Pace's predecessors had been corrupted by the tools of their evil craft.

"Can I believe you?" Featherstone blurted.

"Yes, sir," Pace answered. *On important matters, he thought.*

"Very well," Featherstone said. "I will accept your word." Privately he vowed to double check every word that came out of his CIA director's mouth. "What do the satellites tell you?"

"Something exploded," Pace said.

"What something?"

"It's too soon to tell," Pace said. "Our analysts are comparing the photographs. The initial readings indicate that a concrete structure that originally housed the centrifuges blew up."

"An accident? An Iranian miss-step that the bastards are trying to blame on us?"

"Their reactions seem a little extreme for that, sir. Our initial reading concludes that this is a deliberate provocation, an attempt to justify a future Iranian action."

"Are you referring to that allegation in Jesperson's book?"

"That the Iranians are planning a nuclear attack on us?" Pace waited for the president to react. When he did not, Pace continued, treating his own question as rhetorical. "It's not beyond the realm of possibility that this action is part of the plot that we have previously discussed."

"You are referring to that preposterous operation involving your agent and the alleged Russian suitcase weapon?"

"Yes sir."

"You assured me that was under control."

"It is, sir. Our agent reports that the weapon arrived yesterday and is now hidden in a Fairfax storage depot, but don't worry we have it under complete control."

Featherstone stared at his CIA Director. "You tell me that there is a nuclear weapon hidden in a Fairfax storage depot, and I should not worry because you have it under complete control. Good God, man, the Iranians have just accused us of declaring war with an attack on their nuclear complex, and you tell me not to worry about an Iranian nuclear bomb sitting silently out there in Fairfax."

"The Iranian madman may think he can intimidate us, sir, but I assure you he cannot. The person tasked with triggering the bomb is controlled by us. As of 0800 hours today, we have the bomb under twenty-four hour surveillance."

"What kind of surveillance?" Featherstone stared with disbelief at his chief spook. He assumed that the spooks had assured John Kennedy and Lyndon Johnson that Vietnam problem could be handled with a modest investment of American resources.

"We have a team of our most experienced Directorate of Operations officers stationed in a building across from the storage depot with a direct line of sight to the locker and constant photographic coverage which is forwarded to Langley where we have a relay of officers monitoring the operation."

Featherstone stared at his CIA director. His expression was etched with doubt, but he said nothing. Pace, accustomed to such treatment from this president, patiently waited for the next question.

Featherstone shook his head, turned and looked out his window. In the distance he saw a canoe paddling upriver, presumably heading for the Chain Bridge boathouse. The scene was so peaceful, so orderly, so unlike the unbelievable situation that had been dumped on his desk. The Iranians were accusing him of starting a war; a Russian/Iranian tactical nuke was lodged in a Fairfax storage shed, and his CIA Director was calmly assuring him that the world was under control. Meanwhile, the lathering media had the world staring at the White House waiting for a statement from him. Featherstone had an immediate problem; he didn't know what he could say. Blithely saying that the CIA had assured him that they didn't attack Iran without warning just would not cut it.

The buzz of the intercom interrupted Featherstone's distracted meditation. He turned, fighting the temptation to grab the damned thing and throw it at his waiting chief spook. He glared at Pace and jammed a thick forefinger on the button.

"Yes, Ms. James," the President of the United States growled.

Heather smiled. Whenever the president was in a mood, he addressed her formally as Ms. James. For the best part of the past thirty years, she was Heather.

"Director D'Antonio and Special Agent Cotton are here. They say their little problem is urgent." Heather winked at the FBI director and his senior agent who was nervously pacing back and forth in front of her desk.

"Send them in," Featherstone ordered.

CIA Director Pace rose from his chair, preparing to make his escape. An experienced bureaucrat he could see that this was no time for small talk with this president.

"Sit!" Featherstone ordered.

Pace sat down as the door to the outer office opened. Pace and the president solemnly watched as D'Antonio and Special Agent Cotton stepped between the smiling Secret Service bookends guarding the door.

"Good morning, Mr. President," D'Antonio said.

Featherstone frowned but did not speak. Cotton silently trailed his director who positioned himself in a chair to Pace's right. Since there were only two chairs directly in front of the president's desk, Cotton retreated to the sofa a short distance in the rear. Pace, who was still seated, did not acknowledge the two new arrivals. D'Antonio remained standing, and Cotton wisely followed his example.

Featherstone continued with his silent treatment. He stared at D'Antonio as he tapped the fingers of his right hand on the desk. Cotton assumed that the president was waiting for D'Antonio to explain. The silent D'Antonio appeared to be frozen in place, as intimidated as Cotton had ever seen him.

"I called yesterday evening at a bad time," D'Antonio finally broke the heavy silence. "I apologize, sir, for intruding, but Special Agent Cotton has something urgent to report." D'Antonio turned and glanced at Cotton, acting as if this was the first time Cotton had accompanied him to this office.

Cotton did not react. The president did not glance at him, did not acknowledge D'Antonio's words. He appeared to be waiting for D'Antonio to continue. D'Antonio looked to his left at the seated Pace who ignored his silent appeal for help. Finally, D'Antonio continued with a question.

"Have you talked with AEC or Defense since your return, sir?" D'Antonio asked.

"Just tell me what's so urgent that you have to interrupt my meeting with Director Pace," Featherstone finally spoke.

"As I said, Special Agent Cotton..." D'Antonio began.

"Just get to it," Featherstone interrupted. "And sit down and stop that fidgeting. You're getting on my nerves," Featherstone continued.

D'Antonio and Cotton both sat down.

"Have you heard the news?" Featherstone asked.

"About the attack on Iran?" D'Antonio asked as he looked at Pace who again ignored him.

"The CIA denies they bombed Iran," Featherstone said. "What do you know about it?"

"Nothing, sir, but we can conduct an investigation if you wish,"

D'Antonio smiled thinly at the silent Pace, obviously prepared to enjoy his peer's discomfort.

"Just what I need," Featherstone declared.

Not sure what the president meant by that, D'Antonio waited.

"No, I do not want the Bureau investigating the CIA," Featherstone glowered at his FBI director. "I trust my appointees explicitly," Featherstone said. "Until they disappoint me," the president glared at the silent Pace. "Or lie to me," he turned back on D'Antonio.

Cotton wondered if he could possibly get away with suggesting that it might be best if he waited outside. He quickly decided it would be better if he kept his mouth shut. Maybe they would forget he was present.

"Special Agent Cotton," D'Antonio turned and spoke directly to Cotton. "Please brief the president on the latest developments, particularly as they apply, or may apply, to the current crisis."

Cotton leaped to his feet and tried to collect his thoughts as he waited for the president's permission to report. *You shit,* Cotton thought as he held himself at attention. D'Antonio had thrown him to the wolves, so to speak. Cotton stared at the back of D'Antonio's head and peeked at the president just in time to see him nod irritably in Cotton's direction.

"Sir, the director asked about Defense and AEC because he didn't want to waste your time with a redundant briefing," Cotton said.

D'Antonio turned and nodded his head in approval.

You're still a shit, Cotton thought as he nodded back.

"I returned from New York this morning, and I haven't had a chance to meet with anybody other than those now assembled in this room with their urgent problems," Featherstone said.

"Yes, sir," Cotton said quickly. "As you are aware, we have been tracking an Iranian agent."

"Please don't waste time telling me what I already know," Featherstone interrupted.

"Yes, sir," Cotton said.

"And quit saying 'yes, sir' every time you address me," Featherstone ordered.

"Yes sir," Cotton replied, and then flushed.

Pace smiled.

"The Iranian agent arrived with his cargo yesterday afternoon. He deposited it in a Fairfax storage unit in Fairfax City."

"Do you have the package under surveillance?" Featherstone interrupted, glancing at Pace as he spoke.

Cotton noticed the question seemed to agitate the CIA director who turned to stare at Cotton.

"Yes, but that is only for contingency purposes," Cotton spoke quickly. "Last night a team composed of Bureau technicians and agents, accompanied by Department of Defense and AEC experts, raided the storage company, opened the Iranian's storage locker, and inspected the package."

Ignoring the fact that his comment appeared to agitate the CIA director even more, Cotton concentrated on the president who was smiling for some reason. He waited for the president to explain. He did not, and Cotton continued, "The package contained what the AEC and Defense Department described as a Russian suitcase nuclear device, a tactical nuclear weapon, an old one."

"Where is this device now?" Featherstone demanded.

Cotton hesitated. The president did not seem surprised by the fact that he had just reported the recovery of a Russian tactical atomic bomb from a Fairfax storage locker. Cotton looked at D'Antonio who nodded for him to continue.

"Well?" The impatient Featherstone asked.

"Fort Belvoir, sir" Cotton answered.

President Featherstone broke out into a broad smile. CIA Director Pace pivoted in his chair until he was facing Cotton, glaring at him with a now furious expression on his increasingly red face.

"The experts have disarmed the nuclear weapon. It is now harmless. Meanwhile, the Bureau team assembled a package that to all intents and purposes will pass as the original. We used the green plastic wrapping and canvas bands that covered the original."

"That's very ingenuous, Special Agent Cotton," Featherstone said. In the space of a few seconds his entire demeanor had changed. Now, he appeared relaxed and almost amused.

"We withdrew from the storage site and now have it under constant observation," Cotton continued his now winning report.

"Constant surveillance?" The president asked.

"Yes, sir," Cotton used the two forbidden words.

This time Featherstone reacted with obvious pleasure. Featherstone looked at the CIA director and waited for a comment.

"Where is this surveillance of yours?" Pace demanded of Cotton.

Cotton looked at a smiling D'Antonio who nodded affirmatively.

"We are on the third floor of the building opposite the storage facility with a direct line of sight to the locker."

Featherstone actually laughed at Cotton's response. "You two better coordinate a few things better," he spoke to D'Antonio and Pace.

"When did this big raid of yours allegedly take place?" Pace addressed Cotton.

"We allegedly entered the locker at exactly 1905 hours last night. I was allegedly the first person to approach the package," Cotton spoke sharply with strong emphasis on the "allegedly," his tone making it clear that he was throwing it back into the CIA director's face.

"And your surveillance?" Featherstone surprised Cotton and D'Antonio with his question of Pace.

"Our team was in place by 0800 hours morning, one hour after our asset reported the package's arrival," Pace answered sourly.

"You are surveilling the storage depot at Waples Mill and 29/211?" Cotton demanded.

Pace nodded.

"You are putting our operation in jeopardy," Cotton declared.

"And you are putting our agent and operation in jeopardy," Pace answered. He turned to Featherstone. "I must request, sir, that you order the Bureau to withdraw their personnel immediately. Much more than a simple FBI surveillance is involved."

Featherstone laughed.

"Are you actually trying to describe the seizure of a Russian tactical nuclear weapon on United States soil as a simple FBI surveillance operation?" D'Antonio reacted with considerable heat. D'Antonio turned to the still amused Featherstone, "Mr. President, please."

"Where is your surveillance team, Mr. Director?" Featherstone directed his question at Pace.

"As I told you, sir, we have a team of our most experienced Directorate of Operations officers stationed on the second floor of a building across from the storage depot with a direct line of sight to the locker and constant photographic coverage which is forwarded to Langley where we have a relay of officers double checking the operation," Pace answered as he glared at D'Antonio. "And I should stress that these two gentlemen are not cleared for access to details of our operation."

"Who can authorize them access, Mr. Director?" Featherstone asked, already knowing the answer to the question.

"I can," Pace answered reluctantly.

"And I can also," Featherstone said, making a statement not asking a question.

"Yes, sir," Pace begrudgingly admitted.

"And where is your surveillance located, Special Agent Cotton?" Featherstone turned on Cotton catching him by surprise.

"On the third floor of a building across from the storage depot with a direct line of sight to the locker," Cotton answered.

"May I humbly suggest that someone introduce the two surveillance teams and direct them to coordinate their watchdog activities?" Featherstone said.

D'Antonio and Pace glared at each other. "Yes, sir," they answered in unison.

"Special Agent Cotton," Featherstone looked at Cotton. "Why are you now surveilling the storage container?"

"So that we can track the Iranians when they retrieve their package. We plan to apprehend them when they attempt to place what they think is their bomb, charge them, and bring them to trial as the law requires, sir," Cotton answered.

"Sir, I must request that you order the Bureau to stand down, cease, and desist. We have five years invested in our agent who has a very bright and productive future ahead of her as a penetration of the Iranian nuclear establishment, a potential that we cannot surrender just so the Bureau can garner a few headlines."

"Bullshit!" Cotton was so angry that he forgot where he was.

"This is more Agency nonsense," D'Antonio protested.

Featherstone, who was now enjoying himself completely, smiled. "It is clear that we have a bureaucratic disagreement."

"Sir," D'Antonio lost his Italian temper. "This is more than a bureaucratic disagreement. The Bureau has just foiled an attempt to detonate a nuclear bomb in the nation's capitol, a clear act of war. The law requires that these disgusting criminals be tried and punished and their sponsors clearly identified."

"That sounds reasonable to me," Featherstone said.

"Sir, arbitrary exposure of a critical Agency asset also violates the law," Pace said. "Not only that, the repercussions to Agency operations worldwide would be debilitating. You would be sacrificing the life of a brave young lady who some would consider is betraying her country, but she is no traitor. She is a high minded, principled agent who is cooperating with us in the interest of a higher order, world peace and ..."

"That's still bullshit," Cotton interrupted, now losing his Irish temper. "She's a spy pure and simple."

"But she is our spy," Pace, who seemed to feel he was winning the argument, replied. "You two gentlemen can lose your tempers, but this is one debate you cannot purloin. Our principle agent is our only penetration of the Iranian nuclear program, an agent our government simply cannot afford to lose."

"Enough!" Featherstone ordered. He patted his desk. "As Harry Truman said, the buck stops here. I suggest that the two of you retreat to a secure room someplace in this grand house and work out a compromise. After you reach a reasonable solution, come back; I will hear you out, and I will make my decision."

Not one of the other three agreed with that order, but not one dared table their disagreement with the President of the United States. It would only cost the objector his job and reputation. Unfortunately, or maybe in this case, fortunately, presidents are politicians, and successful politicians are compromisers.

****

Chase moved to the recliner where he followed the television reporting on the alleged American attack on Iran while he watched the crime scene team at work. His mind was not focused on the technicians or the droning CNN newsreaders who kept repeating themselves as they chattered their way through the hour.

"Do you mind, lieutenant, if we take the victims?" the coroner's assistant looked at the still entangled bodies.

Chase nodded approval as he glanced at the Lady in Black one last time. He still could not determine where he had gone wrong. He had investigated every lead, starting with the family, friends, and associates of his first victim, Doctor Jesperson, and it had gotten him nothing, just two more bodies. He was trying to figure out where to turn next, when one of the techs called to him from the bedroom.

"Lieutenant, you better take a look at this."

A relieved Chase pushed out of the recliner. He didn't need to watch the techs untangle the stiffening remains of Secretary Townsend and Sally Kendrick. As Chase approached the bedroom door, he stopped and turned in time to see two techs working on Townsend and Kendrick's bloody embrace. He grimaced as he watched one tech try to twist Kendrick's frozen torso. Chase stared as he wondered what might have happened if President Featherstone had not interrupted his first lunch in the Reston Town Center with the Lady in Black. At the time, Chase had been more interested in the fascinating former fiancée than his investigation.

Chase suppressed a shudder and joined the tech in the bedroom. The bright, flowered orange bedspread with the matching drapes reflected Kendrick's bold personality. The tech stood beside the bed staring into an open chest drawer.

"The bedside weapon, I understand," the tech said. "But the attached silencer catches my attention."

Chase peered into the opened drawer. A .22 caliber revolver with an attached silencer certainly justified the tech's comment.

Chase took out his ballpoint pen and carefully slid it into the trigger guard.

"Be careful lieutenant, that sucker may still be loaded," the tech cautioned. He didn't like it when someone else interfered with his crime scene.

Chase ignored the warning and lifted the little weapon to his nose. He sniffed the barrel and smiled. "This was fired and put away dirty," he observed.

He lifted the weapon above the lamp on the bedside chest top. He carefully studied the cylinder. "If I'm not mistaken, this has been fired twice," Chase said. His smile widened and depression lifted.

Chase carefully lowered the weapon and let it slide from his pen into the drawer.

"Take some pictures and get this weapon to the lab. I want fingerprints to identify the owner and ballistics to compare this baby with the slugs extracted from Doctor Jesperson. Be sure they check the prints with our lady victim," Chase nodded towards the living room.

"Doctor Jesperson, the victim in the GMU shooting?" The tech asked.

Chase nodded. "Unless I'm very mistaken you have found the weapon used in that shooting, and the fingerprints should tell us the identity of the shooter. Tell the lab I want to know what they find yesterday. I stress," Chase said, "I want to know and no one else."

"Yes, sir," the tech said as he watched Chase start for the door.

Chase arrived in the living room in time to see the last stretcher carefully depart through the front door. He did not know who left the room last, Townsend or Kendrick, the shooter or..." Before he finished the thought, his cell phone chimed.

"What?" Chase asked with an unmistakable lilt in his voice.

"Lieutenant Chase," a female voice asked, her self confidence evident.

"Who's this?" Chase asked.

"Lieutenant, this is Heather James, President Featherstone's assistant. "He asks if it would be convenient for you to visit him forthwith?"

"Forthwith?" Chase asked.

"Yes, sir. How soon can you be here?"

"Twenty minutes if I use the siren and lights," Chase said. He assumed that somehow Featherstone had heard of the shooting of his former DHS Secretary.

"Use the siren and lights," Heather said and hung up.

Thirty minutes later a puffing Chase arrived in the reception room outside the Oval Office.

"Sorry, I'm late," Chase smiled.

Heather smiled back and picked up the receiver and poked a button on the box.

"He's here, sir," Heather said.

"Send him in," Featherstone ordered. Featherstone glanced at Vice President Charles Z. Hampton, Secretary of Defense Denver A. Harrison, Secretary of State Harriet Francis Connors and his Chief of Staff Theodore Ted Bertram. "Please give me a few minutes," he dismissed them.

Hampton, Connors, and Harrison exchanged perplexed glances and Ted Bertram stared as he led them out of the Oval Office past a rumpled man not one of them recognized.

As soon as the door closed to the Oval Office, Vice President Hampton asked a question, "Who the hell was that?"

Heather ignored him, and the others shrugged, rendering the vice president's query rhetorical.

"Please have a seat," President Featherstone greeted Chase with a smile. "I apologize for interrupting your busy morning, but I have a few urgent questions that only you can answer."

"I could better answer your questions in a few hours," Chase said.

Featherstone looked up sharply.

"I need to hear from ballistics before I can speak with certainty," Chase said, assuming the president had heard about the shooting of his former Secretary of Homeland Security and wanted to hear the details first hand.

"I suggest, lieutenant, that you let me ask my questions before venturing an answer. I will understand if your responses are incomplete," Featherstone said.

"Yes sir," Chase answered politely while privately he resented being summoned to the White House and treated like one of the president's disciples. Chase did not consider himself one of Featherstone's subordinates and was not inclined to act like one. Common courtesy for Featherstone's position was about as far as Chase was willing to bend.

"Has your investigation developed any information to indicate that the Iranian Government was implicated in any way in the Jesperson murder?"

The question surprised Chase who had expected Featherstone to focus on the Townsend murder. He hesitated because he was not sure what to respond. Chase assumed that the sensational charges in Jesperson's book had caused the Iranian Government considerable heartburn, and the timing of the Townsend kidnapping at the very least appeared to be more than coincidental, but Chase had not uncovered any specific evidence that pointed in Teheran's direction for Jesperson's murder.

"Lieutenant, please don't treat this office like a court of law," Featherstone who was under considerable pressure himself reacted to Chase's silence. "I'm only asking for your opinion, but I have a number of problems on my desk that at first glance appear to be related. Because of my position, my decisions tend to have ramifications far beyond their primary intent. Therefore, when circumstances permit, I try to reach out to many people and acquire as much information as I can before reacting. I definitely am not trying to intrude on your investigation. I know the boundaries of federal and local law enforcement prerogatives, and I am not trying to influence your investigation. I simply am asking you for your help."

The president's candor surprised Chase. "I understand, sir, and I apologize for not responding to your question with alacrity. I expected you to ask about the unfortunate..." Chase almost said murder..."last night's incident involving Secretary Townsend and his fiancée."

That comment obviously surprised Featherstone. He leaned forward and stared at Chase as he asked, "What incident?"

"You haven't heard?" Chase reacted. He knew the double murder had not reached the media, not yet, but had assumed that somehow the president had been alerted and that was why he had been summoned.

Featherstone did not respond, and Chase quickly explained.

"Last evening someone shot and killed Secretary Townsend and his fiancée Ms. Kendrick at her home in Reston," Chase said. "I was at the scene when your secretary called."

"James Townsend? Murdered?" Featherstone reacted. "I didn't know. Who did it? Why?"

"I don't know, sir. The two bodies were found this morning by Ms. Kendrick's maid."

"Jesus Christ! Poor James, his friend murdered, kidnapped by terrorists, and now this. Is there a connection between the Jesperson murder and all this other stuff?" Featherstone asked.

"I don't know, Mr. President," Chase answered honestly. "May I ask what other stuff you are referring to?"

"The Iranian connection," Featherstone answered as he realized the Fairfax Police were not involved in the bomb investigation even though it was happening on their turf. "Do you think the Iranians killed Jesperson and James and why Ms. Kendrick?"

"Again, I must admit I do not know. I can say the same weapon was not used. Doctor Jesperson was shot with a .22 caliber silenced handgun, and Secretary Townsend and Ms. Kendrick were shot with a larger caliber weapon, possibly a 9mm."

"And why Ms. Kendrick?"

"Again I don't know," Chase said. "Do you know how the three were connected?"

"James and Doctor Jesperson were long time friends," Featherstone said. "But I know nothing about Ms. Kendrick."

"Ms. Kendrick was once engaged to Doctor Jesperson," Chase said. "She apparently met Secretary Townsend then. Doctor Jesperson and Kendrick terminated their engagement a year ago when Jesperson took a sabbatical and spent a year in Iran researching his book."

Featherstone stared at Chase as he digested that information. "When did Townsend and Kendrick get together?"

"I can't answer that, not completely," Chase said. "The day Secretary Townsend resigned from the Cabinet, he returned home, collected some clothes, and moved in with Ms. Kendrick."

"I don't know anything that's going on around here," Featherstone complained. He stared at Chase who did not respond and asked, "Was this a surprise to Nancy Lou?" He referred to Townsend's wife.

"Again, I don't know," Chase said. "I have the impression that the separation was mutually acceptable. That is something I will have to explore."

"You think that Nancy Lou shot this Kendrick and James?" The idea seemed to surprise Featherstone.

"I cannot say that, sir. Marital discord has been known to have dire consequences," Chase said.

"Nancy Lou is a formidable woman," Featherstone nodded as he quietly digested the thought. Suddenly he stared at Chase. "Lieutenant don't overlook the damned Iranians in your investigations. Are you handling all three murders?"

"Yes, sir," Chase said, referring to his two investigations but not committing himself on the Iranian comment. Chase waited for the president to ask more questions or to dismiss him.

Featherstone pivoted in his chair and stared out the window. Chase was not sure whether he was expected to leave or remain where he was. Chase was preparing to take the first option when Featherstone abruptly turned to face him.

"Lieutenant," Featherstone said. "There are some things you need to know."

Chase waited for the president to continue, not sure what he was talking about, but Featherstone punched the intercom and asked his secretary, "Heather, are the FBI and CIA still in the building?"

"Yes, sir,"

"Tell them I want them back in here immediately," Featherstone ordered. He looked at Chase and smiled, "Lieutenant, I'm about to make the FBI and the CIA very unhappy."

Despite the uncertainty of the situation, Chase reacted with a smile.

"You will soon learn why I keep asking about Iranians," Featherstone said. "You have a need to know."

"Yes, sir," Chase said. He had enough problems to deal with, but if the Feds knew something about the Iranians that might shed some light on his investigations, he would of course listen with great interest.

"And of course everything you are about to hear is highly classified. I expect one or the other of these two august organizations will insist that you sign a secrecy agreement. Will that trouble you?"

"No sir," Chase said. He rather hoped that news of this briefing would reach Special Agent Cotton and of course infuriate him. Keeping secrets from local police was something that the feds relished.

Suddenly, someone tapped twice on the door to the outer office, and three men entered. Chase recognized CIA Director Pace, who led the somber procession, and FBI Director D'Antonio. Special Agent Cotton brought up the rear, and his appearance delighted Chase, particularly his frown when he spotted Chase in the chair facing the president.

"Sit down, again, gentlemen," Featherstone ordered. "You all know Lieutenant Chase of the Fairfax Police Department."

They all nodded as Pace chose the second chair facing the president's desk and Special Agent Cotton headed for the couch. That left D'Antonio standing. Chase started to surrender his chair, preferring to join Cotton out of the president's direct line of fire, but Featherstone stopped him with five words, "Stay where you are, lieutenant."

A frowning D'Antonio quickly grabbed a nearby chair and pulled it to a position directly in front of the president's desk between those of Chase and Pace. Featherstone waited until his FBI director was seated and then asked, "What have you two decided?" He looked from D'Antonio to Pace.

"Sir," Pace reacted first. He glanced at Chase and then continued. "I must note that Lieutenant Chase does not have the necessary clearances to participate in this discussion."

"Now, he does," Featherstone resolved that issue.

Pace frowned, looked at D'Antonio, who did not react, and then spoke to Chase. "Are you willing to sign the necessary secrecy agreements?"

"He is," Featherstone answered before Chase could answer. "We've already discussed that bureaucratic nonsense."

Pace's expression made clear that he did not like that slap in the face. He swallowed hard and then addressed the president's initial question.

"We've worked out an agreement, sir," Pace said. "I must say that I still believe that..."

"I've already heard your objections, director," Featherstone interrupted. "I don't have the time to waste on reviews."

"The CIA will withdraw its surveillance from the storage unit."

Featherstone looked at Chase and explained. "Lieutenant, the Bureau has tracked an Iranian agent from Niagara Falls to Fairfax City. The agent transported a suitcase containing a Russian tactical nuclear bomb, which was given him by a Canadian contact, to a storage depot in Fairfax City. After the Iranian agent departed the area, the Bureau seized the bomb and replaced it with a duplicate package containing God knows what. The bomb was taken to Fort Belvoir where it was disarmed. Also involved is a CIA controlled agent who was charged with detonating the weapon in our nation's capitol at a yet to be identified location. The CIA learned of the storage site from their agent and placed it under surveillance. Neither of the two organizations saw fit to coordinate with the other, and neither was therefore aware of the other's competing involvement. Our two directors and Special Agent Cotton have just worked out an agreement on how to proceed from this point. I have decided to brief you on this cock-up because both of the Iranian agents are connected with the George Mason University and have been involved in your Jesperson investigation. Hence, I have decided to brief you over certain objections by two bureaucracies who are too stupid to realize how non-cooperation with competing agencies is self-defeating. Now, lieutenant, do you have any questions or views that should be shared at this time?"

Before answering, Chase glanced to his right at CIA Director Pace, was greeted with an angry frown, turned to his left and received the same treatment from FBI Director D'Antonio. He did not bother turning to check on Special Agent Cotton, but he thought he felt a set of eyes burning holes in his back.

"May I ask where this storage depot is located?" Chase asked, stalling while he tried to collect his thoughts.

"The corner of Waples Mill and 29/211," Cotton spoke to the back of Chase's head. "And the surveillance teams are located on the second and third floors of the building diagonally across the intersection."

"Just a few blocks from Doctor Jesperson's apartment," Chase said. "Where two young Iranian men are living, were living."

"Jamshid Afgar and Mansour Taheri," Cotton said.

"Both moved out yesterday," Chase said.

"May I suggest that you two discuss the details elsewhere," Featherstone interrupted. He stared first at D'Antonio and then Pace. "And I hope both of your agencies realize the value of coordination with the local police official conducting two investigations closely related to your respective haphazard operations."

"Two investigations?" Cotton asked, trying to earn credits by taking some of the presidential heat off his director.

Featherstone smiled wryly, a not very friendly response. "A good question, Special Agent Cotton," Featherstone's tone dripped cynicism.

"Lieutenant Chase would you kindly brief our colleagues on last night's developments. Since neither the CIA nor the FBI saw fit to mention them to me this morning, preoccupied as they were with their duplicative and uncoordinated efforts, I can only assume they are unaware of their importance."

Chase took a deep breath and tried to ignore the hostile stares coming at him from three directions.

"Last night, I do not yet have a report from the coroner thus cannot identify the exact time, former Secretary of the Department of Homeland Security James Townsend and his fiancée Ms. Sally Kendrick were murdered in Ms. Kendrick's Reston home," Chase said.

"What?" Special Agent Cotton blurted behind Chase.

Chase did not turn to look at Cotton, and he ignored the FBI and CIA directors on his flanks. He heard D'Antonio take a deep breath, but Chase pretended he did not. He knew the cause; the FBI considered federal officials their responsibility, probably even recently retired ones. Instead, Chase glanced at the president who was smiling thinly as Chase continued.

"A maid discovered the bodies around eight this morning, called 911, and I was summoned. I arrived at the condominium, which I had previously visited, and found the secretary and Ms. Kendrick on the couch, entwined, fully clothed, each with a bullet hole in their heads."

"What was the caliber of the weapon used?" Cotton asked.

"Ballistics is now examining the slugs," Chase answered. "It was probably a 9.mm not a .22."

"A silenced .22 caliber was used in the Jesperson murder," Cotton spoke to his director.

"Gentleman, may I ask that you address details after we adjourn," Featherstone said.

"I should note one thing," Chase said.

"Certainly, lieutenant. I am interested in anything you have to say," Featherstone stressed the "you" as he frowned at his two directors.

Despite his straight face, Chase smiled inwardly as he assumed that he should not consider applying to either the Bureau or the Agency if at sometime in the future he decided to change employers.

"We made an interesting discovery in Ms. Kendrick's apartment," Chase said. He paused briefly for dramatic effect before continuing. "In the top drawer in the table beside Ms. Kendrick's bed, we found a .22 caliber revolver complete with silencer," Chase said.

No one said a word, but Chase heard Cotton behind him shuffle his feet.

"It clearly had been fired recently, twice, and had been put to bed without cleaning," Chase continued. "Ballistics are checking as we speak to determine if it was the weapon that killed Doctor Jesperson."

"I'll be damned," Cotton said. "Need help with the prints?"

"Again, the prints and weapon ownership are being checked. I should know within the hour."

"What do you think, lieutenant?" D'Antonio asked.

"I think that we may have identified Doctor Jesperson's killer."

"Townsend or Kendrick?" Featherstone demanded.

Not one of the other four in the room needed to be told that the president was already calculating how he would deal with the public reaction to Chase's revelation. The murder of the recently kidnapped Secretary of Homeland Security and his paramour would be sensational, but that event coupled with the fact that one of them had previously murdered Doctor Jesperson, the author of the bestselling book linked to the breaking Iranian crisis with its charges of an American act of war, would be world shaking. Even if it did not carry the impact of a level 9 earthquake followed by a tsunami, it would dominate the media for days if not weeks and months.

"If I am correct, we should soon know rather definitively," Chase answered. "Ms. Kendrick, as we discussed earlier, was previously engaged to Doctor Jesperson and was quite disturbed by the fact that he terminated their relationship abruptly before his sabbatical in Iran."

"Gentlemen, I must now terminate this very informative session," Featherstone said. "I have the Secretaries of Defense and State cooling their heels outside," he glanced at the door, "waiting to discuss what we are going to do about the Iranian allegations that are dominating the morning news."

"Do you want me to participate in the meeting?" A shaken CIA Director asked.

"Why don't you wait outside, and I will give you a tingle if we need your input," Featherstone smiled.

As the group started for the door, Featherstone called after them. "Lieutenant Mansfield, I thank you for your contribution. I consider it invaluable and ask that you keep me informed as your investigation develops. I know you, like me, have very much to do right now. Will you be holding a press conference soon?"

"As soon as I hear definitively from ballistics and our fingerprint specialists," Chase said. "We may have one investigation in hand," he referred to the Jesperson shooting, "but that leaves me with another even more sensational one to work on. I assume that the news about Secretary Townsend and Ms. Kendrick is leaking as we speak."

Featherstone shook his head. "You might even push Iran out of the headlines. A cabinet secretary murdered in the arms of his mistress and one of them guilty of murdering a mutual friend, that's God-awful but very attention getting."

Featherstone then looked at his two directors. "And I expect you two, now that you are talking, will work out your mutual little problem without making the discussion about an Iranian attempt to nuke Washington public. I assume responsibility for any public announcements on that one. Keep me informed."

"Christ who would want that job?" Chase asked Cotton as they stepped out in the West Wing hall.

"We've got a lot to discuss, to coordinate, as our lord and master so aptly put it," Cotton said, grasping Chase's arm.

"Later," Chase said as he pulled away with a smile. "I have a few pressing things to do."

Cotton shook his head in dismay as he watched Chase hurry along the hall.

Chapter 32

Chase knew he should report on the latest developments to the chief and Barney—he assumed they were already under media siege—but he had one other obligation first; he had to notify the next of kin for both victims. A major problem for him was the fact that he was acquainted with both victims, and the surviving widow of only one of them. A parallel problem was the fact that he knew nothing about one of the victim's family, Sally Kendrick's, so he was forced to start his misery circuit with Nancy Lou Townsend.

He crossed the Potomac and followed the river towards McLean. He pressed a button on his cell, and Theresa answered.

"CIB."

"Hi, it's me."

Theresa did not respond, but Chase heard her shout. "He's on line one."

"Where in the hell are you?" Barney picked up.

"I'm moving," Chase said, not quite answering the question.

"The chief wants to see you, now. The media have picked up on the Townsend story, and we're all under siege."

Chase smiled but answered as seriously as he could. "I've just left the White House and am on my way to McLean."

"Good for you," Barney said. "The chief wants to know if you remember who's paying your salary."

"I can only deal with one ego at a time," Chase said. "Tell the chief I just got grilled by the president and am now on my way to inform Mrs. Townsend that she has lost a husband. Would you like to relieve me of that burden?"

"Shit, Chase, what should I tell the chief? He, we need something to say before the media eat us alive."

"Tell him I'm simply doing my duty and will see him in an hour."

"What about the media?"

"Stall them," Chase said as he pushed the off button.

Oblivious to the traffic, Chase drove by instinct as he quickly reviewed the Reston shooting scene. It told him just one thing; it did not support a murder/suicide theory; a third person had done the shooting. He speculated on the motives that might have precipitated the murders. He had one victim who had been affianced to two of the other victims. Chase reasoned a disgruntled, discarded Sally may have killed Jesperson, her fleeing first fiancée, but that did not explain who had killed Kendrick and Townsend. One suspect immediately came to mind. Logic suggested that the abandoned Sally Lou Townsend had turned on her husband and her new and younger replacement. Yet, Sally Lou alleged she was more than satisfied with the new arrangement; Chase assumed that could be simple pretense. Chase then asked himself who else had a motive to kill Townsend, a respected civil servant who had climbed to the peak of a successful career, and why now after Townsend 's torturous experience at the hands of terrorists which ended with his resignation. Except for Sally Lou, Chase had no answer. This of course led Chase to consider the Iranians, an option he quickly set to one side. The Iranian involvement puzzled him, particularly now that he knew that the elusive Jalili was a CIA spy. Chase turned to Sally Kendrick, and he asked himself again, why kill her? Engaged first to a prominent academic and then to his best friend, Sally still intrigued him. He understood her motive for killing Jesperson, if she did, but he knew nothing about her business, her personal friends, and other associates. Chase decided to postpone speculation about the killer's motive for killing her in Townsend's arms until he obtained the findings of the ballistic and fingerprint experts. Also perplexing was the fact that all three of his victims had held high security clearances which were granted only after extensive background investigations. If anyone should be clean, the Jesperson, Townsend, and Kendrick threesome should have been; instead they were dead.

"Shit," Chase swore as he turned into the Townsend mansion driveway. These were the most complicated, entangled cases he had ever handled, and his fabled intuitive instincts had apparently abandoned him, leaving him exposed to a raging media army prepared for a rewarding siege.

As he parked his Prius in the deserted driveway near the open garage, Chase asked himself what he had learned this morning. An inner voice told him, Doctor Lyla Jalili is a CIA spy. He slapped the steering wheel. That told him nothing. He would be wasting his time investigating the elusive Lyla. She was CIA's problem. He thought about Afgar who he neither liked nor trusted, and dismissed him. He was the FBI's problem.

Chase slapped the steering wheel, frustrated and angry. The morning's absurd developments had cost him almost all of his suspects. He climbed out, slammed the Prius door, and made his way to the Townsend front porch. Like a preacher, he was left with the chore of delivering bad news to a next of kin.

Chase rapped on the formidable door and waited. Nobody responded. Chase was reaching for the brass knocker to try again when suddenly the door opened.

"Lieutenant, I thought we had seen the last of you," Mary, Mrs. Townsend's secretary, greeted him with a smile.

Chase considered that good news. Mary had showed her independence by confiding that Secretary Townsend had moved on to share his life with a new girl friend.

"Is Mrs. Townsend at home?" Chase asked.

Mary nodded and stepped back, inviting Chase inside.

"How is her mood?" Chase asked.

Mary stared at him. "Same as always," she replied. "Is something wrong?"

"Do you think I could have a few words with her?" Chase answered with a question.

"I don't know," Mary answered honestly.

Chase waited.

"Mrs. Townsend had a late night, slept in, and has just returned from a rather long lunch with friends at the club," Mary said, telling Chase more than she should.

"A late night, out with friends?" Chase asked the obligatory alibi question.

Mary stared at Chase.

"Did she spend the evening at home?" Chase pressed.

"No, I don't think so," Mary answered cautiously. "I heard her call the club and make a reservation for four."

"Do you know who she planned to join?" Chase asked.

"You will have to ask Mrs. Townsend," Mary said as she turned for the stairs. "Please have a chair in the living room, lieutenant, and I will inform Mrs. Townsend that you have called."

Chase shrugged his shoulders and decided that his relationship with

Mary was not as solid as he had thought as he headed for the matching love seats.

A few minutes later, Mary returned and announced, "Mrs. Townsend will join you shortly. Would you like something to drink, a coffee or something stronger?"

"Coffee, black, will do just fine," Chase smiled.

Mary again disappeared. Ten minutes later a maid who Chase had never met silently served him coffee and disappeared. Chase waited. More time passed, and Chase checked his watch. He knew that he had Barney pacing the floor and the chief growing impatient with every passing minute. The media were obviously a very real problem, and Chase realized he was pressing his luck. Finally, he grabbed the delicate porcelain cup, drank half the now luke-warm coffee in one gulp, and stood up. He had given as much time as he had to spare to this mission of mercy. He started for the door and was surprised when Nancy Lou Townsend materialized in front of him. She had obviously taken the time to adjust her makeup and put on fetching clothes. For her age, fifty plus, she struck Chase as having held up to recent life-altering stress quite well.

"Good afternoon, lieutenant," Nancy Lou greeted him with a broad smile.

Chase decided she had not heard the news about her soon to be ex-husband.

Nancy Lou leaned into Chase pressing firm breasts, at least a pointed brassiere, against him and turned her cheek to be kissed.

Chase brushed his cheek against hers and stepped back.

"Good afternoon, Mrs. Townsend," Chase said. "I thank you for receiving me without an appointment."

"You are always welcome, Chase, and please call me Nancy Lou. Mrs. Townsend sounds too formal and quite inappropriate, as you well know."

Nancy Lou waved at the love seat where Chase had been fidgeting and sat down opposite. Chase, not sure if he was the bearer of good news or bad, didn't know how to begin. Nancy Lou appeared to be enjoying her newly regained single status. Certainly, she was working hard to project that image. Ignoring Chase's solemn demeanor, Nancy Lou started chattering.

"You almost caught me in an embarrassing position," Nancy Lou smiled. "Stark naked and heading for the bed in the middle of the day."

Chase flashed the obligatory smile.

"I've been a really bad girl, the past few days," Nancy Lou continued. "Late nights, randy male companions, and not moving from my bed until time to put on some makeup and rush off for lunch with the girls to discuss everything."

"I'm very sorry...." Chase cut to the chase, so to speak. At least he tried.

"And today, I must admit, I indulged my secret weakness," Nancy Lou chirped. "A whole bottle of wine, all by myself, a real good vintage, the wine, not me," Nancy Lou smiled.

"I have some very bad news," Chase tried again.

"One of your many girl friends discharged you," Nancy Lou laughed. "You shouldn't worry, not an attractive man like yourself. I am sure you have to fight the hussies off. If you need any assistance, Chase, don't hesitate to ask. I could be all yours," Nancy Lou winked. "Me and all this," she waved a hand with forefinger extended.

"Last night someone attacked Secretary Townsend and...and Ms. Kendrick," Chase said.

"I hope James was not badly inconvenienced," Nancy Lou shrugged.

Chase noted that she had not included her husband's fiancée in her mild expression of concern.

"Not that I don't think the both of them have earned whatever the future holds in store for them," Nancy Lou continued.

"Excuse me for speaking bluntly, Mrs. Townsend, but both the secretary and Ms. Kendrick succumbed."

"Succumbed?" Nancy Lou stared, the remnants of her smile still frozen on her face.

"Someone shot them, and they both died instantly. They did not suffer."

"Such a tragedy. The lovebirds never got a chance to share marital bliss," Nancy Lou said as bent her head from side to side in an apparent effort to relieve a minor twitch in her neck. "Who did it? A mugger? Sally's little condominium is unfortunately located in that Reston. You know the developer deliberately brought in rafts of poor in a misguided effort to create the illusion of a real city. I worried about James living in such an area."

Nancy Lou's reaction to the news of her husband's death surprised Chase. He had expected her to at least pretend she was affected by the demise of a man with whom she had shared life for twenty plus years.

"I guess I will have to call the boys," Nancy Lou said. She spoke without emotion sounding very much like a mother saying I must remember to call the kids and wish them happy birthday.

"One in Texas and one in California, both married and quite successful," Nancy Lou explained. "I'm quite proud of them. They were not very close to their father, you know. He was more interested in his career than his family."

"They were killed in the living room of the Reston condominium," Chase tried to explain. "There was no sign of robbery. I just left the scene."

"I guess they will want to attend the funeral," Nancy Lou said. "I would prefer a quite family ceremony, but I am sure the president will want to hold some kind of grand event, a tearful photo opportunity. Politicians never miss a chance to impress the voters. Do you think there is a connection with the Jesperson thing?" Nancy Lou abruptly changed directions.

"It's too soon to tell," Chase said. "I will work both investigations, however."

"Poor Thomas," Nancy Lou said with an odd expression on her face. She dumped artificial sympathy on Doctor Jesperson, not her husband or Sally Kendrick.

Chase could not tell if she were feigning sadness or just making small talk to fill in the lapses in their disjointed dialogue.

"I imagine the media will besiege me like they did during that other thing," Nancy Lou referred to Secretary Townsend's kidnapping. "I'll tell you one thing; I certainly will not let that FBI move into this house again and disrupt my life." Nancy Lou paused, giving Chase a chance to comment.

He wasn't sure what to say and discreetly said nothing.

Nancy Lou appeared disappointed in his reaction but did not let it inhibit her. "Do you think you could do one little thing for poor me?" Nancy Lou asked. "I assume I will have to play the part of the betrayed but grieving widow. The media will go just crazy. Imagine what they and my friends will say when they hear my husband died in another woman's bed."

"Not quite in bed, on the sofa," Chase said. "This will be a very difficult time for you, Mrs. Townsend." Chase wondered what little thing Nancy Lou wanted from him and how he would gracefully decline. He was not about to stand before the coffin with Nancy Lou and hold her elbow while she cried her crocodile tears.

"Is there any way you might be able to arrange for some security to hold the media at bay?" Nancy Lou made her very practical request.

"I'm sure we will be able to make some uniformed officers available if the DHS doesn't," a relieved Chase said.

"And you? Can I count on you? On the television the investigating detectives always observe the funeral. They say the killers attend to gloat over their handiwork."

"I certainly will attend the funeral, but do not worry about me causing a distraction," Chase said. "I'll try to meld into the background." Chase recalled the Jesperson funeral and Sally Kendrick's appearance in her sleek black pants suit.

"That's not quite what I had in mind," Nancy Lou smiled.

Before Chase could frame a suitable reply, the knocker on the front door rattled loudly. Chase waited for Nancy Lou to react, but she ignored the distraction. In the distance, Chase heard the click of high heels.

"Oh don't worry," Nancy Lou read his expression. "Mary will handle it."

"Good," Chase said. "It won't be long before the media learns of the shooting."

"A cabinet member, even a resigned one, dying in the arms of his lover, will attract the vermin," Nancy Lou said. "And as we discussed, the poor widow, that's me," she smiled, "will suffer the consequences."

Chase nodded. He considered the poor widow in this instance a black widow, the kind that eat the remains of their prey.

The front door opened and a bevy of voices demanded to speak with Mrs. Townsend.

"See, it's already beginning," Nancy Lou spoke evenly to Chase.

"Tell them I'm in New Hampshire," Nancy Lou called to Mary.

"I'm very sorry, but Mrs. Townsend is in New Hampshire," Mary repeated to the visitors and slammed the door in their faces.

Mary slid the deadbolt in place and joined Chase and Nancy Lou in the living room.

"I'm afraid it's the pests again," Mary said. "Two more satellite trucks arrived while we were talking."

"It's starting all over again, Mary," Nancy Lou announced. "Chase just told me that someone killed Secretary Townsend and his fiancée last night in her little Reston apartment."

Mary reacted with shocked surprise. At least Chase assumed that was what the drawn expression on her face indicated. Mary raised one hand to her mouth and gnawed briefly on a knuckle. She looked like she was about to break out into tears.

"Now don't go all emotional on me, Mary," Nancy Lou chided. "I'm going to need you strong now, more than ever."

Mary looked at Chase. A few tears coursed down her cheeks, and she rushed from the room. As soon as they heard her high heels clacking down the hall, Nancy Lou looked at Chase and grinned.

"I must confide," she said. "I always suspected that James and Mary had a little fling going."

Chase stared at the tough widow and suddenly remembered another caution, one that his grandfather had issued to him when Chase was a naive sixteen year old. "You young men are all the same. You live to pursue the girls looking for the biggest breasts, trimmest waists, and shapeliest legs to go with admiring personalities. My advice to you, young man, is be careful and beware. Those pretty young girls who hang on your every word and pretend to think you are going to conquer the world, eventually grow into round lumps, sour old ladies with white hair who think they have been placed on this earth to tell you how to dress, talk, and eat. In short, they become your masters and mothers, not your admiring cheerleaders."

Chase had obediently nodded his head and immediately dismissed the old man's advice. As he aged he had gradually recognized the wisdom behind his grandfather's warning and in fact was now prepared to add a caveat of his own. Those precious teen-aged girls did not wait until old age to change. By their forties, they had entered a mid-life crisis of their own. That's when their beauty had begun to fade, only to be replaced with a toughness, a sense of life's unfairness, and that is when they turned on their once heroes who suddenly, in their minds, could do no right. Chase feared that those ladies fighting their inevitable transformation were the most dangerous, still enticing but self-centered like Nancy Lou.

"Mrs. Townsend," Chase said as he stood up. "I must continue with my investigation. "If you are lucky, that mob will soon abandon you and turn their focus on the White House and my headquarters."

"Lieutenant," Nancy Lou said. "Don't let me detain you, but I would appreciate your help with some security."

"Of course," Chase promised, noticing his change of status from Chase to lieutenant. "May I ask one question?"

Nancy Lou stared at Chase but did not reply.

"I'm required by regulations to ask it," Chase tried to sound as apologetic as he could.

"Where was I last night?" Nancy Lou smiled thinly.

Chase nodded.

"Correct me if I am wrong. The question has already been asked and answered," Nancy Lou said coldly with no sign of the forced smile.

"Mary said that you were out last night at the club with four friends," Chase admitted.

"So Mary reported," Nancy Lou said coldly.

How quickly they change, Chase thought.

"Goodbye, lieutenant," Nancy Lou said. "Please do not forget the security. I can appeal to the president if the burden is too great for you to handle."

"Would you mind giving me your friends' names?" Chase persisted, ignoring the implicit threat of political pressure.

"Yes I do mind. I do not wish to embarrass my friends," Nancy Lou said. "However it may inconvenience you."

"I really insist," Chase pressed.

"Then insist at the club not here where you are no longer welcome," Nancy Lou said.

"What club?"

"I'm not going to do your work for you, lieutenant," Townsend dismissed him.

"Do you mind if I go out through the garage?" Chase asked.

Townsend shrugged and turned her back on Chase.

As he started down the hall, Chase smiled. That interview turned out a little like his grandfather's version of the female life cycle. It had started with a kiss and ended with rebuke.

As he passed the Townsend home office, Chase saw Mary busy at her desk.

She looked up and asked, "How is she holding up?"

"Better than most," Chase replied. "What club did she go to last night?"

Mary stared at him. "I told her you were asking," Mary admitted.

"I know," Chase waited for her to respond to his question.

Mary took a deep breath and studied Chase. "The Congressional," she finally admitted in a low voice. "I'll have to tell her you insisted, and I told you."

"I would if I were you. You can also tell her that you were doing her a favor," Chase said. "I have permission to go out through the garage in order to avoid the media."

Mary shrugged and turned back to her keyboard.

Chase continued down the hall, turned right, opened the garage door, and found himself facing three cars. He wondered which of the three Nancy Lou drove as her own, but he did not return to the house to ask. They all belonged to the lady of the house now, and she could drive whichever one she chose.

At the open garage door, Chase peeked out. Three satellite trucks were parked a short distance away with antennae turning, and a small cluster of drivers and technicians stood nearby. Other cars lined the curbs, disturbing the ambiance of the exclusive McLean suburb, and a gaggle of at least ten reporters of mixed species were gathered near the porch. Chase moved quickly from the sanctity of the garage for his Prius which he had without forethought but fortuitously parked in a tactical position facilitating a quick exit. He was not spotted until he reached the driver's door.

"Hey," a male reporter shouted.

Chase climbed inside, heard a familiar female voice call, "Lieutenant Mansfield," ignored her, pushed the starter button, and backed on to the manicured lawn. One thing about the keyless Prius, it supported a quick getaway. Chase was racing down the paved driveway before any of the reporters had gotten halfway to him. He glanced in the mirror and smiled when he saw the gaggle give up the chase, or Chase, so to speak.

Five minutes later he was headed down 123 when he ignored the law and punched a button on his cell phone.

"CIB," Theresa answered promptly.

"I'll be there in thirty minutes," Chase said.

"It's him. He's on the way," Chase heard Theresa call to Barney.

"Tell him to come in the back way," Barney called.

"He said..." Theresa started to repeat the message.

"I heard," Chase interrupted and punched off.

Exactly thirty-three minutes later Chase entered the CIB reception room to find Theresa and Barney chatting.

"Where have you been?" Theresa greeted him. "You've got a thousand messages."

"I only want to hear from ballistics and prints," Chase said. "You handle the rest."

"Detective Moscowitz has been talking with them," Theresa stood up.

A smiling but silent Barney turned towards his CIB commander's office and waved one finger at Chase. Chase followed and closed the door behind him. Barney sat down in his chair behind the desk, and Chase dropped wearily onto the couch, a part of Barney's conversational corner.

"I've been busy," Chase said.

"Glad to hear it," Barney said. "The chief just left, mad as hell."

"I guess we'll have to brief him," Chase sighed.

"That's one of life's burdens," Barney chuckled. "I covered for you. I told him I didn't know where the hell you were."

"Thanks," Chase said. "It's always reassuring to have you covering my backside."

"Give me a hint," Barney smiled, obviously pleased to have Chase in the firing line. "Tell me where things stand before we make the chief's day."

"I got the call at 0900..." Chase said before the outer door opened and Detective Moscowitz stormed into the room.

Theresa appeared behind her and took up position in the open doorway.

"Where in the hell have you been?" Moscowitz demanded of Chase. "I've had it with doing his scat shit," Moscowitz spoke to Barney.

"What scat shit?" Barney asked, not at all concerned with Moscowitz's complaints.

"What's a scat?" Chase asked.

Theresa laughed. Moscowitz ignored them all. She tossed Chase two sheets of paper at Chase, which he caught with difficulty. Chase scanned them and smiled. He passed them to Barney, and he smiled.

"What now?" Barney asked.

"I don't think we will need handcuffs for the shooter," Chase said.

"Let's go," Barney said, standing up and heading for the door.

Chase followed.

"What the hell's going on?" Theresa demanded.

Moscowitz ignored her and petulantly followed Barney and Chase to the elevator.

"Mind if I join you?" Moscowitz asked.

"Yes," Chase answered first.

"No," Barney answered, and Moscowitz joined them the elevator, daring Chase to challenge her.

Chase ignored her.

Chief Raymond Arthur's secretary looked up from her monitor when they entered. She glanced at Major Barney Hopkins, winked at Chase, and ignored Moscowitz. "It's about time," she declared and poked at her intercom. "They're here," she announced.

"Frisk them and send them in," Chief Arthur's booming voice ordered.

The secretary inclined her head towards the closed door, and Barney tapped once before entering. Chief Arthur looked up from the memo he was pretending to study, glanced at the two empty chairs facing his desk, and nodded. Chase and Barney with ungentlemanly élan preempted the chairs, leaving Moscowitz the option of standing or taking a seat along the far wall. She chose the wall.

Wasting no time, Chief Arthur tossed the memo to his desk and glared at Chase.

"What the hell's going on?" Arthur demanded.

"One murder down, and two on the board," Chase answered with a smile as he waved the two reports.

Chief Arthur waited.

"Ballistics reports that the weapon that killed Doctor Jesperson was fired from the gun we found in the Kendrick apartment," Chase said.

"And?" Chief Arthur leaned back in his chair and waited for Chase to continue. He knew from past experience there would be more to come. This kind of performance is why he tolerated Chase's idiosyncratic behavior.

Chase leaned forward and slid a report across the chief's desk. Arthur ignored it.

"And the only prints on the gun belong to Doctor Jesperson's former fiancée, Ms. Sally Kendrick, one of our new victims."

"I guess the road of true academic love was filled with potholes," Arthur smiled.

"Look at the bright side," Chase said. "Her murder has saved the county the cost of an expensive trial."

"Certainly the accused is in no condition to understand the charges against her," Arthur said. "Will you be holding a news conference?"

Chase shrugged.

"Do you want me to handle it?" Chief Arthur asked.

"That would be best, chief," Chase said as he slid the fingerprint report across the chief's desk.

"And what do I say about the ongoing investigation?" Arthur asked.

"There's always good news and bad news," Chase answered.

Behind him, Moscowitz shifted angrily in her wall chair.

"Do you have something to contribute, detective?" Chief Arthur stared at her.

"No sir," Moscowitz answered politely. "I'm just here to learn."

"Then listen and quit hopping up and down in that damned chair," Chief Arthur ordered.

Chase turned and smiled at Moscowitz who pretended to ignore him. Chase could tell that she was really pissed, and that amused him more than the chief's positive reaction.

"And the bad news, lieutenant?" Arthur returned his focus to Chase.

"I'm afraid the media will make much of the fact that former Secretary Townsend, who was recently a kidnap victim, left his wife and was currently living with Ms. Kendrick who was once his friend Doctor Jesperson's fiancée," Chase smiled.

Chief Arthur frowned.

"Of course," Chase continued, "Doctor Jesperson is in no position to complain about the intrusion."

"But Secretary Townsend's wife might," Chief Arthur said.

"That might be a problem," Chase said. "At first I thought Mrs. Townsend was comfortable with the arrangement, but after my most recent visit to McLean to inform the next of kin of her husband's most untimely death in the arms of his mistress, I'm not so sure."

"Do you think she offed her husband and his fiancée?" Arthur demanded.

"Mrs. Townsend is a strong minded woman," Chase finessed the chief's question. In Chase's opinion, Chief Arthur, compared to President Featherstone, was a pussycat.

"The Feds still don't know who kidnapped Secretary Townsend or who they paid thirty million dollars to secure his release," Major Barney Hopkins decided the time was propitious for him to join the discussion.

Chief Arthur glared at Barney, not appreciating his contribution. Headquarters staff should know when to keep their mouths shut.

"Somebody is certainly thirty million dollars richer," Chase said in an effort to rescue his friend.

Arthur looked back at Chase, waiting for him to continue.

"And there is always that little matter of the Iranians planting a tactical nuke in downtown Fairfax City," Chase said.

"What?" Chief Arthur, Major Barney Hopkins, and Detective Moscowitz reacted simultaneously to that absurd statement.

"Oh, I apologize," Chase said, not meaning it. "I'm afraid I haven't had time to report the details of an ongoing federal investigation."

"What are you talking about, lieutenant?" Chief Arthur reverted to his original impatient mode.

"My investigation this morning was interrupted by a command summons to the White House," Chase said.

"The White House? Again?" Arthur stared at his sometime protégé.

"Yes," Chase said. "President Featherstone is one of those dreadful hands on managers. He likes to get the full story from field operators."

An intense Chief Arthur waited. Chase speculated that if Chief Arthur were a steam engine, his safety valves would be screaming.

"He wanted to know how my Jesperson investigation was progressing," Chase said. "But I really caught his attention when I mentioned the murder of his former Secretary of the Department of Homeland Security in the arms of his fiancée. That was news to him."

Arthur disappointed Chase by not popping a valve at that point, so he continued.

"I explained the situation and described the interrelationships of the case," Chase said. "And the president was so satisfied that he asked me to sit in on a meeting with the directors of the FBI and CIA who were waiting in the outer office. Special Agent Cotton was also present, and he reacted with high indignation when he learned that the president had asked me to join them."

"I can imagine how he felt," Chief Arthur said.

"Me too," Barney, who did not like the arrogant Cotton, grinned broadly.

Arthur glanced at Barney and then ignored him. He looked back at Chase who continued.

"It was then that I learned about separate CIA and FBI operations targeting alleged Iranian operatives in Fairfax County," Chase said.

Chase paused to give Arthur a chance to admit he had coordinated the federal intrusions without sharing that knowledge with his staff, including CIB.

Arthur did not react, silently admitting that it was all news to him too. Moscowitz, shocked at what she was hearing for the first time, stared at Chase's back with growing respect.

"Stop me if I start repeating something you already know, chief," Chase deliberately rubbed a little salt into the chief's festering bureaucratic wound.

Arthur ignored the unkind gesture. He recognized that Chase was only getting even for some of his callous comments.

"At the president's urging, the Bureau and the Agency confided that the former has been tracking an Iranian graduate student at George Mason University who recently met with a Canadian based cohort who gave him a Russian tactical nuclear suitcase bomb. He transported the bomb to Fairfax County in a car owned by the deceased Doctor Jesperson."

Chase stopped his report, deliberately letting the interest of his audience intensify. His announcement that terrorists had stored an armed nuclear tactical weapon nearby was a real attention grabber. The chief glared in his direction, and Chase wisely continued.

"The Iranian boy, who incidentally was one of my suspects in the Jesperson investigation, deposited it in a storage facility located on the corner of Waples Mill and Routes 29/211."

"You're kidding me," Barney blurted.

"Is it still there?" A concerned Chief Arthur demanded.

Moscowitz, who sat wide-eyed behind Chase, said nothing, too amazed at his performance to ask the Iranian's identity.

"The Bureau last night seized the bomb and moved it to Fort Belvoir where Department of Defense and Atomic Energy technicians defused it," Chase said. "So, chief, there is nothing for us to worry about there."

"The Bureau did all of this without coordinating with us?" Chief Arthur's voice hit a record high note.

"I'm afraid so, sir," Chase said. "And the Bureau created a package that resembles the original and put it back in the storage depot where they have it under surveillance as we speak."

"And we are supposed to ignore that?" Arthur growled as he reached for the phone.

"There's more, sir," Chase said.

Arthur waited with his hand on the phone. None of the other three knew who Arthur intended to call, but Chase tried to dissuade him by telling the rest of his story.

"The CIA is also involved," Chase said quickly.

"The Central God-damned Intelligence Agency?" Arthur shouted.

"Yes, sir" Chase said. "You may find this part of the report amusing."

Arthur took a deep breath; he flushed red, but he did not speak. His reaction tended to undermine Chase's assumption.

"It seems that the CIA and the FBI were tracking this Iranian operation, separately, independently, without telling each other. The president was really pissed when he learned that each had surveillance at the storage depot in the same building, the FBI on the second floor and the CIA on the third, and both were taking pictures of the locker but did not know that the other was present."

Barney chuckled, Moscowitz laughed, and Arthur smiled as they each pictured the irate President Featherstone as they waited for Chase to continue.

"It seems that the Iranian agent's cohort is a CIA agent," Chase said, now truly enjoying his audience's rapt focus on his every word. "The CIA insists that this agent is well placed with the potential to become their primary penetration of the Iranian nuclear bomb program and must be protected."

Moscowitz again laughed, this time louder. "I assume you know the identity of these two Iranian agents, lieutenant," she said.

"A very astute assumption, detective," Chase answered. "I doubt I have authority to identify them. They forced me to sign a secrecy agreement."

"And what happens now?" Chief Arthur rescued Chase for the moment.

"The FBI and the CIA have the package of bricks under joint observation at the storage facility and are trying to devise a plan that lets them apprehend one Iranian agent without compromising the CIA asset," Chase said.

"Lots of luck," Barney said.

"And who are these agents living and operating in Fairfax County?" Chief Arthur demanded.

"Jamshid Afgar, an Iranian national, a GMU graduate student, who has been residing in Fairfax County for the past ten years, and Doctor Lyla Jalili, an Iranian national who last year earned her degree in nuclear physics from the University of Paris. She is currently an instructor on the GMU faculty." Chase's abrupt, frank answer surprised the other three, particularly Chief Arthur.

"Which one is the CIA agent?" Arthur asked softly.

"Doctor Lyla Jalili," Chase answered equally softly.

"Jesus H. Christ," Moscowitz blurted. "I've interviewed both of them."

"Really?" Arthur turned his attention to her.

"But Lieutenant Mansfield knows both far more intimately than I do, particularly Jalili," Moscowitz grinned at the back of Chase's head as she gave particular stress to the "intimately."

Arthur frowned at Chase.

"I've interviewed both Afgar and Jalili quite extensively," Chase ignored Moscowitz's comment. "Both ranked quite high on my lists of suspects in the Jesperson investigation."

"How well did you know these suspects, lieutenant," Arthur asked, clearly picking up on Moscowitz hardly veiled accusation.

"I debriefed Afgar several times at length," Chase said. "I found him particularly interesting because he moved into Doctor Jesperson's apartment as Mansour Taheri's roommate."

"Who the hell is Mansour Taheri?" Arthur demanded.

"A distant relative of Doctor Jesperson's mother," Chase answered.

"And what was your relationship with this Doctor Jalili?" Arthur asked.

"I questioned Doctor Jalili two or three times, including once at her apartment where we had a delicious lamb kabob and Persian rice dinner," Chase smiled. "I think she called it chellokebab or something like that. It's served with raw egg yolks and goat butter."

"Sounds awful," Chief Arthur shuddered.

"Obviously neither is now on my list of suspects for the Jesperson murder," Chase continued. "But I was glad to hear that the FBI had zeroed in on Afgar. I didn't like him and even discussed him with Special Agent Cotton."

"Are you taking credit for putting the Bureau on his case?" Arthur asked.

Chase shrugged, and Arthur knew better than to press for fear he might hear more than he wanted to know.

"Do you have anything else?" Arthur asked.

"No sir. I think we've hit the high spots," Chase smiled.

"Not quite. You succeeded in distracting me, lieutenant," the chief smiled back.

When the chief used that particular smile, Chase knew from past experience that now was the time to prepare to duck.

"This Iranian business is all very interesting, lieutenant," the chief said, "But please tell me where exactly you stand on the Townsend/Kendrick murders?"

"Early days, chief," Chase said, offering his most sincere expression.

Arthur frowned. He stared at Chase, obviously thinking about asking more questions, but to Chase's relief he did not.

"Keep me informed, better informed, on this FBI/CIA thing and your new investigation," Arthur ordered.

"Yes, sir," Chase answered. "And I must stress that the subjects we discussed here today are highly sensitive with some covered by the National Secrets Act."

Chase turned and stared directly at Moscowitz who surprised Chase by responding with a noncommittal wink.

As Chase rose from his chair determined to make his escape, Chief Arthur caught him with another command suggestion. "These investigations are so complicated, lieutenant, I recommend that you discuss how you are going to handle your press conference with Sally." The chief referred to Sally Patrone, the department's director of public affairs.

The chief's comment surprised Chase because it indicated that he had changed his mind about managing the media himself, but Chase replied with a simple, "Yes, sir, good idea."

As Chase and Hoppy were walking down the hall toward the elevator, Hoppy turned to Chase and said, "Christ, you're something else."

"Sometimes these cases develop a momentum of their own and take an interesting turn," Chase smiled at Hoppy.

"And sometimes you are going to have to tell us all about that interesting dinner you had with Doctor Jalili," Moscowitz said with sarcastic sneer.

"How did it go?" Theresa greeted Chase, Barney, and Moscowitz when they appeared at her office door.

Barney gave her a raised thumb as Chase smiled and continued on to his office.

"Special Agent Cotton has called three times in the past ten minutes," Theresa called after Chase.

"Put him through the next time he calls," Chase answered as he closed his closet office door behind him.

Barney retreated into his office, and Moscowitz found herself standing alone facing the curious Theresa.

"Was the chief really angry?" Theresa asked.

"The bastard," she referred to Chase using her favorite epithet for him, "lucked out again," Moscowitz declared as she pivoted and headed back to the detective squad room. "Only Mansfield could stumble over a murder weapon with the shooter's prints at the scene of another crime," she grumbled.

Chase checked his headquarters directory and dialed the number of Sally Patrone, the department's mouthpiece.

"Hi, Mansfield here," Chase said when Patrone came on the line.

"Where in the hell is here?" Patrone demanded.

"In my office, where else?" Chase said.

He assumed the normally unflappable Patrone was suffering from the media siege and desperate for information about the Townsend shooting. It was not often that former cabinet secretaries were found murdered in the arms of their mistresses, particularly not a Secretary of the Department of Homeland Security who was hiding from the media following his ransomed released by terrorists kidnappers.

"Where are you holding your news conference?" Patrone demanded.

Chase noted she asked where not if.

"Where do you suggest?" Chase asked casually. "I can say no comment just about anywhere."

"Bullshit," Patrone erupted. "No comment won't cut it."

"You surprise me, Sally," Chase said. "I thought you were a better wordsmith than that. There's something incomplete about your syntax."

"Bullshit!" Patrone repeated. "Get your ass to my office right now, and straighten your tie."

"Right," Chase agreed.

"And I'll have them set this up in the parking lot."

"The parking lot?"

"There's too many of the bastards to fit anyplace else. We've got at least six satellite trucks out there."

Although he knew the answer, Chase remained an optimist. He asked, "Do you think you can persuade the chief to handle this instead of me?"

"I just got off the phone with the chief. He doesn't want to steal your fifteen minutes of fame," Patrone said.

"See you shortly," Chase said. He was also a realist who was paid to take the heat when the chief so ordered.

"Don't linger, you bastard," Patrone answered.

"Sally, you're going to have to do something about your language," Chase cautioned.

"Screw you," Patrone said and hung up.

Chase put the phone back in its cradle, lifted his feet to the desk, and leaned back in his chair. He was really enjoying himself.

Then, his door opened, and Theresa entered.

"Sir, Special Agent Cotton is on the phone again demanding to speak with you urgently. He said he would send a team to arrest you immediately if you don't pick up. Do you want me to tell him to bring them on?" Theresa smiled brightly. Clearly, she, too, was enjoying herself.

"I'll speak to him," Chase smiled back.

"Line one," Theresa said. "Please give me a second to get back to my desk. This I've got to hear."

Theresa rushed off, and Chase picked up line one.

"Special Agent Cotton," Chase greeted him. "What's new on the federal front?"

"What did ballistics say?" Cotton ignored Chase's feeble attempt at humor.

"The .22 killed Jesperson and it was covered with Ms. Kendrick's prints. We're still checking its provenance."

"Mind sharing the serial number?"

"Yes."

"I assume you're still interested in how our little storage unit saga turns out," Cotton issued a counter-threat.

"I'll have Moscowitz fax you the number," Chase capitulated. "I don't have it in my pocket, and I'm on my way to consult with the media," Chase said. "Do you want me to mention your name?"

"I want them to trample you," Cotton muttered.

"That's a real possibility. You know how inept we local police are."

"What's going on between you and Featherstone?" Cotton demanded.

"You know how politicians are. They like to keep in touch with the common man."

"He certainly selected well when he chose you," Cotton fired from the hip. "I don't recommend that you waste your time by applying to the Bureau or the Agency when your current employer cans you."

"I've got a second career to fall back on," Chase said. "I thank you for your concern."

"Who gave Townsend and Kendrick what they deserved? Was it the betrayed spouse?"

"I can't comment on an ongoing investigation," Chase said.

"Don't try to be smart, lieutenant," Cotton reacted. "I'm sure that little trick is well beyond you."

"Thank you for the advice, Special Agent Cotton, but, as much as I enjoy chatting with you, I must run. The public awaits."

"Don't try to swallow. There's something sticking out of your mouth. You might regret it; the foot is yours," Cotton laughed.

"More good advice. Call again when things get boring in that little office of yours, Special Agent Cotton."

"We could take over that little double homicide investigation of yours," Cotton threatened. "Townsend was a former federal official."

"Be my guest," Chase answered, recognizing that his response was a little trite. He thought about adding that one of the victims belonged to him, but he did not.

"Don't worry. It won't happen. We're impressed with your propensity for tripping over clues while investigating other crime scenes. What's next? A quadruple homicide?"

"Have a nice day," Chase surrendered and hung up.

Not even Cotton and the Bureau could rain on Chase's day. It was not every day that he solved a murder without having to arrest the shooter or fence with defense attorneys at a meaningless trial.

Following his hour long press conference, Chase phoned the Jespersons.

"Jespersons," Doctor Jesperson picked up on the fourth ring.

"Doctor Jesperson, Chase Mansfield," Chase greeted him.

"What's happened now?" The elder Jesperson dispensed with polite formalities.

"Have you by chance been watching television?" Chase asked.

"I only watch old movies and an occasional Patriot or Celtic game," Jesperson said.

"And your wife?"

"She only watches her soap operas during the day."

"Good. Then you haven't seen any recent newscasts?"

"I told you, no. What's happened?"

"I've got good news and bad news," Chase said.

"You've caught Thomas' shooter," Jesperson declared. "Was it the damned Iranians?"

"Yes, sir; No, sir," Chase answered. "I regret to say that your son's former fiancée, Sally Kendrick, was the shooter."

Jesperson greeted that revelation with silence. Chase waited for the old man to react, worried that the news might be too a great a shock for his body to withstand.

"Give me a minute," Jesperson finally ordered Chase.

The old man sounded angry, not shocked. Chase heard Jesperson call loudly to his wife, "Manujeh, Manujeh, Come here!"

"I'm watching my program," Mrs. Jesperson responded, her voice faint, obviously speaking from another room.

"Now, it's important," Jesperson ordered.

"No." Mrs. Jesperson answered.

"It's about Thomas," Jesperson announced.

"What?" Mrs. Jesperson demanded; the volume of her voice indicated she had joined her husband.

"It's Lieutenant Mansfield, and he's caught Thomas' killer."

"Who?" Mrs. Jesperson asked.

"That damned Kendrick person. I never liked her," Doctor Jesperson declared.

"But she was at the funeral? Is he sure?"

"Get on the other line and just listen," Doctor Jesperson ordered.

Chase heard her pick up and Doctor Jesperson say, "My wife is on the line, lieutenant."

"There have been a number of developments. I just wanted to let you know everything before you see it on television or read about it in the papers," Chase said.

"Was it really Sally? Are you sure?" Mrs. Jesperson asked, her voice filled with more doubt than acceptance.

"Yes," Chase said. "We recovered the weapon with Ms. Kendrick's prints all over it from a drawer in the table beside her bed in her home."

"What does she say?" Mrs. Jesperson asked.

"Unfortunately, Ms. Kendrick is not in a position to say anything," Chase said.

"You let her get away?" Doctor Jesperson demanded.

"No sir," Chase said. "Ms. Kendrick is deceased."

"Did she commit suicide?" Doctor Jesperson asked.

Mrs. Jesperson sighed.

"No," Chase answered bluntly. "Ms. Kendrick was found this morning in her Reston home with Secretary Townsend at her side. They both had been shot, fatally."

"With the same gun?" Mrs. Jesperson recovered first.

"What were they doing together?" Doctor Jesperson asked.

"Whoever killed Ms. Kendrick and Secretary Townsend used a different weapon, not the one that killed your son," Chase responded to Mrs. Jesperson first. "Secretary Townsend had left his wife and moved in with Ms. Kendrick. They were engaged to be married," Chase answered Doctor Jesperson.

"Oh my God," Mrs. Jesperson reacted.

"James, Thomas's friend, was engaged to Thomas' former fiancée?" Doctor Jesperson's voice was filled with disbelief and surprise.

"Yes, sir," Chase said. "You will have to brace yourself because the story is going to be all over the media."

"I don't believe it," Mrs. Jesperson said.

"Who shot them? Was it the Iranians?" Jesperson asked. "Was it connected to this CIA attack on Iran?"

"I regret I cannot answer your questions," Chase said, impressed by Jesperson's persistence in trying to blame his wife's countrymen for something. "But you can be sure we are actively trying to find out."

"I don't understand what's happening?" Mrs. Jesperson said. "Is my family in Iran in danger?"

"Are you in charge of the investigation?" Doctor Jesperson asked.

"Yes sir, and I'm afraid that if you turn on the television news you will see my face all over it answering or not answering questions."

"Turn on the television," Doctor Jesperson ordered his wife.

Chase heard the sound of his voice suddenly appear in the background.

"Oh my God," Mrs. Jesperson declared.

"Do you have anything else to tell us?" Doctor Jesperson asked Chase.

"I have a question. Where is Mansour?"

"We already have him enrolled at Boston College and installed in an apartment near campus," Doctor Jesperson answered.

"Does he have a phone? Can you contact him?" Chase asked, distracted by the sound of his own voice in the background. He really didn't like what he was hearing. He made it a rule never to listen to any of the rare interviews he granted. Usually, he limited his responses to no comment, but today had been different.

"He has a cell phone," Doctor Jesperson answered, obviously distracted as he tried to listen to television and talk with Chase at the same time.

"Could you please call him and tell him about developments and alert him to the fact that the FBI will be wanting to interview him."

"Interview Mansour? Why?"

"There have been other developments that haven't reached the public yet. I can't discuss them, and they involve Mansour only peripherally, I think."

"I don't like the sound of that. Do they involve Mansour personally or is it something to do with his citizenship."

"I just can't discuss it," Chase said. "I'm sorry. It's an FBI matter."

"Is it related to this absurd Iranian claim that the CIA attacked Natanz?" Doctor Jesperson asked.

"Is my family alright?" Mrs. Jesperson came back on line.

"Everything will become apparent in a day or so. I don't think Mansour or Mrs. Jesperson's family is directly involved. Please don't mention anything I've said about this to anyone, particularly not to anyone in Iran. Maybe you should only tell Mansour about Ms. Kendrick and not mention the FBI."

"We'll do anything you want, lieutenant," Doctor Jesperson said. "Is there anything else you want to say?"

"No, I'll be in touch," Chase said.

After the call Chase regretted having been too forthcoming. He had merely wanted to caution Mansour to be forthcoming in his future contacts with the Bureau, but obviously he had said too much.

Chapter 33

"There they are," the Bureau agent manning the FBI telescopic camera announced. The surveillance team focused on a tan nondescript Ford that circled through the storage facility and parked directly in front of the locker containing the green plastic wrapped bogus suitcase.

"I hope your boys remember the briefing and are careful where they point their weapons," the officer commanding the CIA contingent worried.

"No problem," Special Agent Tracey Cotton responded.

"They know their target is Afgar not the driver," the CIA officer studied Cotton's face as he spoke. "It'll be your ass if they grab both of them."

Cotton didn't bother to acknowledge the comment. He didn't like spooks and didn't hide it. The spooks tended to treat Bureau officers in the same condescending manner that Cotton and his peers dealt with local police officials, and the federal agents resented it. He watched Jamshid Afgar climb out of the Ford, study the deserted facility, and approach the locker door.

"Are you getting all this?" Cotton turned to the Bureau officer manning the video recorder and monitor.

"No problem," the smiling agent mimicked Cotton's response to the CIA asshole.

Cotton nodded and turned his attention back to the tan Ford. He could not identify the driver, given the fact that night had fallen and the storage facility lights were barely adequate. Cotton had suggested they replace the bulbs, but the CIA had insisted that they not be touched. Cotton had not argued the point. They had Afgar in a box. If anything went wrong, Cotton knew they could always persuade Justice to call the driver, Doctor Lyla Jalili, as a witness whether the CIA liked it or not.

Afgar opened the locker door, turned, and said something to Jalili, probably ordering her to pop the trunk, then disappeared inside the locker.

"Go, Go," Cotton shouted into his radio.

Bureau agents poured out of the dark facility office and from a locker on the far side of the facility wearing jackets with the letters "FBI" stenciled on the back. They carried weapons, mostly pointed skyward.

As briefed by her CIA handler, Doctor Lyla Jalili gunned the engine when she spotted the first FBI agent appear in the doorway of the facility office. She raced towards the Waples Mill exit, leaving the hapless Afgar standing in the locker doorway struggling with the hundred pounds of bricks in a container wrapped in green plastic and bound with thick straps.

The lead agent fired his weapon into the air three times as the tan Ford raced past him, a touch of verisimilitude added at the insistence of the CIA handler.

Within seconds a wide-eyed Afgar was surrounded.

"Set that down carefully," the lead agent ordered.

A defiant Afgar released his burden. A corner of the package grazed one of Afgar's knees and landed on the toe of his right foot. The package slammed to the ground and broke open on one end, spilling bricks out onto the facility roadway.

"Alhamdollilah!" Afgar shouted as he started hopping up and down on one foot, grasping his right Nike with both hands.

It was such a comical sight that the lead members of the Bureau arrest team started laughing as they tried to restrain Afgar long enough to handcuff both of his hands behind him.

"The dumb bastard tried to nuke us with a box of bricks," one of the team members on the right laughed.

"She made it," the CIA team leader in the observation post declared.

Cotton glanced at the spook blowhard and then turned his attention from the locker scene to the Waples Mill and 29/211 intersection below. The tan Ford was nowhere to be seen.

"Wrap things up here," Cotton spoke to the men manning the video recorder and monitor as he headed for the stairs.

He planned to conduct Afgar's initial interrogation himself. The only thing he regretted was the fact that he would not have a chance at Doctor Lyla Jalili. He would have enjoyed the opportunity to question her about her relationship with a certain smart ass Fairfax Police lieutenant. The Bureau's agreement with the Agency stipulated that Jalili would be allowed to flee the country, presumably for Paris. What happened to her after that was the Agency's business; her future would depend on the Iranian reaction to her aborted mission and flight.

****

Chase woke early, wolfed down his burned toast and instant coffee, and hurried to the office where he surprised Theresa with his eight-thirty arrival.

"Please ask Detective Moscowitz to join me," Chase greeted Theresa as he retreated towards his office sanctuary.

"Are you really ready for that?" Theresa asked as she glanced at the wall clock. "She's a real bear before ten."

Chase stopped and stared as he waited for the punch line, but Theresa simply smiled.

"Are you feeling alright?" Chase asked.

"Yes, thank you for asking, sir," Theresa said as she submissively reached for the phone.

Theresa's uncharacteristically feeble responses surprised him.

Chase had barely settled into his chair when Moscowitz appeared with a paper in her hand.

"Yes, sir," Moscowitz said when she entered.

Moscowitz's passive demeanor, coming as it did after Theresa's almost human performance, worried Chase. A subservient Moscowitz would be too much to handle. He glared at her and asked, "Is that it?"

Moscowitz reverted to her old self. She tossed the paper on Chase's desk and waited.

"I'm impressed," Chase begrudgingly reached for the document.

"Don't be. I told Judge Johnson that you were simply carrying out the president's orders," Moscowitz smiled as she sat down without being invited.

"Was he impressed?"

"Not in the least," Moscowitz answered.

"But?"

"But he signed it when I told him that you were pushing your luck and if we encouraged you we would have a good chance of seeing you being shoved out the door."

"Good work," Chase smiled as he pocketed the warrant without reading it.

"I assume you want to handle this yourself as you always do," Moscowitz smiled back.

"As usual, you assumed wrong, Detective Moscowitz," Chase said as he recognized that their combative relationship had not changed. He relaxed; his life had not been permanently altered by a single appearance on national television.

Moscowitz waited.

"Collect the usual search and destroy team and meet me at the suspect's home at eleven," he ordered.

"I assume you realize you don't have a single shred of evidence to justify that," Moscowitz nodded at the warrant.

Chase did not trouble to respond as he headed for the door. To do so would only encourage Moscowitz.

"Where are you going now?" A surprised Moscowitz called after him.

"Motivation, always look for the motivation," Chase called over his shoulder, obliquely challenging Moscowitz while pretending to ignore her question.

The outer door closed behind Chase before Moscowitz joined Theresa in the outer office.

"Where's he going?" Theresa asked Moscowitz as Barney appeared in the door to his office.

"How the hell do I know?" Moscowitz declared as she departed through the same door that had slammed behind Chase.

Barney smiled at Theresa and retreated into his office. Theresa immediately called the receptionist. After a whispered question she listened to a quick answer and announced, "He's heading for the parking lot."

"Thanks," Barney called from his desk.

Theresa turned her attention back to the phone. "Have security check which way he goes and let me know."

Chase with his warrant in his pocket and pleased with his morning thus far climbed into his Prius, exited the parking lot, and turned left. At 236 he turned right to the beltway and then fought the traffic into Maryland. En route, he turned on the radio and was surprised to hear a familiar voice, that of President Arthur C. Featherstone. Featherstone, the man, struck Chase as much more impressive and intimidating when playing the role of Featherstone, the orator, particularly when addressing the nation from the White House.

"The president of the sovereign country of Iran yesterday made some astonishing accusations," Featherstone said. "Astonishing to me, astonishing to every member of this administration, and astonishing to the citizens of the United States of America. On my orders, the Director of the Central Intelligence Agency, the Secretary of Defense, the Secretary of State, and the National Security Council have investigated President Ahmadinejad's allegation that an unmanned aircraft operating under the CIA's auspices mounted a treacherous dawn attack yesterday morning on his country's nuclear research facility near Natanz. Alleging, and I assure you that I use that word deliberately, alleging the loss of countless Iranian lives and the destruction of Iranian property, Mr. Ahmadinejad promised the world irrefutable proof in the form of pictures and on site access to support his charges. Twenty-four hours have passed and Mr. Ahmadinejad has yet to provide this promised proof. I now give you my firm word that President Ahmadinejad's charges have no basis in fact. Your Central Intelligence Agency did not have a single unmanned aircraft operating within five hundred miles of Natanz at the time Mr. Ahmadinejad alleges the attack occurred. Your Defense Department informs me that your Navy had one missile cruiser transiting the Persian Gulf during the same time frame, and the Secretary of Defense assures me that its passage remained passive and routine throughout. Finally, as much as it irritates me to waste time proving a negative, I have directed the Department of State to immediately submit to the United Nations a series of high attitude photographs taken by a satellite which was coincidentally and providentially circling over Natanz at the time of the alleged attack. These time dated photographs definitely show the skies over the destroyed building were absolutely clear at the time of the alleged assault. There were no aircraft of any kind, manned or unmanned, operating nearby when the building exploded from within. I suggest, therefore, that President Ahmadinejad refocus his investigation of this incident and keep his unsubstantiated allegations to himself. The world has better things to do than listen to the ravings of the misinformed."

Chase almost missed the Bethesda exit. At the last minute, he cut across two lanes, enraging a commuter in a red Honda who honked in protest. Chase smiled, waved an apology, and hit his brakes, slowing to crowd into the merge lane. He was now in unfamiliar territory.

"...and I have a rather sensational announcement to make, one that I hope will catch President Ahmadinejad's personal attention because I demand a prompt explanation from that erstwhile gentleman. I will give you the highlights and then turn the microphone over to your Director of the Federal Bureau of Investigation, Mr. Philip D'Antonio, to brief you on the details. I am confident that most of you are aware of the allegations presented recently by Doctor Thomas Jesperson in his best selling study based on a year's sabbatical in Iran. Much attention has been given to his conclusion that Iran is prepared to mount a nuclear attack on our country."

That statement really caught Chase's attention. He pulled to the side of the road, turned on his flashers and listened closely to Featherstone's words.

"...last night a team of FBI agents apprehended an Iranian citizen who was in the process of retrieving a rather large package wrapped in green plastic from a storage warehouse in nearby Fairfax City, Virginia. That Iranian citizen is now in custody. The package has been examined in Fort Belvoir, Virginia, by Department of Defense and Atomic Energy Commission specialists. I am informed that it contained what has been described as a tactical nuclear suitcase bomb. Thanks to alert action by the FBI and the technical expertise of the Defense Department and AEC, the nuclear bomb has been neutralized. While it is premature for me to directly relate its unwelcome appearance on American soil to Doctor Jesperson's exemplary research and President Ahmadinejad's surprising but inaccurate allegations, I am sure that many of you, like myself, have strong suspicions. I now turn the microphone over to Director D'Antonio who will provide more details and address any questions many of you might have. I apologize for having to intrude in this manner on your busy mornings, but I felt you had a right to know."

Chase flicked off his flashers and forced his way back into traffic. Not interested in D'Antonio's self-congratulatory words, Chase muted the radio and belatedly concentrated on the simple task of finding his destination.

Chase knew that the Congressional Country Club was located in

Bethesda, Maryland, and of course Chase was not a member. An astute investigator, he had checked the Internet and learned that the prestigious club opened in 1924, had two courses, and counted 7 former presidents among its past members, including Taft, Wilson, Harding, and, of course, Dwight D. Eisenhower. Chase assumed Featherstone had sponsored Secretary Townsend's membership. A little jealous, Chase wondered if Featherstone, given the apparently growing intimacy of their current relationship, would sponsor him. If he played golf, which he did not, and was willing to fork over $150,000 to join, which he was not, Chase might have seriously considered membership just to enjoy the facilities which included a bowling alley, a tennis club, grand ballroom, one indoor and two outdoor pools, a fitness center, fine dining, and most important of all, a grand foyer to overwhelm guests.

After three impatient stops to ask for directions, a task that always irritated him, Chase found the damned place. He arrogantly parked directly in front of the clubhouse, dropped his "Official Police Business" placard on the dash, and entered in no mood for negotiating with an arrogant staff. He quickly fought his way past an unimpressed receptionist and a snooty secretary to the club manager's nicely appointed inner office.

"I need only one thing from you," Chase confronted a smooth but self-confident male. "I need someone to tell me whether one of your members dined here with friends two nights ago," Chase said.

"I'm sorry, but that will not be possible," the manager answered.

"Do you know what this is?" Chase pulled his Virginia judge's warrant from his pocket.

"Not unless you allow me to review it, sir," the manager answered.

Chase held up a single finger. He pulled his cell phone from his pocket and hit the number for Theresa."

"CIB," Theresa answered pertly.

"Hi, it's me," Chase said.

"Where are you?" Theresa asked. "I know you headed east on 236."

"Let me speak to Special Agent Cotton," Chase ordered rudely.

"What in the hell are you talking about?" Theresa asked.

Chase smiled at the manager while he pretended to wait.

"Have you lost your mind, lieutenant?" Theresa asked.

"Special Agent," Chase said. "I'm out here at the Bethesda Country Club, and I'm getting a runaround just like we anticipated."

"I get it," Theresa reacted. "We're playing games."

"That's right. Send four teams with sirens on and lights flashing; we're going to have to tear this place apart and show these stuffed shirts the meaning of a federal warrant."

"Hey, this is fun," Theresa said.

"Lieutenant, just a minute," the manager reacted as Chase intended. "We are all gentlemen and ladies here. I'm sure we can work something out."

"Hold that," Chase said and glanced at the manager.

"What was the name of the member you were checking on, sir?" The manager asked.

"I'll call you back," Chase said and terminated his call. "Mrs. James Townsend," he frowned at the manager.

"Oh, I understand," the manager said. "This is an official investigation pursuant to that regrettable item on the news."

"This is a confidential inquiry," Chase glared at the man.

"I understand, sir," the now humble manager said. He turned to his computer. "Mrs. Townsend is one of our regulars. She doesn't play golf but frequently joins us for lunch or dinner with her friends."

"Did she dine with four friends the night before last at eight?" Chase said. "That's all I need to know."

The manager studied his monitor. "Mrs. Townsend was here Sunday for dinner and Monday for lunch, but not night before last for dinner. I don't see her name on our list."

"Are you sure?" Chase pressed.

"Mrs. Townsend is not on our reservation list. Let me check with accounting. Our members all sign. We don't accept credit cards."

Chase resisted the urge to comment, "Good for them."

"No sir," the manager said. "We have no record of Mrs. Townsend being in the club Tuesday evening. Does this mean..."

"It means that this is a confidential inquiry, and I advise you to not mention it to another person," Chase glared at the manager.

"Yes sir. We at Congressional know the meaning of confidential."

"I hope so," Chase said as he turned and marched from the office without thanking the officious little man for his assistance.

Forty minutes later Chase turned into the driveway of the Townsend McLean mansion and stopped. Moscowitz climbed out of a patrol car that was parked along the curb behind three police vans and greeted him.

"You're late, lieutenant, where in the hell have you been?" Moscowitz frowned, her normal expression.

"I got delayed," Chase said as he squinted at the Prius's dashboard clock. He loved his little car but hated the cramped dashboard. He resisted the urge to reply, "Only by ten minutes." Chase did not like to over-explain anything to Moscowitz.

Instead, he pointed one finger at Moscowitz and her team and then the Townsend house, indicating she and her party should follow, and drove up the driveway to the garage. He noted that all three Townsend cars were still inside. He parked, blocking the garage as best as the little Prius could, and strolled to the front door. Chase rattled the brass knocker, waited, and was reaching for it again when it opened suddenly to reveal a frowning Mrs. Nancy Lou Townsend, the new widow.

"What?" Mrs. Townsend demanded as she blocked the door.

"Good morning, Mrs. Townsend," Chase greeted her formally.

"Go away," the frowning Townsend started to close the door.

"I'm afraid that is not possible," Chase said, catching the door with his left hand.

"Anything is possible, lieutenant," Townsend said as she put her shoulder against the door and started pushing.

"This is an official visit," Chase said.

As the door started to close Chase raised his right foot and slid it between the door and the jamb. Mrs. Townsend abruptly stopped pushing and stepped back. It flew open; Mrs. Townsend stepped forward, and stamped on Chase's shoe with a spiked heel. Chase hollered in pain.

Behind him, Detective Moscowitz laughed, "Need some help lieutenant?"

Chase frowned and got serious. He pulled his aching foot back and lunged against the door with his left shoulder. It slammed open, barely grazing Nancy Lou.

Chase tumbled into the foyer, barely keeping his balance.

"If it's that important to you," Nancy Lou laughed. "Just come in."

Townsend turned and marched into the living room on the right where she reestablished her blocking position. Chase glanced at Townsend, noticed four packed suitcases standing to his left, and then followed Townsend into the now familiar formal room, limping as he went, determined to regain his lost dignity.

"I have some questions to ask, and I have a search warrant," Chase declared as he pulled a folder paper from his suit pocket.

"So ask and search if you must," Townsend smiled as she held out her hand.

Chase surrendered the warrant. Townsend surprised him again when she pivoted and sat down in one of the facing love seats. She tossed the unread warrant on the table next to her. Unbidden, Chase seated himself opposite.

"Just like old times," Nancy Lou confronted Chase with one of her provocative poses.

Moscowitz appeared in the doorway and stared at Chase.

"Do it," Chase grumbled with a wave of his hand.

Moscowitz nodded and turned.

"Don't make a mess," Townsend, now haughty, ordered as she jumped to her feet and hurried after Moscowitz who was now at the door.

"Wait," Chase ordered.

"Don't get your balls in an uproar, lieutenant," Townsend called over her shoulder. "I'll alert Mary to make sure your thugs don't try to steal anything, and then I'll be right back.

Townsend turned right and hurried down the hall towards her office.

"Stay with her," a still seated Chase called to Moscowitz who was standing at the door watching her search team stream into the room. "She might try to go out the back," Chase added.

Moscowitz chuckled as she turned to follow Townsend. Every member of the entering team of uniforms had a smile on his or her face as each stared at Chase rubbing his foot while they marched past. Chase frowned and tried to ignore them.

Townsend rejoined Chase with a grinning secretary following.

"Good morning, lieutenant," Mary greeted Chase like an old friend. "May I offer you a cup of freshly brewed coffee?"

"Good morning, Mary," Chase said. "Coffee would be very nice."

Mary retreated, and Chase waited for Townsend to sit back down before asking his first question, "Going somewhere?" He glanced in the direction of the hall and the four suitcases.

"I refuse to answer any question until Mary returns," Townsend said as she primly adjusted her skirt over her knees.

"Do you think you need a witness?" Chase forced a chuckle.

Townsend folded her hands in her lap, sat stiffly erect, and silently stared at a spot on the wall to Chase's left.

"We'll start in the office and upstairs," Moscowitz announced from the door.

Chase nodded.

Moscowitz glanced at the stiff Nancy Lou. "Have a good morning, ma'am. This may take some time."

Townsend did not bother to look at Moscowitz.

"The sooner we start the quicker this will be over," Chase said.

Moscowitz got the message and disappeared. Townsend ignored him.

"As you wish," Chase said.

Chase could hear the investigators in the distance chatting, but he could not make out the words. The living room remained silent with the exception of a clock on the mantel ticking away the seconds.

"Did you chance to hear the president's address to the nation this morning?" Chase tried to make small talk.

Townsend did not answer.

"Too bad," Chase said. "He clarified a lot of things."

The ice lady ignored him, and Chase for the first time began to sympathize with the wandering, now deceased Secretary James Townsend. Always before, Chase had been beguiled by the well-preserved and flirtatious Nancy Lou.

"Sorry. I got distracted by the searchers in the office," Mary appeared in the doorway with a silver tray and two cups of coffee. She had a shoulder bag slung over her shoulder.

Mary served her employer and then Chase. She noticed Chase staring at her handbag.

"Not to worry, lieutenant. This is mine, and I don't have a concealed weapon inside," she patted the purse with her free hand.

Chase smiled.

"Detective Moscowitz has already searched it," Mary continued.

Mary turned and started for the door.

"Wait," Townsend ordered

Mary stopped.

"I want you to stay here and be my witness," Townsend declared.

Mary nodded. "Let me get rid of this and collect my pen and notepad," Mary said as she hurried from the room.

"You're making this much more difficult than it has to be," Chase said.

The rigid Townsend again ignored him. They sat in silence until Mary returned with pen and pad in hand. She moved a small chair to a position facing the coffee table that separated the two love seats, sat down, and waited.

"Make a note," Townsend ordered Mary before Chase had a chance to speak.

Mary reacted by touching her pen to the pad.

"I have a two o'clock reservation, and I have to be at Dulles one hour early," Townsend said, clearly enunciating each word. "That means I have to leave here at twelve o'clock." Townsend looked at Chase. "You have exactly fifty-seven minutes to ask your questions."

"Do you have a lawyer?" Chase ignored Townsend's ultimatum.

"Do I need one?" Townsend asked.

Mary recorded Townsend's statement, Chase's question, and Townsend's answer on her pad.

"In situations like this, we always recommend legal consultation," Chase said.

During the silence, Chase had amused himself with the thought that Nancy Lou and Wacky Jacky might make a good team. He hadn't been completely pleased at the way Jacky had treated him during their last outing, and he had decided that putting the two hardheaded ladies together might be a fair reward for both of them. At least he might find it entertaining. He filed that thought away for future reference.

"Are you going to read me my rights?" Townsend asked as she stared at Mary, an action that led Chase to conclude that she was signaling her secretary to make particular note of that observation.

Mary scribbled some more.

"May I ask where you are going?" Chase asked, ignoring the question.

"No, it's none of your business," Townsend said.

"I beg to differ," Chase said even though he was making his best effort not to quibble.

"Beg all you want, lieutenant," Townsend said haughtily.

"Please don't make this any more difficult than it is," Chase said. "I fully understand how difficult all of this is for you, first dealing with the kidnapping, and then the loss of your husband."

Townsend glared angrily at Chase.

Too late, he recognized the ambiguity in his last comment; he had sincerely meant to be consoling. His phrase "loss of your husband" could be interpreted two ways, a reference to Townsend's death, or his abandonment of their marriage.

"Please answer my question, where are you going?" Chase dispensed with his attempt to be considerate. "Four suitcases tell me you are planning a rather extensive stay."

"I'm visiting a close friend in Houston," Townsend relented. "I don't know how long I will stay. I find this place depressing and the visitors intrusive and disrespectful, more insulting than considerate."

Chase assumed Townsend was directly referring to him.

"I'm sorry but I must ask you not to travel at this time," Chase said.

"Is that a legal order or a request?"

"That depends on what happens here during the next hour," Chase said, trying to sound agreeable and not provoking the excitable Townsend any more than necessary.

"Please note the lieutenant did not give me an explicit order, Mary," Townsend directed. "Also stress that he did not read me my rights, and he set a time limit for himself and his storm troops."

"You are not free to go anywhere, Mrs. Townsend, until I am satisfied with your responses," Chase toughened his approach.

"And I find that unacceptable," Townsend declared.

"We could move this conversation to my headquarters," Chase threatened.

"Do that and I will sue you for false arrest and illegal detention," Townsend replied.

"That kind of comment sounds good on television," Chase smiled thinly, "but it means nothing to me."

"We'll see," Townsend frowned. "Why are you harassing me lieutenant?"

"I'm sorry you feel that way," Chase said.

"How can I not?"

"Please be truthful with me," Chase said.

"I am," Townsend shifted her defense from an attack to a poor me mode.

"I visited your club," Chase said.

Townsend glanced at Mary and then stared at her inquisitor.

"They assure me that you did not spend the evening in question there with your four friends."

"Somebody's mistaken."

Chase noted Townsend knew exactly which evening he was referring to, the night someone shot her husband and his fiancée.

"Name the four friends for me, please," Chase asked evenly.

"I'm not going to tell you," Townsend challenged. "I'm not going to embarrass my friends. They are not the kind of people who like to see their names in the papers."

"Then how can I verify your alibi?" Chase asked.

"Alibi? Do you have the temerity to say I need an alibi?"

Chase waited for an answer not a question.

Townsend looked at Mary. "Ask her. Mary knows where I am every night. She keeps track of all my social engagements."

Chase glanced at the secretary who did not react. She stared at her notepad and waited with a poised pen.

"Tell him!" Townsend ordered.

"I'm sorry, Mrs. Townsend, but I was not there," Mary responded without looking up.

At that point, Detective Moscowitz appeared in the doorway. "I've finished with the office," she said. "Should I start in here?"

"Just check the suitcases," Chase replied, pretending to be irritated by the interruption.

"Don't you dare," Townsend reacted. "Does the warrant mention suitcases? Want me to move them out the front door? That's what I was doing when you forced your way into my house."

Moscowitz ignored her and retreated.

"I'll see you in court if she touches my suitcases," Townsend threatened Chase before turning to Mary. "Make sure you make a note of what I just said."

"Where were you last night, Mrs. Townsend?" Chase asked, ignoring the posturing which he found very interesting. He wondered what was in the suitcases that she did not want them to see.

Chase heard the sound of suitcases being dragged into the parlor across the hall.

Mrs. Townsend took a deep breath. "Did you write all of that down?" Townsend glared at her secretary."

"Yes, ma'am," Mary held up her notebook for her employer to see.

Townsend stared briefly at Mary and then looked anxiously at the hallway door.

"Did you visit your husband in Reston two evenings ago?" Chase pressed.

"What is she doing in there?" Townsend demanded as she continued to try to see what was happening across the hall.

"Inspecting your luggage," Chase answered matter-of-factly.

"She cannot," Townsend insisted as she rose to her feet. "My luggage is locked, and I have the keys. If she damages the locks, I will sue..."

"Don't worry," Chase decided to add to Townsend's growing anxiety. "Detective Moscowitz is a superlative locksmith."

"Stop her right now," Townsend demanded as she started for the doorway.

Chase and Mary exchanged surprised looks.

"Oh my, what is this?" Moscowitz exclaimed loudly, almost on cue.

Townsend stopped halfway to the hall. She turned, stared at Chase, and declared, "This is a violation of my constitutional rights."

Townsend returned to her love seat and sat back down. Chase said nothing, just watched. Townsend's aggressiveness and confidence appeared to abandon her like gas escaping from a pierced balloon.

Moscowitz materialized in the doorway with a smile on her face and large pistol dangling from a pencil thrust through its trigger guard. One glance told Chase that it was a Glock, the same brand of weapon used to kill Secretary Townsend and Sally Kendrick.

"And what is that?" Chase asked.

"It's my husband's favorite gun," Townsend declared, her tone plaintive.

"Best have ballistics process it immediately," Chase smiled as he rose from his chair.

"Tell him, Mary," Townsend pleaded as she sank deeper into her sofa. "James loved that gun. How could I part with it?"

Mary scribbled Townsend's words on her pad but did not comment.

"You bitch," Townsend turned her anger on her secretary. "He was sleeping with you, too."

Mary stopped writing and stared at her employer.

"Mrs. Townsend," Chase said, standing above her. "I must order you not to leave town."

Townsend shrugged and ignored him as she pretended to wipe tears from her eyes.

Chase nodded at Moscowitz who hurried from the room with Chase following.

In the hall, Chase spoke to Moscowitz. "I'll be in my office when I finish here. Let me know as soon as they get a match."

"Wait, "Moscowitz said.

Still holding the gun, Moscowitz entered the parlor with Chase following. Chase closed the hall door behind him as Moscowitz retrieved something from an open suitcase. She handed Chase a blank, sealed envelope.

"I didn't open it. Tampering with the mail is a felony," Moscowitz said.

"It's just a paper envelope with no stamp and no address," Chase said as he ripped it open. Inside were two sheets of paper, one a simple list, and the other a detailed itinerary. Chase glanced at the list first and smiled. It contained two lines carefully written in a masculine hand. The first line cited the name of a Panama bank followed by a ten-digit number; the second line cited a different Panama bank and a different number. The itinerary noted the flight to Houston and a continuation the next day to Panama with a twenty-four hour layover and a return to Houston.

"What is it?" Moscowitz asked. "A confession?"

"Hardly," Chase smiled as he put the two sheets of paper back into the envelope and placed it in his suit coat inner pocket. "First things first. Get that," he nodded at the weapon, "to the lab. We can discuss this later," Chase patted his pocket.

Chase followed the frowning Moscowitz to the front door and watched from the front porch as she hurried to her car. Chase returned to the house where he ignored Townsend who was in the parlor opposite the living room frantically searching her luggage. Chase ignored her, briefed the head of the search team who had moved into the living room, and returned across the hall to find Townsend now sitting in a chair staring forlornly at the open suitcases filled with rumpled clothing.

"You bastard," Townsend shouted at Chase. "The president will hear of this outrage. You have stolen my belongings. You'll pay for this."

"Mrs. Townsend," Chase said coldly. "Do you understand my order not to leave Fairfax?"

Townsend glared at him but did not respond.

"If you don't answer my question right now, I will have the officers," Chase glanced in the direction of the hall, "read you your rights, arrest you, and escort you to headquarters."

Again, Townsend ignored him.

"Very well," Chase said. He turned toward the hall and called, "Sergeant."

"Stop it," Townsend ordered. "I give you my word."

"Do you understand the seriousness of my order?" Chase asked.

"I do, you bastard. I thought you were my friend," Townsend said, apparently not sure whether to be defiant or plaintive.

"Good. I am compelled to warn you, Mrs. Townsend, that if ballistics determines that weapon is the one that killed your husband and Ms. Kendrick and if the prints on that gun are yours, it is only a matter of hours before I return to arrest you and charge you with two murders. I recommend you use the time available to you wisely and seek legal advice immediately," Chase said before departing with a smile on his face.

****

In Teheran President Ahmadinejad sat on his artificial throne and glared at his Minister of Intelligence and Security and Brigadier Nasiri.

"How do you explain that scheming devil's lies?" He demanded, referring to Featherstone's press conference.

Minister Behbehani looked at General Obadias Nasiri, the Chief of VEVAK, who answered with a shrug.

"I've only seen the CNN reports," Behbehani stalled.

"We've yet to hear from our people in Washington," Nasiri agreed.

"And you never will," Ahmadinejad declared.

"Sir?" Behbehani spoke softly.

"Because the damned FBI is interrogating them as we speak," Ahmadinejad shouted.

"The president said only one operative was in custody," Nasiri volunteered.

"Which one?" Ahmadinejad pushed back from his desk, stumbled off the platform, and started pacing.

"We assume only Jamshid Afgar, the sleeper," Nasiri said.

"Sleeper?" Ahmadinejad asked.

"Yes, sir," Behbehani came to his VEVAK chief's defense. "We assume that our station chief survived."

"Station chief?"

"Yes, sir," Nasiri said. "Doctor Jalili was supposed to set the device to detonate."

"But this station chief did not complete the mission. Where is he now?"

"She, sir. Doctor Lyla Jalili," Behbehani said. "We are hopeful she is fleeing America as we speak."

"Fleeing? Why do we care?"

"Because Doctor Jalili is one of our most successful officers," Nasiri said.

"You call this disaster successful? How could you trust such a mission to a mere female?"

"Because Ms. Jalili holds a doctorate degree in nuclear physics from the University of Paris," Behbehani answered.

"And how did she accomplish that?" Ahmadinejad, whose only bonafide degree was a BS in Engineering from the Teheran University, asked.

"She was one of our most aggressive organizers," Behbehani finessed the question.

"What am I supposed to tell the media now?" Ahmadinejad changed the subject, getting to the problem that worried him most.

"The Americans always lie. All our friends know that, and such lies are not worthy of a response," Behbehani asserted as he looked at Nasiri for support.

"That's true, Mr. President," Nasiri nodded his head in agreement.

"And the United Nations inspectors who are clamoring for access?" Ahmadinejad asked.

"Tell them that the area is radioactive as a result of the American attack," Behbehani suggested.

"Tell them to wait and we will open Natanz for them to inspect as soon as it is safe," Nasiri agreed.

"And when will that be?" Ahmadinejad asked.

"Never," Behbahani answered. He looked at Nasiri who nodded his head in agreement.

"That might work," Ahmadinejad said as he returned to his desk.

After a lengthy pause, Ahmadinejad glared at his two disciples and ordered, "Tell them to send in the Ministers of Foreign Affairs and Defense."

****

Chase was sipping coffee and casually briefing Barney and a silent but excited Theresa when Detective Moscowitz burst into his office.

"It's the weapon," Moscowitz announced.

Chase raised his coffee cup in salute.

"It fired the slugs that killed Townsend and Kendrick?" Barney asked.

Moscowitz nodded.

"And the prints?"

"Those of Mrs. Mary Lou Townsend herself," Moscowitz said.

Barney glanced at Chase who nodded.

"Bring her in," Barney ordered.

"If she is still there," Chase said.

Both Barney and Moscowitz stared.

"We didn't confiscate her plane tickets," Chase said. "Did we Detective Moscowitz?"

""Shit," Moscowitz exclaimed as she started for the door.

"She has plane tickets?" Barney asked.

"She alleged she had reservations for a two o'clock departure from Dulles for Houston," Chase smiled.

Barney checked his watch. "We have time. Shall I call Dulles?"

"No problem," Chase said. "Let her go. It's a nonstop flight, and Cotton can retrieve her there."

A disbelieving Moscowitz departed.

Barney shook his head and stared at the smiling Chase.

"All the more incriminating," Chase said. "I'm interested in seeing if she actually makes a run for it."

"But?" Barney said.

"I have a little chore that has to be taken care of before we take Ms. Mary Lou into custody."

"Which is?" Barney asked.

"Please bear with me," Chase smiled. "It's quite top secret."

Thirty-five minutes later a frantic Detective Moscowitz called.

Chase broke precedent and answered.

"She's not here, but the four suitcases are. The search team leader said that after we left, Townsend just climbed in her car and departed."

"Not to worry," a relaxed Chase smiled as he checked his watch. "Her flight departed fifteen minutes ago."

"Should I contact Dulles and request they order the flight to return?" Moscowitz asked.

"No, come back in. I have another chore for you."

"Thanks a lot," Moscowitz complained to a dead phone.

Chase looked at Theresa and asked, "Think you can persuade Southwestern to confirm that Ms. Townsend boarded their Houston flight?"

Theresa surprised Chase by saluting and hurrying from the room.

Chase looked at Barney and asked, "What is getting into that girl? She's actually doing something I ask without complaining."

"She has occasional days like that," Barney smiled.

"Rarely, only rarely," Chase said as he leaned back and propped his heels on an open desk drawer.

"Don't you have some unfinished business to take care of?" Barney asked.

Chase shrugged. "I'm working on it."

"I can see that," Barney shook his head. "You seem to have almost everything under control."

Chase gave him thumbs up. "Did you catch the Wizards game last night?"

They spent a few minutes discussing the futility of the local team.

Finally, Barney asked. "Are we ready to brief the chief?"

"Not quite. We still have that loose end."

Theresa rejoined them. "Yes," she pointed skyward with a raised thumb.

"Townsend caught the flight to Houston?" Barney asked.

Theresa nodded.

"That's interesting," Chase said.

Theresa smiled. "I think that's the first time you ever approved of anything I have done or said, and it's when I report a murderess just got away while you two sit here chatting about basketball."

"Listen to her," Chase glanced at Barney. "She sounds like a wife."

"I know the symptoms," Barney agreed. "I think he's working on a loose end," Barney smiled at Theresa.

"Ha, Ha," Theresa countered.

"Since we're all having so much fun, could you do one more little thing for me?" Chase spoke to Theresa.

She waited, not sure if Chase were getting ready to launch another of his little attacks on her or if he were serious.

"Please check Southwestern and find out if Ms. Townsend has onward reservations from Houston to Panama," Chase said as he handed Theresa the note listing Townsend's itinerary that had been in the envelope from the suitcase.

Theresa grabbed the note and snapped at Chase, "Why didn't you mention this when you asked me to check if she had boarded the Houston flight?"

"I apologize. It slipped my mind," Chase smiled.

"Bullshit," Theresa muttered as she left the room.

"She's not wrong, you know," Barney said.

Chase shrugged. "I can't be right one hundred percent of the time."

They heard Theresa in her office speak, "I need to check about an onward reservation..." She began.

Suddenly, the door to the hall crashed open and Detective Moscowitz spoke loudly, "Is the bastard in?"

Chase assumed that Theresa must have pointed towards Chase's office because suddenly Moscowitz appeared in his doorway.

"Are you deliberately letting her get away?" Moscowitz demanded.

"Theresa confirmed Mrs. Townsend is on the Houston flight. What do you want me to do?" Chase smiled.

"Act like a damned cop," Moscowitz responded.

"Listen," Chase ordered as he glanced at the wall between his closet office and Theresa's large reception area.

"Can you confirm that Mrs. James Townsend has onward reservations tomorrow on Flight 247 for Panama?" Theresa asked.

"Panama?" Moscowitz stared at Chase.

"She does? Thank you very much," Theresa said.

Chase smiled silently at Moscowitz and waited.

Theresa did not disappoint him. She appeared in the doorway, stepped around Moscowitz, took a standing position in front of Chase's desk, and said, "She does."

"Thank you, Theresa," Chase said.

Theresa, not sure if Chase was going to continue with a wiseass comment intended to denigrate her, waited, prepared to counter-attack.

Chase disappointed her and surprised all three by picking up his cell phone and consulting his digital phone book. He sorted through the listing and finally found the number he wanted. He hit the dial button and waited.

The curious three, Barney, Theresa and Moscowitz, did not hear what the person on the other end said, but Chase replied, "Good afternoon, Heather, this is Lieutenant Mansfield."

Heather apparently said something that pleased Chase because he grinned and said, "That won't be necessary, but I do have something he will be most anxious to read."

Heather replied.

"No, I don't want to impose," Chase said. "Would it be acceptable if I had the document immediately hand-carried to your office by my assistant, Ms. Theresa D'Angelo?"

Heather replied.

"No, I do not believe she is related to Director D'Antonio. The names are spelled quite differently, though I often make the same mistake myself."

Theresa frowned and put her hands on her hips in what for her was a combative pose.

"And Ms. D'Angelo will be escorted by Detective Jane Moscowitz," Chase continued. "If you would kindly arrange for their clearances, they will bring the document directly to your office."

Chase listened and then replied. "Thank you very much, Heather, and I look forward to seeing you again soon. Please give him my best." Chase smiled and hung up.

"I'm not going anywhere," Theresa declared.

"And who the hell is Heather?" Moscowitz shouted the question that was also troubling Theresa and Barney.

All three stared at Chase who did not reply. He took a folded sheet of paper from his suit coat pocket, opened it, and scanned it. He noted the two lines listing the names of two Panama banks and two separate ten-digit account numbers. Reassured, he nodded and refolded the paper. He slid the single sheet into an envelope from his top desk drawer. Then, still silent but smiling, he wrote down an address:

President Arthur C Featherstone
The Oval Office
1700 Pennsylvania Avenue
Washington, D.C.

Chase sealed the envelope, turned it face up on his desk, retrieved a projector marking pen from his desk drawer, and printed across the top of the envelope in bold red letters:

TOP SECRET
EYES ONLY

Theresa stepped behind Chase and read what he had written. Suddenly the expression on her face changed dramatically. She broke into a huge grin and took the envelope when Chase lifted it into the air.

"Let's go," Theresa spoke to Moscowitz as she headed towards the door.

"Forget it," Moscowitz reacted.

Theresa paused and held up the envelope for Moscowitz to read.

Moscowitz's eye widened; she stared at Chase, and then spun about and followed Theresa out of the office without uttering another word.

Barney waited until he heard the outer door slam shut, looked at Chase, and repeated Moscowitz's original question, "Who the hell is Heather?"

Chase grinned as he answered, "Heather James, a good friend of mine, is the personal assistant to a gentleman named Arthur C. Featherstone."

"The president?" Barney asked with disbelief etched on his face. "What kind of game are you playing? Am I supposed to believe that nonsense?"

"Moscowitz and Theresa obviously don't believe I am playing a game. After the president sees what's in the envelope, I'm confident he'll invite Theresa and Moscowitz into his office for a brief picture taking session."

"You're kidding?"

"Believe."

"What's in the envelope?"

"A concise list."

"What kind of list?"

"The names of two Panamanian banks and two numbers for two separate offshore accounts."

Barney stared at Chase. After a few second of silent thought, he blurted, "Numbered accounts."

"Containing a little less than thirty million dollars, if I'm not mistaken," Chase said.

"Townsend staged his own kidnapping," Barney looked at Chase with awe in his eyes.

"With his wife's and his mistress's complicity and assistance," Chase said.

"And the grieving widow is heading to Panama to retrieve her illicit inheritance," Barney said.

"I'm not surprised she left her four suitcases behind," Chase chuckled.

"Are we going to let her get away with it?"

"She's taking a big gamble," Chase said. "I anticipate it will take about thirty minutes for my messengers to deliver that envelope. They will be escorted quickly through security, taking another five minutes to reach the Oval Office. Heather will interrupt the president, no matter what he is doing, chatting or napping; he will quickly recognize what he holds in his hands, shout Eureka or something less presidential, order Heather to send in the photographer, take three minutes to pose with two smiling Fairfax County Police Department employees, and then get on the green line and begin issuing instructions. I estimate that phone," Chase glanced at his cell now resting in the center of his desk, "will ring in forty minutes, give or take a few minutes delay caused by the traffic, and Special Agent Tracey Cotton will greet me with two demands."

"Where did you get the information?" A smiling Barney said.

"And after I reply, he will ask, 'Where in the hell is she now?'"

"What will you say?"

"Halfway between Washington, D.C. and Houston Texas."

"And then?"

"I will suggest that the Bureau move quickly, have their Panama City Office retrieve the cash before close of business today, and be prepared to apprehend the traveling merry widow when she arrives in Panama tomorrow morning."

"Why not arrest her in Houston? It would be neater that way."

"I wouldn't object to that, but I'm not sure the Bureau will be able to move that quickly. I'll give Cotton her itinerary when he calls, but I don't know where Mrs. Townsend is staying in Houston if they miss her at the airport. I'll suggest, of course, that he confer with Mary, Ms. Townsend's secretary, if he can reach her before she leaves the mansion for the day."

Barney just stared at his friend.

Chase, filled with self-satisfaction, just grinned.

"We have to brief the chief," Barney said, standing up.

"But who will answer the phone?" Chase did not move. "I'm still expecting two important calls and I have one of my own to make."

Barney sat back. "I can't brief the chief," Barney said. "I don't know the details."

Chase nodded.

"Cotton will call. Who else?" Barney asked.

"I expect that the president might ring, just to pass the time of day," Chase said. "And I've been thinking about giving Wacky Jacky a call. I've no plans for the evening and would enjoy a decent fish and chips and some pleasant conversation. "If Jacky behaves herself, I might give her a lead to an interesting client and a high profile case."

"You know what the chief is going to ask?" Barney changed the subject.

"Yes," Chase replied, forcing Barney to say the words.

"Are you going to let the Bureau take all the credit?"

"They can have the media. I've had my fifteen minutes of glory, and now I'm looking forward to seeing how the Bureau and the White House handle the fact they paid Secretary Townsend thirty million dollars to release himself."

Barney chuckled. "Particularly in the face of official United States Government policy against paying ransom to and not negotiating with terrorists."

"And there is also that side issue of Iranian complications featuring tactical nuclear weapons, exploding buildings, and devious little spies," Chase said. "But remember, we have the evidence, the .22 and the Glock, complete with the prints of two of Secretary Townsend's bed partners. Do you think I should suggest to ballistics that they not lose them?"

Barney treated his friend's question as rhetorical. "Do you really want to face Wacky Jacky in court? She caused you a little embarrassment the last time, I recall."

"I know Jacky better now. I'm rather looking forward to a rematch," Chase said. "Besides, I suspect she might find Sally Lou a mean handful. I am looking forward to watching those two spar."

"Don't get overconfident," Barney advised.

Chase and Barney chatted about the case until Chase's phone rang exactly as he predicted.

"Mansfield," Cotton greeted him without preliminaries. "You're a lucky bastard. I'm just giving you a heads up."

"Good afternoon, Special Agent Cotton," Chase said as he smiled at a listening Barney. "I've been expecting your call."

"Why in the hell didn't you give this damned information directly to me?" An irate Cotton demanded.

"Because it's the president's money in those accounts, and I assumed he would want to decide how to collect it," Chase replied.

"Don't expect this to accumulate any credits on this side of the river," Cotton said.

"Not on your end of Pennsylvania Avenue," Chase laughed.

"I thought we were friends."

"That's an interesting subject worth pursuing over a beer," Chase said. "But don't you have a few more important things on your plate at the moment."

"Where did you get this information?"

"It popped up during the course of my murder investigation," Chase said.

"Popped up where?"

"At the mansion of the perpetrator who incidentally is flying towards Panama as we speak. I assume she is on her way to recover her easy earned millions."

"She? Mansion? Townsend?"

"That's right, you know the woman. You spent considerable time enjoying her hospitality while she entertained you and undoubtedly enjoyed a good chuckle behind your back. Did she spend considerable time in her bedroom during you and your teams' occupation?"

"Townsend and his wife staged the kidnapping?"

"Exactly."

"Can you prove it?"

"You can give me a hand. Move the cash now and welcome the good widow when she arrives at the bank to make a withdrawal."

"How much time do I have?"

"Mrs. Townsend is enjoying a cocktail on Southwest heading for Houston where she plans to spend the night before continuing on Southwest Flight 247 for Panama tomorrow morning."

"You knew all this and let her go?"

"I thought I was doing you and the president a favor. I had full confidence that the two of you could handle the Panama end where I have limited resources."

"Bullshit, what's in this for you?"

"I want her back here to stand trial for a double murder," Chase said.

"She knocked off her husband to get all the money," Cotton said.

"She had more motivation than a little cash."

"Thirty million isn't small change."

"She helped her husband to acquire it, and he repaid her by dumping her for a younger model, his long time friend's former fiancée."

"And you have proof?"

"I have the Glock with the resourceful Mrs. Townsend's fingerprints all over it," Chase said.

"Ballistics can prove it is the murder weapon?"

"Of course. Now you understand why I want you to retrieve her for me?"

"You let her go and risked her grabbing the cash and disappearing?"

"I cautioned her not to leave the area, and she took off before I had the ballistics report in hand. It was a slight risk, but I knew she planned to spend the night in Houston before flying to Panama, and I had full confidence in your ability to retrieve her."

"I'm going to charge her with faking a kidnapping and extortion."

"And I am going to see her convicted of a double murder. Are you sure the president is going to want this ransom business to come out in court?"

"I don't give a shit what the president wants."

"Really? I anticipated you might feel that way, so I decided to give the president a first shot."

"I won't forget this," Cotton said.

"And neither will I," Chase said. "Give me a ring when you retrieve her and are ready to turn her over."

"Bullshit!"

"Imaginative phrasing," Chase said. "I'll try to remember and use it myself when the appropriate occasion arises."

Cotton hung up.

"And I will give the president your best when he calls," Chase spoke into the dial tone.

Chase looked up just in time to see Theresa and Moscowitz burst into his closet. Both had broad smiles on their faces and were positively beaming with excitement.

"We were in the Oval Office and the president posed with us for pictures," Theresa declared. "Do you think we will be in the papers tomorrow?"

Chase smiled.

"You set us up," Moscowitz stared at Chase. "Are we in trouble?"

"Only if getting your pictures taken with the president is a cause for concern," Chase said.

Barney applauded.

"Why didn't you deliver the envelope?" Moscowitz asked.

"I'm a very private person," Chase answered.

"I don't care if we are in trouble or not," Theresa announced. "I enjoyed it."

"What was in the envelope?" Moscowitz asked.

"Information that the president might wish to keep private," Chase said.

"I thank you for the experience, but I don't trust you," Moscowitz said.

Before Chase could respond, his office phone rang. Chase glanced at it and looked at Theresa. "Mind getting that for me?"

Theresa reached across the desk and grabbed the phone. "CIB," she announced.

Suddenly, she stood straighter. "Yes, Heather, yes, he's right here."

"It's Heather," Theresa said as she thrust the phone across the desk at Chase.

"Hi, Heather," Chase said casually.

"He wishes to talk with you, lieutenant," Heather said.

"Put the old boy on," Chase said.

After a brief pause, President Arthur C. Featherstone came on line. "Lieutenant, I want to thank you for your discretion."

"No problem, sir," Chase answered.

"Who else knows about these numbers?" Featherstone asked.

"You, sir, me, and Special Agent Cotton," Chase said, not admitting that Barney had also been briefed.

"I shared them with Cotton," Featherstone said. "I assume you understand why."

"Yes, sir, no problem," Chase said.

"And I have your assurance there will be no leaks from your associates?"

"Yes, sir," Chase replied with crossed fingers. "I assume you understand that Mrs. Townsend is a loose cannon."

"Nancy Lou is an intelligent woman," Featherstone said. "She has more to lose than gain if her participation in the bogus kidnapping should leak."

"I'm going to charge her with shooting her husband and his fiancée," Chase said.

"Can you prove that in a court of law?"

"I have the weapon that she used completely covered with only her fingerprints."

"Can you prove that she knows how to use it?"

"I haven't talked with her secretary or former security team, but I'm confident that one or both can establish Nancy Lou's prowess," Chase said.

"You are a good man," Featherstone said. "Just to be sure, I'll have a heart to heart with Nancy Lou."

"Before the Bureau turns her over to me?" Chase asked the key question.

"Of course," Featherstone said. "Nancy Lou is a hard but realistic woman. She knows how the game is played and whose fingers guide the pardon pen."

"Mrs. Townsend was caught in a difficult situation," Chase added, not believing a word that he said. He assumed that Nancy Lou was the brain and the muscle behind the entire plot.

"We think alike, Lieutenant Mansfield," Featherstone declared. "If you ever need anything, please give me a call."

"That would be my pleasure, sir," Chase said. "Please ask Special Agent Cotton to turn Ms. Townsend over to me to prosecute as the law demands." Chase immediately took advantage of the president's kind offer.

After a short delay, Featherstone responded, "Of course."

Chase assumed the president was not quite as happy as he had been when he placed the call.

"What was that all about?" Barney asked.

"Details, just details," Chase shrugged. He glanced at the waiting Moscowitz and Theresa. "The president assures me the properly signed pictures will soon be in your hands."

It was a small prevarication, but Chase assumed the girls would blame the president and not him if Heather did not come through.

"Congratulations, ladies," Barney smiled at Moscowitz and Theresa. "We best give the chief a heads up," he said, glancing at Chase.

Chase nodded and followed Barney into hall as Moscowitz and Theresa applauded behind him.

As soon as they were alone, Barney turned and asked Chase, "What are you going to tell the chief?"

"The truth," Chase responded.

"All of it?" Barney asked.

"Of course not," Chase answered. "The chief only needs the highlights."

Barney looked skeptically at his friend.

"One thing troubles me," Chase admitted.

Barney waited as the elevator started its ascent.

"This case has lots of complications that I don't fully understand," Chase said. "It involves an odd threesome."

"Is that really complicated?"

"I am not sure which threesome is responsible," Chase smiled. "The fiancée, the professor, and the secretary; or the fiancée, the secretary, and his spouse."

"At least you are lucky there was no Holy Ghost complicating either triangle," Barney said as he started down the hall to the chief's office.

"Yes, but the Lady in Black was the same fiancée in both triangles," Chase laughed. "Maybe she was a holy ghost incarnated as a human."

Oh, well," Barney said, "three dead and one heading for jail. You can't win them all. Life's not unanimous."

"And I thought I was the philosopher," Chase said.

About the Author

A graduate of Potomac State College, West Virginia University, and a teaching assistant at the University of Wisconsin where he worked on his doctorate in American History, Robert L Skidmore spent thirty-five years in the foreign service of the United States whose assignments took him to tours in Iran, Greece, New Zealand, Laos, Malaysia, and Portugal. Now, long retired, Mr. Skidmore indulges in two lifelong passions, researching history and writing, both of which enable him to play with his computers and avoid travel at all cost. He has published twenty-two novels.